LAND OF THE FIRST
- SERVANT OF FIRE -

Simon J. Cambridge

Published in 2014 by First Thought Publishing.

ISBN 978-0-9927895-0-3

Copyright © 2013 by Simon J. Cambridge.

First Edition.

The right of Simon J. Cambridge to be identified as the author of this work has been asserted by him in accordance with the Copyright, Designs and Patents Act 1988.

I

- SERVANT OF FIRE -

Kur-ur-ord Um-nalvaagei
Kur-pola Renod-doneis
Kur-logith Ao-aj-lareil
No-unka Iborn-ilmhz
No-unka Deran-od-torz
No-arka Bia-anodsii
Luj-husfam A-de-aozeis

Contents

1

FACE OF STONE

Doho-us Ag-sm-nisan
Nht-tolaa Ors-pir-tapol
Farpa-oth Ramas-nimin
Nissel-sag Ipaj-sosoy
Kamath-aiq Oded-nomkoh
Om-zidaiz Yolod-qasteh
Od-nochis Ipeth-drilaa

The black stepped out of the white and into the grey beyond.

For a moment he stood, sword-sharp and dark, then he held up his hand and the white withdrew. Down it went to a single star, remote but radiant, before vanishing altogether and leaving him to the grey.

He reached over his shoulder and drew out a long stave of crystal. He held it up before him and it sang with blue fire. With a wind out of nowhere the grey fled, tumbling back, ever faster, until all its horizons were achieved. Then the wind died, the light dimmed and the stave was put back into its sheath.

He found himself now upon a low hill: one amongst many that stretched into the distances. Dead stems leaned from every slope, oblique and broken, whilst every hollow cupped a pool, all unmoving as mirrors.

A pale light began, far out beyond the hills. He turned towards it, lifting his head and watching as it grew, swelling and rising. Then it arrived.

Fire fell; water, stone and air all staggered under its weight. Slopes tilted, pools opened like eyes and the dead yearned. Fire crossed the sea of hills and shattered its sleep.

For a moment he drank of it, face raised and eyes brilliant, before turning his back and walking away, off in pursuit of departing night.

On he went, one frozen wave to the next, until the shadow of a mountain reared up before him like an island. He paused a moment as though uncertain, but then moved on again, watching carefully as it coalesced from the luminous air.

The closer he came, the clearer it came, and the clearer it came, the slower he went, and by the time it was fully revealed he had come to a complete stop.

There it was, softly painted in the early morning light, wide-flung slopes and knuckled crags glowering. He stared, scouring it back and forth with his eyes, up the slanted green and over the eroded summits. Disbelief had him, until it darkened to anger.

Black fires swirled – shadows, flames – and he glared at the mountain with blood-drenched sight. Lightning spat and thunders rumbled, but the mountain would not move. As stubborn as its ancient stone, it remained where it was as though rooted in eternity.

His eyes dulled to twin bruises of pain and he turned away. His dark fires failed and his thunders echoed down into silence. For many moments he did not move at all except for his hands, which clenched and unclenched at his sides. Then he turned about and, with a face of stone, strode towards the mountain once more.

He came upon what appeared to be a road, a dark wound slicing its way across the land. He stopped at its edges and bent low. He passed a hand across its surface, feeling with his fingertips and scratching with his claws. The road glistened, a thin film of moisture on its uneven surface, tiny stones nestling in a dark and glossy matrix. He drew back in distaste before turning to his left and then to his right, marking where the road came from and where it went. He bared his teeth at it, almost a snarl, before crossing in a single bound. He did not look back.

Further on he came to a lake. It was long and wide and it barred his way. He glowered at it, standing at its edge and staring into its depths. Then he drew out his great crystal stave and held its tip to the water. Green fire filled it and a deep discordant note shivered the air. With a cracking sound the lake froze from one end to the other. Pausing only to sheathe his stave, he strode out across the ice.

Beyond the lake there was another road, much like the first, skirting the edges of the mountain like a boundary. He crossed it without so much as a glance, and then began his way to the heights.

On the pastures that ran up to the steeper slopes there were small white creatures dotted here and there, feeding upon the abundant green. They ignored him well enough if he kept his distance, but when he came too close they all upped tails and ran. He watched them for a little while as they scampered this way and that, but then he turned to the nearest and his shadow fell upon it.

As if caught on a leash, the beast came to a sudden stop. Then it turned about and walked calmly back towards him, stopping at his feet. He looked down at it and then knelt.

The beast did not move as he studied it; instead it gazed through him, blind, deaf and dumb. After a while he stood again, looking back at the mountain. The beast, forgotten, scampered madly backwards and bleated in panic as it made its escape. Finally, at what it judged a safe distance, it stopped and turned. With rediscovered bravery it stamped its feet and snorted in indignation, but he returned its gaze with cold fire and the beast ran away as fast as it could. He stared darkly after it for a moment and then moved on.

As the way became steeper he found his path crossed by numerous small streams, all gurgling noisily through deep channels and running over half-submerged stones or dropping down soil-carved steps. He turned his head to listen to the music, but he did not linger.

Finally the ground began to level out into a long and wide expanse. To his left reared a shoulder of the mountain, a greater slope than the one he had just climbed, high and steep and studded with boulders. Beyond its guarding heights lay the main mass with its many peaks, all now hidden from view.

To his right a smaller hill crouched, crowded about with rocky walls that led up to a flattened summit. He looked at the steep slope to his left and then at the gentler incline to his right. He weighed up the possibilities and then turned away from the mountain. He would go up the hill instead.

As he climbed the wind grew steadily. A sudden gust, particularly strong, took his long cloak and billowed it out behind him like two great wings. He paused and raised his head. There was a scent on the air, the faintest of odours, and one he knew all too well. He let out a long breath. It was all part of a growing pattern.

When he reached the top he searched the ground, touching rock, fingering soil, smelling the vegetation. He placed his hand against the stone and waited. And waited. Finally he straightened and gave the hill a black look as though it had failed him in some way, then he turned to the wider land about him and looked at that instead.

There were more hills further on, long lines of them stretching into the distance, summits bowed like heads as they marched through the earth. There was a settlement of some kind, low dwellings, enclosed fields, another road. Beyond lay a greater expanse, a wider wilderness that ended at the edge of gleaming waters. It was so like, yet so unlike.

He waited a while, looking, measuring, judging, but as the moments lengthened he grew ever more restless. Finally, with one swift glance at the mountain, he made his way down again.

There was a narrow path that led down from the hill, narrow but well-trodden, so he followed it and let it lead him where it would.

The path eventually joined another, rougher and wider, flattened by many years of use. It took him by a set of fields whose boundaries were written with rude walls of piled up stone. In some places the walls had collapsed, whilst in others thin posts still held everything in place, rusting even as they constrained. He looked with distaste at the broken walls and decaying metal. Such carelessness! Such abandonment! They were like the roads he had encountered: alien, unwelcome and wrong.

He came to a field where a few large and shaggy beasts were penned. They had thick brown pelts which were long enough to hide everything but their legs, snouts and wide horns. He stopped as soon as he saw them, staring in at them whilst they stared back out, uneasy under his threatening gaze.

As before, his shadow fell upon one of them and its eyes glazed over as it trundled calmly towards him. The others drew back as far as they could and watched in fearful silence.

From beyond the wall he looked the animal up and down for a moment, before finally turning away. His eyes filled with anger as he clenched his fists and shook with fury. Was this mockery? Was he being mocked?

With its release the beast ran back to its brethren, bellowing its alarm. But when it found that it was not pursued, it stopped and stared at its summoner, eyes wide beneath its great fringe of hair. It bellowed its displeasure, a challenge perhaps, but backed further away when it caught scent of the stranger's ire. Though he had not moved, the threat of him filled the air like a storm. All the beasts huddled together in the furthest corner of the field, quietly lowing their distress, but he was already gone.

He came to the first of the dwellings he had seen from the hill and found himself a place of concealment where he could watch and wait.

The dwelling, if it could be called such, was crude. Stones were piled carelessly upon one another, knitted together by some strange species of clay. It looked haphazard, primitive and thoughtless, and it was a wonder that it did not all just come crashing down in ruin. A stunted pillar erupted from its roof and he noticed smoke rising from it. Smoke? He sniffed the air. They burned wood? His eyes flickered with a dangerous light.

He looked at the trees around him. Did they take the living for this? Did they cut the living flesh to fuel their fires? Or did they merely take of the dead, the fallen, the cast aside? He hoped it was the latter, but he did not hope too much. The deeper he entered this place, the worse it became.

How sombre his thoughts were now. He tried to distract himself by studying the trees, touching their bark and leaves, following their shape and way of growth, but it was to no avail. They, like everything else, only added to his misery. Like the beasts and the land, the trees were close, so very close to what they appeared to be, yet they lacked in some way. They had the shape and the feel, but there was an uncertain quality to them, as though they aspired to something more but did not know what it was.

The door to the dwelling opened and the occupants emerged. He turned to watch them. Here it came, the final test. Let him see the masters of this world and then he would know how far this went.

Though they seemed familiar at first – their features and the way that they moved and gestured – there were differences also, and he found them as disturbing as he had everything else.

For one thing they were far smaller than he had imagined, and their skin was entirely the wrong colour, as was their hair. Their features were of the right kind, but everything was either subtly out of place or the wrong shape entirely. Looking at them now one might consider them little more than crude copies perhaps, but underneath, below, they were other. He could feel them – unfocused, minds darting this way and that, uncertain even of their own desires.

Suddenly he saw it. This was not mockery so much as memory. He stood in the presence of children, still growing and discovering, unaware as yet of who they were and what they were; the new following the old, remembering but not knowing what it was that they remembered. He had come to a realm of shadows.

He watched as they left in a noisy vehicle of peculiar design. Now it was himself that felt wrong – alien and out of place. He smiled. That, at least, was easily remedied.

He clenched his jaws and folded his arms across his chest. His eyes burned and dark fires erupted. As if suddenly mutable, his clothing and his body rippled. His hair shortened, all but vanishing back inside his head, whilst his height lessened and his skin changed hue. His cloak shrank against him, his armour vanished and in moments he had assumed the likeness of those that dwelt in this place, shrinking, weakening, diminishing as he folded his dark light away. But he could not erase himself entirely. There was still a shadow in the spaces he occupied, and the light of his eyes would not be dimmed.

He unfolded his arms. It was done. Now, to all intents and purposes, he was one of them. He would walk the ways of this world and see what he had come here to see, and though he might now have their look, he must never sink so far as to forget who he was. That would never do. Let the purpose that had brought him here define him only until it was done.

He walked the narrow road from the dwelling all the way to its end. There was a great tongue of water to his left, flat and wide and glistening. Crossing it was a low bridge, a great sweeping curve of stone. Up ahead and to his right lay a scattering of buildings, peaked roofs poking up between tall trees. Seeing them he felt the stir of thoughts coiling in his mind. The world about him was waking up, its children rising from their slumbers, their dreams departing in a blur of forgetfulness as they prepared to go about the day's business. He walked on and went to join them.

She stared at the crowded shelves but wanted nothing of them, nor of anything else that was here. Yet here she was, compelled to remain and resenting it bitterly.

Every few days she came quietly out from her hiding place to collect her due, a brief moment in the light before returning as if to await the next excursion. It was her only rebellion, the only time she rattled the bars of her cage. But no one noticed. She had hidden herself far too well.

Not so long ago she had been free, able to walk the world without constraint. Then she had been beyond all bounds, set apart and revelling in her differences. Now she was trammelled by them.

All lives are shadowed by how they begin, and hers had begun as mystery. Found in a doorway, placed there by persons unknown, there was no clue as to her origins, just a new-born child wrapped in some blankets.

She had been fostered out to a good home and loving guardians, but the seal on her life had been set. She was different and she knew it.

At first she attracted attention. People would stop and stare. "Such a beautiful child," they would exclaim, a tumult of questions following. There were no answers though, or none that might satisfy, and rather than fuelling the fires of their curiosity her very silence doused them. So it became the tale of her childhood, of ever-growing distances, her mystery a wall about her and impenetrable to others.

By the time she came to full flower she found herself walking through her life as though through a parting sea, its waters rearing up about her before closing in again behind whilst its startled denizens stared back at this strange apparition that suddenly loomed in their midst. And though they might follow her with their eyes, none would dare to cross her boundaries, for her wall had grown as she had and now was a circling power, a warding shield to keep the world at bay.

Untroubled by the troubles of others, it seemed she could do as she pleased, but there grew a feeling inside, a sense that became ever more certain as time moved on, that this was not what she was meant for, that this was not where she was meant to be.

There were fantasies, of course, that another life awaited her, that somewhere else was a place to return to, a place where she truly belonged. But she had never found it. Instead she remained gloriously alone and untouchable.

So came the cage when all was revealed as conceit. How naive she had been to think that the world could not touch her. It could. Breaking through her barriers it casually undid her life, turning fantasy to nightmare and forcing her to flee.

He walked through the settlement, following the gently rising road. He watched the people, the few that were up and about, and wondered what it was that he would find here.

A door opened to his left, a little way ahead. He gave it a glance, the briefest of looks, but when she stepped over the threshold he stopped in his tracks. He stopped and he stared and he saw her, saw who she was, exactly who she was.

He watched as she paused to pull her heavy clothing about her, protecting herself against the chill air, and that movement, that simple act, filled him with more hope and despair than he had ever known in his life.

Of all the things he had ever expected to see, she was the last of them. Neither could he be mistaken. Though all else might be a shadow and a sham, in this he was certain. It was her. She was here. She had come again, into this strange place, this shallow resurrection. But how could that be?

He had seen the others here, seen them in their entirety, their crude clay the merest promise of what was yet to come. But now here she was before him, walking amongst them like one of the first. How was that possible?

He had no answer. He had been warned that he would understand when the time came, but he had disbelieved it as he had disbelieved so many other things in his life. Now he had no choice. This changed everything.

Her eyes wandered in his direction. Was she going to see him? He panicked. He was not ready for this. He needed time.

"*Do not see me,*" he told her with his mind, his thoughts falling against her like a wall. "*Do not see me,*" he commanded. "*Do not see me at all!*"

But even so, for the briefest moment – the very briefest – she defied him as though she was still his equal, her eyes catching his and widening in sudden shock as she met his gaze.

He staggered. Was that recognition? Was that accusation? But then, just as quickly, she succumbed and turned away as if nothing had happened at all.

He remained where he was, rooted to the spot and unable to move.

The taste of her, the taste of her thought, was like a knife through his heart. She was exact, brilliant in every detail, a brightness that tore his shadow to shreds. The sense, the touch, the very touch, it was all there, all inside her like a flower awaiting its opening. He watched in broken darkness as she walked away, and then tears fell from his eyes. Nascent fires threatened the circling air and it was all he could do to keep himself from burning to ash.

Should he follow? Should he dare her presence once more? Could he even? He closed his eyes and shook. This was the worst of all, and yet the most wonderful.

He could ignore the mountain, the land, the beasts, the smell of the air and the shape of the trees, but he could not ignore her. Once more Obelison walked beneath a sunlit sky. That she was here meant that he should be here as well. It was fate, written in stone, and on this all would be saved or damned.

He let out a long and shuddering breath. He had thought that he had understood what it was he was meant to do, but clearly that was no longer true. His purposes lay shattered at his feet.

He slowly calmed himself. He would follow her and see where this would go, so he wrapped himself about with shadow and illusion and vanished from the day. Then up the street he went, waiting for the moment when he could act and reveal himself at last.

He watched as he followed; everything that she did, from the way she brushed back her hair to the way she placed her feet upon the ground, it was all as familiar to him as were his very own hands.

Deep she was, pale and beautiful and lit from within with that self-same fire that long ago had claimed his heart. Obelison was written within her with words even a fool could read. There lay the perfection, the grace and the beauty, once born of long-vanished Uriel.

Her hair was just as black, and whilst not so long it still covered her slender neck like a gleam of midnight. She was tall also, far taller than the others that dwelt here, but then how could it be otherwise? She was not as they. She still possessed that beauty, that perilous beauty from before: a form beyond forms, a proportion beyond proportions. He had only to look at her to see once more that wondrous grace he thought never to see again in all the Bright Heavens.

There were differences though, many of them. Being born of this world she had been marked by its taint. Her skin was not the right colour, though it retained a glorious paleness nonetheless and was just as peerless. Her ears were wrong and the tips of her fingers also, but that meant little to him. One look in her eyes told him everything that he needed to know. No other spirit could fill them so. He could drown in them for ever and never again see the light of day. He could die at her hands now and call himself blessed. So he watched her in all her ways, and burned.

At her house, still swathed in shadows, he waited beside a low tree heavy with dark-green foliage.

It bothered him somewhat, that tree. It had a strange, unpleasant smell, something he had not come across before. He fingered the rough black bark and glanced at the thick green needles and the sparse red fruits that dotted the branches. He grimaced. They smelled of poison and death. Why have such a dark and morbid thing here? He felt a sense of foreboding. Obelison would have dwelt amongst drifts of bright flowers, amongst the tall and the shapely. She had liked the air and the light, not stifling shadow. She would not have borne this dark and crouching thing. Had he fooled himself? He turned from the tree to the house, trying to summon up the courage to approach its single door, but he could not move, not yet. Something told him that the time was not yet right.

A grey vehicle, another of those primitive mechanical devices, larger and more intimidating perhaps, entered slowly through the gate. It made a wide circle and came carefully to a stop. A confusion of thoughts tumbled briefly from inside before one of the occupants emerged, all in grey like his vehicle. Looking neither left nor right, the stranger walked smartly up to the door and knocked three times upon it. The others in the vehicle remained where they were, hiding themselves from view. He reached out with his mind, but their tumbling thoughts were oddly muffled, almost as if they had folded themselves away inside. He frowned. What strange play was this?

The door was a moment opening, but even as its locks were lifted the stranger threw it wide with brute strength. He crossed over the threshold and grappled with the opener. It was her.

She fought back, and if the stranger had been alone she would have been successful, but others leapt from the vehicle and were soon upon her. Too many hands came for her, and she was held down and overpowered. Then they slowly dragged her back to their vehicle.

He could not believe it. They were attacking her? Was this supposed to happen? His anger rose up like wildfire and he snarled. How could these crude brutes even dare to touch her? He needed no further goad. He stepped out of the shadows and let his anger speak.

The first she knew of it was a rush of darkness. Her assailants were thrown aside and she was suddenly on her feet again, though how it had happened she had no idea. She stared about in bewilderment. Her attackers lay scattered before her, three of them, all sprawled upon the gravel, faces identical with pain and shock. They were staring, mouths slack, eyes wide, but they were not looking at her.

Now she felt it. There was something behind her, at her back, something hot. For a moment she could not turn, dared not even, but when the hand was laid upon her shoulder she had no choice. Then she looked and instantly froze where she stood.

It towered over her, dimensionless, pale fires in the darkness, threatening wings of air. She could not see and yet she could. A great statue, wreathed in light and shadow. There was a face, a pale face carved of fury, but like no face she had ever seen before. It was as though stone had come to life, beautiful stone, perfect stone. If ever the powers had descended, if ever they had clothed themselves in substance, then surely here was one of them now, immortal spirit caught in imperishable flesh. Living stone stood behind her, Heaven's will set upon the world and filled with its avenging wrath.

She looked at the hand upon her shoulder. It was beautiful and luminous and she caught a fragrance, the scent of it, something delicate and wild. The hand gently squeezed – reassurance, a moment of warmth – and then the statue moved.

It raised its other hand like a judgement, holding up a long shaft of crystal filled with yellow flame. The statue lowered the shaft towards the nearest of her attackers and there came a sharp sound like a distant bell of ice. A heavy flicker of air fell from its tip, a glistening shroud that enveloped him from head to foot.

There was not time enough even to scream. Instead he silently shrank into himself, head, limbs and torso, all curling up into each other as he was crushed down into a ball. But the shroud did not stop; it continued all the way and he continued with it: compressing, shrinking, bones popping, skin bursting. Nothing that was his escaped. As the shimmering cage of air shrank, so did he, too – his features blurring, geometries simplifying, until everything that he was, his body, his flesh, had fallen to a single point. Then he quietly vanished away and nothing remained of him at all.

She stared at the sudden vacuum in disbelief, not daring to think what it was she had seen. She stood now in a still place whilst events about her went whatever way they would.

The shaft of yellow fire moved again and the others were quickly touched. With every touch came that bell of ice and a shroud of crystallised air to crush silently whatever it touched to nothingness. A sense of horror began to grow inside.

The large grey vehicle roared and started to move, its terrified driver only now beginning to understand his peril. But the great shaft of crystal was already there and it touched the vehicle even as it span around to leave. Covered in its entirety, the vehicle came to a full stop as though it had run into a wall. For a moment it shivered, daring to deny its fate perhaps, but then it compressed as well. She caught a brief glimpse of the driver silently shouting at his window, fists pounding against the glass as if he were drowning inside, but then the vehicle folded up around him and he vanished under shattering glass and bending metal. Soon all was crushed from sight and only she and the statue remained.

She stared about her in utter dismay before glancing back at the statue. She had been wrong. Here was no angel. Here was something else entirely. This was one of the fallen instead, darker by far and irredeemable.

The statue looked back at her with eyes of seeing flame and its sight went through her, through her walls, through her horror and dismay. It turned about inside and revealed her thought to itself. It saw what she had seen, saw it through the filter of her comprehension, and the revelation all but undid it. Its flame guttered on its hungry wick and its fiery eyes darkened and shed tears of regret instead. Contrition and grief filled it up: great contrition, greater grief. For a moment it bowed before her as though for forgiveness, and then it turned about and fled.

It moved so quickly that she could not follow, not even with her eyes. In mere moments it had gone and she was alone again. But was she? There was something still inside her, a presence, as though a connection had been made, and there was a peculiar sense to it: a sense of the familiar. But where had she felt this before?

She sat in her accustomed chair and shivered, rubbing her shoulders for warmth. What had just happened? What had she just witnessed? Though it was all there in her mind, every single thing, its meaning eluded her. She even began to wonder whether it had not all been some waking dream, some terrible waking dream.

She started. That was it. She had it. It had been a dream, but it was her dream, pulled from her head and out into the real world. She had been in peril, in peril from the grey, and a protector had come to save her.

The dream first appeared just after she had hidden herself away. To begin with she thought it nothing more than her hopes and fears given form, but then it had come again and again, as though she was being told something. Now she could guess what it was.

The dream would start with fear. She would be in danger, grey horrors pursuing her through some fog-bound labyrinth of broken stone. They waited around each corner, lurking in the shadows or crouching behind the walls. She never caught them clearly. A brief flicker of claws or a brief flash of teeth were all she ever saw. Beyond lay only suggestion and shadow.

Eventually her saviour would come, swathed in potent darkness, a great sword of fire in his hand. Into the shadow he would go and the horrors would flee. Then he would return to her and he would comfort her, shielding her from the world, his arms about her like a wall. Leading her back up into the light he would speak softly to her with words she could never remember when she awoke. But she knew that they were wonderful words of reassurance, gentleness and truth. Though it would start in terror, it would end in bliss with her clasped in the arms of her saviour, the world about them fading into twilight and a crown of ancient stars above like a blessing.

But the dream would not allow her to linger, and with every recurrence the terror seemed to swell and grow whilst the bliss seemed ever more fleeting. She longed to stay, to tarry with her saviour and escape her predicament, but it was almost as if the world had other ideas, closing in over her head and slowly drowning her hope.

She thought again of that face, a thing never seen before in life, so perfect, so still like living stone. Then she thought of what it had done and the old admonition came back to her. Be careful what you wish for. Her protector was not what she had thought it to be. Instead it was some untamed thing, acting in her stead with all the appalling power at its disposal.

She thought of her assailants and shuddered. They had come to her with violence, but a greater violence had taken them in its turn. What terrible force had crushed them from the world? Four people, four of them, had suddenly ceased to exist right there in front of her, right there before her eyes. The memory was cruel in its detail, brutal and appalling. Whatever power it was that had enfolded them, it had been merciless.

Should she tell someone? Should she call for help? Should she tell her tale of assault and rescue? How could she, though? Her assailants were gone, along with her protector, and she had no proof that anything had happened at all. They would look at her as if she were mad.

But four people had died. Four people that had once lived in the world lived in it no longer. That would be noticed, wouldn't it? But that, too, was hopeless. Who would admit that they were gone? They had attacked her. Who would admit to sending them?

There was an answer, an obvious one, but she did not like it. There was one person she knew of that was capable of such an act, and he was the reason she had hidden herself away in the first place.

From the moment their paths had crossed he had pursued her with a will, her unseen shield powerless to stop him. He sent her gifts and she sent them back again. He followed her and she eluded him. He turned up in places she did not expect and she ran from him. She resorted to the law, and though he bowed before it in public she knew that even in this he would not be dissuaded. His last promise to her confirmed it. Someday he would have her. Someday, near or far, she would be his.

Now even her wall seemed to work against her. It was almost as though he was in there with her, caught inside, within a place denied to all others; and as her wall kept out the others, it kept out their help as well. She was on her own.

So she enacted her final sanction, collected up the pieces of her life and hid herself away as deeply as she could. A new life and a new identity, but even in this she had clearly failed to escape him.

Single-minded, obsessive, he knew no bounds. His wealth the engine of his desire, he knew how to get the things that he wanted. She had been a fool. Seeking her out would be child's play to him. She felt again that stifling feeling she had always felt in his presence, of being held down, unable to move and constrained by unbreakable bonds.

Now, though, a protector had come and the bonds had been broken with a single touch. But what exactly was it that had stepped into her life?

He walked to the centre of the bridge, full of sorrow and racked with grief. He looked up at the mountain but did not see it; instead he stared into his depths.

He had acted without thought – it had ever been his downfall. He had been warned so many times in the past, warned not to let his passions rule him, but he had not listened. He had never listened. Once more he found himself surrounded by his failings as if by a great wall of shame.

He could see the mistake now. For all its crudity this land was a far gentler place than he had at first thought. Death by violence was rare. He had come to an island of order set within a turbulent sea and had judged far too quickly. The slaughter he had committed was considered a crime here, but what could he have done? They had attacked her! The answer though was obvious. He could have put them down with his hands and his feet, not his indiscriminate power. There had been no need to kill.

He saw himself again through her eyes, the terror of him and the brutality. That was not what he had intended at all. He should have paid more attention and looked rather for meaning or understanding.

The language here, both the word and the thought, now hummed in his mind. He listened to it with far more consideration than he had before, as he should have from the very beginning. But then it had all seemed like a tangled chaos and he had been far too impatient to try to unravel it accordingly. Impatience! Acting before the time was ripe, jumping to conclusions. It had ever been his fault.

He felt again that sense of return, that dark feeling that the heavens repeated themselves, great cycles of time turning and turning again. He had been down this path before, mistaking the signs, acting without consideration. Now, perhaps, he had one final chance to put things right. The heavens did not offer up such chances blithely.

She gazed out at the world beyond her window but hardly saw anything at all. On a clear day one could see everything from here, from the mountain to the far hills and all the way to the sea, but her mind was filled with the image of a living statue: a fallen angel caught in stone, impossible powers at its beck and call.

Perhaps she had judged too harshly. After all, she had been in danger. Who knew what would have happened if her abduction had been allowed to continue. For all its brutal perfection her protector was still one of the numinous, and surely, surely, it knew more than she did. Perhaps she need not fear. Perhaps this was her way out.

As if summoned by her thought, she suddenly noticed an unaccustomed shadow on the road over the bridge. There was someone down there, alone and indistinct, standing somewhat near the middle. There was nothing else in view, and both the bridge and the road were clear of traffic.

She looked down at the lone figure. How still it was and how unmoving. There were no dimensions to it at all. Was it her mysterious protector? Her breath caught in her throat.

Suddenly reckless, she resolved to find out. The admonition still rang in her mind, "Be careful what you wish for," but she ignored it. She had to know the truth, she had to.

She ran all the way to the bridge, heart beating furiously, hope and fear indivisible. The shape was still there, standing against the parapet and looking towards the mountain, so she stopped a little way off and gathered up the shredded fragments of her courage. Then she approached.

She made her way forwards slowly, carefully, as though towards some wild and wary beast that would flee the instant it saw her. But the shadow shape made no move to leave; rather, it stayed where it was and gazed up at the mountain.

It was tall, very tall and broad, a face of clouded stone above featureless clothing. Even its feet were rumour. There was a wind, a breeze coming down from the mountain, but it passed the tall shape by and seemed powerless to disturb it. It was as she had first seen it, a statue given life, and yet it was more than that now. Something else lay under its pale stone, something warmer, the faintest hint of mortality.

There was a scent riding the air, the same one she had noticed before – delicate, elusive and just out of reach. She thought of flowers, a wreath or crown of blooms, but there was nothing that she could see.

Then it seemed as if she crossed a boundary, for the scent suddenly swelled and the statue moved at last and she could see him. He turned to face her and she stopped in her tracks.

She could see his features, see them fully, and yet they were still veiled to her eyes. His countenance was a mask for something else, she thought, but that was enough. His face that was not a face took her breath away. The sun was suddenly full upon it and all she could see was beauty.

Impossibly perfect, impossibly strong, here stood stone that walked the earth: older than man, older than life and mightier than both. He was as beautiful as in her dream, but here in the light it was a far more terrible beauty, too wonderful, too proud, too sad, too grim. Too much.

The mask shifted a little, softening perhaps. His fine mouth curled slightly into a smile, but it was a sad and regretful smile, the only line in an otherwise unlined face. His eyes were old and filled with time, a deep and curiously gentle darkness from which she suddenly found herself unable to look away. The brutal memory of what he had done was almost forgotten as she gazed up at him, but it did not vanish entirely. It still sat, like a dark warning, at the back of her mind.

"Who are you?" she dared.

He did not answer.

"Who are you?" she repeated.

He still did not answer, but his eyes shifted and sharpened. They peered through her as though they saw something else inside more worthy of their consideration. It was almost as if she was not there at all, that something else occupied the spaces she inhabited, moving as she moved: something of far more consequence. She did not like the inference.

"Who are you?" she demanded, surprising herself. She was actually angry.

"Three times is the way of it, after all," he murmured.

His voice was deep, abstracted, a rush of sound like the slow fall of an avalanche. For a moment he seemed to tower over her, his eyes swelling with force. She backed away, ready to run, but then he retreated and dropped his gaze. She caught a brief glimpse of contrition, before it vanished again into the shadows. He sighed and his face became stone once more.

"I am sorry," he said. "I misunderstood. When I saw them attack you I did not stop to consider. I was angry and acted without thought. I am sorry."

Now his voice was darkly musical, like no other she had ever heard before in all her life. She thought of all the voices and all the accents she had ever encountered, but none of them came close.

"Who were they?" he asked. "Why would they wish you harm?"

"I don't know," she answered.

He looked at her as though he saw deeper, saw guesses, saw truth, but she did not want to pursue that line of questioning. She wanted to know about him. She waited a moment, gathering strength. Her next question would cost her.

"Why did you do it?" she asked. "Why did you rescue me like that?"

His eyes sharpened further. Did he understand this also?

"Perhaps I was wrong," he said. "Perhaps I should leave."

He looked away. She stared at him.

"But why?" she asked.

"I had no right to do this," he replied. "I had no right to interfere again."

Interfere again? This had happened before?

"But you saved me!" she said. "You came here to save me! Why? What am I to you?"

He looked back again. Now his eyes were fiery and they were hard to meet.

"What are you to me?" he asked. "Is it really your desire to know? Is it? For if I were to answer you fully, it would change your life for ever. Is that what you want? Do you truly want to know what you are to me? Sometimes ignorance can be a blessing. You have a life here. I do not."

She looked down. She could not look at him and think at the same time. 'It would change your life for ever!' he had said – and there was the promise. Wonders, marvels, possibilities filled her. Maybe this was her chance. Maybe this was the doorway that would take her on to the places she belonged. She shivered and pushed her fear back down. He was more than the darkness, she was certain of it. She would take the chance. She looked back at him and dared the fire.

"Yes," she told him. "I have a life here, but it is not the one that I want. So if there is a way out, I want to know what it is."

He looked at her strangely and the fire dimmed.

"You do not want your life?" he asked.

She shook her head.

"No, that is not what I meant. I meant..."

She floundered. She could not think of the words. He continued to watch her, his stone softening once more.

"I understand," he intervened. "You mean your life as it is. But that is why I am here. The mistake I made, the slaughter I committed almost made me leave, but I was compelled to stay. I cannot leave this place whilst you are in danger."

He waited while she gathered up her thoughts again.

"What are you telling me?" she eventually asked.

He sighed.

"There is no easy way to answer such a question," he replied. "But even so, an answer must be given." He looked at her and his face gentled further. No longer stone, he was flesh and blood now. His eyes lost their fire and became dark and sad. "You have the face and the form of someone I once knew," he continued. "Seeing you, I wished to speak to her once more before the end. I had hoped for understanding, maybe even forgiveness, but perhaps it was a vain hope. Perhaps you do not remember her. She died long ago."

She went still. She felt a shiver deep inside like the sudden touch of infinite cold. She thought of tombs, of burials and the long, slow sleep of death. It was as though he had awakened such a memory in her, the memory of her very own ending. She shook her head. It could not be true, could it? But her old fantasy of having come here from somewhere else rose back up into the light and now she wondered if she was who she thought she was at all.

"You think I am someone else?" she asked him.

"No," he answered. "You are one, a single soul. I sought only memories."

"Memories?"

"Of other times, other lives. Sometimes they linger."

"They linger?"

"Sometimes we are not washed clean by death," he told her. "Sometimes we remember feelings, visions and voices. Sometimes a face brings it back, sometimes a name."

Did she agree with that – to have lived before? But he said it with such certainty. She looked at him, searched him, but he remained as occult as ever, perhaps even darkening a little as he spoke of death. It was as though he coloured the air about him with his moods.

"What are you?" she asked at last. It was her only possible question. He looked back at her as if he fully understood what it was she was asking.

"What do you think I am?" he asked.

"I don't know," she said.

"But you have guesses," he returned. "Before, when you were attacked, I saw your thought. You saw me then as one of the powers pulled down into the world from on high. But I am not that. Like you, I was born. Like you, I am mortal."

"But the things you can do," she said. "You were in my mind. I felt you there."

He sighed, and his hands made a gesture she did not recognise. They came together, palm to palm, and then parted widely.

"Perhaps we should begin again," he said. "Perhaps we should start with our names, as when two strangers meet?" He paused a moment. "So here is mine," he offered. "At the time of naming, I was given the name Korfax."

His eyes intensified as he said this, flickering over her face, searching and seeking. And as he waited, so did she, waiting for recognition and tasting the name as it echoed through her mind. But there was nothing there, nothing at all.

She looked back at him. 'At the time of naming', he had said. Such an odd way of putting it, but it seemed to fit somehow. Now he was watching carefully. Did he want her to remember his name? She suddenly felt distrustful. He could get in her mind, so who knew what else he could do? She decided to stall.

"Just that? Korfax? Nothing else?"

Was that a glint of surprise she saw? Or was it a trick of the light? She could not tell. He masked himself far too well.

"No," he said. "Once I had both titles and family, but they are no more. Time and tragedy have swallowed them both."

His tone was curiously mild now, but she was not deceived, or so she thought. He wanted her recognition at the very least.

"Titles? What titles?" she asked.

He drew himself up slightly, straightening his shoulders. Was that pride she saw now? Again, she was not entirely certain.

"I had titles once, many titles," he told her. "I was born Noren, destined to become Enay. I achieved Geyad and then became Geyadril. Once I was honoured with the title of Meganza, but in my heart I was ever Faren Noren Korfax, my first title, my first name, the one gift that remained and never changed inside. My memory goes back there when it can."

It was almost as if he had just announced himself, as though his strange titles were momentous and that she would know them. But she did not. Noren? Enay? What words were they?

The light in his eyes intensified as they flicked across her face, but finding nothing to their satisfaction they quickly dimmed again. Was he disconcerted? Had she confounded him? But what could she say? She truly did not know the words.

"Perhaps I should offer a translation," he suggested. "To you, 'Faren Noren' might mean 'Heir to the house of following'."

His eyes darkened as she waited.

"You do not recognise them?"

"No," she said, but that was no longer entirely true. It was only now, now that she understood the meaning of the words, that a curious feeling began to grow inside. She felt a sense of time, of ages long gone, as if something born in the dim and shadowed past had been brought back into the light once more. Now she was the stranger here, not him, as though some elder world had supplanted her own, a world she had once known and whose rules she had since forgotten. Korfax inclined his head, his eyes steady as they held hers. Did he see her? Did he already know what she had only just seen?

"Well?" he said. "You have my name. Where I come from many would consider you to be in my debt. Simple courtesy requires that you give me yours, at the very least."

He gestured at the land, at the mountain.

"So tell me," he said. "How are you called in this place and time?"

In this place and time? There it was again, that sense of ages past, and with it a feeling of profound self-consciousness, only this time it seemed that she had suddenly been transported into a great hall filled with many hundreds, all of them gazing at her in expectant silence.

She thought of her name. That was difficult. She had a new name now. Should she give him the old or the new? She weighed the two in her mind and a strange question came to her. Who was she? Who was she really? Was everything about her a lie? The thought unsettled her so much that she almost didn't answer.

"Helen," she said at last, giving him the new.

He looked at her sharply for a moment as if he knew, or had guessed, even this.

"Just that?" he asked. "Helen? Nothing else?"

Was he mocking her now?

"No," she said, "my full name is Helen MacLeod."

He smiled, but she did not trust it.

"Helen MacLeod," he mused. "That has a music to it. What does it mean?"

Music? And what did he mean by that? This had become as strange a day as any she could ever remember. Abductions, pale statues wielding shafts of light, brutal slaughter and now the import of names! What had suddenly stepped into her life? She looked at him. He was waiting for his answer.

"Helen means 'The Bright One'," she answered.

"I like that," he told her. "That is a wonderful name to be given. But what of MacLeod, what of that?"

Helen felt even more self-conscious. What could she say? 'Mac' meant 'son of'. How could she tell him that?

"Well, MacLeod means 'of the family of Leod'," she offered, hoping that he would not see the shift of emphasis. He appeared not to notice.

"So I was right," he said. "We are closer than I had at first thought."

"Closer?"

"Leod is your house. Does it have a proud history?"

"I believe so, but you have never heard the name MacLeod before?"

"No."

"Then where do you come from?"

She regretted the question as soon as the words left her mouth. So stupid! She would have cursed herself for it, but he clearly did not think it stupid at all. He looked up at the sky for a moment and then looked back at her.

"Distant lands," he said, and Helen felt a sudden chill. How distant? How far had Korfax come to be here? Suddenly the world seemed to shrink about her, dwarfed by the power of two simple words. Distant lands!

She watched him again. The mask was still there, like a cloud about him keeping the world at bay, but now she understood this at least. That was how she lived her life. Like knew like. And with that understanding, and everything else she had seen, she finally saw in his depths the need to trust, the need to know that what he saw was true. He doubted, just as she did.

Seeing it all, and in a single glance, she decided that she would take the next step. It was time to put away her doubts, time to risk all on a single throw and see if what she had wondered all her life was true.

"You said earlier that I do not remember," she said.

"Yes, I said that," he answered.

"Well, that isn't quite true."

His eyes became piercing.

"Not true?"

It was like being pinned in place. It was difficult to continue in the face of such brightness, but she carried on as best she could.

"It's only that I have had these dreams," she told him, "and you were in them, or someone very like you."

Suddenly he was upon her, two hands clasping her shoulders. She gasped at their strength. Two eyes stared into hers and they were so piercingly bright that they almost blinded her.

"You have seen me in your dreams?"

She could only tell the truth before such a demand.

"Yes."

The sudden change in him was profound. For a moment the mask fell completely away and she saw the naked grief and a longing so deep that it was an utter agony to see. Korfax released her and sank to his knees, clasping his hands to his head.

"What is the matter? What did I say?" she asked.

He looked at her again, and now his eyes were full of tears.

"What did I say?" she pressed, her hand half moving to console him.

He smiled, tears coursing down his face.

"What did you say?" he answered. "Why, you said everything. You said everything."

Before she could stop him or back away he took her hand in his and drew her closer.

"Now I know what I must do," he told her. "I must reveal myself to you."

That startled her.

"What do you mean?"

Korfax gave her a careful look.

"This," he said, gesturing at himself, "is not how I am. The face, the form, these are as you have seen them. But I am not as you. I am other."

"I am not sure what that means," she told him, feigning uncertainty.

"But you are," he countered. "You understand far more than you are willing to admit. You already know that I wear a mask. You see the illusion well enough. I see it in you."

He bowed his head slightly.

"But you doubt yourself. I see that also, so let me explain. You see me much as you see the others that dwell here. But I am not as they. Though I have pulled a cloak of deception over every eye, I would lift it for you. Will you permit it? Would you see me as I truly am?"

She thought about his question. When had she crossed into the realms of the fabulous? She suddenly wondered whether she hadn't entered the mad place where all things were possible if one were lunatic enough to think them. But she had no choice now. She had confessed herself to him. She had already stepped over the threshold.

"Yes," she said at last, "I want to see you."

He stood up and smiled, and the smile was so gentle that she was almost overcome by it. How could he contain such brutal power when he could smile at her like that? But then, as if to confound her even in this, he darkened once more.

"You do understand that I am not one of you," he said, "that I come from another place, that I am not of this world?"

She shuddered. There it was, out in plain sight. Distant lands he had said and now she had the truth of it. Childish visions of alien forms swam through her mind, but she cast them aside. What foolishness was that? Hadn't he already said that the face and the form were the same?

"I still wish to see you," she said.

The darkness lifted and he smiled again, but then he closed his eyes and the mask fell away completely.

He grew and she stepped back from him. She was considered tall, but now he dwarfed her. He was huge.

He rippled and changed and his clothes fluttered about his body as though they had a life of their own. His featureless coat became a long dark cloak, heavy, full and voluptuous and of a fabric unknown to her. Underneath the cloak dark armour gleamed, incised with swirls of strange patterns, dark and glowing. Much of his attire seemed to be set with such markings, even his long boots, intricate forms running lengthways from the top to the bottom.

There was a sword over his back, a great long blade crossing from the left to the right. In the opposite direction there appeared to be a long shaft of crystal set in a sheath. The crystal was white and it gleamed with an inner light. She recognised it immediately. This was the implement he had used to kill her attackers.

She watched as his straight black hair grew until it lay almost halfway down his back, dark and luminous, the blackest of blacks. His skin changed colour also, becoming even lighter, if such a thing were possible, but now it took up a subtle hint of violet, the very palest of shades. Then she noticed his ears and put her hands to her mouth in shock.

His ears were longer, stronger than hers, but somehow more delicate also, each rising up from the sides of his head like two fleshy horns. But that was not what shook her. She felt a nervous laugh bubble up inside as she stared at their greatly elongated tips, each ending in a sharp point. They were long and pointed. Pointed? Of course they were! What else would they be? She had entered the realms of the fabulous after all.

Finally she looked back at his face again and watched his features refine themselves. If he had been beautiful before, now he was perilous.

She watched in fearful astonishment and also a strange joy, not quite believing it but wanting it to be so all the same. And when she looked into his eyes she knew that he was real, for they were clear now, the irises a deep, deep purple set in a sea of unbroken white, whilst at each centre an island of midnight sat. He was real, no phantom miracle this. He was flesh and blood.

"What are you?" she whispered, entranced. Korfax looked down at her and his eyes saddened.

"Perhaps the last of my kind," he told her.

She shivered at the naked power of his voice. No longer masked, it filled her up as though sound itself had been reinvented.

"The last?" she queried.

He looked away from her and out over the water.

"There are no more," he said. "Leastways, none that I would call such."

For a moment Helen could not breathe. She felt herself caught in a web, strangling in its threads, held unmoving by its subtle snare. How noble he looked, and how singular. He amazed her. She could see him, but still he was beyond her, her senses unequal to the task of describing him. Something was lost between perception and comprehension.

"What are you?" she repeated.

"I just told you," he said.

"But what are you? What do you call yourself?"

He looked at her for a moment as if he did not quite see her, his eyes distant, looking through her. Then he drew back and took a deep breath.

"I am an Ell," he said.

An Ell? What did that mean? What did it mean to be an Ell, and what did that mean to her? Suddenly she wondered if that meant she was, in some fashion, one as well. Was that the answer to the mystery that was her life?

"I am an Ell," he repeated. "My people were the Ell, the first ever to grace the Bright Heavens. None came before us. We were the first to walk under the light of the young stars, the first ever to name the substance of the world: earth, air, fire and water."

Here he looked about him, marking the mountain, the sky, the sun and the sea.

"We saw the first flowering of the heavens, the first stone, the first wind, the first flames, the first waters. And as we were the first, so we were the most potent. To us were given the greatest gifts, and those that have followed in our wake remain but pale imitations, never to know again the glory that went before. But the echoes of our thought still stir the ageing void."

He looked back at her.

"How do you think it is that we share so much. Your form, your gestures, your customs, even your very thoughts? You have heard our memories in your burgeoning minds, like all the others that have followed in our wake, and as you reach into the fire, so it reaches into you. You even name us in your legends, though we have never met until this moment. You repeat what has gone before, like a dim echo of what once was."

Disappointment filled her. That was not what she had hoped to hear at all. She was an echo? She did not want to be one. Echoes can never be free.

"What is it?" he asked. "You suddenly look sad. What did I say?"

"It's nothing," she answered, rubbing her shoulders. She wanted to go, to leave, to hide. "We should get off this bridge," she continued. "You will be seen."

He smiled.

"Do not be concerned," he told her. "No one here can see me unless I will it. But yes, let us return. At this time it is better to be inside than out. You have been in danger. You might be in danger again and I cannot allow that."

She stood in the doorway and watched as he went about her living room, looking, touching and smelling. It was fortunate that the house was as large as it was, the ceilings high, the rooms spacious, otherwise he would have had great difficulty moving anywhere at all. As it was he had to bend very low just to get through the doors.

Every so often, as he moved, she caught his scent, that elusive and delicate scent she had noticed before of strange and unknown flowers. But that was not all she noticed now. There was a light that was within him, or about him, that moved as he did, brightening or darkening according to his mood. She could not take her eyes from him; she had to watch, though he was far from easy to look at. With his armour and his sword, his great crystal staff and his unearthly beauty, he was an unsettling mixture of the barbarous and the divine.

He was clearly at ease in her house, despite his apparent unfamiliarity with everything he encountered. He tested it all, running his hands over this surface or that, feeling the fabric, touching wood and stone, taking books from her bookshelves and quickly, but delicately, turning the pages. He seemed able to recognise an object's purpose merely by looking at it, but his comprehension was a distant thing, as though he saw how such things could be, but not why they should.

Then her decorative chess set caught his attention and he went to it, kneeling down beside it and peering at it in rapt fascination. He studied it for a long while, not touching, just looking, and then he turned to her.

"What game is this?" he asked.

He knew it was a game? She wondered whether it was insight, or knowledge gained by more occult means. Had he asked the question to confirm what he already knew? She wondered whether she should be circumspect. Who knew what she might surrender if she admitted his assumption was correct? Was he testing the world about him, or was he testing her? Caught by indecision she suddenly noticed how he was looking at her. It was almost as if he was willing her to answer.

"It is called chess," she told him, almost without thinking. Then she felt a momentary dismay as though she had just betrayed herself. He, though, simply smiled back at her before carefully picking up a piece. It was a castle. He studied it for a moment and then looked back at her again.

"A tower?" he asked.

"A castle," she corrected him.

He picked up another piece.

"A sayer?"

"No, that is a bishop!"

She felt a stir of anger.

"You already knew the answer," she said. "You can see into my mind. Don't play with me!"

He put the piece back down again and frowned.

"I was not playing with you," he said. "I truly did not know your name for it. It is just that there is a game I once played which was like, yet unlike, this one. The pieces were set somewhat differently, but the concept struck me as familiar – two sides, two lands set against each other in stylised combat."

He turned to her.

"Nor was I looking into your mind; my people considered it impolite to do such a thing without asking."

"But you have done it before," she accused.

"I cannot help it if you are undisciplined," he told her. "You do not control yourself well."

He raised another piece from the board and looked at it sadly. How apposite, she thought.

"That is a pawn!" she snapped.

He frowned. Her growing anger seemed to spark the same in him.

"Pawn?" he questioned. "Not so! It is a warrior. It must be. And warriors are not 'pawns', not puppets, whatever else you might think. They act, they live, and they die of their own free will. Such a name is demeaning."

He fixed her with a black look that froze her where she stood. A sense of violence filled the air, as though the room, the whole house even, had suddenly been drenched in blood. She thought of her abductors and their brutal ending. Here it was again, his other side, the unmerciful dark.

"Fight a battle, any battle," he told her, his voice hardening by the moment, "and it will change the way you think of such things for ever."

He turned away, his expression almost a snarl.

"Such matters should never be taken lightly. All life is diminished by such callous disregard."

She drew back from him. In mere moments he had gone from beautiful to bestial. It was almost as if he coloured himself with his passions, changing even his physical form to accommodate them. Now he seemed all teeth and claws, like some great hunting beast. She had not noticed before, but his teeth were long and pointed, and his nails also were not nails at all, but claws, strong and sharp. It was an unsettling realisation. She had forgotten how dangerous he could be.

"I had not thought of it quite like that before," she said as she backed out through the door. For a moment he remained where he was, gazing out of the window, then he noticed what she was doing.

His speed was terrifying. As large as he was he was up and across the room in an instant, taking her hand and kneeling before she could do anything about it.

"I am sorry," he said. "I am sorry. I forget who you are and where I am. Let me make amends."

He looked at her, eyes sorrowful once more. Such pain there was in them, such contrition. She found herself breathing hard. Though he held her gently, she could not pull away. His huge hand almost swallowed hers whole. He was too strong, too absolute. She could not compete.

"You doubt me," he said.

"No! I mean yes! I mean..." she said, stumbling over her words as she fumbled for the truth.

"You doubt me!" he asserted. "You do not trust me. I understand. You have seen me slay, you have seen my anger, and to you this is a terrible thing."

He now held her with both hands. She could feel his touch, firm and gentle but trembling, as though he feared to break her.

"I want your trust," he continued. "I want to show you that this is not all that I am. You have seen powers you have never seen before. You see a form and a purpose beyond your experience. These are not what you are used to. I understand. I do not want you to see strangeness. I do not want you to know fear. Let me show you something better."

She didn't answer. She had no idea what she could say.

"Would you see something of the place I come from?" he asked.

That caught her. She found her voice again.

"What do you mean?"

"Would you go to a place of light, a place certain enough to banish all your doubts?"

"I still don't understand."

"I have the power to take you to my world, after a fashion."

"You can take me to your world?"

Competing forces swirled, fear and hope and everything in between.

"There is a way that you could make such a journey," he told her. "It would not be real, not in the sense that you and I are real, but once you are immersed in the illusion you would live in it as though it were."

Not real? Disappointment had her. She would have turned away, but the fire in his eyes would not let her.

"Would you be willing to make such a journey?"

Such need there was, or was it desire? But before she could answer he stood up and went back into the room, taking her with him. She had to follow. She had no choice.

At the centre of the room he released her and turned to the window. Then he gestured with his left hand as if beckoning to something outside. She frowned and was about to question him when the window, and then the entire wall, came apart. She gasped.

The wall of her house fell away from her as though down a well. Vague distances beckoned, and out of them advanced a great crystalline form. It grew and it grew until it all but filled the room, all but filled the house even. It was the simplest of shapes – four triangles, four sides – and, as if to demonstrate its symmetry, it gently rolled about each axis in turn. Then it stopped and waited, almost as though it had just asked a question. It hung in the air, patient and unmoving, but there was nothing that she could say.

Korfax came to her side and gestured at the great white crystal.

"Here lies the doorway to that which is no more. Would you enter?"

She had no answer, neither for him nor for the great crystal. All she could do was stare in astonishment. The crystal dwarfed her. It dwarfed Korfax even, if such a thing were possible. The crystal loomed before her like some ancient and primordial god.

"Would you enter?" Korfax asked for a second time.

But still she did not answer him. She had eyes only for the glorious light that fell from the great crystal; that and the music, for it seemed to her now that she heard a song, infinitely distant, infinitely far. The melody plucked at her. It appeared simple enough at first, so simple that she dared imagine that she understood what it said. But then it turned about itself, revealing subtleties she had not yet considered, and the more she listened, the more complex it became.

"Would you enter?" he asked once more.

The music withdrew and, with a start, she finally heard his offer. Now she understood. Or did she? The music had given her an answer. Or had it? She shook herself. She was being foolish. What was real? Everything was a cage in the end, an illusion of one kind or another. She could not escape; she could only leave one and enter the next. All she need do was choose.

So she turned to him and accepted, a simple nod of her head, and he smiled back at her as though she had given him the greatest of all gifts. He bowed to her and held out his hand. She took a deep breath and held out hers. Their hands joined, hers vanishing inside his, and as they both stepped into the substance of song everything she had ever known quietly disappeared, subsumed by an all-encompassing light.

2

A DREAM OF VANISHED GLORY

Zinzn-a Torz-hil-kormged
Toa-kohar Odtri-dr-pan
Mator-kas Pl-nak-piljo
Oth-loesa Pazen-muh-aa
Nio-basul Sasor-anord
Bia-hozaa Odmap-tolorn
Soi-kamaid Odom-maqaih

Out of the light they stepped and on to another world.

"I must warn you," said a voice at her shoulder, "and you must remember my warning at all times. What you see here is but a dream of what once was. This place no longer is."

It was Korfax. She heard him, everything that he said, but she could not agree. If this was a dream then it seemed more real to her now than her life ever had.

They stood upon the brow of a high green hill amidst a sparse grove of trees. A few scattered clouds hung motionless in the high vault and a scented breeze warmed them both with the gentlest of touches.

The sky was blue and the land was green, but that was all that was familiar. She saw everything, each and every shape, and felt everything, each and every sensation, but it was no longer enough for her to merely see or feel.

First of all, there were the trees.

It was as though she had never seen trees before, that all the others she had ever met were mere dreams themselves, uncertain copies for ever striving towards the paragons that now stood naked before her. She gazed at each in turn but found herself unable to say why she found them flawless. They were trees, that was all. They had root, branch, leaf and flower but, for some inexplicable reason, they surpassed everything she had ever known. A chord far down inside had been struck, and her depths knew that which her reason denied. Unadorned perfection. Forms grew here that could never grow in less hallowed places. She suddenly felt giddy.

She looked down at her feet and found even the grass beyond her experience.

Every single blade, each sword of green, was of consequence. She suddenly wished that she did not have to stand upon it at all.

There were flowers scattered here and there, petalled delicacies reflecting the light. She bent to them but could not look for long. Their simplicity, their beauty, was almost too much.

She turned to the distances to steady herself, but found only more of the same. Beyond the perfect flowers and the perfect trees lay perfect hills and perfect mountains. How was it that such simple forms and colours could so lift her up?

But there they were, rolling shoulders of green and great spires of rock striding across the land. With their roots sent deep into the ground and their proud heads sent far up into the sky, they breathed in the air.

She looked from mountain to tree and back again and suddenly realised what it was that she saw. The trees and the mountains, the hills and the grass, they were all the same, kith and kin, growing together, growing as they should. Nothing had ever marred or broken them. She looked upon a land without stain.

She turned to Korfax and found that even he had changed, the years lifting from his shoulders, the grief from his soul. For the moment he was young again, revelling in what she saw and seeing this place through her eyes, seeing it all as new.

More of the puzzle fell into place. Not only was this land unbroken, but everything around her was in the very first bloom of youth, unsullied and unwearied by time. It was true. She had come back to the beginning, as he had said that she would, to the very first world of all.

He took her hand in his and led her to the edge. She started. Either he had shrunk or she had grown, but now their proportions seemed far more equal.

"How?" she whispered, drawing back.

He smiled.

"Do not be concerned for now," he said. "Allow all things to be. You will understand soon enough."

Then he turned and pointed. Below, upon the plain, a beautiful city waited, tall and ethereal, strong yet delicate.

If she had been asked to describe it she would have failed in the task. As with everything else she had encountered, mere words were inadequate. Though she could see the towers and the walls, the streets and the squares, the gardens and the fountains, sharp and clear as if carved of light, there was so much more to the city than mere form and substance and colour. It unfurled itself before her like the rarest of blooms and it reared up from the plain below like the shapeliest mountain.

So she saw further, her comprehension increasing in leaps and bounds. Some unknown power had woven the city's many towers from the living rock itself. No violence had carved it; instead, it had been coaxed out of the pregnant earth as though obstinate stone could be persuaded to grow and flower. She felt a sudden and painful longing to dwell there and know all its ways for ever.

"Where is that?" she breathed at last. "Who lives there?"

Korfax sighed.

"No one now," he said. "You look upon a revenant. Though I have foresworn such conceits, the temptation is ever with me. It would be so easy to remain in the past and relive it as though it might shield you against all the times that are yet to come."

He turned to her and his eyes were dark.

"I did that once," he said. "I sank back into a reinvented past and wallowed for a time in forgetfulness. I let the real world, the one that mattered, burn in my ignorance. I would not do so again. Once is enough!"

Helen shook her head.

"But it all looks so real."

He darkened further.

"And so you fall into the trap," he murmured.

He took her face in a careful hand and turned her towards him.

"Hear me now and mark my words!" he warned. "This place no longer exists. You stand inside a well-made dream. Your senses can be fooled, but your soul cannot. My people understood this long ago, and they wisely prohibited it. Resurrect no true image. Perhaps your people understood this once, but you have since distracted yourselves and so forgotten it again. Thus you dare to peer back into that terrible abyss, not knowing what it is that you seek but yet seeking it anyway. You still have so far to go."

He drew back, folded his arms and then gave her a searching look.

"There are two ways that a people may understand the world into which they find themselves born. They can unmake it, pulling it apart and putting it back together again to see how it all works, or they can test its substance, taking the knowledge thus gained and pouring it back into the furnace of their thoughts, continuing on and on, generation to generation."

He frowned for a moment.

"Your people have taken this course – neither a good thing nor a bad, as it is just the way that you have been made. But there is another way. You once knew this path also, though you scorn it now."

Helen frowned at the remark.

"What do you mean?" she asked.

He smiled.

"You know what it is. You call it by many names, but one seems particularly apt: magic!"

She turned full about and looked again at everything.

"Magic?"

"Yes, you call it magic and you scorn it. Even the very name implies falsehood to your understanding. I can see it in you, there in your eyes. But what you see here is the truth. The Ell had the great gift. They perceived the word of The Creator, the unfolding act of creation itself. Unlike you we did not need to tear the world down in order to understand it; we were born already knowing. That which was in us became that which was without, and that which was without became that which was within. The simple truth that reveals all."

Helen felt incredulous.

"Then I am seeing magic?"

Korfax laughed and Helen was immediately taken aback. It was the first time she had heard him laugh and, in spite of herself, she smiled because the sound was so clean, so honest. Korfax turned to her and smiled gratefully.

"No," he said. "Not that. You do not see that kind of lie. You have not yet understood. You do not look upon a work of magic; you look upon an act of creation, that truest of acts that comes only from the many ways of creation itself, the will made manifest under Heaven's gaze. We of the Ell were born with our eyes open, as your people are not. You are the distracted. You mistrust what you see. You have taken the long path and submitted to the mask. You have so far to go before you can cross the divide."

"I don't understand," she said, and his eyes brightened as though ignited by some inner fire.

"Is the truth so impenetrable?" he asked. "Here, before you, is the word of The Creator. By seeing the word we open ourselves up to the divine fire within, that fire given to all that lives. From what is within we see how to reshape creation, and by reshaping creation we reshape ourselves. What you see as divided is not divided at all. We act within that unity, becoming creation itself. We are no longer bound by the blind movement of unthinking forces; we stand above them."

She had a sudden glimpse of what he meant but rejected it immediately.

"I still don't understand," she said.

"Yes, you do," he disagreed, "but you reject it. Too long have you been immersed in the waters of a world that would deny such truths – not the belief but the fact. To say a word that would raise up a mountain, another that would subdue time, another that would destroy an entire world? To you that is impossible. In your world such things cannot be. But that is why I have brought you here, so that you can remember it once more and know a better truth."

Korfax turned about.

"Now let us depart this place," he said.

He beckoned to the trees and a beast emerged from within the shadows. She watched carefully and thought that she understood, but when it had fully emerged into the light she knew that she still had so much further to go.

At first she had taken it for a horse, larger, mightier, but still as well-proportioned as the finest of thoroughbreds. Black, all black, it raised its noble head as it came, its laughing eyes proud. But when it saw Korfax it bowed to him, and then she really saw it. She clasped her hands to her mouth in shock, for from its forehead, from the very centre, a single great horn was thrust, a great and curving horn of black, both solid and strong.

"A unicorn?" she finally gasped.

Korfax turned to her with eyebrows raised.

"No!" he admonished. "This is no mythical beast of yours, for this is an ormn: air of earth given flesh. Here is the exact likeness of one I once rode to a ruinous battle, the finest ever to race under the sky. You now look upon his shade, held in perpetuity against that time when he might yet come to the Bright Heavens once more. My father named him Enastul in regret, but I called him Enastul in joy."

He stroked the great flanks for a moment, an unreadable look in his eyes. Then he turned to her again.

"Can you ride?" he asked.

She could only shake her head. Her tongue was tied by the revelation. Korfax smiled.

"Well, that can easily be remedied," he said. "And have no fear, you will know how to do it soon enough. Besides, no ormn would ever let its rider fall. That is not their way."

He gestured again to the pregnant darkness under the trees and glanced back at her.

"Here comes your steed now," he said.

Another ormn appeared, more delicate perhaps, smaller maybe, but just as magnificent with its large dark eyes and its shining coat of white.

"This one is Gahlus," he told her. "I give her to you, though perhaps I should say that I return her."

Korfax stared at Helen with a look in his eyes, as though expecting the name to mean something, but Helen could say nothing. She had missed his intent entirely. She had eyes only for Gahlus. When had anyone given her a unicorn before?

They raced down from the hills, their steeds all but flying over the green. It was as Korfax had said. When he had helped her mount Gahlus she had felt trepidation, but then, suddenly, there it was within her. She could ride.

Now they crossed the great plain, devouring the distances. Her hair streamed behind her, so fast did Gahlus go. Though she held on tightly, she did not need to, because she could ride as though she had ridden all her life. It was both a surprise and a delight to her, like the return of a long-lost memory. Besides, Gahlus was both smooth and still beneath her, almost as if it was the land itself that moved.

As they went, Korfax named the hills around them, and with each name that he uttered, the world to which she had come sank further inside, claiming her a little more with each passing moment.

They came to the city and slowed their pace. At the gates were guards, as still as the stone they served. But as Korfax and Helen approached there was a flash of eyes and the sentries suddenly moved. They came forward and took the visitors' steeds, bowing. Korfax bowed back but Helen could do nothing. She remained spellbound by the ride. She had flown.

For a moment she did not notice, but then the guards caught her attention at last. They were cloaked and caparisoned in red but had argent armour, polished to a brilliance that made it almost glow. They had lances and swords and shields, all treated the same, but underneath they were Ell. She could not help it. She stared.

They were like Korfax, yet unlike him. She wondered if they would speak, but they merely bowed to her and waited for her to dismount.

Korfax came to her side and offered up his hand. She took it and found herself back upon the ground. She looked behind her with longing as the guards took her steed away. Would she ever do that again?

Korfax led her into the city.

"Where is this?" she asked.

"You walk upon what was once called Lon-Gohed," he answered, "the largest of the southernmost lands that lay off the coast of Lon-Elah, the one great land that stretched more than halfway around Uriel, my world that was. Here now is the city of Gar-Asan, last as it was amongst the first, and beyond us lie the eastern edges of the Leein Gellad. North of here, far away, almost on the other side of the world, is the place where I spent my childhood. On the northernmost tip of Lon-Elah is the Lee Izirakal, and on a low hill at its northern end Umadya Losq was built, my home that was, the place where I was born."

She turned to him.

"Those words," she said, "Lon-Gohed, Lon-Elah, Gar-Asan, are they from your language?"

"Yes, they are. You are hearing Logahithell, a language few know, for few have ever heard it. But it is the first speech of all that was ever spoken in the Bright Heavens."

"Can you let me hear some more?"

Korfax smiled a little and looked down.

"Let things unfold as they should," he said. "Do not rush them. There is time yet for such pleasures."

They walked hand in hand through the streets of Gar-Asan, he leading, she following whilst staring all about her with eyes now able to accept anything at all.

She watched the inhabitants as they went by, watched them walk the cities many ways, going about their business as if everything was as it should be. All were tall and graceful, moving with a singular ease as they travelled through the world they inhabited. They were pale of skin and dark of hair, but she could never mistake them for her own kind, as they were far too unearthly and far, far too beautiful. No one she had ever met could walk, gesture or stand like that. She saw one now, simply standing, standing by a wall and looking, nothing more and nothing less. But even that was almost too much. No one from her world possessed such poise, such composure.

She looked away, looked inside. When had she stepped into the ring? She thought of spirits and of wilder powers that dwelt deep in the ancient forests or slept under hills or yet danced on moonlit nights about the standing stones. She thought of being stolen away, carried upon the wings of night to dwell in the places of dream far beyond all mortal knowledge. But now she was here, walking through the dream of the Ell, and it felt as if she had become the dream instead.

They came to a fountain in a courtyard, a gentle spray of water from a stone-carved flower down into a leaf-shaped bowl. She listened to the music for a moment, but then it struck her. The fountain, the courtyard even, showed no sign of wear. Everything looked clean and fresh, as though it had been made only yesterday. She turned to Korfax.

"You said that this place was old, but it looks almost new."

"If you look closely enough you will discover signs of wear," he told her. "The dream we walk through is, at times, almost cruel in its detail."

He paused for a moment as if that was not what he had meant to say at all, but then he gestured at the fountain.

"When we built we used the hardest stone that we could, stone strong enough to withstand the ravages of time for many long ages. But we also strengthened it when it began to fail, rejuvenating it, holding back time itself with our arts. Most of the buildings you see here were made and remade again, by will and by lore. We followed the way of the world in all our endeavours, so if we built a tower like a mountain, should not that tower last as long? We mirrored the world about us, we did not wage war upon it."

He paused again, as if something had just occurred to him. He turned to her.

"Would you go to a banquet?" he asked.

"A banquet?" she asked in reply. That was not what she had expected.

"Yes, a banquet," he said. "And in your honour, no less."

"But why?"

"Because I ask it?"

"No, that is not what I meant. What I asked was, what I meant was, why should it be in my honour?"

"Because you are here again?"

That caught her.

"And who am I?" she asked.

He took a deep breath. Here it came, she thought.

"You are Obelison," he said, taking the plunge. He looked back at her. What did she see? Trepidation? Fear? Need? Desire?

She tasted the name. Obelison. She felt her centre shift as she repeated it. Something awoke, something below thought and memory. What had he touched in her now?

"That was her name, wasn't it?" she asked.

"Yes," he answered.

"Is that how you think of me?"

"Yes."

"Why?"

"Because you are her."

"But I don't remember. Who was she?"

"My love," he said, and he took a long shuddering breath. There were tears in his eyes again. She watched them and did not know what to think.

"Is that how you think of me?"

He bowed his head.

"I dare not presume. Not again."

Then he looked away and gestured ahead, breaking the moment.

"Come," he announced. "The feast awaits."

They came to the door of the tallest tower of all, three spires made one, the Umadya Lusell as Korfax named it. He held out his left hand to the guards that stood there, fingers lightly curled, the hand at a slight angle as though he cupped something. The guards gestured in return, with a sweep of their left hands towards the door. He stepped up to the door and touched a gleaming stone set into the wall beside it. A distant chiming sound came and went.

The door opened and a tall and most beautiful Ell stepped up to the threshold. She looked older than Korfax, much, much older, and outlined by the distant light from within she became the very image of elder memory. Helen saw further again, further than she had yet seen before. It was as Korfax had said. The Ell, all of them, communed with forces beyond her understanding. Whether in the dark or the light, they stood upon thresholds she had not even imagined were there. They occupied places denied all others and burned with fires that would consume less potent vessels.

The Ell in the doorway bowed to them both and held up her right hand, palm forward, fingers spread.

"Zak od zamran," she said.

Helen had never heard anything like it. It was not so much the words themselves, but the way that they were said. The syllables thrummed in the air, like music, like an invocation, demanding an answer. She felt compelled to speak, but did not know what to say. How could she? She turned to Korfax and found him smiling at her. He understood. He turned back to the Ell that waited in the doorway and answered the challenge, his voice transformed by the words, or the words transforming his voice.

"Zirnoqvan Eaijo," he said, holding up his left hand in turn, palm inward and fingers closed.

The Ell smiled and stepped aside, gesturing with a sweep of her arm that they should both enter.

"Pirqaan hoeihte," she said.

33

"Od pirqaan hoauhtekr," he answered back. Then he took Helen gently by the hand and led her over the threshold.

"Those hand gestures, those words," she whispered. "What do they mean?"

He stopped and turned to her.

"Question nothing yet," he told her quietly, "let it all unfold about you. As with everything else here, you will understand it when you need to. I will not let you fall."

He led her in silence through great corridors, climbing wide stairs and crossing many an empty hall, before they came to it at last, the source of the light. It was almost as if it shone through the stone itself, growing and deepening as they approached. Ahead of them was a tall doorway, and beyond it was movement and sound and beauty.

There was a vast hall of stone, but the stone was neither hard nor cold. Instead it was warm and living and filled with light. Pillars grew here like trees, their wide trunks sinking coiled roots down into the floor whilst their luminous branches spread out across the ceiling. Each pillar was set with many living flowers whose varied scents drifted this way and that on the whims of the air. Lights were set amongst the higher branches, caught deep in the vaulted ceiling, flames of red and orange, yellow and green, blue, indigo and violet, captive stars caught in their orbits, the heavens held in abeyance.

Helen thought herself beneath a vast forest canopy at night. The illusion was all but complete and she stared upwards, caught in wonder and in rapture. She would have stayed there for a long while, staring upwards, had she not then noticed the others that had also been summoned to the feast, wandering where they would amongst the pillars.

There were ladies, simply clad in modest robes and gowns, but each seemed tall beyond measure and radiant in their beauty. There were tall lords, armoured or robed, beautiful also, though to Helen's eyes their beauty was of another nature entirely. Watching them she felt like a child again, grown small, caught up in a play of her elders.

She turned to Korfax, her head full of questions, but they fled her the moment she saw what he had become.

Now he looked like a great lord in truth, mighty and proud, bright crystal upon his brow, a great dark cloak of purple swirling about armour that was suddenly brilliant. He returned her gaze and smiled, and then he gestured that she look at herself as well.

Helen gasped and stepped back. Though she had no idea how it had happened, her clothes had suddenly vanished. Instead she was arrayed in paleness, a long gown of a soft and flowing fabric she could not name. It suddenly felt as if she was naked, so lightly did it sit, but yet it flowed from her neck to her feet like the never-ending fall of many waters.

Korfax bowed to her and then took her hand again, leading her gracefully to an annex where there was a tall mirror waiting in solitary splendour. He led her up to it and then stepped aside.

She looked at her reflection and saw another standing in her place. It was like her, this image, for there was her face, her well-remembered face, but as for the rest? Nothing remained. She stared at the transformation in utter astonishment.

On her brow sat a crystal filled with a bright and steady flame, though how it had got there she had no idea. She had not felt it arrive, nor the circlet that contained it. Then she realised that she was taller, that her skin had changed colour, that her hair was suddenly longer, almost down to her waist, that her ears were now long also and that they were pointed. She reached up to touch them.

"How..?" she began, turning away from the mirror to look at Korfax again, but then something moved behind her, flicking gently back and forth between her legs as if to announce its presence as well. Her eyes widened in shock.

She possessed a tail. She suddenly possessed a small tail. She carefully placed a hand behind her and felt it even as it tucked itself neatly away again. She had suddenly acquired another limb. How strange was that?

"I have a tail!" she hissed, almost an accusation. "What have you done to me?"

His expression became the most careful she had yet seen on his face.

"I have made you one of the Ell," he answered, as if that explained everything.

She stared back at him, as if to say it clearly did not.

"I am sorry," he offered. "I should have warned you. All I can say is that we all possess tails, though they are seldom mentioned. They are considered... intimate."

She watched his face. How uncomfortable he looked now. It was such an unexpected expression that she was a moment recognising it. But there was contrition also, as when he had killed her attackers. She saw what it was. He feared he had made another such mistake. But it wasn't like that. She moved to reassure him, though she still felt far from reassured herself.

"I am sorry," she said. "It came as a bit of a shock, that was all."

He stepped closer and bowed his head.

"I am sorry, too. I keep forgetting that you are not born to this. You would know these things otherwise."

His expression was almost one of pleading now.

"Please," he asked, "be one with the Ell tonight? Please, let it all be as it should?"

There was a pause.

"Even the tail?" he continued.

She closed her eyes. It was almost too much, or was it? Something calmed her even as the delirium of her fantasy rolled in to overwhelm her. She felt the brink recede as a semblance of calm returned.

"Even the tail!" she acquiesced at last.

He smiled again, relief flooding him, and he bowed deeply to her.

"Then let the shadows live once more," he said. "Do nothing but watch, listen, know and feel. Allow a world that once was to be again, if only for a little while."

She heard it in his voice. Regret! Such pain, such sorrow. She found an echo in herself and turned away in embarrassment, even as she understood.

Beauty and regret – that was it! She had come to the dreaming lands of beauty and regret. She had seen legend made flesh, light given substance and had herself been transformed into something fabulous. She had been named for an ancient love and had returned to the place where it had all begun, where innocence yet held sway and the words of creation were written across the land with naked fire. How could she not trust this? So she let him lead her away from the mirror and on to the banquet. *"Let it all happen,"* she thought. *"Let everything be."*

First came the dances, dances she thought that she did not know, only to discover that her feet and her body had already remembered them for her. Like the others that swirled about and around, she found herself threading an intricate pattern of delight across the floor. Hands were lightly clasped and parted again as their owners turned and turned about. Many beautiful faces smiled at her in turn as each partner shared a brief moment by her side, but she found herself ever looking for Korfax, waiting for each quick touch of his hands with a longing she would never have believed possible before this hour.

Between the dances there were delicacies, all placed before her like so many offerings – meats and fruits and pastries in abundance, none that she could identify, but yet whose tastes she dared believe she actually knew.

The pastries melted even as they touched her lips, and the delicate sweetmeats within enticed her tongue. Nothing could she name, no flavour, no texture, but neither was it altogether strange either. Something inside her decided that all was as it should be, even though she had never tasted such delights before in all her life.

Wines there were also, served in tall crystal and falling upon the tongue like a gentle ecstasy. But her senses were not dulled; instead, they were exalted, and now she heard the voices about her as a music, a music she dared imagine she could understand. She dined upon pleasure, drank light from crystal and no longer stood upon the world at all, but instead danced above it.

After the dances she was led to an exquisitely carved seat, not beside Korfax, but opposite. His place was set at the other end of the hall. Instead she was to sit between her hosts, a tall lady and her even taller lord. When she was seated the lady spoke to her, strange words falling from her lips like a tapestry of sound whilst her lord looked on with smiling eyes. Helen listened, entranced by the cadences and rhythms until she suddenly realised, almost with a shock, that she understood what was being said to her. And stranger yet, she was able to answer in return.

It came to her then like a reflex, like a long remembered habit, the language of the Ell, filling her up in that very instant, all the rules and all the subtleties.

So she answered, speaking words she had never spoken before, yet understanding exactly what it was that she said. Her hosts did not ask where she came from, or even who she was; rather, it was as though they already knew everything about her, treating her as if she had been away for a very long time and had now returned to her own.

It was at the end, when all had drunk their fill and eaten what they would and danced with whom they pleased, that Helen found herself seated beside Korfax at last.

"How do I know what I know?" she asked him.

"Because knowledge of it was returned to you in this place," he replied.

"But how?"

"Let us just say that you have been allowed to remember it."

"Will I remember it always?"

"Yes," he told her. "Consider it your due. Consider it one of many that I shall return to you."

His arm encompassed her and she sank against him. She no longer doubted anything at all.

Another stepped into the light in the midst of the company, an Ell she had not seen before. This one stood quietly for a moment, looking this way and that, meeting the eyes of all that waited. She bowed to the lord and the lady of the feast and offered up that which she held. It looked something very much like a harp, but it was not. The lord bowed his head just so, and the musician held her instrument close. Then she passed her hands across it and a strange music, like a gentle wind through trees or the slow fall of waves against a shore, filled the air. She let the music speak for itself for a moment, and then she joined it with her voice and sang.

Helen did not know the song, and yet, like everything else, she did. Like a well-loved melody it spoke to her and conjured visions for her amazement.

She saw far cities, riders entering their gates or leaving them. She saw battles between the darkness and the light, each clash of fury heralded with a fanfare of horns, each aftermath sombre with the call of a solitary pipe. She saw mighty heroes, lords and princes both, matching each other with sword and lance upon the field of combat, and she saw the dream of what had been and found herself glad simply to know it at all.

At the end, when the guests began to depart, Korfax led her to a door and turned to her.

"Do you wish to see the night?" he asked.

"The night?"

"Then you will understand why that which you call the universe, we once called Madraxalus instead, the Bright Heavens."

Korfax opened the door and guided her outside. Before her stretched a great lawn set about with tall trees and scented flowers. She walked up to each in turn and gazed at their beauty. He watched her and smiled, letting her take her time. And when she was done he gestured that she look up. So she did, and then all but staggered in astonishment.

Across the black sky were strung stars of every conceivable colour. Above her was a riot of light, a chaos without any apparent order but beautiful beyond compare.

Some of the stars lay in long twisting bands whilst others came together in great groups, some scattered randomly, others gathered in loose circles. Wrapped around many were great cloudy folds, fabulous curtains of fire draped carelessly across the sky. One such concourse, low upon the horizon, even formed a fiery spiral. It was like the spill from some fabulous jewel box. The stars above her were larger and more brilliant than ever she had imagined they could be, and Helen felt tears fall from her eyes. It was a release, a final release from all the wonders she had endured. Korfax came to her side and gently brushed one of her tears aside. He offered her another of his sad smiles.

"As I told you before," he said, "I do not often come here. For me, the memories are almost too painful. But with you beside me, I find that I can bear it all again."

She looked back at him for a moment, before looking up again at the spectacle above. She sighed and wiped away the last tear even as it began its journey downwards. Night on Uriel made all the other nights she had ever known in her life seem dim and paltry by comparison.

As she let her eyes wander this way and that, she noticed a faint luminosity growing above the distant hills where they had first stood. Helen watched in fascination as the limb of a moon rose slowly up into the sky. Larger than she was used to, it seemed unblemished also, a smoother orb perhaps, born not of violence but instead carefully placed in the sky by some god's hand, and as it rose higher, so she saw its colour! It was green, a green globe of spun crystal glittering in the firmament and wrapped around with the naked substance of its birthing. Gently it rode the upper oceans like some great and wonderful vessel of dreams.

She turned to Korfax.

"And this is what you saw every night?" she asked.

"No," he said, "not every night. There were clouds, of course, rains and snows falling from them as they should. But a night of clear skies? Those were always the best."

He pointed to a large group of stars that fell more or less into a rounded group wrapped about by a gauzy nebulosity of faded red. The stars themselves were many shades, some brighter, some darker, but all were crimson, and the largest and brightest looked down at them from the exact centre like an eye. Korfax announced them as if they were triumphant.

"Behold!" he said. "'The Vovin', herald of the rising year!"

She looked back at him.

"You had constellations?"

He smiled.

"Of course! What people now alive or long dead have not at one time or another looked up to the heavens and filled it with their fancies. So here we have 'The Vovin', whilst above it is 'The Mother', then 'The Urn', 'The Tower', 'The Dancer' and then 'The Lamp'."

Having swept his finger across the sky he was now pointing to the horizon, to a great coil of stars that seemed more brilliant than all the others.

"And there lies 'The Gyre'," he said. "The Creator's mark upon the heavens, reminding us all that we are still mortal, no matter how mighty we may think we are become."

She felt herself caught by the idea that they had so much in common. She pointed back to the first constellation he had named.

"I know all the other names," she said, "but what is a Vovin?"

Korfax laughed quietly and the sound of it sent a shiver up her spine. There was a play of light in his eyes now, flickering like a flame but not with any secret humour. He was deadly serious.

"What is a Vovin, you ask? I think the answer to that question might surprise you. You have already ridden an ormn, mistaking it for something from your own myths and legends. You have the language of the Ell inside you now, so can you not guess what a Vovin might be?"

He was right, she could feel the word inside her, but there was no image to go with it. She shook her head. What did it describe? Mythical creatures of all shapes and sizes fell through her awareness, but which one would it be? She had no idea.

"I cannot guess," she said. He raised an eyebrow.

"Can you not? But there are many stories of such a beast, even upon your world."

He smiled and looked up at the sky again.

"Once you believed in a creature that breathed fire, a great and potent monster that prowled through your dreams and your fantasies, your myths and your legends, most fabulous of all – and most deadly."

She widened her eyes.

"Dragons?" she asked. "Do you mean dragons?"

"No," he said. "That is not what I meant. You have not gone far enough. You still judge everything by what you think you know of your own world, but you should not. As with everything else, we of the Ell knew the archetype of your dim dreams. For we knew the Vovin, and they were no mere legend."

He looked at her for a moment, gauging her capacity for wonder perhaps.

"Shall I show you?" he offered, and then, without waiting for an answer, he raised his hand and beckoned to the moon. Immediately, almost as if it had been dragged into the heavens by his finger, a distant form reared up, and Helen stared at the remote silhouette in utter astonishment.

Though it was far, far away, a mere speck of black against a brilliant backdrop, she already understood that it was huge. There was a sense of ponderous immensity in the slow beat of its wings, a sense of vast power held in check. Then, without a sound, it turned upon itself and fell straight towards them both.

Its speed amazed her – that something so big could be so quick! In moments it had reached them, passing low over their heads, claws glinting and wings outstretched. The fury of its passage had her diving to the ground, but Korfax stopped her, holding her firmly against him.

"Do not be alarmed," he said. "It will not hurt you."

His expression changed and became sad again.

"It cannot, not here."

Then he turned her about and gestured. Like a miracle, the Vovin was already at rest behind them, eyeing them both with an imperious lift of its head. Appalled and astonished, Helen stared up at the Vovin, and the Vovin stared back down at her as if she was something it might devour.

She tried to see it, tried to encompass it with her senses, but she found the task altogether beyond her. To see a dragon painted, modelled from clay or pigment, was one thing, but to meet one in the flesh? That was something else entirely.

First there was its scent, a rich odour that rode the air about it, something hot and powerful. She could not place it, for it was unlike anything that she had ever tasted before, but neither would she ever forget it again. Images and impressions came to her as though she had already known them: of fire, of mastery, of power and an indomitable and savage will. Across the landscape of her mind volcanoes were suddenly flung, vast enough to encompass whole worlds, and she found herself flying carelessly between each boiling cauldron, feeling the hot wind across her body like a scourge as she hunted the broken land below for unwary prey.

She blinked and was back before the Vovin again. But now she could hear it, the deep rumble within, the furnace of its life. For the moment the furnace slept, but dare awaken it and the rising would be both swift and deadly. She had a sudden impression of fire as an element – solid, a shaft of flame ejected from the very fount of destruction itself. She could even feel it, the heat of it, enough to undo her completely, to burn her body and even her spirit to ash, whilst that which did the burning looked on with terrible dispassion and dreamed of endings.

And finally, at the last, she could see it; its long head crowned with longer horns, its long jaws filled to the brim with curving teeth. She ran her gaze across its neck and body and watched the slow, impatient coiling of the great bladed tail. With its taloned limbs folded beneath it and its great wings arched up and over its back like a throne, it stared down at her like a lord.

This was no mere beast, she realised, but the element of fire made flesh. The Vovin was absolute. Here was that which knew exactly what it was, the length and the breadth and the height of what it was. Here, waiting before her with immortal certainty, was the master of all hunts. It brooked no rivals. It had none.

Helen turned to Korfax again. She felt herself falling, but he remained to catch her even now. His hands held her and he smiled his most gentle smile yet.

"It is so beautiful," she breathed, like an admission.

Korfax bowed in agreement.

"So give him a name," he urged. "He is yours. I give him to you. A gift."

Helen looked back at the Vovin in disbelief, startled back from the brink.

"Mine?" she asked.

"Yes," he said. "Whenever you are here, so will he be. Give him a name. He is waiting."

She could not think. What was a good name for a dragon? She thought of all the stories she had ever read and the names of all the dragons that she had ever heard of, both the good and the evil. Smaug? Kalessin? Ancalagon? Yevaud? She looked at the Vovin's dark flanks and knew what her choice would be. She turned to face Korfax again.

"Then I name him Ancalagon," she said.

Korfax smiled with approval.

"That is a good-sounding name. I like it. But what does it mean?"

Helen looked at him.

"I don't know that it means anything. It is from a story I once read."

Korfax bowed his head.

"Then so be it."

He gave her a curious look.

"Names come from the soul, after all."

He turned to the Vovin and pointed.

"Ancalagon you are!" he told it. "Do not forget it!"

The Vovin threw back its head in silent assent, before launching itself back up into the sky. In moments it was gone, first a shadow against the moon, and then nothing.

Korfax turned to her after the Vovin was gone.

"Now it is our turn," he said.

"Our turn?"

"To leave."

"Must we?"

The look of pain that crossed his face astonished her. He knelt before her.

"I would like nothing more than for us to stay," he said. "But it cannot be so. The world, the real world, is broken. That is our purpose. Under our hands it must be made whole again. To deny purpose is to deny ourselves."

She did not want to go, and neither did he. She trusted that, more than anything that had gone before. Cage or not, illusion or not, she now trusted everything she had seen and experienced.

Light encompassed them both and they stepped back into the world. Her first impression was how drab it all was, how untidy, how dirty. She had stepped from the pure to the corrupted and she felt like crying again, but this time with bitter disappointment. She wanted to go back to the fantasy; she wanted it with all her heart.

She looked down at herself. She was no longer an Ell. Her body had diminished. She was plain Helen MacLeod again, except that in her mind something else now sat: memories, knowledge and an understanding that had not been there before.

He watched her, and the look upon his face was most eloquent.

"I understand," he said. He reached out and took her hand. Once more her hand vanished inside his. Neither spoke for long moments, but finally he broke the silence.

"Now that you have seen something of my world, I should tell you the rest," he said. "What you have seen is something of the good times, but we were not always at peace. Sometimes we disagreed with each other, violently."

He paused. She watched him, watched how his gaze turned inward.

"There was a time when my people were divided by their beliefs. On one side were those that believed their lore was supreme, whilst on the other were those that believed it was not."

"Lore?" she asked.

"Yes, but it was not just a matter of knowledge – this was a way of life. At the heart of it lay a discipline known as the Namad Mahorelah, and like all such lores it could be used for both good and ill. Unfortunately, those that employed it tended to use it for ill."

She tasted the words. Namad she could work out – it meant something like lore or knowledge – but what of Mahorelah? She had no idea what that word meant at all.

"Mahorelah?" she asked. "What does that mean?"

He looked up for a moment in puzzlement.

"I am sorry, I was forgetting. Even though you now have my language within you, you still cannot hold it completely. You would need to change the way that you are and see the world about you in entirely different colours."

He held her with his gaze.

"Namad Mahorelah would be something like 'the Lore of the Abyss' to you, though that does not fully describe how intimate was the involvement. You have no words in your language adequate to the task. As I said before, you are not born to this, so you see creation in a way we of the Ell never did."

He pointed downwards.

"This place, your world, the Bright Heavens, is not all that there is. Below us, elsewhere, lie other realms. They have never been fully explored and none know them in their entirety, but they are as similar to each other as they are different from the Bright Heavens."

"I am not sure I understand," she said.

"Think of them as abysses, lesser than the Bright Heavens perhaps but older, much older, and based upon entirely different principles. They exist elsewhere, occupying other spaces than the one the Bright Heavens exist in, separated from it by almost unbreachable walls. We live on this side of the wall, and the denizens of the Mahorelah live on the other."

"There are living things there?"

"Living, yes, but not life as you know it. The creatures that dwell in the Mahorelah are born of more chaotic processes than are found here. Many exist in a state of continual flux, their shapes and purposes fluid. In their own realms they are safe enough, quiescent and serene. But take them from the places that they know and they become the very touch of chaos."

She thought about that.

"We have legends that sound uncomfortably close to what you are describing," she said.

Korfax bowed his head.

"I know that you do. You call them underworlds, pits, the abode of demons, and you are not so far from the truth. We called them the same. But we, the Ell, knew them for what they really were. And some of us were their masters."

Helen frowned.

"Masters?"

Korfax looked out of the window for a moment and then back at her. There was a gleam in his eyes now, a dangerous gleam.

"An adept of the Namad Mahorelah, one of the Argedith..." he checked himself and smiled. "I am sorry, you have words, 'sorcerer' and 'sorceress'. Think of the Argedith in those terms."

He paused again, clearly troubled by something.

"But do not be misled, either," he continued. "The Argedith were more than mere workers of wonders, as you might consider them. They could do in an instant what it would take one of your people a lifetime to learn. But such lore comes at a price: the temptation of power. It is insidious, growing within until it consumes you and you are no longer the master but the slave."

He looked at her.

"The best of them were mighty indeed. They knew where their summons reached, and why. They could send their thoughts beyond the confines of the world and through the walls that kept the realms apart. By that very act they momentarily joined what was separated, making inconstant holes in the substance that divided the deeps from the heavens. And from whatever abyss they had access to, they could summon forces, elements, creatures, demons or gods and make them do their will."

"Gods?"

"There is no other word in your language that I know for such beings, so I used the best that I could. What you call God, the Ell called The Creator. But you use the word in so many ways. There are tales I have seen inside you, myths and legends, where you talk of gods many times many. So I use the word as you would use it. And the gods of the abyss are more like the beings that fill your ancient myths than your conception of The Creator. But the Ell knew them by another name, the one they gave themselves. They called themselves the Ashar."

"And these 'Ashar' can be summoned?"

Korfax darkened.

"Yes, they can," he said, "though you have no idea what such an act entails. But even here there are rules governing such things. The more powerful the summoner, the more powerful the entity that can be summoned. But overreach your aim and that which you summon might tear out your heart, or your soul."

Though he had denied it, this really did sound like magic.

"They can be summoned here?" she asked. "But how? It is hard to believe!"

Korfax smiled.

"After all you have seen?" he said, gently chiding her disbelief. "Believe it, for it is most certainly true. The abysses of the Mahorelah exist. Energy can be stolen from them, just as the inhabitants can, and then put to use. In the earliest days, those days that are still remembered by the Ell, many a city was built with the aid of adepts of the Namad Mahorelah."

The smile remained, but there was no humour in his eyes.

"There were other powers of course, powers based entirely upon natural talents. There were the powers of the mind, the ability to see another's heart or even to breach the walls of time, but everything changed when we rediscovered the Namad Dar."

Korfax bowed his head as though he had just offered up a terrible confession.

"And what is the Namad Dar?" she asked.

He was no longer smiling.

"Of all the many lores that we knew, none was more perilous or more glorious than the Namad Dar. With it, an entire world was subdued and unified. With it, the Ell sailed upon the ocean of the heavens itself, the first ever to do so. And with it they committed the ultimate folly – they tried to touch The Creator."

Korfax took a deep breath and shuddered.

"The Namad Dar is astonishing, for with it we learned to make a substance that would echo our very wills."

Korfax drew out his white crystal stave from its sheath as if it was an answer in itself.

"You have seen something of what this can do, but only the tiniest fraction. This is a kabadar," he announced. "From this all but imperishable crystal I can call up forces, forces that I can order and employ in the service of my will."

He lowered the stave and looked at her.

"Let me demonstrate so that you do not mistake me. Come!"

He led her out of the house.

"Where are we going?"

"You will see."

He took her to the moor. They walked for a long while until they were completely hidden from view. There were no roads or houses in sight. He turned to her and bowed slightly, a brief tilt of the head before he stamped the heel of his stave into the ground.

The stave glowed with a yellow light and there was a sound like that of a deep bell. Then the ground shook. Helen could feel tremors passing to and fro beneath her feet. The land about her danced, all of it, from where she stood to as far as she could see. The hills, the pools, all flexed as if suddenly adrift upon a stormy sea. It was as though the world had suddenly decided to shake itself apart. She dropped to her knees, she could not stay upright, but when she turned to Korfax she found that he had not moved at all. He appeared rooted to the spot, he and the earth a single thing. He smiled back at her, lifted his stave again and the tremors ceased. Helen stared about her in amazement. Everything was as quiet as it had ever been. She could stand again.

"What did you just do?" she asked carefully.

But Korfax did not answer. Instead he held his stave aloft. It glowed blue and there was a high-pitched sound, a rising whistle that was almost a shriek. Energies gathered about them both and Helen felt a wind rise up. She looked at him for a moment, but he was not looking at her, he was looking over her shoulder. She turned about and stared in utter disbelief. Bearing down on them both was a whirlwind.

It was huge, a great whirling mass of air that towered into the sky, growling hungrily as it span about its hidden centre. But it stopped before Korfax's outstretched stave and waited like some obedient ogre, grumbling all the while as loose soil and detritus flew up from the ground beneath. Then, after a long moment, Korfax withdrew his stave and the whirlwind subsided, thinning and failing before vanishing completely. Twigs, leaves, clods of earth and everything else it had collected up into itself fell back to the ground again.

Helen had only a moment in which to catch her breath before Korfax raised his stave for a third time, now pointing it at the sky. It hummed, a low sound, angry, like the deep hum of a swarm, and red filled it. Lightning flew from its tip, shattering the day and scorching the heavens. The clouds fled and the land about them shivered under the inconstant brilliance. Thunder rolled about them, peel after peel after peel. She bent over and covered her ears. What a sound. It thundered through her, shaking her, shaking her bones. She could not move.

Then it ceased. Echoes of violence crossed the land until all was as silent as before. She looked up again but realised that Korfax was not done yet. He had one last thing to show her. He turned away from the land and pointed his stave at the sea.

Helen turned with him and watched what he did. There was a chiming sound, a ripple of falling notes, and his stave filled from the inside with a green light. Then the far sea rose up as though pushed from below by some monster of the deep. Soon a great wave swayed in the air, a wall of fish and water. Mighty it grew, towering into the sky and blotting out the light. It dwarfed the land over which it now leaned like some immense fist and Helen stared up at it, dumbfounded. Korfax let it subside again, slowly, carefully, leaving the sea as it was before. He turned to her.

"Do not be afraid," he said. "I would never let anything harm you, ever."

He gestured to a large rock. They went to it and sat down on its wide, flat surface.

"But I had to show you," he continued. "I had to let you know."

She thought about what she had just witnessed and what she had been told. Seeing his power gave his words even more weight; if only she could understand everything that he had said. Though he had given her much, there were still gaps in her mind, knowledge she did not have because she had not experienced it for herself.

"What you have just seen," he told her, "is the Namad Dar made manifest. With it, earth, air, fire and water were ours to command. Energy, freely brought through the doorway in each crystal, was ours to do with as we pleased. We had found the ultimate power, how to split the nothingness from which all creation was birthed. We had found how to reorder creation itself. And in our arrogance we came to believe, in truth, that we had become The Creator's Sword."

"The Creator's Sword?" she asked.

"The act of creation itself," he told her, "slicing through the nothingness, creating everything. It is the endless act, Matheoi, the unfolding word. All things owe their existence to it: matter, energy, light, dark. The sword creates all things, even good and evil, for all things are made known by their opposite. Contention – the action of opposing forces – is the way of the world."

Korfax held up his stave and looked at it with a complex expression.

"Even this pure crystal is of such a nature. It grew out of need, the need for opposition. The Argedith, those who employed the Namad Mahorelah, had to be opposed."

"Why?"

"As I said, they used their lore for ill. They desired too much, and in the end only dominion would do. They became convinced that their way was the only way. Those who would not agree were forced to fight or to bow. There was war and Lon-Elah was soaked in blood for many, many years. Victory was a long time coming, but it came in the end. The world was cleansed."

"Cleansed?"

"You have had it here, though you know it by other names. Call it what you will, cleansing or crusade, as the name does not matter, only the deed. For the victorious it became a necessity, the only way to bring peace. For the vanquished, those that survived it, it became an abomination."

Helen watched his face. Korfax looked angry now, full of scorn for the past.

"Our lives became ruled by dogma," he said. "And for a while we were a blind people, but not all heresy vanished into the night. Indeed, heresy was our saviour, but only for the fortunate few, and only for a little while."

He turned to her.

"I know, I was there."

"During the war?"

"Which one? There have been many."

"The one in which sorcery was defeated."

"No," he said, "I was not present for that. It happened long before I was born. When I was young the world had already been at peace for over six thousand years. I grew up in a world of plenty and order, a world united under the rule of the Velukor. Some called it the long wait, others the blessed pause, for we knew that the next war would come someday. So we remained in the posture of vigilance and waited."

She frowned.

"Now I really don't understand," she said. "You were waiting for the next war? But if the world was at peace...?"

Her voice trailed away in incomprehension and he smiled at her, but it was a sad smile. He reached out to touch her cheek, the gentlest of touches.

"You are such an innocent," he said. "Do not believe that what happens in the past remains there, because it is not so. No act of violence exists in solitude; there are always consequences. Though they may take an age of the world, the seeds of vengeance will always sprout where you least expect them. And that is what we of the Ell understood. Though defeated, we knew that the malice of the Mahorelah would have its day in some far-flung time. And there were prophecies. Karmaraa, once said to be the greatest of us, called Logah Qahn, called Audroh Eithar, said that evil would return and that we had to be ready. So we prepared ourselves for that eventuality. Though there had not been an enemy in all that time, the Ell kept themselves ready for the war yet to come. Blades had to be as sharp as they were when Karmaraa himself rode out to battle, and minds had to be just as vigilant, for Karmaraa demanded that the Ell never cease their watch. And who would dare go against the word of the first Velukor, the chosen of The Creator?"

She shook her head.

"But if this all happened such a long time ago, if there were no more wars, what happened to your people?"

"I did not say there were no more wars. I have not told you everything yet."

He looked out over the moor.

"Karmaraa foresaw it. He said that a war would come, and the seers agreed. He was the only one to oppose the darkness in the beginning. He was the only one that all others would listen to."

He turned back to her.

"Karmaraa was a prince of the west, of a people called the Korith Zadakal. For ages past they had contention with others, the Iabeiorith, who lived in the North. These people had a prince also, Sondehna, and just as Karmaraa was said to be the greatest of us, Sondehna was said to be the worst. The story is long and sad and it ended with the death of Sondehna and the beginning of a terrible war. The peoples of the south and the east allied themselves with the west to defeat the Iabeiorith, but even so the war itself lasted almost a thousand years."

She could not imagine it.

"A thousand years?" she questioned.

"A long time," he answered, "for the Iabeiorith were strong and proud, and even without their prince they were mighty. They used the Namad Mahorelah in terrible ways. Think of it. They could call up armies of demons to do their will. If the west had not employed the Namad Dar, the north would have been victorious, despite their losses."

She thought she detected a certain bitterness in his voice. What was this? She had listened spellbound to names she did not know, deeds she had not witnessed, lore she had only the barest conception of, but here was a suggestion of something else, something deeper, some other, subtler play.

He looked at her.

"I said that when I was born there had been peace for over six thousand years, but that does not mean that there were no more wars. The peace of Karmaraa finally came to an end whilst I was still a child, and it marked the beginning of the last and greatest war of all. It is the reason I am here and the reason you are here."

"The reason?"

Korfax looked back at his stave. There was a strange look on his face now, something she had not seen there before. She could not fathom it.

"I have already told you that no act of violence exists in solitude. Many believed that the powers of the abyss were behind the troubles that came to our world, but I discovered a different tale. Something else caused the fracture, a deeper evil that waited in the background, biding its time."

He leaned back and closed his eyes.

"The Ell had another enemy, a greater enemy, though they knew it not until the end. We fought its servants, thinking we still opposed the malice of the abyss, but we did not. Only at the end did we realise what we were set against. You see, our enemy was not just our enemy. It is the enemy of The Creator, of all creation. And it is this foe, and its servants, that I have striven with ever since, across time and across space."

"The enemy of The Creator?" she asked.

He sat up straighter and his eyes shone.

"I know what is in your mind," he said. "I see your doubt. Your world is full of it – doubt and disbelief. But answer me this. What was it that first moved across the face of the deep?" He gestured at the land. "And if it is proof you desire then look around you. What miracle was it that made all of this? The void was divided so that this, all of this, could be. But what divided the void?"

He looked darkly back at her.

"You have not seen what I have seen. If I have learned anything in this life, it is that no force exists without opposition. For every love there is a hate, for every light there is a shadow, for every creator there is also a destroyer."

He pointed at the sky as though it proved what he said.

"The Ell saw The Creator as a sword, slicing through the nothingness, the non-existent void, cleaving it in two and creating all worlds. But to create light one must also create darkness."

He gestured at himself.

"So it is no surprise that we, the created, do both good and evil. This is the way of all things, everything made known by its opposite. Even the very act of creation itself cannot escape that most fundamental law, for the nothingness from which creation is drawn opposes such an act. And we know this because it has come here to the Bright Heavens, breaking its very own commandments by clothing itself in matter and form. It has taken on the substance of creation in order to destroy it, fighting the heavens with its own weapons. Inevitably, it took a name for itself, and a long time ago I learned what that was."

He waited a moment, watching carefully. He was testing her again, she could see it.

"It is the name of evil. Once you have heard it, then you will know."

Even the day seemed darker now, and Helen felt a rising chill. She should have expected this. No good without evil, no God without a Devil. It was not something she had ever thought about seriously until now. Korfax had done this. He had forced the issue merely by his presence. But this was his world, not hers. She still stood upon the borders, or so she thought, peering over the edge into a world of powers, of absolutes and certainties. She had seen beauty, astonishing beauty, but did she really want to see its counterpart?

She looked at Korfax. To him she was his ancient love, and in the name of that love she knew that he would do anything for her. She had already seen something of how far he was prepared to go, and it made her wonder how much further it would take him. If she crossed over to stand at his side, if she fully entered his world, would she ever find her way back again? Would she even want to? He had taken her to a place of light and beauty, shown her a world without stain. Yes, he was the answer to the longing she had known all her life, but he also had a darkness inside him, a fearful darkness. He could kill without hesitation or mercy, if he so desired.

He was waiting, waiting to tell her the name, but if she heard it, this name of evil, where would it take her? Would his battle become hers? What was she to do?

"Would you hear it?" he asked. "Would you have certainty?"

Helen fought down her fear. Perhaps she was mistaken. Perhaps she was making too much of this. After all, what harm could there be in a mere word? But Korfax had already spoken of the power of such things, and he was a creature of power. Dare she doubt this?

"Surely a name is just a name?" she replied. But even as she said the words she could hear herself. How false she sounded. Korfax looked at her for a moment as if he could not quite believe what she had just said.

"You ask that after all you have seen?" he questioned. "You still doubt?"

He drew a deep breath.

"You must not, you cannot doubt. You must have certainty, you must know."

He turned to her.

"I shall prove it to you. And you shall see," he said.

He leaned closer.

"Qorazon," he said, and the word filled her world.

She fell inwards. A door opened in her mind and she fell through it, and for a brief moment, the very briefest, she was suspended over an abyss, an abyss so vast and deep she knew that it had no ending. She shrank to a mote, the smallest of the small, caught between one moment and the next, caught in the nothing.

Now the abyss was not just below her, it was all around. Impaled upon the substance of nothing she no longer knew up from down. She would have fallen, tumbling end over end, but something caught hold of her and pulled her upwards. The vision disappeared and she found herself in Korfax's arms.

"You were about to fall. I caught you," he told her.

She pulled herself away from him.

"What did you just do?" she said.

"I gave you the name," he said. "What did you see?"

She looked at him. What had he done to her?

"Nothingness," she said. "I saw nothingness."

"Yes!" he smiled grimly. "That is it. Now do you understand?"

She backed away from him. Her world suddenly seemed inordinately fragile, and she could feel its walls crumbling away. She did not want to lose the world, just the cage she was in, but here was Korfax intent on pulling everything down, brick by brick, stone by stone, showing her what lay beyond, whether she wanted to see it or not.

Korfax stayed where he was, watching her with eyes that were now almost black.

"You are frightened?" he asked. "But this is the truth. Would you remain in ignorance all your life? Would you deny what is? You did not deny the beauty that I showed you, as you wanted to linger, to live in the dream of the Ell, but you must understand that beauty in itself cannot stand alone. With nothing to compare it to, it ceases to have meaning. That is immutable. To see one side, you must also see the other. You may run from such things, but in the end you cannot hide. The truth will seek you out."

"What do you mean I cannot hide?" she asked. "What have you done? Is this some sort of trap?"

He stood up, suddenly alarmed.

"No, not that! Never that!"

He bowed his head.

"I just wanted you to know. I wanted you to see. I wanted you to understand and perhaps to remember."

He looked up again, his eyes pleading with her.

"Would you go through your life with a veil pulled over your sight? Or would you know the truth?"

"Your truth?"

"No, this is the way things are."

He gestured with his hands, spreading them wide.

"I am sorry. Fear and pain are the last things that I want for you. Now that I have found you once more I only want to preserve you, to know that you are safe. What happened earlier – you were already in danger here. Those others that attacked you? What if I had not been present? What was their intent?"

He leaned forward.

"You have known of me all your life, in your dreams and in your heart. Now we have met and you have seen a little more. All I ask now is that you see the rest. How can you judge what I say unless you see the truth of it with your own eyes? How can you judge me unless you know my tale?"

He turned away for a moment, suddenly tense. Then he looked back at her again, peering over his shoulder as though beckoning her to follow. And there was an odd expression on his face. He looked almost eager now.

"So we come to the heart of it," he said. "Will you know me? Will you know my story, live it, so that you understand?"

She suddenly saw that everything else had been leading up to this point. This was the question he had wanted to ask all along. She thought long and hard. This was what he wanted. But what of her? What did she want?

She already knew the answer, though she did not want to admit it. He had already seen it in her. Despite her fears, she still wanted a release. She wanted to escape this life and to find a place where she finally belonged.

"Yes," she said at last. "You are right, I want that, you know that I do."

His expression went beyond her. It was as if the last chain had been broken and her simple statement had been the hammer. He came to her and knelt, head bowed. It was a long moment before he spoke again.

"Then I thank you for this gift," he said. "I will show you what no other has ever seen since the very beginning. You have experienced the dream, so now let me show you how it was when I was young, when the birthing fires of the Bright Heavens still raged across the sky and the beauty of the first of all worlds had not yet passed beyond."

Back in her house he took out a single black crystal and held it up before her. She looked at it. The crystal had smooth sides and rounded edges, as though it had been washed in a river for a very long time, but she could tell that it was no ordinary stone. There was a light in its black heart, a dim glimmer that seemed to wax and wane as though some imprisoned flame flickered deep inside.

Korfax laid it in the palm of one hand before touching it, just so, with the other. The crystal erupted into life.

The dim light at its heart now boiled outwards, spinning about some unseen axis. Helen stared at the sudden fires, caught by the play of light. Marvels had her in their grasp again. Korfax watched for a moment and then placed his hand under her chin, raising her face up so that she had no choice but to meet his gaze.

"Do not be distracted now," he told her. "This is of the utmost seriousness."

He gestured at the black and burning stone.

"This is a mapadar," he continued. "You might call it a stone of stories, you might call it a stone of memories, but it is much, much more than that. In here is the memory of my life, my story, my time upon Uriel. In here is the truth."

He looked sadly at the stone for a moment before looking back at her again.

"This is the past. This happened. It was. And if ever anything can truly be said to have been, then you will see it now, if you allow yourself to do so."

He drew back a little.

"Imagine if you will that you hold in your hand a book of stories. Imagine that when you turn to the first page the words rise up about you and become the story itself, that the words become you and you become the words. Suddenly you find yourself there, with the players as they stride across their landscapes, hearing their thoughts, their words, feeling their passions, becoming them and partaking of their lives, their being, their truth."

As he spoke, so the light mounted up in his eyes, until they were almost too bright to look upon at all.

"Here," he said, "naked and unashamed, are the Ell as I knew them. Through the mapadar you will see, for you will live their lives and know their truths. You will know their souls as if you were them."

The stone also grew brighter, its inner fire waxing between his fingers until it became blinding.

"I am in here," he announced behind the brilliance, "and here you will see me at last, body and mind, heart and soul. Accept this stone and you will know me from my heights to my depths, from my innocence all the way to my guilt."

Then Korfax withdrew the light, hiding it away within an enclosing fist. He held up his other hand in warning, his face suddenly grim. The change was frightening; Helen had never seen such darkness in a face before.

"But I must warn you," Korfax said. "There is great evil here also, the worst that you will ever encounter in all your days. I cannot help that. It is the way of the world. For every beautiful thing there exists something equally hideous. Nothing exists without its opposite."

He drew back his hand and revealed the stone once more.

"Yes, there are terrors here, but there is also joy and love in equal measure. So here is my gift to you, held in my hand, loyalty and betrayal, war and peace, love and hatred. But I cannot force you to see this. It is for you to decide alone. It is your choice."

Helen did not move. Choice? There was no choice. No choice remained to her now at all. She had been tantalised by shadows and illusions, lured by possibilities she had only ever imagined in her dreams, and then only dimly. What could she say? She had longed for such truths ever since she could remember, and that longing subdued the very real terror she also felt. The only possible answer was yes.

So she bowed her head and Korfax touched the stone to her brow, and as soon as it touched her she fell, down and down again, falling away, falling completely. And all the while she thought to herself that here it was, her deepest desire at last, that her true life would step out of the past and claim her.

3

THE TOWER

Go-saldor Kar-nor-ialaa
Lap-pimith Do-gei-agi
Nimin-las Kua-jil-tolef
Fal-zadaid Odkon-tasorn
Moz-lonjes Av-belisong
Bao-inho Lai-in-uthar
Kri-do-zid Ino-tello

She dwelt within infinite night. There was nothing that she could see, or hear, or smell, or feel or taste – even time seemed meaningless. She simply was.

After an age or a moment, she could not tell which, she felt a dim stirring, the lightest of touches. But it did not diminish; instead it grew and it grew until it swelled to the movement of immensities, and, like the opening of a great eye, intolerable brilliance enveloped her.

It was too bright, too much all at once, and she cowered from it, but there was nowhere to go. It was everywhere. As blind in the light as in the dark, it took her long moments before she realised that the brilliance had begun to lessen. Structure and form coalesced about her, and she found herself deep within a vastness that her sight could not contain.

She fell through an inferno, ponderous fires and slow eruptions, and passed like a mote into realms of filigree effulgence. Through caverns of light and burning clouds she tumbled, through tempest and rage and endless flame, until all parted before her and she found herself in gentler regions.

Here were stars, many stars, all still swathed in the furies that had birthed them. She passed them by, touching this one or that briefly with her thought until one, mightier than the rest, reared up to bar her way.

Alone, proudly alone, it poured its magnificence out into the night. She understood. Here was the very first, the archetype of all that were to follow. She felt herself caught by it, summoned to it as though it alone was the reason for everything, the very centre of creation.

As she fell inwards she found a shadow blocking her path, the limb of a mighty world, clouds of indigo slowly circling. Over it she went, and over its dark rings, wheels within wheels, dim reflections ever turning. Briefly its sombre mass pulled at her, then, like a leaden weight dropped into the ocean depths, it fell away again, back down into the void.

Another world loomed, banded in blue, even larger than the first. Storms raged across it, great eruptions of light and serpentine coils of clouds. For a moment it threatened her with its wrath, but then it, too, fell away, its storms fading back into the outer dark.

The star drew her in. Huge it grew, a brilliant disc of violet hurling the energies of its burning heart ever outwards. She flew over its surface, through flame and storm, under great bridges of light and over turbulent seas of fire. Around it she went like a world herself, before rising again from the violence and unbearable heat.

Now she came upon a red world, so close to its star that it boiled. Fires glowed and molten rock flowed as its surfaces flexed, made and remade again by the first forge of heaven. Over its rage she went and then on again, back out into the night.

Another world, veiled in deep orange, emerged from the darkness. Serene it floated by, hidden and mysterious, a thing of mists and vapours. Unknown it came to her, and unknown it left her again, turning slowly as it vanished in her wake.

Her speed increased and she barely had time to see the next, a brighter world, smaller, faster, flashing in the light as it span its quicksilver way. A brief glimpse she had of a labyrinth of yellow stone, before it, too, was lost to sight.

And so she came to it at last, her final destination, a world of many colours wrapped about by white cloud and circled by a green moon.

Over the moon she went, as barren as the world below was verdant. But it was not dead, for its unsullied surface smiled with a gentle spirit upon its companion, a ripple of pale greens. Its surface rolled under her and she found herself traversing a vast uncut jewel.

Now the world of many colours drew her in, and she knew that it was all true. Here it was, the first cradle of life, the very well-head of all the stories that were yet to come.

Down she went, dropping through blue air and white cloud to a green ocean, a huge ocean, its ever-moving surface glittering in the light. Over it she went, towards a dark horizon where a storm sat, a wall of fury that roared across the water. She crossed its boundaries and pierced its heart.

She came upon an eye, a calm circle about which the storm turned. Down below her lay the ocean again, but it was no longer empty. A maelstrom span right at the very centre and she could see no limit to its depths. But even as she came to it she went on again, moving back out through the storm and away from the mystery of the great gyre.

A vast land rushed up to meet her, one great continent that spanned more than half the world. Over proud mountains and fertile valleys she glided, over forests that stretched from one horizon to another, over great rolling hills around which rivers wound their questing way, all held in the hand of the ocean like a gift for the air.

There were cities here, great cities carved from crystal or grown from stone, many spires flung proudly at the sky – tall, ethereal, dreams caught upon a single moment, each of a beauty and a form unique unto itself. She wanted to linger but now had only scant moments left to her in which to mark them, for her purpose was quickening and she could feel it pulling her on. So she went her way, leaving everything behind her like a dimly remembered dream.

Her speed decreased. Up ahead lay another great mass of clouds, curling themselves across her path and blocking out the light from above. Though not as potent as that which circled the great gyre, this storm seemed more ominous.

The rain caught her as she flew under the clouds and she felt the water wash through, dissolving her, each droplet taking part of her down with it as it fell onto the hills below. She was merging with the world about her, her story and its story becoming one and the same. What was strange became familiar and what was extraordinary became commonplace. She was both reinvented and exalted, and she finally became one with the Ell.

She knew this place now, seeing the land about her, knowing the rain, knowing the storm. She wanted to wait so that she could take her time, experience this place as it should be experienced and remember what she had apparently forgotten, but the story had her in its ineluctable grasp and would not let her go. Her last sight was of a single tower rushing up towards her, before she came apart completely and drowned in the tale.

Umadya Losq! With its tall tower and its high encircling walls it dominated the summit of Lee Losq, the furthest hill, most northerly of all the heights of Lukalaa.

The tower itself was a single spar of furrowed stone, four sides facing the four directions. The passing ages had blunted its contours somewhat, gentling the sharpness of its youth, so that now it looked more like the trunk of an ancient tree rather than a tower of stone, a great and tapering trunk, still clinging to the hilltop with its old and obdurate roots.

Low about the main tower clustered lesser cousins, the houses and the out buildings. Four square and tipped with smaller spires at each corner, they held firmly to the roots from which they had seemingly sprung, all the way out to the high wall itself. And with its sloping sides curving up into the sky and passing gently down into the ground below, the high wall encircled everything like a comfort, a great bowl of flowering stone, the last flower of the north.

Beyond the tower and to the north the land dropped away to rippling moorland and scattered pools before rearing up again as cliffs, final bastions set against the boundless ocean beyond.

To the west was a wide and flat valley through which a meandering river wound its uninvolved way northwards, meeting at last with a great tongue of water thrust deep inland. Beyond the valley other hills strode across the land in ordered rank, straining towards the north, marching ever on towards the ocean.

To the south reared the seven great peaks of Lee Izirakal, larger by far than Lee Losq. Five lay in a line, a long and wandering ridge set about with many crags and cliffs, whilst the others glowered to the west, their weathered faces bent over the lands below.

To the east was a lake set about with tall and shapely trees, whilst further on a labyrinth of smaller pools and low hills stretched all the way to the far horizon, a frozen sea of soil and stone.

Over it all grey clouds rushed like some interminable herd, for ever spitting their cargo of rain at the ground. The distances vanished in a deepening gloom, and even the warm yellow lights set in the high windows were touched by it, shadowed by the darkening world without.

In the highest room she sat, thin and spare and ancient. Mortality had her in its grasp and the look in her eyes said that she knew it all too well.

She was the naming seer for all the lands between Faor Raxamith and Umadya Losq, between Tohus and Dialsen, a position she had honoured nearly all her long life, performing her duty with both diligence and humility, but she had never encountered anything like this before.

A child lay in blankets upon the floor, as new to the world as she was old, new-born and naked, the sweat of his birth still lingering in the air about him.

Between them both lay four square boards, each incised with the requisite rows and the requisite columns, forty-nine by forty-nine. Here were the seven gates and the four elements – no more and certainly no less. Here, within their exactness, were gathered the proper words, taken from the corners of the world and set out as a mirror to the movements in the heavens above.

Out there, beyond the world, the conjunction moved on, not yet complete. It was the rarest of all, a sword, when all the children of Rafarel came together in a single line. For that was the way of it, above and below, the order of creation, the one reflected in the other.

Seven times had she entered the trance, seven times casting the markers upon the boards in the complex pattern of naming, and seven times the very same name had come back to her, leering up from the stone like a curse.

What evil power had invested this place she could not tell, but she was certain that it was here, holding both her and the child in its vile fist. Though she could neither see nor feel it, she had proof enough. It lay in the name, the dark name that ever came back to her from the trance.

She was caught, huddled about failing flames, for she could not leave this place until a name had been given. Terrible consequences would result if she did, for names were sacred, names were purpose, and to be nameless was to be cursed for all time.

She turned her head from side to side, hunting this way and that with quick movements of her eyes, looking for the footprints of her foe, a shadow, a glimmer, a sense even, but nothing revealed itself, in neither the stone nor the air.

Even after all these long ages of sleep she was certain she would have known it if the Mahorelah had stirred once more. She would have known it, deep inside, that sense of immanence, of lurking immensity. It had been a long time indeed since she had held an angadar in her hand, one imbued with the essence of the abyss, but she had never forgotten the sensation, not in all the years since. Such a frightening and terrible feeling it was, the giddiness of infinite deeps and the dim sense of an almost limitless malevolence. But, colour it how she might, the Mahorelah was not here this night. Something was, though, reaching out over its unknown thresholds, powerful enough to corrupt the most necessary of all rituals.

She looked down. What could she tell the mother? What could she tell the father? They were the best of the north, the best of all, most worthy of honour and service. She remembered naming the father himself, more than one hundred and fifty years ago, and she remembered when he had returned with his young and beautiful bride from the west. She had known them nearly all their lives, and when it had become common knowledge that there would be a naming, that a son was to be born in the time of the sword, many had gone far out of their way to tell her what a wonderful day it would be and what a great honour it was. So how could she reveal this? What could she say to them and to all the others that now waited below to hear her words?

She could have howled, she could have wrung her hands in supplication, she could have rent her clothes, but she did not. Instead she looked at the child nestling in his soft blankets and let rare tears fill her eyes. Two fell together, precious reflections against the parched desert of her face. This one was such an innocent, innocent of everything. How could she stain such innocent flesh with so terrible a name?

She found herself longing to pick him up and cradle him in her arms, desiring to feel his new life like a comfort against her ancient heart, wanting to wrap him about so that she could shield him from whatever it was that lurked nearby, but she did not. Rather, she picked up the markers and threw them at the boards in impotent rage. They bounced and rattled for a moment, and then they came to a stop.

Their movement caught her – the slow tumble, edge over edge, the flash of polished surfaces as they settled like purposeful stone. She stared at the pattern revealed. The markers, by sheer chance, had fallen as if they had been cast from a naming trance. There was even a name there, a good name, a very good name indeed. She stared at the markers and the temptation had her. Dare she, she wondered. The thought coiled seductively in her mind. Perhaps she could use that name instead. But even as she considered it, she stopped where she was. Shame had her. This was false, and not only was it false, it was profane.

She held her hands to her mouth and suddenly dared not even to breathe. Was that it? Was that the real intent here? Was she the one that was being tempted? Now it would be her that corrupted the ritual, not the other, that other that waited within its unseen shadows. She stared all around the room, expecting to surprise an eager grin or a brief flash of satisfied eyes, but she caught nothing unawares.

She looked at the name again. It had not come from the trance, had not been called up by the deepest layers of her being, had not come from her immersion in that holy and primordial water whence all names have their being. Instead it had been born of her rage, born of her frustration and her corruption. By even considering such a name she was betraying everything that she had ever held to be sacred. Her vows of service, her oaths, her acts – all would be rendered meaningless by such a choice. Names did not come by chance, they were chosen! But what of that other, that name from the trance? What did her service mean in the face of that?

She looked at the false name again. It was so good, so true, so rare. Dare she take it? Dare she not? Perhaps she was wrong. Perhaps The Creator had spoken to her with the simplest of answers. As she had been denied the river, was she not now being shown another possibility? Her shoulders dropped and she finally surrendered. She would give the second name to the child and accept the consequences herself. Let the sacrifice be hers, not the child's, and as a penance she would let this be her very last act of naming ever. It was for The Creator to judge her now. The giving of this name was an act of mercy. Let that other, that lie, let it fall back into the depths from which it had so untimely risen. Not until creation had fulfilled itself should that name ever rise again, and then only when the last judgement was at hand.

She reluctantly gathered up her boards and her markers and put them in their wrappings. Then she lifted the child up and held him to her, holding him tight, her thin arms like walls about him. He was asleep now, his lips gently open and his face innocent of any thought at all. She looked at the tiny face and suddenly considered it the most beautiful that she had ever seen.

Tears fell from her eyes again, but she brushed them aside as quickly as they came. It was long past time, long past time indeed, so she gathered up the last vestiges of her authority and carried her charge from the room in a rustle of robes.

Down the narrow stairs she went, down and down, past the fifth level and then on to the great bedroom where they were all gathered, waiting for her, waiting for her words. The mother still lay upon the birthing bed and the father still stood beside her as he had at the birth, still holding her hand. Both looked up with glowing eyes as she entered, both ready to hear their son's name. Around them, and to either side, stood the rest of the household, all eager for the same. They were not a large company, but they filled the air about them with enough passion to make them seem a multitude. She could feel it now, a swirl of love like a caress, an abiding love, a shared love, a love that mirrored the trust and the peace that lay upon the child's face, that self-same face she now held carefully against her breast.

She swallowed hard and handed the child back to his mother, who smiled gently in return before gazing in wonder at her little one's face. The father stood straighter now, quiet pride in his eyes as he stared down at her.

The moment had arrived. They awaited the name, and if she did not speak it soon they would begin to wonder. She cleared her throat.

"Your son has been named," she declared, her voice as steady as a rock. "Into the river I have journeyed and out again, bearing the symbol of his spirit. For he is named Korfax, and he is of the Farenith."

There were gasps of surprise and approval. Hands were clasped and there were many sudden tears of joy. It was done. The name was good indeed, almost too good perhaps, but she did not falter yet. She dared not.

"May his life be long," she continued. "May his spirit be untroubled and may his time amongst us be of great worth. And may he drink of the light of The Creator for all the days that are his."

Many hands were held up in thanks, but the lie stuck in her throat. She looked down and took a deep breath. She must be strong now, stronger than she had ever been before in all her life. Too much depended on this. But when she looked up again, for an instant, for the merest instant, she saw the mother frown. So she covered the falsehood with a mental wall that even the mightiest of the Exentaser would have trouble seeing through, and just to be sure she bowed low to the father, looking away from the mother entirely. Strict formality informed her as she raised her head again and she became stone at last, impervious and unreadable.

"Enay, this naming has tired me greatly. I fear this will be my last naming ever under the Bright Heavens, for the river was unwilling to let me depart this night. I will not impose upon your hospitality, nor upon your joy. Instead, I will leave. The ride back to my home will help settle my thoughts."

They tried to dissuade her, but she was adamant. They said that she must, at the very least, attend the birthing feast, but she refused all the same, even though she risked causing great offence. They were not offended though; rather, she could see that they were all somewhat saddened by it, for their judgements were already written upon their faces. She was old, they thought, eldest of all, and the old had always been stubborn, their lives rooted in a soil of experience so deep that the young could never know it. No one suspected, not even the mother; they were merely concerned, that was all. But even after such an insight nothing they could say would make her relent.

The servants helped her leave, solicitous and grateful, and she rode out of Losq with many a blessing at her back. But she wanted neither them nor the memory of the lie. She only hoped that young Korfax would find a brighter path to follow and that The Creator would forgive her her crime.

The journey home was long, made all the worse by the storm, but she was inured to hardship. One had to be hardy to live so far north. Her steed was almost as old in years as she was, relatively speaking, and it knew the way as well as she did, so she let it decide which path was best to take. She was far too wrapped up in her own thoughts to consider such things.

When she arrived at her tall and lonely house overlooking the Piral Gieris, she took out her naming boards, along with their markers, and looked at them for a very long time.

Though her house might be ancient, built before the wars even, her naming boards and their markers were older yet. They were older than even she dared consider.

Some gifted artisan, far back in the deeps of time, had made them. They were not signed with any famed sigil, but she knew in her heart that their maker had dwelt in the light when making them. All the boards were slightly worn now, and the markers were not as sharp at the edges as they once had been, but they were all still marvellous works, potent tools of the hand, the eye and the mind.

She took them to her place of contemplation, a high crag set above a cliff overlooking the plain below, and placed them all in a pile at the very centre of the stone circle that was set there. She looked down at them, blinking back yet more tears, before she went back to her house to fetch the large stone she used for meditation. It was the hardest thing that she possessed and it was polished to an altogether shining smoothness. She clutched it in both hands as she knelt before the boards and the markers, and her face showed not a flicker of emotion as she raised the stone high above her head. Then she brought it down with all the force that she could muster.

With a flash of light the boards shattered and the riven pieces scattered under the blow. She sighed briefly and collected them all up, and once she had made a pile she raised the great stone above her head and brought it down for a second time, smashing the wreckage into ever-smaller pieces.

She continued at her labour for a very long time, ignoring the pain and the fatigue that mounted with each passing moment. Agony began to consume her, pain upon pain upon pain, but this was her due. This was the price she must pay. Only when she had pounded every last piece to dust could she lay down at last – and then only to die. The reason for her life had been taken from her, and there was nothing else to live for.

Seasons flew by like wind-borne leaves. There were days of joy and laughter, nights of dream-filled wonder and new eyes beheld an elder world and made it young again, repainting it with brighter colours, sculpting it with new-carved shapes. The world, regardless, rolled ever on its ancient way, its path about its mighty star the well-travelled road it had always been, but now that road was seen afresh, and each scar, each well-worn rut, became unknown again, reinvented with expectancy, reinvented as mystery. What pleasures there were, and what discoveries.

All too soon, though, the halcyon days, the golden times, become a thing of fond memory. All too brief they are and all too fleeting, as the world, awakened by knowledge or coaxed by familiarity, turns about its hidden centre and reveals its darker face. Then the dreams of innocence fail, falling away like so many discarded playthings, and harder truths rise up to take their place.

Sometimes awakenings are long and slow, drawn out, savoured and experienced. But sometimes they are abrupt and sudden. Then the world tumbles from its orbit and certainties shatter.

At the great gate they stood, a line of tall riders upon fine steeds waiting in the chill air. Helm and armour gleamed, the dark reds of fury. Cloak and pennant burned, the brighter reds of fire, but all was still. Nothing moved. It was not yet time.

At their head and set slightly apart, two more riders waited, each tall like those behind but one especially so. The shorter was cloaked in red and held a lance also, but the taller did not. He was arrayed in purple and his hands held nothing. They rested instead upon his saddle. Neither did he wear helm or armour; instead, there was a long stave of red crystal in a sheath across his back, and on his brow was a shining stone of the palest violet set in an argent circlet. He was the only one to move, and then only his eyes. They scoured the horizon as if hunting prey.

"Baschim?" he suddenly announced. "I was thinking. It is the eve of Ahaneh once more."

Baschim turned and looked expectantly at his master, bowing his head slightly.

"Yes, Enay," he said, "that it is."

Baschim waited. They all waited. The time for leaving had not yet arrived, but it would be here very soon. Dawn was coming and the east was brightening with every passing moment, but Baschim knew that his master would not move until he was ready to do so.

It was always at this time of year that his master grew restive, his thoughts darkening and turning to strange imaginings. Baschim tried to comfort himself that this was how it had always been, the patterns of their lives repeating themselves, year in and year out, as they ever had. It was the ritual cycle, the smaller rituals joining with the greater, a weight of movements that felt not only right but necessary. There was always that deeper fear, though, that his master's moods might one day turn him aside. It had never happened before, but the possibility always loomed large at this time of year.

"No, Baschim, that was not what I meant," said his master.

Baschim put his thoughts aside and listened attentively.

"I was thinking rather it seems only yesterday that we enacted Kuslah last. The arrow of time flies quicker with each passing season, carrying us ever nearer the end."

Baschim started. The end? That was new. His master really was in a black mood this day, blacker than he could remember for many a year. And was that a certain reluctance he heard now? Surely not! This was Great Ritual they did here, and his master knew it all too well. How could he not? He was Geyad Faren Enay Sazaaim, Geyad of the Dar Kaadarith and Enay of Losq. He was the mightiest in a long line of the mighty, for the Farenith went all the way back to the great wars themselves. Theirs was an ancient and noble heritage. Some even dared call it unique.

Baschim waited a moment in disquiet. What could he say? In some respects his master was an utter mystery to him: a wielder of powers he could never understand, a keeper of secrets he could never fathom. But his moods were the most mysterious of all, and occasionally there was no accounting for them, like now, for instance.

It was at times like these that his one and only nightmare came back to haunt him. Under its infrequent spell he would find himself cast adrift upon an uncharted sea, floundering in its immensity whilst his master stood upon the prow of a great ship above and looked to distances only he could see, speaking words only he could hear, unaware of his servant's turmoil below.

Baschim squared his shoulders and hid his uncertainties behind his mask of duty, as he ever did in such circumstances.

"We should set off soon, Enay," he said. "Time draws on, as you rightly say. Rafarel is near to rising."

Baschim gestured to the east, where the light was now gathering apace. But his master did not look. Instead he offered his servant the faintest of smiles.

"Good Baschim," he said, "you have ever been my goad."

Baschim bowed his head in gratitude and relief, but when he looked up again, he saw that his master's face had an older cast to it now. Perturbed, he dared a question.

"What troubles you, Enay?" he asked. "What really troubles you?"

Sazaaim inclined his head just so.

"So you see me, do you?" he said. "It is as it ever was. Your father was the same."

He leaned closer and his eyes lost their smile.

"I have a sense of foreboding in me, a feeling that has been with me for a while now."

"Foreboding, Enay? But what of?"

"I do not know, but I begin to feel that we should not go out this day. I fear something will happen if we do, something wrong. I suddenly find myself reluctant. I seek a sign, Baschim, a sign that my fears are groundless and that all will be well."

Baschim bowed his head in acknowledgement. So it was reluctance that he had heard. What had caused it? He thought of prophecies and portents and of other, darker things. But that was not his affair, nor his estate, so he pushed it all aside as best he could and told himself that this was neither the time nor the place for indulgences. He had a duty to perform, and his master had said it well. He was a goad, a thing of necessity, as he ever had been.

"Enay!" he announced brightly. "All will be well, of course it will. Why should it not? This is Great Ritual we do here. We must go out. The observances must be kept."

Sazaaim looked sad for a moment, but then he turned his gaze on his servant and fixed him with his hardest look yet.

Even after all their years together, Baschim still felt far from comfortable under that piercing scrutiny. For all his apparent gentleness, there was sometimes a hard fire in his master's eyes, a most unforgiving fire. Now here it was again, and Baschim had no choice but to endure it.

"Yes, Baschim," Sazaaim said, "the observances must be kept. But in all the time I have been Enay, I have never had such a presentiment before. Something has disturbed me, something out of place. I suddenly find myself wishing to seek it out."

Baschim bowed his head. Here was his ingress.

"But surely, Enay," he said, "that is a good thing. That is the purpose of Kuslah, after all, to travel the boundaries and to see that all is well."

Sazaaim gentled his gaze again.

"No, Baschim, no! You do not understand. It is the ritual itself that seems wrong. It is as though this is precisely the wrong time to perform it. Ritual should feel right, necessary, inevitable. But that is not how I feel at all, and if I find no comfort in my thoughts then I shall order that we forgo it at this time."

Baschim opened his mouth as if to speak and then closed it again. He was suddenly struck dumb. Forgo Kuslah? Forgo Great Ritual? But that was unthinkable – and doubly so for his master.

He looked away. Their entire lives were ruled by tradition and ritual. There was a place for everything, and everything had to be in its place. He glanced at the sky, searching it for dark clouds, but there were none to be seen. He looked to the far hills, seeking shadows, but there were none there either. The dawning day was already far too bright for anything to hide from.

Ever since he had become Balzarg, first servant to the Farenith, Baschim had never known his master shirk a duty or miss an observance. Indeed, Sazaaim was far more diligent than many another he could think of. Only those in the west were as attentive, or so he had heard. But Baschim had never travelled that far. He felt a momentary touch of pride. Few other great houses, whether of the north, the west, the south or the east, could equal the Farenith. The Farenith had served with honour for almost seven thousand years, a line that had never wavered and a service that had never faltered. The Farenith were as steady as stone, Enay after Enay, Geyad after Geyad.

So what was his master thinking now? The pride wavered. For the Enay of Losq to put aside his duty was unthinkable, yet this was precisely what Sazaaim seemed to be considering. But before Baschim could say another word, someone else spoke from behind.

"Forgo Kuslah? That is unthinkable! You must not do it. The Velukor himself commands you."

They both turned about and Baschim breathed a sigh of relief. Thank The Creator! His mistress was here at last. Now, perhaps, his master's thoughts would turn to other things, to duty, the needs of his house and Great Ritual itself.

Tazocho, Uren of the Exentaser, Enay of the Salman Farenith and mother of the heir to the Tower of Losq, stood sternly by the gate.

Baschim saw how she bore herself. She had that same sense of power and command about her as that of her sire, but she and her beauty had a sharpness, a seeing sharpness that Sazaaim lacked, as though she saw things unmarked by others.

Beside her stood her son, the heir to the Farenith himself, the Noren of Losq, and for all that he favoured her, he had softer features and gentler eyes.

Sazaaim squared his shoulders and looked down.

"So, you have come to see me on my way after all, even though you said that you would not. Have you become my goad also?"

She offered him the briefest of smiles.

"After a little thought I decided it would be best. Your mood this morning was dark, so I came to reassure you once more that your concerns are groundless. I still see nothing ahead, so gather up your certainty and perform Kuslah without fear. All will be well, you will see."

He smiled briefly again and bowed his head to her. Then, after a brief pause, she bowed back. For long moments they held each other's gaze, before Sazaaim finally turned to look at his son, waiting in his mother's shadow. Sazaaim's expression changed entirely. Now he looked almost happy.

Baschim took the opportunity to glance at the other riders and was pleased to see that all remained stiffly erect, eyes forward, lances raised. There was not a hint amongst any of them that they had marked anything of the previous exchange at all. Baschim expected nothing less, of course, but it was still reassuring to see. He needed reassurance, especially today. He turned back to look at his master, still looking fondly at his son.

"And who is this tall youth I see before me?" asked Sazaaim. "No son of mine, I'll warrant. They said he was still in his bed and couldn't be bothered to see his father on his way at all."

The heir to the Tower of Losq laughed.

"Mother thought it would be best if I were here," he said. "After all, it is only fitting that the old master of Losq be seen on his way by the new."

Baschim allowed himself a careful smile as a few gentle chuckles rose up from the ranks behind. His gloom fled him entirely. Thank The Creator his master now had a son! Ever since the birth Sazaaim had been so much happier.

It was difficult in a world without strife to ever turn your mind to thoughts of war, but that was how it was. They were guardians, and that was even truer for the Farenith. Preparedness at all times, as it was written. Who knew when the inheritors of the dark past would rise again? But so it had been decreed. No act of violence existed in solitude, as it was written. There were always reprisals, no matter how long it took.

Sazaaim looked down at his son, smiling a little wider, a brief flicker of appreciation before raising his eyebrows and drawing himself up in his saddle. Then he leaned over the pommel in mock threat, and his eyes gleamed.

"So that's the way of it, is it? Well, let me warn you now. Your mother is teaching you to desire dominion far too soon. I always suspected that she plotted against me, and now I see the truth of it. I will deal with you both when I return."

He gestured at the tower.

"And though you lock the gates against me I shall storm them and throw them down. Then I will have you and she put in the deep holds until the Velukor comes himself to pass judgement upon you both."

For a moment he smiled his rarest of smiles, a wonderful thing of love and care, before becoming serious again. But it was a happier lord of Losq that looked back at his lady. Baschim saw the resolution in his master's eyes and smiled in return. Sazaaim had finally thrown aside his doubts and would now do his duty. All was right with the world again.

"We will return in seven days, as it should be," Sazaaim announced. "May the light of The Creator shine upon you, my love and my life."

Tazocho smiled gently in return. She came forward and lightly touched his hand.

"And may the light of The Creator shine upon you also, my heart and my whole."

Sazaaim's gaze intensified for a moment, two points of fire piercing her. She waited in turn, cold light consuming the fire. Then the Enay of Losq turned to his son and pointed with a steady hand.

"And you, Korfax, look after your mother whilst I am gone. You are now the master of this place until I return."

He smiled again.

"May the light of The Creator shine upon you, my son."

Korfax swallowed and bowed his head.

"And may the light of The Creator shine upon you, Father."

It was time. Great Rafarel finally touched the edge of the world and the growing dance of fire cast its gentle light across the land. Sazaaim reached over his shoulder and drew out his kabadar from its sheath, that long stave of crystal with which he practised both his art and his holy duty.

Baschim never saw the kabadar without feeling a certain sense of awe. It was an object of power, the will made manifest in stone, and with it a master could command the elements. With it, earth, air, fire and water could be subdued and made to serve.

Sazaaim was a master of fire, so his stave was red: yellow for earth, blue for air, red for fire and green for water. Baschim had never been told why that was so, but that was the way that it was, a holy mystery, as it always had been and always would be.

Sazaaim held his kabadar up before him and tightened his grip upon it. Deep within, along the axis of its heart, a thin line of luminosity waxed, a sliver of light like that between two distant but immense doors.

Sazaaim pointed his stave at the sky. His gaze intensified for a moment and the stave glowed with red heat. A low, angry hum came and went as a shaft of fire erupted from its tip, a great tree of flickering flame that roared upwards, ever upwards, until each fiery branch shattered against the gathering clouds of morning, driving them back again to the four horizons. A brief peal of thunder shook the world and then was gone. Sazaaim lowered his stave and sheathed his power. He waited a moment and then turned his steed smartly about, before riding off down into the west, followed closely by Baschim and the others, the pennants on their many lances fluttering behind them.

Tazocho and Korfax watched them disappear beyond the edge of the hill and then turned back to the gate. They went inside and the great stone doors closed shut behind them.

Korfax smiled as he gazed through the window, sitting in the morning room, his first meal of the day set before him. His father had left him in charge.

It was the first time that he had ever said such a thing – and what a glorious feeling it was! Korfax savoured it, thinking what it meant, whilst at the back of his mind a small voice reminded him that he was still only Noren, heir-in-waiting to a seat of rock and soil, whilst his father was Enay, master of mountain and valley. Losq was not his yet. But one day, one far off day, he would be Enay, too, and then Losq really would be his.

Morning meal done, Korfax went on his way to his lessons. No doubt Doanazin was already there, eagerly waiting for her pupil to arrive. Doanazin was always eager.

He had heard her earlier, just after his father had left, singing the morning prayer from the highest balcony of the tower.

It used to be his mother who sang it, but now Doanazin did it in her stead. Korfax had heard it said that she had asked for the honour when she had first arrived and that his mother had granted it gladly. Not for the first time he found himself wishing that his mother was still the one to sing the prayer. She did it quietly.

He went the way he always did. Now, though, he found it all suddenly different, the familiar reinvented by a few well-chosen words. 'You are now the master of this place until I return.' The words rolled in his mind.

He went along the third landing with its long line of shields, each emblazoned with the sigil of a house of the north. He looked at each in turn as he passed on by and thought of what they meant, of where they had come from, and at what price they had been bought.

He thought of other heirlooms, the special pieces, those marked out by the tale that they told. There were many relics of the past scattered here and there throughout the tower, and Korfax knew much of their history. His favourites, though, made an odd couple. They were of a kind, but as unlike as any two such objects could be. One was an open scroll, but the other was a complete mystery: two fine and beautiful swords.

The first was the great kansehna that was set above the north door in the great hall, its hilt pointing downwards and its blade pointing up to the sky. The blade was longer almost than he was tall, and upon it was inscribed a single line taken from an ancient poem. Korfax knew the words well and always spoke them quietly to himself whenever he walked under the blade.

'Zirdo Soygah Koh', said the words. I am the fall of doom. Korfax looked up. Given the size of the sword, who would dare to doubt it!

In its day, when the sword had been wielded with a purpose, it must have been a terrible weapon. It was said to have been the blade of the Meganza himself, the champion of Anolei, the seventh Velukor. There had only ever been one Meganza, and that had been Noqor, sixth Enay of Losq. Noqor was said to have been tall and strong indeed, but then he would have needed to be in order to wield so mighty a blade.

The second heirloom Korfax favoured was a beautiful and delicate avalkana that hung from the wall in his father's day room. It had the slenderest of blades and the finest of hilts. It had obviously been made for duelling, but Korfax doubted it had ever been used in anger. It looked far too stylised for one thing, and far too new for another. Swords that had seen use in combat never looked so perfect, like the great kansehna of Noqor, for instance.

Korfax did not know the avalkana's history, as no one would tell him, but he had often entertained this fantasy or that as he had tried to account for its prominence. It had obviously been made for his father, but when had his father ever fought a duel? The question always perplexed him, for no one had ever mentioned such a thing to him. His father, whenever he was asked, said that it was a gift, but that was all he would say.

It was hot and Great Rafarel had risen far enough to banish the cool of the morning. Korfax felt both bored and sleepy as he listened to Doanazin drone on and on about the subtleties of service.

Wisdom, fortitude, discipline and justice, his tutor proclaimed, raising her hands dramatically in the air, those were the four pillars that defined the boundaries of the world. Korfax sighed to himself. And how many times had he heard that before? But Doanazin loved such contemplations with a passion. She loved to quote the philosophers, the thinkers and the writers, raising up the acts of the mighty departed, their words and deeds, retelling their lives so that she could bludgeon her pupil with their collective message. Tradition! Service! Ritual! Reason!

Korfax let his mind wander. How much more interesting would it be if his lessons were taken from the house archives instead? There were crystals there that were far more entertaining than his tutor.

There were logadar, as green as deep water, each filled with histories and tales, wars and journeys, stories from the deeps of time. Touch one of them whilst thinking of meaning and the air above would blossom with words. That had been one of his very first lessons in the application of power.

Then there were kamliadar, the colour of the sky, filled with many voices, all recounting the long days of the Farenith. Touch one of them whilst thinking of speech and those voices would speak again, the long-vanished dead sending their thoughts through time so that others might know their wisdom, or their mistakes. Korfax had listened to many.

And then there were oanadar, crystals of the palest violet, each filled with the images of the long-vanished past. Touch one of them whilst thinking of sight and the air above would fill with ancient visions, old shades captured in perpetuity as they went about their business. Korfax had only touched a few, but the images that he had been allowed to awaken were altogether astonishing.

One was a tour of a city in the furthest east, Thilzin Gallass by name, a great port upon the banks of a wide river. Another revealed a duel, clearly a matter of utmost seriousness. Both combatants were fully armoured and their faces were obscured, but the cut and the thrust of combat had Korfax gasp in astonishment. It was fast and furious, almost a dance, and both seemed well matched.

Baschim had told him once that many of the weapons and crystals kept at Losq were unique, that few other houses had such collections in their possession. Once Korfax knew this he was filled with questions. Why was that so? What was their history? Had the blades been used in the wars? Did the crystals tell of the same? But having summoned his curiosity, Baschim would offer little further to satisfy it. So Korfax went looking for his answers elsewhere.

He went to his father, but his father would tell him little either, saying only that he was not yet ready for such knowledge.

He went to his mother, but she said even less, preferring instead admonishments intended to curb his appetite, but it did little good. Korfax remained insatiable. The romance of the long-lost past filled his dreams.

It took him a while, but he eventually discovered that the rarest of all was a great collection of kamliadar that held between them a somewhat unique perspective on the Wars of Unification themselves. They were filled to the brim with the voices of witnesses, those that had been present during many of the great events. Hints picked up from conversations, and from innocent questions, told Korfax that he was not even supposed to know that this great collection even existed, for his father kept it hidden away, only occasionally, on certain days, taking them all out from their hiding place so that he could gaze at them for a while. And once, a few seasons back, Baschim had stood guard outside the topmost room of the tower whilst his father had sat within, listening to each crystal in turn, crystal after crystal after crystal. His mother had been angry that day and Korfax had not dared to ask what it was all about. So, instead, he had crept quietly to the room below the one in which his father sat, and he listened to the sound of distant voices through the stone. It was wrong to do so – very wrong – and he felt guilty even as he did it, but he could not resist the temptation. Stories, especially those from the war, excited him like nothing else.

Korfax could not hear half of what was said, but the little he did glean filled him with a wistful longing. There was a lot that was not common knowledge, and certainly nothing in the histories his tutor taught him. There were many voices, many different voices that spoke from within each stone, the words of the long-vanished dead held in perpetuity by the arts of the Dar Kaadarith.

Korfax had listened as long as he was able to, then he had left quietly with snatches of sentences still echoing in his head.

"It was on the first day of Lahrasom that the forces of Karenor were finally driven back..."

"I was there, I saw it. The ash was still upon the floor and the cold remains of a pyre still lay in the place of the burning. There were bones within the ashes, all scattered about, burnt bones..."

"They fell upon us like demons. If it had not been for the timely arrival of the forces of Zamandas, we would have failed utterly..."

Korfax shuddered with a guilty ecstasy. What a wonder battle must be.

Though some of the words mentioned momentous events from history, like the death of the enemy or the fall of his black city, others were far more cryptic and Korfax could not imagine to what they referred at all.

He was still pondering the mystery of the crystals when Doanazin's voice brought him sharply back to the present.

"Korfax? Korfax! Are you listening to me?"

Korfax looked up. He had drifted away entirely and his tutor had seen it.

Doanazin was glaring down at him.

"Well?" she asked.

Korfax suddenly felt angry. Why did he have to endure this, and on this day in particular. Hadn't his father named him master only that morning? It wasn't the first time he had been brought to task for inattention, and no doubt it would not be the last, but today he would not. Today, he decided, things would be different.

"I was doing what you taught me," he told her in his best matter of fact voice. "I was using your art of memory."

Doanazin deepened her glare, if such a thing was possible.

"Were you indeed?" she exclaimed. "I do not think so. You had not assumed the correct attitude."

"But I was," Korfax insisted.

Doanazin narrowed her eyes.

"Then you should be able to tell me what I just said." She leaned closer. "All of it! Every single word, every single gesture!"

Korfax knew that he could not. He hadn't been listening at all. If he had been, he would have heard and seen everything in perfect clarity and would have been able to repeat it all in exact detail. It was one of the more impressive disciplines Doanazin had taught him – how to still the mind and turn it into a blank piece of parchment upon which everything could be written – but Korfax had not done so this time, and his tutor knew it.

Korfax looked back angrily.

"I do not see why I should," he said. "I heard what you said the first time."

Doanazin frowned.

"So you insist that is the truth, do you?"

Korfax did not waver. He had decided. This would be the day that he defied Doanazin, openly, brazenly. He had had enough. His father had named him master only that morning, so that is what he would be.

"Always you do this," he said. "Always you twist everything that I do."

"Twist?" Doanazin drew back. There was a look of shock on her face now. "That is the one thing that I have never done, in all my life. I hope, for your sake, that was not a serious accusation!"

"But you always look for fault! Nothing ever pleases you!"

"And which one of us is the teacher and which the pupil?"

"So, of course, you are never mistaken!"

"I did not say that!"

"But that is how you treat me! I am the one that is always wrong, always doubted, always at fault."

He was standing now, glaring back at her.

"So you insist you heard everything I said, do you?" she said.

"Yes," answered Korfax. "I am tired of being doubted like this."

He glared at her for a moment and then turned his back upon her, the worst thing he could possibly do.

"So that is the way of it, is it? You dare to dismiss me? I am very disappointed, Korfax, disappointed and hurt. This is not the first time that you have let your attention wander, and if it was only that I could forgive it. But open defiance? Accusations? Wilful lies?"

He heard her sigh.

"You are the son of a noble house," she said quietly, "and with that privilege comes obligation. This is Great Ritual we do here, performed since before the wars themselves. All so blessed have had this honour bestowed upon them, but you especially are favoured. Few indeed have their own tutor these days, but that is how it should be for you, for you are born of a great house."

He could hear it in her voice – the hurt, the reproach. Perhaps he had gone too far, but it was too late now.

"And it is not that you lack in some way," she continued. "You do not. You have great potential, great potential, yet you continue to waste it in inattention. You may well desire to take up the stave of your father and be the master of the forces that he is, but as of now you cannot even master yourself."

At last he turned about to find her glaring back at him from the middle of the room, her eyes bright and sharp with anger.

"All that is required of you at this time is your attention, but instead you dream. And it is not as though you have never been told this before."

She held up a single finger.

"Inattention has ever been a fault of youth. We were all young once, but open defiance? Lies?"

She stepped forward. Korfax was tempted to step back.

"When someone lies," she told him, "they murder a part of the world."

She turned to leave.

"I have no choice before me now. I must speak to your mother about this."

Korfax glowered at her as she left, but he said nothing more.

It wasn't long before the summons came. Doanazin delivered it and left again.

Korfax went to his mother's day room and found her standing in the exact centre. He stood a little way back and waited. She watched him all the while, her eyes shuttered and cold.

"So you were inattentive again?" she asked.

Korfax looked down. His mother did not move.

"I am also told that this time you were openly defiant, that you lied and then turned your back upon Doanazin. Is this true?"

Korfax continued to look down.

"Well?" she pressed.

Korfax looked up, hot with guilty anger.

"But Doanazin makes it all so dull," he complained.

His mother still did not move.

"Dull?" she asked. "Is that all you have to say?"

Korfax looked down again.

"Yes," he told his feet.

"We have had this conversation before, you and I."

Her voice was colder now. Korfax continued to look at his feet.

"And what did I tell you the last time?" she asked.

Korfax took a deep breath.

"You said that those who do not pay attention in their instruction will suffer for it in the years to come."

"Indeed I did," she said. "Those were my very words. It seems that you can attend well enough when it suits you."

Now she moved. Suddenly she was closer.

"And do you think that your father would refuse to do his duty, even if he found it to be 'dull'?"

Korfax had already guessed what his mother would say next, but even so, he still felt a certain shame at the comparison.

"No," he answered quietly.

"No," echoed his mother. "He would not. There are many things he would rather not do, many things. But he does them nonetheless. He does them because it is required of him, because it is his duty and because he serves."

Korfax tried not to look up, tried not to look up at his mother and instead to keep his eyes downcast, but he knew that she was looking at him. He knew it because he could feel the weight of her regard. He could not resist the temptation and glanced up briefly. He immediately looked down again. Her eyes were frozen in place and each was now lit from within by a distant but brilliant flame. She spoke again.

"You are the son of a noble house. You are privileged as few others are, but your privileges come at a price. For you, at this moment, that price is your time."

He heard his mother sigh, but it sounded more like a hiss.

"When your lessons are over you are free," she told him, "but what of your father? What freedom does he have?"

He felt her move away. She had gone to the window. He glanced in that direction. She was looking outside. She was angry now, really angry, and he could feel it even from where he waited. It filled the air about him like a cold wind. He suddenly wished that he was anywhere other than where he was now.

"You have so much time to yourself," she murmured. "Is a little diligence on your part so much to ask?"

Korfax suddenly thought it not. He looked down again.

"Your father did all that you have done," she told him.

"And more," she added, turning about. "He took the discipline he learned as a child and earned much honour with it, great honour. And that is what both he and I expect from you."

Korfax suddenly realised that she was standing over him again. He had not noticed when she had moved away from the window. Though he was looking down at his feet he could feel her closeness. It was at moments like this that she actually scared him. Like his father, she also possessed great powers, but hers were of another order entirely. Her mind was her strength. She was an Uren of the Exentaser, one of the potent few, a mistress of names, of thoughts and of visions. She could see things no others could.

He dared not look up, not now.

She waited a while and then spoke to him again, and her voice all but filled his world.

"At this time in your life you have only one obligation, the obligation to learn. Your knowledge of the world about you should reflect your position within it. You should appreciate all the subtleties, all the details and all the difficulties, for you cannot pick and choose. To each is given their due."

She leaned closer.

"But also, each is expected to pay in turn."

She placed her hand under his chin and lifted his head. He had no choice but to look. Her eyes were terrible, as brilliant as his guilty imagination had already made them.

"Doanazin is here at my request," she told him. "She is here to give you a great gift, yet you scorn it and turn your back upon it."

She paused a moment, gathering herself up.

"Do you realise that by turning your back upon Doanazin you are also turning your back upon me, your very own mother? Was that your intent?"

Korfax could not answer. Shock held him where he was. He had not thought about that at all.

"Your father named you master of Losq until he returned!" she said. "Is this how you would be? Is it?"

Her eyes narrowed as if she were now peering deep down inside him. They became knives of light, carving him up as they sought for the fundamental truth.

"Defiance? Lies? Scorn?" she said, widening her eyes. "I am ashamed of you."

Korfax stared up at her, held in place by her gaze. He could see the cold in her, the ice in her mind so cold that it burned. She reached in and turned his thought upon itself, revealing to him exactly what it was that she saw. Her shame of him became his own. Now he was ashamed of himself, horribly and uniquely ashamed.

Goal achieved, she withdrew her mind and turned away. She turned her back on him, dismissing him just as he had tried to dismiss Doanazin.

"Leave me now!" she told him in her coldest voice yet. "I do not want to see you again this day, not before the evening meal at the very least."

And that was that. Korfax fled her presence and ran all the way to his room.

Korfax sat on his bed and glowered at the floor. He hated Doanazin, but he hated his mother more. She had never punished him like that before. Why, today of all days, had she chosen to do so? Hadn't his father named him master only that morning? His thoughts wandered along the same path they had before. One day he would be Enay, and then no one could tell him what to do, or berate him for inattention. The thought circled in his head until he realised what it actually meant. For him to be master meant that his father was master no more, and the only way that would happen was for his father to be gone.

Korfax felt a chill at the thought. He could not imagine such a possibility. His father gone? It was unthinkable. Wherever had such an unpleasant thought come from? He wondered whether his mother hadn't deliberately set his thoughts along this path as well.

She could do such things, could his mother. Thought was her domain – the mind, its order, the hidden, the buried. It was a rare thing, like his father's ability with stone, a rare gift rarely used, but as far as he could remember she had never used it so harshly before.

He thought about that. She had become hard of late. He remembered back down the years. She never used to be like this. She used to laugh and dance, she used to touch his mind with love, but recently it was as though nothing he did would please her. She had become cold.

Perhaps it was just that the older he became, the more she expected of him. So why couldn't she understand what it meant to him to have his father name him master of Losq? Shouldn't she be pleased by that, that her son was coming into his own? As if in answer, his earlier thought intruded. For him to be master meant that his father was master no more! Perhaps that was something his mother did not want to think about either.

Korfax tried to shake the thoughts from his head, but they would not go. Why was he dwelling on this? This wasn't how he had wanted his day to be at all. But the thought, like an unreachable itch, persisted.

It was much later that Korfax finally emerged again. He had hidden away in his room, shame and resentment battling away inside him, but finally, bored with his own company, he went in search of something to occupy his time until the evening meal. Quietly, he slipped out of the tower and down to the courtyard below.

He tried to forget what had happened earlier, but his mother's words sat upon him like a great weight, as they always did. So he drifted like a sullen cloud until he found himself at the doors to one of the stables. Chasaloh looked up from his work and smiled.

"Noren?"

Korfax bowed his head slightly but did not say anything. Chasaloh widened his smile.

"Now there is a face that would shatter stone," he said.

Korfax still did not answer. Chasaloh folded his arms and lessened his smile.

"And do you believe that you are the first in all the world to find their lessons dull?"

Korfax glowered back.

"Does everybody know?" he murmured.

Chasaloh smiled again.

"Of course not! How could they?" he asked. Then he leaned forward, suddenly conspiratorial.

"But I am a special case," he whispered loudly. "I possess an advantage all others lack."

Korfax frowned.

"What advantage?" he asked.

Chasaloh gestured at the stall behind him.

"Why, I have only to ask old Homral over there what occurs in the world and he tells me everything."

Korfax glanced at the huge gahbal contentedly chewing the grasses in its bier. His despondency started to evaporate. Whatever the weather, whatever the season, Chasaloh always knew exactly the right thing to say.

Korfax considered Homral. Whilst he had been magnificent in his prime, the proud sire of many a gahbal from Umadya Losq to Faor Raxamith, he looked altogether milder now, a behemoth gentled by time. He still kept the appearance of might, but his eyes were less bright than they had once been and his movements were far more considered.

Korfax walked over to the aged beast and affectionately stroked the fringe of hair that lay between his wide horns. Homral raised his head a little and snorted his pleasure. Korfax smiled at last. No, no deep thoughts lay inside that great wide head; instead, Homral dreamed. He dreamed of his youth, of his prime, of the time when his bellow had echoed from the hills to the sea and back again, when he alone had been the undisputed master of the herd.

Chasaloh stood beside Korfax and reached forward to tousle Homral's mane as well.

"Age wearies him, I think," he said. "His end approaches and he knows it all too well."

Korfax looked down. There it was again, that terrible comment upon mortality. What did it all mean? He looked at Chasaloh.

"Chasaloh?"

"Yes?"

"Why does everything have to end?"

Chasaloh turned and looked down at Korfax with bemusement.

"Now there is the question," he said. "You like the hard ones, don't you? Why does everything have to end?"

He paused a moment.

"Could it be," he finally offered, "because that is the way of the world?"

Korfax looked at Homral again and gently stroked his wide muzzle.

"But why?" he persisted.

Chasaloh drew back a little.

"Perhaps it is merely what The Creator has decreed! Let each be given their measure! No more, no less! That way, perhaps, we can all appreciate what we have."

Chasaloh smiled for a moment.

"And I thought you a scholar? Have you not read the works of Talazur and

Jerdess?"

Korfax scowled even as he looked at Chasaloh.

"But they do not answer the question," he said. "None of them do. They all play at the edges. There are no certainties anywhere in all that they have to say."

Korfax looked as hard as he could at Chasaloh, but Chasaloh held his gaze with ease, smiling all the while. Korfax finally relented and looked at his feet instead.

"So that is why I ask you," he said.

Chasaloh maintained his smile.

"Then you have been paying attention in your lessons after all," he said. "I suddenly see that you are the victim of a great injustice. Perhaps I should call Doanazin out and challenge her to a duel so that this dreadful wrong may be put to right?"

Korfax continued to look at his feet.

"And do not make fun of me, either," he said. "Besides, you still have not answered my question."

Chasaloh bowed his head slightly and his smile became somewhat rueful.

"But if you cannot divine the truth from two such great thinkers, how do you expect me to know the answer? You might as well ask The Creator."

Korfax offered Chasaloh another scowl and Chasaloh finally dropped his humour, though it still lurked somewhere behind his eyes.

"Very well then!" he said. "I can see you are in no mood for jest this day."

He turned about and pitched another load of sweet grasses from the pile at his side up on to the bier. Homral turned to it immediately and took it as if it was his due. Chasaloh watched carefully for a moment, gauging the time Homral had left in the world perhaps, then he looked back at Korfax again and his expression was finally serious.

"Noren," he announced. "We live in a world of opposites. To live, one must know death. To be happy, one must also know sadness. To know creation, one must also be aware of destruction. There is no light without dark, no heat without cold, no pleasure without pain and no good without evil. Everything in our world is made known by its opposite. And that is how it is."

Korfax grimaced.

"I know that," he said. "Everyone knows that! But the question I asked was why? Why is it that way?"

Chasaloh pursed his lips.

"I suddenly think that there is no answer that would fully satisfy you. So let me ask you this in return. What other way could there be?"

"I do not know," Korfax answered. "But it all seems so... so... convenient."

Chasaloh suddenly snorted and his face became graver still.

"Convenient, is it? There may well come a day when you find such truth more than you can bear."

Korfax drew back a little. Chasaloh looked fiery now as he held up a single finger in warning. Korfax stared at the finger.

"The Creator's sword slices the void," Chasaloh told him, "making all opposites – the light and the dark, the heat and the cold – in equal measure. The Creator makes opposites manifest, but the contemplation of such absolutes is only for the strongest souls, only for the mightiest, and they do not speak readily of what they have seen."

Chasaloh looked away and breathed deeply for a moment. Then he turned back to the sweet grasses at his side.

"Leastways," he murmured, "they do not speak to me."

It was not long after Korfax left the stables that his mother entered them. Chasaloh looked up and bowed immediately. With her he kept his habitual smile all but hidden away.

"Enay!" he announced. "You are not in good favour with the Noren, I fear."

She dropped her habitual severity ever so slightly.

"He is still a child, filled with all a child's judgements," she said. "He will learn."

Chasaloh let his hidden smile emerge a little.

"And is it really so important that he pay attention every single moment of every single day of his young life?" he asked. "Youth and time are bad companions. He has enough days before him yet to learn what he needs to learn. Besides, his father named him master only this morning, and that is more than enough to stoke the fires of any youthful imagination."

Tazocho dropped her severity a little more and even offered him the faintest of smiles, but Chasaloh thought it still too cold. She had not always been so. There was a time when she had danced, but of late? As Korfax had grown up, so she had grown colder. He wondered about that as he waited for her answer.

"And what did you say to your son when he let the herd wander where they should not?" she finally asked.

Was that an admonition? Chasaloh bowed his head again.

"I told him something of what you no doubt told the Noren. But that was my son I spoke to, not Korfax. He is of another temper entirely."

Tazocho became still.

"Indeed?" she returned, and the ice in her voice was unmistakable. Chasaloh wondered how he could turn it aside. He certainly did not want it aimed at himself.

"Enay," he said, "you may ask yourself what I might know of such things, but the patterns of creation repeat themselves for the high as much as they do for the low. I know it when a young gahbal or achir is ready, and which will be master and which will be servant. I watch it happen year in and year out. And as I have marked the coming and going of the seasons, so I have watched your son as he has grown. I know what he will be."

Tazocho deepened her chill, but Chasaloh carried on regardless.

"Korfax will be alone," he said. "He will not serve as his father does. He, alone of all of us, questions why things are as they are! He does not accept the world as we do, and that is an uncommon thing in these gentler times. Most are happy to dwell in the dream of service, but not Korfax, unless my eyes have deceived me. But I do not think they have. And neither do you, I believe."

She did not answer. Instead she left without another word, but Chasaloh thought he caught something in her eye as she turned. It was sadness. That shook him. He had never seen that in her before.

A solitary figure walked the walls. Korfax stopped and looked upwards. It was Ocholor, old Ocholor, the quiet and the thoughtful, an Ell of very few words. Guarding Losq was his duty, his life and his love, and he took such things very seriously indeed.

Ocholor was the Branvath of Losq, master of all the Branith that dwelt there, and he had been their master for more than a hundred years. Korfax could not imagine such a time, the weight of it, the length of it, the depth.

Ocholor was the oldest inhabitant of Losq now, but even so there were not many who could match him in the contest of arms. Of those the best was Orkanir, his son, one of the very best with a blade in all the north and also a Bransag of Losq.

Korfax liked Ocholor. He could walk beside him for an entire watch and hear nothing more than a few spare comments upon the weather. Ocholor did not waste his words on inconsequential matters, as his time was far too precious, far too concentrated upon the moment at hand. If he had something to say, he said it, otherwise he said nothing at all. And his silence was usually an answer in itself.

Ocholor and Chasaloh – two ends of the very same thread. Chasaloh had an opinion on anything and everything, whilst Ocholor said little or nothing at all. All things made known by their opposite. How true that was. But Korfax was still no closer as to why.

The door to the kitchen was open and the smell of cooking drifted out. Korfax walked by, and though he smelled its delicious air he did not give it a second glance. But then a voice called out to him from inside.

"Noren, you are a good judge of such things! Perhaps you can decide."

Korfax turned back. It was Geziam, wife to Baschim, looking out at him even as she came to stand at the opening.

"Hello, Geziam. Decide what?" he asked carefully.

"Whether my feast cakes are better or worse than last year," she answered.

"I am sure they are as good as they have ever been," he told her.

Another voice came from behind Geziam.

"Now that sounds as if judgement has already been made. It is as I have always said, Korfax has never been fair in such matters."

Korfax smiled. That was Kalazir, wife to Chasaloh. She also never failed to make him smile, whatever his mood.

Of all the retainers in Losq, Korfax liked Geziam and Kalazir the best. As unalike as any two friends could be, they argued over everything, except him of course. Him they doted on. In their company he truly felt like a lord.

Geziam moved back inside and Korfax followed her, but he stopped when he reached the door itself, content instead to stand upon the threshold and just look within.

The light gave the kitchen a certain agelessness as it slanted in through the high windows. Everything was surrounded by a soft glow so that even the simplest pot seemed exalted.

As he stood upon the threshold, Korfax felt himself struck by the sight: Kalazir and Geziam standing at this table or that, the work of their hands scattered about them, all rendered timeless by the light of the passing day.

Then Geziam gestured, breaking the moment.

"Try a cake," she proffered. "See what you think."

Korfax came forward and tasted the one he was offered. He smiled. It melted in his mouth even as he bit into it. Feast cakes had always been one of his favourites, and Geziam had a talent for baking the very best.

"I cannot say," he said between mouthfuls. "This is as good as any that I have ever tasted."

He took another bite and Kalazir snorted.

"But how you can say that?" she complained. "The harvest this year has not been as good as those before."

"That isn't so," Korfax told her.

"Oh yes it is," she said. "Which of us is the elder?"

"And which of us has the better memory?" he countered.

Kalazir wagged her finger at him with a sharp look in her eye, but Korfax gestured at the cakes.

"Or perhaps it is simply that Geziam has made an especial effort this time," he offered.

Geziam smiled at that and came forward. She held out her arms and hugged him.

"You always say the right things," she said.

Kalazir folded her arms in mock displeasure.

"Keep on doing that and his head will swell to such a size that the pair of you will float up and off into the west."

Korfax laughed and Geziam hugged him again.

"And now that we have settled the matter of the cakes," Kalazir continued, "where were you off to in such a hurry?"

"I was only going up onto the wall," Korfax answered.

"Only going up onto the wall? I doubt it was as innocent as that."

Korfax glanced back over his shoulder.

"I was going to walk with Ocholor for a while," he said.

Kalazir laughed.

"With Ocholor?" she exclaimed. "What a glutton for punishment you are! That one never knows when to keep quiet. Talk, talk, talk! Loves the sound of his own voice far too much."

Now Korfax really laughed.

"And have you ever looked in the mirror?" he said.

Kalazir grabbed at him and he dodged out of her way, still laughing.

"By my life," she said. "I will teach you not to mock me, whelp!"

Korfax stopped on the other side of the table.

"Whelp?" he said, standing as tall as he could. "It will not be much longer before I am taller than you."

Kalazir softened her look.

"And is that not the truth," she said. "The years go by so quickly. I remember a time, not so long ago it seems, when you could have walked under this very table without bowing your head."

Korfax paused, suddenly serious. There it was again. Yet another comment on mortality.

"The years go by so quickly," he repeated softly.

"What is it?" Kalazir asked.

"It was something I was talking to Chasaloh about," he told her.

Kalazir and Geziam exchanged glances.

"And what was it this time?" Kalazir asked.

"Why everything has to end!" Korfax answered. "I wanted to know why."

Geziam looked bemused for a moment, but all Kalazir did was laugh.

"That husband of mine has been drowning himself in philosophy again. Such a danger it is, all that thinking. I can see it now. One day he will so blind me with cunning words that I will find myself carrying out his tasks as well as my own."

Korfax laughed along with her whilst Geziam smiled. Then Geziam looked back at Korfax.

"But really, Noren, what do you mean by such a question?"

"I mean... what I mean is..." Korfax struggled for the words. "What I want to ask is why are things the way they are? How did it all come about?"

Kalazir leaned forward and tapped upon his shoulder with a finger.

"Sometimes one can look too deeply. There are some things that can never truly be known."

Korfax looked back at her.

"But I am an Ell," he said. "What can be beyond the reach of my thought? I have the power of imagination, and imagination has no limit."

Kalazir glanced at Geziam for a moment and then looked back at him.

"Give to The Creator The Creator's due," she admonished.

Now Korfax scowled.

"But I wasn't blaspheming," he answered quickly.

"And I wasn't saying that you were. I was merely warning you."

"About what?"

Kalazir sighed.

"Noren, let me answer you with a question of my own. Do you know what it feels like to be an achir?"

"I can imagine it," he said.

"But do you know what it feels like?"

Korfax thought for a moment.

"I think I can see what you are saying. In order to really know what it feels like, I would have to become an achir myself."

Kalazir leaned back.

"Exactly! And now you have the answer to your question. To know why things are the way that they are, you would have to become something other than an Ell. Either The Creator would have to tell you, or you would have to become The Creator yourself. And until such a marvel occurs, things will remain the way they are."

A little while after Korfax had left, Kalazir and Geziam received another visitor. A shadow occluded the light from the door and they both looked up from their work. Kalazir smiled.

"Enay! You are just in time."

"And what am I just in time for?" asked Tazocho.

"For a feast cake," Kalazir said, offering one up. "The Noren has pronounced them as good as they have ever been."

Tazocho glanced at the cake but did not take it.

"High praise indeed," she said. "But what do you say, Geziam?"

Geziam looked down.

"I cannot judge my own work," she said. "I leave that to others."

Tazocho cast a brief glance about the room, eyes searching, marking, measuring.

"And where is Korfax now?" she asked.

She looked at Geziam for a moment, but Geziam's head was down. She turned to Kalazir.

"I think he went up on to the wall to walk with Ocholor," Kalazir told her.

Tazocho smiled, but it was cold.

"Thank you," she said, and then she left as silently as she had arrived.

Geziam watched her leave.

"She is following him!" she said.

"And she has done it ever since the day she bore him," Kalazir agreed.

"But why? Why follow him all the days of his life?"

Kalazir glanced at her friend.

"You have never had a child, have you? You do not understand. I hear that she admonished him earlier. Well, if that was the case, she now feels the guilt of it. It was ever a mother's lot. I know how I felt after I had given Permanal a good talking to. I felt as though I was the one that had transgressed, not him."

"Even so, she is in a fierce mood this day."

"She is in a fierce mood most days."

Geziam glanced at Kalazir.

"What do you think Chasaloh said to her?"

"I do not know," said Kalazir, "but I intend to find out. If he has caused the Noren more trouble by his meddling, then I will teach him better wisdom this night."

Geziam frowned.

"Do not, I beg you. Korfax loves him. And he loves you. He would not see contention between you."

Kalazir smiled, almost laughing.

"And you should be so concerned," she said. "I know my husband's heart. Besides, I am not the only one here that Korfax loves."

Geziam looked down. Kalazir watched as her friend fought with her timidity.

"That his mother should be so cold!" Geziam said at last.

Kalazir agreed.

"All the Exentaser are cold. They sell their passion for power. Did you not know?"

Geziam looked away as if suddenly guilty.

"I did not mean such a judgement," she said.

Kalazir clasped Geziam by the shoulders.

"And you should not be so afraid of your own words. You see well enough, as do many others here. The Enay is ambitious for her son. Think of it as a well-known secret. She desires the gift of power for him, power through action, power through knowledge. Why do you think she had Doanazin brought all the way here from Emethgis Vaniad? Even I, closeted away in the north, had heard the name Doanazin before. The Enay will let nothing stand in the way of her ambition. Remember that she is also of holy blood? The Velukor himself is her cousin. Born of greatness, she desires greatness for her son."

Geziam frowned.

"I had not considered that."

"No, you had not. But then you did not need to either. Instead, you saw the underlying truth, as you should have all along. But that is our estate. We see what lies beneath. Let others seek the lofty, we are of the soil."

Kalazir looked up, her face catching the light.

"And the final truth of it is all that we may ever have. We can watch, but we cannot interfere. Korfax will find his own way in this world, though his mother may not like it. All I have ever wished for him is that The Creator should light his path. Then we will have yet another Enay of Losq. As it was before, so it will be again."

She sighed and then looked sternly at the pots and the trays that had been used for baking.

"But speculation cleans nothing! If we do not clear away before the evening meal then we shall truly drown in chaos."

Back in the tower Tazocho watched her son from the window, standing back somewhat, out of the light. Chasaloh's words had disturbed her. He saw the very same thing in her son that she did, but he drew very different conclusions. Though she did not like to admit it, Chasaloh saw the patterns behind the world much as she did. He saw them in a simpler light perhaps, but sometimes it took a simpler perspective to cut through all the layers and expose what lay beneath. Perhaps it was time for her to look beyond her bounds. It was so easy to slip in a place like this, lulled by the rhythms, by the slow and gentle shift of the seasons. There was a momentum to such things, a weight.

She knew what the others here thought, of her and her son. Him they loved, much as they did his father, but she they had come to fear. They feared her power and her coldness. But they did not understand. None of them, not even her lord, could see the reasons behind what she did. But she had seen beyond these days, and she would not deny her vision.

She turned away and went back to her meditations. Yes, Korfax dreamed, as did so many others here, and that pained her. Such dreams achieved nothing in places where the long, slow sleep of life held sway. She could only hope that the dreams would lead her son on, beyond this place to where he needed to be, the still centre where all truth was revealed and there was but a single direction. Off the straight path lay only failure. It was one of the first lessons she had ever been taught, and it was something that she had tried to instil in Korfax. It was why Doanazin was here. The straight path. But her son rebelled, because of his dreams.

She considered this latest incident and sympathised with Doanazin. Korfax could be so utterly frustrating at times. He certainly did not lack the ability – most definitely not – but he just would not apply himself to his full extent. It was infuriating. If she had been of another temper she might have hated herself for shaming him as she had, but that was how it was done according to the Exentaser. Shame was a most potent goad, its fire turning the will upon itself, healing the mistakes, creating the desire to do better, burning away the imperfections. Her son had to be kept upon the straight path, or he would not fulfil his potential. And as the path brooked no deviation, she had to be just as unyielding. It was her task to see that he become Geyad, like his father, and then more than Geyad. Let him attend the seminary of the Dar Kaadarith and learn the Namad Dar, but let him also be armed with all the advantages that she could give him, and then perhaps her vision would come to fruition and all would come to appreciate the nobility and the power at the heart of the Farenith. Her lord might deny this, but her son would not, she would see to that.

So, in the meantime, she would keep a watch over him and make sure he did not stray.

4

THE INCOMING TIDE

Nim-inan Korm-talunlo
Azon-ring Thar-mya-qasar
Faor-urus Lu-kal-omin
Zad-nisso Norpul-ap-li
Urq-molnis Imul-torzu
Abai-vim Tol-a-dr-pan
Kri-nor-arp Odna-stl-to

Korfax ran across the courtyard and up on to the wall, his feet brushing the fine green fronds that peeped through the cracks in its well-worn surface.

His brief visit with Geziam and Kalazir had lightened his mood, as it ever did. Listening to their words, their thoughts, their laughter, was like listening to the wind and the sea.

He thought back to the morning's lesson and how dry old Doanazin made it sound. No lightness ever entered her orotund speeches. Instead it was all inevitability, all ritual and the undeviating path of service. There was no joy in her world, just the great circle of history, coloured by ritual and tradition, all marching across the sere landscape of her dispassionate mind.

Korfax sighed. It wasn't that he had not listened in the past – he had, and with respect – but today had been different. His father had named him Master of Losq and it seemed only right to him that such a thing should be recognised. Surely Doanazin could have found something more worthy to mark such an occasion – tales from younger times, perhaps, of heroes and villains, of dark princes and bright saviours, of courageous endeavours and the glory of battle.

He leant against the wall. None of the Branith here had seen war. No one had, not in these latter days. Battle was a distant dream, reduced either to ritual or drama. The last flames of the great wars had guttered and died during the reign of Anolei, the seventh Velukor, he that was called the unifier and after whom the wars had finally been named. That had happened over six thousand years ago. Ermalei was Velukor now, but he was the forty-eighth to sit upon the holy throne. How long ago it all seemed. And how very far away.

It was strange to think that the world had once been in upheaval. One look at Losq and you would have thought that the great tower had been standing here since the dawn of time.

He looked back at the tower and the realisation hit him. Old! Everything around him was old! His tutor was old, most of the retainers were old, and even those that weren't were still far older than he was! Everything in the tower was old – the tables, the chairs, the tapestries, the paintings. There wasn't a sword in the whole of Losq that did not have a lineage of less than a thousand years, except, possibly, that avalkana in his father's day room. Some were greater, some were lesser, but all had been handed down from generation to generation to generation, and the collected years of them all suddenly seemed like a great and crushing weight.

He looked up at the tower and saw it as he had never seen it before. Umadya Losq, his home, his beloved home, was the oldest of all, for the tower had been here before the first Velukor had ever sat upon the holy throne, before the great wars even, and the stones that made her remembered times so ancient, days so young and distant that they almost lay at the other end of creation.

It was his father that had started all of this, naming him master of Losq only that morning, and from there it had all sprung. Kalazir was right. There were some things that it was not wise to dwell upon too much. All day he had been consumed by the meaning of those few simple words, and now he had finally learnt a real lesson because of it. He took a deep breath. Was this what it meant to grow up? He suddenly did not want to. Where was the joy?

He leant against the wall again and looked along its great curve. Ocholor was only just visible now, walking along the opposite side and nearly hidden by the tower.

If you could get him to talk, Ocholor did have one or two tales to tell. In his youth he had been both a duellist and an instructor in the Nazad Esiask, one of the seven great guilds, and the only one to teach all the arts martial. Korfax had learnt much under Ocholor's stern but careful hand. He had certainly been attentive then.

Ocholor had even been to the capital, not just the guild house in Othil Zilodar, but all the way to great Emethgis Vaniad itself, the centre of the world. Few others here had gone there, a mere handful. There was his father, of course, along with Baschim, the Balzarg of Losq. His tutor had also been there, serving in the tower of the Erm Roith for many years, but his mother had been born there. She had lived for a while in the Umadya Pir itself, the greatest tower yet reared under the Bright Heavens, until she had met his father and joined with him in its great hall. And it was also in that great city that his father had received his kabadar, thereby becoming a Geyad of the Dar Kaadarith.

Korfax thought about the kabadar, that long stave of imperishable crystal which all the adepts of the Namad Dar carried. As his father's son he was expected to follow in his footsteps and become a Geyad as well. The son became the father, as it was written. Tradition demanded that he go to Emethgis Vaniad and become an acolyte in the seminary of the Dar Kaadarith, just as his father had done. But it was what he wanted, for there he would learn the Namad Dar, the lore of stone. He would learn of the forces that bound the world together and perhaps, if he was successful, become a master in their application. But there was no doubt in his heart that it would be so. Each first-born son of his house, all the way back to Haldos, the very first Enay of Losq, had been of the Geyadith.

It was a heady thought, for the whole world was driven by the Namad Dar. There were stones that made light, stones that made heat, stones for storing words and visions and thoughts, stones for flying and stones for sailing. Then, of course, there was the kabadar itself, the stave of a Geyad. With that an adept of the Namad Dar could command the elements themselves, calling up not only the raw forces that composed the world, but also their essence, their very spirit. The four pillars of creation had been subdued by the art of the Dar Kaadarith, and earth, air, fire and water now did the bidding of the Ell.

Not so long ago he had seen his father use his power to hold back a ruinous storm, turning the air aside and diminishing its force. Afterwards he had watched as a wall was repaired, his father making the broken stone flow back into its many places like water. Only that morning his father had shattered the sky with fire, but it was rarely used, that power, only ever employed for ritual or necessity, as written in the Namad Dar. It was strange, but such events, by their very rarity, made any such act all the more impressive.

He looked out from the parapet above the gate, across to the eastern edges of the hills beyond the valley. Chasaloh had allowed the achir to wander where they would this day. Korfax watched them as they drifted across the slopes beyond like small, wayward clouds, a scattering of white over the rolling green. No doubt Chasaloh was already high up on the slopes of the Lee Izirakal, walking his accustomed way, looking for strays.

The sky was clear and a light breeze played with his hair. Korfax smiled and closed his eyes. How he wished that he had been born into days of excitement and glory so that he would not be troubled by trivial accusations of inattention! But all he could do in these quieter times was dream and imagine the giants of the past as they strode across the world, carving it up with sword and fire.

The distant sound of bleating drifted over the hills. Korfax looked up. He blinked. He did not know why, but something about the sound bothered him. Achir rarely complained, if they ever did at all, and the only time one heard them was during the birthing season, but seldom otherwise. Their lot in life was simple. They went where they were led, they ate the food they found there and they made more achir. But the cries he heard now, they were wrong.

He scoured the land, across the valley to the hills beyond, but there was nothing to see. Perhaps they were down below the lower slopes. Not everything could be seen from the wall.

The cries continued: distant, echoing. Was that panic he heard? Perhaps one of them had disturbed something? He could not think of anything that could so upset even one achir, let alone half the flock. Besides, there were no dangerous beasts here, and only the largest would dare tackle an achir anyway.

He wondered if one had blundered too near the nest of a vabazir as it wandered over the distant rocks in search of sweeter grasses. But he dismissed the thought, even as it came to him. The only nest that was anywhere near to Losq, the only nest that he knew of, was high up on the western crags of the Lee Izirakal. Sometimes its builders could be seen far off against the bright sky, circling lazily out over the lower lands in search of prey, or yet indulging in airy play, claws clasped as they tumbled together from the brightness, only to part at the very last moment with screams of ecstasy. No, such beasts as were hereabouts had better things to do with their time than to bother with the achir of Losq. They preferred easier meat. Whatever had upset the flock was something else entirely. Korfax suddenly dared hope it was a Vovin.

Losq was, perhaps, too far north for that almost legendary beast of the high mountains, but Korfax found himself wishing that today it was not so. He would dearly love to see a Vovin.

He could imagine it, a vast winged shape swooping over the ground, talons outstretched, jaws agape as the fire within it swelled. He had seen many pictures of them, even a stone-held vision of one in full flight, but it wasn't the same. Like so many of the wonders he had heard tell of, he longed to see a Vovin in the flesh. He bowed his head. There were so many things in the world that he had never seen.

The bleating grew louder. Korfax looked up again, glancing from side to side, but there was nothing untoward upon the hills or off them. So what could it be?

Perhaps one of them had fallen and its brethren now echoed its distress.

Korfax was about to run around the wall to find Ocholor when a few of the herd came into view, bouncing frantically over the distant ground in obvious panic, and as they ran they scattered, a semicircle of white forms spreading out over the lower edges of the hill. Korfax watched them stream this way and that, as though the very fire of The Creator was after them, but there was nothing there. All in all, it was most peculiar. The achir were running, but nothing was chasing them. Whatever could it be? And then he finally caught sight of movement. Something was coming after all, approaching the tower from the west.

Several figures emerged slowly, one after another, as if out of a mist. Where they had come from he had no idea, but he could see them now, indistinct forms running lightly up and over the lower slopes. They were not using the road. Korfax watched them for a little while, confused and curious, before looking around for Ocholor, but he was no longer in sight. He had been eclipsed by the tower as he walked the far wall. Korfax frowned in indecision and looked back again. The figures remained indistinct, and it was difficult to make out details, but even at this distance he could tell that they were different.

He stared in rapt fascination. What were they? There were no beasts that he had ever heard of that ran on two legs. After all, it was the one thing that marked out the Ell. Whilst the Ell stood upright so that their faces could be lifted up in praise of The Creator, the beast faced the ground in noble ignorance. So what manner of creature were these?

As they approached he began to see more clearly, and he noticed that they appeared to be carrying things, pale surfaces that caught the light with dull gleams. He frowned. It almost looked as if the running things were carrying shields.

He drew back from the wall. That could not be right, could it? Surely he was imagining it. Shields? They had shields? He looked again, wondering whether he had been mistaken, but he was not. There was something else, too – thin shafts of grey held forwards, each a flicker of dim reflections. They were carrying swords.

Korfax felt the world tilt about him. They had weapons? They were armed?

This was a dream, surely. Strange creatures bearing weapons? What did it mean? Korfax looked behind him, but there was no one else in sight. He was alone, the only one on this side of the wall. He looked back again.

The running things were getting closer by the moment, but he still could not see all that they were. It was like watching shadows.

There were other beasts in the world that were hard to see when they moved. Take the wild yanar of the hills, for instance. Green-eyed, dark and solitary, they stalked their small prey unseen until the very moment that they pounced. But these running things were of another kind entirely, for they defeated his sight in some way, like an advancing fog.

Then he finally saw it.

They were headless.

The running things were headless.

Korfax felt the world go dead around him. Where each head should have been there was nothing more than a crude mound of skin. They had no heads? But it was worse than that, far worse, for each mound, each headless neck was broken by a great black slit, a great grinning wound of a mouth, filled to the brim with gleaming teeth.

Korfax could not move. Shock held him immobile. He had longed to see many things in his short and sheltered life, filling his imagination with what he believed to be their likenesses, wars and battles, cowards and heroes, tyrants and saviours, but he had never imagined anything as wrong as what he saw before him now. The creatures that came towards him were an outrage, an atrocity. They defied the very order of creation.

They defied? He was suddenly outlined in light. Now he understood. Now he knew what they were. Was it not the eve of Ahaneh? Was his father not travelling the bounds even at this very moment? There was only one possible answer, and his learning, a learning given to every Ell almost from the very day that they were born, told him what they were. Here were the products of sorcery, beings called up into the world from the abyss below, demons dredged from the Mahorelah and enslaved to another's will.

All his childish imaginings were overthrown. Demons were abroad in the world again, in the here and the now, running swiftly towards his home, towards Umadya Losq. Like an arrow loosed from a bow, like the tip of a lance that had been tilted and aimed, they were coming straight at the walls as though they intended to pierce the very stone itself with their appalling flesh.

What should he do? What could he do? He could not think. A delirium of panic had him. Monstrosities out of legend were running under the clear light of day once more. Such a thing had not happened for long ages, for thousands of years, and all he knew of it, all anyone knew of it, were the old stories.

The old stories had once filled him with innocent delight, firing his imagination as the bright heroes of the past defeated the terrible darkness of the abyss. But now, here on the wall, he saw how wrong he had been.

The tales had all come with a warning: demons are brutal, demons are merciless, and once summoned they have no remorse, no pity and no will. They go about their summoner's bidding with no thought for the consequences. He suddenly saw how little he had understood. The reality was so much worse. Everyone in Losq was in mortal danger.

As if by a miracle it all came together. He could move again, he could speak. Though it had taken mere moments between sight and comprehension, it seemed to him then that it had taken an age. Fear filled him, and with its shivering fire fuelling him, he did the only thing that he could. He shouted his alarm at the top of his voice.

"DEMONS!" he cried. "DEMONS! DEMONS ARE COMING!"

Orkanir was the first to appear. He looked up at Korfax.

"Noren! Why are you calling out like that? What do you mean by it?"

Korfax pointed over the wall.

"OUTSIDE!" he shouted again. "THERE ARE DEMONS! DEMONS ARE COMING!"

Orkanir frowned. If this was some piece of foolishness then Korfax would find himself in the deepest trouble for it. Such things should never be taken lightly, ever. Orkanir walked up onto the wall so that he could see the truth for himself.

He gave Korfax a quick glance as he came, expecting nothing but play acting, but all he saw was fear. He quickened his pace and came to the edge. He looked out and then stepped back, eyes wide with shock. This was no jest at all. There were horrors on the hill, horrors closing in upon Losq.

He turned about and all but leapt down the steps. He ran to the gates and slapped the locking stone. It darkened and the tiny gap between the gates and the wall vanished as the stone fused. A brief glow of heat came and went. Orkanir allowed himself a shudder of relief. Now the gates could not be opened from the outside at all. He looked back at Korfax.

"Come off the wall, that is no place for you," he said.

Korfax came down and Orkanir went to him, laying a hand on his shoulder.

"Go and find my father, but stay off the wall. If you see anyone else tell them what is happening, but find my father first. When you find him, send him here. Then find your mother and tell her what you have seen. Then you must remain with her in the tower. Do you understand?"

"Yes," replied Korfax.

Orkanir watched the young face before him, saw how it was stretched with fear.

"Go now," he said, as gently as he could. "Go and do as I say."

Korfax turned and ran as if the demons were already at his heels. Orkanir watched him leave and then looked back to the wall again. He needed aid.

"BANAVOAN!" he shouted. "SIHBRUJ!"

Banavoan appeared.

"With me! To the wall!" Orkanir told him.

Banavoan looked up at the wall.

"But why?"

Orkanir pointed at the gates behind him.

"Because there are demons outside!" he answered.

Banavoan stared back in utter incomprehension. Sihbruj appeared behind him, looking as if he had only just awakened.

"What is he talking about?" he said. "Demons?"

Banavoan could only hold his hands out in the gesture of incomprehension.

"Do as I say!" hissed Orkanir.

Banavoan looked at Sihbruj and Sihbruj looked at Banavoan. They both looked back at Orkanir.

"But... demons?"

Orkanir all but exploded in fury.

"COME AND SEE FOR YOURSELF," he roared.

Orkanir grabbed hold of Banavoan and all but dragged him up onto the wall. Banavoan pulled himself away once he had regained his balance, and he would have remonstrated but Orkanir was now pointing over the parapet. Banavoan looked to where he pointed and saw at what he was gesturing. He clutched at the wall to steady himself. He saw them, saw them all. He wiped his mouth with the back of his hand. They were foul. He turned to Sihbruj.

"You had better get up here," he said.

Now it was the turn of Sihbruj to complain.

"Will somebody please explain to me what is going on?"

Banavoan all but spat his answer.

"Just do it, will you?"

Sihbruj drew back. He would have answered but Banavoan had already turned about, drawing his sword.

Sihbruj frowned and turned to Orkanir, but Orkanir was not looking back either. Instead he was standing at the parapet, sword already drawn and shield raised. Sihbruj looked to the gate. It was locked. He swallowed in a throat suddenly gone dry. Perhaps it might be a good thing if he went up on to the wall after all.

Arpanad stepped out of the door that led to one of the many store rooms. He caught hold of Korfax just as he ran past.

"Noren, what is happening?" he demanded. "What was all that shouting about? One should not shout in this place, no matter the cause."

Korfax backed away, pointing behind him.

"There are demons. Demons are attacking Losq."

Arpanad raised an eyebrow.

"Well now, demons is it? If that was a jest then I find it in very poor taste."

"But it is true!" Korfax insisted. "There are demons!"

He sounded almost desperate. Arpanad watched as Korfax ran off towards the outhouses as though his life depended upon it.

Arpanad frowned and looked to the wall where Korfax had gestured. Orkanir was up there now, sword drawn, standing in battle stance over the main gate, as were Sihbruj and Banavoan. The main gate was shut and, by the look of it, locked as well. Arpanad felt a sudden chill inside. Maybe this was no jest after all. Maybe he should go and find himself a lance.

Ocholor had heard the shouting, even from the other side of the tower, and now he marched smartly back to discover the cause. Shouting? No one did such a thing in Losq. He would have stern words with whoever was responsible.

He caught sight of someone running towards him from the northern side of the tower. It was Korfax. Ocholor descended the steps and frowned.

"Noren, what was all that shouting about?" he demanded.

"There are demons!" Korfax told him. "Demons are outside the walls. They are here. Orkanir told me to find you and tell you. He said that you must go to the gate."

Ocholor stared down at Korfax.

"Demons? Join him at the gate? Noren, what are you talking about?"

"I have to find my mother," Korfax answered. "Orkanir told me to tell you and then her."

As though he could stand still no longer, Korfax ran off. Ocholor stared after him, dumbfounded. Was that fear he had seen? Was Korfax actually afraid? He turned about and looked at Losq, his world, his charge. It looked as it ever had. This was some sort of foolery, it had to be.

He strode back the way Korfax had come, back to the western wall. If this was a jest, he thought to himself, someone would pay for it. Whatever this foolishness was it had gone far beyond what he considered acceptable. But as he entered the courtyard and looked up, he saw them, up there, on the wall, swords and shields at the ready, Orkanir, Sihbruj and Banavoan. There was another with them also, Arpanad, keeper of the ormn, a long lance in his hand. Orkanir, Sihbruj and Banavoan had all assumed battle stance, but Arpanad was holding his lance down as though to ward something off on the other side of the wall. Ocholor felt a breath of coldness touch him. This was no jest.

He climbed the steps, keeping his silence. Let him see what he must see first. Then he would say what needed to be said. He looked down.

Below him they stood, a little way off, seemingly looking up at him, except that they had no eyes. All he saw were mouths where their heads should be, and a horrid grimace of teeth. Beyond that it was difficult to tell where one began and another finished, for they seemed to merge together. Everything he looked at seemed wrong – swords, shields, limbs – but it was as though his head had suddenly filled with fog. He took a moment to steady himself before turning to his son.

"Who saw them first?" he asked.

"The Noren," answered Orkanir. "Did you see him?"

"He gave me your message!"

"Good. I told him to seek out his mother also. I told him to go with her into the tower and stay there."

Ocholor frowned and looked back down at the demons below. They had not moved. He felt his skin crawl. Orkanir spoke again.

"Do you know what they are?"

"I have never seen the like," said Ocholor, "in or out of a bestiary."

He glanced to the side.

"Arpanad? What are you doing here? You have no armour."

Arpanad did not look back.

"I am doing what I should be doing," he said. "Besides, there was no time."

Ocholor was about to answer when a voice rang out from across the courtyard.

"Branvath? What is happening here?"

He turned. Tazocho was standing at the entrance to the tower.

"We are under attack!" he called back. "Demons!"

He glanced at his son.

"If they move, call out."

He ran back down to the courtyard and felt the weight of his years almost as a physical thing. Of all that he had ever expected to see in his life, demons from the Mahorelah were the last. Thank The Creator that the Noren had seen them and raised the alarm. The wall was their best defence.

Apart from himself there were only three others of the Branith in the entire tower. Add to that the twenty-two retainers, none of them greatly skilled in arms, and they were in a sorry state to repel any sort of siege, let alone an attack by demons. But then, even with its full complement of arms, Losq had never been heavily populated.

Disbelief threatened him. Demons from the Mahorelah were all but unthinkable, but he had seen the horrors for himself. They stood upright, they were armed with sword and shield and they were headless. Ocholor shuddered as he thought of what he had studied briefly from atop the wall. In all his life, in all his dreams, he had never imagined such abominations.

Putting down his fear and his doubt, he looked back at the wall. Banavoan, Sihbruj, Arpanad and Orkanir remained where they were, watching. They were ready, all of them, and he could almost taste their resolve from where he stood. They waited like warriors, even Arpanad, ready for the foe to make the first move. He looked with especial favour at his son and felt a sudden surge of pride. Orkanir had been the first to act. He had always remembered his teachings.

Ocholor met Tazocho at the centre of the courtyard. She stopped in front of him, her face as hard as it had ever been, her eyes sharp and clear but utterly unreadable. He found himself wondering what thoughts were going through her mind now.

"Demons, you say?" she asked.

"They are just beyond the wall, Enay," he reported.

"And what are they doing?"

"Nothing, Enay. They appear to be waiting for something."

He watched her, saw how well she controlled herself. Not a flicker crossed her face at the news. Only her eyes showed anything at all – and that the cold hardness of stone.

"How many of them are there?" she asked.

"I am not sure, Enay, but there may be at least thirty," he replied.

She looked surprised.

"Can you not count them?"

"It is difficult to tell where one ends and another begins," he told her. By the look on her face, she clearly did not like the sound of that.

"And do you know of what kind they are?" she asked, hardening herself again.

"No, Enay," he told her. "They are of no kind I ever remember reading about. No bestiary that I ever saw described such things. They are armed with sword and shield, but they have no heads, just mouths."

Ocholor suddenly looked angrily back at her, as if his own failures found her wanting instead.

"And here I was thinking that there were no Argedith left in the world," he said.

Tazocho fixed him with an even harder stare.

"Then explain to me why you were trained in the art of war? Was it not to counter such a threat as this? Why does the Enay of Losq enact Kuslah at this very moment? Do I have to remind you of the words of Karmaraa?"

She drew in a great breath, as though what she had to say next required nothing less.

"Though it take an age of the heavens," she intoned, "the Ell shall always be prepared, for evil does not sleep, it merely bides its time!"

Ocholor blinked back his surprise at the rebuke, but there was nothing he could say in answer. She was right, of course, and her words pulled him back to himself. Self-doubt was fatal, especially in the face of battle. He admonished himself with strictures from the Namad Alkar: 'Without constant practice, a warrior will be nervous and undecided when facing battle; without constant practice, those in command will be wavering and irresolute when the crisis is at hand'.

Seeing the effect her words had, Tazocho changed the subject.

"And who raised the alarm? Who saw the threat first?"

"The Noren," answered Ocholor. "He was the one that raised the alarm."

A glint of pride gentled her eyes before a flash of concern sharpened them again.

"So where is he? Where is my son? Where have you sent him?" she demanded.

Her thoughts were suddenly clear upon her face. Ocholor hid his surprise. This was the first time he could ever remember seeing through her walls. Behind her concern for her son lay something deeper. If only Sazaaim were here. Now the defence of Losq lay in her hands, and her hands alone. She had no other to turn to. He was about to answer when another voice interrupted.

"But I am here, mother."

Korfax stepped out from behind her. She closed her eyes for a moment, closing them in thankfulness, and laid a light hand upon his shoulder, holding it, caressing it, before withdrawing it again. That was all she would allow.

"Where have you been?" she asked.

"Looking for you," he replied. "I told everyone that I passed what was happening."

She smiled and then gestured back towards the tower.

"Good, you have done your part. Go inside now – and do it quickly! Lock the doors. This is no place to be."

Korfax looked up at her. Surely they were safe now? Why did he have to go to the tower? He wanted to see. He opened his mouth to object, but Ocholor interrupted.

"Noren!" he growled in his fiercest voice. "Do as the Enay says! And do it quickly!"

Korfax backed away, blinking furiously. Ocholor had never spoken to him like that, ever. Why was everyone so angry with him today? First Doanazin, then his mother, now Ocholor. But as he was about to answer, warning shouts came from the wall.

Korfax span round and stared in horror as grey shapes came over it in horrid profusion. They came almost in a flood, far too many for Sihbruj, who they fell upon and threw back over the wall. He vanished from sight. Banavoan, Orkanir and Arpanad retreated and dropped down to the courtyard, their faces frozen in shock by the speed of the attack.

Time compressed. Ocholor drew his sword and gave a great cry as he rushed into battle. Korfax stared after him even as his mother took hold of him and pulled him back towards the tower. Indistinct shapes dropped into the courtyard from the wall, crouching snarls of tooth and blade.

Ocholor was upon the demons in moments, his sword a whirling arc of metal. It all became a confusion of sound and motion, words shouted in desperation, hisses and roars following them like answering echoes. More demons tumbled over the wall, and more after them, one after another, each lofting a blade gleaming with a hungry light.

Ocholor withstood them for a brief moment, but then even he retreated as the grey advanced like a wall. Then he disappeared from sight. All Korfax could see now were Orkanir, Banavoan and Arpanad, their weapons a flicker of bright reflections.

Korfax watched Arpanad. He was moving fast, faster than Korfax had ever seen him move before, his face twisted into a grimace of the most astonishing ferocity as he impaled one of the demons on his lance, all but lifting it bodily from the stone. Korfax gasped in astonishment at the sight. He had never seen Arpanad look so fierce, or so grim, or so daring. For the briefest moment he saw a hero, a slayer of demons.

But it did not last. As Arpanad tried to withdraw his weapon, a second demon came at him from the side and cut him down with a vicious swipe of its blade. Korfax cried out, a wordless denial. That was not how it was supposed to be. Heroes did not bleed! But Arpanad fell to the ground nonetheless, eyes wide, mouth wider, as his assailant leaned over him and bared its teeth. A tongue lashed out to lick at the blood that now ran from Arpanad's wounds, and then the mouth reached out to take a bite. Korfax could not look away. This was wrong, horribly wrong. Battle was supposed to be glorious, not bloody and vile.

The demon raised itself up again and stepped forward, red with blood. Another joined it. Now Korfax stared at them, and it was almost as if they stared back, their tooth-filled mouths like great eyes. They were coming for him.

Someone raced by, a rush of orange, a flash of blades. Korfax was almost too surprised to recognise his tutor. Was that Doanazin? Was that really Doanazin? Korfax stared at the two blades she held – one high, one low – in the posture of readiness.

"Get the Noren to safety, Enay," Doanazin called back as she ran. "I will hold them off."

Then she was on the demons, her two blades a dance of reflections, notching shields, blocking thrusts, forcing them back again. Korfax felt numb. He had never imagined anything like this at all. That his tutor could fight? That his tutor could wield a blade to such deadly effect? But even as he watched, dumbstruck, he saw others rushing up to join the battle, each suddenly armed with blade, staff or lance.

There went Eilrom, famed for his skill in metalcraft, his hair flying behind him, a large two-handed duelling sword held before him. And there was Permanal, the son of Chasaloh and Kalazir, a long sword clutched in his left hand, a short shield held in his right.

Korfax dwelt in a slow and fevered nightmare, his mother dragging him back to the tower, he following her in a daze. Somewhere out there a battle raged. He heard the clash of arms, the hiss of demons and the cries of the dying. What had happened to his world? The morning had started out so bright and fair. Now, with the end of the day, it had descended into blood and chaos.

As they reached the door to the tower, Tazocho turned to look back. Korfax could see the questions in her eyes. Who was living? Who was dying? He understood as never before. This was where the world turned.

In the courtyard Orkanir appeared to be the only one left, retreating towards them as if fighting his way free from a quagmire. His blade slashed this way and that and for a moment it looked as if he would fail as the demons hurled themselves at him, but he pushed them aside with his shield and then ran on, running hard back to the tower. He came headlong towards them, his blade a-drip with slow, grey fluids, but the demons were after him, picking themselves up or leaping over the fallen, mouths wide, swords pointing like promises.

"ENAY! NOREN! GET INSIDE!" Orkanir called. "CLOSE THE DOOR AND LOCK IT! DO IT NOW!"

Tazocho forced Korfax inside but held the door ready. Orkanir leapt through the gap and the door slammed shut. Thudding sounds came from outside as if things were being piled up against the stone. Tazocho locked the door and a brief heat came and went. It was sealed. Orkanir breathed hard and looked at her.

"You should not have waited, Enay," he said.

"I do what I must," she replied.

"Then you are mine to ward. I am the last."

Tazocho bowed her head as if grateful, but something in her eyes darkened and they became even colder than before.

It was quiet outside now, but there was a sense that something waited just beyond the door, something eager.

The door to the tower began to crack. It seemed only a moment ago that they had closed and locked it, but time was moving quickly now, and its ever diminishing moments were measured out by the eager blows that rained down from outside. The nightmare rushed headlong to its conclusion as the shadows of evening lengthened, beckoning to night.

Orkanir stood to the fore, standing in front of Korfax and Tazocho, his sword in his left hand, his shield in his right. He faced the failing door like a statue, his feet planted on the stone as if immovable.

"How many do you think are left? I counted eight," Tazocho said.

"Eight there are, Enay," he answered.

"Is anyone else alive?" she wondered.

"I do not know," he returned. There was the briefest pause, the slightest tightening of the eyes.

"I saw my father fall."

Another pause.

"Banavoan took many of them before he was caught. Arpanad, Eilrom, Permanal and even Doanazin killed not a few between them. But all now lie in the courtyard and there is no one else that I know of. I think some of the demons went through the outer houses earlier and I thought I heard a cry a little while ago, but I have heard nothing else since."

Korfax stared at Orkanir. He had never heard him speak so. Orkanir seemed perilous now, elemental and deadly, filled to the brim with cold fire. Like the high mountain snow, he was ready to fall down each precipitous slope and crush all that lay in his path. Korfax turned away again. He was not equal to this. Was this what it meant to be Enay, to stand by and watch as others died in your name? It was wrong. He could not do it.

Korfax glanced up at his mother, marking the swift and seeing glance she passed over Orkanir, brief concerns clouding her eyes before she wrapped herself in stillness again. She seemed even more determined than ever, clothing herself in a mantle of the hardest stone. Korfax looked away. He had been abandoned, lost in a world of terrifying absolutes. Orkanir had become an avalanche in waiting and his mother the mountain to which it clung. But where was he?

"They will not be satisfied until we are all dead," his mother announced.

"So it would seem, Enay," Orkanir answered, but he did not turn his attention from the door.

"We must warn others of this danger. Others should know."

"Yes, Enay, others should know." And that was all he would spare. So since he had become her echo, Tazocho said nothing more.

The door cracked further and a fragment fell to the floor. A grey sword thrust its way through the hole before pulling back again. Orkanir glanced over his shoulder and his face was suddenly alight with anger.

"Enay! Why are you still here? Take the Noren and go! He is your care now. Find somewhere! Hide! I will hold them here! They will not pass!"

But Tazocho did not move.

"I must see," she said.

Korfax looked up at her in growing distress. They should go, just as Orkanir had said. What was she waiting for? Orkanir had told them to leave, and Korfax so wanted to obey. He did not want to die at the hands of a demon. But his mother remained where she was. She remained and she waited, watching, her eyes looking beyond the borders of the world. She was seeking for a sign, he told himself, looking for a moment yet to come, a moment that would gain them all an advantage. He had no choice but to stand beside her and wait in ever-mounting panic.

There came another blow upon the door and more of its stone fell. Korfax stared at the destruction in fascinated revulsion. It suddenly seemed that, given enough time, these abominations could even shatter the stone of the tower itself!

The gap in the door widened, more stone fell and under the stone a demon, a noiseless blur of movement that darted through the jagged opening with blade and shield before it. But Orkanir was ready.

He leapt forward and dispatched the creature even before it had a chance to defend itself. The demon hissed briefly and then fell to the floor where it slumped, its body disintegrating with undue haste into a foul pool of grey slime. Korfax felt sick as he watched, unable to look away as the horrid thing corroded onto the flagstones.

The door broke a little more and Korfax looked up. Two more demons surged through the gap as though suddenly boneless, one high, one low. Orkanir repeated his previous move. One demon slashed its sword in response, lightning-fast, but Orkanir, faster still, ducked as it swung, attacking before it could react, taking away its legs with an irresistible sweep of his blade. The second demon brought down its sword in a vicious arc, but Orkanir caught the blow upon his shield and turned it aside, forcing the demon off balance. Then, before it could right itself, Orkanir thrust his sword upwards and the demon shuddered, fluids erupting like a fountain from its mouth. Orkanir leapt back. Now the look on his face was brutal as he watched the demons fail, relishing their demise with dark satisfaction.

An unpleasant sucking sound came from outside and a fourth demon came through the gap in the door like a spear. It found Orkanir unprepared, and its outstretched sword caught him under his right shoulder. Blood spattered the walls and Orkanir gasped with pain. Two more followed, and all three attacked almost as one, blades and shields dancing in strange, unequal patterns.

They were fast, mere blurs of movement, but even though he was wounded, Orkanir still matched them. He took one across its belly, disembowelling it with a great sweep of his sword, before spitting a second with a heroic thrust through its chest. But the third was poised, and it attacked at exactly that moment, returning the compliment a hundredfold. With a jagged grey sword buried in his side, Orkanir staggered, his face filled with sudden mortality.

His shield dangling from his arm, Orkanir dropped to his knees. He looked back at Tazocho and blood ran from his mouth. Then he slumped to the floor like a broken thing and a weak cry escaped his lips.

"Run!" he gasped. Then he lay still.

Tazocho finally moved as if that had been the sign she had been waiting for. As two more demons squeezed through the crack in the door she dragged Korfax away with her. For a moment the last three demons stood over the body of Orkanir, tongues flickering, mouths drooling, and then they danced quickly over his body and followed in pursuit.

They fled grey death. Up many stairs and through many rooms they ran, Korfax following, Tazocho leading, taking as wild a path as she could contrive.

They came to the upper halls, darting through this door or that, along corridors, through adjoining rooms, before dropping back down again and into the main hall, skirting around the great table, aiming obliquely for the door again. As they ran through the hall, Tazocho reached out and flicked one of the lances from its place upon the wall, catching it adroitly in her left hand. Korfax found himself caught by the deftness of her movements. Now it was her turn to surprise him with her speed. She caught his glance and gestured towards the far door with the lance. They ran on, but even as they left the hall two demons entered behind them, silent knots of grey racing over the floor like hungry shadows. Tazocho steered Korfax down the lesser stairs that led to the under rooms. He heard her muttering to herself.

"But where is the other? There were three of them!"

Korfax could not answer. He knew even less than her.

They came back to the ground level, but even as they reached the corridor that led to the outside, the third demon stepped forward out of the shadows, waiting for them as if prescient, a grin of teeth betwixt sword and shield.

Tazocho came to a stop. This one had doubled back to wait at precisely the right place. Now it stood before them, hissing its lust, the shadow of a tongue flickering between its many teeth. They fell back from it and almost into the arms of the others as they danced down the stairs from above.

Boxed, Tazocho pulled Korfax to the side and into an old and all but forgotten room, one only ever used for storage and seldom visited by any. She slammed the door behind her, and Korfax, almost by reflex, set the lock with a single touch of a finger. Outside a faint growl of frustration came and went. Korfax looked up at his mother and allowed himself a sigh of relief. But his relief was short-lived. Their pursuers were not to be so easily thwarted.

A strange sucking sound came through the door, the same sound that they had heard before. It was followed by a momentary silence, and then hard blows began to rain down upon the stone. Each dull thud echoed heavily and Korfax stared at the door with renewed horror whilst his mother looked carefully about her.

There was no other way out. There were no windows and the only light came from a small piradar set in the ceiling. She tested the lance she had chosen, flexing it in her hands, a quick set of movements giving her its feel. Old it might have been, but it was still sturdy and certainly lethal enough in the right hands. It was something at least.

Korfax stood beside the door and gazed in fear at his mother. The filth of the Mahorelah were beating against it now like great hammers, their muffled exertions passing through the stone like curses.

Tazocho remained where she was, erect and commanding, her long lance tilted at the door.

"Get behind me," she said to him. "They will be through soon enough. That door will not hold for ever."

But he did not move. A haze of indecision had him. Before this moment he had never seen his mother wield a weapon of any kind. Watching her now, though, he could see the practised ease with which she hefted her lance. She clearly knew what she was doing. But here he was, a lad of only thirteen years, named master by his father only that morning, and his mother was the only one who could protect them both. He felt worse than helpless.

"Korfax, do as I say!"

Her voice whipped through the air and he had no choice but to obey. His mother still ruled his every horizon, despite his dreams. Korfax leapt over the table so that he could stand at her side. Then he looked up at her and saw her features clench.

The door shuddered and dust fell, but it remained in place, obstinate enough to deny the demons entry just yet. They had only scant moments left.

"I should have a weapon!" he complained.

Tazocho did not look around.

"There are no others," she told him. "This lance is all that there is. Besides, what weapon could you use?"

"But Ocholor told me only yesterday that I was good for my age."

She sighed and looked down. A gentler smile played across her lips and she looked fully at him. She reached out a hand and stroked his cheek.

"But that was just play, young of my heart. We face an altogether harder truth here. So be still now and wait behind me. I will need all my strength for what comes next. There will come a moment when you must run. Seize it and do not look back."

She leaned in and kissed him gently on his brow, but then looked away again. Abandoned once more, he turned about. He could feel tears in his eyes, fear and frustration fighting for control. Run? How could he? There must be some other way. This was not how it was supposed to be – demons and death and carnage.

He searched the room again, desperate to find something that he could use, something with at least a measure of comfort. There was a chest in the corner behind them, an orderly stack of pots in another, several boxes of assorted oddments in a third, and a set of folded banners in the forth. The only other occupant of the room was the table, and there was nothing under that.

He looked around again, before coming back to the chest. It was old, bound about with age-blackened laidrom, darkly nondescript, but there was suddenly something about it, something familiar. A distant memory stirred in his mind and he gasped even as he caught it. Once, a long time ago, he had seen his father lift a great black blade from out of that chest.

How strange it was to remember that now, he thought. It had been so many years ago. But hope lifted within him as he thought of the great black blade.

He had been small, only recently able to walk on his own two feet, when he had found himself by the door to a strange room he had never been in before, watching, wide-eyed and innocent, as his father lifted up a dark sword from out of a small chest, holding it up for a moment before putting it back again with a hard look on his face.

Korfax would have stayed there, watching, but voices from above had called out his name and he had tottered off, his father still unaware that he had been observed at all. Korfax, though, had never thought of the moment again, not until now. It was almost as if the memory had waited for just such a moment as this.

Hope swelled inside. He could use that blade, if it was still there, and if he had strength enough to wield it. He went quickly to the chest and lifted the lid, peering inside as he did so. He frowned. The chest seemed strangely larger within than it did without. How odd was that? But he had no time for such fancies now, as he needed the black sword.

He saw it almost immediately, a thick black blade with a thick black hilt, lying on a bed of scrolls. It was smaller than memory had made it, strangely compressed and oddly shrunken, but then he reminded himself that he also had been smaller when he had first seen it. Memory could play strange tricks, especially when they came from such an early age.

He looked down at the sword. It was so unlike any that he had ever seen before. Like the chest in which it lay, there seemed to be far more to it than met the eye. Korfax suddenly had the odd impression that the black sword had not been forged at all but rather carved from a single block of metal.

He gazed at it in wonder. It seemed all of a piece as it slept in its chest, like a seed deep in its singular dream of resurrection whilst around it the litter of its past lay like old leaves, a curious collection of discoloured scrolls, each impatient for their eventual unfurling.

Korfax blinked. He was dreaming again. He must wake up. He reached for the black sword and his hand fell into limitless depths. He gasped. How far must he go to reach the hilt? He reached downwards, his arm lengthening, his grasp extending. He closed his eyes and tried to ignore the illusion. He wanted the blade, he needed the blade and he would allow nothing else to distract him. He heard a crashing sound, he heard his mother speak, but it was a distant thing, of little concern. He touched the sword. It felt warm. He closed his hand about the hilt. Darkness filled him.

The door cracked from its top to its bottom and fell inwards with a crash. The dust of its demise billowed into the room, but the demons did not follow. Tazocho frowned. What was this now? Were they playing with their prey? Then the strange sucking sound came again.

It was appalling, and for a moment she wished she could stop up her ears, but it did not last long. She wondered what it portended, wondered what new horror the demons were preparing, but then they came into view, stepping slowly through the settling dust as if already victorious, tongues a-flicker as they tasted the air.

Tazocho curled her lips in disgust. Up until this moment it had all been a rush of fighting and fleeing, with the demons things of grey shadow, suggestions of bone and flesh and the grin of wicked teeth. But now, as they advanced slowly, she had time enough to see them in all their grisly splendour. It was almost as if they were displaying themselves to her, that they understood her horror and took delight from it.

At first she thought them the resurrected dead, what with their folded, ulcerous flesh, their withered breasts, jutting bones and famished bodies, but then she saw her error. They were not old, but young, almost unfinished even, as though they had fallen too early or too eagerly from the womb.

Hugely out-sized joints dominated their limbs: knobbed, pitted and seeping. Their legs seemed sturdy enough, built for speed with long taloned feet, but the arms were stranger by far. Each left arm was a shield, a great curling mass of bone that erupted from the flesh like a growth, a clenched fist hidden behind it, wicked with claws. On the right arm, though, there was no hand at all, just a pulsing knot of flesh wrapped around a sword of bone, a jagged sweep of curves that gleamed as though wet with venom.

Hunched over an emaciated belly, each wedge-shaped torso twisted under the dominion of a demented spine that seemingly went where it would. At its base there flexed a tail of sorts, a restless worm of bone, descending from its root as though from rotted gristle.

But the worst thing, the very worst of all, was the absence of a head, for the spine that writhed its way up each crooked back, searching for consummation, ended at the neck as if betrayed. Instead, from the folds of skin that hung between each shouldered pylon of bone, there rose a hump of flesh, a truncated mound broken only by a great wound of a mouth, a grin of teeth like a nest of knives.

Seeing them now, seeing them in all their ways, Tazocho understood the malice of their making: birth as death, creation as cruelty. Thrust into the world in some appalling act of violence, it was all that they knew. Arm wrestled with shoulder, leg collided with groin, tail clashed with spine. Flesh as a battlefield, for ever making war upon itself, and a hunger without end.

They moved towards her – slowly, deliberately – blades and shields lofted and ready. She could feel their anticipation. What had happened before had been quick, a rush of moments and the clash of forces. What would happen now would be slow, the long burning fire of a lust indulged.

The leader of the three extended its mouth and its teeth rolled past each other, riding their rows in a curl of unfurling blades. A hiss, a laugh perhaps, gurgled its way out like slow vomit.

Tazocho gave the leader her full attention and put everything else out of her mind. This was it. She had come to the moment, so she waited, ready, holding her lance down so that its tip was level with the demon's chest, poised for the killing stroke.

"At least I will stop you, slime of the abyss," she told it. But then a shadow filled the room, sucking away the light, and there was something behind her, something dark.

Korfax lifted the fat, black blade up from its resting place in the chest, holding it up before him like some swollen flame. If it had surprised him before, it amazed him now.

When he had first laid his hand upon it, it had felt inordinately heavy, solid and weighty, a weapon that only the very strongest could wield, perhaps. But now that he had dragged it up from its resting place it felt astonishingly light – a mere feather in his hand, almost as if it had been made to rest there. He stared up at it and it darkened the air about him, black upon black, the darkest of fires flickering over its impenetrable surface and beyond.

The sword grew in his hand until it was vast, larger than the largest kansehna, but Korfax did not care. Though it might grow to the size of a mountain he could still wield it, for the sword was a part of him now, another limb, muscled for the act of bloodshed. He turned to his enemies and extended the black sword towards them like a threat, even as the black flames waxed upon its blade. Then the sword began to sing.

The song caught him, a song like no other he had ever heard in his life. It was a song of victory, a melody of blood, and it took him beyond himself and on to another place entirely.

He stood within red mists that curled and drifted whilst the echoes of battles long gone, long forgotten, circled him like distant thunder. He felt himself become mighty, his body reinvented, even as the sword became a fabulous shape in his hand, its surface rippling and flowing as it became both blade and shield.

No sick flesh this; stems and leaves of living metal filled the air about him, darker than midnight, harder than stone. Then either he wielded it or it wielded him, for he suddenly moved and his great black blade moved with him, guiding – or guided by – his willing hand. The one became three, three blades piercing his enemies with liquid ease, drinking deep of their marrow and consuming them in fire before crumbling them to ash.

It was over almost before it had begun, and he suddenly found himself upon the other side, standing over their ruin like some new-born god, smiling down upon them with all a youth's radiance. He raised his sword in the air above him and rejoiced, and the world about him stopped so that it could honour his victory.

Exultant, caught upon the eternal threshold, caught within it, he remained where he was until, from somewhere else, a lifetime's distance, he heard a voice. It was his mother calling to him from some paltry place, her voice intruding on the dream, vying with the song of the sword.

"Korfax!" she called. "Hear me! Hear my voice! Come back to me! Come back! Please come back to me, Korfax! Please come back!"

Come back? He did not want to. Here were miracles. Here lay his heart's desire. No enemy could touch him whilst he stood in this place. But even as he heard his mother's voice, he knew that it was already over. Her desperation touched him, and the moment, fleeting and fragile, moved on.

He stepped reluctantly back out of his dream and found himself beside the ruin of the door. At his feet lay three small piles of ash, and his mother, wide-eyed and gasping, was staring at him from the other side of the room, a long lance clutched in her hands as though to fend something off.

He looked back at her and frowned slightly. Was that fear in her eyes? Was she afraid of him? Surely not! But something was not right here. He felt immersed in cloud, enfolded by impenetrable fogs. He shook his head to dislodge them, but they would not leave.

"Korfax!" she said. "Speak to me, tell me that you are still here."

Korfax deepened his frown. What a strange thing to ask!

"Of course I am here," he said. "Whatever do you mean?"

He glanced again at the ash piles at his feet. Where had they come from? And where were the demons? He looked back at her.

"What happened to the demons?" he asked. "Where are they?"

But his mother did not move. All she did was stare at him.

"Don't you remember?" she asked him in return, her eyes wide.

Korfax felt himself cut adrift. What was happening here? There had been a strange place of red mist, but what was that? Was it a dream? Was it real? He did not know. Did his mother? He looked at her and waited for answers, answers that would make some kind of sense and would anchor him again.

"You killed them," she told him. "You killed the last of them. You saved us both."

Who had he killed? The demons? What was this? Another dream? He gazed at the piles of ash at his feet. Nothing made any sense at all. He looked back at his mother.

"I killed them?"

He shook his head again. His mind had become unruly. He could not think clearly at all.

"I thought there was a dream of red mists," he said, "but I didn't think that I was really there. Then there was a song..."

He looked down and saw the sword still in his grasp, but it was no longer the vast and wondrous shape from his dream; now it was just a great black blade, suddenly incongruous in his hands.

Sounds came from outside. It seemed almost miraculous, but even as they both turned about, Sazaaim and Baschim raced through the door like saviours.

Sazaaim caught sight of them both all in a moment, almost as if they were one and the same, and his expression of uncontrollable rage changed instantly to one of uncontainable joy. He all but sagged in relief as he reached out for them.

"Thank The Creator you are here. I thought you both dead," he said.

Tazocho dropped her lance and went to him. They held each other tight. Korfax though remained where he was, caught between places, caught by his confusion. He lowered the black sword to the floor and let it rest there, a dangle of darkness from his left hand.

Sazaaim turned to his son with tears in his eyes. Though Korfax did not look up, his father looked down at his son and clasped him tight.

"I thought I had lost you!" he said.

Baschim watched the reunion with less joy than he might have. He already knew that his own homecoming would be darker by far than that of his master. He had seen how others had died this day and he feared the worst. But he held himself in place and endured what had to be endured. For the sake of his master he held his duty paramount, so that he could see the world around him as Sazaaim could not. He had already noticed the black sword in Korfax's hand and the three ash heaps upon the floor, so he at least understood something of what had happened. He closed his eyes for a moment in fear, fearing to break his master's joy, but then he hardened his heart so that he could place the hand of warning upon his master's shoulder.

"Enay!" he said. "There is ash upon the floor and your son holds the black sword! Have you not seen?"

Sazaaim half turned to Baschim and frowned.

"What?"

Baschim pointed. Sazaaim looked. Sazaaim looked again. Then he saw it, the ash heaps and the black blade still nestling in his son's hand. He stepped back, eyes darkening by the moment, even as he released his son from his embrace. Baschim turned away and walked to the outer door. His duty was almost done. Now all he had to do was shield the room from others. Sazaaim, meanwhile, had eyes only for his son.

"Korfax?" he said. "Did you do this? Did you wield that blade?"

Tazocho came forward and placed her hand against his lips.

"Is it not enough to know that he saved us both with it?" she asked. "If he had not slain the last of the demons, you would be grieving this day."

Sazaaim held her hand for a moment, kissing it briefly, caressing it, but then he pushed it aside as relief and rage fought for possession of his face.

"But how could he have even known that it was there?" he cried.

"Now is not the time for such questions," she returned. "We are both alive and that is all that matters."

She drew herself up and took a deep breath.

"Now tell me! Who has lived, who has died?"

Sazaaim closed his eyes and shivered.

"The others are looking," he murmured. "I should go and help."

He opened his eyes again.

"As should I," Tazocho agreed. "But our son needs us also. Someone must ward him now. Someone must care for him."

Sazaaim looked at Korfax and his face became hard.

"Yes," he said. "Indeed, someone must attend to Korfax."

Sazaaim pointed at the sword.

"Korfax, put that sword back where you found it!"

The command was almost a demand, but Korfax did not move. Instead he gazed up at his father. Confusion still had him. Surely his father would be pleased by what he had done? He had slain demons, hadn't he? He had slain them with a sword, hadn't he? Wasn't that what he was supposed to do? He had saved his own life and that of his mother. But it had all happened so fast.

Sazaaim's eyes widened as Korfax remained where he was. Was his son defying him? Was his very own son defying him? It was too much. Inconsiderate fury possessed him.

"KORFAX!" he roared.

Korfax jumped back and all but shrank to the floor, his eyes wide as he stared back. His father had suddenly become a storm in his sky, heading in fast, face dark, eyes darker, all filled with the threat of lightning.

"Do as I tell you!" Sazaaim ordered. "Do it now!"

But Korfax could not move. He was terrified. He could not have moved even if he had wanted to. Then his mother stepped between them both and held up her right hand in denial.

"Enough!" she exclaimed. "That is more than enough! Cage your power! Look beyond this moment and think carefully. Consider the innocence of your son!"

Sazaaim backed away from her as though she had struck him. He looked down at the floor, blinking furiously. Tazocho remained where she was for a moment, arm upraised like a shield, but then she turned about again and came to Korfax, her voice altogether gentle, so wonderfully gentle.

"Korfax," she said, "listen to my voice, hear me once more. Do as your father commands and all will be well, you will see."

Korfax could not move. It was all too much. His father had suddenly become terror personified and his mother was now a bright shield of comfort, gentler and warmer than she had been in a long, long while.

"Put the sword back," she said. "Put it back where you found it. Do it, my son, do it for me."

She did not command him, she asked, though it was almost a plea, a hope that all would be well again. Korfax stared down at the black sword in his hand, the strange and shrunken black sword.

He looked up at her and she smiled back at him, a wonderful smile. That was the turning point. He would do it. He would do it for that smile.

He made his way back to the chest. With every step that he took the sword seemed to shrink even further, whilst its weight strangely grew as though it was reluctant to be hidden away again, and by the time he had reached the chest it was all that he could do just to put it back inside. But his mother did not help him and neither did his father. They just watched, carefully, as if this was a task only he could perform. They both followed him with their eyes, his father's dark and bruised, his mother's bright and gleaming as if by hiding the sword away again he did the very best thing he could in all the world. Korfax closed the lid of the chest and looked back at them both. What did it all mean?

Almost as the lid closed his mother came to him, taking him in her arms, holding him tight, enfolding him with her love. She clasped him to her for a moment, and then, without another glance at his father, she took him from the room.

Outside, Baschim still waited, his face carved in stone. He bowed to her briefly but then turned aside again, returning to the side of his master. Without a glance or even a bow of acknowledgement, Tazocho took Korfax swiftly away.

5

THE GREAT DIVIDE

Man-dr-pan Mir-italu
Thil-lantel Tabah-nio-kar
Korm-ger-pa Odus-niljo
Arm-zien-kam Kas-nisel-sag
Teo-pamjo Lap-hommil-pim
Qis-si-uhm Odtol-om-qia
Ipurhon Avdril-piatol

Tazocho led Korfax to his room and quickly took him inside. She closed the door and sat him upon his bed. Then she sat down beside him and took him in her arms again, holding him tightly, holding him close.

"Fear nothing now," she said. "I am with you."

She gently laid her head against his.

"And do not fear your father," she told him. "He has many cares, and sometimes they get the better of him. Think instead that you did what needed to be done. You saved us both, and that is all that matters."

They sat together for a while in quietness. Then she turned to him.

"Nothing you did was wrong," she said. "I am the one at fault."

He looked up at her.

"But you are my mother," he told her. "You are never wrong."

Tears welled in her eyes and she held him even tighter.

"But I have been," she said. "I have been. I have missed many things since you came into the world, and today I nearly lost all that I ever held dear. I thought that I knew how things should be, and I was obsessed by the small, the irrelevant. I thought that I knew what was needed, but I did not. Today you showed me how wrong I was, how blind. You cut through my arrogant belief with one simple act. You are both my son and my saviour, and I find myself more proud of you than I can ever put into words."

Korfax felt the release at last and his tears joined with hers. She was his mother. She loved him after all.

"You will be the mightiest of the Farenith," she told him. "I foresee it. You will rise above all the curses and all the tribulations. They will not contain you in the end. You will be blessed by The Creator."

Korfax could say nothing, do nothing. His mother had blessed him. She had never done that before, ever, and the wine of that blessing made the horrors of the day flee far away on skulking wings.

It was not long before his father came to the door and pushed it wide. He stood upon the threshold, stern and forbidding.

"Come!" he demanded. "There is work yet to do. Let Korfax remain here for now. Whatever else may be said, this has been death's day! There are others that need our attention."

Korfax looked up in fear, but his mother gently caressed his brow and then kissed it, before turning sharply towards his father.

"Will you give me no time," she asked, "even for this?"

Sazaaim glanced away for a moment, his eyes troubled, but then he met her gaze again, sterner than ever.

"I cannot," he said. "Others need you, even as they need me."

Tazocho stiffened, a brief clench of defiance perhaps, but then she looked back at Korfax again and smiled sadly.

"Rest and fear no more," she said. "Stay here, you are safe."

Then she withdrew and the door closed behind her, leaving him alone and deep in bewilderment.

He sat upon the bed and wrestled with himself. When had his mother ever spoken to him like that? When had she ever caressed him like that? When had she ever wept over him? And when had his father been so dark and terrible? His world was suddenly turned upside down.

There were too many questions in his head. What were the grey demons? What was the black sword? Had he really killed with it? Why was his father so angry with him? His thoughts became a tumble of chaos, and for the first time in his life he found himself resenting his father. His mother had blessed him and his father had taken her away.

He heard sounds from outside, raised voices, wordless calls and cries of denial. He went to the window and looked out into the darkness. There were lights below and the movement of shadows.

"Do not look out of the window, Noren. There are things you should not be seeing, not yet at least."

Korfax looked fearfully over his shoulder. It was Baschim.

"But I want to know what is happening," Korfax answered.

"No, Noren, you do not," Baschim told him. "You may think that you do, but I tell you now that you do not."

He waited a moment but then held up the two bowls he had been carrying.

"Come, Noren. Let us sit at the table and eat. Let us eat together."

Korfax looked down.

"But I'm not hungry," he said.

Baschim's face remained as still as ever, but something behind his eyes tightened. "Nonetheless, Noren, it would honour me if you would."

There was an edge to Baschim's voice and Korfax did not miss it, so he bowed his head and joined Baschim at the table. They sat opposite each other.

Korfax looked at the bowls. Both were filled with a thick and wholesome-looking broth. He looked at the broth and smelt its fragrance. It was of the kind Geziam was so good at making. He watched as it steamed gently, almost as if beckoning to him.

Korfax glanced at Baschim, but Baschim was not looking back. Instead he was looking down at the bowl before him, a hint of an expression on his face, a strange look that Korfax had never seen there before, like broken tenderness. Korfax swallowed. What had happened now? But then Baschim looked up again and the strange look was gone.

"I have some things to tell you, Noren."

Korfax waited.

"But first, the broth," Baschim said, handing Korfax a spoon.

They each ate in utter silence. The broth was hot and comforting and Korfax discovered that he was hungry after all. But even as he finished his portion he noticed that Baschim had downed barely half of his.

Baschim was eating slowly, almost reverently, savouring each and every mouthful as if it were his last. Korfax, mystified, waited dutifully until Baschim was done.

Finally, when all had been lovingly consumed, Baschim placed his spoon regretfully inside his bowl and looked back at his charge with sad eyes.

"Things have happened today, Noren, terrible things, things you might never expect to see ever in your life."

Korfax looked away. Visions of grey demons swam in his mind. He saw Arpanad falling before a grey blade. He saw Orkanir cut down by its cousin. He saw a black sword with a mind of its own.

"Where is my mother?" he asked.

Baschim glanced at the door.

"She is helping with the wounded, as is your father. I was sent to be with you whilst they do the things that I cannot. My duties are over for now."

Korfax frowned and looked back. Whatever did Baschim mean? His duty was never over. Baschim, seeing the unspoken question, offered Korfax the slightest smile in answer.

"I know what you are thinking," he said. "You are thinking that my duty is never over, not whilst your father is doing his. But today all things are different. Today all the rituals of our lives have been broken."

The strange look flickered again behind Baschim's eyes.

"But the world still goes on, rolling its way through the heavens as it ever has, as it ever has from the very beginning. The tragedies of this day are, when all is said and done, nothing to the terrors of the past. Though you may not believe it now, even this will come to pass."

Korfax bowed his head. Those were sacred words. Karmaraa, the chosen of The Creator, had said them as he had stood upon the encircling hills after defeating the greatest evil of all.

Baschim leaned forward and gently touched Korfax on the arm.

"I came here to ward you, Noren. I came here to tell you not to be afraid of what has happened. Let no dark dreams fill your head. Today you were brave and strong. Think of that instead. Dwell only upon that. Remember it, even as you remember those that have passed beyond."

It was later, much later, that Korfax finally decided he would try to find out what was happening.

He could not sleep, though he had tried. He sat up in bed and looked about. Moonlight slanted across the room and he could see Baschim clearly, asleep at the table, head upon his arms. His face looked utterly weary. Korfax watched him carefully. Baschim was deep in the dreamless sea.

Korfax looked across to the window. Only the brightest stars could be seen. Fair Gahburel had banished all the others from the sky.

Korfax hugged his knees. There were familiar voices echoing through the door. It was his mother and father in their bedchamber. He listened but could not make out what they were saying. They were the only sounds he could hear.

He carefully got out of bed, watching Baschim as he did so. Baschim did not stir.

Though his mother had told him to stay where he was, and though Baschim had told him the same, he could not do their bidding. None of them had answered his questions. He had to know what was happening.

He carefully left his room, his senses alight for the slightest movement or sound. He went to the door of his parents' bedchamber and found it ajar. He sat in the concealing shadows beside it and immediately felt guilty, but what else could he do?

He could not rest, he could not sleep. How could he do any such thing after a day like this? His mind was awash with demons and black swords and red mists. He needed answers.

The first words that he heard clearly belonged to his mother.

"You look weary."

"And are you surprised? I am no healer. It is a good thing that Orkanir is as strong as he is. He helped me all the way."

"That is something at least. He was valiant."

There was a pause before his father spoke again.

"Someone will rue this day. Someone will curse that they were ever born."

Korfax almost drew back as if discovered. How angry his father sounded. No, he said to himself, that was not anger; that was rage. He remembered his father's look as he had ordered the caging of the black sword. Korfax shuddered. He still could not quite believe that his father could contain such darkness. He listened on. His mother was speaking.

"Do not think on that now. There will be time enough for retribution."

There was a long pause.

"There is one thing I do not understand. How did the demons get so swiftly over the wall?"

"You did not see?"

"I was in the courtyard when it happened."

"When we returned we found a strange growth attached to the stone. It was like a vine and yet it was not. They must have used it to climb up. But where did it come from?"

"A vine? What did it look like?"

"Disgusting! There was something like a clenched fist at the end of one of its branches, and I saw a gaping mouth in its main trunk. It seemed to be composed of flesh and bone rather than wood and bark. Needless to say I burnt the foul thing from the wall, but I was not careful with my power. I scorched the stone. That will have to be repaired."

"I see."

"You know something?"

"Guesses, that is all. I would rather be certain before I say more," she answered.

Another pause.

"Do not fret. You have done all that you could," she continued.

"All? Hardly that! If only I had seen the call of Chasaloh earlier."

"It was fortunate that he was near the old beacon and understood the need. He did what he could, just as you did what you could."

"Hah! I returned only to find that the last act had already been written."

"Well, even then, it was fortunate that you were as close as you were and came as fast as you were able."

There was a pause before she spoke again.

"How is Chasaloh?"

"He is deep in grief. We would not have known of the attack but for him. As soon as I saw it I knew something was amiss. It lit up the sky. I wanted to honour him for it, but he was past caring."

"I had forgotten all about the old beacon."

There was a longer pause.

"And what of Baschim?" she asked.

"He grieves also, though it is far more difficult to tell with him. He masks himself far too well. That is why I sent him to be with Korfax. The task became a duty, and hence a distraction. Baschim has ever distracted himself with his duty. I hoped it would be a mercy on my part. Besides, he guards his tongue well, does

Baschim, no matter the travail."

"And what do you fear that I should say in his stead?"

"You know what I mean. Our son should not be allowed to dwell upon this."

"Not allowed to dwell? Keep him in the dark and he will dwell upon it for ever. I should go to him now. I should watch over him this night, not Baschim," she insisted.

"Spare me a moment. We need to talk, you and I. We need to decide what to tell him, what explanations to give."

"Well, the longer we leave it, the more he will fill himself up with his own imaginings."

"They will be turned aside easily enough once clearer counsels prevail."

"But they will not be forgotten, whatever you or I decide to tell him. Korfax is not of such a temper."

"That is not what Doanazin said."

"And you should take care how you speak for others! We both know what Doanazin thought of Korfax, but what has happened here is not the same at all. I have witnessed another truth."

"Have it your own way then. But were Doanazin here, you might find her agreeing with me."

"I suddenly find myself wishing that our son had picked up that sword earlier than he did, if only so that I could prove to you how wrong you are now."

A sharp intake of breath kissed the air.

"Do not say that. Never say such things. Korfax should never have touched that blade. He should never have touched it at all. What spirit of the perverse sent the two of you into that particular room?"

"Say not perversity, say instead fate. Besides, I consider it a better fortune than the alternatives. And if it were not for that sword, you also would be grieving this day and the Farenith would be no more. Do you wish for that?"

There was a brief silence before his mother spoke again.

"At the end we had no choice. The accursed things trapped us there. Two were behind us and one was in front. We had no choice. We had nowhere else to go."

"Well, what is done is done. But do you honestly think that I regret the gift of your lives? I am so grateful that both you and he live, how could I not be? You are both my life and my love and my son is my one single hope for the future. I love him with all my heart."

Korfax shuddered whilst there was another pause. His father loved him with all his heart? It had not felt like that when he had put the black sword back in its chest. His father spoke again.

"But he should never have touched that sword."

There was another sharp intake of breath.

"I had even begun to believe that the accursed thing had slept so long that it would never awaken again. After all, it has lain quiet in that chest since the time of

Noqor at least. My father touched it once and it did not answer him. I touched it once and it did not answer me. But that was not its intent, it seems. It was waiting for innocence!"

"And you have forgotten that your son touched it in need. Neither you nor your father came to it with fear and desperation in your hearts!"

Korfax hugged himself even tighter. He barely heard his mother's rejoinder; instead, he was almost entirely consumed by what his father had just admitted. Since the time of Noqor? That made it at least as ancient as the great blade that hung in the main hall. The black sword was old! He thought of the elder tales and how they had once fired his imagination. Finding himself upon the other side of the divide, he shivered instead. The black sword went all the way back to the very last gasp of the Wars of Unification, and now he had been gifted with a terrible glimpse of what those times must really have been like. He sat for a moment, lost in a swirl of speculation, before remembering once more where he was and to whom he was listening. It was time to pay attention again. Who knew what else he might hear? His mother was speaking.

"Such things, especially if they are powerful, are said to be able to lie in wait for all eternity. Only those that dwell within the firmaments of wrath possess such terrible patience, and that one is of such a nature. I know. I saw it unleashed."

There was a pause.

"Then you have seen what I have not, so allow me my few remaining illusions. Like my father before me I had merely hoped that the writings were wrong, that was all."

There was another pause and a sound of movement. Korfax made ready to go, but it seemed that the conversation was not over yet.

"No other survived the wars. The rest were all destroyed."

"Or so we believe!"

"And what is that supposed to mean?"

"That you are not the master of all fates. You do not have all knowledge!"

Korfax heard the whip in his mother's voice, and he almost flinched at the sound even though he was not its target. How strange to hear it sent at his father. Up until now he had thought it something his mother only reserved for him.

"I hear what you are saying," his father answered quietly. "But you are not hearing what I am saying."

There was silence. Korfax could imagine them both standing on either side of the room. They suddenly existed in a world of opposites, each staring the other down. It had become a duel between them. Here was a side to his mother and father that he had never imagined.

His father spoke again.

"I entertained a fantasy once that this one would somehow fade away, eventually returning to whatever realm gave it birth. But I always knew, down in my darkest places, that such a thing would never come to pass. Somehow I knew that the accursed thing would always be with us like a black storm on our horizons, for ever circling, for ever waiting its moment to strike. And now the moment has come at last and it has struck indeed. My son has awoken it, and he has killed with it."

"And I say again that he saved us both. Only he could have done so. Besides, you were not there."

"I KNOW I WAS NOT THERE!"

Korfax flinched. His father had shouted at his mother. When had he ever done that before? Korfax drew back from the door. How terrible it sounded.

"Quietly!" hissed his mother. "Do you want Korfax to hear?"

Korfax drew back further. Did she know he was outside?

"Then do not provoke me," his father countered.

"I was only reminding you of what you appear to have forgotten. Only he could open that chest and only he could lift up that sword."

"I know. It is a curse that we share. Only those of the blood can touch it. The black sword will answer to no other. To touch it would mean their death."

"Then you have answered yourself! Fate – as I said at the very beginning."

"A fate you led him to."

"I had no choice."

"As you have said also."

Korfax breathed again. Neither his mother nor his father knew he was there. Another long silence followed until his mother spoke again.

"This has become a debate without end. I shall go to him now and make sure no dark vision disturbs his sleep."

"Stay a while yet, we still have not decided what to do. I would like it if you would."

"Would you? I am not so sure."

"We must be united on this. It will hurt him if we are not."

"Then you should have considered such things earlier. It is too late in the day now."

"Too late for what?"

"Decisions!"

"But we need to decide."

"Then let us decide in the morning. Neither of us is either willing or capable of such a thing now."

"But what will you say to him?"

"And what do you fear I will say?"

There was another long silence before Korfax heard the faint rustle of robes. His mother was coming. He turned about and ran quickly back to his room.

Looking around the door he saw that Baschim was still fast asleep. He went to his bed and lay down, listening.

He heard her approach, heard her open the door. There was a pause and then he heard her move towards Baschim.

"Baschim?" she whispered.

Korfax heard Baschim stir, a sudden set of movements.

"Enay? What is it?"

"It is nothing, I will watch now."

"Of course, Enay."

Korfax chose that moment to sit up.

"Mother?"

She turned.

"Korfax, you should be asleep. It is late."

He looked up at her, expecting a frown, but all he saw was her gentle smile, that very same smile she had gifted him with earlier. She did not suspect anything. She had not even guessed that he had been listening at all.

"I could not," he told her, keeping his answer as careful as he could. Only the truth would do for his mother. She had a way about her, a way of seeing through masks, so he already understood the care he should take, saying only the right things in the right way. Besides, he really could not sleep. Who could? Too much had happened.

Both she and he watched as Baschim left, dutiful but subdued, and then she came to his side and touched him gently upon his shoulder, fingers caressing. He felt the touch like a comfort, like a kiss.

"Lie down," she told him. "I will stay with you now. I will ward your dreams."

"But what has happened? Why have I been told to remain here?"

"That is not for now. There are things that you should not see, not yet, not in the dark. Instead, let the light of day reveal the truth. I will tell you everything in the morning."

Korfax lay back down and his mother sat beside him, her hand upon his brow, like she used to when he was very small. Long-forgotten memories stirred inside, comforting arms, gentle songs under gentle lights, all sending him to sleep, beguiling him with the wonder of dreams.

"Sleep now," she said, her voice almost a whisper in his ear, the faintest caress of all. He closed his eyes and tried to do as she asked, but it seemed all but impossible. Questions and visions flew this way and that in his mind. Then a deep tide of weariness filled him up from inside, and before he knew it he was away, finally lost to the world in a dark and dreamless sleep.

She withdrew from his mind. That had almost been harder than anything she had ever done before. She had never touched his mind as deeply as that, ever, but then she had never needed to until now. Only in exceptional circumstances was it allowed at all, and only then when great need or love caused it.

She remembered back to the day when she had first met Sazaaim. What a day that had been. They had both seen each other across a long hall of stone, eye catching eye, mind catching mind, all in an instant, a flight of gentle arrows. Their thoughts had entangled in mid-flight and they suddenly knew each other with an intimacy neither had ever imagined before. How wonderful it had been, that sharing. They had both understood in a single moment, she seeing him, he seeing her. It was kommah, the touching of souls destined for union, the one joining that could never be broken.

So she had not expected the touch of her son's mind to be so similar. But as soon as she had immersed herself in his depths, drawing up the commandments of sleep whilst soothing the turbulent sea of his troubled mind, she felt again that strange entanglement that went deeper than understanding, deeper than thought, that mingling of waters in some great pool or lake that lay below everything else and yet subsumed it. But this was not kommah, not the joining of souls in blessed union – this was something else entirely.

She had suddenly seen it in his depths, the love he held for her, the love for his mother, with a certainty that shook her to her very core. She had felt it and she could not help it, his love for her, for his father, all of it, everything, that deepest love that lay below all that he was, all of his hopes and fears, all of his concerns and curiosities. Everything that he was came back to this single and sacrosanct place, and she had trespassed upon its borders with her touch. She had withdrawn immediately, but what was done was done. Once seen it could never be forgotten, and now that she knew it the memory would remain with her for ever.

She had not intended to touch such a place at all, only to call up his need for sleep. He had succumbed, of course, almost like the memory of the infant she had once lulled by the gentle rocking of her arms, but that was to be expected. She was the mistress of such powers. What was not so expected was what she had seen. She came closer and laid her head beside his and let the tears flow again. She had been told not to allow this, had been taught how perilous it was to wallow in the deeps, but she could not help herself now. She also had seen horror this day, and only her son had preserved her life, her one and only child, her one and only saviour.

How easy it was to forget. How easy it was to let tradition and ritual and shallow comfort mask all the important things, the things that really mattered. But they had crossed the divide now and she had seen the naked love inside her son, seen how he loved her and his father. Such insights made all the rules by which they ran their lives seem paltry by comparison.

Korfax awoke to find his mother looking down at him, still sitting on his bed with her hands in her lap, her eyes sharp and with no hint of weariness. There was light in the room, bright daylight streaming in through the windows. She smiled warmly at him, and how wonderful that smile was.

"Good," she announced. "You slept long and deep. Sleep is the best healer, the best healer of all. It strengthens us for the days that are yet to come."

He looked up at her.

"Didn't you sleep at all?"

"I meditated, even as I watched and warded. But that is enough for me. You still need the benison of sleep. You are not full grown yet, after all."

He sat up.

"Are you going to tell me what has happened now?"

Her smile faded slightly.

"Yes, I will tell you. I will tell you everything that I can. Then you will dress and we shall both go down and find the first meal of the day."

Korfax sat beside her and tried to understand all that he had been told. For a while he refused to believe any of it, but his mother had said it nonetheless, and he had no choice.

Everyone that had been in Losq during the attack had died, everyone except for him, his mother, Orkanir and Chasaloh. Orkanir had been at death's door when they found him, but he had survived – just.

Korfax could not encompass it. All of them were dead? Kalazir was gone? Geziam was gone? It suddenly sounded strange and far away, a story that had nothing to do with him. Surely all he had to do was to go down to the kitchens to see Geziam again. And would not Kalazir be there with her, as she ever had been? He could see them both in his mind, even now, wrapped about in golden light as they stood at this table or that, discussing the affairs of the day and preparing food, preparing joy.

Tazocho held him close as he cried quietly against her. Now it seemed to her that this was the hardest thing that she had ever done, naming all the dead for her son whilst trying not to see their ruined bodies in her mind. But this was the very thing she would not let him know. He deserved to be told that they were dead, but not the manner of their dying. He was too young for such grim truths.

Later, after the first meal, he sat with his father in his father's day room. Both of them were quiet, but whereas Sazaaim seemed to rest, eyes closed, body unmoving, Korfax fidgeted and stared at his hands. Eventually he looked across at his father. Outside, beyond the tower, clouds were gathering.

"But why must I lie?" he said. "I was always taught that it was a sin!"

Sazaaim opened his eyes and blinked.

"But this is not a lie, Korfax. You will merely conceal, that is all."

Korfax glowered back at his father.

"But it is still deception," he insisted. "Only yesterday I was punished for it."

His father frowned slightly.

"I know you were, but this is different. Between yesterday and today the world has changed. Yesterday you were wilful and it was a trivial matter. Today we stand upon the other side of death and sorrow. You have seen things, done things, witnessed that which is of no concern to any other. So do not mistake me, Korfax, for this is important, more important than anything else you have ever been asked to do. It is utterly necessary!"

His father leaned closer and fixed Korfax with his brightest gaze.

"And now that you know my will, I want you to tell me the truth in return. How did you know about that chest? How did you know about that sword?"

Korfax looked back at his father, unable to avert his eyes. He trembled inside. It was as though he had suddenly been stripped bare, as though his father could suddenly see all that he was, all his secrets, all his memories, every thought that he had ever had, every action he had ever taken. He took a deep breath to calm himself and tried to remember exactly how it had been.

"It was when I was very little," he said. "I followed you to that room and I saw you take that sword out from its chest. Then someone called my name and I ran off. But I had forgotten all about it until now. The memory only came back to me when I saw that chest, and that was when I remembered the sword."

Korfax waited whilst his father continued to look at him. Then Sazaaim dropped his gaze and sighed in relief. He leaned forward and placed a gentle hand on his son's shoulder.

"I am sorry, Korfax, so sorry that I ever doubted you. You did what any brave son would do under such terrible circumstances. You looked for hope and found it in an old and all but forgotten chest. You are as innocent as you have ever been. The guilt is entirely mine and I regret so much that I hurt you with my fears. You saved your mother and yourself. You are a good son, the best a father could hope for. I am just so sorry that it has come to this."

His father's eyes filled with tears. Korfax stared at them, even as they fell. When had his father ever cried before? Korfax felt himself momentarily torn in two, but then almost immediately he rushed to his father and held him tight, burying his head in Sazaaim's robes.

"Please don't cry, please don't! I don't understand, I just don't."

His father returned the fervent embrace, stroking his son's head as the tears continued to fall.

"My son, my son, I cannot tell you this tale yet. It is not the right time. You need joy now, healing joy. Leave the dark tales in the places reserved for them. But when you come into your own, when you are your own master at last, when you are at peace with the world, come to me again and I will tell you the whole truth. You deserve nothing less."

Eventually Korfax looked back at his father.

"Father, what is it? What is the black sword?"

Sazaaim hardened his gaze for a moment as if preparing himself.

"I will say only this. The Farenith are its guardians. It is a burden we do not take lightly or willingly, but we are the only ones that can do it. More than that I will not say, not yet. One day you will understand why. I will tell you everything when you come into your own. But know this, Korfax. There are burdens you cannot yet carry. I will not allow it. That is why I want you to forget all about the black sword.

This is our secret, Korfax, a secret we must keep above all others. It is a matter of deepest trust and honour."

Korfax bowed his head. He understood that much at least.

She came to him afterwards and sat before him. He looked up from his contemplations.

"I know how Korfax knew of the sword."

She returned his look expectantly as if she already knew the answer.

"And?"

He took a deep breath.

"It seems I have a confession to make."

Her eyes hardened.

"Say on."

He looked at her for a moment, measuring, judging, and then looked away again.

"The act that saved you from the demons was set in motion by me. Some years ago, on a whim, I dared to open that chest and take the black blade out. I was feeling strong that day. I had a beautiful wife who had given me a beautiful son and I felt strong enough to face the Vovin in its lair. It was only for a moment and I thought that I was entirely alone, but Korfax saw what happened. He followed me to the door, even though he was the merest speck of a child at the time. He saw me take it out, innocent and unobserved, and the memory remained with him, as it would with any child. But I did not see him because my attention was taken up entirely by the sword. It was pure chance."

She stood up.

"How the wheel turns!" she said.

He frowned and looked back at her.

"And what do you mean by that?"

She remained where she was and folded her arms, setting them like barriers against him.

"You were ready enough to curse me for leading him to that room, but now we discover that it was you all along that showed him the blade."

He stood up and strode towards her, but he did not touch her even though he towered over her like a storm cloud.

"Damn you! Will you twist everything to your advantage, even in this matter?"

She did not flinch.

"I have never twisted anything to my advantage, as you well know. But neither will I stand idly by whilst you blame others for your own folly."

He drew back.

"But it was pure chance, I tell you."

She smiled coldly.

"And was that not my contention also?"

He narrowed his eyes.

"Have it your way then. We have both been the victims of chance."

Her smile widened.

"And more than a few in the past have taken their chance as their fate."

He grimaced.

"You will not let it lie, will you? Round and round you go."

She unfolded her arms and turned away.

"The spiral ever reveals the truth at its centre," she offered, speaking over her shoulder. He deepened his glower.

"And how can I argue with that?" he asked to her retreating back. She turned about again, her eyes now luminous.

"So you finally learn wisdom at last. Creator be praised!"

She came to a stop.

"I have had enough of this argument anyway," she told him.

He gave her his most considerate look yet.

"Well," he said, "if nothing else, I am somewhat easier in my mind. I had believed that the accursed thing had called out to him and that he had submitted to it. I thought that I had lost my son to its power. That was what I feared most."

Her eyes widened slightly.

"Then you are more fortunate than you know. Despite your calling me away too soon, despite your sending Baschim in my stead, our son remains entirely free of taint. I know. I have seen. But your actions could have damaged him even at the very moment of his healing."

She took a step forward and her eyes suddenly blazed.

"I was holding him," she accused, "soothing him, loving him, and you broke the moment. You kept him in the dark. That was entirely the wrong thing to do."

He dared her gaze.

"So now you blame me again?"

The cold fire in her eyes became brighter still.

"Yes, you should answer for that at least. You were far too inconsiderate. He is my son. I know him. I stayed with him during the night. I saw him. I saw all of him."

He hardened his gaze and matched her.

"But he is my son also."

She filled herself with her power.

"And did you nurture him inside you? Did you feel him coming into the world? Did you give birth to him? Did you nourish him? Did you comfort him after the coming of demons?"

He almost ignited with force.

"Enough! He is male! He is of the Farenith! If we have a daughter, claim her! But as far as my son is concerned you will do as I say in the matter."

Disconcerted by how far he was prepared to go, she withdrew a little.

"You will not keep him from me!"

Though he did not advance, the air about him swirled with threats.

"How dare you! I was not suggesting any such thing at all. But he is my son, nonetheless. You know our traditions, and you know them better than most. The son becomes the father, the daughter becomes the mother, or would you deny even that?"

She blinked rapidly.

"I have taught him many things you could not."

He darkened.

"And do you think that I don't know that either?"

He withdrew and sat back down. He looked out of the window.

"There is one more thing I want you to teach him, and it is the most important thing you will ever pass on," he said.

"And what is that?"

"I want you to teach him how to forget."

"Teach him to forget? Now who is guilty?"

"You know what I desire!"

"Indeed I do. When do you want me to show him a hiding pattern?"

"As soon as is possible," he answered.

"You do know that this is one of the most powerful weapons in the entire armoury of the Exentaser? We only teach it to our acolytes in the very final year of their enlightenment. This is the last defence, the one that turns all others aside. I should never have revealed this to you."

"You showed me this because you saw the need. Now that need has returned once more. Do not berate yourself – your foresight has never failed you. Besides, if there was some other way do you not think that I would take it? But there is no other way. I am a guardian from a house of guardians, and we have been guardians for so long that it dominates our every horizon."

"Yes, I know. And I have seen how it tyrannises you," she said.

"I am no tyrant."

"But you have claimed sovereignty over my son."

"And I will say it again. You know our traditions better than any!"

"Do not call up the spectre of dissent before me. I know what moves your heart in this."

"Damn you!"

"And damn you also," she repeated.

"I gave my life to you."

"As I gave mine to you."

"You will defy me?"

"Of course not! It is far too late for that! This game will be played out to its very end, whatever you and I do or do not decide. I will teach him to forget, of course I will, but I offer you this warning. Our son is no fool, whatever Doanazin may have thought. He may well see that a hiding pattern can become a revealing pattern. He has begun to understand the nature of all things that are opposite. He may in time even divine the rest. He has that potential inside him."

"So now we hide one deceit within another? I know which is the greater evil. I wish my son to be safe."

"And do you think that I do not?" she asked.

"I did not mean that."

"Then hear me now. His coming to power must be slow. It must be gradual. The fast-wrought blade breaks soonest."

"But what are the alternatives?"

"In this matter there are none, so let it end here! No more debate, no more contention! I will do as you ask, as I said. I want him to be the best of us. I want him full and strong and mighty, filled to the brim with all that is good in our people."

"And do you really think I do not want that also?"

"Look inside yourself for that answer!"

He looked down.

"So what will you teach him?" he asked.

"I will gift him with the seventh pattern. It is both simple and elegant, and once set in place not even one of the Urendrilith will be able to penetrate it, though I doubt he will ever be in a position where one of my order must look so deep."

"Never underestimate what chances the world may bring."

"Don't you mean fate?" she said as she left the room.

"I hate that word," he muttered.

"I know you do," she returned, just as the door closed.

His mother came to him in his room and sat beside him by the window. She looked out as he did and shared the view. The hills looked lush today, green and vibrant, and there was a warm breeze that was pleasant on the skin.

"Rain is coming," he said.

She looked at her son and saw the unwanted seriousness of him. How things had changed. She reached over and brushed his cheek with her hand.

"There is one last thing to be done," she told him. "I shall teach you a hiding pattern so that you can forget the black sword."

"Father said that it was necessary."

"It is, so this is the last you and I shall speak of it. I know that you are filled with many questions, but you should also remember that the wise wait for their answers before they act, whilst the impatience of fools serve only their own folly. Your father and I have lived in this world much longer than you and we have been trained to recognise the perils of incomplete knowledge. Up until now, for you, no boundaries have existed. Now you have met one at last, one of the worst. For here is something deadly. You have stepped into a new world and been changed because of it. So I will tell you the most important thing of all. Keep the lesson of the fool in your mind always. It is the first and the last catechism of the Exentaser. If you call upon powers you cannot command, then that which you have raised up will claim you in its turn. Do not run towards the precipice with an unseen beast at your back."

She stood up.

"Come, let us begin."

Korfax felt strange. The hiding pattern had already sunk deep into his mind and was still falling deeper with every passing moment. He could feel his memory of the black sword only dimly now. Soon it would be gone for ever, or so his mother had said.

He did not want the memory to vanish, but it was altogether too late now. He had obeyed without thought, caught by his curiosity, setting the hiding pattern in motion by using seven unconnected words of his own choosing even whilst watching his own mind like some abstract observer as the words tumbled his memories down into the deeps.

Then it came to him like a sudden light. The equation his mother had set before him was solved. He suddenly saw how it all worked. He had effectively split himself in two. One part of him would forget the sword, but the other would not, though that part of him would sleep until it was called upon again. And only he could awaken it. He would not actually forget about the sword at all, as the memory would merely be locked away from the sight of others, other minds, other eyes.

He studied the pattern even as it faded away, and he understood it completely. He realised then that this touched upon something Doanazin had striven to teach him, a mystery of numbers and words that revealed the very nature of the pattern. Almost with a shock, he suddenly realised that she would never teach him again. She was gone, dying so that he could live. He turned away from the thought. He did not want to think about it.

It was later in the day that the rites of death were to be enacted. Korfax had never experienced this particular ritual before and he found himself dreading it, but it had to be done nonetheless. The spirit had to be hastened on its way as quickly as possible, and to that end the bodies would be burned and the ashes scattered upon the river below Losq, a re-enactment of the return to that greater river where all spirits were washed clean of their lives so that they could be born again.

The place of the burning was the Tar Telloajes, a room deep underground and set against the east wall. Before now Korfax had always passed its blank doors without a second thought. After today they would finally mean something.

He walked out into the courtyard and went to his appointed place. He stared down before him. Twenty-four shrouded forms lay before the east wall, all wrapped in black cerements, with a single bloom of aovsil, the star flower, placed on each unmoving breast.

Korfax suddenly found his throat tightening. He looked at one of the bound forms. Within those wrappings lay Geziam, Baschim's love for many seasons. He looked to another. There lay Kalazir, wife to Chasaloh for more years than many now here could remember. And beside her lay her son, Permanal, no longer to inherit his father's estate. The house of Chasaloh was ended.

Korfax looked at each body in turn. There was Doanazin, his tutor, and beyond her lay Ocholor, two hundred and fifty years of service suddenly ended upon an unholy blade of bone. Korfax looked to the side and saw Orkanir kneeling, his face racked in pain. He suddenly found himself blinking back his own tears as his breath caught in his throat.

A hand rested upon his shoulder to steady him and he looked up. It was his father. Korfax tried to wipe the tears away, but he could not. They kept on coming and his vision began to blur, softening the world about him into unfocused patterns of light and shadow. His father smiled sadly down for a moment.

"There will be an accounting for this slaughter, my son, mark my words. There will be an accounting. But now is not the time. Instead, we take time to honour the departed, as we should. But swords will be sharper after this day, and eyes will be brighter. We will watch and we will avenge."

Then he looked up again, suddenly grim. Another hand was placed on his other shoulder, and he turned his head. It was his mother. She said nothing, but her eyes glittered sharply back at him. Commandments. He looked back to the front.

Now he felt as if he was suddenly standing upon a fulcrum, his mother on one side, his father on the other, each holding the balance of his life. So he waited, as did all the others, until it was time.

The moment arrived and Baschim stood forward, his face emotionless. He was to conduct the rites. They were simple enough. Each body was taken down to the place prepared for it and the doors were closed. Baschim made the sign of Zinznagah and the rites for the dead were spoken, answered by all at the appropriate moment. Then Baschim held up his left hand and touched the burning stone. A lone piper upon the wall played a quiet lament for the dead as the fires of the Tar Telloajes mounted. And as they stood there, a light rain began to fall as though the world itself now grieved.

After the rites of passing, Losq entered a period of waiting. Now that the messages had been sent out, first to the vale of Gieris, then to Ralfen, little else could be done. The news would flow out across the land, a tale of death, a stark warning. Be on your guard, do not leave the sanctuary of your towers, demons have returned to the world. Only from Ralfen would there be a response, for Ralfen was a fortress, one of the last built during the old wars, and it boasted almost an entire talloh of the Nazad Esiask.

To Korfax it felt like dwelling in the eye of a storm, a treacherous calm that belied a circling wrath. Meals were prepared, Branith walked the walls, but that was all. A quiet grief filled the tower and few were in the mood to talk.

When he wasn't doing this chore or that, Korfax went slowly from place to place, sometimes watching from the wall, sometimes from the tower, but he felt restless and ill at ease. His father was busy at work upon various matters for the Dar Kaadarith and his mother was spending most of her time in a vision state, trying to uncover the power that had summoned the demons. He only saw them at meal times and when it was time to sleep. He found himself looking forward to those brief moments of comfort; otherwise, he spent the most time with Baschim, helping with duties here and there, when needed.

Orkanir was recovering slowly and Korfax went to visit him at times, but they had little to say to each other. Memories of the grey demons seemed to intrude into every conversation and they eventually fell silent.

Silence followed Chasaloh as well. Korfax went to see him just once, but he found him taciturn and joyless. And since Chasaloh clearly preferred to be alone, Korfax did not go to him again.

It was on the seventh day after the rites of death that a great column of riders was seen upon the southern approaches. The cry went up from the wall.

"Riders on the road."

Korfax ran up the stairs to stand beside Orkanir upon the wall. Orkanir had wanted to be there, arguing long and hard with Baschim that it was his right to take the place of his father. Though he was stiff from his wounds and he limped occasionally, with effort he could stand straight, straight enough to perform this duty at least. Baschim had finally relented.

So here he was now, standing upon the right whilst Baodiz stood upon the left, shields held to the front, lances erect. On each lance the banner of the Farenith rippled in the stiff breeze.

Korfax looked down to the south road. There was the column, a great long line of scarlet riders. No doubt Enay Lasidax would be leading them.

Lasidax was a Brandril of the Nazad Esiask, but it was an ill-kept secret that he aspired to become Napei, a full sword. In the days before the coming of the grey demons Korfax had occasionally thought it a little odd, in his more sombre moments, that there was still a guild devoted entirely to the arts of war. There were no wars, and there had been no wars for over six thousand years. But he did not think so now. Now he was glad that tradition demanded the Nazad Esiask should still be here, still the masters of the Namad Alkar, the lore of battle.

Korfax looked for Lasidax and found him easily enough. At the head of the column rode an erect figure, his scarlet cloak flying out behind him.

There he was, Brandril Mamegar Enay Lasidax! Ocholor, were he standing here now, would have had something to say about that. Not noted for his loquacity, Ocholor could wax almost lyrical where Lasidax was concerned. Korfax remembered one particular incident, not that long ago, when one of the Branith had unwittingly opened the door to his scorn.

Korfax had been taking his leisure beside the tower, watching as Ocholor took a lesson in the art of duelling. He had witnessed the whole thing.

"The next move I will teach you," said Ocholor, holding up his sword, "is a twofold movement intended to disarm. It is a rare move known only to a few in the north, and all of them reside within this tower."

"But Branvath, what of Lasidax, Brandril of Ralfen? I heard he was a duellist also. Would he not know this?"

The silence was deafening. Korfax had caught the looks upon the faces of the others. They knew what was coming next, Orkanir especially.

"Lasidax?" Ocholor had questioned. "Lasidax?" he followed with incredulity. "Lasidax is a fool," he finally announced, his face the very picture of contempt. "For all his skill with a sword he is useless, fit only for ceremony. He is worthless and gaudy, a creature of policy, more suited to the Erm Roith than the Nazad Esiask. Enay Lasidax is no sword."

Ocholor's contempt had scorched the air that day.

Korfax smiled in remembrance. Ocholor could no more have hidden his feelings than he could have hidden the nose on his face – both were as inevitable as the seasons. Korfax found his eyes stinging as he remembered that he would never see old Ocholor ever again.

He glanced up at Orkanir, who glanced back down at him. They smiled briefly at each other, almost as if they had both just had the very same thought. But then Orkanir looked stern again and gestured with his head back at the courtyard. Korfax turned about and descended the stair so that he could stand beside his father and his mother in the proper place. Baschim, as ever, stood behind the three of them whilst the rest of the house Branith arranged themselves around the courtyard in the traditional pattern of welcome. Of all who remained of the household, only Chasaloh was not present.

It was not long before they heard a musical voice outside the gate, issuing the ritual challenge.

"In the name of the Velukor, blessed be his name, I require entry to this place."

Orkanir responded, his voice as hard as the stone from which it echoed.

"Move and show yourself."

There was a pause. Korfax could imagine Lasidax holding up a piradar and allowing it to shine. After a moment the ritual response floated up and over the wall.

"I am a true servant of the highest and I hold up the symbol of our power. From stone we come and to stone we go, and in its light we live for ever in the service of the Velukor, blessed be his name."

Orkanir and Baodiz dropped their lances. Now Baodiz spoke, his voice as hard as he could make it.

"Then in the name of the Velukor, blessed be his name, be welcome in this place."

Korfax smiled to himself as he thought of the old conundrum. The right hand forbids, the left hand allows, what follows? The answer had never been found in all the long years since the riddle had first been asked, for all the Ell were left-handed.

The gate opened and in rode an entire parloh, over five hundred in all. Korfax looked at them. They would fill Losq to the very brim!

At their head, stiffly erect and smiling, rode Brandril Mamegar Enay Lasidax. Korfax watched him carefully as he came forward, watching how he dismounted and bowed. It was elegant, a single movement, like a dance. Everyone else bowed in turn, though Korfax noted how his mother and father merely inclined their heads. Korfax was tempted to copy them, but he bowed as he had been taught.

It was strange. Though he had met Lasidax many times before, Korfax now found himself looking at him as if for the very first time.

Something had changed. Whereas before Lasidax had seemed to possess presence, the very image of a Brandril, now all there seemed to be was absence instead. Though as tall as his father, he now seemed smaller somehow, shrunken inside his armour as though it no longer fitted him. He seemed to smile rather too much as well, his mouth wide upon his narrow face, and his eyes kept rolling this way and that as if they did not know where to look next. It was all rather odd.

"Enay Sazaaim. Enay Tazocho. May the light of The Creator shine upon you both!"

Korfax's father said nothing and it was his mother that responded, if a little coldly.

"And may the light shine upon you also."

Lasidax smiled broadly.

"And how do I find you this day?"

"We are as well as we can be, under present circumstances."

Lasidax bowed his head slightly and a more careful expression crept across his face.

"Of course, a most trying time for you both. But that is why I am here, to help alleviate your burdens and to offer the services of Ralfen's finest."

Lasidax smiled again but Korfax was no longer fooled by it. He suddenly understood. Lasidax did not want to be here. He was afraid. Demons had returned and Lasidax would rather they had not. But that was his calling, surely? That was why he served the Nazad Esiask! No wonder Ocholor had thought so little of him. Lasidax was shallow after all, a mask fit only for ceremony.

Korfax realised what had happened. A door had opened in his mind. Before now he had always taken Lasidax at face value. Only now, on the other side of death and tragedy, was he able to see further.

"And here is Korfax!"

Korfax, lost in reverie, nearly didn't reply.

"Enay," he said.

"How you have grown! You are almost the very image of your father and your mother, the very image."

Lasidax bestowed Korfax with a particularly large smile, and Korfax found himself wanting to back away from it, but then Lasidax turned about again.

"Bennass! The parloh may dismount."

Sazaaim gestured at the tower.

"I have had rooms prepared for all and there is stabling enough for every steed."

Lasidax turned back around.

"I am most grateful, Sazaaim, most grateful. But we are, after all, at your disposal."

Lasidax sat back in his chair and frowned, running the long goblet backwards and forwards between his fingers as if seeking for flaws.

"I understand why you sent the message that you did, Sazaaim, but as I told you before, I think you were being somewhat premature," he announced at last.

Sazaaim looked down.

"Premature," he mused.

Lasidax paused a moment and then offered a conciliatory smile.

"The unexpected always takes us by surprise. Indeed, who would have thought it? After all, when was the last incursion by the forces of the Mahorelah?"

Lasidax took out a small logadar and placed it upon the table. Sazaaim glanced at it and frowned as if he did not wish to be reminded, but Lasidax only smiled a little wider.

"Precisely! During the reign of Aligon, blessed be his name. And what did we have? Some fool of an archivist ensnared by an ancient and long-forgotten scroll. Burnt his entire tower down, alas! But that was far from here and very long ago."

Baschim leaned forward slightly, his eyes glittering.

"But that is not what happened here, Enay."

Lasidax stared at Baschim for a moment, all emotion suddenly gone from his face.

Sazaaim smiled a little, but then turned to Baschim and made the gesture of peace with his left hand. Baschim subsided and Lasidax turned back to Sazaaim again, smiling his empty smile once more.

"So you see my point, Sazaaim? This could be the very same thing, another scroll, another fool, another folly."

Sazaaim narrowed his eyes.

"Folly? No! This is far more than mere folly! It is the long-awaited resurgence. Twenty-four of my household lost their lives here, Lasidax. Here, in this place, where my family has dwelt for forty-two generations, my house was nearly ended. If Chasaloh had not signalled us when he did, if those who survived had not lasted as long as they did..."

"Yes, I know all that. If it was not for..." here he paused for a moment, trying to remember the name. Sazaaim's eyes flashed.

"Orkanir!" he rumbled.

Lasidax inclined his head slightly.

"My apologies. Orkanir, of course."

He took a deep breath.

"So, as I was saying, if brave Orkanir had not held out as long as he did, then your wife and your son and heir would also have been slain. But that is not what happened. You arrived in time to dispatch the last of them. The important thing here is that the attack was repulsed and your family survived, is it not? You arrived in time, time enough to dispel the threat. The Farenith were preserved by the grace of The Creator. All I am saying is that we don't want to alarm the people of this province prematurely by calling it 'the long awaited resurgence'."

"I gave explicit instructions that all were to be warned."

"And so they have been, but still I felt it necessary to temper the message somewhat. This, I am sure, is an isolated incident."

"So you took it upon yourself to change what I said? Since when do you speak for me?"

Lasidax took another deep breath.

"It is my task to preserve. I did what I thought best. There have been no other incidents."

"That you know of," Sazaaim retorted. "This is clearly the prelude to something much larger."

"And you do not know that either. I mean, have you even discovered who was responsible?"

Lasidax looked pointedly at Tazocho, who sat unmoving at the other end of the table.

"Enay, were you not of the Exentaser? Could you not turn your abilities to locating the source of this outrage?"

Tazocho allowed herself only the raising of an eyebrow, before letting her voice freeze the air.

"But I still am of the Exentaser, Lasidax. You do not leave a great guild, as you well know, not for any reason, not unless a higher calling comes upon you, like death for instance!"

Lasidax visibly squirmed in his seat.

"Of course, an unfortunate turn of phrase."

He paused and smiled.

"So, will you look?"

Tazocho stared fully at Lasidax now as if his question was only just within the limits of her toleration. He drew back again, further this time.

"I already have," she told him coldly. "But I have found nothing. And that worries me, Lasidax, as it should worry you! The forces necessary to bring such creatures into this world should not have vanished so quickly. Such forces linger, as it is written. Only those most gifted in sorcery could hide themselves from the Exentaser, so my fear is that we have such a one amongst us now. It is in the histories. At the end, only those born to the inner circle were so powerful."

Tazocho continued to punish Lasidax with her gaze, but he did not look up. Instead he preferred to study the contents of his goblet.

"I know how all of this must seem to you," he said, "but I hope you will allow me my own perspective. There are things that you do not know."

Sazaaim and Tazocho glanced at each other.

"What do you mean?" asked Sazaaim.

"Only that this could not have occurred at a worse time," came the answer. Lasidax looked at them both, clearly troubled.

"What I am about to tell you must go no further. It would only inflame the situation out of all proportion."

Lasidax glanced at Baschim. Sazaaim grimaced and slammed his fist into the table. The sound echoed about the hall.

"My Balzarg has served this house with honour every single day of his life. His loyalty to the Farenith is beyond question. What you say here will never be repeated. You dishonour him, Lasidax, as you dishonour us all!"

Lasidax bowed his head.

"That was not my intent, truly it was not, but this concerns the Velukor himself."

Tazocho stood up. Her eyes flashed.

"What is it? What has happened? What of Ermalei?"

Lasidax leaned forward.

"Please! Both of you, you must understand. What I am about to tell you is not common knowledge. I must ask that you say nothing of this until such time as it is formally announced."

Lasidax waited a moment for them both to subside. Sazaaim and Tazocho looked at each other, unspoken questions darting from mind to mind, and then Tazocho sat down again. After a moment Lasidax sat up straighter and his habitual smile was nowhere to be seen. It was clear to all that he had grim news to impart.

"The Velukor is ill," he said, "gravely ill. He has some strange wasting disease that even the best of the Faxith cannot counter. They can hold it at bay well enough, but for how long they can do so even they cannot say. It is as though his life has suddenly turned to water and his body has become a broken cup. Drop by drop it falls from him, and from what I am told they do not know how long it will be before he is drained to the dregs."

Tazocho stood up again, but now she did not hide her fury. Sazaaim reached out a hand to her, palm open. She looked at him for a long moment and then came to him. He took her hand and held it, then he leaned forward himself to gaze at Lasidax. His eyes were cold, bitterly cold and dark.

"Neither of us knew anything of this," he said. "Neither of us! Why were we not told this before?" There was a stillness in his voice, a warning stillness.

Lasidax held up a conciliatory hand, but none could mistake its tremor.

"Please, I beg you. I only knew of this just before I came here. I sent dispatches to Emethgis Vaniad when I was told of what had happened, so imagine my surprise when the Napeiel himself sends a reply straight back."

Sazaaim glowered.

"And why should that not be? This is a most serious matter."

Lasidax held up both hands now.

"Valagar agrees that this is serious, but he does not agree with your summation."

With his other hand Sazaaim made a fist and then slowly opened it again.

"So what did he say?"

"He said that, for the time being, a more cautious approach would serve. Given the situation with the Velukor it would be wise not to disturb the waters of his rule at this time."

Sazaaim glowered across the room.

"Are we not even to prepare?" he grated.

Lasidax made the gesture of placation.

"Of course we are, but carefully – and quietly."

Mollified, but only just, Sazaaim bowed his head in return.

"Let it not be too quiet," he warned.

Tazocho went to stand behind him, resting her hands upon his shoulders.

"Perhaps if I spoke to the Velukor?" she suggested.

Lasidax turned, genuinely startled.

"I am not sure that would be wise, either!"

She stared back at him and gave him her most withering look yet, and from the expression on his face he would have curled himself up into a ball if he could.

"Do not presume with me, Lasidax!" she said. "Though you seem to have forgotten it, the Velukor is my cousin, and I shall speak to my cousin on any matter that I please, unless he says otherwise."

Lasidax was a long moment finding his tongue.

"I can only repeat what I was told," he said.

She looked away.

"Yes, and that is all that you can do!"

Sazaaim glanced up at her.

"He was never the same after the passing of Lavakon."

She looked down to him.

"I should have been there," she said.

Sazaaim stood up and held her. He looked carefully into her eyes and their minds touched.

"It could not be helped!" he told her. "It was your time also."

She gentled her gaze.

"She used to be so strong, did Lavakon, so strong. All loved her, but he especially. She was the joy of his heart. But as soon as she became with child she grew steadily weaker. After her death it seemed to all that the happiness of the Velukor departed with her. Thank The Creator that the Norvel is well."

Tazocho turned around to look at Lasidax again.

"The Norvel is well, isn't he?"

Lasidax gestured emphatically.

"Assuredly, most assuredly."

Tazocho subsided and Sazaaim stroked her hand.

"Do not berate yourself in this. How would you have assuaged his grief?"

He took a long breath and let it out again, breathing out his tension, his anger. He looked back at Lasidax.

"So be it," he said. "You will have our acquiescence. We will keep our silence. Let the Velukor remain untroubled by what has happened here, but I demand that others act on his behalf. I demand that at the very least!"

Sazaaim stared at Lasidax, and his eyes were full of flame. Lasidax bowed, if only to hide himself from that dreadful gaze.

"Of course, of course," he said. "Your report to your order can be as full as you please, tell Geyadel Gemanim everything. It is just that what you say will not come before the Velukor at this time. Maybe in better days?"

He looked up hopefully and was relieved to see that the storm had passed. Sazaaim had turned away and Tazocho stood at his side, staring into the distance.

Lasidax knew well enough when he had outstayed his welcome. This had been the one part of his task that he had not relished at all. Well, it was over now, so he bowed again and left the hall as quickly as he could. All this death, all this upset, it was not good for the soul.

After he had gone they stood in silence for a moment, then Sazaaim spoke.

"That at least explains why it was that the Norvel went to the ceremony of the cursing last year. Many of us wondered when we heard tell of it."

Tazocho frowned.

"For some reason I am suddenly minded of those strange tales I heard from when the Norvel was a child."

"What tales are those?"

"You remember them, surely? Whispers from the Tower of Light. I was told that the Norvel would often be seen talking to himself, and when the Velukor asked him who he was talking to he said that it was his mother. The Velukor was greatly upset by that. It did not please him that Lavakon might not be at rest. After that the Norvel was forbidden to speak of it."

"That? I thought it a fiction. Many a child has invented a companion for want of company. He had lost his mother. That is never an easy thing for a child. Besides, there were many tales after the death of Lavakon, many tales inspired by nothing more than grief and fear."

"But the Velukor was not the same afterwards."

"Who would be? But why do you think of this now?"

"I do not know. Demons appear once more, the Velukor is unwell and all I can think of are tales from the Umadya Pir."

"Do not dwell upon it. It is your feeling of guilt that has done this, but there is no guilt. How could you have known? No one saw it."

"Perhaps, but there were other things. What of all those that attended the birth? Of them all only Osidess is still alive. Even Samor is gone, going into exile, to Lonsiatris no less, and no news ever comes back from there. I imagine she has entered the river by now. She was already old when she departed."

Sazaaim frowned.

"Those were days of great sadness and great joy both."

"Yes, they were."

"And where is Osidess now?"

"The last I heard she was still at her estates outside Othil Homtoh."

He leaned closer and took her hand again.

"So what happened to all the others?" he asked.

"The chances of the world took them. Many were old, it is true, but most died before their time. You know of one at least, Urendril Zirad, wife to Geyadril Abrilon. She was lost at sea – a mighty storm born out of the furthest west, if I remember rightly."

Sazaaim leaned back.

"And now the Velukor himself is dying?"

"Yes, that was my thought. I will send word to Osidess."

"I doubt she will tell you anything you do not already know."

"Perhaps, but I would still like to know why it should bother me."

"And you have already heard what I think. After the events of the last few days there are more pressing concerns. Give it no more thought."

"No more thought? Even the smallest scratch can become an open wound if left untended."

6

A JOURNEY BEGUN

Onchan-jiz Vohim-torzu
Krin-nora Heijon-zadaih
Nimin-eol Dorfal-eil-jes
Dril-detol Krih-li-iqo
Li-omtra Odmeg-torzu
Nis-basa Av-moz-iad-jes
Zien-renaih Dr-pan-ral-ji

It was a strange thing, but in all the upheaval since the attack upon Losq the sudden news that a foal had been born seemed to attract everyone's attention. The mother was Hellus, the steed of Tazocho. Many came to the stables to marvel at this fine new arrival, but only Sazaaim did not take heart from it.

"There is no other mark upon him?" he asked, staring down at the foal.

Chasaloh looked back sadly.

"None, Enay, nor will there ever be. I know my lore. He is black, black from head to foot, black all over. And he will be mighty, I think."

Sazaaim dropped his head.

"I was not questioning you on that. I was merely seeking some sign of hope."

"Hope?"

"A cloak of darkness without a chink of light is not a good omen."

Chasaloh frowned.

"But, Enay, his mother is the steed of Tazocho. This is the child of Hellus. And Tazocho chose Hellus herself."

"And you are sure who the sire is?"

Chasaloh sighed.

"Yes, Enay, without a doubt. The sire is your steed. Norimeh is the father, and you know how he is. He would permit no other the honour."

He gestured at the black foal.

"Look at him. His father is Norimeh, his mother is Hellus. Kalazir would have approved."

Sazaaim looked unhappily at Chasaloh.

"Maybe she would, but she took joy from everything. I just do not like this sudden clash of events. When Korfax comes of age this dark child will be ripe for the riding."

Chasaloh glowered back at his master.

"Exactly! And I can think of no better rider for this steed. Even though it is only a few hours old, this one is the best that I have ever seen in all my life, and I have seen many, Enay, north, west, south or east. This one, when he is ready, will be a mighty mount for your son."

"But he is all in black!" Sazaaim complained.

Chasaloh snatched up his pitchfork and turned away.

"Then blame the parents, Enay, this one is innocent."

Chasaloh then fled the stables and was gone.

Blame the parents? What did Chasaloh know? Sazaaim felt weary as never before. It had all gone so wrong. So many things had happened, so many that were unplanned, unforeseen and unfortunate. He already carried many burdens, and the coming of the black foal seemed yet another weight upon his back. He looked down sadly at the child of his steed.

"Well, if you are to be mighty, then you should have a mighty name. I name you Enastul."

Cantering here and there in the stable, the foal seemed to laugh back at him with its eyes as if it already knew exactly who and what it was.

Sazaaim sat alone in the highest room of the tower, the room of observances. From here he could see the four quarters – north, west, south and east. He sat at the centre, as he ever did, but he did not look out over the land. Instead he looked inside and pondered hard words.

'Blame the parents,' Chasaloh had said.

Sazaaim shuddered. Demons crossed his lands, his son had touched the black sword and his steed had sired a black foal. The confluence of events was too much for him to ignore. Visions coiled in his mind like dark roots. There was a doom upon him, on him and his house, a doom he wished he could be rid of for ever.

He served the Velukor. He served the line of Karmaraa the saviour, and there was no greater calling. But now the old doubts came back to haunt him, doubts he thought he had put down many years ago. It felt almost as if the world around him had decided to pull itself apart. All he had ever wished for, all his hopes, all his dreams, lay shattered at his feet.

He knew what he should do. He should bury himself in his duty. He had done it before when his world had threatened to crumble, and he could do it again easily enough. But what would the others say? He grimaced. Let them say whatever they pleased. He had walked this road many times many, keeping silent, keeping humble.

He closed his eyes. How easy it would have been to rise further. He could have been Geyadril, one of the highest of the Dar Kaadarith, not only a master of fire but a master of all the elements: earth, air, fire and water. He could have been one of the mightiest in the entire world, but he knew in his soul that it was not meant to be, because it would place him to the fore and he had never wanted that, then or now.

But notoriety had sought him out nonetheless, as though fate had other plans for him, in spite of all his attempts to extinguish its revealing light. It did not help that his house was already a byword for service, the Farenith having served faithfully and steadfastly for forty-eight generations, nearly seven thousand years in all. Few other houses, few even in the west, could say as much. They all waxed and waned, rising and falling as The Creator ordained, but the Farenith were as constant as the northern stars and they never, ever, failed of their seed. Only the house of the Velukor could match them, but then the Salman Zilodar had a far mightier pedigree.

Ever since the first days of their house, ever since Haldos, the Farenith had been blessed with potency and with power. Though their seat was one of the furthest from the centre, their name was known throughout the world. Few did not know of the Farenith.

Sazaaim thought it a curse and understood all too well why his father had thought the same. No doubt all his ancestors, all the way back to Noqor, had thought as much at some point in their lives. He felt the weight above him almost as a physical thing, the weight of service, the weight of honour. They had all walked this line, keeping the Farenith humble, but not so humble as to deny the gifts of The Creator, for to deny The Creator was the worst sin of all. He bowed his head. It was hard, but it was the only way to continue.

Fate, though, had made his journey particularly difficult. The one, the only one that he would love was of holy blood. Tazocho was of the house of Zilodar, cousin to the Velukor himself. If all Sazaaim had wanted was a quiet life then that was certainly not the way to achieve it. But he had been young at that time and he had not thought about the future at all. His mother had been overjoyed at the joining, but his father had warned him afterwards of the dangers. That had been a strange time, both happy and sad. He had found his love, known the greatest happiness, and then paid for it with burdens he could never have imagined. His father's stern face was ever there before him. Stay humble, remain a guardian and keep to the faith. Tazocho had not liked it, but she at least understood the need.

So what of his son?

Sazaaim feared for Korfax. Tazocho had told him how Korfax dreamed: of battle, of conquest. Sazaaim thought about that. What child reared upon the glorious past did not? They peopled their imaginations with the great, the good and the vanquished, and if the great had been warriors, then the child would see themselves in their place. But this was different. Korfax was already born of a mighty house, and the dreams of youth that were born in the places of power often came true.

There was only one answer. His son would go to the seminary this year. Get him away from this brooding place, get him to a place of light and joy, of safety and learning, so that he could discover what worth there was in service and humility.

With the ending of Ahaneh came the ritual of joy. Nimah Kleiun arrived, the time of celebration, but this time it was a subdued affair. Only those from Ralfen were in any mood to give it its due. The tree of light was made, food prepared and waters drunk, but Korfax drifted through the preparations as though through a badly remembered dream. Too many were missing from the feast.

It was at the ending of the seventh day that Sazaaim told Korfax of his decision.

"Korfax, I have a gift for you," he said. "You are to go to the seminary of the Dar Kaadarith in Emethgis Vaniad. Your training to become a Geyad begins this year."

Korfax stared up in amazement.

"The seminary? But I thought that wasn't until next year."

"That would have been the way of it, but things have changed. Messages have already been sent and I have made arrangements for you to start at the beginning of Lahrasom."

"But that is only a few days from now!"

"Yes, it is. Nevertheless, that is how it will be. We will ride to Ralfen, but then we will take a sky ship to Leemal. From Leemal the wings of the wind will take us all the way to Othil Zilodar, then to Emethgis Vaniad, and once we arrive at the capital you will begin your education in earnest. Demons have returned and they have found us wanting, so you must grow up all the sooner because of it. The north needs all its sons and daughters."

Korfax watched his father leave. That was that! He sat and he thought. How fast his life had suddenly become, the wings of the wind indeed, and the last few days had only added to the confusion welling up inside. Losq was full of Branith. They were everywhere – on the wall, in the courtyards, in the halls and galleries, strange faces that watched him whenever he went by. He could see the looks in their eyes – concern and curiosity all in one. He understood their curiosity at least; he had seen demons, they had not.

Of those that were left of the house Branith, he saw Orkanir the most. Orkanir and Baschim were always there now. They had always been glad to see him, but now their friendship was fervent. They spent more time together than they ever had before.

His mother and father were the same. Whenever he came near, they stopped whatever it was that they were doing and concentrated entirely on him, his mother especially. The survivors of Losq had come together it seemed, like many strands of rope joining together in a knot. There was one loose end, though. Chasaloh. He was the only one Korfax saw little of, but Korfax found himself not minding too much. He could not bear to see the change in him. There was no joy there any more.

The day came swiftly, just as he feared it would. There seemed to be no time left for anything now. He sat in his room and stared out of his window.

"Korfax, come now. It is time."

He looked around, suddenly fearful. His mother was at the door. This was it. He was to leave his home.

Not so long ago he would have been overwhelmed with excitement to learn he was finally to travel all the way to Emethgis Vaniad, there to enrol in the seminary of the Dar Kaadarith. But now he no longer thought so. The death of so many he had known in his short life had suddenly made him acutely aware of loss. Now he was scared he would lose his home as well.

"Do I have to?" he asked.

His mother crossed the room and looked down at him, her expression suddenly sad. He had seen that expression many times since the coming of the demons.

"Yes," she said. "Not only is it wise, but it is also your time. You are almost of an age, after all."

Korfax frowned.

"Almost?"

She frowned slightly in return and he felt her touch his mind, the lightest, most fleeting of touches. Ever since the attack she had done this, reaching out, touching him, almost as if she needed to reassure herself that everything was all right. She withdrew again and smiled. Her eyes softened even further, becoming almost as soft as they had been after the attack. She came close and held him to her as she had before, her arms enfolding, her head against his. He closed his eyes and his mother spoke, her voice suddenly unsteady.

"I know what it is that you fear."

She pulled back and stared intently into his eyes. He saw the love there and the concern, and he found himself thinking how cruel life could be, if it so chose. The coldness that had grown in her, the remoteness, was utterly gone, and now he had to leave. It was so unfair.

"You fear that you will lose us," she said.

She touched his forehead gently, caressing it as only a mother could. Korfax closed his eyes at the touch.

"That will never happen," she told him. "We will always be with you."

She looked sad again.

"You have learned a hard lesson, one few others have ever had to learn since the dark times. Remember it as you remember those that are gone. All things have their season, but all things move on. The world changes about us, as we change with the world. The time of childhood is ending for you, quicker than it should perhaps, but that cannot be helped now. The time of maturity approaches and you must face it as only one of the Farenith can."

They embraced once more, and Korfax laid his head at her breast whilst she held him to her. Her eyes became the only bright clouds in his heaven, their gentle rain falling on his head.

They rode out of the gate, leaving behind them a considerable garrison under the command of Baschim. Korfax said goodbye to Baschim and Orkanir as best as he could, but their obvious grief at the parting hurt him in ways for which he was not prepared. Baschim, knotted into a clenched fist, hardly held him at all, but Orkanir almost squeezed the life from him, so passionate was his embrace.

"May the light of The Creator shine upon you always, Noren," said Orkanir.

"And may the light of The Creator shine upon you, Orkanir."

Orkanir then lifted Korfax onto his ormn, perilously close to weeping. Baschim stepped forward.

"Enough now," he said. "The Noren has a great journey to undertake, the journey of his life."

Baschim looked up then with proud and gleaming eyes, the only passion he would allow.

"You will do well in the seminary, Noren. You will follow your father."

It was almost a commandment. Korfax blinked at the words. But then Baschim turned quickly about and led Orkanir away. The gates closed behind them. It was all Korfax could do to stop his own tears.

Seven honour guards rode in front, led by Lasidax, whilst Sazaaim and Tazocho rode behind them, he upon Norimeh and she upon another steed. Hellus remained behind to be with her foal, Enastul. Korfax rode between his parents, astride Famdir, his very own ormn, given to him by Chasaloh on the eve of his twelfth year. Behind came the rest of the forces from Ralfen.

Korfax looked back many times as they followed the long road down to the wide plain on the east side of the Lee Izirakal. It didn't take long for the spire of Umadya Losq to vanish behind its greater slopes. Soon, too soon perhaps, all Korfax could see was the long ridge of the hill, with its great lumps and bumps, frowning over the quiet lands beyond. His home was gone from his sight and he had a sudden premonition that he would never see it again.

They took few stops on their journey across the brown plains of the Piral Rossjil, though there were frequent way stations maintained along the road. Korfax had been this way many times, journeying at least once every year to the city of Leemal. Then the journey had been a more gentle adventure, each familiar view, each well-remembered bend in the road eagerly anticipated. Now, though, Korfax did not watch the world about him. He was immersed in his own thoughts.

He was off to a strange place and an uncertain future. All that he had ever known was to be left behind, even his family. His father and mother would take him all the way to the capital, but then they would leave him there and return home again. He would have to make his own way in the world from now on.

As they stopped on the approach to the Leein Haea, beyond the Piral Rossjil, his father came up behind him and touched him lightly on the shoulder. Korfax turned and looked up.

"Let us talk, you and I."

Korfax looked down and let his father guide him to one side. He suddenly felt as though all eyes were upon him, but when he glanced about he saw that no one else was watching him at all. Most of the Branith were seeing to their steeds, and Lasidax was speaking to his mother. Korfax looked up at his father again, but Sazaaim was looking ahead to a small hillock. He took Korfax to the top, where they stopped. There were two flat boulders resting there, so Sazaaim sat on one and Korfax sat on the other. Sazaaim turned and breathed deeply, scanning the horizon with his eyes.

"Korfax."

"Yes, Father?"

"We need to speak, you and I. We need to speak of what troubles you."

"But nothing troubles me!"

Korfax folded his arms and looked hard at his father, but it didn't work. Instead Sazaaim fixed him with a hard stare of his own, and Korfax quickly looked away again.

"It has been as plain as Great Rafarel in the sky," said Sazaaim. "You have been unhappy ever since we left Losq. Before even! Did you not speak with your mother about this?"

Korfax looked down. Sazaaim leaned forward.

"And what did she say?"

Korfax swallowed. An echo of his misery entered his voice.

"That the world changes, that all things have their season," he said.

"That all things have their season," his father repeated gently. He looked into the distance for a moment. Then he looked back at his son.

"And would you stay a child for ever?"

Korfax frowned.

"No," he said.

"Good," said his father. "Now you begin to follow The Creator's path. And would you stay always at Losq and never see the rest of the world?"

Korfax deepened his frown.

"No," he said again.

"Even better. Now you go further."

Sazaaim took a slow breath, smelling the air.

"It is a hard thing to do, to grow up. And it becomes even harder when death and loss come upon you before you are ready for them. But that is the nature of our life here. I remember going out with my father to the great cliffs to help rescue those that had foundered upon the rocks. I remember the shattered bones of the vessel, I remember the cries of the fearful."

There was a pause.

"But we rescued them, my father and I."

Korfax knew the tale, knew it well, but somehow it no longer moved him as it once had. He saw again the grey demons in his mind. He saw people he had known all his life dying on their blades. He saw Orkanir weeping beside the body of Ocholor. He looked up to find his father smiling at last, a gentle smile of reassurance.

"This last season has made yours the harder road, I think," said Sazaaim. "But things move on, as they should, and it is now time for you to do the same. Your mother and I will not always be here, and you know this in your heart. So now you must prepare yourself. You must find your own way in this world, just as I did when I was your age. In other circumstances this should have been a joyous time for you, where the only thoughts in your head were those of excitement as you contemplated a bright future. Instead, you have seen death, face to face, and so you think of loss, of the past, fearing what may yet be ahead."

Sazaaim placed a hand on his son's shoulders.

"But think on this," he said. "You are born of a great house! You are going to the greatest city in the entire world, and there you will train to become one of the mightiest, a Geyad of the Dar Kaadarith. So have no fear for the future, my son, I see a glorious one."

He stood up.

"Come now. We should go."

The road wound its way through the Leein Haea, rising gradually as it followed the gently sloping contours. Following his father's advice Korfax looked up now rather than down, and he let his gaze wander over the hills past which they travelled.

They appeared gentle, these slopes, but Korfax knew that they kept their more forbidding faces hidden from travellers upon the road. The slopes above were like an enticement, for beyond the ridges, higher up, frowning cliffs broke the curving symmetry of the Leein Haea, sudden and unexpected drops whose gullies were filled with shattered stone, precipitous slopes covered in boulders and scree that tumbled down to lonely pools and deep lakes, each caught by the enfolding land as though cupped within a great hand. Strange tornzl, long and lightning-fast, lurked within those lakes, and no doubt the few wild yanar that lived hereabouts filled their lonely bellies with such delights, if they could but catch them.

Korfax looked about him. With all that had happened he had forgotten how much he loved this land, almost as much as he loved his home. Its peace, its gentleness, showed him how all things could be healed in time. He knew that great armies had once rampaged across these hills, and that these valleys had once burned with the fires of war and sorcery, but little was now left of anything. The bones and the ashes had long since sunk into the earth, and all that remained were memories.

Korfax smiled as he thought of an older tale, that of the giant under the ground. All the mountains were its bones, or so it was said: all the mountains its bones, all the seas its blood and all the soil its flesh. And though the giant slept, it heard all the stories, the woes, the joys, the hatreds and the loves, and the giant remembered them. But the giant slept even as it listened, never to move until The Creator said otherwise. Then, in that far off time yet to come, the lands would change and the giant would shake off its slumber. It would rise up to gaze, just once, upon the Bright Heavens themselves. Then, having witnessed the glory, having filled itself to the very brim with the beauty of creation, it would lie back down again to die at last. Korfax looked at the land about him. Even now he could imagine the hills as great folded limbs, each cast upon the land in careless slumber, here a shoulder, there a knuckled fist.

With Lahrasom passing, the first snows had reached the tops, painting the raw crags with white. Below the white fields, though, naked stone still stretched, red stone that glimmered in the light, and when Rafarel sank into the west or rose in the east, the hills blushed with reflected fire as though they burned.

The company reached the highest point by midday. To their right rose the slopes of Lee Ormei, a gentle enough hill if one kept away from its northern edges where a wasteland of shattered rock fell quickly over a crumbling cliff. On the left lay a high valley caged on either side by Lee Tiomia and Lee Halus, companions that could not be more dissimilar.

Lee Tiomia was a long low hump, featureless and barren, while Lee Halus stood proud and naked, a shapely spire somewhat like the prow of a ship. Korfax looked at its distant summit, the highest point of all on the Leein Haea, and he thought of that far off day when he would climb it. He knew that his father had, as had his father before him. All the Farenith had, at some time or other, stood upon its summit, adding yet another votive stone to the ever-growing pile. Forty-one stones lay there now, and Korfax would add the forty-second.

On they rode, passing over the Leein Haea and down into the Piral Gieris, a wide land lined with hills on either side. Beyond Gieris the road threw itself southwards in great curves, avoiding the many foothills of the Adroqin Vohimar, and that was where Ralfen lay, another day's ride at least.

The Piral Gieris was green, a sharp contrast to the omnipresent browns of the Piral Rossjil. It was more sheltered for one thing, set about by high hills, and many streams flowed quickly across it. But though its soil was well-watered, there were no pools or lakes, for the streams did not linger. There was a gap in the hills to the south where they all joined together to flow into the great long lake of Zlminoaj.

Many scattered houses, tall and thin as towers, dotted the land. The largest lay on a low promontory in the centre, and it was there that they were going, to the Faor Raxamith.

Inside dwelt Raxam Nar Granvor and his family. They cultivated the entire vale and had done so for generations. These were Chasaloh's people, and like all the families between Dialsen and Tohus the Raxamith gave their allegiance to the Farenith.

But Granvor was very old now, and his son, Heiral, dealt with the order of the day – the planting of crops, the rearing of beasts, master in all but name. Heiral was younger than Sazaaim, but he looked much, much older, his hands stained by the soil and his face weathered by the wind. Even his son, the young Gildir, looked older than his years.

Korfax had often helped Gildir doing this task or that, whenever he came to stay. The families often visited each other, either at Faor Raxamith or at Umadya Losq, and there Granvor would sit and dream in the great hall while Sazaaim and Heiral spoke of the passing seasons with Paniss, wife to Heiral, and Tazocho. Meanwhile Korfax would go off with Gildir, off to the long tongue of water that stretched inland below Losq, in the hope of catching a few vasah.

But all that was changing now. He was leaving his home, he was growing up and demons had returned to the world.

Paniss met them all at the gates and ushered them into the courtyard with the traditional greeting. After the greeting and the shutting of the gates, Paniss led them all inside, into the main hall, where the table was already set with food and drink.

Korfax watched his father place a gentle hand on the shoulder of Granvor, who looked up from his chair and smiled sadly in return, bowing his head as he offered up his sorrow for the dead of Losq. Sazaaim said nothing in return but merely bowed his head as well.

Then Sazaaim clasped arms with Heiral, before reciting the names of all who had entered. Heiral then named all within the hall, before gesturing to the table and saying the customary words.

"Honoured guests! Eat and drink your fill."

Korfax smiled at the salutation. Comforting words. Heiral never changed. Not even the threat of demons could alter his path. Like the Farenith, the Raxamith could trace their line all the way back to the wars, and they held their traditions just as close to their hearts.

Korfax found himself beside Gildir, suddenly surprised to discover that his friend was now betrothed. Gildir was young for such a thing, and it had only just happened, but Korfax wondered whether recent events had not thrown Gildir and his intended closer together. Another touch of chaos to the hallowed rites of the Ell.

Usually, when they came to visit, Heiral and Sazaaim would talk deep into the night and there would be long silences, meditations where both stared into the distance. Sazaaim would stand with his hands clasped behind him, Heiral with his arms folded, a bottle of old Apilazin between them both and two small crystal goblets in attendance. Every so often each would partake of the golden liquid, such a well-practised ritual that neither need say a word. Occasionally Granvor would join them, sipping slowly from a third goblet, rare snatches of wisdom falling from his lips at apposite moments.

But that ritual was not followed this night. There were far more serious things to discuss.

Korfax lay in the place he always did whenever he came here. Faor Raxamith was large, with many spare rooms, much like Umadya Losq, but Paniss always kept this particular one aside for him, knowing how he liked to be as high as possible. 'Close to the stars', she always said, smiling fondly.

Paniss was very like Kalazir, or so Korfax had always thought, but the comparison was painful now. It was as though the spirit of Kalazir still walked the world, unable to rest.

It did not take very long for Paniss to divine the truth. Like his mother, she also had a seeing way about her, though she was not of the Exentaser. So, when she led him to the room she always kept for him, she sat beside him on the bed. It was what his mother had done after the attack at Losq, and Paniss had never done anything like that before.

Korfax looked at her and she at him. Then, after a moment, she spoke.

"You are growing up. Your mother tells me that you go to the seminary of the Dar Kaadarith."

She smiled.

"I cannot imagine what it is that you saw. None have ever seen anything like it since long ages past."

She looked down and Korfax watched her carefully.

"They say we are coloured by our experiences," she continued. She looked up again and shook a finger at him. "So you must not think that the world is a place of death, for it is not! There is life here also, much life, the ever-unfolding circle itself. The world is so much bigger than you can possibly imagine."

Korfax smiled back in reassurance, but inside he remained sad. It was as his father and his mother had said. The dark tale had drifted down from the north like a stain, infecting all who heard them with fears and doubts.

After Paniss had left, Korfax looked out of the window, watching as the great constellation of 'The Vovin' rose into the sky.

In the past he had always enjoyed watching such events, thinking it as much a ritual as that of his father's enjoyment of the Apilazin. But now there was an odd sense of foreboding in the sky, and the red fire of the stars felt like an omen. 'It will all end in fire and blood', they seemed to say. Korfax watched them for a long time, and right in the centre, in the middle of the constellation, great Vepanil stared back at him, glowering like an angry eye.

Sazaaim and Tazocho stood together under the stars and let the light gather about them. But a shadow lay at their feet, and they stood separately.

"I saw you speak to Korfax on the road," she said.

"Yes," he answered.

"And?"

"I told him the comforting fiction expected of me."

"Fiction? What fiction? Do you see the future at last? Well now! Here is a talent the Dar Kaadarith have kept hidden from the rest of the world for many an age!"

"And that will be more than enough of that," he told her. "You know what I mean."

"Yes, I do," she said. "And I also know how superstitious you can be. Demons? A black foal? Where now the famed rationalism of the Dar Kaadarith?"

Sazaaim sighed.

"And you know the truth of that also."

"Yes, and I know you. I know your hopes and I know your fears. I know everything. But that is why I came to you. You entrusted me with your soul. I have never been given a greater gift except, perhaps, for Korfax."

He looked at her and came close.

"Tell me your thoughts," he said.

She came closer and smiled.

"You know my thoughts. You always have."

They held each other tight and became entangled.

The next day they took the road to Ralfen across the wide fields of Damintor. To their right rose the beginnings of the foothills of the Adroqin Vohimar, said to be the mightiest mountains across all of Lon-Elah. It was difficult to say which of the four great mountain ranges was actually the greatest, but one thing was certain – the Adroqin Vohimar were the highest. In the midst of the range tall Kasaveh was set, highest of all, abode of Vovin, eternally crowned with snow. Few had ever tried to climb its perilous heights to the very top. None had succeeded. The Vovin kept their own.

They arrived at Ralfen late in the day. Korfax looked across the valley at the four towers that made the fortress so imposing. The towers were joined at their bases, four as one, or one becoming four, depending upon your point of view. Around the towers many ancient trees grew, whilst around them circled a long high wall. Ralfen was one of the last fortresses to be built, raised during the final siege of Nalstul.

Whenever he had travelled to Ralfen before, Korfax had always wondered what it would be like to stand upon its walls and weather a siege, but now he found himself grateful instead for its solidity and strength. He did not want to think about sieges at all.

They went to the waiting sky ship near the second tower, on the wide green swath set aside for such things. Korfax had seen sky ships before, but this was the first time he would get to ride in one. Before now the journey to Leemal had always been by road, but not this time. This time they were to travel by sky ship all the way to Emethgis Vaniad, stopping at Leemal and then at Othil Zilodar before going on to the capital itself.

The sky ship was of the smaller kind, built to take no more than a hundred at best. Korfax looked up at it, a long gleaming seed, with its tapering tail and rounded hull. Very little disturbed its symmetry, not even the furled wings tucked neatly away on either side. It rested lightly upon the grass, barely bending the blades, but it was rooted to the spot.

He felt a curious sensation as he came closer. Something tugged at him, almost as if he was being pulled towards the ship. He knew what that was. It was the power that lay in the vessel's depths, the niadar.

Korfax understood well enough how it could do what it did, as he had been told as much a long time ago, but what he did not understand was why it worked the way that it did. Niadar cancelled mass, lifting the sky ship up, and once the wings were unfurled they could be filled with winds by zongadar. Air and earth subdued. Simple. But it seemed a strange thing that the heavier an object was, the easier it was for the niadar to lift it, and that there was a limit to how small a sky ship could become. Beyond a certain size they became uncontrollable.

On either side of the main entrance of the ship two Branith stood in the posture of forbidding, whilst another, the Raxen, the master of the vessel, stood between them, waiting to welcome his passengers aboard. Korfax thought he looked the very image of a master of the air, with his swept-back hair, his long thin eyebrows and narrowed eyes.

"Welcome aboard," said the Raxen. "May the light of The Creator shine upon you all."

Sazaaim smiled.

"And may the light of The Creator shine upon you and yours, Raxen Liexar."

Liexar bowed to both Sazaaim and Tazocho and they bowed back, then Sazaaim gestured to his side.

"Now may I present my son, Raxen. Here is Faren Noren Korfax. He goes to the seminary of the Dar Kaadarith."

Liexar smiled and bowed.

"Many are the times I've taken your father on my ship. I hope I will have the pleasure of doing the same for you, Noren."

Korfax bowed in return. He liked the smile.

Korfax stood upon the viewing platform, his heart beating hard. He could barely contain himself. He was about to fly! He no longer cared how it worked. Standing here now, such knowledge seemed irrelevant. He was about to fly!

Boarding the ship had been curious. Once he crossed the boundary the tugging sensation shifted, holding him to the deck. It was like, yet unlike, walking upon solid ground. One took the sensation of weight for granted, but here it had been reinvented. Gentle hands held him in place.

He saw, rather than felt, the ship rise. It was so smooth that if your eyes were closed you would not notice it at all. The ship cleared the tower and its great wings unfurled. They filled with summoned wind and now Korfax could feel the vessel move, a great surge of power. It was such a glorious feeling that he could only laugh. Up the ship went in a great curve away from the tower before levelling out again. Then it headed south. The speed! The power! Standing there upon the platform he felt like a giant as the land flew by below.

His mother and father watched him but said nothing. Instead they smiled at his joy and were content.

Leemal sat in a wide vale at the edges of the Leein Ises, a long line of hills that wandered gently up from the south. Walled and gated, Leemal was almost a hill in itself, and the collection of high towers at its top, the Garad, was nearly as high as the two hills that flanked the city on either side, Lee Pas and Lee Nor, the so-called 'guardians'.

Many steep lanes wound their way between the tall houses that clustered about the Garad, but one in particular stood out – a straight line that went all the way from the city walls to the gates of the Garad itself. It was justly famous, a proud eccentricity some said, and few visitors left the city without at least walking part of it, considering the touch of its stone to bestow good fortune. There were those, though, that came only to sample its many hostelries, drinking deep of the cup as they slowly climbed all the way to the top. Only a few could achieve it, for it was long and arduous, and most would fall to either side to dream of wonders until the morning light brought them back to The Creator's realm again, a painful enough awakening by anyone's reckoning, especially if it had rained during the night.

Korfax thought Leemal one of the best places to be in the entire world. He loved the steep roads, flanked as they were by gleaming towers of crystal and stone. He also thought its people amongst the finest – always calm, never hurrying, dignified but not aloof. Friendly and courteous, it was like being part of a huge extended family. You could never feel alone in Leemal.

There were other noble houses in the city, some even as high as the Farenith, and occasionally, in the past, he had visited them with his father and mother, but he had always noticed how deferential they all were. The Farenith were held in the highest honour in Leemal.

The ceremony, the honour, those were all fine and good, but Korfax always looked forward most to walking through the great market.

Here were all the wares one could wish for, each gathered from the remotest corners of the world. Savoury local breads were in abundance and their mouth-watering smells wafted across the market square like a beguilement. Many kinds of tornzl were here as well, both the large and the small, freshly caught from the great sea to the north, the Zumdril Lukal. There were rich fabrics from the east, perfumed woods and incenses from the south and cunningly-wrought jewellery from the west. There was always something new to see, and there were also many tales to hear, stories from the great ports of Lon-Elah and gossip from her mighty cities. Stand outside one of the open windows of any hostelry and you would hear all the songs and all the tales of many a distant land.

Korfax looked out of his window and smiled. He was in the family apartments in the Garad, the best place to be outside Losq, or so he thought. Seven towers made up the Garad, and the Farenith had apartments in one of those, the northern-most. From here, all of Leemal was spread out like a finely wrought jewel, and since all the towers were tipped with piradar, they lit up the night like so many stars.

Korfax could think of no finer sight than the city of Leemal at night. So here it was again, laid out before him like a feast, a feast for the eyes, a feast of light.

Since journeying south, his mood had begun to lighten. A visit to Leemal was always a pleasure, but now at last a real sense of excitement was beginning to grow inside. He had flown for the first time, and that had been a great delight. He would soon fly again, off to see even greater wonders. He would see Othil Zilodar, greatest city of the north, before coming to Emethgis Vaniad itself. Paniss was right. The grief and the terror of the recent past could not compete with the wider world. Looking out over Leemal now he could not imagine the grey horrors that attacked Losq daring its high walls. Against such mighty works of stone they were reduced to beggary.

He thought of where he was to go. He had heard many say that Othil Zilodar was the largest city of the Ell, a city of authority, the will of the Velukor made manifest under heaven's gaze. Of the other great cities, Othil Homtoh to the west was said to be the most steadfast, the most pure, unflinching of service, sacred and the birthplace of Karmaraa. Othil Admaq to the south was said to be a feast for the senses, rich beyond dreams, a vast jewel set at the edges of the great desert. Othil Ekrin, the cup of the east, was said to be the most beautiful, balm for the eye and the soul, a vision of astonishment. But above them all reared great Emethgis Vaniad, holiest of all, most powerful and most potent, for had not The Creator blessed it?

Come the following day they boarded the sky ship for the second time, walking along the ornate stone gangway to reach the main deck. Others would make the journey with them this time and the vessel was fuller, but Korfax still found room enough on the observation deck to see the sights.

He waited for the great rush of power and laughed again as the craft sped away. The world fell back as they rose higher and soon Leemal could no longer be seen.

They crossed wide plains, great expanses of grass and forest. It seemed interminable. The world was getting larger, moment by moment, and Korfax began to appreciate its scale. How small the furthest north now seemed.

They came to a barren region, in the middle of which there appeared to be ruins, the dim outlines of walls, scattered stones and broken foundations. He turned to his father.

"What is that down there? Are those ruins?"

Sazaaim looked to where Korfax pointed.

"Yes, those are ruins. And you of all people should know what they are; you have heard their name often enough."

Korfax looked at the sparse and scattered remains. They lay like ancient bones lifted from their resting places, crumbling and bereft.

"Is that Peis-homa?" he asked.

"Yes," said his father, "that is Peis-homa."

Sazaaim turned to Raxen Liexar and gestured at the ruins below. Liexar bowed his head and turned to the great bell which hung above the stone that steered the ship. He struck it with its hammer and a single clear note rang out. All stopped what they were doing and looked back. Sazaaim held up his left hand and every face turned to him.

"It is not often that we pass such a place," he said, "but since we are here, we should pay homage to the lost."

All heads bowed. Korfax bowed also, but he kept his eyes on what passed below. Peis-homa must have been splendid in its prime, much like Leemal perhaps, a tall and a proud place filled with people and full of beauty. Now it lay in ruins, a monument to the horror of war, one of the very few that still remained in the world. Sazaaim raised his head and pointed a finger at the mute wreckage below.

"So that no one ever forgets, here lies the worst of it. Here it was that the Black Heart committed his most evil crime. Here he revealed his true self before the world and before The Creator. Here it was that he broke the ancient covenants of war, tearing Peis-homa and its people apart without mercy, raising first an army of demons and then an army of the dead to do his hated will."

Korfax stared at the mute piles of stone. The Black Heart, Sondehna, tyrant of the north. He knew the story well, everyone did. It lay at the heart of the world. It was the reason for everything.

Sondehna was born of the old people of the north, the Iabeiorith. He was their prince, of the house of Mikaolaz, and like many of that people he was mighty in sorcery. Some said that he was the greatest of all, that there was no demon he could not summon and no power of the abyss too intractable for him to command.

The lands of the Iabeiorith were said to be dark, for they loved the night – not the stars but the darkness itself – and many of their towers were built in the valleys, in the shadow and rendered with the blackest stone.

Karmaraa was born of the west, of the Korith Zadakal. He also was a prince of his people, but he was unlike the Black Heart in all other ways. As with many of the west he understood the lore of stone and was said to be the greatest in its practice.

The lands of the Korith Zadakal were wide and green, and they built their pale towers upon the hilltops. They loved the high mountains and the rolling hills. They were a people of the air.

It was said that there had always been contention between the Korith Zadakal and the Iabeiorith. How long it had been so no one could say, but the borders of their lands were drawn in blood and neither side ever gave quarter.

When Karmaraa and Sondehna were born there was a heavenly event, a great conjunction of the outer spirits in that rarest of occurrences, the sword. Seers took note. Something momentous was about to occur, but they could not say what it might be. On that day all oracles failed and the world held its breath.

The two princes grew: Karmaraa virtuous, Sondehna dark. Each was a reflection of the other, in that they were born almost at the same hour, their fathers died at almost the same time and they ascended to their respective thrones on the very same day. It was clear that fate was speaking, but no one, not even the best of the seers, could tell what was being said.

Eventually it came to pass that the two princes would finally meet. It was a long held custom to sign treaties and make agreements in the presence of the seers at the Rolnir, the centre of the world. In those days the Rolnir was forbidden territory. Dark storms raged inside the encircling hills and there was an unspoken belief that to cross the boundary, to climb over the hills, was to invite doom.

So here it was that Karmaraa and Sondehna met for the first time, and there was immediate contention between them. They were utterly opposite in all things but one. Both of them came to desire a young seer called Soivar.

It was said that Karmaraa had kommah with Soivar – that blessed state of souls destined for union – the very first time that he saw her, but being a humble soul he did not presume. Sondehna, though, had no such qualms. Instead, enamoured of her beauty, he beguiled her and stole her away under cover of darkness, imprisoning her in his dark tower, right at the very centre of his great city, whose name must never be spoken.

The seers sent embassies, entreating of the other great powers of the world, the Korith Ial and the Korith Zinu, saying that one of their own had been taken against her will, but Sondehna would only answer that it was not so, that it was Soivar's desire to be with him and with no other. If proof were wanted, they were invited to come to see for themselves. Many suspected sorcery, though, for Soivar did not seem to be herself when they spoke to her and she ever looked at her dark lord with fearful adoration. Soivar told them all that she would remain in the north, that she would bare the children of Sondehna and that this was her choice. Few believed her words.

Karmaraa confessed his kommah to the seers, and they urged him to go to war, for kommah was a blessing from The Creator. But he would not. His was not a spirit of violence. Instead he mourned for what could not be and let it pass.

Sondehna, though, was not so easily satisfied. Having taken one jewel, he wanted more. It was said that he had a hole within him, a great and hungry hole that would never be filled, and believing that the rest of the world would not stand in his way, he decided to take whatever he would.

There was an old prophecy, one of the oldest of all, how a ruler would come, one who would unify the world, remove all divisions and bring down The Creator's word to all. Sondehna decided that he was that one. But there was a test. The unifier must dare the Rolnir.

So Sondehna slowly gathered all his forces to him. When he was ready he would march south in panoply of war and take the Rolnir by force. Only one people in all the lands of the north refused his summons, and they were the Korith Peis.

They dwelt in the city of Peis-homa, peacefully and proudly alone. But Sondehna would not tolerate any dissent, no matter who they were, and he decided to make an example of them. Then the rest of the world would know how foolish it was to defy his will. Peis-homa, alone of all the cities of the north, was laid waste and her people were slaughtered to the last. Heralds were sent to all the great powers, showing them the price of defiance. This is what will happen to you if you reject the demands of our prince, they said. Many were cowed by what they saw. This was a darkness and a power they knew they could not match.

But Karmaraa was of another temper. He now saw that there would be no stopping Sondehna in his mad desire to rule the world, so he reluctantly decided to defy the might of the north and make himself protector of the holy centre.

The forces of the west finally met the forces of the north at the Rolnir, and it was here that Karmaraa revealed his destiny. By the power that was in him he changed his stave from that of fire to that of spirit, from red to white, changing the purpose of stone itself and re-forging it with his will. No other had ever done this, before or since. It was the mark of the word, the word of The Creator. So Karmaraa, armed with the holy white, the white of spirit, the grace of The Creator and with full mastery of all the elements stood forth. He defeated the Black Heart and burned him from the world.

It was said that Soivar, at the death of Sondehna, was finally released from his power. Overcome by the horror of her enslavement, she killed herself along with her two children, burning together upon a great pyre, and the Iabeiorith, hearing the news that the house of Sondehna was no more, that even his children were dead, went mad with rage and vowed eternal vengeance upon the rest of the world. From that moment on, the name of Soivar was a curse in the north and she was ever afterwards called the 'Great Betrayer'.

So began the Wars of Unification, even as the house of Sondehna ended. Karmaraa and his forces held the line against the north, even finding another that would love him, but it was said that he ever grieved for Soivar and the promise of what might have been.

Korfax looked back down at Peis-homa. When he had first been told the story he had tried to conjure in his mind's eye what he imagined must have happened. He had pictured the Haelok Aldaria, the elite guard of Sondehna, those who spoke only the will of their master, riding across the plain. He had pictured Sondehna himself, riding at their head, tall and mighty but with the face of a demon – black flesh, long teeth and burning eyes. He had imagined Sondehna raising a black hand over the plain that stretched before beautiful Peis-homa, and he had imagined the dead rising up, each corpse filled with horrid life. But now, as he looked down upon the ancient ruins, he saw misshapen things erupt from the ground instead – grey things, headless things, things armed with sword and shield. He saw grey horrors storm the gates and the walls, and he saw Peis-homa erased by tooth and bone.

The story he had been told seemed far too innocent now, a tale fit only for a child. He found himself wondering what had really happened on that day. What horror had the people endured, and what terror?

Korfax wanted to be the first to see Othil Zilodar, so he stayed at the front on the main deck and stared ahead, watching the great sweep of the land as it flattened and widened into the wide plain of Zilodar.

But he did not know what he was looking for. His mother came to stand beside him, and without a word she pointed to the hazy distance. Korfax looked where she was pointing but could not see what it was that she meant. She smiled and gestured that he look again. Then he saw it. What he had taken for a low line of hills was not a line of hills at all. It was a wall.

They began to descend, and Othil Zilodar grew in size. Korfax moved from surprise, through delight and on to utter astonishment. How could a city be so big? To see such sights in a projection was one thing, but to see it with your own eyes? He stared ahead and tried in vain to encompass its immensity with his sight. But it was just too big.

First there was the great wall. He could see no end to it, for its mighty curve vanished into the misty distances on either side. Straddling the wall and spaced equally around it were the great watchtowers, each set with the traditional four spires apiece. They rose up like mountains set above a cliff, challenging the world without. But for all their size the wall and its towers merely described the limits of the city, not what stood proudly within.

Othil Zilodar's huge northern gates yawned below, great mouths of carven stone, and behind them rose the city itself, hills of stone and crystal, tall towers, taller spires, each leading the eye ever onwards to the centre, where one single and immense citadel dominated.

There, in the misty distance, was the Umadril Detharzi, a huge cluster of towers named for the peace that came in the wake of their building. Korfax stared at them in awe, for he could tell, even at this distance, that the Umadril Detharzi would have swallowed little Leemal whole.

And there was another wonder, for a greater sky ship was rising up from a tower on this side of the citadel. Korfax stared at it in delight. The sky ships that came to Leemal, like the one he currently rode in, were small indeed compared to this giant.

He watched intently as the huge craft sailed upwards gracefully, rising far above them and away from its moorings. And when it had reached the requisite height it unfurled its great wings at last. Then it picked up speed. Somewhere inside, one of the four Raxenith, each a sky master in their own right, stood over one of the four zongadar, the wind stones, and summoned the forces that would send the ship on its way across the heavens.

Korfax turned to his mother.

"What would it be like to travel in something so big?"

Tazocho smiled.

"You'll find out soon enough. Some things are better left as surprises."

Korfax turned back to watch the departing ship, watching as it swiftly disappeared.

"How long does it take to get to Emethgis Vaniad?"

"At best speed it takes just under a day. If you were to ride to Emethgis Vaniad, it would take considerably longer."

Korfax turned back and stared at the city. His brow furrowed.

"I was thinking. Why don't we use sky ships to go everywhere?"

"Until now, there has not been the need," said his mother. "Besides, you would miss the land itself. We are stewards here. We should care for the land and know its ways. So if we spent all our time hopping from one place to another in sky ships we should soon forget that there was anything in between. Having a destination is a good thing, but most of the time the journey is an end in itself. Only when the distances involved are great do we resort to sky ships. We should appreciate the land."

Korfax looked up at her.

"Has anybody ever made an earth ship, one that travels over the ground, so that we can appreciate it closer?"

His mother laughed, and another laugh joined with hers. It was his father, standing behind them both. Korfax smiled. It was good to see them laugh. Away from the north their moods had lightened, especially that of his father.

"So that we can appreciate it closer, you say?" his father said, smiling broadly. "Speed is speed, my son."

"But that is not what I meant," said Korfax.

"I know it is not," answered his father, "but you do pose an interesting question. So let me tell you a tale. A very long time ago, when Valgan first had the idea for a sky ship, he also gave thought for an earth ship. And not only did he conceive the idea, he actually built one, and you can still see it in the archives of the Aldon Zna. The idea was sound, of course, Valgan being who he was, but it was soon realised that a sky ship could go much faster than an earth ship. Besides, you would need special roads for the earth ship, but the sky ship can go anywhere. So Valgan lost interest in the idea."

"Are there other means of travel?" Korfax asked.

"There are the ships of the rivers and the seas, of course," said Sazaaim, "but you mean something as fast as a sky ship, don't you?"

"Yes."

"Well now, there have been experiments of all kinds in the forges of the Dar Kaadarith. One idea that gained currency for a while was to make a gateway that would allow you to travel anywhere, anywhere at all, instantly."

Korfax looked on in astonishment.

"Anywhere? In no time at all? How can that be?"

Sazaaim smiled.

"It goes something like this. You have two special crystals, one in Emethgis Vaniad and the other in Othil Zilodar. You step onto one and immediately you are transported to the other and you step off it. The theory is that travel from one place to another takes no time at all."

Korfax stared with eyes wide open.

"Has anybody ever done that?"

"A few brave souls investigated it a long time ago. One called Sidiu even created two such stones. The idea was considered interesting, but again the objection was raised that such a device would have us ignore all the land in between. As your mother has already said, we are stewards here, stewards of the lands in which we dwell. An agile mind and the works of subtle thought are all fine and good, but not when they transgress the meaning of our place in the world. But do not worry, you will hear about all kinds of things when you get to the seminary, and you will learn why many such ideas, even though they are recorded in our archives, are never employed. The knowledge is not lost, of course, but neither is it ever used."

Korfax looked back to the front, his face a picture of concentration. Both Sazaaim and Tazocho watched him, waiting for the next question with faint smiles on their faces. It was not long in coming.

"But how would that work?" Korfax asked. "How could you disappear from one place and reappear in another?"

"The secret," said his father, "as always, lies in the heart of the crystal. Inside them, at their very centre, there would be a store of power. And that power would help each crystal breach the walls of the world, opening a gateway to another place. The gateways of the two crystals would then be made to overlap, so as you leave one, you enter the other. But also the crystals would be identical, down to the smallest detail; otherwise, they could not communicate at all."

Korfax thought about this for a moment, trying to imagine what it would feel like to cross such a boundary.

"What other things have they done in the Dar Kaadarith?"

His father smiled again.

"There is still research, but little of it is practical. Besides, what is the need? We have achieved all that we were ever meant to achieve. The last really great foray into the unknown took place many years ago and ended in accusation and recrimination. Not all such explorations are good. You see, my son, the world has two sorts of people in it. There are those that are content with the way things are, and there are those that are not. For the last few thousand years the contented have held sway over the counsels of those that govern and order our world. And those that are not content seek out Lonsiatris and remain there. Some might consider that a sad thing and some might say that the fire has gone from our hearts, but others might counter that we have matured as a people, because there are no wars, there is plenty for all and everyone has their fair share."

Korfax looked up at his father, catching the wistful expression.

"And are you content, Father?" he asked.

Sazaaim, caught off guard, glanced at Tazocho. She tilted her head back at him slightly, eyebrows raised. Korfax had seen that expression before. It meant 'answer the question'. A quick flash of emotions passed over his father's face, regret and determination in equal measure. Korfax frowned. Suddenly, or so it seemed, his father had lost that special clarity, that special certainty he had always had before. Korfax wondered whether the attack on Losq was not the reason. That seemed to have upset so many things, intruding where it should not. But his train of thought was broken when his father smiled back down at him gently.

"I thought that I was, my son, I thought that I was."

7

THE LARGER WORLD

Hedaa-si Ahz-pi-vargim
Fenaih-iam Lanouch-ors-ji
Ip-sb-ho Taljiz-luzh-aid
Sib-zarurq Iolki-alkar
Bas-depam Pao-kasan-jes
Aovin-far Impatol-ihd
Odurq-pim Nimjiz-nisan

The sky ship came to rest on one of the landing fields beside the northern sky tower. All alighted, steeds were led from their stabling and those that were to ride mounted. For the rest there were finely-wrought carts.

Korfax rode between his mother and father and held his breath as they entered the main thoroughfare. He had seen pictures of this, the wide avenues, the tall towers, constructions seemingly hewn from the mountains, but the images had lacked scale. Here, amongst them, lay another tale entirely.

He felt as though he had entered a city of giants. Everywhere he looked there were buildings that dwarfed him. Othil Zilodar was a place of immensities.

The city had once been one of the oldest of the five great cities of Lon-Elah, though it had been called by another name then. Only Othil Ekrin was said to be older. Othil Ekrin still stood, but the city of the princes of the Iabeiorith had been utterly destroyed during the Wars of Unification, her every stone removed and shattered until all traces of her had been wholly erased from the world. So Othil Zilodar had been built in her place, and it became as if the city of Sondehna had never existed at all. She vanished from the world and her name was never spoken again.

Of the four great cities of the four great provinces, Othil Zilodar was said to be the largest. Some said that she was also the mightiest, mightier even than Othil Homtoh, capital of the west. Her walls were thicker, her gates stronger and her foundations were rooted deep within the ground, like those of mountains. But many in the west said that Othil Zilodar was all show and that Othil Homtoh was stronger yet. First city of Sobol, heart of the lords of the west, Othil Homtoh had one final claim to fame – no army, whether that of Ell or demon, had ever conquered her.

They rode to the Umadril Detharzi, along the great northern road and past huge arches, towering spires and great cliffs of stone. But the immensities around them did not oppress, they uplifted. The sense of power and permanence was glorious, and Korfax felt as though all things were possible in such a place.

They eventually arrived at their destination and were escorted through the gates. They were to meet with the Tabaud himself, Geyad Kaldaray Tabaud Abinax.

Korfax felt horribly and uniquely visible as he walked with his mother and father into the presence of the Tabaud. The hall was lined with Branith, each holding a long lance set with the pennant of a noble house of the city. Behind them stood counsellors, petitioners and officials, and all looked on as Sazaaim, Tazocho and Korfax approached the seat of the Tabaud. In front of them marched Abinax's Balzarg, an ancient-looking Ell with a sharp glance, an imperious manner and an unsmiling face.

They arrived before Abinax, the word of the Velukor in that place, and bowed. Korfax almost overdid it, first with a slight hesitation and then by bowing so vigorously that he nearly lost his balance. No one seemed to notice, though. The Balzarg presented them to his Lord.

"Tabaud, may I present Geyad Faren Enay Sazaaim, Uren Faren Enay Tazocho and their son, Faren Noren Korfax."

Abinax leaned forward and smiled. Korfax found himself almost instantly liking him. His smile was warm and there was humour in his eyes.

"It is good to see you both again," he said.

Sazaaim smiled in return and inclined his head.

"And it is good to see you also, Tabaud," he replied.

Abinax turned to Korfax.

"And so I meet your son at last!"

He leaned forward.

"And how do you like my city, young Korfax?"

Korfax suddenly found himself without a single thought in his head. He tried desperately to think of an answer, suddenly aware that not to answer at all would be the height of disrespect. He offered the first words that came to him.

"It is so very large, Tabaud."

There was a ripple of quiet laughter around the hall and Abinax looked somewhat taken aback for a moment. Korfax blushed and wished he was anywhere else but there. But then Abinax smiled again and looked keenly at Korfax as though he saw something deeper in his simple statement.

"That it is, young Korfax, that it is indeed, a most careful observation. For we need always to be reminded of what stares us in the face."

He turned back to Sazaaim.

"It is my pleasure that you will join me in the inner chambers. There we will discuss what brings you hence. When do you leave for Emethgis Vaniad?"

"Tomorrow morning, Tabaud, at the hour of Safaref."

Abinax glanced at his Balzarg.

"Then we shall eat as well," he said.

The Balzarg bowed.

"Come," Abinax said, rising. All in the hall bowed. Abinax bowed in return and walked down from the dais. With his steward in front of him, and Sazaaim, Tazocho and Korfax behind, he left the hall.

They sat upon fine chairs on a high and wide balcony overlooking the northern quarter of the city. Beyond the balcony was a wide forest of towers and walls. Before them was a low table set with many dishes, each filled with delicacies the like of which Korfax had never before encountered. There was no one else present, just himself, his father, his mother and Tabaud Abinax.

Abinax leaned forward and took a small dark fruit from a pale crystal bowl. He peered at the fruit speculatively, before placing it delicately into his mouth. He looked at Sazaaim.

"You should try the kwanis, you really should. This year the harvest has been particularly good."

Sazaaim smiled fondly.

"You and your kwanis. All the years have been particularly good according to you. You were for ever making that claim at the seminary, as I recall."

Abinax smiled in return and turned to Korfax.

"Your father and I studied at the Umadya Semeiel together. I hear you are going there yourself."

He leaned forward, almost conspiratorially.

"If you do as well as he, you will go far indeed."

Sazaaim laughed quietly as though at a private joke and Abinax sat back again with a speculative look on his face as he reached for yet another kwanis. Then he gestured at all the food that lay upon the table.

"Come, all of you, eat and drink and tell me of the north."

Sazaaim took a small cake, his mother took a goblet of wine and Korfax looked for something he recognised, failed miserably and settled for one of the bright red confections that sat nearest to him. He placed it in his mouth and found that it had a gentle sweetness that all but melted on the tongue. Its flavour was a delight. He was reminded of the avasil that bloomed during the season of Axinor. Their perfume could be heady if there were a great many of them collected together, but here it was like a delicate infusion. He finished the cake and took another.

"You wish to know of the north?" Sazaaim looked down. "What can I say? What is there that you do not already know? The north, until recently, was as it has ever been – peaceful and at peace with itself."

161

A troubled look came into Abinax's eyes.

"Is this a wise topic?" he said. "That was not the intent of my question."

Sazaaim smiled gently enough, but his eyes flickered with another light. Tazocho did not move at all.

"I know," said Sazaaim, "and I do not intend to mention it other than in passing. But I will say this at least. My son was there, one of only four to survive."

He reached out and took Tazocho's hand. He squeezed it for a moment and then turned back to Abinax.

"My wife was another, along with Bransag Orkanir and Chasaloh, warden of the lands about Losq. We have spoken of what occurred, all of us, and my son has learned a hard lesson, one of the hardest of all. You can say anything in his presence. He knows when to speak and when to be silent."

Korfax looked at his father. A hard lesson indeed. But then he noticed Abinax. The Tabaud of Othil Zilodar was staring at him as though Korfax had suddenly become a wonder. Korfax did not know where to look, but then his father broke the moment by leaning forward and holding out a small green crystal. Korfax glanced at it. It was a logadar. Abinax stared at it briefly before leaning back and looking away. He suddenly looked sad.

"It is all in there?" he asked.

Sazaaim placed the crystal upon the table.

"All of it," he said. "You should know everything I know concerning this matter. These were creatures never before seen: new demons, new threats. I fear that one of the Argedith has arisen again, one of great power."

He gestured at the crystal.

"I will be giving copies of this stone to Geyadril Fokisne and Urendril Andispir before I leave, but this one is for you."

Abinax looked sombrely at the crystal. After a long moment he took it up in his hands before placing it to one side. Then he smiled again.

"Now I want some real news," he said. "What of Gieris? What of Leemal? Tell me of the Raxamith and the Saqorris. Tell me all the good news."

"Of course," Sazaaim answered.

And for the next hour Sazaaim, Tazocho and Abinax spoke of the north while Korfax listened, occasionally answering when Abinax asked him about this or that. But the subject of the grey demons was not raised again.

Later Korfax found himself with Abinax once more, but this time they were alone. Abinax wanted to show him the city. Korfax thought that he meant that they would ride through the streets together, but instead Abinax took him up to one of the many observation rooms. He found himself wondering how Abinax could spare the time. Wasn't the Tabaud of such a great city busy all day? Clearly not.

They arrived at the room after the long climb. Most of their conversation to this point had been about the many places Abinax had visited. Now, though, Abinax turned to his city as it stretched out before them both.

"Now you can see Othil Zilodar in all its glory," he said. "Few have ever stood where you stand now."

Korfax went to each great window in turn. It was a spellbinding scene. He could just make out the city walls in the distance, far, far away, but in between was an ordered riot of towers, gardens, walls, roads and movement. There was a sky ship lifting up and another coming down. The roads below were scattered with the dots of people, riders and wagons of various sizes. On the river that wound its way through the city there were ships, some very large, moving to and fro or simply berthed at one of the many wharfs. Korfax watched it all in silence. Eventually he turned back to Abinax and thanked him. Abinax smiled in response.

"Your mother was right, I think."

Korfax waited. What did he mean?

"You needed a renewed sense of proportion," Abinax told him.

Korfax did not know what he meant by that either.

"I don't understand, Tabaud," he said.

"What do you see out there?"

"The city, Tabaud."

"Yes, but it is so much more than that. You see life, Korfax, life in abundance, great and glorious life. You see its power. You see what it is capable of."

Now Korfax understood at last. This was the point Paniss had tried to make to him. Abinax continued.

"This city was finally completed just as the old wars came to a close. It is the very seal of our victory. In this place, with voices mightier than the manifold winds, we said 'no more'. Now Othil Zilodar stands as living proof of the words of Karmaraa. Compare what you saw at Losq with this."

He gestured out of the window.

"Can such as that even begin to compete with this?"

Korfax could only agree. The sheer force of the city, its sheer magnitude, made such terrors insignificant by comparison. The world was so much larger. Abinax looked at it all as if thoroughly satisfied, and then he turned to Korfax again.

"Now let me tell you something else. From this window you see order. Because of your experiences you now represent something outside that order. You have seen demons, everyone else has not. You will become an object of curiosity. Not your mother, not your father, but you. Be aware of it, but treat it as you would any matter of small consequence. Contrast it with what you see of the world, the vast against the small."

"My mother asked you to do this, to show me this?" Korfax asked.

"Yes," Abinax said, pausing a little. "And no. I wanted to do this as well. You see, Korfax, when you achieve your stave you will be amongst the highest in the land. You will come here often and you and I will get to know each other very well, just as I know your father. I wanted to show you what you fight for. We are guardians.

That is our purpose. We hold this world for The Creator and guard it against evil. Here, in this place, that has special meaning, for here the hammer fell hardest. And you, first amongst many, now know exactly what it is that we defend against."

Korfax felt a lump in his throat and a sudden desire to bow low before Abinax and pledge his eternal loyalty. The world had turned again. He did bow to Abinax, but only to thank him, and Abinax looked deep into his eyes in return.

"I think we will be good friends, you and I," he said.

The sky ship they were to take was immense, a huge streamlined shape seemingly better suited to the sea than the clouds. But here it waited for them now, a leviathan of the winds rather than the deeps, ready to ride an airier ocean. All its wings were furled for the moment, folded at its sides, except for the great fin on its back and the other that was its tail. Korfax stared up at it in wonder. His excitement had grown as they had ridden to the great mooring tower, one of the four that were set within each quarter of the city. Each of the Umadya Izorax was tall, lofty spires of stone set about with many platforms, and they were to go to the very top of this one.

They arrived at the platform and Korfax could now read the name of the craft they were to take. The words were emblazoned proudly on her side. She was the *Mondril Zilodar*, the great heart of the city.

Unlike the small ship from Leemal, Korfax felt lost as soon as he entered the hall of boarding. It was huge, a great cavern of a place, full of gleaming pillars and curving walls. Above and below it stretched, with many layers, balconies and stairs leading this way and that. There were people everywhere, and Korfax, along with his mother and father, seemed to be just another three amongst the many hundreds on their way to the capital. But when his father led them up to the great observation deck, the most privileged position of all upon the vessel, he saw the difference. Only a few were there, a Brandril with dispatches, two nobles of the house of Namadiol and a Raxen. But all bowed as they entered. They bowed back, of course, but not a word was said. Korfax noted that a subtle space was made around them as his father led the way forward to the balcony, his great stave held up before him like a badge of authority.

Ever since they had left Leemal, Korfax had noticed a change come over his parents. Slowly, inexorably, as they drew ever nearer to Emethgis Vaniad, both had seemed to grow. Then Korfax realised that it wasn't so much that they had changed; rather, it was the world around them that had changed. He could see the deference in the eyes of those they met. Now he began to feel the weight of his heritage. His family, though small, was a power. And doubly so, because his father was a Geyad and his mother was both Uren and of holy blood. He looked up at his father. How stern he looked. Korfax looked down again. An echo of the fear that had come upon him at Losq returned.

Sazaaim touched him lightly upon his shoulder.

"And what does my son see now?" he said.

Korfax kept his gaze down. How could he answer that? But Sazaaim leaned over and spoke quietly in his ear.

"Do not speak of it if it troubles you. But I can guess what it is. Now you see the power, my son. In Losq it is hidden. In Losq I am only your father and only its lord, nothing more and nothing less, but as we approach Emethgis Vaniad, so we approach the source of all power, where all things assume their truest nature. There, in that place, your mother and I are of consequence. There, in that place, we become what we are, powers of the highest, powers made manifest. Notice it, my son, notice that it exists, but never give it more than its due. Power is also temptation."

Korfax understood that much at least. Power was temptation. Power was a servant, but it tempted as well. One denied the temptation, but the temptation could never be erased. His father continued.

"The deference you see about you is the result of seven thousand years of tradition, of untrammelled service to the Velukor, blessed be his name. And the closer we get to Emethgis Vaniad, the more you will see it. I am Geyad and your mother is Uren. We are both Enay, nearly the highest of the high, but there is more, for your mother is of the blessed line and you are born of such blood. Such things carry great weight in the places where you will tread. So never forget it, but do not let it rule you either. Always remember from whence you came. We are humble at the last."

The ship moved away from the tower, gliding gently up as it turned to face the south. Soon it had risen to a height sufficient enough that its wings could be unfurled.

Above them and below them the outer decks of the ship came alive with movement as the great wings unfolded from each side. Korfax watched as huge jointed pinions swept outwards, great webs of imperishable fabric stretching between immense limbs of metal. As soon as they were fully extended, the four great wings swept out and back, each twice the length of the ship and twice as high. Then came that barely perceptible change in the air as winds were summoned to fill the wings.

Korfax looked about and noticed that the ship was already picking up speed. Beneath them, Othil Zilodar was spread out in all her glory. There was her proud centre, the Umadril Detharzi, sparkling in the early morning light, and there were the great roads, radiating out like the spokes of a vast wheel, leading all the way to the many gates in the high city wall. Over the wall the sky ship flew and Othil Zilodar diminished with ever-increasing rapidity. All too soon the city became a shadow upon the horizon, eventually swallowed by the curve of the world itself.

Now they were flying over the south lands of Lukalaa, over Ladassir with its green valleys and hills, some of which were tipped with ancient masses of rock that seemed as though they were simply taking their ease, whilst others were surmounted by fair towers brightly watching over the valleys below. The wide valleys themselves were scattered with fields and estates. Here was a small part, the very smallest, of the great food bowl of Lukalaa. Everything was grown here on Ladassir's fertile soil, everything from kwanis to hunak, from piuko to rohsil. Korfax found himself thinking of the Piral Gieris and how tiny it was in comparison. You could have tucked it all away in just one small valley here.

Great rivers wound their way here and there below, the occasional ship riding their waters, perhaps on their way to join one of the mighty three. Two of them, the Nyakal and the Pihrsem, were destined to reach the great ocean itself, but the third, the Zadha, would not. Korfax peered into the east, hoping to catch a glimpse of that great landlocked sea, the Zum Risson, into which the Zadha ultimately flowed, but he was too far west. The Risson was said to be immense, a great sea the size of an entire province. Korfax had heard that the tornzl in its depths were so huge and the waters they swam in so clear and so calm that to sail a boat upon it one would think that one was floating at the limit of the heavens whilst sky ships passed blithely beneath.

Come midday, Sazaaim, Tazocho and Korfax ate a sparse meal together of kwanis and silath, a parting gift from Abinax. The kwanis were bitter-sweet and not entirely to the taste of Korfax, but the silath, the flat and heavily spiced bread favoured throughout Othil Zilodar, he thought wonderful. Packed inside it were strips of cured meat mixed with fresh herbs of varying sorts, along with slices of dried kwanil, the bright red fruit beloved of the people of southern Lukalaa. The journey lent the simple meal a special savour, and Korfax ate everything with delight, even the kwanis.

Sazaaim and Tazocho watched their son between mouthfuls and they smiled, but only Sazaaim smiled in remembrance. He had once undertaken this journey himself.

After the meal Korfax went back to the railings, just in time to catch another spectacle. If Peis-homa had been the most terrifying reminder of the Wars of Unification, then below him lay its proudest. The Great Wall!

Even after all this time it showed little sign of wear. Few of the watchtowers upon it were occupied, of course, and it was seldom that any walked the road on its top, but a greater work of the hand and the mind it was harder to imagine.

From mountain range to mountain range it was spread, spanning the land, over hill, over plain, over river, one single stretch of wall. Built during the Wars of Unification, it had been the cage that kept the remnants of sorcery locked away in the north. It marked the limits of Lukalaa. Now they were coming to Ovaras, the province that held the centre of the world.

Mountains appeared to the south, west and east. To the west lay the last of Adroqin Vohimar whilst to the south and east loomed the Adroqin Perisax. The two ranges would join up ahead, coming together at the Leein Komsel, the hills that encircled the Rolnir, but first they had one more landmark to cross.

So they came to the Nazarthin Ozong, the pillars of the wind, great towers of rock carved by the elements into fantastic shapes and all set about with mighty forests that stretched from the east to the west.

There was little wind now and a mist hung across the jagged spires. With Rafarel moving into the west, the land took on a golden glow. Caught by the mystic distances, Korfax watched in wonder as the world drifted by, dreamlike and silent. With the Nazarthin Ozong set out before him he thought that he now stood upon the balcony of the highest tower ever built, looking down at a great city gentled by time, her eroded towers still proud with elder majesty. He had come to the borders of legend, that fabulous place where dream vanquished the waking world and memory and vision took on a life all their own. The beauty of it pierced his heart and he vowed to himself that as long as he lived he would never forget this day or this place. He would keep it in his heart and would remember it always.

The great craft landed at one of the four wide assembly areas beyond the Leein Komsel. They were to ride the rest of the way.

Korfax knew what he would be seeing – the walled hills, the city within like an offering of stone – but standing here now with his steed, standing upon the landing field, he felt trepidation. The hills were huge and the walls upon them greater than any he had yet seen. He had thought nothing could be as mighty as Othil Zilodar, but now he saw otherwise. There was power here, great slumbering power hidden away behind encircling heights.

They rode slowly along the road towards the northern gate, following one of the many curling ridges that led up to the hilltops. Here the land had been turned upon itself, a huge spiral of stone created by four curving and interleaving folds of land, the great ring of hills that was the Leein Komsel. Within lay the Rolnir, a wide bowl of stone and soil in which Emethgis Vaniad had been built.

In ancient times the Rolnir had been shunned as a place not meant for mortal sight. It was said to be The Creator's mark upon the world, a place of ever-circling storms and darknesses. Only seers had dared to live close by; all others kept away in fear. To enter the Rolnir was said to invite damnation, but then Sondehna had come and everything had changed.

After Karmaraa defeated the Black Heart, he sealed his victory by walking within the Rolnir itself. It became a gentle place at his touch, and all the seers proclaimed him the chosen of The Creator and Velukor of all. The unification of the world was begun.

Korfax took a deep breath as he approached the gates. He felt small, insignificant and yet uplifted. Legend, and the mighty stone about him, reduced him to a mote.

They rode through. It was dark inside, a darkness said to be a reminder that all had been dark at first. Then, after a moment, the walls opened out and great Emethgis Vaniad was revealed in sudden light.

Korfax stared in awe. Here at last was the first city of the Ell, majestic Emethgis Vaniad, the seal of The Creator upon the world. The sight held him. He looked about him now with eyes capable of accepting anything. If Othil Zilodar had been a revelation, then Emethgis Vaniad was beyond compare.

The hills of the Komsel spread out on either side, a high ring circumscribing the immense bowl that was the Rolnir. Within this great curving bowl Emethgis Vaniad had been built, seven mighty walls in the fashion of seven wide circles. There were spires, mountains of crystal and stone leaping proudly upwards, flashing in the failing light of the day. There were domes, earthbound orbs of many-hued stone, all set within frozen seas of glittering crystal. There were roads and squares, bridges and archways, gardens and avenues, all circling the centre at which stood the greatest assemblage of all – seven mighty towers surrounding one, the mightiest of all, the Umadya Pir.

There was no greater city, for none rivalled her. Great Emethgis Vaniad, spread out like a mighty jewel within a necklace of hills.

They rode slowly down to the nearest gate set within the seventh wall. No one spoke. Korfax glanced at his father and was surprised to find a look of peace upon his face. He wondered whether his father was remembering his first view of the city. Korfax glanced at his mother and found her smiling back at him. It was radiant, that smile, and he immediately knew what she was thinking. This was where she had been born, in the Umadya Pir itself. She was coming home.

They approached the first gate, and Korfax stared up at it in wonder. Its walls looked as though they had grown up from the earth, at one with the gentle grass, immense and venerable like ancient mountains. He felt humbled by their size. If giants had made Othil Zilodar, then gods had made Emethgis Vaniad, raising it up with huge hands so that their children could play within.

They halted at the gate. Upon it were great words, inlaid with gleaming metal and crystal. Korfax read them:

'Karhusas. Arpas. Od Trinan Eoi.' 'Here I came. Here I conquered. And here I will sit for ever.'

They were the very words Karmaraa was said to have spoken after his great victory, when he took his ease within the Rolnir itself. Korfax stared up at them and then lowered his head. He felt their weight upon him. With such words the world had been remade. With such words the Ell had been recreated. With such words they had been redeemed, saved from the darkness. Here the first Velukor had spoken with the will of The Creator, as all his heirs had ever since.

The thoroughfare beyond the gate was huge, easily taking all the traffic that crossed it or passed beside them. So many things there were, great wains piled with fragrant woods from the south, covered wagons filled with rich fabrics from the east, proud cavalry from one of the outlying watchtowers. But the city was curiously quiet, as though all movement was subdued by the immensity around them. One trod quietly in Emethgis Vaniad.

So on they went, passing through the circles of the city as though through a dream. Korfax could see where they were going, straight to the Umadya Pir itself. But when they reached the second gate they turned aside. To the second circle they went and up onto the wide wall that circled it. Once there they stopped and dismounted. Korfax would have questioned this, but his father gestured that he look about him.

"Look at the city, my son," he said. "Look at it all and remember this moment."

It was strange, but with the words of his father Korfax suddenly felt as though it was he that was returning home. There was a quietness to the air, a stillness that reminded him of a far northern evening at the fall of the year. There was no one else about, and if it wasn't for the great city about him, the sense of home would have been all but complete.

Korfax looked about him. With the advent of evening, the lights of the city had begun to shine forth. It was an astonishing sight to one who had never seen it before. Every tower was tipped by a piradar, some greater, some smaller, much as the stars above. But there, on the high wall, it felt as though they now stood within the heavens themselves, the stars set about them, not above.

He looked to the Umadya Pir. Brightest of all was the immense crystal that rested upon the highest spire. Yet for all its power it was a gentle light, and the many colours that filled it ever moved, like drifting clouds or waves upon a sea, never the same twice. To either side he could see many of the great towers that made up the seven guilds. He knew each of them, their place and their nature, for Doanazin had told him much about them. They were the order of the world.

To his right lay the first of the first, the Umadya Semeiel. That was where he was going, to the seminary of the Dar Kaadarith. It was a mountain of stone, ridges and spires, precipices and cliffs. If not for the Umadya Pir it would have dominated the city.

Further on stood the Umadya Zedekel, the tower of his mother's order, the tower of vision. There were many layers, towers wrapped in towers like the layered mind. Here the Exentaser had their being, the oldest order of all. There had always been seers. They were the eyes of the world and little could be hidden from them.

Beyond the Umadya Zedekel lay the Umadya Korabel, the Tower of Commerce. Here were the doers of the world, the Prah Sibith. By their hand all things moved. Commerce was their province, through which the world was ordered and kept in balance.

Further on would have been the Umadya Madimel, but Korfax could not see it, as it was hidden by the Umadya Pir. This was the red tower, the Tower of War and home to the Nazad Esiask. He had seen images of it, a collection of towers like many swords raised in salute.

Following along the second circle, the next tower was the Umadya Sabathel, a curious mixture of the heavy and the slender. This was the Tower of Healing, home to the Faxith, the most serious order of all. They stood at the gates of death and

169

were invariably silent. Almost as old as the seers, it was said that once, long ago, the Faxith had been coeval with Exentaser, but a schism had split the disciplines. Now there were two where before there had been only one.

Next to the Umadya Sabathel was the Umadya Levanel, a single tower like a finger pointing at the heavens. This was where the Balt Kaalith had their being. 'Eternal vigilance' was their catechism, and those words were said to be carved into the stone over every door in that place. Korfax had been told that they settled disputes, but he had never knowingly met one of their order. Their dark green cloaks were rarely seen outside the great cities, for they liked to move quietly. Far more importantly they dealt with heresy whenever it reared its ugly head. Doanazin had taken great care to explain this to him, but even so, Korfax still found it difficult to accept. It seemed that there were some, born into each generation, that chose not to follow the rule of the Velukor, and it was therefore the duty of the Balt Kaalith to seek them out. It was traditional to offer recantation, but if they refused they were to be banished lest they upset the order of things. To this end there was a place set aside for them, the land of the exiles, Lonsiatris.

Last of all, and to his left, lay the Umadya Nogarel, the square and orderly tower of the Erm Roith. If the Prah Sibith were the doers of the world, then here were the sayers. By their word all things stayed the same, the many rituals observed. One saw their orange robes everywhere, for they watched everything and made sure that everything occurred as it should, at the right time and in the right place. This had been Doanazin's order.

They mounted again and rode towards the Umadya Semeiel and soon they arrived at the tower gates. Korfax gazed up at the tower itself, lost in confusion. The closer he came to it, the more complicated it became, and now he did not understand what it was that he saw at all. The great tower looked to him like one spire made up of many spires, or a mountain of many summits and ridges. But yet it lacked a mountain's spontaneity. There were peaks and pinnacles, valleys and gorges, plateaus and cliffs, but they were arranged so cunningly that they bewildered the eye.

"Do not be confused, my son," said his father, seeing the look on his face. "We of the Dar Kaadarith are the true masters of stone. Only we can understand what has been wrought here. One day soon, when you are ready, you will look up at the Umadya Semeiel again and know what it is that you see."

Korfax waited to enter but then noticed that his mother and father were looking at him.

"What is it?" he asked.

"It is time," answered his mother.

"Time?"

"I must leave you here. I shall not enter the Umadya Semeiel with you. I go now to the Umadya Zedekel."

He took a long breath. Then he went to her and held her tight. She held him tight also, and she smiled at him. But she was not sad, not now. Now there was joy in her, unalloyed joy, and he understood, even though it was hard.

"Go now," she said to him. "Go and fulfil your destiny. Be as one of the Farenith. Find joy and purpose and serve as only those of the Farenith can."

"But that is what I always wanted to do," he said.

"I know," she answered. "And I love you for it."

She kissed him and then drew away, mounting her steed. Then she turned about and rode slowly into the west. Korfax and his father watched her go. As she vanished into the distance Sazaaim turned and looked at his son.

"Your mother is so very proud of you," he said.

Korfax looked back at his father. Again there was a flicker of emotion across his face, a curious mixture of love and regret.

"As am I," he said finally, like an affirmation. Then he looked down at his son and smiled. He was almost his usual self again.

"So come now," he said. "Our final destination awaits us."

Through the gate they rode and up to the great door, where they dismounted. Their steeds were taken by a Geyad who bowed to Sazaaim and smiled at Korfax. Korfax bowed in return, a little taken aback that a Geyad would be stabling his ormn. His father leaned closer.

"That one has only just attained his stave," he said. "It is usual for a newly forged Geyad to spend some time serving the needs of the tower."

"Did you do that?" Korfax asked.

"Of course," said Sazaaim. "As will you, seven years from now."

They went up to the great door and here was another Geyad, offering up the ritual challenge and then bowing to Sazaaim as the door opened. Sazaaim looked at Korfax.

"One of the wardens," he explained. "You will get to know them as time goes by. They keep the observances."

Inside, the tower was as confusing as it was without. If his father had not been there Korfax would soon have been lost. There were halls and stairs and corridors in great abundance, and even the stone itself seemed to shift as though it could not keep still in the presence of so much collected might.

His father led him on, up to a high place, three high corridors coming together in a large chamber with one great door. There were others here, a great many of them, doing this or that, talking, standing or listening. But they all looked up when Sazaaim arrived, and every one of them fell silent.

Korfax waited outside the door alone, sitting upon one of the great stone seats that lined the walls. Around him were statues and carvings and pictures of such richness and intensity that he found he could not look at any of them for long. Even the floor, with its beguiling patterns of inlaid stone, was too much for him. He felt dwarfed, inadequate and out of place.

Here was power, real power. It beat in the air about him and it thrummed in the stone. He shut his eyes. He felt overwhelmed. He sat at the heart of the Umadya Semeiel and he knew it all too well.

Given the sigil upon the door, the room into which his father had gone belonged to the Geyadel himself, first of the Dar Kaadarith. All the others that had been coming and going or simply standing had disappeared. Another, a Geyadril by his insignia, commanding and tall, had asked them all to leave by order of the Geyadel. This they did, though one or two of them passed a quick glance at Korfax as they left. Most, though, did not. Then the Geyadril had asked Sazaaim to enter before departing himself. Korfax had been left alone.

After what seemed an age, the door to the inner chamber opened and a bowed and ancient Ell emerged. By his robes Korfax knew that this was the Geyadel of the Dar Kaadarith. This was Gemanim.

Korfax stood and bowed as he had been taught. Then he waited whilst Gemanim walked towards him slowly.

Gemanim might have been tall once, but something weighed him down now, bending him to the ground. He walked deliberately, leaning upon his great stave. It was a kabadar, just like his father's, but this stave was as white as the purest snow.

Gemanim's eyes were the saddest Korfax had ever seen. In them lay a deep sorrow, a vast grief that almost made Korfax want to burst into tears himself.

Gemanim approached Korfax and put forward his left hand. Then he laid that hand upon the head of Korfax and closed his eyes. Nothing was said. Korfax waited. He felt nothing in his mind. Was this a blessing?

Gemanim withdrew his hand and smiled gently at Korfax. There was still the sadness in his eyes, but it was muted now. Korfax thought it the most reassuring smile he had ever seen in all his life. It wrapped him up in arms of comfort and told him that all would be well. Korfax again almost felt like bursting into tears. Gemanim bowed his head slightly as if satisfied and went back into his inner chamber. The door closed behind him and Korfax was alone once more.

Except that he wasn't.

Around him the outer chamber suddenly took on a different light. The statues that had at first been stern now smiled at him, and the paintings, the portraits, suddenly seemed to fill up with light. Even the power that beat in the air was gentler now – warmer and less forbidding. It was as if the very touch of the Geyadel brought blessings with it.

It wasn't until much later that Korfax realised it wasn't the chamber that had changed, it was himself.

After his time with the Geyadel his father took him to one of balconies looking out over the city. There they stood. It was quiet about them.

"My son," said his father, "there is one more thing that needs saying before I go."

Korfax waited quietly as he had been taught to do. One waited for answers. His father looked at him carefully.

"These last few days have taught you much," he said. "There was a time when you would have answered before you knew what was coming. You have learned a measure of patience since then, I think. Silence is to be desired at all times, until all is finally revealed."

He smiled.

"There are many forces at work here, and I do not mean just in this tower. There is a hidden game within the ritual of the great guilds. They vie with each other, seeking advantage. There is rivalry, and more than rivalry. Though the Dar Kaadarith are the first of all the guilds, the first amongst equals, there are others that covet our pre-eminence and the power that comes with it. Of these, the Balt Kaalith are the hungriest. It is an old hunger, for they have always considered their rightful place to be ours, ever since the days of he who made them, of Efaeis, blessed be his name. Now that demons have stepped back into the world they seek to increase their influence once more. The Balt Kaalith vie with us and with the Nazad Esiask, and the Erm Roith side with the Balt Kaalith. The Prah Sibith petition the Dar Kaadarith and the Exentaser for their support, while the Faxith keep their own counsel and hope to remain unaffected by the waters that flow around them."

"But I thought that had been going on for years," Korfax said. "It is part of the greater ritual that is Emethgis Vaniad, or so Doanazin told me."

"No, my son," Sazaaim answered. "What Doanazin once considered to be true, is actually true no longer. Before the demons came it was as she told you – a dance of words, one ritual amongst many. But now passions have been inflamed by fear, and old memories have started to awaken. There is much more to the dance now, and the Balt Kaalith have decided that they should be the ones to order it. Be wary of them, my son, be very wary. All of the highest come from the noble houses of the west, unlike many of the other guilds. In the Dar Kaadarith and the Exentaser one advances by merit, but in the Balt Kaalith one advances by patronage. They have remembered that which they had all but forgotten in the long years of peace, their age-old desire for primacy and power. You are of the Farenith, a house whose voice is listened to. Some may attempt to influence what is said."

He turned about.

"Now for the last act. Come."

His father led him through more corridors until they came to a small hall where another was waiting for them. His father gestured.

"Geyad Sohagel, may I present my son. This is Faren Noren Korfax and he is now of an age to take his place in the seminary."

Sohagel was old, possibly as old as Gemanim, but that was the only thing they had in common. Sohagel was upright, stern and almost bursting with vigour.

"So I was informed," he said, bowing to Sazaaim. He then turned to Korfax.

"And I am pleased to meet you at last, young Korfax."

To Korfax, he looked anything but, with his powerful voice and demanding eyes. Korfax bowed in return, keeping his face straight, his demeanour correct, but deep down inside Sohagel already terrified him. He suddenly had a vision of an old and stubborn tree, proudly clinging to life, its roots delving deep into the earth to crush rocks for their pleasure.

He looked back up again, but Sohagel had already turned back to his father.

"I take it you will be with us for a while yet?" Sohagel asked.

"I have business with Geyadril Abrilon and then I must leave," said Sazaaim.

"Nothing beyond what is already known, I hope."

"No," said Sazaaim. "But I must speak with Abrilon and only with Abrilon. There are certain 'affairs' to clear up before I take the next sky ship back to Othil Zilodar."

Sohagel fixed Sazaaim with a most seeing look for a moment, before looking away again. Korfax had the impression that a brief battle of wills had just taken place, a battle his father had won all too easily. Sazaaim had returned the gaze of Sohagel with ease, and there was now the vaguest hint of a smile upon his lips. Korfax began to feel a little less daunted by Sohagel.

"You were ever a closed box, Sazaaim," said Sohagel. "This haste is unseemly."

Sazaaim kept his smile.

"But it is, nonetheless, most necessary. I must return to the north. And you know why."

"Not all agree with you on this," said Sohagel.

"Then it is time that they did," returned Sazaaim.

Sohagel sighed as if only partially satisfied, and then he turned to Korfax.

"Do not believe that I think less of your father because I disagree with him," he said. "I do not. Like many here, I believe him to be the best of us. His unflinching service is a shining example and one you would do well to follow. Did you know that your father should have been a Geyadril? It is a mystery to many of us as to how that did not come about..."

"Sohagel!"

Korfax stared back at his father. Here it was again, that commanding voice. But in this place it assumed even greater power, for it echoed from wall to wall and Sohagel had no choice but to bow his head.

"Of course, I am sorry, but I still think it would clear the air. Gemanim has not appeared in council for many a year! Abrilon handles everything now. He is Geyadel in all but name. Sometimes I think that you and Gemanim are two of a kind."

Sazaaim raised an eyebrow.

"And that is not a subject for your speculation!"

Sohagel made the gesture of acceptance.

"So be it! Keep your secrets, as you ever have."

Sazaaim turned to Korfax. He had become grim again.

"I must leave you now. All your belongings are with the wardens. Sohagel will show you where you are to go."

He half turned for a moment as if to leave, but then he looked back. There was a look of sadness on his face, of sadness and regret, and Korfax sank at the sight. He ran to his father and clutched at him. Sazaaim held his son tight. This was it. Here came the last parting of all.

At last Korfax let go. He looked up to see his father smiling down at him.

"May the light of The Creator shine upon you, my son."

Korfax swallowed.

"And may the light shine upon you, Father."

Sazaaim turned about and strode off. This time he did not look back. Korfax watched him go, and gloom descended. After Sazaaim had turned the corner and disappeared, Korfax knew he had truly gone. He felt a gentle hand on his shoulder and turned to see Sohagel looking down at him carefully.

"Well, young Korfax, here you are, misery incarnate. I seldom see such sadness in this place."

Korfax looked away. He did not know what to say.

"Do not fear," Sohagel continued. "You will be cared for here. We whose duty is the seminary consider it our most solemn commandment. You are in our hands now, and those hands will be gentle. So put away your fears. You are in the safest place in the world."

Korfax looked up and found Sohagel smiling at him. The old Ell's face had almost completely changed shape. Laughter lines fanned out across the parchment skin and Sohagel all but beamed.

"Come, let me show you the sights of the seminary. Let me show you sights enough to make your heart leap with joy."

And with a gentle hand on Korfax's shoulder, Sohagel led him away down the corridor.

8

LESSONS

Lan-sontol Ban-ren-q-don
Fam-od-arm Muh-aa-qahljo
Qi-relaa Buseoi-ors-eas
Si-laajon Git-org-mirk-loes
Nt-imad But-pim-roqa
Zar-ipak Banim-gahjon
Goh-hulim Ippla-te-ed

Korfax sat in his new room and pondered. Sohagel had taken him through the seminary, all of it, and though it was only one small part of the tower, it was still immense – a labyrinth of corridors, rooms and halls.

Every wall had its mural. Some were obvious – the process of forging, stone entering the furnace, crystal emerging in light – while others were less clear, representations of concepts and relationships, a dance of sigils and angles of force. But there was an overall design, with the corridors favouring stories and pageants and the halls favouring historical events. One in particular had stood out, a representation Korfax had never seen before.

In it was Karmaraa, standing upon a rock, stave raised up but pointing down. At his feet lay his enemy, Sondehna, bound in chains and burning with fire. Karmaraa was all light and radiant, brilliance streaming from the sky behind him, but Sondehna was all darkness, staining the ground with his shadow, black face, black eyes, all stretched in agony. For some reason Korfax found it too stark and too merciless, but he did not say so to Sohagel.

Sohagel had pointed out many things on their journey, a whole litany of places and purposes, and Korfax had quickly realised that this was a test, a test of his powers of concentration and memory. Though the tour seemed gentle and friendly, he knew that Sohagel expected him to remember exactly where everything was afterwards. There were no maps or directions. Once shown, one should not forget.

There was a knock upon the door.

"May the light of The Creator shine upon you."

Korfax looked up and then frowned. It was another acolyte, and from the look of him he was roughly the same age as Korfax.

"And may the light of The Creator shine upon you also," Korfax said.

He waited for a moment.

"What do you want?" he asked.

The other was clearly uncertain.

"I was told that you would be here," he said.

He looked Korfax up and down.

"You are Korfax, aren't you?"

Korfax started. What was this now?

"Yes, I am. But who are you?"

The other smiled.

"I'm sorry. They told me that you would be coming, but I almost forgot. I should have remembered. There is so much to remember here. Yours was almost the last name on the list. I thought I was the only one to arrive late."

Korfax waited. The other looked uneasy.

"They told me that you would be here," he repeated.

"Who told you?" Korfax asked.

"Geyad Omagrah," came the reply. "He is one of the teachers. I met him when I arrived. Everyone is met by one of the teachers. But I was lucky in that regard. Geyad Omagrah is a friend of my father. He showed me where to go. Who met you?"

"Geyad Sohagel."

"Oh, he is the eldest. He always takes the first lesson."

"Did you say that you arrived late?"

"Yes, I wasn't expecting it, but then they told me that I was ready and that I would be coming this year. It all happened very suddenly, but my father was very proud. I am the first of our house to come to the seminary."

"And what is your house?"

"Forgive me, I forgot to say. I am Erinil Noren Tahamoh."

Korfax bowed.

"And I am Faren Noren Korfax," he said.

Tahamoh finally looked a little more at ease.

"Yes," he said. "Good."

He looked speculative now, as though something was on his mind.

"You arrived even later than I did," he said. "You are only just in time for the first lesson. That is tomorrow. Most of the others have been here for days."

Korfax became still. Here it came.

"It was not by choice," he said. "The decision to come this year was somewhat forced upon us."

Korfax watched Tahamoh carefully. This was what he was really after.

"Oh!" Tahamoh said simply.

Korfax continued to watch. Was that fear he saw? What did this one know? He waited in trepidation for the inevitable, and then Tahamoh finally asked the question that was clearly consuming him.

"Did demons really attack your home?" he said, an almost breathless rush of words. Korfax looked away.

"I did not know that it was common knowledge," he replied.

"But of course it is," Tahamoh insisted. "Such an event like that cannot be kept secret. No one has experienced anything like it for thousands of years. I must say that it was fortunate that your father was at hand. Ever since I arrived here I have heard nothing but praise for him."

As Korfax thought back to the attack he was suddenly aware of a dark wall in his mind, a dark wall in which a door was set. For a moment he felt as though he had been split in two, part of him watching in confusion as another part hurriedly tested all the locks and guards. Tahamoh, meanwhile, catching something of Korfax's internal struggle, looked down.

"I'm sorry," he said. "All I seem to be doing at the moment is offering my apologies."

He stepped forward.

"I can see that the memory of it pains you. There is another tale to tell here, clearly. Forgive me for speaking without thought."

The dark wall vanished and Korfax had the worrying impression that he had just betrayed himself in some way. But he could not think why. Then Tahamoh came further forward and bowed again.

"Do not worry. On my honour, I will not tell another soul that there is more to this tale. I do not know what horrors you saw and what you had to endure, and I dread to think that any others might suffer the same. It is just... well... I did not think that this would ever happen. I don't think anyone did."

Korfax looked away. There were several answers to that, but he suddenly found himself not wanting to speak of it at all. He tried hard to still his inner turmoil. There was something he had forgotten, something he needed to forget, but he could not think what it was. The very act of trying to hide it again, though, had stirred it up, like a revealing lie. His mother had warned him of this, another admonition from the Exentaser. Guilt will always point to itself. He looked up to find Tahamoh watching him carefully.

"I am sorry," Tahamoh continued. "I should not have talked of it at all. They told me not to, but I could not help it."

Korfax smiled.

"It's all right," he said. "I understand, but it is why we are here, after all."

Tahamoh brightened.

"Yes, that is true, isn't it? I must remember that, but there is so much to remember here."

He looked about the room.

"Have you eaten?"

"I ate earlier. Geyad Sohagel took me to the eating hall. He took me about the tower and showed me all the places I would need to remember, and then he brought me here and said that I should rest and prepare myself for tomorrow. He also gave me new robes."

"That is what Geyad Omagrah did with me, too," Tahamoh said. "It happens to all the new acolytes."

Korfax watched Tahamoh. How nervous he was. Then he realised the truth. As unsettling as he found this change in his life, Tahamoh found it even more so, and now that demons were back in the world the truth had become something harder than it had been before. Like a stone dropped in a still pool, the ripples were going where they would, not caring what they upset or what disquiet they would create. Tahamoh had only heard a tale, and yet his imagination had run riot because of it, whereas Korfax had seen the real thing. It was an advantage he had not expected at all.

After a restless night, the first day of learning dawned. As Tahamoh had said, the very first lesson would be delivered by Sohagel, and since this was the first day, there would only be four lessons in all, with plenty of time in between for each acolyte to consider what they had been told.

Korfax went with Tahamoh, and as they went Tahamoh introduced him to two others that he had befriended, Thilnor and Oanatom. Though neither of them said anything about the attack upon Losq, Korfax could tell that they, like Tahamoh, were burning with questions. But instead they talked mainly of where they had come from and what they would be learning.

Thilnor came from Othil Ekrin. It was easy to tell that he came from the east, for he had the eastern look – narrower eyes and higher cheeks. Thilnor seemed happy and ebullient, and Korfax found himself warming to him almost immediately.

Oanatom was quiet and thoughtful and came from the west, from Othil Homtoh, much like Tahamoh. But he was friendly also, much like Thilnor, and Korfax decided that perhaps life here would not be as lonely as he had feared.

When they entered the room Korfax felt more than one pair of eyes following him. It was as Abinax had said. He had become an object of curiosity. He decided that he would do as Abinax suggested, and pay it no heed.

As he went to his seat he noticed how many there were from the west and the centre, along with not a few from the east. There were two from the south, easy to see because of their darker skin, and though he looked carefully, Korfax saw no one else from the north. It seemed he was the only one this year.

It was just as Korfax reached his seat that Sohagel entered the room. They all stood and bowed to him. He bowed back and then smiled at them all.

"Welcome to your first lesson at the seminary of the Dar Kaadarith. Before this day you could only have said that you were going to the seminary, to become acolytes and to learn the Namad Dar. But today you have arrived, you have become acolytes and you are learning the Namad Dar. From this day hence, all will change. Now your lives begin in earnest!"

He looked about the room, marking each and every face, and then he began.

"The first question!" he announced. "Why are you here?"

There was silence. No one was certain if the question was rhetorical or if it required an answer. Sohagel, though, did not wait.

"You are here for one simple reason: to learn the lore that rules our world."

He looked at them all again, this time as if measuring their capacities.

"The Namad Dar is a lore of peace," he said. "With it we command the elements: earth, air, fire and water. With it we create light and heat, the means to travel, the means to store thoughts and memories. With it our world is made to work. But let us not forget that the Namad Dar was born of conflict. We, the Dar Kaadarith, were created to preserve, to save the world from that which would destroy it. That is our final purpose, to guard against the powers of the abyss."

He made the gesture of warding.

"All of you have heard tell of the Namad Mahorelah, the lore which details the powers and the properties of those realms collectively known as the Mahorelah. But how many of you know how extensive that lore is? Although we have destroyed all the grimoires, all the means of expressing that lore, we have not destroyed that which it is needful to know concerning it."

Sohagel paused and took a pace towards the window. He turned away for a moment and then turned back again, his hand at his chin, where a single finger stroked back and forth, back and forth, as though coaxing the words from his mouth.

"We have bestiaries that catalogue the known beings of the abyss and we have descriptions gleaned from practitioners of the art of still more wonders that dwell there. The Mahorelah is vast beyond mortal imagination and of a depth unknown."

Someone stood up.

"Yes, Thilnor?"

All turned to look at Thilnor.

"Wonders, Geyad? I thought it was all a terror, both evil and wrong."

Korfax felt envious. He should have been the one to ask that question! He looked to the front and was puzzled to see Sohagel with a slight smile on his face. The assumption was wrong?

"Not so," said Sohagel. "Though the denizens of the Mahorelah are dangerous when summoned here, most are mere beasts, creatures with little or no knowledge of this place. If you take a beast and place it where it should not be, that is an evil thing to do. But if you leave a beast in its natural surroundings then you do The Creator's bidding, for that is where it should be. It merely is. Left alone, we believe that the denizens of the abyss live out their lives as The Creator originally intended. Would you call an izchar evil? Or a churneh? Of course you would not. No, the evil lies entirely with the summoner. Each practitioner of the Namad Mahorelah, those of the Argedith, makes whatever they summon work their will, and thus you have the very nature of the evil, for to dominate another's will and force them into servitude is surely a terrible wrong. The summoned beast has no say in the matter, it must comply."

Another stood up.

"Yes, Aduret?"

"So it is the Argedith that are always wrong, Master, no matter what?"

Sohagel smiled.

"Nearly always," he said. Then he waved the finger that had been stroking his chin.

"And that is a better question than you know."

Korfax glanced at Aduret. Aduret looked pleased with himself as he sat back down again.

"Though there are beasts in the abyss," Sohagel continued, "there are also sentient forces there, and they, like us, can walk the line between good and evil. I will illustrate the point with three beings that none of the Argedith should ever, ever summon."

They waited and he let the pause lengthen.

"The first of these are the Vovin," he announced.

Korfax sat up straighter.

"Now the Vovin are interesting, for they still abide in our world, on the Adroqin Vohimar, on the heights of Lonsiatris and in a few other places. Someone, in the long distant past, brought them here and allowed them to stay. How that was accomplished we do not know, but it is certainly true that they are still here, children of children of children, still remaining after all this time."

Sohagel smiled broadly.

"They are magnificent creatures, as you all well know from their many likenesses scattered about the world in this archive or that. But to hunt one is supremely dangerous, for they are not only powerful, but also extraordinarily cunning. It is even believed that they can communicate with each other with their minds, but on what level that might be is uncertain. Let us just say that you could not have a conversation with such a beast. On more than one occasion they have been driven to the brink of extinction, and it was only by an edict of Anolei, the seventh Velukor, blessed be his name, that they were preserved at all. For the Vovin are not, in the end, evil. They have chosen to live and let live, like all other beasts that yet dwell in our world. But here is the thing. They ill-endure the domination of another, and any of the Argedith that summon them must pay for the privilege with their life. Though they are fatal, they are not inherently evil. In this, they are like much that dwells in the abyss."

Sohagel looked about the room at a sea of rapt faces and felt a great swell of contentment. This was what he enjoyed the most. The tales that welled up inside like ancient springs, the lore that fell from his lips like a sudden cascade and an audience ready to drink every drop. He could see them all now, hanging on his every utterance, swallowing every word. The first lesson was always his favourite, for here he could indulge himself and let the topic go where it would. It was never the same twice, but today it seemed apposite that they should dwell somewhat upon the dangers of the Mahorelah.

He turned to the window again, looking out at the tall oezong that grew in the courtyard and watching its many branches as they waved in the wind. Then he turned back to his audience.

"The Vovin are one thing," he continued, "but there are others that dwell in the abyss, others that have far darker natures. Of these, the first of note are the Gaaha."

Sohagel was intrigued to hear a sharp intake of breath. Interesting. At least one of his charges had heard of the Gaaha. He wondered what they had been told. He hoped it was not too much.

"And what are the Gaaha?" he asked. "They are beings of shadow," he told them all, before anyone could proffer an answer. "They do have a form, one they return to when at rest, but when they fight they are savagery incarnate. They, we consider, are evil. They have minds, they have thoughts and they are said to have a love of cruelty. To give you a measure of their depths, it was even said that Sondehna had certain dealings with them, and you all know who he was!"

Every single head bowed, and every single face was identical. Sohagel looked at them all with complete satisfaction.

"And so, the Gaaha, like the Vovin, will actively avenge themselves upon their summoners. But they will do so with a purpose."

Sohagel fixed them all with his brightest gaze.

"I will tell you the tale of the Arged of Unchir. Has anyone here ever heard it before?"

There was complete silence, which pleased him. No one knew the tale. It remained purely within the domain of the Dar Kaadarith, for no other guild remembered it and no other member of the Dar Kaadarith dared repeat it in full, for it was far too disturbing. But for these acolytes, a gentler version would do for now. And it would sit within them like a dark and fearsome goad, as it was meant to, until they were ready for the real truth.

"There was once an Arged who lived deep within the Unchir. Her tower was in a clearing, set upon a large hump of rock and surrounded on all sides by barren ground and treacherous, shifting marshes. She had not participated in the Wars of Unification, as she was too young, which was a fact of great annoyance to her. It made her cruel, for like all the followers of the Namad Mahorelah her temper was short and her memory was long. Hate festered within her, and when any embassy from the west came to her gates, she ensnared them with sorceries and slaughtered every one of them with great deliberation.

For long years she held sway in that place, aided by her servants and guarded by a remnant of the vile Haelok Aldaria, the old warrior elite of the Black Heart.

So there she was, carrying on the old fight long after Sondehna's death. But inevitably, one distant day, it came to pass that Achoin, a Geyad of the Dar Kaadarith, passed her demesne with two parloh of the Nazad Esiask.

Now Achoin was a master of fire, one of the strongest at that time, and he had heard tell of the tower of this Arged. He well knew the stories that were told around many an encampment in that part of Rasayah, how it was dangerous to travel too far into the depths of the Unchir. For it was whispered that a terror dwelt there, something born of sorcery. So Achoin resolved to put this tale to the test, and thus, when he saw the tower, he knew what manner of peril it was that dwelt in that untamed land.

So Achoin led his troop to the gate and demanded entrance. The Arged refused, laughing at the assembled might at her doors, and with studied cruelty she had prisoners brought up from her dungeons so that her servants could slit their throats in front of Achoin. And as this happened she cast an illusion, letting her gates appear as though they were faulty and poorly maintained.

The death of the prisoners enraged the Nazad Esiask, and they were ready to charge through the gates but Achoin stopped them. He could see the trap, and he knew that the Arged had greater powers at her disposal, so he taunted her instead, inviting her out.

Seeing that her ruse had failed, the Arged became enraged and ordered out the Haelok Aldaria. So out they rode wearing Qahmor, sorcerous armour that enveloped them in shadow, and bearing Qorihna, dark swords of fire. But Achoin was too good for them – he burnt them even as they emerged from the keep, and the swords of the Nazad Esiask finished them off.

Then the Arged sent a dark cloud to smother her enemies, but Achoin was equal to that task, too. He called up a wind to blow the poison from the air before it could touch any of his people. Then followed an assault upon the keep, and the Nazad Esiask at last forced their way inside.

But the Arged had been busy, for in her extremity she summoned a company of Gaaha, and at her bidding they fell upon the Nazad Esiask like formless demons of shadow. If it hadn't been for Achoin, none would have escaped.

So it became a stand off. The Gaaha could not close with Achoin, and Achoin could not pursue them and leave the Nazad Esiask without his protection.

But like all things, the standoff was not permanent, for the Arged became tired, unable to hold the minds of those that she had summoned. So they awoke from the power of the summoning and fell upon her in turn, torturing her to death before departing back to whatever realm from which they had been plucked."

Sohagel looked up with an expression of utter satisfaction.

"And that is the moral of the tale," he said. "The Namad Mahorelah is fatal. The Gaaha are just like the Vovin, for they ill-endure domination by another. The Arged of Unchir must have been mighty indeed to call up so many. But even so, at the end, she ultimately failed."

There was silence for a while until someone at the back stood up.

"Yes, Nederess?"

"You said there were three beings that should not be called, Geyad. If you please, what is the third?"

Sohagel frowned, but not at the question.

"We believe that no one has ever attempted this, but the assumption is that to summon the ones of which I am about to speak would be more than fatal, for not only would death result, but also one would lose one's immortal soul. The beings I speak of are the gods of the lower deeps themselves, the Ashar, the most powerful forces in all the many abysses of the Mahorelah."

Sohagel was gratified to see every eye upon him. Good, they understood the seriousness of the subject. Not all Ell had heard of the Gaaha, but every Ell had heard of the Ashar. They lay below everything – all the darkest nightmares, all the foulest dreams. Of all the Ell, only one had ever had truck with them, but even she had not dared summon them directly.

"From what we know," Sohagel continued, "the Ashar are various and singular, each of an aspect distinct from its brethren. Of the ones we can catalogue there are Ash-Tel and Ash-Mir. Ash-Tel is obsessed with death in all the forms that it takes, whilst Ash-Mir, we think, enjoys sacrifice and pain. Others there are whose natures we can only guess at, each with enough power in them to wreak havoc across the width and breadth of Lon-Elah, if unopposed."

Sohagel leaned back and folded his arms. He gazed at the floor as though staring into some personal abyss where the Ashar disported for his pleasure.

"What we know of this matter comes mainly from one source. I imagine you all know of whom I speak."

Everyone bowed their heads. All knew the name of the greatest seer ever to live.

"Indeed," said Sohagel grimly, "which of us has not heard of Nalvahgey. She it was who created the Exentaser and set the Ell upon the road to discover the secrets of the Namad Dar. And she it was who could call up the foulest demons from the Mahorelah and not suffer the consequences. She is the most enigmatic of all the great ones that ever walked our world. The four princes bowed to her, whether they did her will or no, and when the time came, she eschewed the Namad Mahorelah, saying only that it would bring doom upon the Ell. For at the last she was filled with the fires of prophecy, and she foresaw Karmaraa and Sondehna. But her name does not sit easily upon our lips. Much evil did she do, as well as good. She embraced the Namad Mahorelah and yet she founded the Exentaser."

Sohagel became even grimmer, if that was possible.

"Yes," he said, "Nalvahgey was a complex soul. Thank The Creator that Karmaraa came afterwards to show us the way."

He paused again, and then stood taller. Now he held up his right hand in warning.

"So do not mistake me. Though the Ashar are the worst of it, the Namad Dar is equal to the task. The Namad Dar could lay low even one the Ashar, if the wielders be of sufficient power. And that is the answer to my question: why are you here? You are here to become guardians. The world is your charge and your sword will be the lore of stone."

Korfax sat and pondered all that he had heard, especially the tale of Achoin. Though he had listened to everything Sohagel had said, he was certain there was something he had missed. There was an itch in the back of his mind, a memory he could not quite touch.

He berated himself for not listening as Doanazin had taught him, as then he would have remembered everything about the lesson, both word and deed, in perfect detail. With that he immediately felt guilty. The last time he had been with his old tutor he had lied about precisely this point.

Korfax pondered the story. Sohagel had mentioned two things especially, Qahmor and Qorihna, names he had heard before but to which he had never been able to put an image. Was that it? He wasn't sure. There was plenty of time before the next lesson, so he decided to find out.

He went to the archives. Sohagel had shown him where they were only the day before, so he knew the way well enough, but once he walked through the door he stopped where he was and stared about him. Inside it was not how he had imagined it to be at all. The archive occupied one of the larger spires that made up the tower, and there were circular galleries going all the way up, all the way to the distant top. Each gallery was filled with shelves, many times many, and the shelves themselves were stacked high with small boxes. There was so much. He was still staring at the sheer volume of material when an archivist approached him.

"Can I help you?" asked the archivist.

Korfax started and then quickly remembered his manners. He bowed to the archivist.

"I am Faren Noren Korfax," he said.

The archivist bowed back.

"And I am Geyad Ethudis Nar Paladir. So, what are you interested in?"

"The tale of Achoin and the Arged of Unchir," answered Korfax. "I was told it in my last lesson, but there were some things Geyad Sohagel mentioned that I was curious about."

Paladir smiled.

"And I wouldn't mind a cup of good wine for every time an acolyte comes down here looking for images of Gaaha. Happens every year, without fail. But we don't have any, truly we don't."

"I'm sorry Geyad," Korfax told him, "but that wasn't what I was after. I was wondering if you have anything on Qahmor and Qorihna."

Paladir drew back a little in surprise. Then he smiled.

"The weapons of the Haelok Aldaria, is it? Let us see what we can find."

It turned out that there was much more, and much less, than Korfax had expected. Paladir led him up one of the sets of stairs to the third gallery and then took him a little way along it. There he went to one of the shelves and pulled out three boxes. He gestured to a nearby seat.

"When you have finished, bring the boxes back to me and I'll put them back again."

"I can put them back for you," Korfax offered, but Paladir held up his hands in denial.

"Thank you," he said, "but that is my task. Everything must be put back exactly as it was."

As the archivist left, Korfax opened one of the boxes and found three logadar, each in an individual compartment. With them came a small tablet containing a description of their contents. Korfax read each description carefully before awakening its accompanying crystal. Then he perused its contents.

There were long histories of various campaigns, each mentioning the things he was interested in, but little on their qualities, merely that they had been defeated in such and such a manner. There were images of the Haelok Aldaria in their baroque armour, but no one had ever told him that it had been called Qahmor. He looked at it. It was armour, and that was all. He read that it could summon energies from the Mahorelah to protect its wearer and that it could resist the power of a Geyad for a time. Its strength directly reflected that of its wearer, so the stronger the wearer, the greater the power of the armour. There was a warning as well. Some of the best of the Haelok Aldaria had apparently learned how to make themselves partially, or wholly, invisible. That was impressive. Korfax thought about that. How could you stop something that was invisible? He read on and found precise details on how the armour could be breached, and the forces necessary to achieve this end. There was little else, though. As far as the author of the treatise was concerned, Qahmor was a problem to be solved, not one to be comprehended.

Qorihna were treated exactly the same way, great sorcerous swords that burned with energies torn from the abyss. Again there was a warning concerning their nature, how they could apparently anticipate an attack and change their nature to deflect it, so making their wielder better at sword craft than they would otherwise have been. Again it was described how they could be thwarted and destroyed, but there was little more on their nature than that. The images showed large dark swords that were as baroque as the armour, but that was all.

Most of the information he read was far beyond him, descriptions of forces that could be pulled from the stave of a Geyad, their application, modes of thought, visualisations, references to other writings on related matters, speculations upon the nature of matter and energy, geometries of summoning, angles of elements, sub-angles of elements. The list went on. Korfax put the stones back in their boxes.

There was little more he could learn here.

The itch remained and he had not found what he sought, and since the time for the second lesson was fast approaching he took the crystals back to Paladir. Paladir took one look at his expression and laughed.

"Not the easiest of subjects, is it?"

"There was much I did not understand," Korfax said. "But I thought there would be more on the nature of these weapons than there actually is."

Paladir took the boxes and checked their contents, making sure that the stones were all in their correct compartments, along with their descriptions.

"What we have here in these archives," he said, "are exact records of all the acts of the Dar Kaadarith throughout the ages. I am not surprised you found it difficult. You have a long way to go before you achieve your stave. Then you will understand what is written here. But as to the art of the enemy? What if I were to tell you that there are no grimoires left in the world? What would you say to that?"

The light dawned.

"To study the devices of the enemy is to become the enemy," Korfax quoted.

"Exactly so!" exclaimed Paladir. "We keep no record of anything that could possibly unlock the door to sorcery. We detail the acts of the profane, we detail how to stop them, but we do not keep their words or copies thereof."

He smiled again.

"And just so you don't forget, we don't have any images of Gaaha, either."

With the next lesson it was the turn of another Geyad named Asakom to instruct them. Korfax decided he would not miss another opportunity here. If something important was to be said or revealed, he would catch it.

Asakom strode into the room and they all stood. Korfax was surprised. Asakom was far younger than he had expected, with a sharp glance and quick movements. From what Korfax had been told by Tahamoh, Asakom did not enjoy questions whilst the lesson was in progress. In this, he was utterly unlike Sohagel.

Asakom stopped at the front and looked at them all. They all bowed to him and he bowed back smartly, but with Asakom there were no further preliminaries. As soon as they sat back down again, he was off.

"Earlier today you met the enemy, so to speak. Now you will meet your ally, the Namad Dar. We shall start with a question that you have all doubtless asked yourselves. Where does a Geyad's power come from? Does it come from the stave? Or is it inherent within the Geyad himself?"

Asakom paused only a moment, just enough time for his glance to flicker over every face.

"The answer," he continued, "is not as simple as you may have believed. All Ell have inherent power, some more than others, and the power of the mind has been known and understood since the earliest days. But when a Geyad employs the Namad Dar, it is more than just the mind that is involved. A Geyad interacts with the very substance of creation itself, with its underlying nature no less. Here is where the law is written. Here is where we find the word of The Creator."

He glanced at his audience again. There was expectancy on every face.

"Each stave, each crystal forged by our lore, contains within it a flaw. This is deliberate. That flaw, and its nature, pervades the entire work."

Now the room was filled with frowns. Asakom smiled slightly. It was the same every year. They always assumed perfection. Then he noticed Korfax.

Asakom knew all the faces, had seen their likenesses and committed them to memory, had been told their qualities and committed those to memory also, so none here were strangers to him. He had kept an eye out for Korfax especially, given what had happened, but now he wondered. Either Korfax was not listening or he had already seen the truth. Asakom could not decide which it was.

"So, you might ask," he said, "why make something that is marred? Why make something that is not perfect? And therein lies the paradox."

Was that a hint of sadness he saw on Korfax's face? Asakom walked over to the window. No other in the room matched his expression. Asakom allowed himself a second glance. The sadness was not there, he had imagined it. Or had he? The expression on Korfax's face was enigmatic at best. Asakom spoke on, but now he watched Korfax carefully from the corner of his eye.

"That flaw, that happy accident, is the key to the very heart of the Namad Dar, for it divides creation, opening upon a void, a nothingness, a place of infinite potentiality. Think of this, if you will. Inside each crystal that we make is an opening – the tiniest portal, infinitely small – that leads on to an area, a region, that is altogether nothing. But being nothing is not enough. This nothingness has potential. It has the potential to be something."

He looked at all of them in turn.

"The Word!" he announced. "The Word of The Creator!"

There was utter silence, as there should be.

"Yes, the Word!" he said again. "Here resides that primal state from which all things arise. Here, everything is possible."

He glanced at Korfax again. Was that revelation he saw? Did Korfax understand? So why the continuing sense of unhappiness? Asakom looked at the others. None of them appeared to have it. Most looked confused, some even dumbfounded, as though their expectations had crumbled about them, but Korfax kept that very same expression upon his face. It was most unsettling. Asakom moved on.

"Many of you, no doubt, believe that I am describing pure chaos, but that is not the way of it. The stone, by its very nature, brings order."

He gestured around the room.

"With most of the stones that we make it is the nature of the flaw that dictates the form the Word will take. Some flaws curve back upon themselves, unending rivers of power in which we can store things, sounds, thoughts and visions. Others flow outwards like springs, emanating eternal heat or light. Over the many years we have learned to create stones of many kinds. There are stones that cancel mass, stones that mark time, stones that preserve and stones that destroy. But once made, each stone is locked to the task for which it has been created; it cannot be changed from its course. It speaks the Word it has been given and will not stop until the day it is unmade."

He held up his finger.

"Then, of course, there is the kabadar!"

Asakom reached into his robes and took out a short blue stave, a child stave of air. He weighed it in his hands.

"The kabadar lies at the heart of the Dar Kaadarith, for with a stave the elements themselves can be subdued. The kabadar is special, for it exposes the naked schism itself. But do not believe that the stone is mutable, for it is not. It is the mind that is mutable, for it alone is the agent that reaches in and pulls out possibility from the void and gives it certainty. This is what we of the Dar Kaadarith are trained to do. We intercede between each void within and creation without, letting the mind shape the chaos that has been called up and bringing it back again to the here and the now."

He held up the stave. A dim blade of light was now awake at its heart.

"So," Asakom said, "once the adept has shaped the chaos and brought it to order, what then? Can he forget about it and move his mind to something else?"

There was a brief pause before Asakom answered his own question.

"No!" he said. "The adept must take hold of the energies he has summoned with his mind and control them, moulding them to his will."

He walked over to the window and held up the stave. It waxed brilliant in his hand and with a whistling sound a wind rose up, a coiling wind that flew in through the window and circled the room, just above the heads of everyone. It was easy to see, for leaves were caught within it, a wobbling ball of orbiting leaves imprisoned between invisible bars.

It circled the room three times, Asakom guiding it with his mind. Then he sent it back out of the window again, where it vanished. The leaves fluttered this way and that for a moment and then dropped out of sight. Asakom lowered the stave and its light went out.

"A simple enough task for me," he said, "but for the rest of you? You face a mountain."

He looked at them all again. Korfax had watched the ball of leaves like all the others, but even then his expression had not changed. Asakom walked back to the front and frowned to himself.

"Control is the key," he told them. "Only a disciplined mind can master a stave. You have years of work ahead of you, theory and practice to master, knowledge and skills to learn. And you have many preconceptions to throw aside."

Oanatom stood up. Given that Asakom had a reputation for disliking interruptions, it was a brave thing to do.

"And you wish to ask what, Oanatom?"

Asakom folded his arms while Oanatom summoned up the courage to speak.

"Would not the same discipline of mind apply to those who practiced the Namad Mahorelah, Geyad?" he asked.

There was deathly silence for a moment as Asakom's gaze intensified. Then he smiled, if a little dryly.

"Normally I do not approve of questions whilst the lesson is in progress," he said. "I have often found it to be the case that the question is either irrelevant or that the person asking it has not given my words the attention they deserve. In this case, though, you have raised a very good point. You have already been told that the Namad Mahorelah is no longer studied and that even though we still possess the catalogues, the bestiaries and the commentaries, we no longer hold any records of how the Namad Mahorelah was actually expressed. That does not mean, though, that we are safe. Accidents occur. Even those who do not go looking for the art sometimes stumble upon it, and that is why we must be eternally vigilant, for is not the very first commandment of the Logah Dar 'Suffer not the Argedith to live'? So, in order to keep temptation from the path of the innocent, all the grimoires have been hunted down and destroyed."

Though he was answering Oanatom, Asakom spared a glance at Korfax once more. Such an enigmatic expression on his face! Was that guilt he saw now, or was it something else? What was going through the youth's mind? He was beginning to find it most distracting. He looked away again and gestured at the stave in his hands.

"There is one major difference between the Namad Dar and the Namad Mahorelah that is certain," he continued. "With the Namad Dar we speak with the Word of The Creator. Here is the act of pure creation, a mirror of the one true act, utterly holy. But the Namad Mahorelah? That is not a lore that creates. Instead it is theft and destruction! We believe that the profligate theft of energies from the abyss has laid waste to entire regions. And, if such wanton and selfish destruction is not enough, the lore enslaves."

He raised his hand in the gesture of denial.

"Beings whose natural function it is to dwell in the abyss have been summoned here, to this place. They may be unlovely to our eyes, but The Creator made them and populated the abyss with them, so who are we to question the will of The Creator? No, the sin is to bring them here and to set them tasks that may well prove fatal to them. No matter that they are dangerous in themselves, to kidnap them and suborn their wills is an utter evil."

At the end Korfax remained seated as the others left. He reviewed the lesson again, letting it all run through his awareness once more. He was particularly surprised at the fact that asymmetry was the way of it, and the form of that asymmetry, its geometry, dictated the form of the energies that were born of the void within. How unexpected and how marvellous it was! He made to leave, but as he stood up he found Asakom standing before him, a stern look upon his face.

"All throughout my lesson," he said, "it seemed to me that you were not listening at all. Your expression hardly changed, even when I summoned a net of winds, a marvel that surely should have caught your interest. I would like an explanation, if you please."

Korfax swallowed.

"I was listening, Geyad. I heard everything."

Asakom folded his arms.

"That may have been true of the others, but I remain unconvinced by you. I have never had one of my charges so apparently unmoved."

"But I was interested... I mean I am interested... I mean..."

"Enough! I want a full and detailed account of the entire lesson. You will sit in this place and write it out now. Your midday meal can wait."

Korfax sat and wrote. He wrote furiously, his mind a sea of fire. Why had he been picked on? He had listened. He had heard it all. It was Doanazin that had showed him how to do it, how to turn the mind into a blank scroll so that he could let others write upon it. He had been accused of inattention before, and that did not merely rankle now, it burned.

He finished and looked at the scrolls before him. It was all there, every single bit of it. He stood up and walked over to Asakom.

Asakom took the scrolls and read through them slowly. He began to frown, and the further he went, the deeper his frown became. Then he looked back at Korfax in amazement.

"It is all here, every single word that I said, every deed that I did. It is exact!"

He leaned forward, holding up the scrolls.

"Who taught you this?"

Now Korfax was really confused.

"Geyad?"

"I know what this is," said Asakom. "The Erm Roith use this art. Who taught you how to do it?"

"My tutor."

"And who was your tutor?"

"Doanazin."

"Doanazin!"

Asakom let out a long breath.

"I see," he said, smiling at last. "Well then, that puts an entirely different perspective on things. Now you will come with me and I will make amends. I can at least make sure that you eat well this day."

Meal eaten, they sat together in Asakom's room.

"So Doanazin was your tutor?" Asakom asked.

"Yes," said Korfax, looking down.

"Astounding," said Asakom. "I did not know that."

Korfax looked up again. He swallowed.

"Geyad, did you know her?"

Asakom laughed out loud.

"No," he said. "That was not what I meant at all. I have heard of her, though, as have many. She used to be a debater of great subtlety, one of the best. That you had her for a tutor is an utter astonishment to me. The 'art of memory' she gave you is one of the more impressive disciplines of the Erm Roith. They rarely pass on such things. You must have been a great joy to her. I must tell the others..."

Korfax bowed his head. He suddenly felt dreadful.

"Please do not," he asked. "She died. She died at Losq. I was a disappointment to her. I did not value her gifts until she was gone."

Asakom stopped where he was.

"I am sorry, Korfax, truly I am. I seem to have spent this day making one false assumption after another. Everyone thought that Doanazin had decided to retreat from the world. It is not common knowledge that she ever became your tutor. She died during the attack upon Losq? I see. I will inquire no further."

After a long silence Asakom leaned forward.

"Korfax, I have some advice for you. I think you should be more circumspect with this gift of yours. I understand your need to prove yourself, but do not try too hard. Though there is much to learn, you have time enough to appreciate it without worrying about every single thing that you hear and see. Besides, the disciplines of the Erm Roith are for the Erm Roith, not the Dar Kaadarith. You will learn soon enough what to apply and what not."

Then he looked up.

"Now it is time to go. The next lesson is upon us."

It was the turn of Sohagel again.

"In the last lesson you saw the Namad Dar in action and learned what lies at its heart. Now you will discover how it is we learned of it, how the word was revealed."

Sohagel looked about the room.

"At the heart of every stone, at the heart of every creation of the Dar Kaadarith, lies what some have called the flaw, but a better name for it would be the infinite work."

Every face stared up at him, many looking expectant, and not a few thoroughly mystified. This was as it should be. They were about to hear something that they had never heard before.

"In making the Bright Heavens, The Creator left many signs pointing the way. We of the Dar Kaadarith have found a few of them and, in all due humility, we have taken them up and used them. What I speak of are the movements of numbers, numbers not only formed by the very act of creation itself, but that also define it. Take, for instance, the relationship between a circle's width and its circumference, or the number that defines the path of the gyre. Neither has an end, for both stretch off into eternity. Here is the order of creation, the finite and the infinite, both caught in each other, an order we can only feebly grasp. For we are but the created, shadows of that which created us. Do not be deceived, though. To us has been given a great gift – the greatest – that vital spark of comprehension, for we are lights in the grand design, placed here to see and to know. For in knowing what we know, we can better care for the world and so follow the word of The Creator."

He held up a piradar in his hand.

"A piradar, a simple light. We take them for granted, but we should not. I hold in my hand infinity. Here is nothing and everything. Within this stone is the order of creation, matter and energy in perfect balance. Here the world is folded upon itself, falling down into the places where all things are possible. Here is the beginning of the path – and its end."

And so, with the light in his grasp, he told them of the laws that ordered the world, how everything grew from simplicity, unfolding upwards with ever greater complexity, proportion built upon proportion, self-repeating geometries that became the very pillars of the world. He then told them how the Dar Kaadarith took what was laid out before them and turned it back into the furnace of their thought, reapplying the great proportion to the work of their hands and folding the world back down again into the flaw that lay in the heart of every crystal. And so they reworked the laws of creation, remoulding the geometries so that they fell downwards and inwards, back to the infinitely small.

Here was the Word, that terrible, wonderful Word that made everything. So simple, so profound.

Here was the power to take the Word and reorder creation with it, earth becoming air, air becoming fire, fire becoming water and water becoming earth. The Word!

As he spoke his last, so Sohagel held up the piradar once more, holding it up as if bathing in its light. It lit his face and the light seemed to hang there, held in place. No one moved. They were transfixed by the image.

The last lesson of the day followed immediately, giving them no time at all to think on what they had just heard. And as unexpected as its timing was, its subject was even more surprising. Asakom entered the room, bowed to Sohagel and then gestured that all the acolytes should follow him. He took them through the seminary and then on to the gardens that surrounded the Umadya Semeiel. He said nothing, but simply led them all to one of the wide open spaces and then turned to face them.

"You have now seen something of the task before you," he said. "You have heard of that which you are here to defend against and learnt something of the nature of the lore to which you will commit yourselves. You have begun to appreciate just how daunting that task is. But this last lesson is intended to place it all in perspective. Turn around."

They all did so. Behind them reared the Umadya Semeiel, and from where they now stood it seemed as if they could see it in its entirety.

"Behold the agent of revelation," Asakom announced, "pouring down the continual fires of life."

Korfax stared up at the tower and looked carefully. Then he saw it. An image came to him of Sohagel holding a piradar in the palm of his hand. There it was now. What had confused him before was suddenly laid bare, and the secret of the tower's proportions leapt out at him. It was a prayer of stone, proportion built upon proportion, the ennoblement of the humble by the divine.

He thought back to a view seen from the deck of a sky ship, of the Nazarthin Ozong, golden in the light of failing Rafarel. This was the same, a beauty that could never be put into words, a symmetry that could only be felt by the mind, a feeling that would remain with him for ever.

Asakom walked to the front and looked at each and every face.

"Now you truly begin to see," he said. "You begin to understand how it is you come to be here, what powers have been laid out before you, what you must master and what you must serve. The tower of the Dar Kaadarith, the tower in which you now have your being, is the Namad Dar made manifest. It is the hand, the hand of revelation, the centre about which all thought turns. To see is to know and to know is to see."

And that was that. The day's lessons were over. Korfax sat alone for a while, thinking. The others drifted off, back to their rooms, singly or in small groups. No one spoke. There was too much to think about.

He found his head spinning with realisation. Nothingness and infinity, nothingness and infinity. So simple, yet so utterly profound. He realised then that there could be no other way of expressing it. He thought back to a conversation that now seemed to lie on the other side of the world, him asking Chasaloh why things were the way that they were. But here was the answer. It was how creation was and it could be no other way. Draw a line. How many points composed it? An infinite number. Draw a longer line. How many points composed that? He lay back and stared up at the sky. Everything was infinite and yet it was not, and the Dar Kaadarith dwelt within that schism, within that word, a splinter of stone caught between what was and what was not.

The next day it began in earnest, seven lessons a day, every day, except for the seventh, which was set aside for prayer and contemplation.

The lessons built in intensity, Sohagel teaching theory and Asakom teaching practice, both interleaving and complementing. It was a dance, a careful and complicated dance, and all were caught up in its rhythm, stepping where the dance dictated. They were given no time to do anything else.

There were lessons in the order of creation: earth, air, fire and water, the composition of matter, the disposition of energies, how all could be expressed in numbers and how those numbers could be used to order the world.

There were lessons in mental discipline: visualisations, the holding of thoughts and their release, the mind as a landscape with thought its occupant, cause and effect, solitude, even absence and the nothingness of the void, the most difficult of all.

It had but a single aim – to prepare the acolyte for the supreme test, the touching of a stave with purpose.

Come the day and Asakom stood before them all and offered up a proud smile.

"Now we come to it at last," he said. "This is your first real test. Here you will find yourselves upon the shores of a far greater sea. You will see the surface, the waves, the rise and fall of waters, but you will find yourself realising that far more lies in wait for you in the depths."

He held up a child stave of earth.

"There is a certain sense, a certain feeling you will experience when you use a kabadar, but it is not the same for all. Some consider it too personal and know that they can never talk about it to another. Some find that their minds compress to a point, others that they are both moving at great speed over a featureless plain whilst remaining stationary all the while. But I assure you, you will all experience something and know what it is that you experience. Whatever it is that you feel, though, that is the moment when your naked self comes into contact with the void inside a kabadar. That is the first stage."

Asakom turned the child stave this way and that in his hand.

"The second stage is the opening of the void. Again, you will know it when you feel it. As when a door is thrown open in a lightless room, letting what is without enter in, so it is with each void in a kabadar. For some it opens like a flower in their hand, for others it is a hole beneath their feet or a star above their heads. Before now, not a few have even become dizzy and fainted at its first touch, so potent was the sensation. But be that as it may, this too is a personal thing and you will know it when you experience it."

He held the child stave up to his eye as though peering deep inside.

"The third stage is entry. The void is entered by the mind. Here is the realm of pure creation. All things can be imagined in this place."

He lowered the stave again and frowned.

"I must warn you, though. There have been instances where a few have lost themselves for days in a state of unfettered possibility. So let me reassure you. The third stage is not, in itself, dangerous. Only the weak can succumb to its lure and none of you are weak, otherwise you would not be here."

He smiled.

"Now it is at this point that all accounts agree. Everyone experiences the sensation of motedom. You feel as though you hold the heavens in your hand. But do not be deceived. You hold nothing in your hand at all. It is an illusion, except for one singular fact. The nothingness that you perceive has the potential to be everything that you can imagine."

Asakom let a certain satisfaction settle over his features.

"And so we come to the fourth stage, the creation of energies. This is, surprisingly enough, both the easiest thing to do and the hardest. For now you are become the fulcrum. You must visualise what you desire and only that. Any lack of discipline on your part and you will fail utterly in the attempt. The mind must be focused and concentrated and clear. Your will becomes the key that unlocks this particular door."

Asakom clenched his jaw for a moment and then released it.

"The fifth stage is the withdrawal of the mind, taking with it the created energies out of the void. This takes strength and it takes practice, years of it. Just as a child must learn to walk, you must learn to harness these energies with your mind."

He made an expansive gesture.

"The sixth stage brings the energies created in the void into manifestation. This is not so much an act of strength but more akin to a reflex. Once you learn how to do this, you will never forget it again."

Finally he looked at them all in triumph.

"The seventh stage is the unleashing of those energies. Some are easy, whilst others take great control, and it all depends upon what has been called up. Air of air needs constant vigilance, whilst earth of air can be freed and forgotten. All will drain your strength a little when you summon them, so here is the final danger. It is easy to over-exert oneself. But once it is done, it cannot be undone. Be as a peizin and so bend before the storm. If you are rigid, believing you have limitless strength, you will fall."

Korfax waited. Each went in and then they came out again, a strange look on every face – revelation, confusion, uncertainty. He wondered what they had experienced, but he did not have to wonder too long. His turn came soon enough.

He went in and found Asakom waiting for him. Asakom gestured at the stave, but no words were said.

Korfax took a deep breath, touched the child stave and instantly felt a strange sensation in his mind, like a memory of an experience he knew he had never had. He still stood in the room of staves, could still see and hear everything around him, but his mind had split in two. Another part of him had appeared, and now it flew over a landscape dotted with strange geometric forms. It wasn't so much that he saw the landscape, but rather as though he felt it, as though he and the landscape were one and the same and that he now travelled over himself. Up ahead of him lay a destination, something glorious, something potent. He approached its borders, shrank, diminished, crossed the boundary to confront it and then found himself in another place entirely, a red place, a place of rage. He quickly let go of the stave and looked down.

"And what did you experience?" Asakom asked.

Korfax thought hard, wondering how to describe the speed, the landscape, the oncoming glory. But what of the rage? He quickly looked for it, but it was gone, back to wherever it had come from. He found himself reluctant to say anything about it at all. Rage was a thing of darkness, a product of the Urq, the unreasoning beast that dwelt in every breast. Far better to embrace the Saq, the light, but here he was now, staring into his own personal abyss. He had no idea what to make of it. He looked up again to find Asakom smiling, mistaking his reluctance for something else.

"Do not describe it if it is difficult," Asakom said. "And I suspect you would rather not do so anyway. But that is as it should be. The important thing is that the stave awoke in your hands. I saw it. Well done, you have achieved the first stage."

Korfax waited as Tahamoh walked up to him. Tahamoh looked worried.

"You did it then. What was it like?"

"It is not easy to describe," Korfax said.

"That is what Aduret said. And Oanatom."

Korfax watched as Tahamoh looked down, scowling at the floor. Despite his own uncertainties, Korfax found himself wondering what was wrong with Tahamoh. He had not even touched a stave yet.

"What is it? What is the matter?"

"Everyone is different after the test," said Tahamoh.

Korfax stepped back.

"What do you mean?"

Tahamoh became even more worried.

"I suppose I did not think it would affect everyone like that."

Korfax tried to put a simpler gloss upon the experience.

"But what did you expect? Everyone changes. Each day brings change."

He paused a moment.

"We all grow," he added simply.

"It isn't that," said Tahamoh. "You all entered a room and came out different. It scares me."

"I don't feel any different," Korfax told him. "I am still me. It's just that the experience is not quite what I expected, that is all. But you shouldn't be scared. This is what we came here for, isn't it?"

Tahamoh now looked as if he doubted even that.

After he had taken the test Tahamoh brightened somewhat, but it was clear he was upset about something. Korfax tried to find out what it was, but Tahamoh would not talk. They went to the evening blessing in silence and parted with few words. Korfax wondered what had upset his friend and remained deep in thought all the way back to his room, so it was a moment before he realised that there was someone waiting for him outside his door. It was one of the wardens.

"You have a visitor," he said.

Korfax started.

"A visitor?"

The warden beckoned.

"Come with me."

The warden took him to the courtyard of Hais, a place of high walls with views over the lower towers. Here he bade Korfax enter. Korfax could see that someone was waiting for him, but they had their back to him. Then they turned and Korfax laughed with sudden happiness.

"Father!" he shouted, as he ran into his father's arms. The warden smiled, bowed his head and withdrew.

Sazaaim embraced his son.

"And how are things with you? Are you working hard?"

Korfax looked up happily.

"Of course! I have risen to the first level. I touched my first stave today."

He proudly displayed the single stripe on his shoulder and the insignia upon his chest. Sazaaim's smile widened.

"I know," he said. "That is why I am here. But I had expected you to have achieved the third level by this time."

Korfax laughed gladly.

"And you cannot fool me. The third level is two years away. Everyone knows that!"

Sazaaim lost his smile and Korfax drew back.

"Did I say something wrong?"

Sazaaim reached out a hand and placed it on his son's shoulder.

"No, my son, you did not. It is just that you are growing up now, growing up fast, and neither I nor your mother are here to see it."

Korfax looked down.

"But you cannot help that. That is simply how it is. All those at the seminary are absent from their homes. You have to be at Losq. You are its guardian. And this is the only place I can be if I am to follow in your footsteps and become a Geyad of the Dar Kaadarith."

He looked up again and caught a look in his father's eye.

"What is it?"

Sazaaim sighed heavily.

"Come over here and let us sit by the wall. I have many things to tell you, things I could not tell you with a message in a stone."

They went and sat on a long stone seat. Behind them were arrayed many of the lower spires of the Umadya Semeiel, and beyond them was spread the west side of the city. Sazaaim looked out at the view for a moment and then back at Korfax.

"Firstly," he said, "we are no longer living in Losq."

Korfax did not know what to think. His family no longer lived in Losq? But the Farenith had always lived in Losq. He felt again that premonition of loss, that sudden sense that had soured his mood as he said goodbye to his home and watched as it vanished behind the bulk of the Lee Izirakal. He looked back at his father with hot eyes.

"But why?" he said.

His father looked down as if ashamed.

"Because it is no longer safe," he replied. "Losq is old and not easily defended. We have moved the entire household to Leemal and now occupy our apartments in the Garad."

Korfax stared hard at his father. He suddenly felt burned and confused. What did his father mean? Why was it no longer safe?

"I do not understand," he said. "What has happened to our home?"

Sazaaim tried to smile, but the sadness did not depart.

"Nothing has happened," he answered. "And do not fear for our home. Losq is still there."

Then his eyes darkened.

"But so are the demons. More of them have appeared."

More demons? Korfax found himself breathing hard as he thought of them.

"Do you know where they come from?" he asked.

"No," replied his father. "That remains a complete mystery. But we have given them a name and added them to the lists. We have decided to call them Agdoain, for want of a better word."

Agdoain! Korfax did not like what that implied. There was a long pause before his father spoke again.

"They have been making ever more frequent appearances since you came south, and their numbers have been increasing. It is possible they are returning to the places they come from after being summoned, but I think not. Someone is building an army."

Korfax felt a sudden surge of outrage. How dare they keep secrets from him? Losq was his home.

"But no one has told me anything of this," he said at last, barely able to contain his anger.

Sazaaim leaned back and looked sternly at his son.

"Nor will you hear anything of it after today. And I want you to promise me, Korfax, that you will say nothing of this to anyone else," he said as he leaned forward. "Not to anyone! Do you understand?"

Korfax bowed his head reluctantly, impelled by his father's gaze. But his eyes were still hot as he looked back.

"This is between us," Sazaaim continued. "It is not for other ears. Do you understand what I am telling you?"

"Yes!" Korfax answered, looking down. "But do the teachers here know, do Geyad Sohagel and Geyad Asakom?"

"Only those that need to know are so privileged," his father said, "and you are one of those. This is why you must remain silent."

Korfax remembered the grey horrors leering at him as they came through the door of his memory. He gazed at his feet. He suddenly felt cold.

"What has happened?" he asked. "How bad is it?"

A gentle hand touched his shoulder.

"Bad enough. It is no longer safe to travel north of Leemal without armed escort. There have been attacks. From Dialsen to Tohus these Agdoain have gone, swarming down from the hills to wreak their abominations. But then they disappear again and cannot be found. It is like duelling with shadows."

Korfax could not believe the enormity of what he was hearing.

"But that is almost the whole of the furthest north," he said.

His father looked tired now, as if the weight of his duty had become a physical thing.

"Yes, it is," he said. "Which makes avoiding these attacks, or predicting them, almost impossible. These Agdoain seem able to come and go as they please."

Korfax pictured the distances involved. Dialsen was in the east, almost as far from Losq as Losq was from Leemal, and Tohus was in the opposite direction, nestling amongst the gentle hills of the western coast.

"How many have died?" he asked.

If his father's eyes had been dark before, they became almost black now and Korfax suddenly wished he had not asked the question. There was a stillness about his father, a caged stillness as though he had locked himself away from the world, letting nothing in or out.

"Many thought that the attack upon our home was an isolated incident," he said quietly. "I counselled against this but was not listened to. The towers of the north were fortified with many Branith from Leemal, and a few more from Othil Zilodar were called up to patrol the hills and vales. Would that some of the Urenith and Geyadith could have been spared from regular duties. For a time your mother and I were the only ones looking, riding around the outer settlements, seeking for the foe. But we found nothing and we were told that our diligence was unwelcome. I even heard some say it had all been a waste of time. Then Tohus fell silent."

He passed his hand over his eyes as though to wipe away the vision.

"I will not darken this day with tales of what I saw. Suffice it to say that nothing had been left alive."

His eyes became distant and Korfax saw in them the many dead of Losq.

"We are fighting monsters, my son, monsters summoned by a monster. Out there, somewhere, in the hidden places of Lukalaa, one of the Argedith lurks. And when I find this creature I will kill it, for though it may look like an Ell it is one no longer. Then, maybe, the slain of Tohus and the Umadya Beltanuhm can find rest at last."

Korfax looked down at the ground, not knowing what to say, whilst images ran riot through his mind.

It was almost time for his father to go, so Sazaaim turned to his son and delivered his last piece of news.

"I have one other thing to tell you, and it will not be easy to hear, either. Chasaloh has passed into the river."

Korfax looked hard at his father and clenched his jaw.

"How?"

Sazaaim drew a deep breath.

"When we decided to leave Losq, he refused to go. I was stern with him but it did not sway him. Your mother tried gentleness, but that did not sway him, either. It was only later that we discovered he was missing. We searched and Orkanir found his ormn fleeing the northernmost headlands. Chasaloh was nowhere to be seen. I fear he jumped from the high cliffs. I doubt his body will ever be found, as the currents there are swift."

Korfax looked down. Chasaloh was gone?

"It was the loss of Kalazir," he said, trying to hold back the sudden ache in his throat and chest. Korfax hugged himself and closed his eyes whilst his father watched him wrestle with sudden grief. Finally Korfax looked back at his father.

"Everyone is going. Soon I will be the only one left."

Sazaaim frowned and looked away.

"That is not so, my son," he said, but his voice carried little conviction. And as if to give the lie to his words he stood up to leave. Korfax stood up with him.

"Now I really must go," Sazaaim said. They embraced and Korfax watched with sullen eyes as his father left. There had been too much bad news, too much loss. Things used to be so much happier, but now it was all forebodings, like a presage of nightmares. A darkness was coming, he was certain of it, a terrible darkness and there was nothing anyone could do to prevent it.

9

HERESIES

Mad-zaasi Tolzen-urais
Bus-od-bao Odzor-odkom
Von-od-loa Zimhel-talu
Ipaj-muh Onath-for-don
Iksho-a Dr-pan-lanihm
Oachors-ain Ipom-soiaih
Nuhm-ipang Odpam-gahaih

It was not long after Korfax's father had returned north that Tahamoh suggested they visit a place he had been told of. Since they rarely ventured out into the city, most of their time being spent in the seminary, Korfax welcomed the chance to explore. Besides, it would help take his mind off things.

Tahamoh took him to a tall house in the fourth circle. Korfax did not know what this place might be, as Tahamoh had said very little about it, but when they arrived he could see why his friend was so interested.

Korfax stared up at the house. It seemed out of place, crowded about as it was by greater towers. He had the odd feeling that it had been built long before the city, like a solitary and aged tree that suddenly finds itself surrounded by a new forest.

Korfax read the naming pillar and drew back in surprise. The house declared itself to be a 'haven of rare antiquities', but since there already was a tower of archives where all the tales of history were kept, what was the point of this place?

The Ell were preservers, not misers. The past was gone and should never be resurrected, or so he had been taught. There were archives of ancient writings, devices and weaponry in the requisite guilds, but they were purely for reference. This, though, seemed to be something entirely different. Korfax wondered what it was like inside. Would it be a gallery of the unquiet dead, restless shades unable to enter the river because one of the living selfishly kept their thoughts alive?

Tahamoh walked to where Korfax stood and looked at the pillar.

"It is strange, isn't it?" he said.

Korfax agreed.

"Yes, it is. Who told you about this place?"

"Geyad Omagrah. He suggested that you and I visit."

"Me?"

"Aren't you interested?"

Korfax looked back at the house.

"Yes, of course," he said. "I wonder what is inside."

"Then why don't you both enter and see for yourselves?" intruded another voice. "I am sure that two such youthful seekers after the rare and the intriguing could find nothing but diversion within."

They each turned to find another smiling at them both. He was dressed in the robes of an archivist, for who but an archivist would own such a place? However, Korfax was not reassured. Though the stranger's voice was gentle and his manner friendly, there was an obscure sense of threat in the air as though his spare frame was a mask for something else.

"May I introduce myself?" asked the stranger. "I am Athzur Rom Matchir. I am the keeper of this place."

He offered them a wider smile and then bowed. Korfax and Tahamoh bowed in return. Tahamoh spoke first.

"I am Erinil Noren Tahamoh," he announced.

Matchir inclined his head.

"You are the heir to the Erinilith? I am most honoured."

Tahamoh smiled somewhat smugly in response. Matchir turned to Korfax.

"And your name is?"

"Faren Noren Korfax," said Korfax.

Matchir looked momentarily taken aback.

"The heir to the Farenith? Surely not!"

His eyes gained in intensity for a moment, but then he seemed to remember himself.

"But of course you are. Did you not just say so? I am most honoured. Who has not heard of the Farenith? No one, I should think."

Korfax felt a sudden heat rise to his cheeks. He caught a clenched look on Tahamoh's face and suddenly wished that his name was not so well known after all. Matchir bowed yet again.

"Well now!" he said. "Two great houses, both on the same day? I am doubly honoured."

He gestured to the door.

"Please, enter. Are you both students of history? Yes, yes indeed you are!"

He clasped his hands before him.

"Would you like to see? It is certain that you would, otherwise why would you be here at all? Perhaps you will find something of interest? I am sure that you will."

Korfax found himself struck by Matchir's mannerisms. He seemed far too eager for one thing, answering his own questions before anyone else could, and he bowed his head too many times. It was like a dance that was also a distraction.

Korfax distrusted it immediately. He glanced at Tahamoh, about to suggest that they move on, but his friend clearly wanted to have a look.

"Why don't we go in?" he suggested. "I have never heard of a place like this. Why don't we go inside and look? It cannot do any harm."

Korfax smiled as best he could, but now he felt on edge.

"Whatever you like," he said. "But we must be back in time for the evening blessing."

Matchir smiled again.

"Of course you must. But we have time yet, plenty of time. Come and see that which I am sure you have never seen before."

And that was that. Tahamoh gestured that Matchir lead the way, and then he followed him through the dark doorway while Korfax came slowly after, reluctance in every step.

The haven, at first glance, turned out to be something of a disappointment. There were many items on display, ancient artefacts from long before the last wars. There was armour that had all but rusted into shapelessness, there was a long misshapen blade of curious design and a lance that was no more than a broken shaft, but none of it was startling. There were some oddities concerning the arrangement, but Korfax did not ask Matchir why the items were placed so, as he decided he would work it out for himself.

The first thing of note was that each item had in front of it a tablet giving both a location and a tentative date, and that all of the dates went further back than recorded history. That meant that they came from the dark times, from before the building of the great cities and before all the famous names of history.

The dark times were not considered worthy of serious study. Little had survived from those days and they had become a repository for all the myths and fables that still circled the world – fertile ground for weavers of dramas and parables but of little real use.

Korfax eventually came to a line of pots, each getting older as the line progressed, increasing in decrepitude until the very last exhibit was nothing more than a few broken fragments. At first he wondered why they had such prominence, but when he reached the end he went back again and looked harder. The older the pots became, the simpler was their design. But the very last and oldest fragments looked, oddly enough, far more sophisticated.

Matchir stepped forward from where he was lurking in the shadows.

"You see it, don't you? Of course you do! I see the light of comprehension in your face."

Tahamoh came over to look as well.

"A pot is just a pot, surely?" he said.

Korfax gestured at the long line.

"But these tell a tale. They become simpler the further back in time you go until you get to the oldest. It is different. It appears far better made."

Tahamoh looked suitably surprised. Korfax turned to Matchir.

"Where did these come from?" he asked.

"From exactly one place," Matchir told him. "When they rebuilt the Umadya Garanku in Dolteos they had to remove the foundations. These were all found underneath, at various layers. The ruins of Garanku are known to be very old indeed, older than memory or record. The dates are estimates, obviously, but I have every reason to believe they are as accurate as they can be."

Korfax looked at Matchir.

"And what does this tell you?"

Matchir's eyes glowed with eagerness.

"That there was a fall," he said. "That the Ell were once mightier than they have since become."

Tahamoh looked up.

"There was a fall?" he asked.

Matchir oozed sincerity.

"Think of all the tales that have come down to us from the dark times. Always there are hints of ancient greatness. And why are the dark times called so? Because there was a fall."

Tahamoh stared back at the pots with new respect, but Korfax was dismissive now.

"But the evidence is so flimsy," he said. "If that is the purpose of this place, to illustrate such a belief, then I think it needs far more evidence to tell its tale. One set of pots, a few swords and a stone tablet?"

Matchir looked less than pleased.

"That is not all that there is. There are many mysteries from our past that have never been explained. Who built the valley of the towers upon Lonsiatris? Where did the Namad Dar originate? I am not alone in my speculations."

Shocked by the assertion, Korfax was a moment speaking again.

"The Namad Dar?" he exclaimed. "But that was given to us by Risatah. Everyone knows that."

"But where did he obtain it?" Matcher returned.

"It was given to him by The Creator," Korfax answered.

"Divine inspiration? Or a rediscovery?" Matchir retorted.

Korfax backed away.

"But that is not what we have been taught. Are you saying that you know better than those of the Dar Kaadarith?" he accused.

Matchir held up his hand. There was a flicker of consternation for a moment and something else Korfax could not identify. Then Matchir seemed to collect himself and merely looked somewhat graver than he had before.

"It is merely speculation, that is all," he said. "I do not state it as fact."

"And are these just your speculations, or are there others of like mind?" Tahamoh asked.

Matchir paused as if he was taking a huge risk in answering.

"There is the Sal Kamalkar," he said.

"I have heard of them," Tahamoh said. "I was told they are dissenters."

"Dissenters?" Korfax asked.

"Those who do not agree," Tahamoh explained.

"I still do not understand," Korfax said. Then he lowered his voice.

"Are they heretics?" he asked.

Tahamoh looked surprised at the question. He would have answered, but Matchir was quicker.

"No!" he said. "That is not what they are! They debate, that is all. They do not reject the rule of the Velukor, they merely wish to pursue other inquiries than the more usual ones. They ask, they probe, they debate."

"What is their aim?" Korfax wondered.

"The truth! Enlightenment!"

"Enlightenment?"

"The truth of The Creator," Matchir said. "By studying the world about us, we discover the intent of The Creator. By holding opposing views, we find the truth between us. Dissent is the way of it."

Matchir looked at Korfax for a moment, measuring him.

"You have a questing mind," he said. "Why do you not come and see for yourself?"

It was clear who the invitation was aimed at, but Korfax was having none of it.

"It sounds very much like something only an archivist would be interested in," he said.

Matchir disagreed.

"No," he replied. "There are many there that have nothing to do with our guild. There are merchants. There are artisans. There are poets and thinkers. They allow anyone through their doors. All are welcome."

Fed up with being ignored, Tahamoh folded his arms.

"I have also heard tell that their heart and soul is Dialyas."

It was almost a sneer. Matchir started, clearly startled by the interruption. Then he glared at Tahamoh as though he had just said something he should not. Korfax, though, concentrated on the name of Dialyas. He had heard it before. They all had. Dialyas was the only Geyad ever to have been expelled from the Dar Kaadarith. In all its history he was the only one that had ever left its service, and all the acolytes had been explicitly warned to avoid him.

"I think it is time for us to go," Korfax said.

"I could not agree more," Tahamoh answered.

They both bowed to Matchir and made their way out. Matchir watched them leave in silence and glowered in the shadows.

Time moved on. Now that they had touched a stave with purpose there was more to learn, much more. Korfax forgot all about Matchir and the haven of antiquities, but it seemed that Matchir had not quite forgotten about him, for as Lamasa passed to Axinor, Korfax found himself on the receiving end of an invitation.

"I met Matchir yesterday," Tahamoh told him. "I was asked to give you a message. He was wondering if you had reconsidered his offer to go to a meeting of the Sal Kamalkar."

Korfax looked carefully about. No one else was near.

"I thought you did not like him?"

"He sought me out," said Tahamoh.

"Well I can't," Korfax told him. "There is an edict. We were told to keep away."

Tahamoh smiled in agreement.

"That is what I said to Matchir, but he said that I was being far too literal. The edict actually applies only to Dialyas, not to us. We can go where we please. It is Dialyas who is not supposed to seek us out."

"But the result is the same," Korfax returned. "After all, he was the one that was cast from the Dar Kaadarith."

"True," said Tahamoh. "But I have had a thought about that. Think what you could learn. He was supposed to be brilliant, was Dialyas. I think it would be interesting to meet him."

Korfax looked carefully at Tahamoh.

"Then why don't you go?" he said.

"I am not the one that has been invited," Tahamoh retorted. Then he turned smartly about and walked away. Korfax thought he caught a resentful look on Tahamoh's face.

It was not long before the next message arrived. This time Tahamoh looked regretful, almost conciliatory.

"I met Matchir again," he said. "He still wants to meet with you. He wants to take you to the Sal Kamalkar."

"And I have given him my answer," Korfax returned. "Why does he persist?"

Tahamoh looked down.

"I think I know the reason. I do not think it is Matchir who is asking this time, but Dialyas."

"Dialyas?" Korfax asked.

"Matchir told me something," said Tahamoh. "It explains why he is so interested in you. Dialyas knows your father. He would like to meet you."

Korfax started and then stared in utter surprise.

"He knows my father?"

"That is what Matchir said, that he was once a friend of your father's."

Korfax felt dumbfounded. His father knew Dialyas? Dialyas was once his friend? He felt dim, dark stirrings inside. Should he ask his father, or should he find out for himself? Certainly his father had never mentioned anything of this before. More secrets? More things they had not told him? Korfax suddenly found himself wanting to find out what these secrets might be.

Korfax stood with Matchir outside the house of the Sal Kamalkar and wondered whether he had made a mistake.

They had walked all the way to the southern edges of the third circle, a long journey of narrow streets and walled paths. They saw few as they went their way, and Korfax wondered whether Matchir had chosen such a route for precisely that reason. Such thoughts only increased his discomfort.

He looked up at the house. Though it was much like all the others thereabout, four spires leaning towards each other and joined by four great walls, it was also set apart from them. Korfax thought of the haven of antiquities. That had seemed out of place also, but whereas the haven was hidden away in the shadows of greater spires, this house almost shouted its presence to the world. It was the stone from which it had been made. Rather than carefully matching each block against its neighbours, its builders had decided to make the house using stone of different shades. It made the place seem almost gaudy.

Around the house there appeared to be many courtyards and gardens, whilst the walls were covered with fragrant vines and blossoms. The beauty and the order of its surroundings seemed to contrast with the house itself, and Korfax found himself disconcerted by the clash. He looked at Matchir unhappily.

"I am not sure about this," he said quietly.

Matchir smiled.

"You are uncertain?" he asked. "Good! That is precisely how you should feel. Uncertainty and doubt fuel the fires of understanding. Without them we do not look beyond our borders. Beware the closed mind."

Korfax turned as though to leave.

"I do not have a closed mind," he said. "I am just concerned what my masters might think. If I break faith with them they will not look kindly on me in return. Last year Geyad Sohagel was quite insistent that we should have nothing to do with Dialyas. An edict was placed against him when he was cast from the Dar Kaadarith."

Matchir watched him with glinting eyes, his face suddenly hard.

"No closed mind, you say? Yet here you are, thinking of leaving before you have even looked! What is it that you fear, truth or censure? What if Dialyas has been falsely accused? What if this edict you speak of is the result of jealousy and pride? What if an injustice has been committed? Surely it is your duty to right the wrong?"

Korfax looked away for a moment, thinking furiously. Matchir smiled.

"Do you have no answer?" he asked.

Korfax looked back angrily.

"I was thinking about what you just said."

It wasn't quite a sneer, and it wasn't quite contempt, but there was an expression on Matchir's face now that Korfax did not like at all.

"Take all the time that you please," said Matchir, "but I know which one of us awaits revelation!"

Korfax was about to walk away when a figure, unseen by either of them, detached itself from the shadow of the wall. It came towards them both and spoke in a deep, rich voice.

"And I think I had better intervene before matters take a turn for the worse."

They both looked around. The figure came into the light and Matchir immediately dropped his head in deference. From his reaction, Korfax guessed that this must be Dialyas.

Dialyas was not as tall as Korfax had imagined him to be. He was instead broader than was usual and very pale of skin. His eyes, though, were dark, so dark in fact as to be almost black, and yet they burned with a light that was fearsomely bright.

"Greetings to you, I am Dialyas," he said to Korfax.

He bowed and Korfax bowed in return.

"I am Faren Noren Korfax," Korfax returned.

"Yes, I know who you are. Matchir has told me on many occasions that he might persuade you to come here."

Dialyas turned to Matchir.

"Presumption is ever your way, isn't it? You always seem to think that you know my mind better than I. This was not well done."

Matchir started. Korfax looked from one to the other in confusion.

"But I heard your desire quite distinctly," said Matchir. "What was it you said? 'I would very much like to meet the son of my old friend Sazaaim.' Did I misunderstand?"

"No," Dialyas answered, "but you have conveniently forgotten everything else that I said as well. Always you give your attention only to the things that please your vanity."

Matchir looked hurt. He took a long, deep breath and then answered with exaggerated restraint.

"I was not thinking of myself in this, I was thinking only of you. I thought this would please you."

Dialyas pursed his lips and looked at Korfax.

"It does please me," he said. "Of course it does, but Korfax also needs the good will of his masters at this time. He is right in this. They would not look with favour on his coming here."

"Then I shall leave it in your hands," Matchir said curtly, before walking off through the gate and on to the house. They both watched him go for a moment and then Dialyas turned back to Korfax.

"Please forgive him," he said. "Matchir means well, but sometimes he can be a little single-minded. And of late I have detected a certain impatience in everything that he says and does. I expect he will be leaving us soon."

"Leaving?" Korfax asked.

"To be blunt," sighed Dialyas, "voluntary exile. Reconciliation is not a word that sits easily in his heart these days."

Korfax was shocked. Matchir considered himself a heretic? That was as serious as it could be. He was suddenly conscious of Dialyas studying him.

"You are very like him in some ways," Dialyas said.

"Matchir?"

Dialyas smiled.

"No," he said, "your father."

Korfax looked down.

"He never mentioned you. How do you know him?"

"We were at the seminary together. We were friends for a long while."

Dialyas paused a moment.

"So he has never mentioned me?" he continued.

"No, should I ask him?"

"I think not. When he chooses to speak of it, he will. Then you can ask."

Korfax looked back the way he had come.

"I should leave," he said.

Dialyas stepped forward and gestured at the house.

"Perhaps, but I would be remiss if I did not at least offer you some refreshment before you did so. It is a long way back to the Umadya Semeiel."

"But I should not be here," Korfax said.

"And neither should I," Dialyas returned. "Yet here we both are despite our misgivings. The lure of the forbidden, how sweet is its song."

Dialyas laughed quietly and looked back at the house behind him. Listening to that laugh, Korfax pictured the rustling of leaves in his mind. He suppressed a shiver.

"Do you mock?" he asked. "I came here in all honesty, yet here you are laughing at me. Do you mock?"

Dialyas smiled sadly and Korfax was caught by the look. Now it was Dialyas who looked like his father.

"No," Dialyas answered. "You misapprehend me. I would never do that. Mockery is the sin of the arrogant and the prideful. I was merely reminiscing, that is all. I once did the same as you."

His sadness drifted away and something harder took its place.

"So you are curious? Do you wish to hear what I have to say? Is that why you have come?"

"Matchir told me that you knew my father, but my father has never mentioned you. I think I would like to know why."

"You think, but you are not certain. Perhaps I should not tell you this tale."

Dialyas waited a moment as if listening, then turned and gestured towards the house again.

"But this can be left until later. I am being a poor host."

Dialyas went to the gate and opened it.

"Please, enter freely of your own will and leave behind some of the wisdom you bring with you."

It was an odd welcome, but Korfax said nothing. Instead, he followed Dialyas to the house and the subtle scents of the garden rode the air about them both like an augury of secrets.

As they came through the main door, Korfax looked up. A sigil hung there, the sigil of the hand. He stared up at it, intending to ask why that one in particular, but Dialyas did not give him time. Instead he urged him on.

Korfax found the inside of the house as distinctive as the outside. Like the haven of antiquities, it also seemed to have been left behind from some older time. Built, no doubt, for a long-vanished noble family, there was a sense about it that its original occupants were still here, still drifting through its stone and unwilling to depart. Usually, when a house or a tower was reoccupied, the new owners remade it in their own image, but not here, where little appeared to have been touched at all.

Korfax found the bright murals on the walls to be of interest. On his left, one in particular caught his eye. In it a lone figure stood, a long scroll in one hand, a stave in the other. Against him were arrayed a dark collection of demons, jeering things that reached out to him but were not yet able to touch. Korfax thought the depiction familiar, but he found that he could not name it. Dialyas noticed where Korfax was looking, and he smiled.

"Do you recognise it?" he asked.

Korfax glanced at Dialyas and then looked back at the mural.

"I am not sure," he said. "It does seem familiar."

Dialyas raised his eyebrows.

"I imagine that it would. Try harder."

Korfax looked back at the mural whilst his memories played hide and seek with him. The lone figure had a serene expression, totally at odds with those of the demons or his peril. Korfax recognised some of the nastier creatures the artist had added to the scene. There were five Pataba for a start, immense and brutal, all crowded together, leering faces, sneering mouths. Usually they were depicted as stupid, shambling things, but here they had been gifted with intelligence. Their eyes looked peculiarly bright, as though each of them shared a secret knowledge known only to themselves, passing it from one to the other with subtle whispers and knowing looks. Of the others, there were Iladoal, Rinpia and Barmor, and each of them had been given that self-same intelligence by the artist.

"It still eludes me," Korfax said.

Dialyas tilted his head slightly.

"And what if I mention the name of Risatah?"

Korfax sighed. Now he had it.

"Of course! The Temptation of Risatah. This must be a copy of the work by Rodellus. I have heard of it, of course, but never seen it," he looked at it again. "I wonder how old it is."

He turned to Dialyas.

"It is a copy, isn't it?"

Dialyas laughed.

"Yes, it is merely a copy and not the original. I should be so fortunate! But it is very good, nonetheless."

Korfax turned back to the mural.

"It looks old."

Dialyas gestured at the whole.

"It is quite recent. I had it put in a few years ago. The artisan who placed it here blended it well with its surroundings. It seemed the right thing to do."

He gestured to the opposite wall.

"Now, seeing that one, what can you tell me of this?"

Korfax looked to where Dialyas gestured. Here again stood Risatah, but this time he was surrounded by a mighty assemblage of nobles, each striking a different dramatic pose as though they argued. In their midst, their lord sat upon a tall throne with his left hand fingering his chin as he stared down at Risatah in wonder. Korfax smiled.

"Knowing one, you know the other," he said. "This is 'The Gift of Risatah', also copied from Rodellus. That I do know, for the original is kept in the Umadya Semeiel. Here he is confronted by the Korith Zadakal, giving their Audroh, Nerroh, the key to the Namad Dar."

Korfax looked at the mural for a moment longer and then turned to Dialyas.

"So why should I not know these works?"

Dialyas put his arms behind him.

"It occurred to me that you might not expect to see such holy and noble works in this place. Think of it as a gentle test. Sometimes we do not recognise the familiar, especially when we see it in such unfamiliar surroundings."

Dialyas flicked a hand at both works.

"Now, can you tell me why you think the Sal Kamalkar would have such as these in its main hall?"

"You were once of the Dar Kaadarith," Korfax said.

"True, but that is not the reason."

Korfax looked from one mural to the other. He thought of the usual interpretations, of temptation and revelation, denial and enlightenment. For some reason Matchir's words from before came back to him, something about looking beyond borders.

"Boundaries?" he asked.

Dialyas looked surprised for a moment.

"And why do you say that?"

"It was something Matchir said, how uncertainty fuels the fires of understanding."

"I see. Nothing else?"

"I did think of temptation and revelation, of denial and enlightenment, but that is how the two works are usually seen, and I was thinking that you meant something else."

"Why would I?"

Korfax was at a loss for a moment.

"You mean that it is?"

Dialyas smiled.

"You see how your expectations colour your thoughts? Were you expecting something a little more unusual, perhaps? I do not think you properly understand what it is that happens here."

"Then what does happen here?"

"I suppose you could call this house an open door. All are welcome. Those that come here come to debate and discuss. They are here to learn, to disseminate, to criticise and to know. From a single idea to an all-encompassing philosophy, they come to this place with whatever inspires them. But that is all."

"You debate?"

"Yes."

"And nothing else?"

"No."

"So why are you held in such disfavour?"

"Because some ideas are more dangerous than others."

They sat in one of the many large halls and drank of a pale wine that Dialyas did not name. It was, as he had promised, refreshing. Dialyas also furnished Korfax with a plain and voluminous robe to cover those that he wore. Others sat or stood in the hall in little groups, some quietly discussing, others in heated debate. Korfax could not tell where any of them came from, whether they were merchants or artisans or servants or nobles, as all of them wore the same nondescript robes as Dialyas had given to him. All he could see were faces, pale, dark, animated or thoughtful. He caught sight of Matchir in one of the groups, but Matchir was clearly engrossed in the discussion at hand.

Korfax looked at his own robe and then back at the various groups. Dialyas, catching where he looked, explained.

"It brings us all down to the same level," he said.

"Why?" asked Korfax.

"Equality is important in a debate," Dialyas explained. "It is preferable to concentrate upon what is being said, not who is saying it."

"But none of the great guilds debates in that way," Korfax countered.

"I know," said Dialyas, "and I consider that a flaw. If an idea has merit, then it should be able to stand on its own. If the person delivering that idea understands it, then that should be apparent also. No one should be able to say 'I am right because of who I am'. They must instead be able to prove it. Nothing should be taken for granted."

"But what of truths that are self-evident?"

"Are there any?"

"Yes!"

"Such as?"

"The duality of existence."

Dialyas raised an eyebrow.

"The illusion of separation? The myth of the sword?" he asked.

"But it is not an illusion, it is reality," Korfax answered.

"It is a perception," said Dialyas.

"But a perception that rules our every horizon," Korfax insisted. "It is our reality, whether we will it or no. We are caught within it. If we were to exist outside it then we would not be who we are. And so it is a self-evident truth."

Dialyas gave him a strange look then, both quizzical and curious.

"I have heard that argument before. So what if I say that all truths are one truth, the single truth of The Creator?"

"Then I would answer that The Creator divided the void so that the one truth could be revealed by the many, all things made known by their opposite."

Dialyas smiled now.

"Which is exactly what I was expecting."

He looked hard at Korfax.

"I seem to have had this conversation before."

"Who with?" Korfax asked.

"It was a long time ago," Dialyas told him. "And I think I know where this will go."

"Do you concede the point then?"

"No. Neither of us will gain the upper hand. You will argue from the position of the rising spirit, of the ennoblement of the humble, whilst I will counter with the fall into the realm of matter."

"You believe we are fallen then?"

"Yes, I believe that we are, but not in that way. The belief in the fallen spirit has been adjudged a heresy, and I am no heretic."

"But you were prepared to argue from that position."

"Yes I was, but that does not mean that I agree with it. Debate brings enlightenment, as any such exercise of vital powers should. You are entirely correct when you say that all things are known by their opposite."

"So what do you gain?"

"A challenge to my assumptions."

Dialyas smiled a moment.

"Do you understand now?" he asked.

"I think so," said Korfax. "It is something the Erm Roith do – arguing from every position so that a consensus can be achieved."

Dialyas dropped his smile.

"That wasn't quite what I meant. We are not interested in consensus here but enlightenment, plain and simple."

"There is one thing, though," Korfax said after a moment.

"And what is that?" Dialyas asked him.

"You said that we have fallen. What did you mean by that?"

"I meant that it is my belief that we have strayed from the path."

"You deny the balance then? You deny the great ritual, the great cycle?"

"No, I do not deny it. It is self-evident."

Korfax frowned at that, but Dialyas smiled back fondly.

"It was a jest, Korfax," he said.

"Then what do you mean?"

"That this is not all that we are. We could be better than this, greater, closer to The Creator."

"Give to The Creator The Creator's due!" Korfax warned.

"But what is The Creator's due?" Dialyas retorted. "How do we know what that might be unless we test it? I believe we were meant for something more than this!"

"You want more than this?"

Dialyas became very still.

"I believe that the Ell are not all that they should be. We are a glorious people, the favoured of The Creator, but we have lost our way. Like our bodies cage our spirits, tradition and ritual cage our minds. Each holds us in its grasp and will not let us go. We are meant for more than this. That is what I believe."

He stood up.

"Now it is well past time that you went on your way."

Dialyas escorted him back to the gate of the house.

"What of Matchir?" Korfax asked.

"He will leave later."

Dialyas gave Korfax another of his quizzical looks.

"I would like it very much if you would visit with me again. I did not expect to, but I have enjoyed our words together. Perhaps there are things I can tell you, things it would be needful for you to know."

Korfax thought about that. Dialyas watched him carefully as if judging what he would say next.

"Come only when you are ready, though," he said.

Korfax looked up.

"I would like that, I think. You are not what I expected either. And you have been both courteous and considerate."

Dialyas smiled once more, a regretful smile that was yet warm and fond.

"Thank you, Korfax. That was kind of you to say so. Many would not. You know, you remind me very much of your father when he was your age. You have his fire."

He gestured to the road outside.

"When you wish to return, be circumspect. Do not let it be widely known what you are doing. Remember that there is also malice in the world. Farewell."

Tahamoh sat on his cot and looked up expectantly.

"So what was he like?"

"Interesting," said Korfax. "Not at all how I imagined he would be."

"What did you talk about?"

"This and that. He was being careful, I think."

"Are you going again?"

"Yes, I think so. He was kind and fair-minded. There are many that go to his house. They debate."

"What kind of debates?"

"All kinds. There is no restriction."

"That is all?"

"Why? What did you think it would be like?"

"I don't know. More than that, though. Did you talk to him about his time as a Geyad?"

"No, it did not come up. I am not sure he would discuss it anyway."

"You aren't being very forthcoming," Tahamoh accused.

"No, I suppose not," replied Korfax. "I need time to think."

He gave his friend a sharp look.

"Anyway, if you are so interested, why don't you go?"

Tahamoh did not answer.

It was a little while before Korfax went again. Lessons were harder now and there was far more to learn and many more tasks to master than he would have guessed, but the words of Dialyas ever sat in his mind: 'Perhaps there are things I can tell you, things it would be needful for you to know.'

Things it would be needful for him to know! He had already experienced something of that, the news given him by his father, for instance. Demons rampaging across the land, Losq abandoned and Chasaloh gone. How that burned. What else had they not told him?

So eventually Korfax found himself back beside Dialyas again, back at the Sal Kamalkar.

He arrived just as quietly as before. Dialyas met him at the door, a mixture of surprise and delight on his face, which he quickly hid. Then he furnished Korfax with a robe as he had the last time, and they walked together in the garden for a while and talked of this and that. Eventually they went back inside for refreshment.

As they entered the main hall, they saw only one debate in progress. Matchir was there, talking earnestly to a few others.

All turned to look at Dialyas before bowing, then they bowed to Korfax, all except Matchir, who smiled instead.

"So here you are!" he said. "Back again! I am somewhat surprised after our last conversation. You seemed most unwilling to come here then."

Dialyas frowned.

"He is my guest here, as you well know. I will not have him harassed in this fashion."

Matchir kept his smile.

"I was merely curious to see whether he still possesses a closed mind, that was all. There is only one way to test it."

Korfax held up his hand in the gesture of division.

"I think I know what Matchir desires," he said. "He wishes to debate with me."

Matchir bowed his head.

"Yes, I do," he said. "I was just discussing something with the others here, my beliefs if you will. I find myself wondering whether you can accept them also."

"I can only listen," said Korfax. "What is it that you were discussing?"

"That we, the Ell, have taken the wrong path."

Korfax frowned. That was what Dialyas had said at their first meeting.

"I have heard that before," he said. "But what do you mean by it?"

"That we do not understand our true purpose," answered Matchir. "That we do not fully understand the world into which we have been born."

"But we do understand the world," Korfax countered.

"And I think we do not," said Matchir. "I think we have lost our way. We are no longer the partakers of the secret wisdom."

"The secret wisdom?"

"The Creator's intent!"

"But we do. We are here, in the world, and the world is the word of The Creator made manifest."

"Many say the words," Matchir sighed, "but they do not fully appreciate what they actually mean. Yes we exist here, yes we are born of the substance of the world, but we go no further than that. We do not know everything, and only by knowing everything can we truly know The Creator."

"So you are saying that by pursuing all knowledge, whatever form it takes, you will then understand The Creator?"

"No, I am not saying that at all. I am saying that we will then be The Creator."

"Be The Creator?" Korfax asked, incredulous.

"Yes," said Matchir. "Divinity will be ours. We will return to the source of all creation, back to the place from whence we came."

Korfax thought for a while.

"You did say all knowledge?" he asked.

"Yes, I did," answered Matchir.

"That nothing is forbidden?"

"Absolutely nothing."

"Then what about sorcery?"

There was silence for a moment.

"I meant knowledge of this world," Matchir said at last, "the one we are born into. Sorcery is of the abyss."

"But The Creator is The Creator of all," said Korfax. "The Creator made the abyss. Would there be knowledge and The Creator not know it?"

Matchir looked a little startled by that.

"What are you implying?"

"You just said that to know everything is to know The Creator, but how can you do that if you limit yourself to this world alone? You will fail in your intent. For us the Creator is unknowable. Better that we understand who we are rather than reach for that which we are not. That is why we are here. To each is given their due."

There was a laugh from one of the others.

"The child has had an education it seems, straight from the Namad Vaney."

Korfax gave him an angry look.

"I am not a child!" he said. "Do not mock me!"

"It was merely a jest," said the other.

"A jest with the intent to distract, I think," retorted Korfax. "If you cannot gainsay it, you mock it!"

The other withdrew a little. Matchir looked at him.

"I agree. That was unworthy," he said.

He turned back to Korfax.

"You say that each is given their due. But what if our 'due' is knowledge of the divine, the spark of divinity? What if we already have what we need within us? What if we can know the unknowable? Our imaginations can cross the highest heavens, plumb the deepest chasm and disregard the tyranny of time. We can imagine eternity. The Creator is eternal. With our imaginations we can surmount the heavens. With that divine spark we can touch The Creator. It is for us to decide. The choice is given to us, by The Creator. In your world we do not move. We remain where we are."

Many bowed their heads in agreement. Korfax took a deep breath and thought hard about his answer.

"That is not so," he said after a moment. "We move with the world. Each generation sees it afresh. Each new pair of eyes sees something different, something never before seen. We are here to discover who we are, not to deny ourselves. We are here to live and to understand what that means."

"To advance is not to deny," said Matchir.

"But you would have us touch The Creator. If we were to do that then we would no longer be of the Ell."

"Then perhaps that is what The Creator is telling us. By giving us the power of imagination, by showing us our limitations, The Creator wants us to transcend them."

"But what if The Creator has already spoken to us? What if we have already been shown the way and told our purpose."

Matchir frowned.

"Say on," he said.

"Karmaraa was the chosen of The Creator. He became The Creator's sword on that fateful day and defeated the greatest evil this world has ever seen. From that moment on our fate was written in stone. Karmaraa and his heirs are the word of The Creator made manifest amongst us, and by that word we are to be the best that we can be with the gifts that we have. We are to keep the world and to guard it against evil. To meddle with the way of the world is surely to go against the word of The Creator."

"I did not say that we should meddle, only that we should transcend our bounds."

"Yes, by trying to touch The Creator. But Karmaraa has already done this for us. His intercession brought salvation. The Creator descended on that day. What then is the need to ascend?"

"Not ascension, but growth. We should become more than we are. Within us is the divine spark, our own personal intercession, and to know it is to know The Creator."

Korfax paused once more. Whatever did Matchir mean? Debating with him was like grappling with smoke.

"Now I am confused," he said. "Our own personal intercession? But we have the Velukor, the word of The Creator amongst us. He is who he is. We are who we are. What need is there to look inside ourselves for The Creator when The Creator is already here?"

"That is not what I meant at all," said Matchir. "I am talking about the here and the now. Karmaraa is no longer among us. The world has changed, we have not."

"But the world has not changed. The word of Karmaraa, the exact word, is as relevant now as it was then. I know. I have seen the truth of that word. I was at Losq."

It happened all at once, the rise of a slumbering fire. Korfax saw again the grey demons at Losq, the evil tide sweeping towards the wall and then over it. How dare Matchir deny such things?

"I was there, at Losq," he said, "when the Agdoain attacked. I saw them. I saw what they did. If you doubt the word of Karmaraa then go to the furthest north and see for yourself."

There was a deafening silence. Many stared at Korfax as if seeing him for the very first time. For a brief moment Matchir looked delighted at the outburst. Very quickly, though, his expression shifted to one of shock instead, as if he had not expected such an answer at all.

Dialyas stepped forward and held up his hand.

"I think this debate is over," he said.

Korfax sat with Dialyas. They were alone. Dialyas looked troubled.

"It never occurred to me that the debate would go to such a place," he said. "I am sorry. I should have intervened earlier."

"But why? It was the truth," said Korfax.

"Yes, and now you have told everyone present exactly who you are. I have no doubt that word will spread. There will be trouble."

"Trouble? Why?"

"Many will ask why I have allowed the son of such a faithful house to come here. They will be angry and fearful."

"But I do not know who they are. What do they think I will do? I am just an acolyte."

"Fearful, I said. Fear makes the world other than it actually is."

Dialyas sighed.

"We live on sufferance here. Our debates can sometimes push the boundaries of what some would consider acceptable. I have no doubt that were one of the Balt Kaalith here, we would all be called to account."

"I am sorry," said Korfax. "I did not think."

Dialyas laughed quietly, more leaves rustling in the wind.

"Do not be sorry," he said. "It is entirely my fault for not foreseeing such an outcome."

He came a little closer.

"You handled yourself well against Matchir."

Korfax sat back and thought carefully about that. Something had burned inside, as though a flame had risen up, and yes, he had answered Matchir fully each time. There had been no preparation and little hesitation, the words coming to him as if they had already been said.

Memories flew by in a rush – his home, his family, his life that had been. In amongst them lurked Doanazin, his tutor. It was Doanazin that had taught him this, long before he had come to the seminary of the Dar Kaadarith. How the world was and how the world should be, what was the truth and what that truth meant. He had taken it all for granted, until now.

He had been a trial to Doanazin, inattentive, constantly dreaming of something else instead of paying attention to what his tutor said. But now she was dead, and Korfax could neither thank her for the instruction nor apologise for his lack of appreciation. But the learning remained, nonetheless.

Dialyas leaned forwards slightly.

"It is not often Matchir is held at bay. I doubt that anyone else here could have done better. Who was your tutor?"

Korfax looked up, astonished. It was as though Dialyas had just peered inside his head.

"You think I had a tutor?"

Dialyas laughed.

"Korfax, please! It is obvious! Your answers were immediate. You did not have to pause over much or think too hard and you knew the counterargument to every point raised. You did not learn that in the seminary. You have been prepared. Your father is Enay of the Farenith and your mother is of the holy line. Of course you had a tutor! So tell me, who was it?"

Korfax took a deep breath.

"Goniras Nar Doanazin."

Dialyas closed his eyes.

"I knew it!" he said. "I knew it!"

"You knew her?"

"Oh yes."

"How? When?"

Dialyas looked into the distance for a moment, but his eyes were sharp and dark.

"When I was cast from the Dar Kaadarith and stripped of my stave, the Balt Kaalith took it upon themselves to try me for heresy. They are very good at what they do, but they could not find a single thing with which to charge me. So they brought in an inquisitor, someone who already knew me and who was fully acquainted with both ritual and the law."

"Doanazin!" said Korfax.

"Yes," agreed Dialyas. "She and I had crossed swords before on numerous occasions. As I am sure you are aware, one of the many dances between the great guilds involves a number of debates, all held during the festival of Bialah. That was where we met."

He looked sideways at Korfax.

"So imagine her relish when she sat across from me in one of the inquisitorial chambers deep inside the Umadya Levanel."

He smiled.

"She debated with me for seven days, seven long days of twists and turns, of accusation and counter accusation. But in the end she failed, and I was released."

"You were vindicated?"

"No, it was declared void. I did not surrender, but neither did she or the Balt Kaalith. They still regard me as suspect."

Dialyas gave Korfax a long hard look.

"So Doanazin was your tutor! And if I read things aright you resented her. Interesting. She was your tutor and you did not like her. Yet you debate like her echo. Not only interesting, but astonishing also."

Korfax felt uncomfortable. Dialyas was very good at seeing behind the masks of others, it seemed.

"And how can you tell that I resented her?" he asked.

Dialyas smiled gently.

"Because it is written all over your face. There is one thing you do not do well, Korfax, and that is to hide your feelings. It is not in your nature. But I see more. You feel guilty about Doanazin also. Was it because you did not pay her the attention she thought she deserved?"

"Is it that obvious?"

"Korfax, whether you know it or not, we have all walked this road. There were times in my life when I did not pay attention either. But be of good heart. I think you paid far more attention than you give yourself credit for. I think Doanazin would have been proud of her pupil this day."

Dialyas looked studiedly at the ground at his feet for a moment and then back at Korfax.

"I would very much like to know how your mother managed to entice her all the way to the furthest north. She did not offer her services lightly, and rarely to others outside her order. She considered her duty to the Erm Roith sacrosanct."

"I believe she thought it an honour to tutor one of the Farenith."

"And what do you think?"

"I think I did not appreciate her gifts."

Dialyas looked fondly at Korfax.

"I have a particular delight for candour, Korfax. Thank you for sharing that with me."

"But that was one of her lessons. When a lie is uttered a part of the world dies."

Dialyas drew back a little.

"I was taught that also," he said carefully.

Korfax heard the complex honesty in Dialyas's agreement, and he wondered what it meant. He waited for a moment and then looked at Dialyas again.

"So you agree with Matchir?"

"No, I do not. I think he goes too far."

"But I thought..."

"He is pursuing his own vision, his own belief."

"And you tolerate that?"

"Of course I do. No one has a monopoly on the truth. I encourage free thinking here."

He smiled as if that was a jest.

"It seems you still have not entirely grasped the purpose of the Sal Kamalkar yet," he said.

"Clearly not," said Korfax. "And what is free thought? What does that mean? There are no strictures on what we think. There never have been. We are Ell! Our world is free."

"You are certain of that?"

"Yes."

"Then what of heresy? What of Lonsiatris?"

Korfax paused. Here it was again. It loomed over everything in this house. Heresy! He thought of Lonsiatris, that distant land to the south. He had been told of it many times, a great island, one of the largest, set within the greater ocean and large enough almost to be a separate province all by itself. It was where the exiles went. Some went there voluntarily, taking themselves to Lonsiatris and never returning, but others had been sent forcibly, banished for all time by the powers of the day. Korfax looked back carefully at Dialyas.

"Lonsiatris is necessary," he said. "It is for those that reject the rule of the Velukor. But that is their choice. They are free to make it, just as they are free not to make it. This is how the peace is kept. This is how we remain a single people. It is the price of unification. Anolei, blessed be his name, drew up its charter, the Logah Siatris. And the Logah Siatris is written in stone."

"Indeed it is," Dialyas agreed. "But how can you say that there are no strictures on what you can think or believe whilst Lonsiatris exists?"

"But they are free to think whatever they like there."

"Are they?" he asked. "What is the first commandment of the Logah Dar?"

Korfax answered immediately.

"Suffer not the Argedith to live."

He looked back at Dialyas.

"You cannot mean that!" he said.

"But I do," returned Dialyas, "and the Logah Dar precedes the Logah Siatris. There are some things in this world that it is indeed perilous to think."

"Do you believe then that the practice of the Namad Mahorelah should be allowed?"

"No, Korfax, of course I do not. I am merely pointing out that there are philosophies and practices and beliefs that it is not safe to contemplate at all. Therefore you are not as free as you believe yourself to be."

"But that is an issue of choice and of morality."

Dialyas spread his hands in the gesture of agreement as if to affirm the point.

"Indeed it is. So now you discover how your choices confine you."

"But that was not the tenor of the debate," Korfax said.

"No, it was not," Dialyas conceded. "But you must also understand that sometimes we have to weigh morality and truth in the balance. What happens when they clash?"

"That has never occurred."

"Has it not? Are you sure? The Iabeiorith once believed themselves to be right, as did the Korith Zadakal. Both thought they had The Creator on their side when they went into battle. The war hymns of the Korith Zadakal are remarkably similar to those of the Iabeiorith. Have you ever studied them?"

Korfax looked down again. What could he say? He could not argue with that, no matter how he played with the meanings of the words. Very well then, he decided, he would not argue at all, not until he knew better. He looked back at Dialyas.

"Does this have anything to do with why you were cast from the Dar Kaadarith?"

Dialyas became dark for a moment, his eyes lidded, his expression withdrawn. Then he smiled again and looked back brightly at Korfax.

"You have an admirable directness. Not many would dare such a question with me," he said.

Korfax suddenly felt far from comfortable under that searching gaze, but Dialyas looked away soon enough. Now he gazed into the distance, into the past, into memory.

"The answer is yes, it does. But in order to understand that, you need to understand why I was cast out. The entire story could take days to tell or mere moments. Which do you prefer?"

"Whatever you wish," said Korfax.

Dialyas offered him a careful expression.

"Whatever I wish?" he mused. "You are generous. Then let me say only this. I was expelled for declaring that all stones made with the Namad Dar communicate with the very same void. I was expelled for saying that the same void sits within each and every stone."

Despite himself, Korfax was shocked.

"Just for that? But that is nothing. Who was ever cast from our order for being wrong?"

"You do not see it yet, but you will," said Dialyas. "So you think I am wrong?"

"Unquestionably. Each stone, be it piradar, oanadar or kamliadar, gets its energy from its own internal void, a void that is created during the actual forging. They lie inside like a minute pool, caged for ever by imperishable walls."

"Do they, though? Let us pursue that, you and I. You have already faced down the admirable Matchir, so why not dare the Vovin in his lair? Debate with me."

Korfax looked hard at Dialyas.

"But how can I debate with you? I am just an acolyte. You were a Geyad!" he said.

Dialyas smiled easily in return.

"But you have been well-educated, Korfax. Having heard you now, I have no fear that you will hold your own against me. I have a desire to duel with Doanazin once more, her or her ghost. Besides, it is theory we will discuss here, not practice."

"Even so, you know far more than I do. You have had years of experience, whilst I have only just begun!"

Dialyas stared into the distance once more, eyes glittering.

"But it is a long time since I studied as you do now. Though I remember that time with great fondness, it is all that I do remember. The details have all but vanished

surprise written all over his face.

"You think the void is the nothingness from which The Creator took creation?" he asked.

"Follow that thought," Dialyas said. "Then you will see."

Korfax thought a moment.

"No," he said eventually.

"And if I say to you that since all stones open up onto the very same void, the purpose that is set into each stone at its forging is now a limit of the stone, not the void it communicates with."

"I still do not see it."

"That someone of sufficient strength could change the purpose of stone merely by the power of their thought. But in order to do that you would need to make stones of far greater refinement than those that we make now."

Korfax understood at last. It was so outrageous that he had to stand up.

"You were trying to explain Karmaraa!" he accused. "You were trying to explain how his stave could change during his battle with Sondehna!"

He looked down at Dialyas in amazement.

"No wonder they cast you out! That is blasphemy!"

Dialyas took a deep breath and looked a little disappointed. He had clearly met such a reaction before.

"It is not blasphemy," he said. "It does not detract from the intercession at all. Grace was given on that day, and I do not contest that. But what I do contest is the manner in which the miracle occurred. I may never be able to study the stave of Karmaraa, but I believe that if I could it would prove to be of exceptional purity."

"But you are trying to explain away the miracle," Korfax insisted. "The implication is obvious. You believe that anyone could have done what Karmaraa did, given the right circumstances."

"Korfax, we have already explained a great many miracles of the world, but that does not detract from them. Grace was the intercession, not the act."

He held up a hand and clenched it into a fist.

"What if I told you that I once made a stone of such power and of such a nature that all were amazed to behold it, for it did something no other stone could do – it changed the nature of its communication with the void according to its need. It changed its purpose according to how it was used. How do you answer that?"

"But that is not miraculous. Kabadar do the same."

"No, Korfax, they do not, and you know it. With kabadar it is the mind that is mutable. Kabadar only extract raw power. It then falls to the Geyad to use that power, summoning earth of air, or fire of water, with their mind."

Korfax looked hard at Dialyas.

"So what was this stone?"

"Is, Korfax, is. It is the Kapimadar!"

"But we were told that it was a glorious failure. It is on display in the lowest level of the archives. Though I have not seen it I am told that it does nothing."

A flicker of anger ran this way and that across the face of Dialyas like a ripple across still waters, only to vanish just as quickly. He drew himself up and Korfax thought he did so with a certain pride.

"Few had the wit to understand it at the time, and those that did subsequently turned away rather than admit to the truth, so I suppose I should not be surprised if no one understands it now."

Dialyas turned to Korfax and his eyes were shadowed, hiding their light.

"Let me suggest something to you," he said. "Stand alone before the Kapimadar, at either sunrise or sunset, it does not matter which, and then you will see a thing."

"I was told that it keeps time," said Korfax, "but we have other crystals that do that, and they are far simpler."

"Then try touching the Kapimadar when it changes. You will soon discover how much of a 'failure' it is then."

"No one is allowed to touch any of the exhibits in the archives. It is forbidden."

Dialyas narrowed his eyes.

"Forbidden, is it? How your freedoms diminish!"

His eyes brightened again.

"But that changes nothing. I have proven, to my own satisfaction, that the void in each crystal is the same void. And the lack of acceptance of that singular fact, in the face of all other proofs, convinces me more than anything else that I was right to create the Sal Kamalkar. Any governance that embraces dogma over truth should be exposed for what it is."

Korfax frowned.

"But you have proven nothing to me."

Dialyas pointed at the north wall.

"Then go back to the Umadya Semeiel, touch the Kapimadar and discover the truth for yourself."

"It is forbidden," Korfax insisted.

"You wanted proof. Do as I say."

"You ask me to do something that I cannot."

"And so you waste your gifts. I think they would rather not teach you how to think at all. I think they would prefer that you were only taught how to keep the world the way that it is."

"But I want to be Geyad. If I disobey my order, if I disobey my guild, not only do I dishonour my calling, but I also dishonour my family and myself."

"By that measure you are already disobedient. Are you not here, with me?"

Dialyas sighed.

"But let that pass. Are there not higher callings? What of the truth? Are you prepared to build your life upon lies?"

"How arrogant is that?" Korfax asked.

"Arrogant?"

"You believe you are right and that the rest of the world is wrong. But what if it is the other way around? What if you are wrong and the rest of the world is right?"

"But I have proof."

"Demonstrate it to me then."

"Touch the Kapimadar."

"This is not a debate," said Korfax, "this is a temptation! Is this how you recruit new followers? By temptation? By subversion? Cleaving them to you by guilt? I have to break an edict given to me by the powers that I serve in order to see your truth? I see through you."

Dialyas almost beamed with pleasure.

"Now we come to it!" he said. "You see it at last. Here is the true nature of discovery. Not temptation, not subversion, but the breaking of laws."

His face was all but beatific. Korfax thought of the mural in the hall, of Risatah as he faced the demons of the abyss.

"Think, Korfax, think!" implored Dialyas.

He was almost beside himself now and his eyes were like lights in his head.

"If we do not test the limits, if we do not look beyond and think the unthinkable, we will end up in a sealed room with nowhere else to go. We will imprison ourselves."

Korfax could not agree.

"You describe chaos," he accused.

The light diminished a little.

"I advocate change over stagnation. Laws should and must be rewritten."

"You would deny the word of Karmaraa?" Korfax asked.

Dialyas laughed sadly and the light vanished altogether.

"Korfax, Korfax! Listen to yourself. That is not what Karmaraa said at all. Besides, Karmaraa was my inspiration. He changed his stave!"

But Korfax was thoroughly entrenched now.

"That was a holy act!" he said. "Would you even subvert the single greatest event in the history of our people to your cause?"

Dialyas drew back and his eyes were now dark and shuttered.

"No, Korfax, I would not. But instead I would ask you to think on what I have said."

Tahamoh listened in complete silence as Korfax told him what had happened and what had been debated. When Korfax was done, Tahamoh immediately took out a logadar, his ever-present copy of the Logah Dar, and awoke it. Words flickered in the air above the stone and he read rapidly through the layers of text, his attention shifting from page to page. Korfax watched him for a moment and then turned away.

"I am not sure I should go there again," he said. "If the wardens ever find out..."

He looked back at Tahamoh.

"Can you imagine the reaction of Sohagel?" he asked.

"If they don't know about it, what can they say?" Tahamoh returned.

Korfax turned away. Not a lie, but a concealment. Where had he heard that before? He looked back at Tahamoh.

"I looked it up in the archives," he continued. "When Dialyas was cast from the Dar Kaadarith it caused much trouble."

Tahamoh waved his hand impatiently and then gestured.

"Here we are," he announced. "I knew there was something. There are one or two passages that are ambiguous, especially in the testament of Risatah."

Korfax frowned.

"Risatah? Dialyas has two murals set within the walls of the entrance way to his house. One is 'The Temptation', the other is 'The Gift'. Perhaps he has a reason for them other than the one he told to me."

He looked at Tahamoh.

"What have you found?" he asked.

"Here!" Tahamoh pointed. Korfax looked at the passage Tahamoh had indicated:

'Of latter years I have started to think that perhaps all furnaces are but one furnace, that all stones of the art are but one stone, and that all flaws are but the same flaw, reflections of the one truth given to us by The Creator.'

Korfax held his hands up in the gesture of dismissal.

"I know that passage," he said. "He is talking about sub-creation, the many acts that reflect the single act. It is a metaphor, nothing else."

But Tahamoh was not convinced.

"I don't know," he said. "It does possess a certain ambiguity, especially in the light of what Dialyas said..."

Korfax wagged a finger.

"No, I don't believe it! Who came first, Risatah or Dialyas? Dialyas has reinterpreted the past to suit the present. No one before Dialyas has ever given any other meaning to that particular passage. The Dar Kaadarith have always understood what Risatah meant by it. Besides, look at it in context."

"Yes, I know," said Tahamoh. "He talks about the many flaws containing the many principles. But where does he actually say that there are separate voids?"

Korfax took a deep breath to offer a rejoinder, but then he thought better of it. He drew out his own copy of the Logah Dar and skimmed through it. He started with the works of Risatah but then moved on to later writings.

"As I thought," he said eventually. "Look at the words of Heddor, Zamdia and Doarol. They are explicit on the matter."

"But Risatah was the first," Tahamoh countered. "There is a definite ambiguity here."

Korfax suddenly laughed.

"This is madness!" he said. "We have been acolytes for less than two years. We are not even close to becoming Geyad, let alone Geyadril, and here we are, questioning the very writ of the giants of the past. The words of Risatah have been known for thousands of years. Are we experts? Are we experienced? No, we are not!"

Tahamoh looked hard at Korfax.

"And what else did Dialyas say to you? Challenge all assumptions? What if it is all an assumption?"

Korfax got up to leave.

"I want nothing more to do with this," he said. Then he walked away.

It was later the next day that Tahamoh came to Korfax again.

"I want you to take me to see Dialyas," he said.

Korfax started. Tahamoh looked excited, enthused.

"Me?"

"I asked Matchir, but he said no."

"Matchir said no?"

"This is your fault," Tahamoh said. "You knew that I wanted to go, yet you refused to take me. Now you have set others against me."

"I have done nothing of the sort. What do you mean, it is my fault?"

"Apparently you debated with Matchir and the debate got out of hand. Nobody liked what you said."

Korfax took a long hard breath.

"I knew this would cause trouble," he said. "I knew I should never have gone to the Sal Kamalkar."

He turned now to look at Tahamoh.

"I only went because Dialyas invited me, because he knew my father. But he never spoke of that. All anyone there wanted to do was to prove to me how wrong the world is. I can't help it if they failed to do so."

Tahamoh looked angry now.

"You are my friend, so I ask you in the name of our friendship. You owe me this."

"I am not sure what you think this will achieve."

"Truth!" said Tahamoh. "I already have some of it. Now I want to know the rest."

"What do you mean?"

"I went down to the low archives and looked at the Kapimadar. I wanted to know about it."

"But it's a failure!"

"Is it?"

Korfax looked carefully back at Tahamoh.

"What have you done?" he asked.

"I touched it," said Tahamoh.

Korfax lowered his voice.

"That is not allowed," he hissed.

Tahamoh smiled.

"No one saw me. But now I know why it is forbidden. We have been lied to."

He leaned closer, his voice almost a whisper.

"Do you remember what happened when you first touched a stave? How singular it was?"

"Yes."

"This was utterly different. It was like standing in two worlds, not one. It was fleeting, a brief flash, but I saw so much."

"What?"

"I cannot say. I need to speak to Dialyas."

"Tahamoh, this is dangerous," Korfax told him. "He was thrown from the Dar Kaadarith for precisely this."

"I don't care," said Tahamoh. "I have to know."

Korfax stood in the hall of the Sal Kamalkar and waited for Tahamoh. Dialyas had not been pleased when they first arrived, but when he heard what Tahamoh had to say, he took him aside and told Korfax to wait.

So here he was now, standing in the hall, waiting, alone and silent. And as he waited, another walked out from one of the side doors.

She was not the tallest lady he had ever seen, but she made up for her lack of height with sheer presence, something she seemed to possess in abundance. She was not dressed as those of the Sal Kamalkar either, though her robes were just as plain, just as nondescript, but as soon as he saw her Korfax could not take his eyes away from her. It was almost as if she compelled him.

Her face was at odds with her figure, cold hardness set above sensuous curves. It was a strange combination. Though she was older, much older than he, Korfax found himself watching her, watching her curves as she swayed out into the hall, owning it and dismissing it in equal measure. Korfax felt himself impressed. He had seen few in the city to match her. She was certainly a commanding presence.

After a long moment he finally remembered himself enough to bow, and it was only as he lowered his head to her that he came to her attention at last. She looked at him in studied surprise, but then bowed her head in return, a slight tilt of the neck, before looking up again and running her sere glance over him. Korfax felt far from comfortable under that cold gaze.

A child of perhaps thirteen years stepped out from the same door to join the lady, but she kept her face downwards. Korfax guessed they were mother and daughter. There was a more than common resemblance.

Korfax met the eyes of the mother and all but caught his breath. Her gaze was inordinately powerful, as though she had suddenly filled the air between them with phantom knives, each stabbing at him through the stillness of the hall.

Dialyas emerged carefully from behind the lady, delicately insinuating himself between her gaze and that of Korfax, shielding him from her even as he broke the moment. He smiled crookedly at Korfax.

"Ah, Korfax, there you are! Tahamoh will be with you shortly."

He gestured to the others.

"You have not met my wife, or my daughter, or have you?"

"No," said Korfax. "I have not had the pleasure."

This time he tried a gentle smile. Dialyas smiled back but his wife and daughter did neither.

"May I present my wife, Naman Rom Ovuor."

Ovuor did not acknowledge the introduction, nor did her eyes move.

"And this is my daughter," said Dialyas, "Naman Pasrom Doagnis."

The daughter did not move either.

Korfax bowed to them both in turn.

"I am Faren Noren Korfax," he said.

For the second time the lady Ovuor looked surprised, but this time it seemed genuine, as though his name had caught her unawares. She laid a hand against her throat to cage her consternation and then looked hard at Dialyas, unspoken words writhing in her eyes. Finally she turned back to Korfax again, and her voice whipped through the air.

"You are Enay Sazaaim's son? Extraordinary! And what would the heir to the Salman Farenith be doing within these walls, I wonder?"

Dialyas answered before Korfax could open his mouth.

"He comes here to debate," he said. "And a most formidable disputant he is."

Having regained her composure, Ovuor stepped forward.

"How interesting! And do I surmise that you do not entirely agree with the precepts of the Sal Kamalkar, Faren Noren Korfax?"

There was a most seeing look to her now. Korfax gazed into the depths of her eyes and found himself caught within them, locked inside, alone and naked behind bright windows. It took all his self-control to put the feeling down and he was a moment in answering.

"No," he said, "I do not agree with any of its beliefs at all."

She suddenly smiled a cold smile and lifted her gaze back to Dialyas.

"Then you and I are allies, I think. I, too, disagree with much that is said here."

With that she walked smartly from the hall and out into the garden. Her voice came sharply back.

"Come, Doagnis. Attend your mother."

The child followed quickly, only daring a furtive glance back at Korfax. Korfax caught a brief glimpse of wide eyes and a face that was a simpler copy of her mother's, before she too was gone. The door into the garden closed and Dialyas coughed.

Korfax turned back as Dialyas approached, walking slowly, his head downcast.

But when he was within a pace, Dialyas lifted his head and stopped. There was a sad look to his eyes now and a wry smile upon his lips.

"Take my advice, Korfax," he said. "When you are eventually joined with another, make sure you fully understand the consequences."

Korfax gazed back to the closed door that opened upon the garden, his face colouring with embarrassment. He suddenly felt that he had stumbled upon some private tragedy, one that had never been intended for others. Then he heard Dialyas laugh darkly from behind. He turned around but Dialyas was already gone, and only the echo of his self-mockery remained.

Korfax left the house of the Sal Kamalkar with Tahamoh and together they walked back to the Umadya Semeiel. Korfax found a sense of uneasiness growing on him. Tahamoh was deep in thought and clearly did not want to talk, but Korfax felt something was wrong and he itched to enquire. Eventually it became too much.

"You're very quiet."

"I don't wish to talk."

"What's wrong?"

"Nothing."

Silence. Korfax looked at his friend for a moment and then, for want of something to ease the tension, he looked around. The path, the trees, the walls, all were unremarkable. The sky was clear and the air warm. He glanced behind. Someone was following them. Korfax turned fully and the figure disappeared. He nudged Tahamoh.

"There was someone behind us," he said.

Tahamoh turned.

"There's no one there now."

"They were there. They were following," Korfax insisted.

Tahamoh frowned.

"So they were following us. What does that matter? Besides, they obviously aren't very good at it because you saw them."

"But if they tell others where we have been..."

Tahamoh made the gesture of dismissal.

"That doesn't matter now," he said.

Korfax looked back at him. What did that mean? But Tahamoh kept his silence all the way back to the seminary. Korfax looked behind occasionally, but the follower did not reappear.

It was a few days later that the summons came. Korfax was to present himself before Paziba, first of the wardens, at the hour of Safaref. He felt the beginnings of fear. This was something to do with Dialyas, it had to be. He felt his heart sink at the prospect. He went to find Tahamoh to warn him, but he was nowhere to be found.

In the rooms of the first warden Korfax found himself under hard scrutiny. Paziba was tall and broad and powerful, intimidating at the best of times but especially so now.

"You have been visiting with the Sal Kamalkar, I hear, and have met with Dialyas on many occasions. Is this true?" he asked.

"Yes, Geyad," said Korfax.

"Have you any idea how serious that is? He was expelled, disgraced and even accused of heresy! Did you know that?"

"Yes, Geyad."

"You knew this and still you met with him?"

Korfax held himself very still. He could feel his heart beating against the walls of his chest, and it was a moment before he could speak.

"Yes, Geyad," he said. "But I wished to..."

Paziba held up his hand in the gesture of denial.

"Do not volunteer information, Korfax. Give me only what I ask for. I will decide what I need, not you."

Paziba lowered his hand again.

"How long have you been with us?" he asked.

Korfax swallowed and stared straight ahead.

"Nearly two years, Geyad."

Paziba stood up and paced around the table.

"Nearly two years, is it? Long enough to know what is expected of you then."

"Yes, Geyad."

"And in all that time how many other edicts of the seminary have you disobeyed?"

Korfax shot a frightened glance at Paziba. All he got in return was a burning glare. Even Paziba's eyebrows seemed to be on fire. He quickly looked away again. An image of his father came unbidden to his mind: enraged, closing in like a storm. He tried to calm himself so that he could answer.

"None that I am aware of, Geyad," he said.

Paziba glared a little longer and then returned to his chair. He sat back down and steepled his hands together, just under his chin.

"None that you are aware of!" he repeated. "What a careful answer that is!"

Paziba slammed a hand into the table. Korfax jumped.

"Then tell me why you 'consciously' broke this one?" he snarled.

Korfax swallowed again. What should he say? That he was invited? That would get Dialyas into trouble. That he was curious? That would get him into trouble. That Dialyas had known his father? He could only imagine the trouble that would cause. He thought of Matchir. That was where this had all started. But it was Tahamoh that had taken him to the house of Matchir. Everywhere he looked he saw consequences.

"Well, Korfax? I am waiting?"

Korfax tried to suppress an inner tremor of fear, but he found that he could not do so.

"Geyad, I had hoped to find fault with their arguments," he answered at last. Was his voice shaking? It certainly felt like it.

Paziba paused, looking down for a moment. Then he gazed back again, and the light in his eyes increased in intensity.

"And why would you want to do that?" he asked.

Korfax looked away again and thought furiously. He did not want to implicate Tahamoh. He turned back.

"Geyad, I thought their ideas were wrong and disrespectful both to the Velukor and to the Dar Kaadarith."

"Really?" pondered Paziba. "Is that so? You may believe that now, but what was in your mind when you first went to see Dialyas? Was it something else?"

Paziba leaned forward. Korfax kept his head down. Paziba tapped a finger upon the stone of the table.

"No answer? Then let me help you remember. What would you say if I told you that Tahamoh has left the seminary? He has returned to his family in Othil Homtoh in disgrace. I am told that you are the cause. What would you say to that?"

Korfax looked up in shock. Tahamoh was gone? Disgrace? He stared bleakly back at Paziba, who merely returned his stare with one of his own.

"Me?" Korfax asked.

"You!"

"But... why?"

"I have been told that you were the one that led him to the Sal Kamalkar. It was at your instigation that the edict was broken."

Korfax felt stunned. The lie was as brazen as it was bold.

"But I didn't. He was my friend, he asked to go."

"Are you saying that he instigated the meetings?"

"No, it was not like that."

Paziba pounced.

"No? Then how did this come about?"

The tale poured out. He had no choice. Paziba listened quietly, intently. Korfax did not mention everything, said nothing about the Kapimadar, but he did mention Matchir and the haven of antiquities, the invitation, Dialyas knowing his father, the debates that he had taken part in and their outcome. At the end, when he at last fell silent, Paziba sighed.

"Quite a story," he said.

He sighed again.

"Earlier today I spoke with Geyad Sohagel and Geyad Asakom. They both told me that you are one of their best, with a gift for discipline and attention to detail, qualities highly prized by the Geyadith. You work hard, are diligent and are very capable. Which makes this all the harder."

Paziba held up a dark stone in his hand. Korfax looked at it.

"Do you know what this is?"

Korfax could guess, though he had never seen one before.

"An angadar?"

"Yes," said Paziba. "It will show me the truth."

Korfax felt fear. Angadar were rarely used in such a manner. Mainly they were used to store thoughts and feelings, but occasionally they were also used to determine true intent. It was a measure of how serious this was that Paziba was considering using one at all. It was far more usual to employ a seer.

Korfax could not think. What was he to do? Angadar were indiscriminate. All sorts of things could be sucked out of his head if he submitted to this test. Besides, from what he had read, the process was said to be unpleasant.

He looked at Paziba.

"Do you submit?" Paziba asked.

"But I am telling the truth," Korfax insisted.

"And I have been told another tale."

Paziba drew himself up.

"Do not fool yourself that this is a small matter, Korfax, for it is not. An acolyte has left the seminary, and not because of failure. You have been accused of subversion, and the Erinilith are demanding justice. This matter is before the high council even as we speak, and I am to have an answer for them as soon as possible. So, do you submit to the examination, or do you wish me to pronounce summary judgement?"

Korfax could see where this was going now. If he did not submit he was to be ejected from the seminary. He was to be disgraced. He had no choice. He bowed his head.

"I submit," he said. "I am telling the truth."

Paziba pointed at the stone.

"Take up the angadar," he said, "and when I ask you a question, answer it immediately and as concisely as possible. Think only of your answers."

Korfax reached out and touched the stone. There was a curious sensation in the back of his mind now, as though something was waiting there.

"Did Tahamoh lead you to the haven of antiquities?" asked Paziba.

"Yes!"

A brief tugging sensation came and went.

"Did Matchir, the keeper of the haven of antiquities, invite you to the Sal Kamalkar at the behest of Dialyas?"

"He thought Dialyas wanted to meet me," Korfax answered.

The tugging sensation came again. It was longer this time.

"Why did you eventually go to the Sal Kamalkar?"

"Dialyas said that he had once been a friend of my father. I was curious."

The tugging sensation was accompanied by another, as though his father suddenly stood at his shoulder. He resisted the temptation to turn around.

"Do you subscribe to the views of the Sal Kamalkar?"

"No!"

Another brief tug, very fast this time, like the snapping of a twig.

"What do you think of Dialyas?"

The question threw him for a moment. All sorts of things tumbled through his mind – courtesy, gentleness, wit, humour and friendship.

"At first I liked him," Korfax said. "He was kind and courteous. He was gentle."

The tugging sensation came and went, slower, a roll of emotions. Dialyas the gentle, Dialyas the tempter, Dialyas the prideful. It was a curious feeling, like being sucked dry.

"Did you take Tahamoh to the Sal Kamalkar at his behest?"

"Yes!"

Not so much of a tug this time, more of a regretful release. A sense of betrayal went with it, fading away and down to nothing.

"Put the stone down," said Paziba.

Korfax did so, breathing hard. That had been difficult. Paziba watched him for a moment and then picked up the stone. He enclosed it in a fist and closed his eyes. He smiled and his expression was almost one of relief.

"Well, that is as clear as it can be. You are true. Your story stands."

He looked at Korfax.

"Ah, Korfax," he said, "you had us worried. You had us worried indeed. Let me tell you now that our concerns were severe."

He held up the angadar.

"But here is the truth of it."

He looked at the stone for a moment and scowled.

"The accusations against you will not stand. I do not know what lies at the back of this, whether it was honest misjudgement or malice, but as far as you are concerned your honesty and your loyalty to your friend have been noted, as has your distaste for the Sal Kamalkar."

Paziba gestured to the door.

"Come now, we are to go before the high council. You and I are summoned. They will want to know your story also."

Paziba took Korfax to the chamber of the high council. They did not pass many on their way, but those that they did stopped and stared. Korfax felt horribly and uniquely visible. When they reached the chamber they found another before them, barring their way. Korfax gasped. It was his father, and his face was the very image of fury.

"I am not pleased, Paziba," said Sazaaim. "I should have been told about this from the very beginning!"

Paziba took a step back, clearly intimidated. Korfax, though, wanted to run away and hide. His father fairly rippled with anger and force.

"I had no choice," Paziba said. "I was told to proceed with all due speed. This matter could not wait. The charges against your son were severe."

"But an angadar?"

"There was no time! But why the concern? Your son has been vindicated."

Sazaaim took a long hard breath, calming himself. Then he held out his hand.

"Give me the stone. I will see this for myself."

Paziba took a step back.

"But that is impossible," he said. "I was directed to give it straight to the council."

"At whose behest?"

"Geyadril Chirizar."

"As I thought," said Sazaaim. "He will answer for that. But first you will give the stone to me. I take precedence in this matter. I have already spoken with others on the council and they have agreed. Give me the stone, or both you and Chirizar will regret the day you were ever born!"

The threat blackened the air. Paziba was clearly shocked speechless. Reluctantly he handed over the stone. Sazaaim snatched it and crushed it in his hand, closing his eyes. There was a moment of pause and then he opened his eyes again. His expression gentled somewhat. He looked at Korfax.

"Good," he said.

He handed the stone back to Paziba.

"Now we may proceed."

Korfax waited outside the chamber. He was glad there was no one else about. He wanted to be alone. Standing outside the chamber of the high council was bad enough, but standing outside in the presence of others would make it far worse.

He had told the council his tale. They had all listened carefully and not a word had been said. He knew them all by name, but he had never met any of them before, so he could not put names to faces. But he could guess.

To the left sat Tonaon, Chirizar and Vatamath, to the right sat Ponodol, Samafaa and Zildaron, but in the middle sat Abrilon, standing in for Geyadel Gemanim. Behind him was his father, along with Paziba. To Korfax it felt as though he was at the bottom of a long dark well.

Standing before them was hard. Telling his story was hard. But watching their faces as he spoke was the hardest of all, for it was like staring up into unflinching judgement. When he had finished Geyadril Abrilon had inclined his head slightly.

"Leave us now and wait outside," he had said. "We must deliberate on what we have heard this day."

It was a long time before the door opened again. Some of the high council came out, walking slowly. None of them looked his way. Paziba came out, glanced briefly at Korfax and then went quickly off down one of the corridors. Then his father emerged with another of the high council, Ponodol. They bowed to each other and then his father came over to him. He was calmer now perhaps, but still not at peace. The anger remained. Korfax wondered what had been said and what had been decided.

"Come with me!" his father commanded.

Sazaaim took him to a small courtyard off the main corridor. There he turned on Korfax, his eyes blazing. The anger was back.

"Why would you do such a thing?" he demanded.

Korfax could not look up.

"I was curious."

"Curious?"

"Dialyas said that he knew you. He invited me."

"Yes, but you were told to stay away."

"But the edict says..."

"I know what the edict says. But you were told to stay away."

Sazaaim drew back and looked up at the sky.

"You have been cleared of all charges," he said. "I should also tell you that the use of the angadar was deemed regrettable. The services of a seer should have been sought instead."

Korfax felt himself breathe a little easier. He had been cleared of all charges. A weight was lifted, but then, in its place, others descended.

"What of Tahamoh?" he asked. "He was my friend."

"Hardly that," came the answer. "But he is gone. He has been withdrawn from the seminary, so you are to have no further contact with him."

Sazaaim looked sharply at his son.

"Do you hear me, Korfax? No contact."

"Yes, Father."

"I do not know exactly what occurred, but know that it was from his house that the accusations first came."

Sazaaim held up a hand in the gesture of warning.

"There will be trouble over this. There are many both here and in the west that do not look kindly on such things."

There was only one thing left to ask, and Korfax dreaded it, but he had to know.

"Dialyas said that you and he were friends once."

His father turned about.

"And that is the saddest thing in all of this. Whose testimony do you think was instrumental in his expulsion from the Dar Kaadarith?"

Korfax looked down. Dialyas had said nothing about that. His father stared at him for a long time and there was silence. Korfax endured the scrutiny as best he could. Then his father turned away.

"You have been noticed," he said, "so from this moment on you will keep your head down. I do not want to hear of anything like this ever again."

His father swept from the courtyard. Korfax stared after him. This was the first time he had seen either his father or his mother in more than a season. Rage and pain swirled inside. A tear rolled down his face and he wiped it away. Another followed and he brushed that away as well.

10

CONSEQUENCES

Zor-aisaa Iaman-sm-ias
Dial-pir-je Gah-korm-viupol
Von-ava Odbalt-imteo
Aud-orfen Pl-a-dr-pan
Koh-ippra Lanin-teosor
Oach-zurji Avna-injir
Ia-komaa Ip-chis-anooch

Paziba walked to the great temple on the Piodo Holk, lost in thought. He had not enjoyed this day. The seminary had lost one acolyte and nearly lost another, and his confrontation with Geyad Sazaaim still sat in his mind like a rumbling storm. Sazaaim's anger, the coiled power of it, had been a thing to behold. His demand for the stone had been irresistible. Only a Geyad Sazaaim might have been, but Paziba found himself wondering whether there were any others in the Dar Kaadarith that could match him at all.

Damn Chirizar! This was all his fault. If he had not ordered the use of the angadar none of this would have happened. But he had so ordered it, and what was Paziba supposed to do in the face of that?

Then of course there were the questions he was asked after Korfax had given his testimony. Why hadn't the wardens been more alert? Why had no one seen what was occurring? There were no answers that he could give. It was utterly unprecedented. No one had foreseen this. At least they had not lost Korfax. Paziba dreaded to think of the repercussions from that.

Thankfully it had all calmed down at the end. Sazaaim's anger had abated as his son was cleared of the charges, and everything would get back to what it had been. Now, though, he felt weary.

A voice called out to him from behind, stopping him in his tracks.

"Paziba! May the light of The Creator shine upon you!"

He turned and smiled at the tall and slim figure that had hailed him.

"Okodon!" he said. "I would know that voice anywhere. And it has been a very long time since I wished the light of The Creator to shine upon you also."

She smiled in return, stepping out into the light, wrapped about in the dark robes of the Balt Kaalith.

"Too long, I think!" she answered. "How is it with you, cousin?"

It took him a moment to reply.

"Not as good as it might be," he said. "If it wasn't for the trouble in the north, and in the seminary, things would be better than they are."

Okodon raised an eyebrow.

"The trouble in the north I know all about, all too well I think, but what could possibly trouble the seminary of the Dar Kaadarith?"

Paziba gestured to the temple gate.

"Let us do our duty within," he said. "Then, if you have the time, I will gladly share a cup of wine with you and tell you what I may. But only if you have the time, of course."

"I always have the time," she smiled. He turned away. "For you," she whispered in his wake.

They sat upon two carved stone seats by a window that looked out over the Piodo Holk. A low table squatted between them on which two long cups were set, along with a round bottle of pale blue crystal, half-filled with liquid darkness.

It was getting late and the wide square before them was now outlined in a gentler light. There was a glow to the air and the distant towers seemed to float on the evening mists.

"So tell me," Okodon asked, "what disturbs the seminary of the Dar Kaadarith?"

"The dark touch of heresy!" Paziba said.

"Heresy? In the Umadya Semeiel? Surely not again!"

Okodon leaned forward.

"And who has been speaking heresy this time?"

Paziba held up his hand in the gesture of denial.

"No one, but we have lost an acolyte nonetheless. We thought we had lost two, but the other was merely indulging his curiosity, ever a fault of youth."

Okodon leaned back again and frowned.

"Curiosity?"

"The Sal Kamalkar," came the answer.

"Dialyas?" she said. "But I thought there was an edict? Has that been broken?"

Paziba looked uncomfortable.

"Not as such," he said. "Think of it as a long slow slide of events, one merging with the next until the participants are in deeper than they intended. Unfortunately one of them became too enamoured of Dialyas and was ensnared."

"Who was it?"

"A young acolyte named Tahamoh."

"Tahamoh? Who is he? I do not know the name."

"He is the first-born son of the Salman Erinil."

"Ah, the Erinilith. I have heard of them. Are they not one of the newer houses to have risen up in the west?"

"They are."

"Then I am surprised that one of them has managed to gain entry to the Dar Kaadarith so quickly."

Paziba took another sip of wine and waved a hand in the air.

"Sometimes the young shoot is sturdier than the old. The Erinilith have proven themselves to be strong, so much so that they were recognised for it. And it is most certain that Tahamoh is strong, which makes his loss all the more vexing. But what complicates matters slightly is that the Erinilith have the support of Enay Yamandir."

"I understand completely," said Okodon. "The house of Sosatar once had both power and prestige."

Paziba agreed.

"They did indeed. But no more, alas! It has been many long years since any of its sons passed the doors of the Dar Kaadarith. Sosatar was once truly great, though they still have the respect of many. That weighs little in the scales of the Dar Kaadarith, though. One only enters our tower through merit. Now Sosatar hopes to regain what they have lost by an alliance with a younger house."

Paziba looked at his cup.

"It should not have happened, but I can see how it did," he said. "Dialyas is charismatic, amongst other things. If the friend had left well alone, none of this would have occurred."

"And who is this friend? I take it he still sits within the Umadya Semeiel?"

"May we be struck down if we ever lost that one!" Paziba exclaimed. "That would have been a sore blow indeed."

"Why?"

"Because the friend of Tahamoh was none other than Faren Noren Korfax!"

Okodon looked suitably impressed.

"The heir to the Salman Farenith? Now there is an unlikely union. Erinil out of Sosatar allied with the Farenith? Few houses are as strong as that one, or so they say! Small but potent, as it ever has been. And their loyalty is without question, or so I thought. Does the young Korfax entertain the notions of the Sal Kamalkar? Surely not!"

"Have no fear on that account," Paziba told her. "I assayed him myself. No, Korfax was told of his father's association with Dialyas, and so his curiosity was aroused."

"Sazaaim and Dialyas?"

"It was Sazaaim's testimony that caused Dialyas to be expelled."

"And how did Korfax learn of this association?"

"He was told of it by another, one Matchir, keeper of the haven of antiquities, whatever that might be."

"I have not heard that name before."

"Neither had I, but Korfax told me that it is hidden away on the third street of Neilis in the fourth circle. Tahamoh had heard of it, though. He was the one who told Korfax about it."

"An interesting turn of events then."

"You could say that."

Noqvoan Naaomir stared out of his high window and pondered.

"How did this happen?" he asked.

Okodon felt a little surprised at the question.

"Noqvoan? It happened as I said."

Naaomir looked back at her with a frown.

"No, that is not what I meant," he said. "I do not trust this tale. There is far more to this than you have said – of that I am certain."

"Do we move against the Sal Kamalkar?" she asked.

He turned around fully and walked back towards her.

"We should certainly pay them more attention than we have of late," he said, "but that is not what bothers me here. There is something wrong in this matter, something that does not make sense."

He looked down.

"That Dialyas still has influence enough to corrupt even one of the Dar Kaadarith is sad news, even if it is only an acolyte, but even that is not the issue here. What bothers me is that neither the Salman Erinilith nor the Salman Sosatar have demanded action of us."

He turned about and walked back to the window.

"Why were charges of subversion given to the Dar Kaadarith but not to us? It is our task to solve disputes, not theirs. At the very least we should have been consulted."

He clasped his arms behind him.

"And there is another thing," he said. "Who is this Matchir?"

"All I know is that he is keeper of the haven of antiquities," Okodon told him.

"And what is that?"

"It is a house on the third street of Neilis in the fourth circle."

Naaomir glanced sideways at Okodon.

"Do you know exactly which house?"

"No, I do not," she said.

"I wonder," he murmured.

"Noqvoan?" she asked.

"There is something I must look into," he told her, turning about.

"I shall take this report to Noqvoandril Uchanir. No doubt a watch will be put upon Dialyas, him and his followers, to make sure that this never happens again, but I doubt that it will."

"Could we not see if the law has been subverted?"

Naaomir made the gesture of dismissal.

"From what you say," he said, "Tahamoh went to the Sal Kamalkar of his own free will. It was his choice. Besides, this is not the first time we have duelled with Dialyas. His philosophies and those of the Sal Kamalkar are cunning. They are dissenters, skirting holy writ but hiding more than they reveal. They never openly oppose, and they dissemble when challenged. When the Dar Kaadarith ousted Dialyas, many wondered why he was not declared a heretic forthwith and duly banished. Then we discovered just how gifted he was. A towering intellect, but the foundations of his thought lie in fog and quagmire. They remain impenetrable. We are sure that even his followers do not know the heart of it. That is how Dialyas has managed to avoid banishment, by keeping just inside the law. No doubt he will avoid censure on this occasion as well."

"So what is it that you do not trust, Noqvoan?"

"The story, the way it happened. There is something awry here. You say there were accusations of subversion against Korfax?"

"Yes, but according to my cousin they were utterly unfounded."

Okodon waited as Naaomir pondered again. Then he raised a finger.

"The heir to the Farenith," he mused.

"Do you wish him watched also?"

Naaomir smiled.

"No, you mistake me. But this affair does bring him to our attention, and we would be remiss if we did not listen out for news of his progress. Remember that business with his father?"

Okodon stirred.

"Do you mean when he was to become Geyadril?"

"I do."

"But that was many years ago. And wasn't the thinking that Gemanim refused the position of Geyadril to Sazaaim?"

Naaomir was not so sure.

"That was the rumour, certainly. And whilst the Dar Kaadarith do not speak of the matter, a few of us are still not so sure that is the truth. Remember that Sazaaim married holy blood. Tazocho is cousin to the Velukor, the only one of two that remain. That one from the north should gain such prestige caused consternation in more than a few of the great houses of the faithful. Certainly Audroh Zafazaa was said to be furious over the matter, and there was even a rumour that he opposed it vigorously. I think, and I am not alone in this, that Sazaaim refused the position of Geyadril for precisely that reason. He did not wish to rise too far or too fast."

Naaomir stopped where he was.

"You said that Korfax was invited by this Matchir at the beginning?"

"I did."

"Find out all that you can of the affair, when it happened, how it happened and who was involved. Go back to before their arrival at the seminary, if you have to. Look for influences and confluences, but be discreet. Do not let anyone know what you are doing, and do not let it interfere with your other duties. Be mindful, though. This could be important. Meanwhile, I will look in the archives."

Naaomir duly took the report to Uchanir but said nothing concerning his doubts. Besides, Uchanir would be more interested in Dialyas anyway. To the Balt Kaalith, Dialyas remained unfinished business.

After delivering his report Naaomir went back to his room to continue his duties. To all intents and purposes his report to Uchanir was just that, one of many. Important, but not especially so.

At the end of the day he took himself to the archives and went to the shelves that housed reports from particular years. He wandered to and fro, reading the succinct commentaries one by one. There was something in the back of his mind, something that had been awoken, something heard or read, and he needed to find it again. He went through the reports on the expulsion of Dialyas. One of the witnesses called had been Sazaaim, which he had known. It was not common knowledge that Sazaaim had spoken out against Dialyas, but it was well-known in both the Dar Kaadarith and the Balt Kaalith. Next he found the report that described how Sazaaim would not become Geyadril as had been expected. He read it all the way through. Many in the Dar Kaadarith had been deeply upset by this, and the report detailed how isolated Geyadel Gemanim became because of it. Sazaaim was popular, highly regarded and had the favour of the Velukor.

He put the report back. That also was interesting, but it wasn't what he was looking for. He went further back, searching for reports upon the Farenith. The next he found detailed the joining of Sazaaim to Tazocho. He read through the report but found no mention of the opposition of Audroh Zafazaa at all, which was strange. Beside the report was a stone marker, indicating the place of a sealed report. The seal upon the stone was that of Laizid, predecessor to the current incumbent, Noqvoanel Vixipal.

His interest quickened. This was it. This was what he was after. He sat and thought, events clicking through his mind. Something had happened before the joining of Tazocho and Sazaaim, something that had incurred the wrath of Audroh Zafazaa, and it was of such a nature that a report had been sealed. Sealed reports were rare. He smiled. Now he could see his way. This stank of conspiracy.

Something had happened to create contention between Sazaaim and Zafazaa, and Zafazaa was not one to forgive or forget. For him it would become a matter of the blood. Vengeance. It was his nature. He would plot and plot until the right moment came.

Sazaaim, though, remained a difficult target, out of reach in the north. So what of his son? Now that Korfax was here, at the seminary of the Dar Kaadarith, Zafazaa could act at last.

Think on it. Tahamoh became the friend of Korfax, but Tahamoh was of the Erinilith, allied to Sosatar and favoured by Zafazaa. Zafazaa would know that Dialyas and Sazaaim were once friends, so why not direct Tahamoh to guide the son of his enemy into the arms of the disreputable? Though the accusation of subversion against Korfax was easily disproved, that was not the intent here. The Farenith were to be brought down, and how better to do it than by an association with heresy? The faults of sons were so often the regrets of fathers. The target here was Sazaaim, not Korfax. Dialyas was the one flaw in an otherwise flawless life. Guilt by association – that was how it worked.

It was tenuous, but Naaomir liked the progression. He now had two choices before him. He could petition the present Noqvoanel and so reveal his hand, or he could pursue the matter by other means. The answer was obvious. Advancement in the Balt Kaalith came from patronage or from initiative. Naaomir had no great house at his back; he had worked his way up through the ranks, so all he had was his initiative. Given the great houses that were involved, this affair, he was certain, would see him rise again.

Korfax waited alone outside the teaching room. He found that he preferred it that way. Ever since the departure of Tahamoh, life had become somewhat harder.

Harsh things were being said about him by many, especially those from the west. The loss of Tahamoh was being taken personally by more than a few, even some of the teachers. Omagrah especially had become cold and remote.

Of those closest to him only Thilnor remained unchanged. Korfax could talk to him. Indeed, he explained everything that had happened at the earliest opportunity and found Thilnor both sympathetic and understanding, but there was little that he could do or say in return. Things were as they were. Korfax asked him whether he had heard from Tahamoh, but he had not. Neither had Oanatom, but it was difficult to talk with Oanatom, as he was clearly uncomfortable being seen with Korfax at all. It was as though he had become tainted in some way. So rather than push the matter, he decided that he would remain alone.

"So, you are Korfax, are you not?"

Korfax turned about and found another acolyte standing over him, of the sixth level by his markings. Two others stood behind him, one at each shoulder. They both had expressions of concealed amusement upon their faces, but their leader did not. He merely looked scornful.

"I am," Korfax answered carefully.

"I hear tell that you are a heretic," said the other.

Korfax frowned.

"I am not," he answered hotly.

"But you have consorted with them."

Korfax kept himself still. No need to guess what this was about.

"No, that is not true," he said.

"But you went to the Sal Kamalkar!"

"They are not heretics."

"Do you defend them?"

"No, but if they were heretics they would not be allowed to remain in the city."

The other sneered.

"I am also told that you met with Dialyas. Are you aware that he was cast from the Dar Kaadarith?"

"My reasons for speaking with Dialyas are none of your concern," said Korfax.

"Anything that brings the Dar Kaadarith into disrepute is my concern! That is why you, and everything about you, is my concern. You should not be here. To walk where a heretic has trodden? To sit where one has sat? To talk with one? You are a poisoned thorn that should be pulled."

Korfax kept his silence.

"Have you no answer?" asked the other.

Korfax still would not speak. The other came closer, and there was now a threat in the air, a sense of violence. Korfax tensed.

Things might have taken a turn for the worse but it was at that moment that Asakom strode around the corner, shadowed by many more. The acolyte leaned closer.

"Just make sure that you keep out of my way, Korfax of the Farenith," he hissed. "If our paths ever cross again, you will regret it."

Then, with a swirl of his cloak, he walked quickly away, along with his two companions. Korfax remained where he was in stunned silence. He had not imagined such a turn of events at all.

"Korfax?"

He turned about to find Asakom behind him.

"Lost in thought?"

While Korfax tried to find something suitable to say, Asakom merely smiled and gestured at the door.

"Come! Stand aside now and let me open the door. After all, we cannot enter unless you let us."

As they went to their accustomed places Korfax turned to Thilnor.

"Did you see that acolyte just now?" he whispered.

"The one you were speaking to?"

"Yes, do you know who that is?"

"I think that was Simoref. Oanatom knows him slightly."

"Simoref?"

"Zadakal Noraud Simoref, surely you have heard of him?"

Korfax was shocked.

"The son of Audroh Zafazaa?"

"Yes, why?"

"He accused me of being a heretic."

Thilnor widened his eyes.

"Then I would keep out of his way, if I were you."

"But what have I ever done to him?" Korfax asked.

"The house of Sosatar has had the ear of the Audroh since the earliest days, and you know that the Enay of Sosatar blames you for what happened with Tahamoh. They take such alliances very seriously in the west."

"But that wasn't me – I had nothing to do with it!"

Thilnor made the gesture of unknowing.

"I know," he said. "But you were named in association with Dialyas, and that, I think, is all that they care about."

The voice of his father rang in his ears.

'There will be trouble over this. There are houses in the west that do not look kindly on such things.'

Prophetic words.

Korfax walked to the temple on the Piodo Zilodar. It was the turning of the hour of Ragaroel on the day of Adelparna, the one day set aside for prayer and contemplation, but it was not usual to be at worship so early. Korfax, though, had found it wise to change his daily routines to something a little more eccentric. If he kept himself scarce, he would keep out of trouble. And though he did not like to admit it, even to himself, it also meant that he could avoid Simoref.

He did not know what to do about Simoref, for Simoref had begun to take more than a simple interest in him. After the first confrontation he seemed to be everywhere, timing his appearances with worrying precision. He always found a way to contrive an encounter when there were fewest around, and he made the most of his opportunities, openly cursing both Korfax and his house.

Not for the first time he berated himself. He had brought this disapproval down upon his own head.

The halls of the Umadya Semeiel were never empty, but at the Siaon Lukal he could sit in silence with little fear of interruption. Perhaps a few others in the seminary chose this course of action as well, visiting this temple or that, but even so, none chose the Siaon Lukal, preferring instead the grander temples that sat upon the great highways, filling each vaulted hall a thousand strong.

Korfax had with him a number of logadar. He had started re-reading some of the old tales he had read when at Losq. He found them comforting. No doubt if some of the others knew that he liked to read such stories they would make it their business to spoil one of the few remaining pleasures he had left to him. So rather than spend all his time in prayerful meditation, he combined pleasure and duty by contemplating some of the more mystical tales.

He fingered one of the stones in particular. In it were tales from the dim and distant past, myths and legends, tales breathed to life by Faminor, a master storyteller. Today he would read one of his favourites, the tale of 'Endril and the

Great Gyre'.

That the great gyre existed at all was a mystery, and the only time a sky ship had verified that it did in fact exist was many, many years ago. Nor had anyone repeated the journey, for it was a voyage fraught with the utmost peril.

The great sea did not give up its secrets easily, and the sky ship had encountered many dangers, not least of which was the eternal storm, a permanent barrier about the still and ominous calm of the great gyre. But they had eventually breached the walls of wind and water, cloud and lightning, and so came upon the gyre itself, where they had stared down in awe at its terrible immensity, turning for ever about its dark centre, sucking the ocean down into a mighty hole that dropped away into impenetrable darkness. The sky ship had not remained long, only long enough for her crew to catch their breaths before chancing again the immense storm that boiled about them. And so they had returned with the loss of nearly all on board and the wrecking of the sky ship, but all they brought back with them were questions, for no one knew what the great gyre was. A few speculated that some engine, some vast power deep within the world, had taken the great ocean in its fist and then turned it about its dark axis. Others said that it was The Creator's mark upon the waters, much as the Rolnir was said to be The Creator's mark upon the land. But no one knew, not really.

Korfax walked down the narrow lane that led to the temple. Usually the lane was empty at this time of day, but as he approached the temple he thought he could see someone ahead, lying against the wall. Korfax stopped and stared. Were they hurt? Were they ill? But even as he went to find out, an arm was raised up and a bottle was waved to and fro. The sound of dim singing came and went. They were drunk!

Korfax had seen this more than a few times in Leemal upon the long road – a night of hard drinking followed by a painful awakening. It was one of those odd traditions he had never quite grasped, and though a common enough sight in Leemal, he had never seen anything like it in Emethgis Vaniad. He walked carefully around the prone body.

"Greetings to the pair of you."

He turned about. The body was up on its feet. Whoever they were, they were quite young, perhaps even the same age as Korfax. Korfax noted a dark skin, a lopsided smile and a red cloak. This one appeared to be an acolyte of the Nazad Esiask. That being the case, he would be in trouble if any found him in this state. Those studying the Namad Alkar were not allowed the fruit of the vine. It was explicit.

The acolyte came over and rested an arm on Korfax's shoulder, looked straight into his eyes, looked elsewhere, then back again.

"Where did your companion go?" he asked, frowning.

"My companion?"

"Yes, there were two of you. I saw him."

Korfax did not know what this one had been drinking, but he stank of it. Heady fumes rode the air. Korfax disengaged himself and stood back a pace.

"I think you should find somewhere to hide," he said. "If they find you like this, you will be in trouble."

"I don't like them," the drunk said, waving his free hand in the air. The other still clutched its bottle. He looked at Korfax.

"I think I like you," he announced. "You seem to be a caring soul."

Korfax moved away.

"I have to visit the temple," he said.

The other stayed where he was, swaying as though caught upon a breeze.

"Is there anything to drink in there?" he asked. "I'm almost empty!"

He held up his bottle and waved it back and forth.

"I really think you have had enough," Korfax told him. "You should get off the streets. You will be in trouble if anyone else finds you like this."

Korfax continued on his way, conscious all the while of the other watching him go. He felt the stirrings of guilt as he walked on. This day, more than any other, was a day for service, service to The Creator, service to those in need of it. Perhaps he should have helped the drunk. But how?

Just as he came to the temple square, someone grabbed him from behind, and before he knew it he was being dragged down a small pathway between high walls.

"So here we are again!" came a voice.

He was thrown against one of the walls. There were three others standing over him. His heart sank. It was Simoref, along with his followers, Solfaia and Zanbal.

"I told you what I wanted, Faren, so I can only assume that this is wilful disobedience on your part."

Korfax pushed himself away from the wall only to find himself pushed back again. Both Solfaia and Zanbal were smiling.

"What are you talking about?" Korfax asked.

"I told you to stay out of my way!" Simoref retorted.

"Not an easy thing to do when you insist upon following," Korfax said.

"I am following you?" mocked Simoref. "I don't think so. My place is here. Yours is not!"

"My place is here also."

"No, I don't think that it is. You are a heretic."

"I am not."

Simoref was about to reply when he was rudely interrupted by a hand pushing him away. It was the drunk.

"Leave my friend alone," said the drunk. "He was showing me where I could find another drink."

He turned and peered at Solfaia.

"I don't know you, do I?"

Simoref grabbed hold of the drunk and threw him aside.

"How dare you touch me? Be gone with you!"

The drunk tumbled to the floor and rolled. Simoref looked down in disgust.

"Shameful!" he said, turning back to Korfax. "Your choice in friends does not improve, it seems. First the disreputable and now the dissolute!"

Korfax tried to leave again, but Solfaia and Zanbal grabbed hold of him. They pushed him back against the wall once more. Korfax stared at them both.

"Let me go!"

"Not until you learn your place, heretic," said Zanbal.

There was a cry of pain. Simoref was on the ground, holding his head. The drunk had struck him with his bottle. Both Solfaia and Zanbal left Korfax to intervene, but then the drunk put them down as well, with two well-placed kicks. Drunk or not, this one could fight. Simoref stood up again and received a hard punch to the face. Solfaia and Zanbal tried the same and were put down once more in short order. Soon, Simoref, Solfaia and Zanbal were all lying on the road, clutching their heads or their stomachs, depending on which hurt the most. The drunk stood over them, pointing at each in turn with his bottle.

"And let that be a lesson to all seven of you," he announced. "If there is one thing I cannot abide, it is violence."

He turned to Korfax and held the bottle up in the air once more.

"I don't suppose you know where I can get another one of these, do you? This one has been in a fight."

Korfax grabbed him and pulled him away. Perhaps it was time to do them both a service.

"Come with me," he said. "I know just the place."

"Wonderful!" announced the drunk. "You are the best friend anyone could possibly ever have ever!"

Korfax took his charge back to the seminary. It seemed the safest thing to do, and by the time he had arrived his drunken companion had quietened into a somewhat more tractable state and did exactly what he was told. Korfax covered him with his robe and led him through the gates and into the tower. No one gave them a second glance. As far as they were concerned it was just another pair of acolytes.

Korfax was fortunate that it was still early in the day. Few were around, so getting his new-found friend to his room was easier than it might otherwise have been. The only thing he could think of was to keep him out of the way until he sobered. It would also be better to keep out of the way of Simoref as well, though after the beating he had taken he imagined Simoref would be lying low also.

He laid the drunk upon his cot and watched him sink down to sleep. Given the darkness of his skin he was clearly from the south, but beyond that Korfax had no idea who he was. He watched for a little while and then sat down in his chair, looking out of the window.

What was he going to do about Simoref? It was getting out of hand. Simoref was making his life a misery. Perhaps he should tell one of the wardens or one of the teachers, Asakom for instance, but he was reluctant to do so. His father had told him to keep his head down, and this would only cause more trouble. But he had to do something; otherwise, who knew what Simoref would do next.

He took out his logadar, the one with the tales of Endril, and awoke it. He stared at the words but could not concentrate. He sat and he thought, and his thoughts circled around his head as though caught in the great gyre itself.

Midday came and went. Korfax went for his meal, and when he returned he found his guest finally risen. Korfax watched as he looked around blearily, moving his tongue about his mouth as though thoroughly dissatisfied by the taste.

"I don't suppose there is anything to drink, is there?"

Korfax gestured to the water room.

"There is water," he offered simply.

His guest grimaced.

"Water? Have I wilted? Do I need watering? Do I look in need of rain? No! I meant a real drink!"

Korfax raised his eyebrows as he met the other's glower.

"A real drink?"

"Wine, you dullard!"

Korfax opened his mouth and closed it again. Now that he had sobered a little, his guest had seemingly lost his manners.

"Wine?" he returned quietly. "In the seminary of the Dar Kaadarith?"

The other turned about and looked all over the room again.

"I am in the Umadya Semeiel?"

Korfax gestured at the walls in reply. His guest grimaced and then slumped back onto the cot.

"Gods below!" he declared as he stared at the floor for a moment before turning back to his host.

"And whose hospitality am I accepting today?"

"This has happened before?"

"It has not been unknown. So, who are you then?"

Korfax suppressed a frown as he stood up and bowed. Yes, this one needed a lesson in manners.

"Faren Noren Korfax," he said.

Now it was his guest's turn to raise his eyebrows.

"You are of the Farenith?"

"Yes, I am. So who are you?"

"Badagar Nor-Tabaud Ralir."

Korfax started. That was the house that ruled the south. All of it. This Ralir belonged to one of the most powerful families in all the world.

"Badagar?" he asked.

"Yes!" said Ralir. "Badagar! What of it?"

Korfax looked warily at his guest.

"You are a son of the house of Badagar?"

Ralir breathed deeply and looked heavenward for a moment. He then cast a sceptical eye back at Korfax.

"Yes!" he said. "The house of Badagar! Look, I thought you of the Dar Kaadarith were supposed to have quicker wits than this. I thought I was slow in the morning, but you seem to crawl whereas I sprint. How many times do I have to say it! I am of the house of Badagar!"

Korfax took a deep breath.

"Well," he said, "for one thing it is not morning; it is well past midday. For another you are rather a surprise. I suppose I am just not used to finding the son of such a great house in the gutter!"

Ralir looked down again.

"That was where I was?"

Korfax stood up and walked to the window.

"Somewhat, or at least that is where you started!" he said. He looked over his shoulder at Ralir. "And you were singing."

Ralir screwed up his mouth.

"Ah!" he said. "Singing! Yes!"

He looked back reluctantly at Korfax.

"And what was I singing?"

Korfax smiled faintly.

"'I have set my feet in the South', I think. The words were difficult to make out, but the tune was there, most certainly."

Ralir ran his hands through his hair.

"'I have set my feet in the South'?"

He looked down.

"That cannot be. That is the last thing I would be singing!" he said.

Korfax smiled unkindly in return.

"Well, I am sorry to say that you were."

Ralir stared at the floor.

"Why in the name of all the stones would I be singing that?" he asked. "I hate it!"

He stood up, somewhat painfully. He winced.

"I seem to be bruised," he said.

He looked at Korfax.

"Was I in a fight?"

Korfax smiled. He could still see the image in his mind – Simoref, Solfaia and Zanbal all lying on the floor and Ralir standing over them, waving his bottle in the air.

"Yes, you were," he said. "I am not sure I should tell you who it was, though."

Ralir thought for a moment.

"Did I win?" he eventually asked.

"Yes."

"Well, that's all that matters then."

Korfax looked down.

"It may not. You fought with Simoref, son of Audroh Zafazaa. You also fought with his friends, Solfaia and Zanbal. I think they were in some pain when you were done."

Ralir scratched his ear and looked at Korfax.

"Simoref?"

Then he frowned.

"Wait, I remember something."

Now he stared at Korfax as if he had just seen him for the very first time.

"Were they attacking you?"

"Simoref does not like me," Korfax explained. A look of delight crossed Ralir's face.

"You have enmity with the house of Zadakal?"

"So it seems."

Ralir laughed.

"And I intervened?"

"Yes, you did. You hit Simoref over the head with your bottle."

Ralir laughed again, and then kept on laughing. Korfax was bemused by this for a moment, but then started laughing, too. Ralir's laugh was infectious. Both of them ended up laughing for a very long time. When they were done Ralir looked happily at Korfax.

"So tell me what happened. Tell me the whole story."

He did not know why, but Korfax suddenly felt an immense upwelling of trust for this Ralir, so he told him all of it, even explaining about Tahamoh and Dialyas. By the end of the story Ralir was looking at Korfax with shining eyes.

"Dialyas, is it? Well now! It must be fate!"

"Fate? Whatever do you mean?"

"A tale for another time, I think."

He looked down for a moment, pondering perhaps, and then smiled back at Korfax.

"But the first thing I must do, the very first thing, is to thank you."

"Thank me?"

"For taking me in and letting me sleep it off. No doubt if I had been found by another they would have taken me back to the Umadya Madimel and I would have been disciplined. That would have involved my father, and I am already in enough trouble with him as it is."

"But you saved me. I should thank you," countered Korfax.

Ralir smiled.

"No," he said, "that part was easy. It's what I do best."

He looked back at Korfax.

"So I hit Zadakal Noraud Simoref over the head with a bottle, did I?"

"Yes!"

He laughed again for a little while.

"I don't know how this is dealt with in the Dar Kaadarith, but in the Nazad Esiask I would involve one of our wardens. You should speak to someone, someone you can trust to do the honourable thing. I will confirm your story."

"But you were drunk!"

Ralir smiled.

"We won't tell them about that."

"But Simoref will."

"Then I will call him out, a duel, bottles at dawn."

Korfax peered intently at Ralir.

"You would do this?"

"Yes," he said. "I know what it is to be held in contempt. Sometimes it is good to fight back."

"You are held in contempt? Why?"

"I am not of a fighting house. I am often told, especially by those of the west, that I will never be a sword, that I will always be a merchant, no matter how good I am with a blade. And that is what rankles, I think. I am better than all of them, and they know it. Even my instructors know it."

"Not of a fighting house? Does that matter?"

"In the Nazad Esiask everything matters," Ralir answered, and then he sighed.

"I am of Badagar," he explained. "We are merchants. That is what my father wanted for me, but I would not have it. He wanted me to join the Prah Sibith. Commerce? Trade? I loathe it! My only joy is the sword."

"You rebelled against your father's wishes?"

"Yes, he and I are not on good terms at the moment."

He looked meaningfully at Korfax.

"Rather like you, it seems."

Korfax looked down.

"I would it were not so."

"So do many," Ralir said, offering up a short, sharp laugh of derision.

"There is an answer, of course," he said. "You should learn to drink. It makes the world a brighter place."

"It makes the world a brighter place?" Korfax asked.

Ralir looked back darkly.

"Sometimes the loneliness and the hostility get the better of me. How do you face it?"

Korfax looked away.

"I turn my back upon it," he said.

Ralir frowned.

"That will never do," he said. "Never turn your back on anything. Confront it. Someone should teach you how to fight. There were only three of them, none of them skilled. I should never have been able to put them down armed only with a bottle."

"I learnt some swordplay when I was at Losq," Korfax told him, "but there has been little chance of continuing it here."

Ralir stood up.

"Then I shall teach you, and not just swordplay."

He grinned.

"I consider it my solemn duty," he continued. "By the time I am done with you, you will be able to take on entire armies armed with nothing more than your bare hands."

"I am not sure what my teachers would think of that."

"We won't tell them about that, either."

Ralir stretched.

"But first, though, let us do something about Simoref. Come. Take me to someone in authority here, someone you can trust to do the right thing. I think it is time for a little justice. The prestige of my house must be good for something."

Korfax led Ralir to Asakom. Asakom was a little surprised to be confronted with the Nor-Tabaud of Badagar, but when he heard what Ralir had to say he was furious. He looked long at Korfax.

"Simoref has been attacking you? Why did you not say so immediately?"

"I had hoped it would not continue, Geyad," Korfax said.

Asakom gestured to the door.

"With me, the pair of you. This must be set before the first warden."

They went to Paziba, and Asakom let them tell their tale. Paziba looked as though he wanted to be anywhere but listening to this, but with Asakom standing over him he had no choice.

Simoref was duly summoned and asked to give an account of himself. His story, not surprisingly, was markedly different from that of Korfax. Ralir laughed long and loud when he heard what Simoref had to say.

"This fiction would not fool a child," he said. "That is not what happened at all."

Simoref sneered back at him.

"And I will not be mocked by a liar and a drunk!"

Ralir stepped up to Simoref and looked him straight in the eye.

"That cannot be borne," he said. "Such slurs, especially from a coward, demand an answer. I will have satisfaction. I call you out upon the field of combat."

Simoref went very still.

"I am not of the Nazad Esiask," he said.

"Then name someone to fight in your stead. Name anyone, I do not care. But you will not stand here and call me a liar."

Paziba held up a hand.

"This has gone far enough. You are acolytes, all of you. None of you shall say what shall be."

Ralir turned sharply about.

"But in the Nazad Esiask such words as these would be met with an instant response."

"But this is not the Nazad Esiask! This is the Dar Kaadarith. You would do well to remember it."

"Then do your duty, Geyad!" demanded Ralir. "Call a seer! Discover the truth! Unlike you I do not shake in fear in the presence of the house of Zadakal!"

Korfax stared at Ralir, utterly amazed. He seemed completely fearless. Paziba, eyes blazing, would have answered, but then Asakom held up his hand in the gesture of division.

"Enough of this, all of you. There is only one matter of concern here. Korfax has made accusations against Simoref, Simoref has made accusations against Korfax and Ralir has vouched for Korfax. That is all we need to consider. I think Ralir's suggestion a good one. We call upon the services of the Exentaser and let a seer determine the truth of the matter."

Ralir smiled.

"I have nothing to hide," he said.

Simoref swallowed hard. He was trapped.

"I withdraw my accusations," he said.

Asakom scowled darkly at Simoref.

"Then I am very disappointed. You have achieved the sixth level, Simoref. I expect better than this from such as you. So here is my judgement. From this point forward you will have nothing more to do with Korfax. You will leave him alone and make no further accusations against him or his house. Korfax has already been exonerated by the high council in the affair concerning Tahamoh, so your continued enmity is in direct contravention of our word. We take a very dark view of such things in this place, so go now and think long and hard upon your vows of service."

Simoref turned to leave.

"One more thing," said Asakom.

Simoref turned back and waited.

"Tell any others that are of like mind that the next time anything like this comes to my attention there will be serious consequences."

Asakom then turned on Ralir.

"Now you will apologise to the first warden for your remarks."

"Of course, Geyad."

He bowed low to Paziba.

"I regret my words and the offence they may have caused, but I was concerned only for my friend. I desired justice for him. My fear was that he would receive none."

Paziba took a long, hard breath and inclined his head ever so slightly. The apology was clearly nowhere near as full as he would like it to be, but there was nothing he could do. Asakom was still present, and Asakom clearly sided with Korfax and Ralir. Apology given, Ralir turned smartly about and left the room. Asakom looked at Paziba.

"Now, I think we should go back to whatever it was we were doing before this matter came to our attention. Let no more be said upon it."

He left also, leaving just Korfax and Paziba. Korfax turned to go but Paziba held up his hand.

"A moment, Korfax."

Korfax waited.

"You have a talent for choosing troublesome friends, it seems."

Korfax said nothing in reply.

"This is twice now that you have appeared before me. I am wondering whether to send a message to your father. There is a rumour I have heard that there is contention between him and Zafazaa. Do you know anything about that?"

Korfax was shocked. Contention between his father and Zafazaa? That was a surprise.

"No, Geyad," he said. "I do not."

Paziba looked hard at him for a moment.

"No, I am sure that you don't."

He took another deep breath.

"Your father enjoys his secrets far too much, I think."

Here it came again. Secrets! Korfax decided that he did not like what he was hearing. What else might be stirred up by this? He would have left, but Paziba clearly had more to say.

"Well, perhaps it is best that we say as little as possible on this matter from this moment forward. Let everything return to what it should be."

He paused a moment.

"I also think it best that you do not appear before me again. Ever! That is all."

Korfax walked from the room feeling that he was the one that had transgressed, not Simoref.

The seasons turned and turned again: Izirakal to Axinor, Axinor to Lamasa and then Lamasa to Adzinor. Now every day was so bright that everything looked black against the sky. The towers gleamed and the roads sparkled. The wide parks of the second circle were filled with people, lords and ladies of the court, children of the noble houses, members of the great guilds, all taking their ease in the shade of the many trees or yet walking slowly along the cool avenues in between.

Each day was like the next, as was each night. Great Rafarel travelled alone across a cloudless sky, followed each time, without fail, by fair Gahburel. And only in its waxing and waning was the passage of time seen at all.

Ralir kept his word to Korfax and taught him all the ways of battle that he knew. In return, Korfax tried to teach Ralir something of the Namad Dar, but Ralir had little ability in that direction. Certain mental disciplines, though, not taught by the Nazad Esiask, he did find useful, especially ways of stilling the mind, a floating awareness that promised an increase in his abilities, particularly with those of the sword.

They became firm friends but were as unlike each other as any two friends could be. Ralir was always of the moment. He never thought of the past or the future, only of the now. With him it was eat, drink and be merry, and usually the last two in abundance. Korfax despaired of it occasionally, especially if Ralir drank too much, and he wondered what lay at the back of it, but Ralir never spoke of anything unless he could make a jest out of it.

After one particular duelling session, as they lay upon the grass in the private courts of Bathrin, Ralir caught an odd look in Korfax's eyes. He leaned over and prodded his friend with the tip of his practice sword.

"So what has got you thinking now? Surely not that last move I used to disarm you with?"

Korfax sat up.

"No," he said, "not that. I was wondering, though. Are we doing a proscribed thing here – me teaching you about the Namad Dar and you teaching me the Namad Alkar?"

Ralir looked a little surprised.

"Proscribed? You worry about that after all that has happened?"

"What do you mean?" asked Korfax.

"Tahamoh? Dialyas? The Sal Kamalkar?"

He leaned in closer.

"Me striking the son of Zafazaa over the head with a bottle?"

Korfax smiled.

"Those have already happened. This is still happening."

Ralir shrugged.

"Then, to answer your question, I don't think so. Nothing in the precepts of the Nazad Esiask disallows such a thing. Each guild can be very jealous of its inner lore, but neither of us is passing on such things to each other. Besides, I am not a Napei and you are not a Geyad. I would guess that there are secrets that you are only told once you have attained your stave, just like the ones I will be told once I earn my sword."

Korfax lay back and stared at the bright vault above. A sky ship drifted across his sight, high up and alone. The only other thing in the heavens was Rafarel itself. He watched the light catch upon the unfurling wings of the sky ship, a series of brilliant flashes, one after the other, as it went ever faster on its way. He watched it vanish into the distance, a fading sliver of brightness. He leaned over to look at

Ralir.

"I have never been told not to do it, either. But you are right. The guilds can be very jealous. There is a certain rivalry, I think. I was just wondering what our masters would say if they knew."

Ralir laughed gently.

"We won't tell them!"

Korfax stared at Ralir, his face suddenly complex.

"In the Nazad Esiask you do not have to guard your thoughts. In the Dar Kaadarith it is a different matter entirely."

Ralir looked back coolly.

"But they must have something specific to look for. At least you are not in the Exentaser."

Now it was the turn of Korfax to laugh.

"Then you would really be in trouble! That is especially prohibited."

Ralir grinned in return.

"Very true, but what I meant was that there is usually more than one way of obeying the spirit of the law, even whilst skirting its intent!"

Korfax looked shocked and Ralir grinned even wider.

"Oh don't look so scandalised," he said. "Visit with me at the courts of Badagar, and you will soon change your mind."

His expression suddenly soured.

"They deny me nothing," he said, "except for the very thing that I want."

Korfax watched his friend, puzzled by the sudden change in his demeanour.

"What do you mean?" he asked.

"Nothing," came the reply. Ralir raised himself from the ground and stretched.

"It is time to be going," he said. "I have a lesson I must attend."

He walked off and Korfax followed, wondering again what had disturbed his friend.

It was as he was crossing the Piodo Gellin that a salutation stopped him.

"Well now, if it isn't Korfax of the Farenith! May the light of The Creator shine upon you."

Korfax turned and looked behind him. He stood back in shock. Dialyas was standing there.

"And may the light of The Creator shine upon you also," he answered carefully.

Dialyas smiled. To Korfax, he seemed both older and younger. His face looked more careworn, but his eyes sparkled with youthful energy.

"You look well," Korfax offered.

"I am well, thank you. And you have the makings of a fine Geyad about you. I see the beginnings of power stirring in that youthful frame of yours."

Korfax looked for double meaning, but there was nothing of which he could be certain. Dialyas, as ever, had managed to put him off balance. He waited to see what Dialyas would say next, but Dialyas just smiled warmly at him and gestured towards a narrow street that led off from the Piodo Gellin.

"I was on my way back home, but when I saw you I found myself wondering whether you would care to join me for some refreshment?"

Korfax looked nervously about and Dialyas's smile widened.

"Do not worry, Korfax," he said. "This is no den of iniquity to which I would lead you. I merely offer my company and the chance of good conversation. I find that I miss our debates together."

Korfax stayed where he was.

"I was told not to seek out your company."

"But you haven't. This is a chance meeting. Besides, I have been shackled also. I must not speak of the Sal Kamalkar in public, and we are in public, you and I."

Korfax dropped his head.

"I am not sure others would draw that distinction."

"What do you mean?"

"I was nearly dismissed from the Dar Kaadarith, did you know that? That was when I learned of the choices that lay before me – to consort with heresy or to continue my calling. I chose to continue my calling."

Dialyas narrowed his eyes.

"You have changed," he said. "What has happened to the quiet and deferential youth I once knew?"

"I have had to travel a far harder road because of you!"

"Ah, now I see it. You have discovered yourself within the hierarchy. No doubt those above you still receive your deference but pity those below. They receive nothing but your scorn, I think."

Korfax felt the heat rise in his face.

"You are wrong," he said. "I have been told to keep my head down. I have received nothing but scorn from many at the seminary. This year has been hard and I have had to adapt. Change has been forced upon me."

He leaned forward a little to emphasise his point.

"I lost a friend because of you. Tahamoh is gone."

"And I dared dream that we could still talk, you and I," said Dialyas.

"If you would like us to talk together then perhaps you should listen more carefully to what I say."

"I listen, of course I do!"

"And what of Tahamoh? What of my troubles? Have you nothing to say of that?"

"Only that which is worthy is born of pain. Your experiences will serve you in the days yet to come."

"What a comforting thought. I must remember to tell myself that every day from this moment forward."

"You know, listening to you now I think that we are almost two halves of the same being."

"Two halves?" asked Korfax. "I am honoured. Or am I? So which half has me? Am I the Saq or am I the Urq?"

"No, Korfax, no!" exclaimed Dialyas. "What makes you say such a thing? That is not what I meant at all! I was only contrasting our lives. We have both become outsiders, it seems."

"Ah, yes, the shared covenant of misery. But I am clearly not your equal, so what am I then? Your echo?"

"Korfax, please! You are deliberately misunderstanding me. That is not what I meant at all. I was merely offering a contrast of aspects. You have all your time before you."

Dialyas smiled.

"When I was young," he continued, "my imagination spread out from me like two great wings. But when my wings were clipped by the powers that I served, it all gradually contracted to a fist. Looking at you now I am wondering whether you have not already assumed that condition."

Korfax scowled.

"So now I am reduced to a mind's tool, am I? A mere appendage?" He half turned away. "Play your games as you wish. I, for one, have had enough of them. I am innocent no longer, and neither am I a toy for your amusement."

Dialyas dropped his smile.

"How like your father you have become. At the end he spoke to me much as you are doing now. The son becomes the father, or so it is said."

"So that is it," Korfax hissed. "You cannot berate my father, so you berate me?" The anger rose up; he could not help it. "This was a mistake. I knew it in my heart even as you called out to me. I should have walked on by but I did not, even after all that has occurred. Another hard lesson to be learned, or so it seems."

Dialyas looked down.

"Such bitterness in you now, and you are still so young."

"But that is the point, isn't it?" Korfax returned. "I am young. What do I truly know of the world, or the Namad Dar? Yet you insisted that we debate. You lavished praise upon me and I was pleased. But then I learned my lesson, even whilst I was nearly disgraced. So here I am again, still the plaything of the great Dialyas. Why is that, I wonder? Could it be that the mighty Dialyas can only duel with his intellectual inferiors? What if the Geyadel stood here now? Would you dare your theories on him? Could you even?"

Now it was the turn of Dialyas to become angry.

"How dare you! None of them equalled me, none of them at all. I remember Gemanim. I remember Abrilon. I remember all of them. None of them could see the truth, not even those that shared my vision at the beginning. There were four of us: myself, your father, Ponodol and Virqol. We had the proof, in our hands, the Kapimadar. But I was betrayed. The others left me, even though they could see it there, right there in front of them. They denied what they had achieved and sought refuge in dogma instead. They are hollow, all of them."

Korfax turned away.

"I was right! This is about revenge, isn't it? You blame my father!"

Dialyas took a step back, a sudden look of horror on his face as though he had gone too far.

"No!" he cried. "Never that! All I ever desired was restitution! All I ever desired was justice! Don't you see that?"

"You are right and the rest of the world is wrong?" Korfax mocked. "We have had this conversation before. My answer remains. The prideful ever lock the doors to their towers."

Dialyas shook a finger at Korfax.

"But you know that I am right! You know what Tahamoh did. I know that he told you! He has accepted what your father denied."

Korfax pulled his cloak about him.

"Do not dare ask me to choose between you and my father! There is no choice. We have nothing more to say to each other."

There was a fire in his eyes now, and his mouth had become a thin and hard line. He turned his back on Dialyas and strode away, back towards the Umadya Semeiel.

Out of the shadows of a pillar opposite, a face looked up to watch him. Then it watched carefully as Dialyas made his weary way in the opposite direction. The face waited until Dialyas was out of sight, then it followed after Korfax.

Korfax sat in his room until he could bear it no longer. He would go out. He was tired of the anger that coiled inside him and would not lie down. He would go out, walk and calm himself.

He left the Umadya Semeiel and went out to the third circle. He stared up at the heavens as he went. The lights of the city made the glories of the night sky less than they had been at Losq, but it was still a splendid sight. He walked to a nearby square, the Piodo Heifal, where he could sit beneath the trees and stare up at the sky in relative darkness.

As he crossed the road to enter the square, a shape emerged from the shadows. Korfax felt his heart sink. He recognised who it was immediately. It was Simoref. And, as if to confirm it, Simoref's voice came to him from out of the darkness.

"Well! And here you are again!"

"You were told to have nothing to do with me," Korfax said.

"But you are the one coming here, not me!"

"Nonetheless, here you are in front of me."

They looked at each for a moment.

"I will move on," said Korfax.

"I do not think so," Simoref told him. "I think I have had more than enough of you. Your name is continually ringing in my ears. Korfax this, Korfax that, Korfax the other. I am sick of it. They have given you and your house far too much licence, whilst others are put down for even the slightest of failings."

Simoref gestured about him as though describing the empty square. He turned back to Korfax.

"Your friend called me out, challenged me to a duel, but that should be between us. So let us see how you stand upon your own two feet, without others to hide behind!"

Korfax wondered what exactly Simoref meant by that, but then he caught a gleam of light in Simoref's hands. He was holding a child stave of air. Korfax stared at it. Now he knew where this was going.

"Such things are forbidden," he said.

Korfax turned about but found Solfaia and Zanbal blocking his way back. He span around again to look back at Simoref.

"If you are proposing a duel, I have nothing with me. You could lose your position here if they find out. This is forbidden."

Simoref sneered.

"But what do you care if it is forbidden or not? You are the one that loves to mock the law. Well I for one have had enough of it. You are caught and there is nowhere else to hide. And you do love to hide, don't you Korfax, behind the wardens, behind the rules, behind anything but the truth?"

"And what truth is that?"

"That you are a heretic! What other truth could there be? You do like to keep their company after all, even when expressly forbidden to do so!"

Korfax took a step back. There was a dangerous feeling in the air now. This was no mere humiliation Simoref had planned; this was something far more serious. And Simoref had chosen his moment well. There was no one else about, the Piodo Heifal was quiet and dark and they were far enough from the Umadya Semeiel for the power raised by a child stave to go unnoticed. They were effectively alone.

Simoref stepped forward and smiled unkindly.

"But I will be merciful," he said. "I will give you a moment in which to gather yourself."

Korfax looked about.

"I have no stave. How can we duel if I have no stave?"

Simoref held out a second stave. He threw it to Korfax. Korfax caught it. It was a child stave of earth.

"I refuse," he said, putting the stave down.

Simoref tilted his lips in a slight snarl.

"Coward!" he mocked.

"It is forbidden!" Korfax said.

"And when has that been your concern?" Simoref countered. "Ever since you came to the Dar Kaadarith you have done as you saw fit, consorting with heretics at every available opportunity. Who knows what other iniquities hide within you. Your very life seems a catalogue of the forbidden, and yet here you still are, walking free whilst others pay dearly for the merest trespass. But not you, Korfax, not you! This cannot be allowed to continue. Pick up that stave!"

"I shall not. And I do not consort with heretics!"

"Do not? A brazen lie! You went to the Sal Kamalkar at every available opportunity before they found you out. But still you see them in secret. I know this, Korfax. I know that you met with Dialyas this very day! It cannot be borne! Pick up that stave!"

"How do you know that?"

"So you do not deny it? Good!"

Simoref clenched his stave. There was a brief glow from inside it and the merest hint of a sound, like a distant whistle. A small blast of air struck the ground just in front of Korfax. He stepped back.

"Pick up that stave."

"I will not."

"Then I will make you."

Simoref clenched his stave again, and this time the whistling sound was far more certain. A punching thrust of air passed over Korfax's head. Korfax ducked and rolled. Another blast came and dust boiled upwards behind him. Korfax looked frantically about and saw that both Solfaia and Zanbal had staves too, and like Simoref they were both child staves of air. Korfax ran in the opposite direction, dodging the twisting knots of force that Simoref sent after him. He bounced against an invisible wall and was thrown back. Solfaia and Zanbal had surrounded the two of them in a net of winds. Physically, it was impossible to escape.

His sudden pause allowed Simoref to land his first blow. A blast of air rammed into Korfax's back, knocking the breath from his body and sending him sprawling to the ground. He heard laughter as he struggled to stand up again. Another blow came, this time obliquely across his legs. His right thigh throbbed with pain and his left leg went dead below the knee. Simoref kicked the stave of earth in his direction.

"Pick it up!"

Korfax rolled away and managed somehow to get to his feet, but he was limping now. Simoref walked slowly after him, sending delicate flicks of air at his head. It was like being slapped by unseen hands. Simoref played with him like this for a little while, but then seemed to tire of it. He sent a much stronger blast of force from his stave and a blow like the kick from an ormn landed across Korfax's stomach. He fell backwards, gasping. The pain was immense. His innards were on fire. He tried to catch his breath, but even that was difficult. Simoref stood a small distance away, watching and waiting, clearly relishing the pain he was inflicting. Once more he picked up the stave of earth and threw it towards Korfax. Korfax stared at it. If he touched it now he would be complicit. He looked at Solfaia and Zanbal, but they remained in the shadows, their faces hidden. Korfax found himself wondering whether they were enjoying this or regretting it. Whatever the outcome, they would be held just as responsible as Simoref. He looked back at his tormentor.

"I will not duel with you," he said. "It is forbidden."

His breath back, Korfax stood up once more, only to be slapped across the head by another blast. This one was stronger than before and it tore the skin. Korfax felt a trickle of blood run across his cheek.

"What do you want?" he asked. "Me beaten to my knees? What joy is there in that?"

Simoref held up his stave.

"A considerable amount," he said. "But I do not want you beaten to your knees, oh no. I want you beaten to the very edge of life itself! You upstarts from the north should learn who you are, once and for all. You are the dregs of the Haelok Aldaria, planted amongst the rest of us to lessen our purity. Only those from the west should aspire to the highest estates in the land, not grovelling slime such as you. You should have stayed in the north, Korfax, and wallowed in filth like your ancestors."

Korfax stared back at Simoref in horrified disbelief. He could not believe what he was hearing. The dregs of the Haelok Aldaria? Was that what the west really thought? What sick hatred was this?

"What have I ever done to you?" he asked.

Simoref drew himself up, power gathering in his stave as he clutched it with both hands. His eyes seemed to light up with a cold fire, a fire that sent a shiver along Korfax's spine.

"You were born, idiot! Excrement such as you should never have graced this world. That your mother ever married your father was an outrage. That you even exist is an affront to The Creator. That you have come here to study the most sacred lore cannot be borne at all. Prepare to enter the river, Korfax, for I have sworn to rid the world of such as you."

Korfax went still inside. Now he understood. His death was in Simoref's heart. The revelation should have stunned him, held him immobile in shock, but instead he found himself split in two.

Against the backdrop of the square, with Simoref standing over him like an executioner, he saw another image superimpose itself across his sight. He was back again in that long-forgotten room at Losq. His mother was there, a lance in her hands, as were three grey demons, Agdoain, headless horrors dancing. But for some reason he was not scared. There was a power somewhere, a power he could use to burn the demons from the world, if only he would grasp it. For a moment he was confused as though the memory was incomplete, but then he understood what it was he had to do. He had to reach out and grasp the power before him in both hands.

Ignoring the stave of earth, Korfax came straight for Simoref, a mighty leap off his good leg, hands outstretched. Simoref tried to complete the killing blow, but Korfax had already laid his hands upon the stave of air. Then, even as he quietened its power, he tried to wrest it from Simoref.

Backwards and forwards they went, Simoref mouthing wordless sounds of outrage as he struggled for mastery of his stave while Korfax, face unmoving, drove his mind deeper and deeper into the crystal heart, seeking for the well of power he knew to be there.

If it had been just a physical contest, Simoref might have had the advantage, for whilst Korfax was large for his age, Simoref was older and stronger. But even as Simoref tried to wrench the stave away from Korfax, using his weight and his strength to good effect, he found that Korfax could not be thrown down so easily. Power joined the pair of them together now, the power in the stave.

A gathering of forces rose up between them and rose again, thrumming in the air, vibrating in the ground, the sounds of summoning. Discordant chimes rang from the stave as random blasts of force spat outwards. A few connected with the wall Solfaia and Zanbal had erected and shattered it as if it was suddenly paltry.

Solfaia lowered his stave, released his power and ran away. This had gone so much further than he had thought it would. All he had expected was that Simoref would knock Korfax around a bit and so leave it at that. But Simoref had threatened Korfax with death and things had suddenly become as serious as they possibly could. And if that was not enough, Korfax had seemingly defied all the odds and got inside Simoref's guard so that he could wrestle for possession of the stave. Now powers were being unleashed out in the square, deep powers that the adepts in the Umadya Semeiel would surely notice. Solfaia did not want to be there when they arrived.

He ran on, casting occasional glances back over his shoulder as though worried that the forces being unleashed behind him would follow. He could see a gyre back there now, a gyre of turbulent air flickering in and out of existence, boiling into the quiet sky above, a beacon that marked the very spot where Korfax and Simoref still struggled with each other. Solfaia gaped up at it and ran on, only to collide with another.

He fell to the floor and looked up, straight into the face of Asakom. And not only Asakom, for Sohagel stood beside him and at his back were many wardens. All had their staves with them and each of them stared down at him with dark eyes. But amidst them all stood another, a Geyadril, his white stave blazing in his hand. Solfaia had decided to flee the battle too late, so he sank down into a deep pit of fear instead.

Korfax and Simoref had finally reached the heart of the matter and the outside world no longer existed for either of them. Their duel for mastery of the stave consumed them both.

Within each of their minds an emptiness pulsed, a thin artery of nothingness like a river down which energy was pouring in ever-increasing torrents.

Korfax could feel his opponent's possession of the stave like a sphere, a sphere that his mind could actually taste – metallic and bitter, but fast. Its surface ever eluded his touch. It was difficult to catch and it was receding all the while, so Korfax balanced upon his thought like a moving blade, long and thin, a thrusting corridor within which he stood alone and in which his mind was constrained. Towards the ever-receding sphere he raced, his mind compressing as he fell across a landscape of dim geometric forms. Ever simpler his world became, whilst the point of force upon which he balanced rode in with him as though upon the crest of a wave. It felt as though he had an ocean at his back, an ocean of power, driving him on to the climax, that wonderful climax where glories awaited.

The wardens fanned out across the square. Seven stood to the fore, their staves like barriers before them. There were brief shouts of power, brief flickers that danced through the turbulent air. Whichever warden happened to be the closest caught each chaotic blast upon their stave and extinguished it with earth of air, but occasionally the force was so much that a warden would stagger back. One or two were even knocked off their feet.

Sohagel watched it all with mounting fury. Finally, unable to contain himself, he turned to Solfaia and Zanbal who waited behind, heads down, eyes to the ground.

"And this is a duel, you say?"

Solfaia mumbled something unintelligible. Sohagel deepened his scowl, if such a thing was possible.

"Then please tell me why there is only one stave?"

Neither answered. Sohagel all but snarled at them before turning back, glancing at the Geyadril beside him.

"Ponodol, are you absolutely certain that there is only one stave? Even I cannot penetrate the power that is being unleashed here now."

Ponodol pointed at the swirling forces before them.

"Look at them both. Can't you see it? They wrestle for mastery of a single stave. All the power comes from a single point. If there are any others present, they are not being used."

Ponodol turned to Asakom.

"Has either Simoref or Korfax ever done anything like this before?"

Asakom made the gesture of astonishment.

"Fight over a stave?" he asked. "When has *anyone* ever done anything like that before?"

"That is not what I asked," said Ponodol. "I seek understanding here."

"Then I have none to give," Asakom replied. "All I can tell you is that there is an edict upon Simoref. He was told to keep away from Korfax. Clearly he has not done so."

Sohagel spluttered.

"This is all well and good, but we must find a way of stopping this."

Ponodol held up a hand in warning.

"Foolish to try! Dangerous also! This affair must run its course. The forces they have unleashed are yet contained and we are on hand to catch them both. If I read it aright they now approach the fulcrum. So let us be ready, shall we?"

Then Ponodol peered intently into the gyre of air that surrounded the combatants.

"Beware, all of you," he said, "the crisis is already upon us."

Korfax felt the sword of his mind pierce the shield of Simoref whilst the cry of his enemy assailed him from all sides like a wail of fading light. Korfax laughed. He had won. He had the stave in his hands and Simoref was defeated. Korfax pulled back, away from the rushing places and back to the world he knew.

The winds died down and the air became quiet again. He looked down.

Simoref lay at his feet, writhing in pain, sobbing like a child. Korfax felt a sudden rush of anger, a fury that begged for release. He was in that red place again, that place of rage, of blood-drenched mists. He clenched both his hands about the child stave, feeling his passion mount within it and preparing to summon fire, preparing to burn his foe to ash. But a heavy hand landed upon his shoulder and stopped him dead in his tracks. He turned about to find another standing behind him, a being of far greater power, holding up a great white stave and a look like thunder on its face.

Once again, Korfax was summoned to give an account of himself, but this time it was to Geyadril Ponodol. They were alone. No other was present.

"So, Korfax, tell me about the duel," said Ponodol.

"It was no duel, Geyadril," Korfax told him.

"But I distinctly remember seeing you and Simoref engaged in a contest over a stave. Are you telling me that I am mistaken?"

"It is not what you think, Geyadril."

"Not what I think? And what is it that I think?"

"That it was a duel, Geyadril. I refused."

"Well now, if that was a refusal I cannot imagine what your acceptance might look like."

Ponodol leaned forward.

"We found a child stave of earth at the scene," he said. "Simoref said that it was yours."

"It was not," said Korfax. "I did not accept it when he tried to give it to me."

"Korfax, you are injured. There are bruises and cuts upon you. Are you telling me that you just stood there and let Simoref hurt you without striking back?"

"If I had picked up that stave I would be complicit, Geyadril."

"What changed your mind?"

"He was going to kill me."

Ponodol paused.

"So why did you not pick up the stave then?" he asked. "Why did you get inside Simoref's guard instead?"

"Because the power had already been raised in that stave, Geyadril. It would have taken too long to use the other."

"That was quick thinking on your part. But it was not the only reason, was it?"

"If I had picked up the other stave, I would be complicit, Geyadril."

Ponodol studied Korfax for a moment. He was a picture of abject misery. Reduced to his essentials, he had shut himself down. Ponodol could see the thoughts written on his face. He would be expelled. He would be disgraced. And all because of the unreasoning hatred of another. Except that it wasn't unreasoning at all. Ponodol already knew the truth.

"Korfax, I have summoned your father here. He should arrive tomorrow. You will need to speak to him concerning this, I think."

"I am to be expelled, Geyadril?"

Ponodol smiled.

"On the contrary, you are to be commended. I have never seen the like, and neither has anyone else. What you did, what you achieved, is an astonishment to many of us. That you, an acolyte of the third level, could take the stave of an acolyte of the sixth? We did not even know that such a feat was possible. It was an act of great power, young Korfax. You demonstrated both bravery and discipline in your willingness to follow the commandments of our order. None could ask any more of you."

The astonishment on Korfax's face was a picture. Ponodol had to control himself. He so felt like smiling.

"I already had some idea of the truth of this," he said, "but I had to speak to you to confirm it. I am almost entirely satisfied. Once I was told your history I understood what it was that had happened. You are the victim here, Korfax, the victim of a hatred you knew nothing of. It is not something I can speak about openly, as I must let your father do that, but what I can say to you is that you are without stain in this, without any stain at all."

Korfax seemed to clench himself and Ponodol was shocked to see tears on his cheeks. That was not what he had expected.

"What is it?" he asked.

"I try to do my best, to follow, to do what is expected of me, but always it goes wrong."

Ponodol watched carefully. What was this?

"No, Korfax, no. You did nothing wrong. There is no fault. You have been the victim of appalling malice, that is all."

He stood up and went to Korfax and put a hand on his shoulder.

"Yours has been a hard road, I think. But remember this: everything you have achieved here has been noticed and approved. Of those that matter many speak highly of you. Do not believe you are alone. You are well-loved."

Korfax looked up and wiped his eyes. Ponodol smiled.

"You should rest. Nothing more for you until your father arrives."

On the morrow Korfax found himself summoned to the courtyard of Hais. His father was there before him, waiting. They embraced.

"How are you?" he asked.

"Still a little shaken by all that has happened. Simoref said some terrible things. I think they hurt more than the blows he landed with his stave."

Sazaaim looked down. Korfax could feel his anger.

"Simoref is gone," Sazaaim said. "He has been sent back to Othil Homtoh. Solfaia and Zanbal have gone also."

"Have they been expelled?"

"Not exactly."

"Won't they be punished?"

"Yes, and no. They are no longer to be at the seminary, but they have not been expelled from the Dar Kaadarith. You see, their houses are powerful and exert much influence. An accommodation has been reached."

"An accommodation? I don't understand. Geyadril Ponodol said that you knew the truth of this and would explain it to me."

"And I will, my son, I will. You see, it was Audroh Zafazaa who set these events in motion; his son was merely his instrument. Consider it his revenge upon me."

"On you?"

"There is something you do not know. I once shamed him."

"You...?"

"Yes, it is a story I should have told you long ago, but there never seemed to be a good time to tell it. And now you have suffered because of it."

Sazaaim gestured to the seats by the wall. They sat.

"I first met your mother in the Umadya Pir. When I saw her, and she saw me, it was the most beautiful moment of my life. Our eyes met, our minds met, our souls entwined. It was kommah, souls destined for union, a state of utter bliss. What I did not know at that time, and what you do not know, is that your mother was already promised to another."

Korfax could guess who that was.

"Zafazaa," he said.

"Yes, and he did not take the news well. He raged at her, he raged at everyone, but it was kommah and he knew well enough what that meant."

Korfax bowed his head. kommah was one of the most sacred states, and it was unlawful to break it. That was the spark that had started the Wars of Unification themselves. Sondehna had taken Soivar from Karmaraa, breaking kommah itself so that he would not be denied his desire.

"What happened?" Korfax asked.

"Zafazaa appealed to the Velukor, but in vain. Ermalei loved your mother dearly.

273

They had grown up together, knew each other's hearts. He would have done anything for her, so he annulled the betrothal. Zafazaa appealed to the courts, and they sided with him. Zafazaa, like all the princes of the Korith Zadakal, had the ear of the Balt Kaalith. A betrothal is a betrothal, they said, and they ruled that it could not possibly be kommah. Such a ruling would have been ridiculous if it had not been so serious. The Velukor may have been angry, but your mother was furious. That was a sight to behold. She would have taken up a sword herself and called Zafazaa out if she could, but she could not. The law would not permit it, so she did the next best thing. She asked me to be her champion. I challenged the verdict of the court and called Zafazaa out."

Sazaaim looked at his son.

"Do you remember the avalkana that rested in my day room at Losq?"

"That was the sword you beat him with?"

Sazaaim sighed.

"Yes, a gift from Ermalei. Zafazaa did not like that, either. Zafazaa was good with a sword, very good, but I had an advantage he knew nothing about. You see, during my time at the seminary I took lessons in the art from a friend, one who taught sword craft in the Nazad Esiask."

Korfax marvelled at the parallels. He was taking lessons from Ralir even now. How strange it was. He wondered who it was that had given lessons to his father. He could only think of one.

"Was it Ocholor?"

His father smiled.

"Yes, it was Ocholor. With his aid I beat Zafazaa and won the hand of your mother, but Zafazaa felt humiliated because I did not kill him, though I could have done so easily. That was not my way and he did not understand it. Zafazaa does not look into the hearts of others, only his own. So, as a consequence, he has hated your mother and I ever since."

Korfax did not know what to say. That his father had fought a duel for the hand of his mother was astonishing. He sat and thought about it.

"You are very quiet," said his father.

"It is a lot to think about," said Korfax.

He pondered what had happened, both recently and in the past. All the good things that had happened were suddenly wiped away and all he could think of were the bad. He thought of his visits to Dialyas and his father's subsequent anger. Then he thought of the malice of Simoref, all because his father had once beaten Simoref's father in a duel. Simoref had nearly killed him. It all began to hurt inside, a pain that would not relent. He looked at his father.

"This is twice now that something from your past has been visited upon me. First it was Dialyas, because you testified against him, and now it is Zafazaa wanting revenge for his humiliation. Is there anything else I should be aware of?"

His father looked as if he had been stung. He stared back at his son in disbelief.

"My son," he said, "none of this was foreseen."

"And yet it happened, not to you but to me."

The anger came.

"You do not know what you are saying. You do not know what I have had to endure or the choices I have had to make. I will not be held to account like this."

Korfax drew back but did not submit.

"I was not holding you to account," he said, "but I still have to ask if there is anything else I should know?"

"I am no seer!" his father exclaimed. "How can I know what the future will hold?"

He stood up and left without another word. Korfax stayed where he was. What should he do? Should he apologise? But for what? There were other things inside, things he had not confronted his father about, like his refusal to become Geyadril. What else might there be? What else might rise up out of the past to strike out at him?

It was later in the day that Korfax was summoned by Ponodol. He entered his rooms but found only his mother there. She immediately came to him and put her hands on his shoulders, looking fully into his eyes.

"You have hurt your father," she said.

He looked down but said nothing.

"And you have been hurt," she continued.

"It wasn't my fault," he said.

"I did not want this," she murmured. "I did not want contention between you."

She took his face in her hands.

"Your father has already returned north. I doubt he will come south again. He will hide himself away after this."

"What must I do?"

"There is nothing you can do. Continue your studies. I will talk to him. As with everything else he blames himself for what has happened. Let time heal him. It is over for now."

Korfax looked at her.

"Is it?" he asked.

She frowned.

"What do you mean?"

"Secrets!" he said.

She smiled sadly.

"Secrets," she agreed.

They spent the rest of the day together, talking of simple things, happy just to be in each other's company. His mother finally left in the evening and Korfax watched her go, with a lump in his throat. There was something unexpected inside him, something he had not known before. He found himself hating another.

The hatred boiled up inside like a poison, even as he watched his mother pass through the far gate. But it wasn't Simoref he hated, it was Zafazaa. One did not hate the hand that held the whip, but the mind that ordered it.

He turned from the gate to find Ponodol standing behind him.

"You should make peace with your father," he said.

Korfax started.

"It was not my fault."

"I know, but you should still make peace with him.

He paused.

"One more thing. As of now you are to receive special tutelage."

"Special tutelage, Geyadril?"

"From me," he said. His gaze deepened.

"When I interceded at the end of your contest with Simoref, what was in your mind?"

Korfax blinked. Had Ponodol seen his anger? He had not mentioned that before.

"There was anger," he said.

"Yes! Anger! And what were you prepared to do with it?"

There was a long silence.

"I do not know what would have happened, Geyadril."

Ponodol waited a little longer.

"Would you have killed with it?" he asked eventually.

"I don't know," Korfax answered, looking down, looking into his deeps. Ponodol took a deep breath.

"Well I do. I saw it in you. Remember this the next time you are called upon to use your power. You showed great discipline up to that point, but come the end your anger got the better of you. That cannot be allowed. Talent such as yours should dwell in the light, not the dark. This, above all else, is why I have chosen to watch over you."

"But you are a Geyadril and on the high council. I am just an acolyte. What of your duties?"

Ponodol gestured at the tower behind him.

"This is my duty. The Namad Dar is my duty. You are my duty."

He smiled a little.

"Besides, your father is my friend. It is long past time you heard a different tale."

"A different tale?"

"We have been remiss in our duty of care to you. We have stood too far back. Now it is time to step closer and show you better answers, instead of letting you seek them out on your own."

Korfax understood immediately. Ponodol was referring to Dialyas.

"Dialyas!" he said.

"Yes," Ponodol answered. "And remember, I was there, too."

Naaomir gazed out of his window while Okodon waited calmly behind. There was a brief fluttering of wings and a small napanah alighted on the window ledge. For a moment it twitched its head this way and that as though listening to their thoughts, and then, just as quickly, it was gone again. Naaomir turned about and sat back down in his chair.

"So then, a conclusion!"

"Indeed, Noqvoan. Do you have any special orders?"

"No, this affair now passes from your hands and into mine. I will take it to the Noqvoanel."

Okodon showed only a slight downturn of her mouth, but Naaomir did not miss it. He looked at her.

"You disapprove?"

"I am the one that brought this affair to your notice in the first place. I am the one that has watched and reported. So have I not done my duty well? Is my service of so little worth?"

Naaomir smiled.

"Good, very good," he said. "We need such as you to swell the ranks of the Noqvoanith."

He let the words hang in the air. Okodon absorbed them, tasted them and suddenly held herself straighter.

"Then I apologise for my words, Noqvoan. They were ill-considered, spoken in haste."

Naaomir smiled.

"No," he said, "they were not. You thought your service was being ignored. If you were indifferent, if you did not care, then that would say one thing, but if you cared, as you clearly do, then that would say something else. Only the fastest vines reach the light, and only the hungriest worry about their next meal, do you not agree? You have revealed all that I needed to know with a few simple words. Learn the lesson and discover the deeper truth behind the Balt Kaalith, the truth few outside even suspect is there."

Okodon bowed and her eyes shone. Then she looked troubled.

"But, if I may ask, what now of Korfax?"

Naaomir tapped the table with a finger.

"I imagine that he will become the concern of the Noqvoanel. Every so often, every generation or so, one is encountered who clearly has a destiny. Through no fault of their own they become the focus of events. Korfax is such a one, I think. And since these matters touch some of the highest in the land, they become matters only the highest of our order can safely contemplate. It is said that the Prah Sibith hoard wealth against times of famine and that the Exentaser hoard vision against times of need. Well, we of the Balt Kaalith hoard knowledge, intelligence to be used only in times of peril. Korfax may yet fail to become Geyad, or he may die in the struggle against the Agdoain, but whatever fate has in store for him we will be there, ready to act when the time is right."

Vixipal, Noqvoanel of the Balt Kaalith, looked at the logadar in his hand and smiled.

"I approve the elevation of Okodon," he said. "She has performed her duties well."

He looked at Naaomir.

"You also have done well, and it was right of you to wait to bring this to my attention."

"It was difficult to untangle the web, Noqvoanel," said Naaomir. "I had to be sure."

"Indeed."

Vixipal put the logadar upon the table.

"This will enter the archives under seal. Both you and Okodon will bind your tongues in the matter. No one is to know this for now. What we have here is a lever, a lever that will lift the Balt Kaalith up and make us a power again."

He looked at Naaomir.

"You seem troubled by this."

"The law has been subverted by one of the highest. Vengeance is one thing, but I find I cannot approve of the use the house of Erinil was put to."

"No, I cannot approve that either. But Tahamoh was the one that fell, not Korfax."

"Proof, if proof were needed, of his strength and the strength of his house."

"No one suspects who the agents were?"

"No one, but the plot was obvious once the connection was made."

Vixipal narrowed his eyes.

"From Zafazaa, to Yamandir, to Omagrah, to Tahamoh and then to Simoref. Not many fathers would spend their sons so."

Naaomir agreed.

"Simoref was eager to do his father's will, by all accounts. Too eager, perhaps."

"And there we see the contrast," said Vixipal. "Look at the strength of Korfax. Your summation is correct. It is clear we should take an interest in him. Sazaaim is a lost cause, for all his staunch defence of the north, but what of his son? The good graces of the Salman Farenith would be desirable."

Naaomir paused.

"There is one matter that is not within that stone. It is troubling."

"And what might that be?"

"The involvement of our order."

Vixipal looked up. His eyes flashed.

"Explain!"

"It is something else I have discovered. I think I have found out who the mysterious Matchir is."

"A heretic, surely? His disappearance is easily explained. He has taken himself voluntarily to Lonsiatris, and good riddance to him."

"No!" said Naaomir. "I think he is still amongst us. I think he is a Noqvoan, and a Noqvoan by the name of Voanam, no less!"

Vixipal started.

"Are you certain?"

"As certain as I can be. The evidence is purely circumstantial, but I can match them up. It was Voanam became the heretic Matchir. When one appeared, the other disappeared. I believe his purpose was to ensure that Korfax visited with Dialyas, using any means that he could. And it was a subtle piece of work, from what I can tell."

"You know who Voanam is?"

"He is the hidden hand of the first Noqvoandril of Othil Homtoh and an archivist of the Umadya Gonaa. Who better to falsify documents and create a fictitious individual?"

Vixipal frowned.

"Yes, the hidden hand of the Noqvoandril! And the loyalty of Soqial to the house of Zadakal knows no bounds. I see why you have been so circumspect. You did well not to include it in your report. If another saw this it would have damaged us beyond recall. Subversion of the law is one thing, but subversion of our order? We must be above reproach! This cannot be allowed."

Naaomir paused again.

"Something for the future, perhaps? Another lever?"

Vixipal smiled.

"Exactly so! Another lever indeed. Come the right time, Zafazaa will bow to us, not us to him."

He stood straighter.

"Assemble your evidence but keep it locked away and separate from everything else. Something tells me we shall need it."

11

SONS AND FATHERS

Ialho-aa Qur-odavon
Nor-odnoq Chisoth-iaais
Tolzaf-holq Od-drol-vasdril
Banip-vim Salluj-pamim
Diz-norid Odfen-dr-pan
Ialho-nuhm Tapil-prd-zior
Maq-charaih Odtrin-hozaa

As after the affair with Tahamoh, things changed again. Korfax felt different inside now, as though his centre had shifted. It did not help that others saw him differently as well. Word had spread of the duel and, wherever Korfax went, eyes were upon him. No one knew quite what to make of the tales that were being told, so they watched and waited.

Thilnor was supportive, admiring even, when Korfax would let him be so, but Korfax felt more alone now than he had ever felt before. His other friend, Oanatom, was as unsettled by this matter as he had been when Tahamoh had left the seminary. Korfax was set apart from the others and everyone knew it. It would take time for him to make his way back again.

It was Ralir that helped the most, and that was because he did not care what it was all about anyway. To him it was simple. Simoref was his enemy and Korfax was his friend. Ralir was the first to make Korfax really laugh again.

"Do you know what I think?" he asked one day.

"What?"

"I think it was my fault!"

"Your fault?"

"I must have caused more damage than I thought."

Korfax frowned.

"Whatever are you talking about?" he asked.

"Well," said Ralir, "I did hit him over the head with that bottle, didn't I?"

The time for festival approached, when burdens were lightened and duties were relaxed. Korfax would have remained aloof from it all, but then Ralir came to him with an invitation.

"Korfax, I have a surprise for you."

Korfax looked at his friend. Ralir was smiling his happiest smile.

"For me?"

"Yes, you are invited to Othil Admaq. You are to accompany me there."

"When?"

"The festival of Soytal."

Korfax was surprised.

"But that lasts for seven days!" he exclaimed. "I am expected to attend temple during that time."

"I asked my father to speak to those that needed to be spoken to." Ralir told him.

"Your father? But I thought that you and he did not have much to say to each other?"

"Well, actually, it was my mother I spoke to and she spoke to him. I expected him to refuse me, as he does with everything else, but he acquiesced without even an admonishing word. Astonishing, isn't it?"

"Why?"

"I have no idea. Or perhaps I do. But enough of that. What is important is that you are going."

"So I will get to see the south?"

"Yes, and father will even send his personal sky ship to bring you there."

"His 'personal' sky ship?"

"My house is rather wealthy, after all."

"But not even Tabaud Abinax has his own personal sky ship."

"Maybe not, but the house of Badagar relishes wealth above all other things. And so we display it. For what is wealth if it is not put on display?"

Korfax had no answer.

Time passed, and in what seemed moments the day of departure dawned. Korfax rode to the southern landing field, as Ralir had directed. There was only one sky ship waiting upon the green, a beautifully crafted affair, gleaming in the morning light. As soon as he dismounted, a waiting attendant appeared as if out of nowhere, bowed lavishly to him and then took his steed. Another appeared from out of the sky ship, bowed in a similar fashion and then hurried him on board. Korfax would have returned each bow but they gave him no time to do so. It was all rather confusing.

Once inside Korfax found himself ushered into a luxurious cabin and then on to a luxurious seat. The attendant bowed again, as extravagantly as before, and left in a whirl of robes. Korfax was alone. He took a moment to catch his breath and then looked about him.

The cabin was magnificent, almost overpowering. Reds and golds chased each other across the floor, the ceiling and the walls. Inlaid with rare stones and hung with beautiful fabrics, the sky ship seemed more like some glittering confection than a vessel of travel. He felt himself oppressed by the opulence.

It was not long before Ralir entered with great fanfare. Many accompanied him, clearing his way and guiding him to his place, but as soon as he saw Korfax he shrugged them off and made his way to the seat opposite. Then he clapped his hands sharply and they all vanished again as if sucked back through the walls.

He turned to Korfax.

"I made sure that you came on board first," he said, "otherwise you would have had to endure that with me." Ralir gestured at the empty doors and then offered Korfax his sweetest smile. "And I do so know how you like to remain humble."

Korfax folded his arms and glowered back. They remained that way for a moment and then both burst out laughing.

The sky ship was in the air before Korfax had even noticed that they were moving. He looked outside and watched as the land fell away below. They picked up speed and were soon engulfed by cloud.

The cloud gradually thinned and then vanished. Below them now lay the northern borders of the Piral Jiroks, the great sea of sand that stretched nearly all the way to Othil Admaq. Korfax went to the viewing platform for a better look.

"That place below," he said, "I have never seen the like. Look at it! It is so barren, so sere."

"Barren indeed!" replied Ralir. "Behold the Piral Jiroks. But it does possess a certain beauty, don't you think?"

"A simple beauty perhaps, but it looks perilous down there. There is nothing but sand and heat."

Ralir leaned back from the rail and closed his eyes.

"And for that reason they built the great road. No one travels the Piral Jiroks any more. It has been left to itself for thousands of years – as The Creator intended, I think."

Korfax watched the seemingly endless sea of sand and wondered what it would be like to walk there. It would be lonely, he thought.

Refreshments were served formally at the hour of Ialaxan, though Ralir said that they could have had them at any time.

"It is odd, though, isn't it?" he commented. "Having been away all this time I find that I miss the traditions."

"The comforts of home," Korfax offered quietly.

Ralir caught the wistful tone in his voice.

"Korfax?"

"I was just thinking," he said. "That is the one thing I cannot do."

Ralir stopped what he was doing and stared. All the attendants stopped what they were doing as well. Korfax looked up.

"What? What is it?"

Ralir shook himself and gestured furiously to the others that they continue doing whatever it was they had been doing before.

"I'm sorry," he said. "I did not think what I was saying."

Korfax shook his head and smiled.

"Why should you even?"

He thought about it for a moment.

"But it is odd, isn't it?" he continued. "Here we are, life carrying on as if normal, whilst they hunt the far north for demons."

"I hear the news," said Ralir. "Some are almost avid for it in the Umadya Madimel. But you are right. It seems a very distant thing when you are so very far away."

He waited a moment and then peered at Korfax.

"Any word from your father?"

Korfax looked down.

"We haven't spoken since the affair with Simoref. We argued. He was angry."

He looked up again.

"But I speak to my mother."

"Speak to him, Korfax, don't let it pass."

"I have tried, but he does not hear me."

Ralir went back to his wine and the rest of the journey passed in silence.

Othil Admaq gradually emerged from the haze ahead. Korfax first thought that he would see a city much like Othil Zilodar, but he soon realised that Othil Admaq had a flavour all its own. Whereas the tower dominated Othil Zilodar and Emethgis Vaniad, in Othil Admaq the dome reigned supreme.

There were many towers here, of course, a great many of them, tall and white and shapely, but domes – great domes – occupied much of the city. And the greatest of them all was the vast dome of the house of Badagar itself, the hereditary home of the lords of the city for more than ten thousand years, the Rax Izikal.

Korfax looked about him and marvelled. What a place he had come to.

The sky ship came to rest on a platform jutting from one of the many sky towers. Again, with great fanfare, Ralir was preceded by his servants. Korfax followed quietly. He alighted from the vessel and gazed about him. The city stretched in every direction, as far as the eye could see, but the distances were hazy, hidden by the heat. It was so unlike the clear air of the north, where the horizon was marked by what stood upon it or before it. But here? Infinities beckoned.

Korfax took a deep breath and caught a scent to the air, a taste of fragrances he did not recognise. He turned to Ralir, who smiled in return.

"You smell the air?" he asked. "Wonderful, isn't it? Ah, the scents and the sights of home! It will be good to have you here Korfax, as you make me see this place anew."

The honour guard stepped forward, all forty-nine of them. There were forty-two

Branith, all proudly bearing the sigil of Badagar upon their shields and armour. Then there were the Branvath, six of them, each holding aloft a banner proclaiming the suzerainty of the Tabaud. Finally there was a single Brandril, tall and very dark of skin. Only the single sigil upon his helm proclaimed his allegiance. He stopped before Ralir and bowed.

"Nor-Tabaud, we are here to escort you to your father."

Ralir waved his hand airily.

"I have a guest with me. I present Faren Noren Korfax. You will be escorting him also."

"So I was informed, Nor-Tabaud."

The Brandril turned to Korfax and bowed again.

"Noren!"

Korfax bowed in return and the Brandril raised an eyebrow. Ralir laughed.

"Korfax, that is not necessary here. Customs differ."

Korfax frowned back.

"That may be so, but from where I come from it is considered polite."

Ralir wagged an admonishing finger.

"But have you ever considered that what some might think polite, others might think rude? When in the south, be as the south. That is good advice, I think."

He smiled and gestured to the Brandril.

"Enough of this now. Lead on!"

Ralir placed a hand on Korfax's shoulder as the Brandril turned away.

"Things are different here, my friend. You know what they say, don't you? There are only two directions – the south and everywhere else! And here, especially, you will find that saying particularly apt."

They walked amidst the honour guard and descended the tower. Korfax found himself caught by the sumptuous decoration that adorned its walls. Here were scenes from the glorious past of Othil Admaq: battles, victories, treaties and triumphs. He would have stopped to look closer, but Ralir ever urged him on.

So they reached the bottom at last and found an equally sumptuous chariot awaiting them, a glorious ornament of white, red and gold, drawn by four ormn, all white, all magnificent. When he saw it Ralir stopped in his tracks and cast a glance at Korfax.

"Well now, will you look at that! My father honours us indeed. That is the Chariot of Enshe."

Ralir seemed genuinely surprised. Korfax was about to inspect the chariot more closely but Ralir steered him inside before turning sharply to the Branvath who held the reins.

"When are we expected?" he asked.

"At the turning of the hour, Nor-Tabaud," answered the Branvath.

"Which one?"

"Nor-Tabaud?"

"Which hour?"

"Agahpon, Nor-Tabaud."

"Then take us by the best route you can devise in the time allowed. I wish to give my friend here a taste of all the sights of the city, at the very least."

Ralir looked away for the moment and then looked back again.

"And make it leisurely," he ordered.

The Branvath bowed his head.

"And make it scenic," Ralir ordered again.

The Branvath bowed for a second time.

"And make sure we pass all the important places."

The Branvath bowed his head for a third time.

"Well? What are you waiting for?" Ralir cried. The Branvath looked away at last and stared stonily ahead. Korfax thought that he heard the grinding of teeth, but he was not entirely certain.

Ralir entered the chariot and sat himself down beside Korfax. He grinned at his friend and gestured about him as he lay back upon the sumptuous seat.

"I tell you now, Korfax, this is just the beginning. And when we achieve my father's house? There you will see things that you will never have seen before, not at all."

Korfax did not answer. He was already consumed by the sights about him. But then the chariot began to move, so smoothly and so perfectly that it took him a little moment to realise that they were even moving at all. Ralir smiled again.

"Those that pull the chariot of Enshe are specially trained. I even think that they know how special they are, they take such care. Only the ceremonial chariots of the Velukor can boast as such. And the Branvath that drives them? He possesses a skill and an understanding of such matters that it is all but beyond mortal comprehension."

Korfax smiled. How Ralir loved to exaggerate. Then he looked at his friend a little more seriously.

"Ralir, I know you have said that you and your father do not see eye to eye, but this welcome is marvellous. He clearly wants to honour you."

Ralir shrugged.

"I know, I know, my father tempts me once more, as he has ever done so. But don't let it worry you. I shall be as mild as Losq achir with him."

Korfax raised an eyebrow.

"Then you know little of achir," he said. "Come the season for mating and they are anything but mild!"

Ralir laughed happily and leaned forward. In front of them both was a cabinet filled to the brim with rounded crystal flasks. Below them two wide and golden goblets had been set in solitary splendour. Ralir handed one goblet to Korfax and then took the other for himself. Then he passed a searching finger over each of the flasks, before selecting the one that was darkest. He lifted the stopper and sniffed.

Then he smiled.

"Ah, Father, you know my tastes far too well."

He turned to Korfax and grinned.

"My friend, you must relax whilst you are here, I command it. No, I demand it. And you must try this."

Korfax looked at the bottle Ralir held in his hand.

"What is it? I have never seen a wine so dark."

Ralir poured some into Korfax's goblet.

"It is no more and no less than well-seasoned Pelarr. It is the best of the best. It has a nobility that is unequalled anywhere else in Lon-Elah, and it has many virtues, not the least of which is its taste. Drink of this and it will convince you that you have left this life altogether and been transported beyond the river itself."

More exaggeration? Korfax sipped cautiously. Then he drew back in surprise. Ralir was right. The taste was indeed like nothing else he had ever experienced before. It was both rich and potent, complex and simple, but also astonishingly mellow. He took another sip as though not quite believing what his tongue had told him the first time.

Like all good wines, this one changed with each taste as if its long-vanished maker now stood at his shoulders in order to educate him in its subtleties. But Pelarr especially, like no other before it, sat upon his tongue like an awakening dream.

Korfax leaned back in his seat. The wine seemed to drift through him, an evocation of elder things: fond memory, lost pleasures. For a moment he was transported to the balcony of a sky ship, with the Nazarthin Ozong spread out before him, immense rocky pillars like the crumbled towers of a city out of ancient times, each dreaming in the golden light of a sunset. Korfax savoured the vision briefly before turning back to Ralir.

"This is so unlike the wines we got back home. I don't ever remember seeing any in Emethgis Vaniad, either."

Now Ralir really laughed.

"My dear Korfax," he said, "sometimes your ignorance frightens me, it really does. No one 'gets' Pelarr at all, except for the Velukor and my family. It is the rarest of the rare. Outside of the Rax Izikal the only other place you will find it is the Umadya Pir. I thought you knew your history. Need I mention the consort of Karmaraa?"

Korfax stared at his goblet.

"I was forgetting that," he said. "Zorvu was of Badagar. She would have ordered all kinds of things from the south."

"It is why the Wars of Unification had so little effect here," Ralir told him. "Zorvu was the only one who could tell Karmaraa how things should be. Even the fanatics of Othil Homtoh could not gainsay the first Sapax."

Korfax looked up.

"Fanatics? I have heard you say that on a number of occasions, but I have never really asked you about it. What do you mean by it?"

Ralir dropped his smile.

"You've met a few, I think."

"Who?"

"Need I mention Simoref?"

Korfax gaped.

"But that was because of his father! He at least had a reason!"

"A reason, yes. But there are others that do not, and you will meet them soon enough, I think. Once you rise in the ranks of the Dar Kaadarith, you will meet them. It is one of the very few things that I learned from my father for which I am truly grateful – knowing where the power really lies."

Korfax thought back to a past conversation with his own father, words of warning he had forgotten until now. He looked sideways at Ralir, who merely smiled in return before wagging his finger again.

"Yes, if you rise far enough you will discover them, in the Erm Roith, in the Balt Kaalith. But do you know what? I think that they will leave you alone. You are the heir to the Salman Farenith after all, and I do not think there is anyone on Lon-Elah that has not heard of your house."

Ralir stopped himself suddenly and frowned.

"Actually, that might be the reason why Father sent the Chariot of Enshe in the first place."

He grinned again.

"If that is why he did it then I forgive him. Nothing is too good for my friend Korfax. Here, have some more Pelarr."

He refilled Korfax's goblet and then attended to his own.

The journey to the Rax Izikal was indeed leisurely, and Korfax found himself transported by the wonders of Othil Admaq.

They crossed many great squares, distances drifting on the hot and hazy air, the scents of unknown perfumes wafting about them. They passed many ornate temples, wrought of pale stone and set about with fine crystal, spires reaching upwards and domes basking in the light. They journeyed down wide avenues set with statuary, carved from the finest pidai, each as white as snow. They passed by gardens all set with fountain or waterfall, filled with the eternal music of water. They traversed beautifully wrought bridges that leapt majestically over the many rivers of Othil Admaq, and they looked down upon the wide and stately barges going slowly to and fro with their myriad wares.

Everywhere he looked, Korfax saw colour and movement and beauty and riches. He travelled the heart of glory, drank of the finest Pelarr and gazed out at the splendour that was Othil Admaq, floating in the dream of the Ell, a dream of perfection, of order, the divine made manifest.

Eventually they arrived at the main gate to the Rax Izikal. But they did not have to stop or even slow down, for the immense stone doors parted before them even as they approached. It was a dance of perfect movements.

Once inside they found themselves in a vast courtyard, on the opposite side of which awaited a perfect arrangement of spectators. There were drifting hues of blue and red, violet and orange, each rising to a plinth upon which a single person stood, cloaked in bright and gleaming yellow. Ralir nudged Korfax, his voice barely concealing his surprise.

"My father is here to greet us, and he has summoned the entire court to attend him. What game are you playing now, Father?"

Korfax stared ahead.

"He wears the cloak of the first of the Prah Sibith. I thought that was Tochior."

Ralir pursed his lips.

"It is hereditary. The house of Badagar initiated the Prah Sibith. Hence, as a singular honour, we are allowed to wear the colours. My father, being who he is, remains nominal head of the guild – as I will be when I succeed him."

Korfax sat back in his seat and pondered for a moment.

"You are right. There are indeed only two directions – the south and everywhere else. What else is different here, I wonder."

Ralir gestured at the waiting crowd and smiled cryptically.

"Many things, as you will soon discover."

They stopped before a platform of white and yellow across which a deep-red carpet had been laid. Ralir went immediately to his father, whilst Korfax followed at a slower pace. Both bowed, and the High Lord of Badagar smiled in return. Korfax found himself watching Ralir's father carefully. Tabaud Zamferas was not how he had imagined him to be at all.

Zamferas was tall, and certainly had the look of a city lord. He had that imperious gaze, his eyes burning brightly within his dark skin, skin that was darker even than Ralir's. But he possessed a subtle look to his face, a look alien to that of his son. It was an expression Korfax had never seen upon Ralir's face at all. Ralir did not care for consequences; he lived only for the moment. But his father was of another temper entirely.

Tabaud Zamferas cared for many things. He cared for the moment at hand, for his appearance, for what others thought of him, for policies, for advantage. And so Korfax saw the gulf between the father and the son. They were not, and never would be, of like mind. The only time Ralir ever came close was when he duelled. Then the fires of his ambition, to conquer and be victorious, burned fearsomely in his eyes. But, by comparison, his father's flame was an altogether subtler affair.

Zamferas smiled considerately at his son but then turned to Korfax all too soon, breaking the reverie.

"Faren Noren Korfax," he announced. "We are honoured to have the heir of such a noble house as our guest."

By the tone of his voice, it sounded as though Zamferas had proclaimed him Velukor, so Korfax bowed again. After such a proclamation, it seemed the only sensible thing to do.

"Tabaud!" he answered. "To arrive in no less than the Chariot of Enshe. It is I who should be honoured. I am deeply in your debt."

Zamferas smiled just so, as was the custom, but his eyes gleamed his pleasure. Then he gestured towards the great doors behind him.

"Well now, I imagine the journey was tiring for you both. Come, let us go inside and partake of refreshment together."

In his given apartment at last, Korfax walked to the great balcony and looked out at the view. A more luxurious set of rooms he had never seen. Othil Admaq was awash with riches, within and without. Even the rituals.

Of them all, the ritual of pleasure was by far the most widely practiced. The merest swirl of a cloak seemed to precipitate the sudden appearance of trays of delicacies and goblets of refreshing wine. Othil Admaq was a continual dance of sensual distractions.

Korfax found himself the centre of attention, not something he was entirely used to. Many watched him, especially some of the younger ladies of the court. He remained courteous and reserved, though he caught a look on Ralir's face occasionally, that of barely concealed amusement when the conversation took a certain turn. Then there was Ralir's father, who seemed to take especial delight in honouring him. He felt embarrassed even thinking about it.

As they had entered the great hall of the Rax Izikal, Korfax had noticed a number of delegations from Othil Homtoh, each headed by a representative of one of that city's noble houses. But Tabaud Zamferas had been almost offhand with all of them. Korfax had noticed the banners of Idzar, Zamandas and Laplkur, each a mighty house in its own right, with ears in the court of the Velukor himself, but that did not seem to mean anything to the lord of Othil Admaq. He dealt with them as if they and their embassies were of little or no consequence at all. But when the trade delegation from Othil Ekrin crossed the floor with petitions in their hands, Zamferas became all smiles, even passing a few light comments with the steward of the house of Athzin, far more than he had with those of Othil Homtoh. Korfax caught a sour expression on the face of Zamandas Enay Dorass, whilst the face of Idzar Noren Hamanur could have almost been set in stone.

Korfax mulled Ralir's words over in his mind, as well as his dislike of the west. He wondered. The west had a right to be proud. All of what was now Sobol had fought with unswerving passion against the evil of the Iabeiorith. Perhaps it was jealousy he was seeing, a resentment of the continuing pre-eminence of the lords of the west? Korfax suddenly wished his mother was here. She would have seen through the masks on display here today and perhaps revealed to him a deeper play. But Tazocho was far, far away in Leemal, helping in the search for whomever, or whatever, was summoning the Agdoain. It seemed a far call from the wealth and beauty of the Rax Izikal.

The climax of the day was a feast in honour of Ralir, which he accepted with far more grace than Korfax might have expected. But then Korfax found himself set in the highest seat of all, right between Tabaud Zamferas and his wife, Tabaud Tharah, whilst Ralir was seated to one side, beside the first sword of the city. Ralir seemed happy enough, but Korfax was immediately put on his guard.

Ralir had not said much about his mother, and Korfax found himself taken by her dark beauty, but as she spoke to him on this matter or that, he soon realised how cleverly she turned the conversation back to the one thing that concerned her most, namely Ralir and his refusal to join the Prah Sibith.

The matter clearly weighed on her mind, but Korfax began to suspect that her care was other than that of her lord. She only wanted peace between father and son, whereas Zamferas wanted conformity through tradition, ritual, service and the long unbroken chain of continuance. Though Zamferas said nothing, Korfax could tell that he listened intently to all that was said, and so all he could do in return was defend his friend and explain his love of the sword.

At the end of the feast, after the songs had been sung and the dances danced, Zamferas and Tharah had stood before him and both had smiled at him.

"Your loyalty to my son has not gone unnoticed," Zamferas had said. "It warms my heart that he has found such a friend."

Korfax had looked down in response.

"Thank you, Tabaud," he said. "I also know what it is like when there is tension between father and son. There is never any peace on either side whilst it lasts."

Zamferas had frowned.

"There is contention between you and your father?"

"Yes, Tabaud, and I wish that there was not."

Here he had turned to Tharah, and bowed to her slightly.

"But my mother intercedes between us, much as Tabaud Tharah does between you and your son."

Zamferas had glanced at Tharah then, seeing how she smiled gratefully at Korfax. Zamferas had then turned to Korfax once more.

"Tell me what is in your heart," he said.

"That your son is truly gifted with a blade. There are few who can match him even now, and when he becomes a Napei I doubt any will. It is not my place to say in this matter, but I was always taught that it is a sin to deny the gifts The Creator gives us."

Zamferas had tightened his gaze for a moment, but then gentled it again.

"So what would you have of me?" he asked.

"It is not my place to say, Tabaud."

"But it is. I have listened to your words and I have seen that you speak only with the deepest honesty. Rightly are the Farenith honoured if all their sons are such as you. So tell me your desire. I would greatly value the friendship of your house."

"In that case, Tabaud, that there be a reconciliation."

Zamferas had then bowed his head slightly in acknowledgement. There was the hint of a smile in his eyes.

"We shall see," he had said.

There came a knock upon his door. He looked up even as it opened. In came Ralir with the widest smile on his face that Korfax had ever seen. Ralir positively radiated joy.

"Korfax, my wonderful friend, bringing you here was an act of unmitigated brilliance on my part. You have charmed my parents into the most agreeable mood I have ever seen them assume in all my life."

Korfax offered a wry smile in return.

"I did nothing," he said. "I merely spoke the truth as I saw it."

Ralir laughed.

"But your work is now done, my friend. The rest of your stay here shall be as you will it. We spoke, my father and I, and reached an accord. He will no longer oppose my desire to become a sword, just so long as I am properly prepared to take his seat when he no longer occupies it."

"Then you will become the first of the Prah Sibith after all?"

"Yes."

"So there is peace between you now?"

"Yes, that too."

Korfax looked away.

"That is good," he said.

Ralir dropped his smile.

"Now all that is needed is for me to speak to your father and sort things out between you."

Korfax turned quickly.

"Do not, I beg you. You do not know what he is like when roused."

Ralir paused a moment as if considering a retort, but then he seemed to change his mind.

"As you wish," he said, before producing a large crystal bottle from behind his back.

"Now to more important matters. I thought that you and I could sit out upon your balcony, gaze down upon the sights, smell the evening breeze and drink of the very best Pelarr of all, because, if nothing else, you have earned it this day."

Korfax looked at the bottle.

"The very best Pelarr? Is there such a thing?"

"Oh indeed there is," said Ralir. "Here, from the family vaults, I bring you a gift. This bottle is nearly four hundred years old and the wine within it has seen three ascensions. I give you the eighth bottle of Ertil Pelarr. There are only seven left now."

Ralir tapped with a finger the table that divided them.

"Wine such as this never leaves the Rax Izikal, ever, and very few outside my family have even suspected that it exists at all."

He leaned closer, lowering his voice.

"And even fewer have tasted it."

Ralir gestured to the long chairs set before the low table. There they both reclined and took their ease. Ralir slowly released the stopper from the ancient bottle and sniffed at the unsealed air. He closed his eyes for a moment before pouring the liquid darkness within into two waiting goblets. They each raised their goblets to each other, the scent rising about them, mellow, yet potent. Then each took a sip, and each sighed in turn. The taste fell upon their tongues, wonder unbounded, seducing them with sweet memory, whilst about them both the Jewel of Badagar threatened the lights of heaven with its captured stars.

The next day was leisurely, quiet and peaceful. Korfax was content just to wander, but Ralir had other ideas.

"Korfax?"

"Yes?"

"You know, you have told me an awful lot of things about yourself, but I do not think I have repaid you in quite the same way."

"I haven't even thought about it," Korfax answered.

"It doesn't bother you?"

"No, we are friends. What passes between us does not need words."

Ralir smiled.

"There is something I want to tell you though, something you should know. It might help explain a few things."

Korfax watched carefully. Ralir's demeanour had changed. What was coming, he wondered, what did Ralir want to say?

"There have been many who would have liked me to call them friend," Ralir continued, "but there is only one other that ever mattered to me as you do, and he is gone."

Ralir seemed to be struggling with something now, something deep and difficult.

"Don't tell me if it causes you pain," Korfax said.

Ralir looked up and smiled reassuringly.

"You are a true friend," he said. "I will tell you everything, but not here."

He beckoned.

"Come, I have something else to show you."

Ralir took Korfax through less well-travelled parts of the Rax Izikal, down to the vaults and then to a hidden door at the back of one of them. Behind it there were stairs, stairs that went down into the depths.

It was a tunnel, old and forgotten, that went all the way from the centre of the city to beyond its walls. It did not deviate but ran its course true all the way. Ralir would not speak as they walked along it; instead, his eyes stared straight ahead. Korfax followed behind and wondered.

It took a good hour to reach the end. Then they started climbing, old stairs that took them back to the surface. The stairs ended at a blank wall. Ralir put his ear to it and listened. Satisfied, he drew back and pushed at a particular place on the blank stone. The stone slid outwards and sideways and they stepped out into the light. They were in the forest to the south of the city, just beyond the walls, and around them lay the last stones of ancient ruins.

"Now we can talk," said Ralir.

They sat inside the ruin of an ancient tower, in the cool of its darkness, and Ralir began his tale.

"I once met a Napei here, when I was young. He was heading, by secret ways, to Lonsiatris."

"Lonsiatris? Was he a heretic?"

"Perhaps, but his exile was not voluntary. You might know more of this than you realise. He was friend to Dialyas."

Korfax started.

"A friend? What happened?"

"He was being hunted by the Balt Kaalith."

"Hunted?"

"They wanted him so that they could bring charges of subversion against Dialyas. Odoras would not tell me what happened, or what he knew."

Korfax leaned back against the stone of the old tower.

"Odoras?"

"That was his name."

"How did you meet him?"

"It was pure chance. He was hiding in one of the gardens near the outer wall, wounded, cuts to his arms and one across his midriff. They were deep and he had lost a lot of blood. But the biggest problem was a dart they had thrown at him, covered with some sort of poison or drug. It made him sluggish and he could not move his left arm at all. I helped him hide in a little-used annex, just as two Noqvoan came over the wall in pursuit. They were following the blood. It didn't take long for the guards to get involved, and soon there was all sorts of confusion going on. It was actually quite funny to watch – lots of shouting, lots of pushing and a great deal of shoving. The guards were determined to detain them and the Noqvoan did not want to be detained. I used the distraction to help move him to a better hiding place. There are lots of rooms in the Rax Izikal that have rarely, if ever, seen the light of day. I got him to one such, though it was difficult. He kept drifting in and out of consciousness. More by luck than anything else I managed to help him through the worst of it. He was very grateful."

"That cannot have been easy. Did anyone notice?"

"No. No one paid too much attention to what I did. So long as I attended my lessons and did what my father and mother asked of me, there was no other call on my time."

"How long did it take for him to recover?"

"A very long time. Almost a year, perhaps. But think of it! He was here, a fugitive from justice, in the Rax Izikal itself. I found that I rather liked the idea."

"He remained here? That was risky, surely."

"Yes and no. I could not chance bringing in one of the Faxith, so I had to nurse him myself, smuggling in food and healing herbs at his direction. But as I said, no one noticed. There are many secret ways and unused rooms. Hiding him was easy. We became friends. It was he who taught me how first to fight with a sword. Think of it. I owe my skill to an exile."

Korfax felt caught in a swirl of conflict. Ralir, his friend, had done a proscribed thing. He thought back to Losq and a memory of a memory that was hidden. Such a confession deserved a response.

"How long did he stay?"

"Longer than he intended."

Ralir looked up.

"I think he came to care for me deeply. I certainly cared for him. He was alone, had lost all that he loved and his name had been dishonoured. I was the only one to care."

Ralir looked down.

"He is the reason I do not trust the west."

Korfax frowned.

"What do you mean?"

"Lies. They told lies about him so that they could get to Dialyas. He was a means to an end. They falsely accused him of heresy. He would not tell me what they had done, only that the charges against him were false. He said I must remain innocent in the affair so that its taint would never stain me."

"Can any of this be proved?"

"No! They hid their lies as they hide everything else. He never told me who was behind it, but it was clear that some of the Balt Kaalith were involved."

Ralir looked up again.

"Be wary of them, Korfax. Not all of them can be trusted."

He continued with his tale.

"When the time came and he had to leave, I got him a steed. That was difficult. I sent him out through the tunnel I showed you and brought the ormn to him the next day. I nearly got caught."

"Caught?"

"I very foolishly stole the ormn. It was a scandal at the time. The possibility of theft? My father was in a foul mood for the next three days. Theft in Othil Admaq?

Unthinkable. He cursed everybody: frequently, visibly and loudly."

"You were not caught?"

"No, they had no idea who had done the deed. The Balt Kaalith decided that it was Odoras, fleeing after lying low somewhere in the Rax Izikal. My father was even angrier and he cursed them, to their faces, for even daring to suggest it."

"Was there anybody he did not curse?"

"In order? The Creator, the Velukor, my mother and me. Everybody else at least three times each."

Korfax smiled.

"I think I understand. Odoras showed you another way. That was why you wanted to become a sword."

Ralir looked up.

"I knew you would see. It was difficult, but I managed to persuade the Nazad Esiask that I was serious, especially when they saw how good I was."

"Did they not suspect?"

"No! Leastways, no one said anything to me."

"Have you ever heard from Odoras again?"

"Never. He would not risk it. A message from Lonsiatris? Unthinkable."

Ralir looked away.

"I hope he found a measure of happiness at last."

There was a long silence. Korfax thought hard for a moment and then looked up.

"My turn now," he announced.

Ralir gave him a curious look.

"Your turn?"

"The telling of tales."

Ralir smiled a somewhat superior smile.

"What tale? I know everything there is to know about you."

"No, you don't."

"So what is it you think I don't know?"

"The attack upon my home – what really happened."

Ralir paused and the smile dropped from his face.

"Are you sure you want to tell me this?"

"Do you want to hear the tale?"

"Helping heretics is one thing. Fighting demons? That is something else."

"You may be called upon to do it. I know that I will."

"Are you sure about this?"

"I'm sure. You have told me your tale, so you deserve to know something in return."

Korfax told Ralir everything, right up to the point when he and his mother were caught in the small room. Then he paused. Something inside him was urging him on, speaking to him from the other side of his mind. *Tell of the hidden*, it said, *you owe it to your friend. Share the secret. Share the burden.* He was suddenly scared.

Ralir was waiting. It was obvious that something was wrong, as Korfax was trembling, fighting himself. He leaned over and put a hand on his arm.

"Don't say any more. This hurts you," he said.

Korfax closed his eyes and opened them again, a long slow blink.

"I have never spoken of this to another soul," he said. "I should speak of it now."

But he could not cross the boundary, he could not. The walls of the hiding pattern rose up before him like a denial. He could see what lay beyond them, but he could not say the words.

"They broke down the door," he said. "They stepped into the room and we were moments from death. I remember them opening their mouths wide, their tongues, their teeth."

He paused and took a deep breath.

"Then fire caught them and they burned to ash."

Korfax breathed out. That had been hard. He had been so close to telling Ralir his secret, so close. But Ralir had already missed the omission.

"Your father!" he said. "Gods below, Korfax, but that was close. No wonder you have not spoken of it. The tales I have heard are nothing like that, nothing at all."

Ralir stood away from the wall. He looked angry now.

"And then you have had to endure the likes of Simoref? What does that pampered fool know? What do any of them know? The north is at war and the rest of them sit in their towers and spout platitudes!"

Korfax remained looking down, staring into the stone at his feet.

"I had forgotten how terrible it all was," he said, "the death, the horror. And my father saw it all again at Tohus, though he arrived there far too late. The Agdoain had already done their work."

Ralir came back to Korfax.

"Now do you see why I value your friendship? I knew it from the moment I met you. We share a covenant, you and I."

"Yes," agreed Korfax. "I think that we do!"

It was not long before Korfax and Ralir were buried once more in the long rituals of their respective guilds. Time moved on, ever-repeating movements like the long slow turn of the seasons, and then came the day the great bells of the Umadya Telloah echoed across the city.

They always sounded mournful, ringing quietly at each ceremony of ending, ringing the departed soul on its way back to the river. But now they hurled their grief even out to the furthest quarters of Emethgis Vaniad. Mourn they cried, mourn for loss, mourn for the departed.

Korfax leaned out of his window and looked down at the scurrying figures below. Something had happened, something terrible. He knew it, he could feel it. He turned back to his room and went to the door. He looked out and saw one of the wardens coming towards him. It was Kurapan.

"Geyad, what has happened?"

Kurapan looked at Korfax and smiled sadly.

"Ah Korfax, this has become a grim day. Prepare for sad tidings indeed. The Velukor has died. Ermalei, blessed be his name, is no more. His shell is empty and the stone of his life has finally been broken."

Korfax was shocked. Velukor Ermalei was his father's age, still young by Ell reckoning at only a little over a hundred and fifty years old. Ermalei's father had nearly reached three hundred.

Korfax bowed his head and uttered the only response that he could.

"May he find his way back to the river so that he can come amongst us again. The world is diminished by his going."

Kurapan came forward and stood beside Korfax.

"May The Creator's light shine upon him," he said, bowing his head also, "and may he once again be as a stone in the greatest of all rivers."

They looked at each other. Kurapan's eyes suddenly glistened.

"You said that with true feeling, Korfax. I have heard those words many times this day, but never were they uttered with such honesty. Honest grief is always a blessing to the departed."

Kurapan leaned forward.

"I am sure he will return to us in future times. You, though, should prepare yourself. You will be one of the few journeying to the Umadya Pir."

Korfax looked up, astonished.

"Me?" he asked.

"That is why I was coming here," Kurapan said. "Neither your father nor your mother are here. I am told that your father is out of contact, scouring the distant north. It may well be that your mother will come, but I cannot tell you with any certainty whether that will be so. You, though, are here and you should be ready to represent your house. It is a shame perhaps, for your father and the Velukor knew each other well, or so I am told."

"Yes, Geyad. My father and my mother were joined together by the Velukor himself. My mother and the Velukor were cousins."

"That I did know, but it does not change things. You are still to the fore. You will be numbered amongst the blood. Be ready. The ceremony will be tomorrow."

Korfax stood beside Audroh Usdurna and waited. It seemed only moments ago he had received the news from Kurapan. Now here he was, in the Umadya Pir, standing at the front of the Hall of Remembrance and looking up at the covered body of the Velukor, draped in black.

He had ridden to the Tower of Light, lonely and subdued. Though all the high council of the Dar Kaadarith would be there, they would come at different times and by different routes. Being of the blood, he had to travel another way, the most direct – the path of the arrow. Few others would go that way.

He wore robes of mourning, freshly provided by Kurapan. No other decoration was allowed, and even his steed was simply arrayed.

He arrived at the tower, and the imperial Branith took his steed without word. He walked to the Hall of Remembrance, head bowed, utterly silent, and went inside. There were few others present as yet, as he was early. He went to the place prepared for him and assumed the Eoan Telloah, the posture of respect for the dead.

So here he was now, beside Usdurna, prince of the east, waiting for the rites to begin.

Usdurna had not long arrived from Othil Ekrin by sky ship, but somehow everything about him, everything that he did, seemed slow, deliberate and filled with aged dignity. He seemed to take for ever to walk the length of the Hall of Remembrance, marking out each long step with a single swing of his great staff. When Usdurna eventually reached his place, Korfax had bowed deeply to him and Usdurna had bowed back. Then they had regarded each other.

To Korfax, Audroh Usdurna seemed the very paragon of nobility. Tall, taller even than his father, Usdurna stood proud and straight, his high brow set with an argent circlet of Izen, itself set with a single green crystal of water, the ancient crown of all the princes of the Korith Zinu.

It was not permitted to speak during the rites of Telloah, but Korfax felt a brief touch upon his mind. Usdurna had placed a message there. *You are Faren Noren Korfax*, it said, *and we will talk afterwards*. Korfax bowed again, and sent one word of his own. *Audroh!* Usdurna had smiled lightly in response.

The hall began to fill, a gentle swelling of numbers. Korfax kept his posture and tried not to feel the movement of minds behind him, but then he felt the presence of another and could not ignore it. The prince of Othil Homtoh had arrived.

Audroh Zafazaa strode the length of the aisle as though to stamp his authority upon its stone. He went straight to the place reserved for him, bowing to no one and nothing. But then he caught sight of Korfax, and they locked eyes.

Korfax could not help it. Memories of Simoref flooded back into his mind full force, and his thoughts were suddenly naked upon his face. Utter hatred. Zafazaa drew back, clearly disconcerted. He was used to servility and care, not unfettered hostility. He looked away again and faced the front. Korfax watched him for a moment more and then turned to the front again.

He seethed inside until a gentle thought touched his mind. It was Usdurna, a timely reminder of where he was and what was expected of him. Korfax took a deep breath and calmed his mind.

More great houses appeared, each taking their place to this side or that, but always behind. At one point Korfax felt Tabaud Zamferas and Tabaud Tharah arrive. He turned to acknowledge them and they both touched his mind as they took the places prepared for them, careful thoughts returned in kind. Ralir followed them with a face of barely concealed discontent, which lessened when he saw Korfax, and they passed a quick bow to each other before Ralir went to stand by his mother and father. Korfax turned forward again and began to feel rather alone. He was right at the front, up amongst the very highest in all the land, and he was certain that he was being scrutinised from behind by every single eye.

Few were of the blood. His father, were he here, would have represented the Farenith, but he would have been in the second row, not the first. Korfax, by right of birth, could stand to the front, but only if his father was not present.

His mother came very late, like a cold wind from the north, and he felt her approach, even over all the other great ones assembled there. The great hall seemed to echo to her step. He waited, unmoving, until she came to stand beside him. Usdurna made way for her and bowed slowly and with great deliberation. She bowed back and returned his sad smile with one of her own. But Zafazaa did not move at all and stared steadfastly to the front. She clearly knew he was there, but she did not look or even acknowledge his presence; instead, she turned to Korfax and her expression gentled even further. He looked at her and she looked back at him. They touched minds, a brief mingling of love. Then she came to his side and kissed him lightly upon his brow, though now she had to stretch somewhat to do it. It was only then that she glanced in the direction of Zafazaa, a brief look of cold.

None missed the act. It was an uncommon thing to do on such a day, but her intent was obvious – an act of challenge and defiance aimed straight at Zafazaa. Usdurna allowed himself the merest hint of satisfaction, but Zafazaa did not move at all, clenching himself even further into stillness.

Korfax remained where he was. He stood tall beside his mother as the dark rites of death were enacted and the Velukor's body was burnt back to the substance of its making. When the fire reached its height, and all was burned back to nothingness, it stopped with a suddenness that made Korfax jump. Although he knew what would happen, its abruptness still startled him.

Now, where the flame had been, a figure in white stood. It was Onehson, Velukor-to-be. He held up the stave in his hand, the stave of Karmaraa, and it blazed with light. The light was met with a single peal from the great bell. An awesome silence fell. Onehson spoke.

"Here I came. Here I conquered. And here I will sit for ever, dwelling in the brightness of the heavens."

Four heralds appeared, two to the front, two to the back, each facing the four directions. Upon their breasts were the four sigils of the spirit, brilliant in the light.

"Here stands the Velukor of the Ell," they cried, "Onehson, forty-ninth and first, blessed be his name."

All bowed their heads.

It was done.

Korfax walked the high balcony, Usdurna at his side. His mother had left him almost immediately after the rites so that she could be with the only one left of her family, Enay Osidess.

Korfax had only caught the briefest glimpse of Osidess. She had arrived alone, hooded and veiled. Having taken the oaths of grief she would never show her face to the world again. It was a hard thing to do, and a blow for Zafazaa. In doing this she would leave his side. He would be alone from this point onwards. Though he should not have done so, Korfax found himself relishing the justice of it.

Usdurna looked down at his young companion.

"To be able to meet you at last, young Korfax, is an unlooked for pleasure on such a sad day."

Korfax bowed, unable to think what to say in response. The day had been such a contrast – the solemnity of the rites, the quiet pageant of honour, the assemblage of the mightiest in the land. His confrontation with Zafazaa, brief as it had been, still burned in his mind and he had wandered through the gathering after the rites as though alone.

Many had bowed to him as he had passed, and he had bowed back. But then he had drifted on again, catching snatches of conversation here and there. Many from his order were here, but he did not feel he should seek out their company. He felt out of place, a wanderer, listening to conversations on matters that did not concern him and to which he was not privy. Then Usdurna had rescued him, guiding him out onto the great east balcony.

Now here he was, with the Audroh of Rasayah smiling down at him.

"I know your father well. We have met many times."

Usdurna leaned closer.

"Of all the great houses, yours is, I think, the most steadfast."

Korfax blushed.

"Audroh, I am sure, were my father here, he would remind you of your own great heritage. I but follow in his footsteps."

Usdurna let his smile widen.

"And it is well that you should. A finer example of service I cannot imagine."

Usdurna turned to Korfax and fixed him with his kindly gaze.

"And when you attain your stave, you must do as he did. You must travel the world, take a peregrination, see our land for yourself and marvel at its beauty."

"I would like to do that, Audroh, if duty allows. But there is strife. Demons walk the land once again. I am sure that I will be sent north, to help in putting an end to them."

Usdurna dropped his smile altogether.

"And it is very right and proper that it should be so, but your father fights the evil ere we speak. I do not doubt that he will defeat it at the last. Then the world will return to its accustomed ways, as was intended from the very beginning."

A slim figure approached them both, flanked by many of the imperial Branith. Korfax bowed low, as did Usdurna. It was Onehson, resplendent in the crown of Karmaraa, unmistakable in his cloak of white, the cloak of the Velukor.

Even for an Ell, Onehson was uncommonly beautiful, the light within him shining for all to see. But there was also something uncertain about him, something doubtful, as though his spirit was yet wary of fully claiming its perfectly formed vessel. The eyes especially never seemed to fill with the objects placed before them, but rather drifted across their surfaces like fleeting clouds. And they were pale, the lightest of purples, uncomfortably pale.

"Audroh."

"My Velukor."

"And you must be Faren Noren Korfax."

Korfax bowed again.

"My Velukor," he replied, as the only thing he could think of was to speak when spoken to. The words ran through his mind as though on a wheel. Speak only when spoken to, speak only when spoken to.

Onehson looked at Korfax carefully, weighing him up perhaps. Everything Onehson did he seemed to do with great consideration.

"I have heard much about you," he said.

Korfax could not say the same. He knew very little about Onehson. Onehson kept himself to himself. He was aloof, some said, while others considered him quiet and thoughtful. Korfax wondered which it was, and what he could say in return.

"Much has happened since the attack upon my home, my Velukor."

A look of concern drifted briefly across the Velukor's face.

"Yes, it has. You have had quite an eventful life, I think. I cannot imagine what that would be like."

Korfax had no idea how to respond, but he was spared the trouble of answering as Onehson turned to Usdurna.

"Audroh, I would speak with you."

Usdurna bowed.

"Of course, my Velukor."

Korfax bowed as Onehson left with Usdurna. He watched carefully. How self-contained the new Velukor seemed, how controlled. Korfax wondered whether it was the loss of his father. Loss! He thought back to Losq. He understood how that felt.

He remained upon the balcony, looking out over the city, until his mother found him again. She came to stand beside him, her expression severe.

"I have heard a thing," she said. "I was told what you did."

He looked at her.

"What I did?"

"Many saw how you looked at Zafazaa. You are fortunate it went no further. Most understand and are sympathetic, but you must never do such a thing again. He is Audroh, and despite what you may think of him, he remains a great power in the land. If anything happened to the Velukor he would become regent."

Korfax looked away.

"He does not deserve his position."

"No, he does not, but that is not for you to decide."

"He set his son against me!"

"Yes, but that is now over and done with."

"Not for me!"

She reached over and turned his face towards her. Her expression remained severe, but it was a far gentler severity than before.

"Do not hate," she told him. "That is their illness, not yours. Hatred is the unbalanced mind. I will not have you submitting to it. Clear your head, my son, and remember who you are and where you come from. In this matter you have prevailed. Be magnanimous."

Life would have moved on much as it had done before if not for news of another death. This time it was that of the Geyadel, Gemanim.

The news came a few days later during the evening meal. Korfax was sitting with Thilnor and Oanatom as usual, all eating in customary silence, when the sharp crack of stone on stone echoed around the hall. Geyadril Abrilon was standing at the centre. He had struck the floor with his stave.

"Hear me, all of you," his voice rang out, clear and echoing. "The Geyadel has entered the river. Be prepared."

He turned about and strode from the hall.

The rites of Telloah were to be the next day. Lessons were suspended so that all could attend. There was no need to ask who the new Geyadel would be, as Abrilon had been Geyadel in all but name for the last thirty years. Korfax stood with all the others of the fourth level, waiting respectfully, waiting for Abrilon to call up the fire that would burn Gemanim's body from the world.

He watched as Gemanim's stave was handed with reverence to Sohagel so that it could be placed back into the furnace from whence it came. He watched as Abrilon came forward to burn the body, and then he started. His father was there, right at the front, and his face was dark.

It seemed only a moment later that he found himself once more in the courtyard of Hais with his father, ever the place for their confrontations. But there was something different this time. Something had changed. His father appeared more open, less restrained, as though something within him had been unleashed.

"Hello father," he said.

His father smiled, but it was a cold smile.

"You have grown," he said.

"The seasons pass."

The smile wavered.

"You are still angry, I see."

"And what of you?" asked Korfax

"The seasons pass."

"You did not answer any of my messages."

"There was nothing I could say."

"Yes, there was."

"Korfax," Sazaaim said, "it took me a while to realise it but now that I see you here before me I know it to be true. We are too alike for our words together to change anything between us. There was nothing I could say, and there is nothing I can say now. I see the anger still within you, and I know what it is, for the same beast lives in me."

Korfax looked away.

"Secrets!" he said.

Sazaaim agreed.

"We all have them," he said. "Some must be kept, others revealed. But only at the requisite time."

"So you will tell me nothing more?"

"No."

"Then there is nothing further to say."

"You intend to keep your distance?"

"Only because you keep yours."

"You do not trust me?"

Korfax looked up at that. Trust?

"YOU ARE MY FATHER!" he raged.

Sazaaim sighed.

"Yes," he said, "I am. And I am sorry that it has come to this. One day you will understand, and then all will be clear. But until then?"

He came forward and embraced his son. Korfax hesitated, but then he returned the embrace, holding his father tighter and tighter as the rage fell away. Down and down it went, back into the depths, but it did not entirely die.

12

THE FURNACES OF TRUTH

Bruj-pildih Ip-ged-torgin
Get-relihd Odmirk-kaoji
Vonod-qur Logah-kompah
Ti-biru Drm-nipilihd
Teo-duhnith Aisan-urqihs
Bs-ianio Krih-nisula
Paf-anihr Odpam-atel

It was time to serve the furnaces. All those that reached their fifth year in the seminary were expected to do this: to learn the art of forging and to master it accordingly. The furnaces were kept by Tabitem, spare and taciturn. Like most of the others in the seminary Korfax had only ever seen Tabitem in the great Hall of Forging. It was rare to see him anywhere else. The furnaces were his life. He and those that worked beside him kept them in continual use, and when he was not busy he would sit and stare into them as though divining strange truth in their fires. As a consequence his eyes had taken on something of their fury, so it was not easy to meet his gaze if you were unprepared for it.

Those of the fifth level were expected to spend much of their time in the Hall of Forging, as much as could be allowed in fact. It took time to get used to the heat and few had the stamina for prolonged exposure at first, so other, lighter duties were provided. As with everything to do with the furnaces it took time, lots of time.

The great hall itself was intimidating. The furnaces were huge, great cauldrons of power, and everything in the hall seemed to radiate their force, even the stone of which it was composed. Dark and fiery, it had been specially chosen to withstand the power that beat against it. Maintaining the hall took dedicated skill and a certain imperturbability, so those that worked here, like Tabitem, were all masters of earth.

"Here is stone!" Tabitem announced, standing before them and marking each with a sere glance. "You will find no impatience here. This is a time-honoured place, a slow place, and it is slow for a reason. The powers that we deal with cannot be hurried. To do so is to invite failure. Forging is a slow art, but it is precise. One misstep will spoil the entire work and it has to be started all over again, from the very beginning. There is no other way. Like the slow growth of life, you cannot go back and amend your mistakes or try to mould your error back into the shape it should be. That will not work. And though I have some tolerance for mistakes, as we all have to learn after all, I do not tolerate impatience. Be warned."

He gestured at a row of smaller furnaces, all lined up against the southern wall. They were large enough to sit inside, but tiny when compared to the behemoths that did the real work.

"Here are your furnaces," he told them, "one for each of you. Your first task is to learn how to create a constant heat. You might consider that a somewhat trivial undertaking, but it is not. You must learn consistency and attention, for a forging can take anything up to seven days. I have even heard tell of forgings taking an entire year."

He looked at them all once more, as if measuring their stamina.

"Imagine it," he said. "An entire year of concentrated focus. You cannot believe such a thing now, but when you leave here at the end, every one of you will be capable of helping in such an endeavour."

The long slow preparation went on, day in, day out, and when each was sufficiently capable of maintaining a consistent heat they came to it at last. They were to perform an actual forging.

They were to make piradar, the eternal lights that were the delight of every Ell. Like all the other acolytes Korfax tended to take piradar more or less for granted. They were ubiquitous. But to actually make one?

After setting his furnace in motion and letting its fury mount to the requisite height, Korfax placed his portion of base material, a large stone, dark and heavy, into his ladle and lowered it carefully into the fire. Everything had to be done by hand. Power could not be used, as the furnaces themselves were sensitive and volatile.

He watched the stone fall into the centre and withdrew the ladle. After a moment the stone began to liquefy, then to burn, then to collapse in upon itself as the impurities were scoured from its substance. Soon there was nothing but an incandescent sphere where the stone had been. Korfax felt his way into the furnace with his mind and set the change in motion. Mere heat was not enough. The fires of his mind had to change the fires of the furnace and set them on a new path. He held the shape and the substance he required in his thought, and then let it transmute the base material, gently coaxing it towards his intent.

He decided that the process was akin to devotional meditation, the visualisation of light coming down from above and filling the vessel of his desire. It was neither peaceful nor restful, though, and the discipline of such singular attention took its toll. Only one forging a day was to be allowed.

Korfax almost missed the transition, the moment coming so quickly that he could not quite believe that it had happened at all. The furnace died under his hand and its heat dissipated. Inside it a glorious light swelled. He reached in with his ladle and withdrew the light. He looked at it in satisfaction. He had done it.

The piradar was a brilliant white. It shone in the vaults like a star, and many others turned to look, those that tended the furnaces, and they smiled.

Tabitem was at his side in moments.

"You are successful?" he asked.

He looked at the stone in the ladle.

"Perfect," he said.

"You are the first!" he announced, as if that was no surprise at all. He looked at Korfax and his eyes gleamed.

"Your father was the same. He was first also. It is good to see a tradition upheld."

Tabitem leaned in closer.

"Now the question. He understood – do you?"

Korfax saw Tabitem's meaning immediately. He was asking if Korfax had understood the process. Though it had happened in a mere moment, the final stages of the forging were there inside him, the intricate folding that went down and down into the appearing void, faster and faster, down to where the nothingness was divided and light was born.

"Yes," he said, and he meant it.

Tabitem smiled.

"Then I am content. You are truly on your way."

Korfax watched as the others quickly followed. Lights were born, one after another. There were smiles of success, and puzzled expressions also, as each of the new-born forgers fought with their experience and tried to understand it.

It was during one of the prescribed moments of rest that Thilnor came to kneel beside Korfax.

"I have something to tell you," he whispered.

"Tabitem will not be pleased if he sees that you are not in your place," Korfax whispered back.

"But this is important," Thilnor insisted. "Oanatom told me only this morning."

"Then why doesn't Oanatom tell me himself?"

"Because he knows how sensitive you are where Tahamoh is concerned."

Korfax turned fully to Thilnor.

"What?" he hissed.

Thilnor was about to speak again when another voice intruded.

"It is called 'rest' for a reason."

They both turned to find Tabitem leaning over them both, his expression severe. Thilnor went back to his place.

After the day was done, Korfax found Thilnor waiting for him outside the Hall of Forging.

"So?" he said. "What is this about? Why couldn't Oanatom say it?"

"He asked me to speak to you on his behalf. He didn't want to upset you." Thilnor took a deep breath. "You know," he said, "you are not exactly the easiest person to talk to these days."

"I have learnt to keep my own counsel," Korfax told him.

Thilnor looked down.

"I didn't blame you for what happened to Tahamoh."

"I know, and for that I thank you, but many others did. Some still do, though they remain silent about it."

"As to that, are you surprised? After what happened with Simoref?"

"From an object of contempt to an object of fear! I am not sure which I prefer. The only good to come from all of this is my friendship with Ralir."

Thilnor suddenly looked crestfallen and Korfax frowned.

"I didn't mean it quite that way. You are a good friend too, Thilnor."

Thilnor brightened, but only a little.

"I can be nothing else," he said. "Whatever others may think, I know who you are."

Korfax returned the smile.

"So what did Oanatom want to say?"

"That he met with Tahamoh when he went home to Othil Homtoh last. It was quite by accident. Tahamoh told him things, things I don't think he was meant to tell anyone else."

Korfax stared at Thilnor for a long moment. Finally he gestured ahead.

"Let us go and find Oanatom then. He can tell me the tale himself. It is long past time that we made peace over this."

They found Oanatom in his usual place in the archives. He was sitting alone, reading what appeared to be a treatise on forging, its origins and its evolution. He looked up as Korfax and Thilnor approached. Both of them sat opposite him.

"Thilnor tells me that you have something for me," said Korfax.

Oanatom glanced at Thilnor.

"You didn't tell him?"

"Korfax wanted to hear it from you," Thilnor said.

Oanatom turned back to Korfax.

"We have been friends for a long time now," Korfax told him. "Only this issue stands between us. I would clear it away. I cannot be angry all my life."

Oanatom looked at the logadar he had been using.

"Then this might not help," he said. "Tahamoh told me things that make me question all I have come to trust."

He took a long breath as though steadying himself for what was to come. Then he dimmed the light of the logadar and turned fully to Korfax.

"There is no easy way to say this," he said. "But it seems you were deliberately placed in the path of Dialyas so that you would be dishonoured by your association with him."

"Tahamoh knew?" asked Korfax.

"No, not at first," answered Oanatom. "Nor was he supposed to find out. But he inadvertently overheard a conversation that was not meant for his ears. After that he went looking for answers."

"Zafazaa!" Korfax hissed.

Oanatom bowed his head.

"So Tahamoh was innocent?" Korfax asked.

"Yes, his father was ordered to spend his son; otherwise, patronage was to be withdrawn and they would be outcast and dishonoured."

Korfax took a long slow breath to calm himself.

"And what of Tahamoh?"

"He is still studying to become a Geyad, but in Othil Homtoh," said Oanatom.

Korfax drew back in surprise.

"I thought he was supposed to be in disgrace," he said.

"It was withdrawn. Part of the bargain, I imagine."

Oanatom looked unhappy now.

"But, Korfax, he is so bitter. He hates his family, he hates the west and he hates the Dar Kaadarith most of all."

"He was my friend," said Korfax. "I still feel an obligation. There must be something I can do!"

"If you stir things up, there will only be more trouble. Tahamoh is not supposed to know about any of this. Besides, he remains at the mercy of his family and those to whom his family answer."

"So who else is involved?" Korfax asked. "I know only of Zafazaa. Who else played a part in this?"

"Tahamoh's father and Yamandir of Sosatar, as far as we know."

Korfax went still as thoughts boiled through his awareness, a series of images and places, a journey of mind and memory he did not want to take. It all made sense. Tahamoh was to lead Korfax to Matchir and then play no further part. Matchir was to lead Korfax to Dialyas and let events take whatever turn they would. Korfax was to be dishonoured by association. That part had worked and Korfax had been shunned. Then came the second part, humiliation. Korfax was to be broken. Enter Simoref. But that part of the plan had gone badly awry. No one had counted on Ralir. Korfax almost smiled at the memory, of the drunken Ralir wielding his empty bottle like a sword.

Then he remembered it. When he had first gone with Tahamoh to the haven of antiquities, someone else had suggested that they go.

"There was someone else!" he hissed, clenching his fists.

He wrestled with his passion as he grappled with his memories, and the others watched as he slowly controlled his temper.

"When I first came here," he told the others, "Tahamoh was sent to befriend me by another Geyad, by Omagrah. It was Omagrah who suggested the haven of antiquities to Tahamoh."

Both Thilnor and Oanatom looked shocked.

"Geyad Omagrah? Are you certain?" Oanatom buried his head in his hands.

"Tahamoh told me he was a family friend," Korfax said. "A seer would prove this, beyond all doubt."

Oanatom looked up again. He looked frightened now.

"Omagrah returned to Othil Homtoh when Simoref left," he said. "Some of us wondered why at the time."

"I will talk to Geyadril Ponodol," said Korfax. "I should be guided by him in this matter, as he is on the high council."

Now Oanatom looked even more frightened.

"But won't he ask how you found this out?"

Korfax paused and looked at Oanatom. Consequences! What good would come of this? What would accrue? What would he gain if it all came into the light, and what would be gained by silence? He struggled with it, fought with it. There was a part of him that wanted more than mere restitution, but then his mother's words came back to him: 'Do not hate,' she had said. 'That is their illness, not yours.' He took a deep breath. She was right. He must not hate.

"It would all come out," he told Oanatom at last. "It would have to."

With an effort he pushed it all back down again, and then he leaned forward and put a hand on Oanatom's shoulder. "And the innocent would suffer along with the guilty. I imagine that this would cost you, as it would cost Tahamoh and his family. I will keep it a secret for now. After all, what is one more amongst so many?"

Oanatom bowed his head.

"Thank you, Korfax."

"I have had enough of this anyway," said Korfax. "But there will come a time when there should be an accounting."

There was a moment's silence, and then Thilnor looked carefully at Oanatom.

"One thing I do not understand," he said. "Why does Tahamoh hate the Dar Kaadarith?"

"He did not tell me," said Oanatom. "Complicity, I imagine, if Geyad Omagrah was involved."

Korfax looked at them both for a moment.

"No," he said. "Not that. I know the reason."

They both turned to him.

"Here is something else to keep secret," he said. "I want your word on this."

"Yes, of course!" they answered in unison, both bowing emphatically.

"Tahamoh told me that he touched the Kapimadar."

Thilnor and Oanatom looked suitably shocked.

"But that is forbidden!" exclaimed Thilnor.

"Yes," agreed Korfax, "but he also told me that it did exactly what Dialyas said that it would. He felt it change. He believes that Dialyas was wrongly ejected from the Dar Kaadarith." Korfax looked at them both. "This is dangerous knowledge. Keep it to yourselves. Perhaps when we join the Geyadith it will be safer to contemplate what it actually means, but not now."

Thilnor looked worried.

"But what does it mean?" he asked.

"I don't know," Korfax answered. "Leastways, not yet!" he added.

During the festival of Soytal his mother came to visit. He met with her in the circular gardens that meandered through the second circle. Around them stood shapely osaagaa, trees greatly prized for their beauty. Behind them rose the Umadya Zedekel.

They embraced and then looked at each other.

"You wanted to see me?" she said. "It sounded important."

"Yes," he answered. "There is something you should know."

He gestured that they sit. She waited a moment and then sat beside him. She watched his face all the while, clearly marking the conflict within.

"What is it?" she asked.

"I have learned a thing: it seems that my visits to Dialyas were part of a larger plan."

She did not move, but her eyes intensified and she became cold.

"Zafazaa? Again?"

"Yes."

"Tell me the tale," she said, her voice quiet and still.

Korfax told her everything, even the part about keeping his own counsel.

"I made a promise to Oanatom," he said. "This would cause him trouble as well, and I do not want that, but somebody else had to know and I could only think of you."

Tazocho remained still for long moments. Korfax could tell that she was ordering her thoughts, placing everything in its own little compartment in her mind. When she was done, she sighed. She had clearly found it difficult. Like him, a part of her hated Zafazaa. Unlike him, though, her hatred was cold, an icy hatred that she could crush down and control.

"When will we have justice?" he asked.

She looked up, surprised.

"You know, I was so expecting you to say vengeance then."

"It is true, I still hate him. But as you told me, I must not submit to it. Hatred serves only itself."

She smiled, a warm and proud smile, and it banished the anger and the bitterness.

"You have grown. You understand."

She reached forward and touched his cheek, stroking it gently with her fingers.

"My son, strong and true." Her smile became sadder. "So let Zafazaa and his thralls sink back down into their petty darknesses. We shall not talk of this unless he acts again. Then, perhaps, all the secrets – all of them – can come into the light so that justice can finally be done."

He started at her words.

"*All* the secrets?" he asked

The words were out before he could consider the consequences, and seeing the look on his mother's face, Korfax suddenly wished he could call them back.

Tazocho looked hard at her son for a moment, a great heat in her eyes.

"So you have not entirely forgotten, I see."

"No," he said. "It stirs inside me occasionally, like a dark dream."

Tazocho looked away again, her expression sad.

"You should not even be aware of it," she told him. "How long has this been the case?"

"Since the beginning," he answered.

She looked back, a snap of the head. Her eyes were hard now.

"How?" she demanded.

"I found that I understood it. You taught me well, as did Doanazin."

"And you should have told me there and then. There are ways to amend such things, if one is quick. It is too late now."

"I did not know that I should," he said. "Anyway, what is one more secret amongst so many?"

"That depends!" she returned. "Not all secrets are equal, though I see that you think they might be. Neither are all secrets schemes and stratagems either, but they are secret until they become ripe, if the conspirators are wise. This, though, is of the blood and the past. You are a guardian, as is your father, serving with loyalty and with honour. Zafazaa serves only himself, and there lies the difference. One day you may know the truth of this, but until then you should learn to think with a little more consideration before you speak."

Korfax bowed his head, accepting the quiet rebuke. But he wondered about it, as he wondered about a lot of things.

Work in the furnaces went its own slow way, but it was by no means a dark work. Though they toiled away in the depths of the tower, the work itself had a curious joy to it that lifted the spirit. It was an act of creation, a fusion of forces to make something new, something wonderful, the calling down of light.

So it was left to Sohagel to bring them all back down from the heights. Now that they were beginning to understand the very essence of the Namad Dar, a necessary reminder was needed of their essential purpose and the threat they were all here to guard against.

All thought the lesson was to be yet another adjunct to the art of forging, but as soon as Sohagel stepped out in front of them, they could tell, just by his demeanour, that this was to be a very different lesson indeed.

"It has always been our custom," he announced, "since the beginnings of the Wars of Unification, to record campaigns by various means, whether by sight in oanadar, by speech with kamliadar or with the written word in logadar. There are many such recordings in our archives and many more of them in the Umadya Namin."

He looked at them all sternly, passing his glance over each and every face.

"As you have been told before, the chaos of war brings with it two things of note. It brings desolation and it brings renewal. You might consider them curious companions at best, but, if you think upon the matter, you will also understand why it is so. War is the prosecution of an aim. It is the most violent force for change that we know of. Think of it as a process of making. Two forces clash and seek victory over the other. They strive for mastery, look for advantage and know only the desire to succeed. Such conflict crushes friend and foe alike, both the innocent and the guilty, under its headlong rush for consummation. Here is desolation. But along the way great leaps are made that are judged worthy of the price that has been paid. Here is renewal. Such a reward was the Namad Dar, and the Wars of Unification were the crucible in which it was forged."

He held up three oanadar.

"Here are three of the many records of that forging. In these are three visions from those times, three visions of the consequences of sorcery. This is what you have come to see today. It is against such fire that you will be set. Here is your furnace."

He placed the oanadar upon the table.

"First, let me show you one of the Pataba. You have all seen the paintings and the illustrations, but to see such a beast as a living and breathing entity is, I think, something that you will not easily forget."

Sohagel touched the oanadar and a wide plain appeared above it, hanging in the air like a bright and sudden cloud. On that plain stood a single figure, immense and brutal. They all stared up at it, and a few scattered gasps passed around the room.

The great beast seemed to glower back at them all, its small black eyes glinting with bestial hatred beneath its horned brows. Its arms hung almost to the ground and its thick curved claws scrabbled at the earth around its wide feet. Though there was little enough to gauge it against, no one could mistake its apparent size. It was huge, and even this evanescent image seemed to compress the air of the room with its bulk. It stood before them, the height of many Ell, and exuded strength like an element.

For a moment it waited, shifting as it breathed, a glaring hulk, but then it opened its great jaws in a silent bellow and rushed forward with horrid speed. Fire splashed its hide and the vision ended.

Sohagel looked at his charges. One or two were visibly shaken. He marked them carefully. Most of the others exchanged nervous smiles, pretending that they had not really been scared at all. Sohagel smiled at their bravado. Things never changed. Then he noticed Korfax. Of them all only Korfax remained essentially unmoved. Sohagel frowned for a moment but then reminded himself of one salient fact. Korfax was the only one here that had seen demons, real demons, and their work in the flesh. Even Sohagel could not say as much. He picked up the next oanadar.

"Now let me show you an attack of Barmor. And let me warn you also. This particular vision is bloody. Those who wish to leave may do so now."

No one moved. They could all taste the test in the air about them.

"So be it," said Sohagel.

He set the crystal in motion. A scene set in mountainous pastures unfolded above them all.

Past them and over them went a cavalry in ancient livery. There were wagons filled with supplies, there was a tall Ell with a stern face riding up the weary lines and back again, talking with this one or that, checking that all was in order. Then fingers pointed at the sky and mouths were opened with warning cries. The view swung upwards until it was filled with a great wide sky framed by stony heights. But the sky was not empty, for down from it circled great coiling forms, gliding to the attack on wide and outspread wings.

The view shifted again to show the cavalry scattering. One single figure stood his ground, a Geyad holding up a stave of blue. The stave seemed to flicker with power, gathering force, but then, all too soon, one of the demons tore past the Geyad, its long blade of a tail like a scythe, and he fell in pieces. Blood drenched the ground and the vision ended.

There were no nervous laughs now. Few hid their shock and none could mistake what they had just seen. That had been a Geyad, and the Geyad had fallen. What they had seen had actually happened. It was already history.

Sohagel looked at them all carefully.

"That particular vision was lifted from the first campaign to retake the lands about Ladassir," he told them. "It, as the histories relate, was a disaster. The Kolorsith had the mastery that year. Then Efaeis himself came north and bent the entire power of the west to the task. So the forces of the Kolorsith were beaten back at last, though that campaign lasted seven hard years. It took the combined might of almost every Geyad of the Dar Kaadarith to achieve it."

Sohagel glanced at Korfax again and saw the expression on his face. Korfax had been moved now, deep memory filling him, bodies failing on bone blades, loved ones dying under the claws of headless horrors. Sohagel shuddered. He could suddenly see it as well.

There was only one stone that contained a vision of the Agdoain, but it was so disturbing few had ever dared unlock it. Sazaaim himself had retrieved it from the ruin of Tohus and sent it south with a warning: 'Do not see what is in this stone unless you wish to know horror.' The admonition was so stark that few had ever dared it. One foolhardy soul, though, a young Geyad who should have known better, had unlocked the vision for a dare. Unmarked by any he had awoken what was within with a light heart and had promptly fainted. He was discovered much later, both pale and ill, whilst the vision still floated above his head like a nightmare. The Faxith had tended him for a long while.

But Sohagel was made of sterner stuff. He was one of the few that had dared the horror. He had looked upon the Agdoain and their works, and seeing Korfax now, he suddenly wished that he had not. Korfax had witnessed this? No wonder he was unmoved by what he had seen here today. He had seen far worse.

Sohagel shook himself and continued, as was his duty, holding up a third crystal.

"Now I will show you a Babemor," he announced. "This was a last desperate gambit to forestall the siege of Nalstul. It failed, of course, as all of the Argedith did eventually. And the rest, as they have ever said, is history."

He touched the crystal, and a column of dark boiling flesh filled the scene. Before the walls of Nalstul it flexed itself, a spinning, bloated column of glistening black, studded with luminous green eyes and yawning mouths. It rolled here and there, wherever it would, and slaughtered indiscriminately, flowing over each victim and leaving little behind other than a few bleached bones.

Four Geyad fell before it. No element could contain it, whether of earth or air or fire or water. The demon seemed impervious to everything.

But then a lone figure stood before it and challenged it with his stave of water, pulling down the snow from the high mountains and covering the Babemor in an air-bound avalanche. The Babemor failed at last, freezing to death, the one thing that it could not withstand. Its black flesh cracked and crumbled, and it died slowly under a mounting hill of snow and ice.

The room was silent. Some had not watched at all. Sohagel sympathised. Babemor were a horror. But he saw one thing which lightened his mood. Korfax at least seemed to have taken some hope from what he had just seen. He at least had seen that demons could be defeated in the end. It all depended upon application. It was the Geyad's choice and Korfax had understood the lesson and taken heart from it.

"You may wonder why you were not shown this when you first came here," Sohagel said. "But then you were children. You needed to be led gently to the truth. You needed to learn strength."

He picked up one of the oanadar and looked at it.

"You are nearing the end, all of you. Another year will see you attain your staves. Each of you will become Geyad, if you merit it. Then you will serve as you should. But you should also be prepared, as you may experience such dangers as you have just witnessed here today."

Sohagel bowed his head to them.

"We do not hide such things from our charges. We show you the truth. The

Namad Mahorelah is a terrible lore, both in offence and defence. To defeat such evil, the Namad Dar has proven itself the only answer that suffices. And it is the only lore sanctioned by The Creator. His chosen, Karmaraa, blessed be his name, showed us the way. So remember – stick to the path of the Namad Dar and you will always have The Creator at your shoulder."

After Sohagel's lesson Korfax went back to the archives with renewed fire. He had read the acts of many Geyad from the war, but now he wanted to read them again because he wanted to understand what he had not understood before – applicability.

He found it best to go late in the night, when Paladir was there. Paladir was not a talker, like many of the other archivists, and Korfax liked that.

So it was that he eventually came upon a history of the Black War, as unexpected as it was surprising. It was in a stone hidden away upon a high shelf in the far reaches of the archive. Most of the stones on that shelf were on fairly obscure matters, but this one was set slightly apart, and when he read the summary he took it down.

The Black War? That was almost legendary. Few records remained of it. All that could be said was that long before Karmaraa and Sondehna, long before the Wars of Unification, there had been another war, a darker war of sorcery that overran the north, namely the Black War. Only one name stood out from that time: Nalvahgey, seeress and sorceress, creator of the Exentaser, most powerful and most mysterious.

Korfax stared at the stone. Why was this here? Surely this had nothing to do with the Namad Dar? He set the stone in motion and read what it had to say, and then he went back and read parts of it again, and again. Finally he put the stone back in its box and sat for a very long time, deep in thought.

Paladir came by, doing his usual hourly walk around the levels, a cursory check that everything was in order.

"The night is almost gone, Korfax. Shouldn't you be in bed?"

"I can't sleep," Korfax replied.

Paladir smiled.

"Can't, or won't?"

Korfax gestured at the scattered boxes about him.

"There is too much to do, too much to know."

Paladir looked at the boxes also, and without any trace of irony he added, "And not enough time in the day. Life is hard."

He walked on and Korfax watched him leave.

'Life is hard.'

Now what did that mean?

Korfax walked into Ponodol's room and stopped just inside the door.

"Well now!" said Ponodol. "This is the time set aside for relaxation and meditation, so what are you doing here?"

Korfax frowned.

"I need guidance, Geyadril. I am uncertain."

Ponodol looked back at him with a brighter look in his eyes.

"And what are you uncertain about?"

"The Agedobor."

Ponodol smiled.

"So it was you, was it? I did wonder."

Korfax looked carefully at Ponodol.

"Geyadril?"

"I was told that someone had been in the archives, studying the histories of Fimon on the fifth level, but I did not know who it actually was."

"But the Wardens knew I was there, as did Paladir."

"Yes, Korfax, I know that. But as I said, I was told that someone had been there not who it actually was. I wished to be surprised, that was all."

"But why?"

Ponodol's smile became somewhat fonder.

"Allow me my few small pleasures, yes? I like mysteries. I like revelation."

Korfax could only frown in return.

"Very well then," said Ponodol. "Let me give you a sop for your impatience. You are the only one to touch that particular stone this year. Most would have expected Oanatom, perhaps even Aduret, but not you."

Korfax deepened his frown.

"Why not me?" he asked.

Korfax thought Ponodol strangely triumphant now.

"You are so like your father," he said. "You have power and ability, you possess insight and the wit to use it well, but you hide yourself. You do not declare yourself. Your father is the same. He was ever thus. So attend me now, whilst I explain."

Ponodol gestured at a chair.

"Sit," he said.

Korfax waited where he was while Ponodol collected his thoughts. Ponodol looked up again and then gestured at the chair once more.

"Come, Korfax, sit! And let me tell you a thing."

Korfax fully entered the room and sat in the proffered chair. He waited while Ponodol sat himself on a wide bench, resting his arms upon the sides.

"How did I know?" he asked. "Sooner or later, someone from each crop of acolytes discovers that stone. We do not lie to our charges, Korfax; we only reveal what we think they are able to understand at the time. We provide comforting tales until they are ready for the real truth, but the true nature of the Agedobor we do not reveal unless we have to, not until an acolyte comes looking."

"I never imagined that it would be like this," Korfax said. "All I ever knew of the Black War was that it took place in the time of Nalvahgey, and that she put an end to it. It was a war of sorcery against a terrible foe that was eventually beaten, but more than that, I did not know."

"Few do," said Ponodol. "And few go looking. Many consider it enough to know that the war took place, and that out of it arose the line of sorcerer princes that ended in Sondehna. As the Wars of Unification forged the Namad Dar, so the Black War forged the Argedith and made of them a power to threaten the world."

Ponodol looked down, gazing at the floor.

"Nalvahgey understood this," he continued. "She foresaw much and did all that she could to prevent it. She told the princes of the west that doom would befall them unless they took up the Namad Dar. That is where the Dar Kaadarith had its origins."

"But I thought that was Risatah!"

"It was, but some say that Nalvahgey had a hand in it. I would not be surprised if that were true. She left behind her many warnings, many visions that revealed what would come. She foretold Sondehna, Karmaraa, even the Wars of Unification. Since that time her prophecies have become the stuff of legend – the prophecies of Nalvahgey. So much she saw, and so much of what she saw was lost."

He looked at Korfax.

"I have seen them, you know."

"The prophecies?"

"Yes, and though many of them were destroyed, some remain still. They are kept in the Hall of Sight in the Umadya Zedekel. Imagine a hall of stone, filled with vision after vision after vision, and then you come to the end where the scrolls are kept. Here they stand, suspended in imperishable crystal, a few solitary pages and all that remain of the prophecies of Nalvahgey. The others were never deciphered because of the damage."

"Damage?"

"Yes. Just after she died, her prophecies were found by one of her followers. They were kept safe and secret until another came and, for some untold reason, burnt them. Only a few survived intact. It is all that I know of the tale."

He paused a moment, gathering his thoughts.

"Of those that do survive, a few are startling in their accuracy, once you appreciate the language and the imagery. Then you begin to understand why she is venerated as the greatest seer that ever walked this world."

"How were you able to see them? I thought that was a privilege reserved for the Exentaser alone."

Ponodol smiled.

"A friend took me during happier times. I am one of the fortunate few."

"Is it true that they are difficult to unravel?"

"It depends on what you mean by difficult. The language she employed is certainly open to interpretation, and it is often the case that the prophecies themselves are not to be fully understood until the events they describe have already come to pass. From what I saw of them I had the distinct impression that Nalvahgey liked to play games with her audience."

"I thought they were masked, that one could not read them."

"No! The originals were, certainly, but no one can see them, as they are far too dangerous. I saw the translations only."

"Too dangerous? Why?"

"Because Nalvahgey employed what has since been decreed a forbidden art when making them. She hid her verses behind unspeakable words."

Korfax did not understand.

"Unspeakable words? I have never heard of such a thing!"

Ponodol did not answer; instead, he took out a piece of parchment and wrote something on it. He then passed it to Korfax. Korfax looked long and hard at what was written there. It was a word, yet it wasn't. The arrangement was all wrong. It took him a while to even work out that it was in fact a word at all, not some strange scrawl. It was not something you could say, though. Ponodol took it away from him and then placed it in the firebox that sat in the corner of his room. Flames came and went.

"Do you understand now?" he asked.

"No," replied Korfax. "What you just wrote does not make sense."

"It is a technique employed by the Argedith," Ponodol told him. "From my understanding of it, certain sounds, certain words, can reach into the abyss more easily than others. The more impossible the word and the harder it is to say, the greater its effect upon the mind. The overall intent is to break through barriers, break rules and create chaos."

"But that does not make any sense either," insisted Korfax.

"And that is precisely the point," said Ponodol. "It is chaotic, without reason, speaking to parts of us better left undisturbed. What I have just shown you is wrong. It is a blasphemy. Be aware of it, but never try to study it or understand it."

Ponodol paused a moment as if remembering something, staring into depths only he could see. Korfax watched him but then looked down himself. Unspeakable words? He thought of Dialyas and his musings on the freedom of thought. Then it had been thoughts you were not supposed to have, but now it was sounds you were not supposed to make. Korfax frowned and then looked up again to find Ponodol watching him.

"Don't think too hard upon the matter," Ponodol told him. "Remember that to study the ways of the enemy is to be tempted by them, and that is why we watch and ward. You saw how easy it was for me to create such a thing? Imagine what would happen if I did so with a purpose – what would be stirred by such an act? The Namad Mahorelah is ever at our throats, yet we never see its hand."

He smiled for a moment and then sighed.

"Well, enough of that. Back to what we were originally talking about, Nalvahgey and the Agedobor, two foes pitted against each other much like Sondehna and Karmaraa. The Black War."

His expression became grim.

"The Agedobor appeared like a sudden plague whilst Nalvahgey was still young. Some say they were a curse from The Creator, planted as a torment to the wicked. They killed, they despoiled, they conquered and they ruled. They were a terrible breed. Every single one of them had the power of summoning within it as if born to it, and only the best of the Argedith could ever match them. They possessed an undying hatred for all that went on two legs, and woe betide any that they conquered, for all that fell under their dominion received only torment and death in return. They were beaten back, of course, beaten back to the dark places, to caves and pits that knew no light. For long years they ruled the darkness into which they had been driven, a terror to all that chanced upon them, until the Wars of Unification finally swept such wreckage from the land. So the forces of Karmaraa vanquished them at last and they passed from the world, falling back into the darkness from whence they came. Nalvahgey gave them their name, the Agedobor, for that is how she saw them, but what they called themselves was never discovered. Only one name has come to us out of the dark years, that of Arzulg, their ruler, but nothing more than that."

Ponodol sighed.

"It was thought that they were the products of strange and powerful sorceries, that their small and hideous bodies had been culled from the stuff of the great abyss itself and filled with potent spirits of malice. But that was only a comforting lie, a pretty fantasy we told ourselves so that we should feel no remorse after their extermination."

He looked grimly at his charge.

"You see, Korfax, the stark truth of it is that we know nothing of their genesis, even now. They appeared, they fought us and we fought back. By necessity the north had to become strong in sorcery in order to oppose them. It was that or extinction; there was no other way. So at last the Agedobor were defeated, but at a price. Their taint entered the north and it became a place of darkness for a while, until the coming of the light."

Korfax swallowed carefully. Headless horrors danced in his head. He looked away.

"I have a nightmare," he confessed.

"I know that you do," said Ponodol. "Having seen what you have seen, this was all but inevitable. You went looking for answers, comforting answers, but found only further distress instead. I have only to look in your eyes, Korfax, to know what it is that you think you have discovered. Such considerations, such contemplations, have always been hard, but for you, I imagine, they are even more so. You are, after all, one of the few of us that has ever seen the Agdoain about their business!"

Korfax kept his head down. He clenched a fist and then slowly loosed it again. Ponodol watched the fist.

"I had already anticipated your guess," he said, "but what you think might be the truth remains uncertain yet. So let me tell you what we of the council think. And once you have heard that, then perhaps you will learn better judgement."

Ponodol leaned forward and his eyes were suddenly bright. Korfax looked up again and met that gaze, setting his inner darknesses against that light, testing it. Ponodol watched for a moment but then brightened his gaze even further. Korfax drew back a little. He had no choice, for Ponodol did not spare him.

"Do not mistake me in this, Korfax," he said. "Here is the final lesson that we teach. You are here to learn judgement. You have power and skill, but they must be tempered, tempered for all time by careful judgement. That – and only that – is the final lesson you have to learn. To know when to act, to know how and when to forbear."

He withdrew a little, lessening the force of his gaze, and Korfax breathed easier. The lesson in power over, Ponodol continued, speaking quietly and carefully.

"Like the Agdoain, the Agedobor were masters of hiding. But do not be fooled. The Agedobor are as unlike the Agdoain as they possibly can be. Even when they came into the light they hid themselves, clothing themselves in fabrics and shadow. They let none see them for what they truly were. But the Agdoain? When they reveal themselves they are utterly naked. I know. I have seen the stone that was lifted from the wreck of Tohus. I, like you, have seen the Agdoain at play."

Ponodol bit at the words as though to match the ferocity of the memory.

"To know a thing," he said, "you must ask yourself 'what is it, what is its nature?' The Agedobor and the Agdoain are not the same."

Korfax thought for a moment.

"But does not the abyss also obey the fundamental principles? Do we not find opposing forces there also? Could not the Agdoain be a counterpart to the Agedobor, a dark shadow like a revenant?"

Ponodol almost smiled at Korfax's reasoning.

"A good question, but I consider it unlikely," he said. "There is no record of the shape of the Agedobor, merely reports. They were rarely seen, and they never removed the strange skins in which they clothed themselves. A few have conjectured that even they could not stand the sight of themselves. Some of those that pondered longest on the matter even considered them to be the true spirit of the Mahorelah, its underlying truth made manifest. They said that the Agedobor had no form at all, that they were utterly shapeless in the end."

Ponodol spread his hands wide.

"From what we know of it the Iabeiorith fought them for a very long time, for they were both tenacious and devious. But after many long and ruinous campaigns they fled at last to dwell in the caves below certain mountains in the Adroqin Vohimar. The Agedobor were here to stay. Like the Vovin, they were now a part of our world, for good or for ill. But the north was not unaffected by this, and a darkness entered the hearts of all that lived there, a black stain that gradually revealed itself as the taint of the abyss.

"There were incursions from time to time, battles and forays, but the Iabeiorith were ever ready. Akiol, third of the line of sorcerer princes, created the Haelok Aldaria, the warrior elite, with the express purpose of seeking out and destroying any nest of the Agedobor that they came upon. All were of the Argedith, and all wielded potent and sorcerous weaponry. The Agedobor could not counter such forces, so they hid further away, even deeper, and kept themselves to themselves in their underground kingdom. But damned were those that dared enter their demesne unprepared. No tale of their suffering ever made it back to the ears of the living.

"Then Sondehna did that which set the north on its final path to ruin. He subdued the Agedobor at last, daring the depths of the Adroqin Vohimar and travelling its dark ways to the very centre. And there he named the Agedobor as allies of the Iabeiorith. Peace, he proclaimed, and the Haelok Aldaria took his message to the rest of the world, speaking with their dark master's voice, claiming that everlasting peace was theirs. But that was not what lay at the heart of their alliance. The north now dreamed of empire, and they would attain their peace through subjugation, domination and by tyranny. The taint of the Mahorelah had consumed them at last and they became conquerors and usurpers all. As Sondehna subdued the Agedobor, so the abyss subdued him and his people in turn. And there you have the dark price of power."

Korfax stared at Ponodol.

"What are you telling me?"

"That this is what really started the wars. The Agedobor desired ascendancy, they desired the world, they desired the Ell as their slaves, or worse. But they miscalculated. Their plans were undone by Sondehna himself, and they became his slaves in turn, whilst he took their dream to his heart and nourished it."

"I have never heard that before," said Korfax. "Every tale that I have heard tells of Soivar and how Sondehna stole her from the side of Karmaraa. Little or no mention is made of the Agedobor at all."

"That is so," agreed Ponodol. "And those tales do not lie. That also happened. But where did Sondehna's dark desire come from originally? It came from the abyss. Soivar was nothing less, and nothing more, than the stone that started the avalanche. The abyss has ever been the source of all woe in this world."

Ponodol leaned back.

"Now we come to it. Think on this. The Agedobor made this alliance with Sondehna because he frightened them. He was darker than they, mightier than they. He was the darkest Ell ever to walk the world. The Iabeiorith loved him in abject fear, a hideous reversal if you think about it, whilst the Haelok Aldaria would willingly slay themselves at his command. The north had learned the worship of power long ago, and now they beheld its ultimate expression in the body and soul of their last prince.

"Karmaraa and his forces killed all the Agedobor, they could do nothing else. They were utterly evil, twisted beyond any hope of redemption. But such an act is not undertaken lightly and we can only hope that we fulfilled The Creators purpose by removing them from the world."

Korfax looked down, his face pensive.

"So why is this kept hidden away?" he asked. "I thought I was reading something that could be relevant to the war we now face in the north, but you tell me that isn't so. I understand that some knowledge is uncomfortable, but this? This I don't understand."

"Some knowledge is uncomfortable." Ponodol mused.

He looked darkly back at Korfax.

"There is something you will not find in the archives, no matter how hard you look. It was found on a certain scroll lifted from the ruins of Nalstul. Now it is on a single logadar in the private archives of the high council. Knowledge of it is passed from generation to generation for those that come asking, but only to those that find. This is not for everyone. The Agedobor cannot be summoned!"

Korfax frowned.

"But everything from the abyss can be summoned. Even the Ashar."

Ponodol smiled darkly.

"Yes. But not the Agedobor. It is even written into their name."

"But I thought that meant they came to us unbidden."

"No! Their name has two meanings, the truth hidden in plain sight. Yes, they came to us unbidden, but also, alone of all the creatures that have ever climbed out of the dark pit, they cannot be summoned. We have it from the archives of Gandao himself, along with a stark warning. Do not touch their flesh or try to see it, nor allow them to touch you or show you what they are."

Ponodol made the gesture of denial.

"Why you would want to see something so avowedly hideous," he exclaimed, "let alone touch it, is beyond me. But then, as it is written, the mind of an Arged must be a terrible place. They allow themselves no constraint, no bounds. They are creatures of chaos."

He sighed.

"So there it is. We do not understand it, not what it means nor what it implies. And now the Agedobor are no more, and we shall never know."

There was a long silence as Korfax wrestled with what he had just been told.

"How many such secret tales are there?" he eventually asked.

"Many times many." Ponodol told him. "What we have though is small compared to what we have lost."

"What of the tale of the Arged of Unchir? Is there another version of that?"

"And why do you ask?"

"Because Fimon mentions the Gaaha when he talks of the Agedobor. He seems to consider them differently to all the other creatures that dwell in the Mahorelah. He refers to them as 'Toqoth'. I was wondering what he meant by it. I have never come across that word before."

"Toqoth!" Ponodol mused. "Yes! That is the only instance of it that we know. Fimon never mentions it again, not in all his other writings. He obviously knows what he means by it, and clearly expects his reader to do the same, but whatever it is he is describing it has passed beyond recall. In some respects I think we have fallen, losing that which it was once needful for us to know."

"That sounds like something Dialyas once said."

Ponodol smiled.

"He ever skirted the bounds. The mysteries from the past consumed him. He wanted to know everything, explain everything."

Korfax felt uncomfortable.

"Even Karmaraa."

"And so he went too far," said Ponodol. "He told you about that, did he?"

"We debated the nature of the flaw and the nature of the void in each stone," Korfax told him.

"I guessed as much, but do not be misled. I was there when he was at the height of his powers. Though he was brilliant, he was also mistaken. I was there when we forged the Kapimadar. I did not agree with his interpretation of the result. It proved nothing."

Korfax would not argue with that. It was the first time Ponodol had mentioned his association with Dialyas, and Korfax could hear regret in his voice.

"I am sorry I mentioned him," he said.

Ponodol looked up and smiled.

"Don't be. It is long past time we talked of him. If you have any doubts about the things he said to you, you can always ask me."

He took a deep breath and then clasped his hands together.

"Now, back to the matter at hand. The point I am making, Korfax, is that there are powers we do not understand, even now. We have, in our time, defeated the greatest wielders of the lore of the abyss, but that does not mean that we fully understand what it is that we have destroyed."

He paused for a moment.

"And so to the Gaaha and the Arged of Unchir. You are correct. There is indeed another tale to tell."

He looked sharply at Korfax.

"Why do you think Fimon draws the distinction? Why do you think he considers both the Gaaha and the Agedobor as different?"

"They are Toqoth?"

Ponodol smiled.

"You like that word!" he said. "No, it is something far more explicable. Think about it."

Korfax pondered. What was the one quality the Agedobor possessed? They could not be summoned, but the Gaaha could be. They were beasts of the abyss, as the Agedobor had been, but the Agedobor also had speech. They had been a community. Korfax looked up at Ponodol.

"The Gaaha have speech?" he asked.

Ponodol smiled.

"Very good, they have speech. Just as we are ignorant of the nature of the Agedobor, so we are ignorant of the nature of the Gaaha. Always we strive to understand the world about us, and always it eludes our grasp. Even now, grey demons walk the north, the Agdoain, a fresh insurgence from the Mahorelah, one never seen before. Karmaraa warned us all those long years ago."

Korfax waited for Ponodol to continue.

"While the Agedobor have never been seen in the flesh, while their form can only be guessed at, the Gaaha are another matter entirely. Achoin saw them at the end, and though he did not speak to them, they spoke to him."

A revelation was coming, Korfax could feel it.

"Think of it! They spoke to him. But that leads us to another question. How was Achoin able to understand them? Surely they would have a language of their own."

There was another pause.

"There is a stone," Ponodol continued, "a dark and bloody stone that Achoin used to record the truth for all time. The Gaaha know the written word. Like the Agedobor, they know a form of Logahithell, a barbarous form to be sure, but still quite recognisable to a Geyad of the Dar Kaadarith, for they left behind them a message on the floor of the summoning chamber, after they had strung up the Arged by her own entrails. And the message was this: 'Never summon us again, or there will be undying hatred between the Pallar and the Pollar until the end of time.'"

Korfax stared at Ponodol, his eyes wide.

"I am not sure that I understand," he said. "The 'Pallar' and the 'Pollar'?"

"Very few know of this," Ponodol replied, "so I will ask you to keep this to yourself, unless specifically asked. This knowledge can only be known safely by the Dar Kaadarith and the Exentaser, but no one else!"

He paused a moment.

"It is clear that they think of us as 'the Pallar', whilst they call themselves 'the Pollar', and many of both the Dar Kaadarith and the Exentaser have pondered the riddle ever since. Why should we, the Ell, be the divided whilst the Gaaha be the unified? But the riddle deepens beyond even that. At the end Achoin saw the Gaaha, and he wrote of their likenesses. He said that they were somewhat like us, as they stood upright, wore clothing and carried weapons."

Korfax frowned.

"Clothing and weapons?"

"Yes."

"They look like us?"

"Yes, except for one thing."

"What is that?"

"They have the heads of beasts."

Korfax thought long about what Ponodol had just said. There was something here, something he could not grasp, an elusive pattern that lay just out of reach. The Agedobor were small, little more than the size of a head perhaps, but they hid themselves from sight. The Gaaha were upright, like the Ell, but they had the heads of beasts. Then there were the Agdoain standing upright also, but entirely headless.

"The Agdoain have no heads," he said, and Ponodol smiled.

"Yes! But what does it mean? Something is happening here, something dark and terrible, but we cannot see what it is." He leaned back in his chair. "There is an influence at work, reaching out from whatever realm contains it, sending horrors against us as and when it can."

"To know a thing," Korfax murmured, "ask yourself 'what is it? What is its nature?'"

"So what is it that you see?" Ponodol asked.

"That this is the work of the Ashar?"

Ponodol waited a moment.

"And why would you say that?" he queried.

"Because each of the Ashar has a consuming passion," Korfax answered. "The Agdoain are so shaped because of the influence that made them."

He paused a moment.

"But is that true?" he continued. "Surely, somewhere, there is one of the Argedith summoning these creatures?"

"And who are the agents of the abyss? Whose hands do the work that others cannot?"

"Then it is the Ashar that are our enemies."

Ponodol looked satisfied at last.

"Now you see the truth of what many of us have come to understand. We believe that every so often the Ashar build up their powers enough to reach out to the world, so that they can influence their agents here or those that are susceptible. The Black War was one such incursion, the Wars of Unification another. How many there have actually been we do not know, but always the dark powers are beaten back and their agents defeated."

"You said those that are susceptible?"

"Yes, there have been instances, few and far between, when even the innocent have become overwhelmed by some external influence. They change and become the focus for dark powers. There was an incident at Geddial during the reign of Aligon. The official story is that an archivist uncovered a scroll and was overwhelmed by the knowledge he read within it, but that is not the whole story. Another power intervened, something dark and dreadful."

"But that would mean that the war can never be won! Always evil will return!"

"Now you see the wisdom of Karmaraa. He foresaw this, understood it and planned against it. Few realise just exactly what the task involves. For many it would be far too uncomfortable, especially for those that have lived all their lives in peace. But the Ashar are eternal and their malice is eternal."

"Unless we take the war to them," Korfax said.

Ponodol started.

"What do you mean?" he asked.

"Invade the Mahorelah. Seek them out and put an end to them."

Ponodol stared for a moment and then roared with laughter.

"I am breathless at such audacity," he said finally. "What a glorious answer!"

He laughed a little more and then held up a hand.

"No, Korfax, no!" he said. "That is not our purpose, and nor should it be. We keep this world. We are here to defend its borders, not to go marching with war into other realms. We are guardians."

Korfax looked up. It was as his father had said: they kept guard against eternal powers. Except that hadn't been quite what his father had meant. A dark memory writhed in the distance and then fell away again.

"I am a guardian," he murmured.

Ponodol made the gesture of acceptance, a lowering of cupped hands.

"Yes, you are," he said. "And you are well on your way to becoming a Geyad."

He held in his hand the sigil of the sixth level.

"Tabitem asked me to give you this and I was going to give it to you tomorrow," he said as he handed it to Korfax. "Your work in the forges has been judged as exemplary."

Korfax took the embroidered sigil and looked at it. He was almost Geyad. Only one more year to go. Ponodol leaned forward.

"You know, Tabitem is rarely so impressed. He said to me that it would be an honour if you decided to serve the furnaces after your making. You have done well. I am proud."

13

VISION

Til-arged Eil-de-nilzid
Ath-orahz Ip-zak-od-ran
Si-vorkas Ursal-mannuhm
Pild-veh-ial Nt-gon-lairo
Nis-nio-aa Ortol-id-fen
Od-ar-ith Aj-ald-maano
Ors-torzan Stl-ku-an-ie

Korfax sat alone beside the window and stared out over Emethgis Vaniad. Three logadar waited beside him. Two were quiescent whilst the third gleamed with a dim light, ready for that final and awakening touch. But the touch never came. The stones had been forgotten. Instead, other words absorbed him.

'We do not lie to our charges, Korfax, we only reveal what we think they are able to understand at the time.'

Ponodol's exact words. But Korfax had heard another tale. He thought again of Tahamoh.

'I touched it.'
'That is not allowed.'
'No one saw me. But now I know why it is forbidden. We have been lied to.'

The Kapimadar! The challenge Dialyas had given him all those years ago still sat in his mind like a splinter, an itch he could not reach. Temptation.

Ponodol was one of the stone's forgers and he had said that the stone was not what Dialyas thought it to be. But he had also denied Dialyas, as had all the others that were involved, his father and another Geyad named Virqol. Korfax wondered, not for the first time, what the truth actually was.

He looked up at the sky. There were a few clouds up there, a few thin clouds. They were doing nothing, just as he was. But for him, it was a rare luxury. That he had nothing he needed to do for almost half a day was virtually unprecedented.

He thought about that. How fast the last six years had flown by. It seemed only yesterday that he had been a child, blissfully unaware as he ran through the ancient courtyard of Losq, sprinting over its ageing stone and dreaming of a future yet to be. But then the Agdoain had come and everything had changed under their corrosive touch.

His world had broken then, and everything he had ever known had shifted to accommodate the fracture. Now here he was, six years on, an acolyte of the Dar Kaadarith, an acolyte of the sixth level no less and a veritable Geyad in the making.

They had told him that he was strong. They had told him that he was powerful. They had filled his ears with praises and warnings in equal measure, but now, now that he had time enough to stop and think, he realised that he no longer belonged to himself at all. Instead he spent his days dancing to the tunes of others.

Another boundary had been crossed. Everything that he had taken for granted was suddenly unknown to him. That he was no longer free, no longer the master of his own destiny, was a regret. That he no longer knew what the truth was, was deeply troubling.

He let his eyes wander around the old room. It was one of the oldest parts of the Umadya Semeiel, untouched ever since the tower itself had been built. Few ever came here, if at all, and it remained an all but forgotten annex to the great debating chamber.

There was to have been a debate here this day, one that he was supposed to have attended, but it had been cancelled early that morning for some unspecified reason.

And that was how he had found himself with nothing to do. When he had been told that the debate would no longer be taking place he had been momentarily at a loss. How should he fill the time? So he had dutifully picked up the three logadar he had been studying, before coming to this old and empty room in order to be alone. He had intended to continue with his studies, but he had fooled himself. Even when he had been freed from his tasks, he had fallen back upon the semblance of duty. But that was how he was now – dutiful. Even his rebellions were small and personal, unseen by any other but himself. So here he was, in the one place no one else would be, alone with his empty rebellion.

Quiet noises came from outside. Others had entered the great chamber without, their uncaring voices disturbing its silence. Korfax grimaced at the door and looked back out of the window. He did not want to be disturbed.

But the sounds continued, and they increased in volume. He turned to the door, his curiosity aroused, and looked out to see what all the fuss was about. But then, just as he looked through the widening crack, he realised that through no fault of his own he was in entirely the wrong place at entirely the wrong time.

Below him were many from both the Exentaser and the Dar Kaadarith, most sitting in the first circle, a few in the second. The rest of the great debating chamber remained empty. Asvoan, Urenel of the Exentaser, walked to the centre. All turned to her, they could not help it. She was as she had always been, a demanding darkness, commanding their attention simply by being.

"So here we all are at last," she announced, as if this gathering had come about through some hard-fought battle. "Though you do not show it," she continued, "I feel the doubt in you, the questions."

She looked about her, judging her audience with her dark gaze.

"Is this yet another false trail, you ask? Are the Exentaser so bereft of vision that they have started chasing dreams?"

She turned away, almost as if she dismissed them all.

"I know your doubts, so spare me your denials."

Though she spoke quietly, her words, every single sound that she uttered, could be heard perfectly. Clever design of the chamber gave any speaker that occupied the floor of the hall the ability to reach all the way to the outer walls without unduly raising their voice.

Another stood. Korfax held his breath. It was the Geyadel himself, Abrilon. Korfax was tempted to retreat from his vantage point. What exactly was it that he was witnessing? Abrilon spoke.

"No, Asvoan," he said, "you are wrong. That you have called us here and told us that it is a matter of import is all that is needed. But may I remind you also that this has not been done blithely. The order of the day has been greatly upset."

Asvoan looked back over her shoulder.

"And Creator forfend that the order of the day ever be upset," she said.

There were smiles from some of the Exentaser. Abrilon folded his arms carefully.

"And that will be enough of that," he told her. "I know how important you consider this matter, but what of the rest of us? We cannot judge the evidence until you show it to us. All we ever have from you are cryptic statements; you say neither yes nor no! But consider this. We have done you the courtesy of attending, so please say what it is that you wish to say and so spare us all your well-considered theatrics."

Asvoan turned around fully and gave him a searching look.

"I fully intend to," she said, "but I think it worth saying that there are many among the Dar Kaadarith who prefer their own counsels to those of others..."

Another interrupted.

"Not so! We have come here at your behest, have we not?"

The voice echoed around the chamber like a subterranean growl. Korfax could not see who it was that had spoken, but he knew of only one who sounded like that. It had to be Geyadril Samafaa.

Asvoan looked pointedly at the speaker and raised her voice accordingly.

"Yes, you have come," she said. "But only as far as this chamber. We are the ones that had to leave our tower, not you."

Before any answer could be made she held up a milky-white crystal in her small hand, like a shield. Korfax stared at it. It was an uranadar, a seeking stone. He had heard of them, of course, for they could only be made in the great furnaces in the deeps of the Umadya Semeiel, but he had never actually seen one that had been used before. When they were made they were clear, but when a vision filled them they became opaque. A sudden desire to touch it and to know what it contained filled him.

"Here is the record of the divination," continued Asvoan, looking this way and that, "and we are as certain of our interpretation as we have ever been of anything."

"Which, I think, is not saying very much at all," came a deep rumble.

It was the same voice that had interrupted before. Korfax had been right. It was Geyadril Samafaa. Korfax watched as he raised his not inconsiderable frame from his seat. He stood tall for a moment, gathering himself up before advancing. All things considered he was a most imposing figure, seemingly cast from the same heroic mould that had made Napeiel Valagar, the first of the Nazad Esiask. The two could almost have been brothers but for the colour of their skin. Whilst Valagar was quite pale, almost as pale as those of the north, Samafaa was of the darkest hue.

He towered over the diminutive Asvoan, dwarfing her, a mountain peering at a tree. But Asvoan was not daunted. She looked up at the giant and sneered back at him instead.

"And you, Samafaa, seem to be saying far too much at this juncture!"

There were more smiles from amongst the Exentaser. Samafaa, though, had not finished.

"Whether you know it or not, Asvoan, I am one of the few that has heard something of this vision, and what I have heard makes me doubt its import. Besides, Payoan is young."

Korfax wondered at the name. Who might Payoan be? He looked back at Samafaa.

"To consider changing our direction on the word of an untried Uren is asking much of the rest of us."

Asvoan sighed. She glanced at the ranks behind her.

"You may ever lead them to water, but you can never make them drink," she said.

Korfax saw many of the Exentaser broaden their smiles, and he smiled as well. That was a heavy insult. But then Asvoan compounded it by turning her back upon Samafaa altogether. She made a gesture to those who sat close by. Though Korfax could not see what she did, it clearly caused some hilarity amongst many of the younger seers. Their elders merely bowed their heads in appreciation before turning sharpened glances back at Samafaa. Samafaa flapped his hand in dismissal, a dark cliff denying a darker sea, before stepping further forward as though to offer a rebuttal. But Asvoan was there before him, hot with sudden passion. She pointed a diminutive finger up at him.

"You may indeed consider Payoan to be young and untried, but what do you truly know of such matters? I have assayed her myself. Do you consider me young? Or untried? Or inexperienced?"

"Asvoan, there is no need for..."

Asvoan quickly held up her right hand in denial to silence him.

"As I said before, I would not have called for this meeting if the matter was not of the utmost import."

She extended her finger again, like a threat.

"Dismiss the counsel of the Exentaser at your peril!"

Samafaa frowned for a moment, folding his arms across his wide chest whilst glaring back down at Asvoan. Then he unfolded his arms and made an exaggerated gesture to Asvoan that she had the floor again. She bowed extravagantly in return. Samafaa turned about and sat back down.

Asvoan looked at all in turn and then took in a great breath.

Korfax waited. Whatever it was that Asvoan was about to say, she was preparing herself for it, both physically and mentally. Abrilon had been right – her preparations did indeed seem somewhat theatrical – but Korfax wondered whether there wasn't some deeper reason. He remembered the teachings of his mother. She had shown him something of this when she had taught him the courtly dances during his tenth year. So here came another dance now, one intended to lead the eye or the mind. Korfax smiled at the memory. He wondered how many below were thinking the same as him. Where might this go?

Asvoan finished her beginning, and after she had looked in every eye for the second time, she spoke again, marking each and every one of them with the tip of her finger.

"As you are all aware, there have been no visions concerning the Agdoain. None! This is unprecedented. Every other incursion from the Mahorelah, every one that we know of, was accompanied by some sign, some warning that not all was well. Many of us came to believe, in our comfort if not in our hearts, that the best of the Argedith entered the river long before the end of the Wars of Unification. But someone," and here she looked significantly at Samafaa, "has not only rediscovered the craft, but they have also mastered it to a most formidable degree."

There was a pause while Asvoan gathered herself further up, as though drawing strength from the stone upon which she stood.

"And what is more," she added, "they have achieved all of this in secret."

There was another pause.

"Until now."

The hall became utterly silent, and even Geyadel Abrilon sat with increased erectness, his face daring to betray his interest at last. Only Samafaa remained as he ever had, a glowering hill of intransigence.

Korfax ran his eyes over the assemblage. He should leave now, he really should, as this was not meant for his eyes or ears.

He considered his options. He could stay where he was, hidden, but if they found him it would look bad. There was no way to leave at the moment without attracting someone's attention, but let their attentions wander and he might be able to sneak past them without any being the wiser. Oh, for a potent distraction.

Asvoan continued from below.

"A recent and most welcome addition to our ranks, the now famed Uren Payoan, has been gifted with a vision of a most powerful Arged, powerful enough to escape the combined attentions of the Dar Kaadarith, the Exentaser and the Balt Kaalith all together."

"That being the case, how then can we be certain that this vision is true?" It was a voice from the back. Korfax could not tell who it was that had spoken.

"I am certain!" replied Asvoan. "So I ask again. Do any of you doubt me?"

There was silence, and a certain satisfaction crossed her face.

"So, without further ado," she said, "I will show you the distillation."

There was a pause while she turned to one of the Urendril nearest to her. Without a word something passed between them, from hand to hand, something wrapped in dark fabric.

Asvoan held up a large blue crystal. Korfax stared intently. The crystal was an oanadar of exceptional power, a stone of sight made for the express purpose of containing a vision, and Asvoan was about to call up the image that was stored within. From uranadar to oanadar the vision had gone. Korfax understood the process well enough, but he had never witnessed its application. Fascinated, and despite his fears, he dared to move a little so that he could see what might emerge. His curiosity was getting the better of him. Like the others below, he also wanted to see what was held within the stone.

Asvoan set the crystal in motion, touching it just so and awakening its stored sights. For a moment there was nothing, a stillness of the light that seemed to hold the air within it, but then the vision emerged and there were several sharp intakes of breath. A few of the Dar Kaadarith even stood up to stare. Korfax, though, could not move at all.

Rising up from the oanadar was a vast face, a powerful and proud face. Coldly beautiful, as though carved from clouded ice, it hung in the air above the crystal like a summoned spirit. But around the visage there circled a hint of shadow, a sinister darkening of the air.

If this was a vision then it was the strangest Korfax had ever seen. It was almost as if someone had captured the element of life without its substance. No wonder the others were surprised. Usually visions were chaotic, images tumbled together in a riot of shape and colour, but this singular floating face?

Korfax stared down at it with a growing sense of panic. It was, in some strange way, seductive, as though it promised things, forbidden things – terrible fulfilments and vile rewards in equal measure. He found that he could not look away from those black, black eyes that glistened like midnight pools, beckoning him in, pulling him down and sucking at his essence. *Come to me*, they said, *bathe in me,* they commanded, *though it all burn and blind you*. Korfax felt himself falling, tumbling towards them as if his spirit had been torn loose from its moorings by those twin wells of night. He flung himself away from their terrible seduction, jerking his mind aside, but he did it with such force that he lost his balance and staggered back against the wall. But now he realised that he had seen that face before, and he knew to whom it belonged.

The shock of recognition brought him back to himself. He should not be here. He was suddenly back outside his parents' bed chamber at Losq, listening to a conversation not meant for his ears. He heard again the rustle of robes. But it was too late. He had already been seen.

"You there! Stop where you are!"

The call froze him where he crouched and in moments he was surrounded. Two of the chamber guardians had him hemmed in with their staves whilst the others of the council arrived even as they pointed at him. Samafaa came to one side, his arms folded across his mighty chest yet again, his face a picture of stern disapproval, whilst on the other side stood Ponodol, resolute and sad, all at the same time. But in front of them both stood Geyadel Abrilon, and he looked absolutely furious.

"What is the meaning of this?" he demanded. "What are you doing here? Did you not read the signs? How did you pass the guards?"

Korfax could not think of anything to say. Abrilon glared at him, demanding answers. Korfax said the first thing that came into his head.

"I thought this place was not going to be used today, Geyadel. I sought a place of solitude..."

His voice tailed off. Abrilon darkened and turned to Ponodol.

"This one is under your tutelage, is he not?"

"Yes, Geyadel, he is," said Ponodol. "But if you are wondering whether there is any malice here, I would argue strenuously against it. I think this a genuine mistake. We have here one of our brightest and best, after all."

Abrilon drew his lips into a thin line.

"I know all of that, Ponodol," he said, "and I wasn't about to attribute any malice to him either – an occasional mischief, perhaps, but never any malice."

Abrilon softened his expression ever so slightly as he regarded Ponodol for a moment, but then he became stern again as soon he looked back at Korfax.

"Nevertheless, whilst I might agree that this may well have been an honest mistake, you have seen things here that you should never have seen at all."

Abrilon drew himself up and his eyes became pinpricks of light.

"So hear my words, Faren Noren Korfax. You shall take yourself to the first of the wardens henceforth. Tell Geyad Paziba that he is to escort you to the Hall of Judgement on the order of the Geyadel. You will neither pause nor will you deviate, and believe me when I say that I will know it if you have. Once there, you will both await my arrival – Paziba to bear witness, you to hear my judgement, once you have given as full an account of yourself as you are able. I will expect nothing less, either. Then we shall see what we shall see. We do not allow spies in the Dar Kaadarith, inadvertent or no."

Abrilon raised a finger like a warning.

"And one more thing! You will bind your tongue from this day forwards. You will never speak of what you have seen here, not to anyone, not ever. Is that clear?"

Korfax could do nothing but agree.

"Yes, Geyadel."

"Good! Now you will leave."

Without further ado, Abrilon turned about and made to start back down the stairs, but Asvoan, who had been waiting at his shoulder, stopped him. She placed her hand gently against Abrilon's arm.

"But did you not see?" she asked.

She turned to Korfax and held him with her gaze. Her eyes were large and very dark, but there were no pits of blackness lurking in their depths; instead, they were filled with a fearsome brightness and they burned with a seeing intensity that Korfax found he did not like at all. He felt a shiver ripple up and down his spine, even as he looked away. If only he was anywhere other than here, anywhere other than under that fearful scrutiny.

Abrilon looked sharply at Asvoan before turning back to Korfax.

"See what?" he demanded.

Asvoan looked heavenwards in frustration.

"You know, Abrilon, I think you wilfully blind at times."

She pointed at Korfax.

"He knows that face!"

Abrilon gestured at Korfax.

"Him?" he said. "Impossible!"

He turned fully on Korfax.

"Is this true?" he asked.

Korfax kept his head down. He had rarely seen Abrilon, let alone spoken with him. The last time of any consequence was when he was being judged by the high council over the affair with Tahamoh. Now here he was again, confronting the first of the Dar Kaadarith and in bad favour once more.

"Well?" Abrilon insisted.

Korfax kept his gaze to the floor. What was he to do? What was he to say? Consequences tumbled through his mind.

"Look up and answer me!" Abrilon commanded. "By the powers, was this how you were taught?"

Korfax looked up, but still could not answer. He was caught by too many competing forces.

"Gently, Abrilon, gently," said Asvoan as she tapped the Geyadel upon the arm. "If my eyes do not deceive me there is a revelation to be had here. And if I know anything at all, I know revelation."

Asvoan leaned forward, now touching Korfax upon his arm. He started and looked at her, eyes wide. She looked back at him and smiled in reassurance.

"Though it may not seem so," she said, "we are not quite as terrible as you fear us to be. So tell us what we need to know and have no fear for the consequences. Honesty is its own reward."

As if by a miracle, clarity returned and Korfax found that he could speak again. He swallowed and looked back at Abrilon.

"Geyadel, the Urenel is right. I have seen that face before."

He pointed at the vision as it went through its never-ending cycle back at the centre of the debating chamber, turning and smiling coldly at something just beyond the field of vision.

"You know who she is?" Abrilon gasped, looking utterly astounded. "Now what in the name of all the created does an acolyte of the Dar Kaadarith know of an Arged? Explain yourself!"

For all the reassurance Asvoan gave him, Abrilon did indeed sound terrible now. Korfax closed his eyes and tried to marshal his thoughts. He must be clear, he must be focused.

"Some years ago," he said, "I went with a friend, Erinil Noren Tahamoh, who was attending the seminary at the time, to the Sal Kamalkar. I was waiting for him when I saw her. She is Ovuor, wife to Dialyas."

Gasps filled the air. Abrilon stared at Korfax as though appalled. Then he turned to Ponodol, but Ponodol could only make the gesture of astonishment in return. Asvoan, though, offered no reaction at all, and her face became a mask. Korfax found himself looking back at her, just as she looked at him, both caught in the vision of the other. They locked eyes, and it became a reluctant battle of stares, until Ponodol intervened and so broke the moment.

"Korfax?" he asked carefully. "Wife to Dialyas?"

Korfax turned to Ponodol and bowed his head.

"Yes. I only met her the once, but she was not easy to forget. Besides, I believe that she and Dialyas had come to a parting of the ways. I had never come across such a thing before. It stuck in my mind."

Ponodol frowned.

"But Dialyas has never had a wife – ever!" He made the gesture of appeal. "You must be mistaken!"

But Korfax did not answer. He already knew that he had said more than enough. He kept his gaze steadfastly on the floor now. There were so many standing around him: Abrilon, Samafaa, Ponodol, the rest of the high council of the Dar Kaadarith and many of the Exentaser. They crowded about him in a confused circle of stares and he could feel them all, all of them, their eyes like so many demanding and doubting stars. He could not face them all.

Asvoan intruded, pushing the others back with her upraised hands. Small though she was, the others gave way before her. She was like a hard and knotted fist, punching her way through the fog of their disbelief.

"Korfax?" she asked.

"Korfax!" she demanded.

"Look at me," she ordered.

He did so, he had no choice. Asvoan was intense now, filled with her power. And once he caught her gaze, no matter the intensity, he found he could not look away again.

"There is only one way to settle this," she said. "I must see exactly what it is that you have seen. Will you permit it?"

Korfax drew back, even as Asvoan stepped forward. She had changed. Now she seemed to be stalking him, like a hunter.

"Do not be afraid," she said, but Korfax was indeed fearful, even more so than before. He was caught now, caught in a trap of his own making. But Asvoan had filled herself with her purpose, and she pursued it as if nothing else mattered. She wanted a resolution to the vision, an understanding of its truth, and she would let nothing get in the way of that desire.

"Hear me, Korfax," she told him. "I will look at nothing else in your mind but your memories of Ovuor. I must have the answer in this matter. This is of the utmost importance."

Korfax heard Abrilon speak behind him.

"Asvoan! This is unprecedented. He is an acolyte! I am not sure that I can sanction this. Surely his father should be present, at the very least?"

Korfax started at the suggestion. His father? Complex emotions swirled. He was tempted to say yes, look within, look at it all, take it, none of it belongs to me, but Asvoan was no longer looking at him; she was looking at Abrilon, her eyes filled to the brim with passion and force.

"But these are unprecedented times, Abrilon. This is our only lead. I must know the truth of this matter, and I must know it immediately. If this vision fails, if we do not know where we must aim ourselves, what follows? Up until this moment we have had precious little to go on. But now we have a face and a name, a name that we must pursue. This is no act of blind chance. Korfax was meant to be here."

Abrilon frowned and his eyes darkened.

"Korfax was meant to be here? Do you know what you are saying?"

"Of course I do," replied Asvoan. "We have here a chain of events following a single glimpse. The way has been shown. That is how it works. How else should I interpret it?"

She turned to Korfax again and her gaze was soft once more. She seemed able to change herself from moment to moment, light to dark, hard to gentle.

"Do not be afraid," she assured him. "Many of us fear the surrender of our secrets or the trespass of another upon that which is private or sacred. Do not fear that I will see anything other than that which you wish to show me."

But Korfax did feel fear. Though he saw her, saw her honesty, he was afraid. For all his rebellion there were secrets in his head, things he did not want revealed. He wished now that he had never risen from his bed this day.

"All you need do," she continued, "is think of this Ovuor, and only of her. Let me do the rest. I am bound by oaths, Korfax, all of the Exentaser are. I will reveal nothing of the thoughts I might find in your heart. They are not for me. They are for you alone."

Korfax felt the pressure about him. All were eager to know the truth of this matter, even Abrilon, though he still would not admit as much. Korfax waited until the pressure became unbearable and then submitted at last. He found himself bowing to Asvoan.

"You may look within," he told her, and almost immediately he regretted his weakness.

Asvoan did not waste any time. Her mind was like a knife as she took his gaze and held it. Then Korfax found himself reliving the moment, that very same moment where he had first met with the wife of Dialyas and endured her cold regard. Again it was as though he was caged by it, lost in a darkness without surcease, but now there was a strange duplicity within and without. He was held by Asvoan and by Ovuor, and the similarity between them both did not escape him.

He watched again as Ovuor left the house of Dialyas, her daughter beside her, the quiet laughter of Dialyas following in their wake like an echo of self-mockery. Then the moment passed and he found himself back again in the great debating hall. Asvoan was standing before him, others clustering behind her. For a moment he caught a look of astonishment on her face as though she had suffered a revelation herself. But then it was all but gone and her face was a mask once more, a stone mask like a wall.

"Thank you, Korfax," she said. "Even one of the Urenith could not have done better."

She looked at him carefully for a moment, but then she quickly turned back to Abrilon.

"I am impressed, Abrilon, truly I am. You train your acolytes well. Not only do I have this 'Ovuor', but I have her imprint also, her essence, the very feel of her spirit. This can be sought out."

Asvoan licked her lips as though tasting the information she had just gleaned.

"Korfax is true. He has seen. Dialyas and Ovuor were indeed husband and wife."

There were a few scattered oaths, but Asvoan held up her hand to silence them.

"But there is more – much more. There was a daughter also, a daughter named Doagnis. We have a dynasty to consider, a nest of Argedith in the making."

More words and not a few sharp intakes of breath.

"But Dialyas never showed any interest in such matters," said Abrilon. "He was always busy, always researching, always thinking. The moment he left our order, after we cast him away from us, he immediately set up the Sal Kamalkar. We always thought that its business took up his every waking hour, that and defending himself against the many charges of heresy that came his way."

Abrilon looked hard at Asvoan.

"I just cannot see it, Asvoan. It is so out of character."

Asvoan smiled.

"Then perhaps you do not know Dialyas as well as you think you do. This was no ordinary joining. There was an arrangement between them! I can feel it. I can see the signs," she said as she glanced at Korfax again, a speculative glint in her eyes. "Such detail from this memory," she murmured.

Abrilon let a spasm of disgust twist his features, and that self-same look spread to the faces of the others that had gathered around. Korfax glanced at each in turn and felt their stern disapproval. Then he looked at Ponodol and saw only regret. He dropped his gaze, even as Ponodol looked back sadly at him. He had intruded into matters he should not have. He thought back to when he had last listened to a conversation not meant for his ears. The world ever repeated itself, or so it seemed. His sins had caught up with him.

Abrilon broke the shocked silence.

"But this is appalling," he said. "I do not know what to say."

Even he looked unhappy now.

"And what was the nature of this arrangement?"

Asvoan smiled as though she had just won some close-fought game.

"Each wanted something that the other had," she said. "That much is certain. I think Ovuor wanted a child, and she chose Dialyas to be the father. Perhaps she divined him. It is not unknown."

Asvoan closed her eyes and opened them again.

"I think that is what I see here. Yes, she wanted a child. I could be mistaken but I believe Dialyas did not know what she was. I think that she fooled him. That also is not unknown. I think that she caught him in a trap, used him and then walked away when his purpose was done."

As Asvoan said this, Korfax found himself remembering long-forgotten words, the words Dialyas spoke after his last meeting with Ovuor.

'Take my advice, Korfax. When you are eventually joined with another, make sure you fully understand the consequences.'

Asvoan must have seen those very words in his head. She was right. There had been an agreement between them. He wondered what Dialyas had gained from the union, but then his reverie was broken by the intervention of Samafaa.

"Dialyas has been many things in his life, even a fool, but to wed with one of the Argedith? Preposterous!"

Asvoan drew herself up.

"Then I will say it again, and I will say it slowly. It is a known trait of the

Argedith, one of the worst. They use others to do their will. It is their nature. I do not believe that he knew who or what she was, even at the end. Think, all of you. None of us have ever seen her until now. The best of the Argedith were said to be the very essence of deception, and who amongst us here has had actual experience? There are the records, of course, but how often is the difference seen between the written word and the waking moment? Perhaps we have revealed a fatal flaw within ourselves."

Abrilon sighed.

"Then I suppose I must be satisfied," he said.

He turned to the Urenel.

"I must respect your judgement in this matter. I find myself greatly swayed by it. Dialyas shall come before us and he shall submit to our scrutiny."

And that was that. The Geyadel had spoken. Abrilon turned to Korfax and his stern gaze finally lessened into something a little less forbidding.

"Korfax, I apologise for my earlier displeasure. Rather, I thank you. It is clear to me now that without your presence here today we would never have been able to solve this conundrum. It is so unlikely an answer that none of us would even have thought of pursuing it. Your presence here has saved us much time. But now I think you really should leave."

Abrilon straightened his shoulders.

"And I rescind my judgement," he continued. "You are free to go with no penalty upon you at all except for one. You will bind your tongue on this matter, and you will make sure you do not do such a thing ever again. Remember the tale of the listener."

Then he leaned forward, pitching his voice so that only Korfax could hear it.

"And I shall not forget this day, either, nor your part in it. You have been noticed, Korfax of the Farenith. When you achieve your stave, come and see me. We shall have words together, you and I."

And with that, he turned around, gesturing to the others about him that they resume their seats.

They held a council. Though Korfax was not there, Ponodol told him much of what passed within. Korfax would have questioned the wisdom of this as the Geyadel himself had told him he was not to speak of the matter ever again, but Ponodol dismissed his concerns before he could even raise them. Korfax had not yet heard the reason why he was being told.

Dialyas had been summoned to stand within the great ring itself, the great ring of the highest, surrounded on all sides by the first council. In judgement sat the Geyadel, second only in authority to the Velukor himself, whilst all the others – Torzochil, Asvoan, Vixipal, Tochior, Pirzia and Valagar – took the lesser seats.

But Dialyas remained undaunted, even in this matter. He refused to submit to their demands and he held them all at bay. He defied the council, all of them.

Noqvoanel Vixipal had even threatened him with death at the end, but Dialyas would not bend. His knowledge of the law was enough to save him, and how that grated with the first of the Balt Kaalith.

Ponodol had bowed his head as he recounted how Dialyas had hidden himself away. It was as though he clutched some great secret close to his breast, a secret he would not reveal to any other, even under the greatest possible duress. He had denied knowledge of sorcery, he had denied that he was traitor, but he would not submit to examination. The only charge he would accept was that of denial, denial of the Velukor's authority. So, with little evidence of anything else, the council had recourse to but one action. Dialyas was to be declared a heretic and banished.

Korfax looked down at the news. Dialyas would be exiled. With all due speed he was to be sent to Lonsiatris, the land of the heretics, where he would spend the rest of his days. In the meantime, he was to be incarcerated in the Umadya Levanel.

The Balt Kaalith took what pleasure they could from the outcome. That Dialyas would come under their hand at last? It was a victory of sorts. They would have liked to have kept him for all time, or even put him to death, but the law was specific on the matter. By denying the high council, and there being no actual proof of wrongdoing, Dialyas had merely declared himself recreant. He was not a candidate for recantation for there was, as yet, no proven crime to answer. His only misdemeanour was one of denial, an act of heresy, and for that he must go to Lonsiatris forthwith.

Korfax felt both guilty and sad as Ponodol recounted what had happened. Dialyas had reached his end. It was the final step in his disgrace, and he, Korfax, had brought it about.

Ponodol finished his tale with tears in his eyes. Korfax almost could not bear to watch.

"So having heard all of that," he said, "you will now hear why you are being told it at all. Dialyas wishes to see you."

Korfax clutched at the arms of his chair with barely concealed panic.

"Me? He wants to see me? But why?"

Ponodol smiled sadly.

"He did not give his reasons. But it was his last request, and both the law and our traditions require that the last wish of the condemned be honoured to the fullest possible extent."

Korfax bowed reluctantly. He did not wish to meet with Dialyas again, now or ever, but as Ponodol had already said, this was a matter of duty. He had no choice. He found himself wondering what his father would say.

Korfax stood before the final gates of the Umadya Levanel and gazed up at its straight lines and stark simplicity. Each of the great towers of the great guilds revealed something of their underlying nature, and the Umadya Levanel was no exception. But whereas the others tended towards a certain subtlety, the Umadya

Levanel revelled in its bluntness.

Korfax looked to his left and studied the nearby Umadya Sabathel, floating still upon the early morning mists. Tower of the healers, he saw slender spires rising gently from their dark foundations, hope rising from leaden mortality. Then he looked to his right, to the Umadya Semeiel. Now there stood an exultation written in stone, a leap into the void, a great hand calling down the fire of creation itself. But if the Umadya Semeiel was a hand, then the Umadya Levanel was a fist, forbidding and sombre, its purpose indelibly inscribed upon its sheer walls and tall windows.

Here it declared itself: loyalty without question, duty without compromise. Here dwelt a devotion that the careful called unwavering. Others, less careful, called it fanatical. But not openly. Never openly, as the Balt Kaalith were excellent listeners and they had very long memories. Korfax thought of Ralir as he gazed upwards. Ralir had never been careful with his opinions. Had he been noticed?

Korfax walked up to the great northern gate and stopped before one of the Baltarith that stood on guard. The Baltar did not speak but instead held out an expectant hand as if he already understood all purposes. Korfax swallowed. He felt daunted. He was tempted to draw back, but then he reminded himself that this was mere ritual he confronted here, ritual in its most naked form, the mind and the spirit reduced to a series of motions. It saw nothing but its own blind wants. Korfax had not been seen at all. As yet, he remained just another word upon the great scroll that was the Balt Kaalith.

As if a fire had suddenly ignited inside his mind, he realised that he was of the Dar Kaadarith, the first of the first, so he held himself as tall as he could and gave the Baltar the kamliadar wrapped in cloth of authority, the seal of the first council writ large upon it. Acolyte or not, Korfax was on official business, and there was only one higher authority than that of the first council.

Korfax mentally dared the Baltar to test him as he waited, narrowing his eyes in preparation, but the Baltar did no such thing at all. Instead he handed back the stone and the cloth and bowed as if utterly submissive. Korfax bowed in return, as was expected, and so the gate opened. It was all as it appeared, just a ritual. Korfax entered.

He had little time to look about him, for behind the gates a Noqvoan was already waiting for him.

"Welcome to the Umadya Levanel, Faren Noren Korfax. May the light of The Creator shine upon you."

The Noqvoan bowed and Korfax bowed in return.

"And may the light of The Creator shine upon you also," he replied promptly.

The Noqvoan did not smile, but the glint in his eye told Korfax that he was very pleased by the speed of the response. Korfax smiled inside. He now had the beginnings, the veriest glimpse, into the inner workings of the Balt Kaalith. They required rectitude, adherence to tradition, unswerving, unwavering and unquestioning. Korfax felt easier in himself. That was how he had been taught as well.

The Noqvoan spoke again.

"I am Noqvoan Therendis Nar Naaomir," he said, "and I am honoured to escort one whose family has served the line of Karmaraa so faithfully for so long."

Korfax bowed again, suddenly unsure as to what to say next. It was not that he had been wrong-footed, for there were many responses that he could give, but it was just that he was suddenly at a loss for the best one of all. He finally decided that the words of the covenant would be the most apposite.

"The praise of the praiseworthy is as a garland to the righteous," he quoted.

Naaomir allowed himself a wider smile.

"You honour me greatly!" he said. "So let me repay your favour and show you our heart in all its glory. Few others outside our order have ever been gifted so."

Naaomir led him on.

"Have you ever been in the Umadya Levanel before?"

Korfax remained careful with his answers.

"No, Noqvoan, I have never had the pleasure."

Naaomir cast his hand at the vast spaces about them both.

"And what do you think of it all now that you are here?"

Korfax made the gesture of looking about him in consideration, but he had already seen. There were vaulted ceilings high above and great alcoves in between, each containing a statue lit by many piradar. It was a great circular space, vast and unoccupied, addressed only by the great statues in their alcoves, and the many diminutive figures that walked calmly to and fro across its wide floor seemed dwarfed by the immensity. Korfax was impressed by the scale, but the place already felt cold to him. The Umadya Levanel was too large and too empty, but he understood enough now to know what he should and should not say, so he offered up the words he knew Naaomir was already waiting to hear.

"I see before me a celebration of service," he said.

Naaomir all but ignited. Korfax had judged it well. It was almost exactly the right thing to say.

"And so few see that, Korfax, so few! I am gratified that the heir to one of our most revered and noble houses is of such a temper."

His smile widened further and his eyes gleamed.

"So come with me now!" he said. "Come see our heart and rejoice in the sight of it."

Naaomir took Korfax on a brief tour. The tower was impressive, built upon a scale that dwarfed its occupants, but everything seemed all of a piece – the stone, the statuary, the corridors, the halls and meeting places. Korfax decided that once you had seen a part of it, you had seen it all. It was exactly as he had described it, a celebration of service, but it was cold, sere, single-minded, the word but not the spirit. Korfax thanked Naaomir afterwards and Naaomir was pleased, but inside

Korfax suppressed a shiver. He could not imagine serving in such a place.

Naaomir led him back to the main hall.

"Now to your purpose," he said. "You are here to see Dialyas, are you not?"

"I am, Noqvoan. I was told by Geyadril Ponodol that he has asked for this."

"Indeed," said Naaomir. "But it is a strange request."

He looked carefully at his charge.

"I will be entirely open with you, Korfax, because I think you deserve nothing less. I know you to be an innocent in this matter, but I believe the seducer still desires one last seduction."

Korfax was instantly on his guard. How much did the Balt Kaalith know? He thought of Zafazaa and his plot to discredit his house, he thought of what Oanatom had told him concerning Tahamoh. It was a strange irony that Dialyas was also very much an innocent in that matter, but he did not say so.

"I am not sure that I understand," he offered.

Naaomir returned a brief smile.

"No, I am sure that you do not. You have already denied him. His strategies, as cunning as they are, will never gain you. You are of the Farenith. You are altogether too pure for him."

Naaomir dropped the smile.

"But there is something else I must tell you. You are not the only visitor Dialyas has had this day."

Korfax felt a clench of uncertainty.

"But I thought that those about to be banished were allowed only one visitor so that they could claim a witness to their exile, one witness to the justice meted out upon them."

Naaomir did not change his expression in the slightest, and Korfax felt his uncertainty deepen.

"So did I, Korfax, so did I. But it seems that sometimes the law is not quite so rigid as one was originally led to believe."

Korfax could not contain himself.

"Who was it?" he asked.

Naaomir held his hand up in rigid denial, but his expression remained gentle nonetheless.

"That I am not allowed to divulge," he said. "I am sorry, but that is the way of it. But if you will follow me now, I will take you to your destination and there you might find out for yourself. Though what good it may do you, I do not know."

Naaomir inclined his head slightly and then became all but unreadable.

"But let it not be said that the Balt Kaalith are entirely lacking when it comes to the interpretation of the law. We understand all too well what games can be played with its spirit and its intent."

His expression hardened somewhat.

"So as I bring you to the heretic, meditate upon the nature of mirrors. Think of reflections, not just of the body but also of the mind. Think of need and the answers to hard questions. Think of the price of knowledge and the bargains made to obtain it."

And with that cryptic and bitter statement, Naaomir took Korfax to the lower levels.

Mirrors? Reflections? Need? Hard questions? Korfax frowned. He looked involuntarily at Naaomir, but then looked away again. Naaomir would not explain himself again, not even to one that he favoured. He had bound himself about with his oaths – oaths of office, oaths of duty – so Korfax pondered the conundrum alone as he followed Naaomir to the lower levels.

As they came to the cell where Dialyas was being held, someone approached them from the opposite direction. Korfax was utterly taken aback to see that it was Asvoan.

"Urenel!" he exclaimed.

"Korfax!" she answered, as if also caught unawares. She even placed her hand against her throat as though to cage her surprise. Korfax was reminded of Ovuor. It was almost exactly the same gesture.

He bowed to her to hide his insight. He was not sure, but he thought he caught a most seeing look upon her face as he did so. Then she quickly bowed to him in return, before moving on again, her gaze as hard and as cold as it had ever been. In moments she had passed him by and was quickly gone.

Korfax watched her leave, wondering what business she had with Dialyas. Whatever it was, it must have been urgent. Perhaps it had something to do with the whereabouts of Ovuor. Korfax suddenly thought of bargains and strange alliances. Was that what Naaomir had meant? But a firm hand landed on his shoulder and Korfax found Naaomir looking back at him sternly. Naaomir gestured ahead with a flick of his hand and they walked on. It was almost as if he had said 'Now you know!'

They arrived at the door of the cell and Korfax waited whilst Naaomir opened it. Inside all seemed dim and spare. Then Korfax saw Dialyas.

Dialyas slowly hauled himself to his feet. He looked older now, as though many years had suddenly fallen upon his shoulders, but there was still that same heat within his eyes, that well-remembered fire that smouldered darkly as it gazed back out of its prison. Korfax felt far from comfortable under that gaze.

"Well, Korfax, here you are at last." Dialyas smiled slightly. "I understand that it is you I have to thank for my present circumstances."

To any other it would have sounded like a reproach, but Korfax knew better. Dialyas did not reproach, he mocked instead. He mocked himself, as he ever had. He mocked himself, his fortune, his life. But now, inside, beneath the self-mockery, something else had been stirred, something elemental. Korfax could hear it all – the dreams, the hopes, the pinnacles and the betrayals – but he knew that Dialyas did not blame him for his misfortune. Korfax still stood on the outside. He suddenly understood, though he did not understand why, that Dialyas would never blame him for anything. It was both curious and confusing. He wondered if this was yet a deeper game that was being played out here, and he locked eyes with Dialyas, wondering if he might provide an answer, but then Naaomir interrupted with reproaches of his own.

"You have only yourself to blame for this, heretic! You were the one to associate yourself with one of the Argedith. Korfax did his duty as befits any loyal subject of the Velukor."

Naaomir passed a swift look of contempt over Dialyas and then left, shutting the door behind him. Korfax was alone with the tempter. He looked down, suddenly unable to speak at all. His questions had fled in a flurry of uncertainty and there was nothing else he could offer. But then Dialyas laughed quietly to himself, and Korfax listened to that instead. It was such a well-remembered sound. Korfax looked carefully back at Dialyas again and found new questions to replace those that had already become stale.

"Why was the Urenel here?" he asked.

Dialyas dropped his quiet laughter and went very still. His eyes had a look to them now, a look of strange knowledge, as though he had seen possibilities, other realms, other hopes, and found strength therein.

"We had business, she and I. It was a private matter," he said.

Korfax bowed his head again, before looking this way and that, marking the stark simplicity of the place in which Dialyas had been incarcerated. It seemed the very mirror of the Balt Kaalith. All that they stood for was suddenly present in this small and all but empty room. He looked back at Dialyas.

"This was no wish of mine," he said.

Dialyas stepped in front of Korfax.

"Korfax," he said. "I do not blame you for this, of course I do not. You did your duty as befits any loyal subject of the Velukor."

Again, Korfax did not miss the mock in Dialyas's voice, but just as before it was not aimed at him. Now it was aimed at Naaomir, at the Balt Kaalith themselves.

"You saw Ovuor and you named her," Dialyas said. "What else could you do? You are entirely innocent in this affair."

Then Dialyas dropped his shoulders and turned away. He sat down upon his cold stone bed as if utterly weary.

"It was inevitable that they would come for me," he said. "The only sad thing about it all is that it happened before I was ready for it. But that too was seemingly foretold. Now all I have left is my trust that everything will unfold as it should."

Before Korfax could question what he meant, Dialyas looked straight into Korfax's eyes and held his gaze.

"Korfax, I have two things to ask of you. One is a requirement, the other is a boon."

"I have little power to grant such things," Korfax answered.

Dialyas laughed again, but this time he did not avert his gaze.

"Do you not? And can you see all ends? You have more power than you know, both of the spiritual and the temporal. And you will gain more, I think. You are almost a Geyad now, I see the markings of the sixth level upon you. It will not be long before you are made over in your own image, and not long after that I think you will become Geyadril. I see it all in you, written in your flesh, written in your spirit. So do not discount your ability to grant me what I ask."

He held up a kamliadar.

"This is my requirement. Please give this to Ponodol. It is for him alone and contains my testament. Only he can unlock it."

He gave the stone to Korfax, who looked at it for a moment until Dialyas took him by the hand and held on firmly. His gaze never faltered in the slightest.

"And of you, all I ask is this. When the hard times come, as they must, when you find all hands turned against you as they are turned against me now, do not forget your old friend Dialyas. Visit with him on Lonsiatris, for he might have a proposition for you."

Korfax walked away slowly from the Umadya Levanel, the words of Dialyas circling in his mind. What did he mean by hard times? What did he mean by all hands turning against him? That sounded too much like prophecy, but Dialyas was no prophet, and only those of the Exentaser could pronounce on such things. Then Korfax thought of Asvoan. Was that it? Was Asvoan saying less than she knew? What did she have to do with Dialyas? He considered the words of Naaomir.

Mirrors and reflections, need and the answers to hard questions! The more he considered the matter, the less he liked it. He began to think of conspiracies, of secret words and secret thoughts passed from one generation down to the next. He was tempted to turn about and voice his concerns to Naaomir, but then he heard his father in his head, warning him to keep away from the Balt Kaalith.

And that was when he realised that he had reached another turning point in his life. The decision was ultimately his to make. He could ask those who knew more than he did, or he could keep his own counsel and wait for the answers that were yet to come.

For the past six years he had been taught to think and act within a rigid framework, following the higher calling, the discipline that was the Namad Dar, following the straight road without deviation and accepting all without choice. But here it came, that strange and unforeseen freedom that lay at the end. No one could tell a Geyad how to summon power from stone, when to summon it or what to do with it once it was summoned. It was in the province of each individual, theirs alone. Indeed, a more personal relationship between mind and matter did not exist. Even the Exentaser were not so alone. Their greatest gift, that of prophecy, had to be verified by others. But it was not so for a Geyad. At the end a Geyad stood alone. The decision was his. How he used his power was up to him, and none could gainsay him. It was a terrible freedom surrounded by adamantine bars; he was free and caged all at the same time.

That was it then. He made his decision. He would keep his own counsel. But he would watch, wait and listen, and he wondered how long it would be before the answers came his way.

Back in the Umadya Semeiel he gave the kamliadar to Ponodol, who looked at it sadly.

"I know what is on here," he said. "Many is the time he has asked it of me."

He turned to Korfax. He looked both broken and sad.

"I am sorry," Korfax said.

Ponodol smiled in reply.

"And what do you have to be sorry for?" he asked. "None of this was your choice, none of this was your fault."

He held up the stone.

"Do you know what is on here?"

"No, Geyadril."

"Would you like to know?"

Korfax looked shocked.

"But that is for you, surely?"

Ponodol smiled and bowed his head.

"Quite right, quite right. Ignorance is bliss, after all."

Tazocho went straight from the sky ship to the Umadya Zedekel. Usually her visits followed the ritual paths, the times of celebration, the times of remembrance. She had never been summoned before and she wondered, not for the first time, what it could mean.

Once in the tower she went straight to the Urenel's rooms and there announced her presence. Asvoan took a little time to respond, which also was unusual, but once she did, Tazocho entered.

"Tazocho!" Asvoan declared.

Tazocho bowed.

"Urenel! You sent for me?"

"I did. How are things in the north?"

"As they have ever been since the coming of the Agdoain."

"No further insights then?"

"I still see nothing, if that is what you mean."

Asvoan frowned.

"Whenever you are asked that question you always say the very same thing, but what exactly do you mean by it?"

"I mean what I say," Tazocho answered. "I look and there is nothing there."

"But the sight within is never so still, not even for the best of us. There is always some distraction."

Tazocho narrowed her eyes.

"If I go looking for the origin of the Agdoain then that is what I see. I see nothing."

"An active principle?"

"Not even that."

"Then why have you not said as much in your reports?"

"But I have, I have always described it so."

"Your reports are invariably terse," said Asvoan. "They are open to much interpretation."

"I report as I was taught – concisely," Tazocho replied. "If there was anything else, I would tell you. Do you doubt me?"

Asvoan looked out of the window.

"No other in the north says the same as you. And only you, of all of us, have ever met the Agdoain in the flesh. I find myself wondering why that is."

Tazocho fixed Asvoan with her coldest gaze yet and waited. Asvoan looked back.

"You are displeased?"

Tazocho did not relent.

"You have had many times many to consider what I do or do not see. So why am I here now, at this very moment?"

Asvoan looked down at her hands for a moment, but then she looked up again and her eyes were bright.

"You are here because of your son."

Now it was Tazocho's turn to frown.

"My son?"

"He has provided us with an answer to a most difficult problem and, I might add, a most intriguing insight into his education."

"I do not understand," Tazocho said.

"You heard the tale of the vision of Payoan? Your son was instrumental in solving the riddle. Without him, we would never have known about Ovuor. He even allowed me to look within. I must say that I was impressed by his clarity. He is a credit to you."

Asvoan leaned forward, her eyes brightening a little more.

"But that is not why I called you here. What I really want to know is why does Korfax have a hiding pattern in his head?"

Tazocho did not move. Now it was Asvoan's turn to narrow her eyes.

"What have you helped him to hide?" she demanded.

Tazocho did not flinch.

"And must I remind you of your oaths?" she asked.

Asvoan drew back as if suddenly slapped, but all too soon she leaned forwards again.

"Play no games with me, Tazocho," she warned. "Why does he know a hiding pattern? There is only one person in this world who could have taught it to him."

Tazocho drew herself up and folded her arms.

"So, if you will not abide by your own oaths, how can you expect me to abide by mine? I thought we were all meant to lead by example."

Asvoan spread her fingers wide.

"I could take the truth from you, you know, I have that right."

"Only if I was the one that concealed," Tazocho said. "But that is not me."

Asvoan scowled and exerted a modicum of force.

"You had no right to share our secrets with an outsider, be he your son or no. We reserve the hiding patterns only for when an acolyte awakens the inner light and becomes Uren at last. They are amongst our most potent tools of defence. You ask if I doubt you? Are you surprised? What else might you have shown him?"

Tazocho matched the power of her mistress.

"I will not explain myself in this matter," she said. "You have looked where you should not. That in itself is not a crime, as such things can be inadvertent, but having seen what you saw you should never have spoken of it to another, not even to me. Of what worth are your oaths now, or the sanctity of our order, when the highest can make and break the rules with such impunity?"

Asvoan hurled the full force of her mind at Tazocho and Tazocho flinched, leaning back, almost averting her gaze, but she withstood the Urenel nonetheless. For a long time they held each other at bay, a long and weary time of inner fencing, of measure and countermeasure, but it was Asvoan who desisted first, dropping her gaze as though with sudden disgust.

"You are not held in high favour at the moment, Tazocho, not with any of us. We expected you to become Urendril, but you did not do so. Instead you ignored the needs of your order and followed the path of your mate. What a waste! There are only two, in all the Exentaser, who have any insight into this affair. One of them has dark abstracted dreams that make no sense, whilst the other sees nothing, literally nothing at all."

"I cannot help what I see!" said Tazocho.

"Really? My doubts remain! Our only hope now lies with Payoan. She we still own, but what of you, Tazocho? Where does your allegiance lie now?"

"To the throne, where it always has."

Duel over, Tazocho drew herself up again and refolded her arms.

"Do you mean to tell me now that you consider the throne to be of less importance than your own desires or those of the Exentaser?"

Asvoan scowled.

"I know your heritage, Tazocho, and do not for a moment think that I don't. But you have less influence now than you once had."

"Then you should look to the future, Urenel. I might well gain it again."

Asvoan looked back darkly.

"You were always proud. I remember when your choices humbled Zafazaa. I remember what you did. Beware, daughter of Rageiol, fate has never been kind to such as you. Put your blood before your loyalties and the world will turn its back upon you."

Tazocho smiled.

"But you forget, Urenel, the world has never turned its back upon the blood that runs in my veins. Never! Not in seven thousand years." She waited a moment. "So, will you speak of this to others? Will you break your oaths further?"

Asvoan smiled back.

"Your secret is safe with me, have no fear, but I shall be watching you from now on, Tazocho, be certain of it. You may go."

Tazocho marched away, full of fury. Asvoan had broken her oaths. The matter of the hiding pattern should never have been spoken of, not to anyone. Fear and anger fought inside her – fear of discovery, anger at its manner. There was only one other she could talk to in her order: Kukenur, second Urendril and Asvoan's bitter rival.

Tazocho found her on one of the high balconies overlooking the eastern side of the city.

"I have just come from the Urenel," she said. "I have a concern."

"Then perhaps you should have mentioned it to the Urenel when you spoke to her," said Kukenur.

"The Urenel is my concern."

Kukenur blinked slowly.

"Say on."

"The breaking of oaths, the bending of rules."

Kukenur widened her eyes slightly.

"That has long been known," she said.

"You will do nothing?" Tazocho asked.

"She is Urenel."

"But you have no love for her."

"My likes and dislikes are no concern of yours."

"You opposed her elevation."

"Yes, I did, and I made no attempt to conceal my feelings in the matter. But we are where we are. I may regret that Samor left before her time, and I may resent the rise of one who should never have gained such heights, but that is all I will ever do."

"Well, it may comfort you to know that you are not alone in that at least."

Kukenur turned around fully.

"But you resent nothing, Tazocho. Your path is already set before you. Your son will fulfil your desires. You have already named yourself for him and are already blessed. You have become one of the fortunate few."

"Do you have no ambition?" Tazocho asked.

"We all have to shift with the times," Kukenur replied.

"I faced her down, and I can do the same to you," Tazocho warned.

"Then why did you come here? To gloat?" Kukenur did not hide her displeasure.

"I seek those of like mind, that is all," Tazocho told her.

"No," said Kukenur. "You are altogether far too proud to seek allies. The mere mention of your bloodline is all that you will ever need."

"Then you will not act?"

"Why should I? We have all at one time or another skirted the intent of the law by subverting its spirit. You are no different."

"But I seek justice."

"Then be careful what you wish for, Tazocho, as you may be granted it."

She looked hard for a moment and then sighed.

"What's done is done. Samor's final vision remains beyond us all. No one knows why she did what she did, and only Asvoan had her ear at the end. We have divisions enough within us as it is, so it would be well if you did not widen them any further with your rebellion."

"I had no intention of doing so," Tazocho insisted.

"Good!" replied Kukenur. "As to justice, you should be patient. We will gain it in the end."

"Then you ally yourself with me?"

"No, but you will ally yourself with me. And that is how it shall be, Tazocho, or you will stand alone until you enter the river. Now leave me."

Still dissatisfied, Tazocho had one last place to go – to her son. She went to the Umadya Semeiel and met with him in the courtyard of Hais.

She asked him what had happened, and he told her all that he knew. She looked at him for a moment and then told him about her encounter with Asvoan.

"Do not tell your father anything concerning this matter," she said. "I would not burden him with more worries than he has at present."

"But she saw the pattern!" Korfax hissed.

"She did not penetrate it," Tazocho replied. "All she knows is that something has been hidden, but she does not know what it might be. She tried to look into my mind also, but I denied her."

Korfax was horrified.

"Can she do that?" he asked.

"In the Exentaser one is tested all the time," Tazocho told him. "But you already know this."

He looked down for a moment.

"So what of her oaths? That was the only reason I allowed her to look in the first place."

"Asvoan has always been a law unto herself," said his mother. "She, alone of the Exentaser, was chosen by Samor, and Samor, alone of the Exentaser, went to Lonsiatris. None knows the reason. All we can be certain of is that Samor was guided by a vision and that Asvoan is the only other that knows what it is. And since she has never spoken of it she is distrusted."

"What shall I do?"

"Do nothing. Asvoan will not speak of this again, but be certain that she will be watching you."

"I will confront her," he said.

Tazocho stood tall and her eyes blazed.

"You will not!" she commanded. "You will do nothing of the sort." She gentled again. "Leave it to me," she said. "Besides, things will go the way that they go. Asvoan knows that she stands upon delicate ground in this regard. If she speaks out, breaking her oaths for all to see, that will be that. She will no longer be Urenel. If she moves against our house she will incur the wrath of many. Remember that your father saw down Zafazaa."

"But what if she does speak out? How do we explain the hiding pattern?"

"We do not, it is no one else's affair. And now let there be an end to it."

14

INTO THE FIRE

Pol-honli Pi-sil-saaje
Kaamoz-chis Od-bl-konihr
Viu-noli Zo-unlus-u
Kommaa-nei Siba-ippal
A-gos-alk Aj-an-dr-pan
D-nimin Tri-an-zafaa
Kurg-tolzim Zin-zn-agaa

Korfax waited in the Gardens of Becoming. His forging was at hand. Others had fallen by the wayside, failing in this task or that, but he had stayed true to his course.

It was strange to think that of all those that began as he did, less than half had reached their forging. It was the last year that had whittled the numbers down – the tests, the pressure to perform each and every time you were asked, never to flinch or break, no matter how hard the challenge.

Aduret was one of those that had failed. Aduret the keen, the able, who had shown such promise in the first few years, but even he had fallen at the last, unable to make the correct choice when it mattered most. An incorrect summoning could be fatal.

Those unable to achieve their stave moved on to become sky masters, or water masters, or builders or smiths. But never again would they touch a stave. It was sad and for some heart-breaking, but that was the way that it was.

Someone came towards him from the south and he looked up expectantly. It was Ralir, smiling and full of joy.

"It is done?" Korfax asked.

"It is done!" Ralir answered, whereupon he drew out his sword and displayed it in both hands. It was a miamna, not as large as a kansehna but just as deadly. He held it up with his left hand and all but devoured it with his eyes as he ran his right hand up and down it, from the tip to the hilt and back again.

"Here is Ilpazar," he sighed, "my badge of office."

He turned to Korfax again, eyes aglow.

"Is it not glorious?"

Korfax smiled carefully. He looked enviously at the long shining blade, suddenly wishing that he could wield it as well.

"It is a fine blade indeed, and rare. But what is its heritage?

Ralir swept it around him in a brief arc of metal.

"It has slept within my father's house for nigh on six thousand years. It was used in the wars themselves, but I am the first to claim it in all the times since."

"Has it been re-forged?"

"Yes, it has been made over, like its master. Now it has a chiraxadar set within its hilt."

Korfax looked at the great blue stone set where blade and guard met.

"Not a weapon to be used lightly then," he offered.

Ralir smiled back.

"But knowing how to use it is all part of the test of a true Napei."

He span the sword about his head and then brought it down in the attitude of waiting.

"And it strikes with the force of a falling hill. No demon would dare survive such a blow."

"You have a shield to match, I see," Korfax said.

Ralir raised up his shield and looked at it with pride.

"Yes, the mate of Ilpazar. This one is Malanar, also re-forged and set with a kusadar, as it should have been from the very beginning rather than pining away in the vaults of the Rax Izikal. Now it sits upon my arm, as light as air, but a veritable wall when set before the foe. I almost feel invincible bearing such weaponry."

He looked upwards.

"I AM BECOME NAPEI!" he declared, shouting the words at the heavens and holding out his sword and his shield as though to offer them to the sky. Then, full of himself, he assumed the very first stance and all but danced his way through the first and second motions in an instant. Korfax drew back and applauded.

"And I, for one, would not like to be on the receiving end of such skill."

Ralir smiled back at his friend and quieted himself. Then he put his shield over his back and sheathed his sword again.

"But it is a great joy to me, my one true friend, a great and glorious joy," he said. "I have achieved my heart's desire at last. I am now where I was meant to be, and it is all because of you. You have been there for me, helping me when I needed help the most, and I love you for it."

Ralir clasped his friend by the shoulders. Then he drew back again carefully as if suddenly embarrassed.

"But what of you? Aren't you also happy that your moment is about to arrive?"

Korfax looked down.

"Yes and no. I must confess that I am more than a little scared. No one has told me anything about it."

Ralir leaned closer.

"But that is the way that it is with all great mysteries. Though you may doubt it now, you will soon be Geyad in truth. And then we will be together, Geyad and Napei, masters of all we survey."

Korfax smiled nervously and then looked up again. At least he could bathe in the reflection of his friend's joy, but he found himself wishing his own upcoming ordeal was already over.

Before long they came for him, two wardens, Paziba and Kurapan.

"It is time," said Paziba.

Korfax followed them back to the tower. Paziba and Kurapan held up their staves before them, lighting the way, and Korfax walked behind them, dressed only in the simple robe of an aspirant.

Those others that waited watched as well. This was the day of making, when all the great guilds harvested their acolytes and made them over in their new image.

They entered the Umadaya Semeiel and went straight to the Hall of Making. Korfax stood before the door and waited. Paziba and Kurapan left him. He was alone.

The door opened and he entered the hall. It was dark, except for one place, the place reserved for him. It was set at the centre. He went to it, feeling the weight of eyes as he did so. Out there, in the darkness, others watched. He arrived at his place and knelt, his robe spreading out around him. The light shone down on him and he felt almost naked under its glare. The light went out and it was deathly silent. For how long he knelt there he did not know, but as he began to wonder what would happen next, the stone on which he knelt rippled with force. It cracked and opened. He would have moved but winds suddenly assaulted him from all sides, pummelling him and holding him in place. Then fire swirled about him, brilliant flame, so even if he had wanted to move there was nowhere to go. Next he heard the rush of waters, a great roar like the emptying of a sea. The stone around him fell away and dark waters swirled under the fire, rising up as if hungry for him. He was alone in the night, caught by the elements – earth, air, fire and water – and he had no other choice but to endure.

"So, what was it like? I have never seen the making of a Geyad," Ralir asked, his eyes eager for an answer. Korfax frowned.

"Nor will you ever, just as I will never see the forging of a Napei," replied Korfax.

"But I told you everything that happened," said Ralir.

Korfax smiled carefully.

"But I did not experience it. Its mystery was not for me, just as the mystery of the making of a Geyad is not for you. But I will tell you what happened, if you truly wish to know."

He paused a moment, gathering his thoughts.

"First came the darkening, when I was cleansed by the elements. I was crushed by stone, racked by air, burnt by fire and drowned in water. I was reduced to my essential substance and I became a residue of what I had been."

Ralir stared back at Korfax as if he could not quite believe what he was hearing.

"What are you saying?" he asked. "You describe it as though they were trying to kill you! Surely not!"

"And did I understand why they fought you to exhaustion and then threw you into the waters of Leiath?" Korfax answered.

"No."

"Well then, you should not be surprised if you do not understand the mysteries of the Dar Kaadarith in turn."

Korfax looked down, his eyes unfocused as he thought back to what had happened.

"I became black," he continued, "and they buried me. But I felt no pain or distress, as I was already on my way to my very own becoming. And so, within me, the seed grew like a flower, opening up, widening and ever seeking the light. It seemed to take an age of the world, as though I had entered a timeless place. To me it felt as if I had already rotted in the earth and that some slow furnace leached away those substances that barred the way from the impure to the pure! But then I was turned in upon myself and that which I had been feeding became that which I would become. At times I felt solid, at others fluid. Sometimes it felt as though I sat upon the earth like a mountain, or that I flew up into the air on sudden wings or that I flowed like a river. Many colours flashed before me, colours like the plumage of the shial, but then my world turned red at last and fire entered me. The mountain erupted, the air ignited and the river burned."

Korfax smiled and closed his eyes.

"It was utter bliss. I had been made over. I had become red. I had chosen fire."

He held up his red stave and brandished it above his head.

"And here it is, the language of creation revealed in stone. Kabadar Bitem! I am become Geyad, Geyad Bitem, as my father before me and his father before him, as all the others of our line have ever been, all the way back to the very beginning. For the Farenith have always chosen fire."

Korfax clenched his hand tight about his stave and awoke his power. The stave glowed briefly and a low note, almost a hum, came and went. Then fire erupted from its tip.

Red lightning flew upwards into the sky, a multitude of brilliant blades shattering the calm of the day. Great thunders rolled this way and that, echoing across the city. The air staggered about them both, and the few that took their leisure about the wide gardens at that time turned to stare at the sudden display. A column of fire briefly pierced the heavens and all looked up at it in awe or satisfaction. Then Korfax withdrew his power and the heavens growled back at him for a moment before falling silent again. He looked with utter joy at his stave.

"So here is my power," he said, "here, in this slender shaft of crystal. I have but to command it and all the elements will bow down before me. I hold the very forces of creation in my hands."

Ralir stared back at his friend, breathing hard and eyes wide.

"I suddenly think that I have been well and truly put in my place," he said. "You say that you would not like to face my sword and my shield? Well, you have nothing to fear from the likes of me, nothing at all. I would not last a moment against such power as you just revealed."

He looked back carefully at Korfax.

"Tell me something, though, as I have often wondered. Why have the Farenith always chosen fire? I know of other houses where the son does not follow the father. Do any of the other houses remain with the same element always?"

Korfax looked up. He frowned a little.

"Some, I think. Certainly there was no surprise at my choice, so I imagine that the predilection for a certain element does run in some families, but it is not something that is ever really discussed. Oanatom is of the Ziranur, and they have always chosen air. Thilnor is of the Hamindoh, and they have always chosen water. So, I suppose it should be no surprise that I would choose fire, or should it?"

"I suppose not." Ralir said, looking down. For a moment he was silent, then he looked back at Korfax again.

"But now that you do have a stave of fire, why is it that you can command more than the one element?"

Korfax smiled.

"You know, I did once try to explain this to you. You quickly became bored, if I remember rightly."

"Well, I promise you now I will never be bored with anything you ever say again."

Ralir gestured at the kabadar and Korfax laughed.

"You can be as bored as you please," he said. "But how to explain it? The fire I call up is not fire as you understand it; it is the element of fire, its essence. Look about you. Rarely do you see the elements naked, as they are nearly always masked by whatever receptacle contains them. All you perceive is their effect only, how they react with each other to make the world. And that is the important point. They interact, flowing from one state to another. Now you might wonder how fire can flow into air, or earth into water, but they do it all the time. The underlying truth is that even they are masks for something else, something that lies even deeper. Below everything else there is only the word. But you never see it, only its effect."

"Yes, so I have been told, but I am still not sure that I fully understand."

Korfax reached down and touched the stone of the path.

"Normally my hand cannot pass through this stone. Why?"

Ralir frowned and gave Korfax a quizzical look.

"Because it is solid," he said.

"No," Korfax told him. "That is not so. My hand is not solid, and neither is the stone of the path. Nothing is. My hand cannot pass through the stone because the forces that make them both will not allow it. What you see here is the word of creation made manifest, the continuing word, the interaction of the four elements creating order out of chaos. My hand cannot pass through the stone because the word will not allow it to do so."

Korfax stood up again.

"But imagine if you were able to reach the underlying word, the source. Then you would be able to call upon the very essence itself and control it."

He glanced down again.

"Then it would be possible for my hand to pass through the stone."

Ralir looked down at the stone for a moment.

"That would be a useful trick," he murmured. He turned back to Korfax. "You keep talking about the word, but you once told me it was all angles and geometries."

Korfax laughed again.

"Did you ever listen to anything that I said?" he chided. "Both statements are correct. When a Geyad summons the elements, he does so by speaking the words that began creation. A word, in this case, is the act itself. Think of it as a movement within the fundamental geometry that underlies everything. A Geyad who speaks the word can bend that geometry to his will, which is why stone can be made to flow like water, or air to solidify like earth.

"Think of it like this. For a moment, a very brief moment, a small part of the world is returned to a state that it once knew, when everything was in flux and order had not yet been imposed. In this singular moment the world itself can be reordered. It is like remaking a tower. No fundamental law is broken in the process, but the tower itself has been changed. Such workings, though, do not last for long, because creation has a momentum all of its own. It is itself a far greater word. As soon as a Geyad expresses his power, that power is gradually subsumed again into the greater word that is being spoken continuously about you. You have already seen this. Once fire of air is unleashed, it quickly dissipates again. Others linger, like earth of air, remaining in the world for perhaps no more than a day. But all decay in time."

Ralir thought on that for a moment, before turning back to Korfax once more.

"So what is the difference between a Geyadril and a Geyad then?" he asked.

"Mastery and power," said Korfax. "To be a Geyadril you must demonstrate complete mastery. And to have complete mastery you must be strong."

"Just that? But I was always told that the white stave signifies spirit."

"But it is true," Korfax said as he smiled. "The white stave signifies spirit: spirit of earth, spirit of air, spirit of fire and spirit of water. There is even spirit of spirit, but only Karmaraa was said to have been such a master. That was how he destroyed Sondehna and then his vanguard. Seeing such power unleashed, the remaining forces of the north retreated. Karmaraa, Logah Qahn, Audroh Eithar, whose works shall be a song of honour for all time, single-handedly turned the battle by the power that was in him. No other has matched it since."

Korfax looked at his stave, eyes bright as he held it up to the light so that many reflections ran across and through it. Then he looked back at Ralir again.

"We know how to make white staves," he continued, "given the stave of Karmaraa himself, but not how to call up that fundamental spirit that lies beneath everything. Only to Karmaraa was that grace given. Some say that at the heart of it lies the power to overturn creation entirely, for if you say the word that began it all then surely creation itself will be subsumed, to begin again."

Ralir stared for a moment.

"Is that true?"

"Some have considered it so."

Ralir looked at Korfax's stave for a moment.

"That is a terrifying thought," he said.

"And an impossible one," Korfax told him. "In order to speak such a word you would have to become The Creator, so I would not worry about it, if I were you. This world is more than enough for all of us, I think."

"You know me," Ralir said. "I never think over much on anything. But things are different in the south. You are either of the Prah Sibith or you are not. All the other guilds are subordinate. And so it has been ever since the time of Karmaraa."

Korfax looked away, his eyes suddenly abstracted.

"Zorvu would have seen that it remained that way, I imagine."

"What do you mean?" Ralir asked.

Korfax looked back at his friend.

"Just that there are two directions," he replied, "as there ever have been – the south and everywhere else."

Ralir opened his mouth in surprise for a moment and then roared with laughter.

"Well said, my friend, well said indeed! Time was when I would have caught you with the differences, but not any more. My good friend Korfax comes into his own at last."

Ralir came forward and held out his hands. Korfax saw the gesture and came to his friend. They embraced, but even as they touched Korfax felt a sudden sadness. Ralir was right. The days of his youth were finally ended. He was of the Geyadith now, and the world that had nurtured him for all these years expected its due in return. The time for play had passed and now he would be given cares and responsibilities. In the shedding of his fears he had lost something precious. Change was ever the way of the world.

A cynical thought came to him then, something Dialyas had once said a long time ago. The longer you lived, the more compromises you made. Korfax had not understood at the time, and the conversation had lain forgotten inside him like a seed. But now it came to him again as if he had heard it only yesterday.

"Do you like the garden here?" Dialyas had asked.

"Yes I do, it is a fine garden and rare. Was it laid out by a master?"

"I am certain that it was, but I cannot tell you who, as I do not know. We tend it, of course, and try to maintain its original design, but the world about us has plans of its own, as it ever has. Sometimes the blossoms arrive late, or the fruit comes early or a foreign seed will land here or there and grow unnoticed for a while, spreading a little more chaos amongst the established order. That is, naturally, until it is noticed and rooted out."

Korfax had looked up with surprise at Dialyas's statement.

"Rooted out? I hope it is not wilfully destroyed. In the gardens at Losq, Mohbul always planted the strays in other places."

Dialyas had offered up a regretful smile.

"And do you think so badly of us? Of course we do not do that. All life is precious. No, all I meant was that the trespasser is taken elsewhere."

"Trespasser?"

"One who goes where they should not – a trespasser!"

"I am sorry, I did not see what you meant. Is this a parable you tell me now?"

Then Dialyas had laughed.

"You begin to read me well, Korfax, indeed you do. Very well then, I will reveal my thought to you, though I doubt that you will truly appreciate it until you come into your own."

"Into my own?"

"You are of the Salman Farenith and attend the seminary in the Umadya Semeiel. Now you are Noren and a mere acolyte, but one day you will be more than that, I think, much more."

"Oh, I see."

"No, Korfax, I do not think that you do. But you will, given time."

Dialyas had given him a sharp look then, sharp and most seeing, before looking away again with a smile.

"What I meant to convey to you was how the world keeps changing about us and how there is a continual struggle to hold it back. But one can only keep such forces at bay for a little while. Flesh fails eventually."

"That is true enough, though I do not see why you make so much of it."

"Do you not? But my point is simple, Korfax. Not only does the world change but we change also. We learn, we age, the world changes and we change with it, whether we will it or not. But you cannot fight a war on two fronts for ever."

"Now I see what you mean. You argue against the stability brought about by the Wars of Unification."

Dialyas had almost laughed at that.

"You are far too absolute," he had said. "No, all I am suggesting is that we should embrace change, as we cannot continue this way. To stand still is to stagnate, and to stagnate is to eventually face extinction. The rock is ever worn down by the wind and the rain and the sea, and that is the danger I see for the Ell. Ever since the wars, the Ell have become the obstinate stone."

"And what if that is the will of The Creator?"

"And you truly think you know what that is?"

"And you do?"

"No, Korfax, I do not, but it strikes me that those who believe otherwise are like the word that thinks itself the entire sentence, or the note that thinks itself the entire song."

Dialyas had then smiled.

"My young friend, it ignores the nature of the Ell themselves. To grow older is to change, to lose what one had before. If one was virtuous, one becomes compromised. If one was innocent, one becomes guilty. The unthinking rituals of the past are suddenly revealed for what they truly are, a cage in which to contain us all. Though it be called wicked, still we rattle the bars of that cage, for we know in our heart of hearts that to remain inside goes against our very nature. We were once born free."

The smile had then gradually fallen away.

"Do you see what I am saying? In our world, as it is now, to grow older is to grow more wicked. It is the way things have become. The longer you live, the more compromises you make. The more compromises you make, the more guilty you feel. And to live in this world is to know guilt."

Others approached. Korfax looked up and saw his father and mother walking slowly towards them both. His father was looking at him with a stern eye.

"Was that you that just lit up the sky?"

Korfax bowed his head.

"I wanted to show my friend what it meant to be Geyad," he said.

Sazaaim glanced at Ralir.

"I have been informed that the pair of you have been displaying your skills to one another. If it was not the day that it is, you would both have been reprimanded by now."

Then he smiled.

"But it is the day that it is. First a Napei and then a Geyad, both made over in their own image. The powers that be understand all too well what has occurred here."

Sazaaim leaned forward and looked carefully at his son.

"But don't ever make a habit of such proud displays. One should always tread carefully in Emethgis Vaniad."

Tazocho gestured to Ralir.

"I believe that your mother and your father await you in the seventh grove. They stand there even now, ready to give you their blessings. I told them that I would send you thence."

Ralir bowed to her.

"Thank you, Enay, and thank you for your friendship. I have attained my heart's desire because of you."

She frowned slightly.

"Because of me?"

"You brought Korfax into the world. You and your sire have given me a gift beyond price, the best of all friends."

Ralir turned to Korfax and they embraced once more.

"I will see you again."

"I am sure that you will. Be well, my friend."

Then Ralir was off, running swiftly across the green towards the seventh grove. Sazaaim turned to his son.

"Kneel," he said.

Korfax did so, wondering what his father was up to. But then Sazaaim extended his hand and placed it upon his son's head.

"Receive now my blessing," said Sazaaim. "As when you were born, so I wish it for you now. May you drink of the light of The Creator all the days that are to come. I am so very proud of you, my son, so very proud."

Korfax looked up and his eyes filled with sudden tears.

"But I am proud to be your son," he answered.

Sazaaim raised Korfax up and they embraced. Then Korfax smiled.

"We are of the Geyadith."

His father held him close and smiled in return.

"We are indeed," he said.

They laughed together, and their shared tears became their shared joy. Then it was his mother's turn. She embraced him.

"Now you are one of the mighty," she said. "Now you fulfil your promise."

Korfax dropped his gaze, suddenly embarrassed.

"No, Korfax, look up," she told him. "Do not turn away from the truth. On this day, at the very least, let your humility take second place to your pride. And you should be proud. You deserve to be proud. You are the mightiest of the mighty now."

Korfax raised his face and smiled at her. She smiled back at him and her eyes were bright with joy.

"You have become all that I could wish for, and your father is the happiest I have ever seen him since the days of your birth. You are a gift to us both, the brightest gift that we could ever ask for."

He knelt before her and she kissed his brow. Then she held him against her and closed her eyes.

"You have become the very essence of all my dreams. You have become the very image of all my hopes."

With the ending of the ceremonies of making, many farewells were said. For Korfax that meant saying goodbye to Thilnor and Oanatom.

"Well, here we are," he said. "The parting of the ways."

Korfax looked at Thilnor.

"Where are you going?"

"Back to Othil Ekrin to become the aide of Genadol."

"You are to serve the second Geyadril of the east? That is a great honour!"

Thilnor looked down.

"Yes, it is. I am not sure that I am worthy."

Korfax smiled.

"Of course you are. I am happy for you."

He turned to Oanatom.

"And Oanatom? What of you?"

"Back to Othil Homtoh, of course. I am to serve in the archives. But what will you do?"

"I do not know yet," said Korfax. "The Geyadel wishes to see me at the hour of Ialaxan. I do not know where my service will take me yet. Most are staying here to serve the tower. No one has spoken to me."

"But you are to see the Geyadel," said Oanatom. "That is an uncommon thing in itself."

"Yes, and it makes me wonder."

The door opened and Abrilon smiled.

"Come in and be welcome, youngest of the Geyadith."

Korfax bowed and entered, glancing this way and that as he did so. Though he had once waited outside, he had never been inside the Geyadel's apartments before. He found himself entranced.

The apartments were the Umadya Semeiel in miniature, a place of proud stone redolent with meanings. There were not too many comforts here, nor too many works of art, but that which had been set in this place seemed powerful in its solitude. Though Abrilon was something of an ascetic, he was a most careful one.

He gestured to a pair of fine seats set either side of a small table on which were set two long crystal goblets and a tall bottle of wine. The goblets sat exactly before each chair and the bottle sat at the exact centre of the table. Korfax did not recognise the bottle.

"Sit, Korfax, and together we shall drink to your making."

Korfax felt himself caught by the gesture. How many others that had been made this year had been accorded such an honour? Precious few, if any at all, he thought.

He sat in the proffered chair and waited for Abrilon to lift his goblet. Korfax did the same and they both drank, almost as one. He had already been warned by Ponodol concerning this meeting. The Geyadel enjoyed both symmetry and precision.

The wine was light and refreshing and it sparkled upon the tongue. Korfax thought that perhaps it was a stimulant. Things certainly seemed brighter after he had swallowed it.

"You asked to see me, Geyadel?" he said.

"Yes I did," said Abrilon. "As I told you after you revealed to us the name of Ovuor, you were to come to see me when you achieved your stave. We need to talk, you and I."

"Geyadel?"

"You have led an interesting life, I think."

"Interesting, Geyadel?"

"Interesting, Korfax! You survived the massacre at Losq, you dared face Dialyas in his lair and you defeated an acolyte of the sixth level in a battle of power whilst you were still only of the third. You have the friendships of the houses of Badagar and Zinu, and whether you know it or not, you are already a power in the land. Many care what happens to you, and many care what you think. Though you can be daunted by hard words and hard judgements, you do not flinch. You are gifted with humility and a loyal and loving heart. That is a rare and potent combination."

Korfax did not know where to put his face. He felt as though his entire life had suddenly been laid out before him in astonished praise. How could he answer? Sincere gratitude seemed the only option. He bowed his head.

"Thank you, Geyadel."

Abrilon smiled warmly.

"I do not mean to embarrass you, Korfax, though I have also been told that it is easy enough to achieve. I understand this. Nor do I intend to mention the past over much. You are now one of the Geyadith, newly born to the world and made over in your own image. No other of the great orders experiences anything quite like it."

Korfax remained careful.

"But we do not know their secrets, either," he said.

Abrilon tilted his head slightly in acknowledgement.

"That is true enough. Each order does indeed possess arcana known only to itself, but whereas we can duplicate the powers of others, none can duplicate ours. Only we can make stone. Only we can communicate with the void in each crystal. Only we can bring back the created energies. That is why we are the first of the first."

On hearing the Geyadel speak so, Korfax felt both humbled and proud all over again. Here was a secret covenant that was his alone to know. The Geyadel was right. The Namad Dar was employed by every other guild, but none were its masters except for the Dar Kaadarith.

Abrilon placed his long goblet carefully back upon the table. Korfax did not miss the precise way in which it was done. He copied the gesture, placing his goblet just so upon the table. Abrilon smiled slightly for a moment and then took a deep breath.

"Korfax, we must discuss some things, you and I. No doubt you are aware that there are rifts and schisms in our order, as there are in all the great guilds, and I have done much to heal the ones that I know of, but there is one remaining wound that I would see healed before I pass into the great river itself, because, you see, it affected me personally."

Korfax looked up and became still. The wine made him bold.

"I think I can guess which one, Geyadel," he said.

"You can?"

"I believe you are referring to my father."

Abrilon waited, but Korfax added nothing further. He was waiting in turn. Abrilon steepled his hands before him, each finger leaning against its opposite in a brief ripple of motion.

"That has long been a mystery," he said. "Your father should have been a Geyadril, yet he did not become one. Many believed he was refused by Gemanim. A few believe otherwise. It has become a thing of sadness in our order."

Korfax became still.

"Have you spoken to my father concerning this?" he asked.

Abrilon bowed his head sadly.

"Many times," he answered.

"And has he told you how it was?"

Abrilon sighed.

"No, he has not."

So this was what it was all about, Korfax realised. But there was nothing he could say. The Geyadel would remain disappointed.

"I am sorry, Geyadel," he said, "but until my father speaks of it and tells me that he has, I will not speak of it either."

Abrilon did not move, but now his face betrayed a deeper concern.

"I know of the contention between you," he said.

"There has been," Korfax told him.

"That is a thing of sadness also." Abrilon leaned forward and looked with regret at Korfax. "I understand. It is one of the reasons that I asked you here – Dialyas and Zafazaa."

Korfax clenched and then unclenched his fists. Abrilon watched for a moment and then sighed.

"Let me tell you something about your father," he said. "He is one of the most honourable in all the land. I know, as I was there when Dialyas was dismissed from our order. There was hatred between them at the end, but your father did not submit to it as Dialyas did. Instead he fought to defend the honour of his friends, even Dialyas. He would only do that which was right. It was quite remarkable to see."

Abrilon smiled and then continued.

"Ponodol told me, in later days, that he thought your father the most powerful Geyad he had ever seen, stronger even than any on the council. Think on that, Korfax. Ponodol is one of the mightiest of us, but he says that your father is mightier still. That he is not Geyadril is a source of great regret to many."

Abrilon took another sip of his wine, placing the goblet back in exactly the same place from where he had lifted it.

"I find myself wondering if it was your father that refused. It would be like him. It is my guess that he felt guilt over the dismissal of Dialyas. Perhaps he sees it as a flaw in himself and considers himself unworthy."

He looked up.

"What I am saying to you, Korfax, is that I do not wish this to be the way of things with you. I see the worth in you much as I see it in him. Do not let his guilt become yours, for as I see it, there is no guilt. Your house is one of great worth and honour. I would see you rewarded for your service."

Korfax stared at Abrilon.

"Thank you, Geyadel, but I cannot answer for my father. I truly do not know anything."

"No, I see that. And if you did know, you would not tell me anyway. You honour your house, as you should. It is for your father to say in this matter. I understand. Gemanim did not tell me everything either, and we were very close in his last years. Did you ever meet him?"

Now that they were off the subject of his father, Korfax found himself relaxing, just a little. He looked down.

"Just the once, Geyadel. When I first came to the seminary, my father went to see him. I waited outside, but then Gemanim came out to me. He did not say anything; he just walked up to me and placed his hand upon my head. Then he smiled and went back to my father. I never understood why."

Korfax looked back up to find Abrilon staring at him, unmoving, his eyes wide.

"Was it his left hand?" he asked.

"Yes, it was."

"He blessed you?"

"I suppose it was a blessing, I wasn't sure."

Abrilon drew back and blinked.

"Geyadel, what is it?" Korfax asked.

"I am just rather surprised at what you have told me," Abrilon said. "That was a rare thing that happened, a very rare thing. I know of only one other who received such a benediction."

"And who was that, Geyadel?"

"It was I," said Abrilon.

Abrilon sat alone. What a revelation. He had not imagined such a thing. It was a shame that he still had no idea why Sazaaim had not become Geyadril, a source of great regret to him, but to discover that Korfax had been blessed by Gemanim? He remembered when it had happened to him. It had been just as unexpected, just as enigmatic.

He had been an acolyte of the third level, engaged in a contest of wills with another. It had been a small thing, nothing like the duel between Korfax and Simoref, but at the time it had inflamed his passion. It had come to blows, his opponent lashing out with his fists and his feet. Abrilon had skipped back, defending himself but not retaliating. It was his way. Let your opponents exhaust themselves in futility. It was the cliff set against the sea. Being tall and strong, Abrilon had always seen himself as a cliff. Let others spend their passions in extravagance; he understood a different song.

The wardens had stopped it, of course, and both were to be disciplined, but then Gemanim had intervened, saying only that it was a matter of no import and that no harm had been done. Then he had dismissed everyone except for Abrilon. He had stood there for a moment and then he had come forward and blessed him in exactly the same way that he had blessed Korfax. It was only at the onset of his death that he had explained himself.

"It is the hardest thing in all the world to pick a successor," Gemanim had said, almost his last words. "But there will come a time when you truly see the one to follow you, truly see who he is, and the light of your choice fills you."

Abrilon had wept when Gemanim had died, the gentlest of souls and one of the most misunderstood. So he had become Geyadel in Gemanim's place, and he did his duty as Gemanim had taught him. But he had never seen another to catch his eyes. Until now.

That Korfax had told him that he, too, had been blessed by Gemanim was a sign, a sign that said Korfax was the one to watch. Not that he hadn't been watched, as Korfax was special in many regards, but Abrilon had never thought of him as a potential first. It changed everything.

All who were chosen, willing or not, knowing or ignorant, had to be tested. Gemanim had tested him, and tested him mightily, so he would test Korfax in turn. Korfax was of the fire, so into the fire he must go. Only The Creator would know the outcome, but Abrilon was as certain of the conclusion as if he had suddenly risen to the very last realm itself and seen for himself the final truth!

The summons came the very next day. Korfax was to see Geyadril Samafaa and so receive his first orders of service.

Samafaa looked up as he entered.

"Korfax? Good! You are prompt. A fine beginning."

"Geyadril," Korfax bowed.

"I have your first orders of service before me," said Samafaa. "They are as follows. You are to proceed to Piamossin with Enay Onizim. He is returning there after long-needed rest. You will travel with a force of two parloh. Once at Piamossin you and he will relieve Enay Bienchir and Geyad Angalam. Angalam will supply you with whatever intelligence you will need to fulfil this duty."

Korfax let nothing show in his face, but inside he felt more than a little surprised. They were sending him north? So soon? He had barely been made a Geyad. He had always been told that only the seasoned were sent out into the world, and if there was one thing he was not, it was seasoned. That was another seven years away yet.

He had expected to serve in minor ways, perhaps in the Umadya Semeiel, perhaps in Othil Zilodar, whilst his preparedness for the wider world was judged. But now here he was, new-made and being sent on a mission almost immediately.

"How long will I serve at Piamossin?" he asked. It was the only question that he could think of.

"Two seasons," Samafaa announced, and he drew back a little in his chair. "I understand that your father knows Enay Onizim well."

"My father knows all the nobles of the far north," answered Korfax. "I do not know them as well as he, but I have met many of them, usually in Leemal but sometimes at Losq."

Korfax kept his face as motionless as he could, but inside he boiled. He was going to serve in a fortress in the furthest north. He was certain his trepidation was written all over his face, but Samafaa did not indicate whether or not he had noticed.

"Good," said Samafaa. "So you understand why it is you have been chosen. We have need of both knowledge and skill to defeat the Agdoain threat. You know the Namad Dar, without question, but now you need to gain experience in its application. Only with such duties can you attain it accordingly."

Samafaa glanced at the logadar before him. Then he looked back at Korfax.

"There is one thing further I will add. It is unusual to send an untried Geyad into the fire. Usually you would take lighter duties, but these are unusual times. The answer then is simple. You know the furthest north, being one of the very few that do, so therefore we send you."

Standing beside each other, Abrilon and Ponodol watched from a window. Samafaa waited behind, waiting upon the word of Abrilon as he ever did.

"I do not like this, Abrilon."

Abrilon looked askance at Ponodol and raised an eyebrow.

"So you have said before. Have you so little faith in your pupil?"

Ponodol took a deep breath.

"He is not just mine. Many hands helped Korfax on his way. Speak to Asakom. He was a great influence in the beginning, and I often went to him for counsel. Sohagel and Tabitem also account him one of their best."

He looked at Abrilon for a moment and then at Samafaa waiting behind. Neither of them moved. He took another deep breath, this time in exasperation.

"Very well then, let me state it as plainly as I may. The sword forged in haste breaks soonest in battle."

Samafaa tapped his stave upon the floor.

"And where have we been hasty?" he growled.

Ponodol turned away from the window.

"You know me, my friend," he said. "Korfax is the son of his father. I do not have any doubts that he will face this duty with fortitude and with strength, but I still feel that he is too young, too raw. He needs the weight of years for this task, the weight of certainty. Remember, both of you, that he witnessed the massacre at Losq. I would hate to discover that he is the hot crystal suddenly thrust into frozen waters. I have always believed that the slow way is the best way."

Abrilon raised a hand and turned around as well.

"And many would agree with you," he said. "But in this instance Korfax is the ideal candidate. We have few enough from the north as it is. He knows the land and he knows the people. And they know him. They will follow him. He is of the Farenith and we could ask for no one better."

Ponodol sighed.

"But he is still a child, in some respects."

"Not so," Samafaa disagreed. "He is Geyad now."

"And I saw no child when I spoke to him after his making," said Abrilon.

Ponodol looked up.

"So that was when you decided. I did wonder. What was it set you on this path?"

Abrilon held up his hands in the gesture of dismissal.

"No, that is for me alone," he said. "Suffice it to say that Korfax and I spoke together. Much was revealed."

Ponodol leaned forward.

"What do you mean?"

Abrilon held up a warning finger.

"And you should know better than that. What passed between the two of us was for our ears only. My decision stands."

Ponodol turned to leave.

"Then I must see to it that your will is carried out."

Abrilon looked surprised.

"But it already has."

Ponodol reached the door.

"You wish to test Korfax?" he asked. "So be it! I wish him to survive."

Then he was gone. Abrilon frowned for a moment and then turned away and looked out of the window again. Samafaa glanced at Abrilon briefly and then left the room quietly. Once outside, he ran after Ponodol.

"Wait!" he called as he sped down the corridor. "Ponodol, I would have words."

Ponodol stopped, looked back and waited.

"More?" he asked. "That is most uncommon of you. And what do you have to say now that could not have been said before the Geyadel?"

"But there you have it!" answered Samafaa.

Ponodol let his surprise show only by the widening of his eyes.

"Do not go against the Geyadel in this matter," Samafaa told him.

"I have no intention of doing so," Ponodol retorted. "He knows that."

"Then tread carefully. I have seen Abrilon like this only once before," Samafaa warned.

Ponodol waited.

"I believe I know what it was that Abrilon and Korfax discussed," Samafaa offered.

"And?"

"Gemanim!"

Ponodol drew back.

"That? Are you sure?"

"As sure as I can be. It is the only answer that satisfies."

"Well then," said Ponodol, "I suddenly find myself agreeing with the Geyadel. That is a matter for Korfax and Abrilon alone."

"But all those years of mystery?" Samafaa asked. "Can you not at least understand why? Abrilon had to deal with the repercussions alone. He had to mediate between Gemanim and the rest of the Dar Kaadarith for so many years. That Sazaaim remained a Geyad became a wall between Gemanim and everyone else. There cannot have been a day or a night when Abrilon must not have asked himself why."

"And it is not your affair or mine," said Ponodol.

Samafaa admitted defeat at last and held up his hands in surrender.

"I know, I know!" he conceded. "But what if it had been you? Or me? Such a thing would have played upon the mind of any of us."

"And do you believe I do not understand that?" asked Ponodol. "I most certainly do, but this is the Geyadel's affair, and his alone. Thank you for the warning, but your fears are groundless. I merely wish to make sure that Abrilon does not come to regret his decision, that is all. Regret damages the soul, and I would wish that pain on no other."

Ponodol rode to the Umadya Madimel and strode inside. Many watched as he walked through the tower, asking directions as he went. It wasn't often a Geyadril of the Dar Kaadarith was seen in the Tower of War. First he sought out Valagar, Napeiel of the Nazad Esiask. After a brief meeting he emerged again and sought out another. Eventually he found the one he was looking for.

"Enay Onizim," he said, bowing slightly.

Onizim turned and bowed in return, his face a picture of surprise.

"I understand you are going back to Piamossin soon," said Ponodol.

"That I am, Geyadril."

"Could you use a Napei, by any chance?"

Onizim looked up.

"Geyadril?"

"I was wondering if you could use a Napei when you return to Piamossin."

"I have already asked for one," said Onizim, "but was told none were available at this time."

"That is not strictly true, I believe." Ponodol told him.

Onizim narrowed his eyes. Ponodol's expression did not change in the slightest.

"What game is this?" Asked Onizim.

"No game, Enay, I assure you. I merely wish to help."

"Who did you have in mind?"

"Ralir of Badagar."

"I have heard of him," said Onizim. "They say he is peerless with a blade. But why should the son of such a mighty house choose such service? Surely he will be going back south, will he not?"

"Napei do not choose." Ponodol reminded him. "They go where they are sent, or needed."

Onizim drew in a deep breath.

"Well, I want no posturing fool at my side!" he said. "We already have enough of those in the north as it is!"

"I do not believe you will be dissatisfied." Ponodol told him. "Besides, he is good friends with your new Geyad."

Onizim subsided and then laughed.

"So that is it. You wish someone to watch over your precious pupil."

Ponodol became very still.

"I have a fear in me. I wish to allay it."

Onizim bowed his head.

"I think I understand. I was surprised when I was told it would be Korfax. I was expecting someone far more experienced. But be that as it may, he is now Geyad, and a Geyad is needed. I will see if it can be done."

"No need," said Ponodol. "It is already arranged. But I thank you, Enay, for your understanding."

Korfax looked at his belongings. How meagre they were. In his years at the seminary he had accumulated very little. There were two logadar and a kamliadar. The two logadar held between them a copy of the Articles of Unification and a copy of the Namad Dar, while the kamliadar held all the messages between himself and his parents, all condensed into one stone. There were his clothes, his stave, a sword - a large kansehna given to him by his father - but precious little else. He strapped his sword to his back and then crossed it with his stave. The rest he put in a travelling bag. That was it. He was done.

He looked about his room. He had lived here for the past seven years. They had not been the easiest of times, as the work had been hard and the demands great. There had been friends to ease the burdens and enemies to increase them, but now it was done. He did not know what to think as he stood there, staring about him at such familiar stone. When he was gone, another would take this room and that would be that.

He felt odd, distracted. He did not want to go, and yet he did. That was it, then. Time to leave.

He made his way from the tower without looking back. He had said his farewells earlier, especially to Ponodol, Asakom, Sohagel and Tabitem. Now he made his way to the landing fields outside the city walls, there to join with Onizim and so travel to the north.

At the landing field he found Onizim already waiting for him. Tall, far-sighted and sere, Onizim was the very image of a lord of the north.

"There you are, Geyad," Onizim said, bowing his head. Korfax bowed in return.

"Enay," he said.

Onizim looked at him for a moment.

"And are you ready to return home?" he asked.

Korfax took a deep breath.

"It has been seven years."

"A long time to be gone," Onizim said. "Much has changed. Are you prepared for that?"

"My father and mother tell me what occurs."

"Good."

He gestured to his left.

"I believe you know my new Napei."

This one turned about and grinned from within his hood. He drew the hood back. Korfax gaped.

"Ralir?"

Ralir laughed.

"So here you are at last!" he said. "Well now, it seems that you and I are destined to suffer each other's company for a little while yet."

Korfax laughed in return and grasped Ralir by the shoulder. Then he gestured about him in bewilderment as if he still doubted his eyes.

"But how are you here?" he asked, looking at his friend.

Ralir gestured up at the pennant that flew above them both.

"It seems that Enay Onizim requested a Napei. I was available, so here I am – my very first service to the Velukor!"

He smiled back at Korfax and his eyes sparkled.

"And finally, finally I get to see something of the north."

They alighted from the sky ship on the fields before Leemal. Korfax stepped down from the gangway and stopped, breathing in the air in long, slow draughts. He smiled. Onizim watched him carefully for a moment and then bowed his head in satisfaction.

"Home!" he announced.

Korfax looked back gratefully.

"Home," he agreed.

Ralir joined them both, his eyes jumping this way and that, eagerly drinking in the sights about him. Now it was the turn of Korfax to watch.

"Welcome to Leemal," he offered.

Ralir smiled in return.

"Korfax, my friend, what a marvellous place this is. I can see why you love it so. So green, so mountainous. And Leemal? There are no cities like this at all in the south. It is like a mountain itself, but so small and compact. I feel as if I could pick it all up in the palm of my hand."

Onizim leaned forward and tapped Ralir on his shoulder.

"And I would not say such things within the hearing of others here, if I were you, Napei."

Ralir raised an eyebrow as he looked back at Onizim.

"But why ever not?" he asked.

"Because, come the morning, you would find them all waiting outside your door, lining up in droves to fight you for the honour of their city."

Ralir frowned.

"But I did not insult the city. I think it beautiful."

"You also called it small, and many here would consider that the greatest insult of all."

Korfax laughed and wagged a finger at Ralir.

"Now there are three directions," he said.

Ralir's frown deepened.

"And just what do you mean by that?" he asked.

"The south, the north and everywhere else, of course!"

Ralir narrowed his eyes.

"Am I ever going to live that down?"

Korfax gave his friend a knowing smile.

"Not if I can help it!" Then he looked up at the city himself. "Now, before we leave, I must go find my mother. She will have news for me, perhaps."

Onizim's face almost gentled at that.

"And when did you see her last?" he asked.

"At my making, one season back."

Onizim gestured towards the city.

"Then go to it, young Geyad. I must gather up my own people and order them for the ride to Piamossin, so you have two hours at least. But then we must leave indeed, or we will lose the day."

Korfax bowed to Onizim and ran off.

He arrived at the tower and stared up at it. How small it seemed. Then it struck him; Leemal itself had shrunk. He thought of what Ralir had said, but that wasn't it. It was he that had grown. He had been to Emethgis Vaniad, had lived there for seven years, so no wonder Leemal appeared small in comparison.

He went to the door and touched the chiming stone. The door opened and there was Baschim. They looked at each other for a long moment and then Baschim bowed deeply.

"Noren!" he said. His eyes glistened with joy. "It is good to see you once more."

They embraced. Korfax found himself happier than he had been in a long while. He was home at last, back in the places that he loved, back with those that he loved.

"I have missed you," he said.

They drew apart.

"I have missed you also," he said. "We heard all the news, of course, but it was not the same. Now you are returned and you are Geyad, like your father."

"Is he here?"

"No, he is at Ralfen."

"But why are you not with him?"

"I keep this tower in order; it is your father's wish. Besides, Orkanir is ever at his side."

"Is mother here?"

Baschim smiled.

"Yes, but there are others here also. They will be happy to see you."

"Who?"

"Heiral and Paniss and many more beside. The tower is quite full."

Korfax thought about that. No doubt they had come here after the clearances, when the furthest north had been emptied following the tragedy of Tohus. He suddenly felt guilty. There he had been, comfortable in Emethgis Vaniad, when the people here had been suffering.

Baschim looked at him.

"I know what you are thinking, Noren, but there would have been nothing you could have done. Besides, you were in the one place that you needed to be. How else could you have achieved your stave? And now you have come back to fight. Many are grateful for that."

"How did you know?" Korfax asked.

"All who come north wear that very same expression when they realise what is happening here, and what the consequences are. Those who are not here do not understand. Whether they know it or not, whether they admit it or not, we are at war."

He gestured inside.

"Now, how long do you have before you leave?"

"A long hour at most."

"Then let me take you to your mother now."

"Mother!"

"Korfax!"

They embraced. Then she stood back and looked at him.

"Look at you," she said, standing back and gazing at him in obvious astonishment.

"How you have changed, yet again. Who would have thought it in such a little time? Now you are Geyad in truth. You are so like your father when I first saw him."

Suddenly there were tears in her eyes and she came to him and held him close once more.

"I am so proud of you. If only your father were here to see it – it would lighten his heart ever more."

Korfax looked down.

"Baschim told me that he is still in Ralfen."

"Yes, but he spends most of his time scouring the lands, hunting for the enemy," she said while sighing deeply.

"I barely see him. Though it gives heart to the people to know that he is out there, ever seeking for the foe, I worry for him. This travail has become a whip across his back."

"But I am here now. Surely I can help."

She looked at him and her smile was both sad and grateful.

"Of course, of course you can. That is why you were sent, I am sure."

She cupped his cheek with her hand.

"When it was announced that you would be coming home to join in the hunt, many were all but overjoyed. All are most glad that they have the Farenith to ward them."

Korfax smiled carefully.

"So that is why they were all bowing and smiling at me as I made my way here. I did wonder. I have never been so welcomed in Leemal before."

"But look at you," she said. "You are a Geyad now. You are full grown and in the service of the Velukor at last."

She gestured to the door.

"Now, you have a little time. There are others here that would see you."

The reunion with Paniss and Heiral was not what he had expected. Though they were happy to see him, their joy masked something else. There was a sadness in them, a despondency that he had never seen there before. It took him long moments to realise what it was.

Without their land, without their purpose, they were bereft. In their own eyes the clearances had deprived them of their worth.

There were others of the far north here, besides the Raxamith. There were some of the Illiforith from the south east, some of the Golor Aelith and the Leor Aelith from the west and even some of the Saqorris from the east.

As Baschim had said, the tower was full. There was a brief moment of joy, like a sudden banquet of celebration, as word spread that Korfax had come home, but all too soon he had to leave again. Many blessed him as he went, almost as if he had already defeated the foe and restored them to their lands. He found that hard to bear and wondered whether he would be worthy of their hopes.

Last of all he said goodbye to Baschim and then his mother. That was the hardest to do, but the resolution he saw in her eyes gave him heart. Both she and Baschim understood fully what was to come next.

15

FORTRESS

Nis-ho-pi Amos-in-jon
Bo-dar-od Branluh-kal-aa
Ipsol-koh Urzaa-vanjes
Zim-oag-iul Relors-deqao
Zak-od-ran Azon-torzu
Alkar-vim Zil-od-arp-zien
Krih-iks-a Tolno-chan-bas

His first view of Piamossin was glorious. The road rose up through the trees to a high wall that curved to the left and to the right. A second wall rose up behind that, and behind that rose the tower itself, all nestling at the end of a steep valley set deep within the high peaks of the Adroqin Vohimar.

Tall and proud, Piamossin looked every part a great fortress. Rebuilt after the taking of Leemal, it had been the furthest outpost until the building of Ralfen. Then the wars had ended and silence had fallen upon the place of horns. Now war had returned and the walls of Piamossin once more echoed to the sound of arms.

They stopped before the gate. Korfax rode forward with Onizim. He had been waiting for this moment; it was his task to answer the challenge.

"Move and show yourselves," came the cry.

Korfax held up his stave and called up fire of air. His stave hummed and lightning flew up into the sky, rising higher than the tower itself. The walls echoed to their thunder. Then he ceased his power and there was silence. Onizim raised his head and called out.

"I am a true servant of the highest and I have with me the symbol of our power. From stone we come and to stone we go, and in its light we live for ever in the service of the Velukor, blessed be his name."

The answer was prompt.

"Then in the name of the Velukor, blessed be his name, be welcome in this place."

The gates opened and in they rode.

There was only the merest honour guard to greet them, and Enay Bienchir was nowhere to be seen. Onizim scowled, but then another stepped forward, a Geyad, and he welcomed Onizim warmly.

"May the light of The Creator shine upon you," he said.

Onizim's mood lightened.

"And upon you, Geyad. But where is Bienchir?"

The Geyad gestured towards the tower.

"I imagine he is within the main hall."

"Still? He was there when I left. Has he moved at all since?"

Korfax noticed one or two murky smiles on the faces around him; clearly Bienchir was not held in high regard.

Onizim dismounted.

"Then, I suppose, if he is incapable of coming out to see me, I should go inside and see him."

He beckoned to his Branvath, Boavor, and to Ralir. Then he strode off. Ralir glanced at Korfax, made the gesture of confusion and followed the others inside.

As the rest of Onizim's troop dismounted, the Geyad came up to Korfax.

"You must be Korfax," he said. "Or should I say Geyad Korfax!"

Korfax bowed. The Geyad was tall and spare, with a gentle face and smiling eyes. His accent was broad. Korfax guessed that he hailed from the north-east. This had to be Angalam.

"Geyad Angalam? May the light of The Creator shine upon you," he said.

The other returned his bow.

"And upon you," he said, and his eyes shone with a glad light.

"It is good to meet you at last. I have heard a great many things concerning you."

Korfax drew back a little, but Angalam laughed.

"Do not worry, it was nothing bad. Quite the opposite, in fact." Angalam's smile slipped a little. "I am sorry I was the only one here to greet you, but it seems Enay Bienchir has more important things to which he wishes to attend."

Catching the note in Angalam's voice, Korfax was immediately put on his guard.

"What do you mean?" he asked.

Angalam smiled again.

"Think nothing of it. I am afraid that I have been serving alongside the Enay for longer than I would like, that is all. Have you ever met him?"

"No," said Korfax, "I have not yet had that pleasure."

The smile became somewhat crooked.

"Pleasure? I would not call it that, if I were you. Whilst your courtesy serves you well, it would be entirely wasted upon the likes of Bienchir and his kin. He comes from the west, the furthest west, out from his cultivated fastnesses to play a little in the wild lands."

Korfax frowned. Here it was again – resentment of the west. Every so often it reared its ugly head, or so it seemed.

"I understand," he said, looking down and hiding his thoughts.

"I am sure that you do," Angalam said quietly. "Now, since Enay Onizim is ensconced with Enay Bienchir, you and I have some time to get to know each other. And whilst I show you around the tower and tell you all the news, you must tell me of the Umadya Semeiel. I so wish to see it again."

Angalam looked darkly at the gate.

"And I have need of it. I have dwelt under the dark shadow of the foe for far too long."

After Angalam had helped him stable his steed, they explored the tower together, walking its many ways. The tower was much in the manner of the north, with many rooms, corridors, corners and surprises, a labyrinth of stone. In some ways it reminded Korfax of Losq.

Finally they ended up on the outer wall, back over the main gate where they both stood at the edge and looked down into the valley below. Korfax lifted his head to the cool breeze. There were scents upon the air, scents he had all but forgotten since he had left his home. They were such well-remembered fragrances: the resin of the trees, the musty aroma of the undergrowth and the faint perfume of opening flowers.

Angalam looked at him.

"Seven years is a long time to be away," he said.

"Yes, it is," Korfax agreed.

"Strangers do not understand," said Angalam. "The beauty of this place escapes them. But this is the land of my heart also. My family watch over the fields and hills about Peinothar. I go back there when I can."

Korfax looked out over the wall.

"I wish I could go back to Losq," he said.

Angalam placed a gentle hand on his arm.

"But you will, Korfax, you will. Did you know that I once visited your home?"

Korfax looked up.

"No, when?"

"Long before you were born. I went there with dispatches for your father. I had not long been made a Geyad myself and had not travelled much. I well remember my first sight of the Lee Izirakal, so rare and so beautiful. But then I saw Losq itself. I have never seen anything to compare. So ancient it seemed, so rooted in the ground. How long has it stood upon its hill? I have never heard."

"No one truly knows," Korfax answered. "The records go back to before the time of the Black War even."

"Ancient indeed," said Angalam. "The north remembers times like few others."

He looked wistfully at the mountains that rose behind the main spire of Piamossin, but then he turned about again and gestured at the pass beyond the walls.

"Something is happening out there," he said. "Something new."

Korfax looked carefully at Angalam, but Angalam was not looking at him. Instead he was pointing at the long and winding road that dropped down into the dark forest beyond.

"I have seen things," Angalam continued. "Disturbing things. The last was down there, in the forest, not two seasons ago, something I have never encountered before."

Angalam shuddered as though a sudden chill had caught him unawares.

"It was at the turning of Alohan," he went on. "I was exploring, as I like to do. By all accounts I should not have been out on my own at all, but Bienchir does not care what others do, just so long as he gets to do what he wants. And what he wants to do most is to spend his time drinking, hunting and boasting of his prowess to his followers! Yes, Bienchir loves to hunt. If it was not for the ancient edict, I think the fool would have gone up into the mountains behind us to seek out the lair of a Vovin."

Korfax frowned.

"But there are no Vovin here," he said.

Angalam gestured to the heights.

"Actually, I think that there are, but only a very few, and all of them are wary. I believe I saw one of them last year, but it was very far away, a distant speck beyond the furthest peak. But the way that it moved!"

Angalam's eyes brightened as he stared at the peaks beyond. He took a deep breath.

"From what I could see of it I think it was large, very large. I think it was a Vovin."

Korfax watched Angalam for a moment and then gazed in wonder at the mountains above.

"I would give much to see one," he said.

"And I hope you are granted your wish," Angalam told him, "but you will be lucky if you ever do. They have learned, over the long years, to stay well away from us. The west has got its way in the end."

Angalam drew himself up and turned back to the forest.

"Now, let me continue my tale and tell you what I saw down there."

Korfax looked to where Angalam was staring, down at the trees below, down at their shadows.

"I was in the forest," he said, "exploring its many ways. Ever since I came to this tower the forest below has fascinated me. I am not sure why, but I think it a long-lost part of the Peisith Tatanah, estranged from its southern cousin by many long years."

"But Tatanah is far from here," said Korfax.

"It is," answered Angalam, "but the forest below us is like its southern neighbour in so many ways. Have you ever been there?"

"Not to Tatanah," Korfax said. "I only know of it from what I have read."

Angalam smiled.

"Well, I have. I went there three years back, along with your father. We were on our way to the dark places, heading for the Forujer Allar."

Korfax shuddered.

"I have never been there either."

"Nor do you want to," added Angalam. "It is an evil place." He looked up. "A tale for another time, perhaps. But what of Tatanah? In the depths of that forest the trees are huge, and the distances between each trunk are so great that you might believe yourself a child crossing some vast hall of giants. The forest below us is much like that when you leave the beaten track. Then you enter an echo of the ancient dream of green."

Angalam's smile slipped away entirely.

"But that is not what I wanted to tell you, for it was as I was admiring the vast beauty around me that I caught sight of it, a distant shape running in the darkness beyond the shadows of the furthest trees, moving quickly and furtively, like a guilty thing. But it was not quick enough for me to miss it."

"What was it?"

"I do not know, but it was big, as big as an ormn, though far bulkier. At first I wondered if it was a monujer."

Korfax was surprised.

"But there are none here, or so I was always told. They dwell only in the west, or am I wrong about that, too? If there are Vovin hereabouts, then why not a few monujer? They are hardy, I have heard, but they are not swift and neither are they particularly furtive."

Angalam smiled at Korfax.

"Then you understand. You see the strangeness. Good."

He looked at the trees again.

"I was all for following. I wanted to see, I wanted to know, but then it stopped for a moment as if it knew that someone was watching. It moved into the light a little and I saw something of its nature. Then it turned away again and ran on. I did not follow; I was too shocked to move."

"So what was it? What did you see?"

"A great beast, far larger than one of the Agdoain. It ran on four limbs and had a great heavy tail. But the worst of it was, Korfax, the worst of it was that it had no head. I saw a great mouth full of teeth, but no head."

Korfax stepped back.

"No head?" he uttered as he looked darkly at the forest below.

"Yes," continued Angalam. "And I could not be mistaken, either. So I warn you now. Do not go out there alone. They are down there even as we speak, in the forest, in the shadow, gathering themselves together. They are waiting beyond our thresholds, lurking in all the lonely places. Since my encounter I have felt them at the edges of my mind, and though it may be dim and uncertain, I cannot be mistaken."

"Have you told others of this?" Korfax asked.

"I have sent messages to Leemal and Ralfen. I am not certain many believe my tale. Only your father answered me. He at least understands. He bade me keep watch, so ever since that day I have been on my guard, and whilst Bienchir has drunk his fill of wine I have stood upon this wall. The Agdoain are hiding down there now – and something else besides."

Korfax was sad to see Angalam leave, but Onizim was not so sad to see the back of Bienchir. Once the gates had closed he turned to his Branvath, Boavor, and grimaced.

"How can Angalam put up with that fool?"

Boavor said nothing, but Korfax felt a sudden need to defend the gentle and quietly spoken Angalam.

"He does it because that is his calling," he said.

Onizim raised an eyebrow and glanced at Korfax.

"Well, if that is what it takes to be a Geyad, then all I can say is that your order is possessed of the patience of mountains. Were I alongside Bienchir, I would soon show him the meaning of service."

Onizim turned about and studied the tower.

"Come," he announced, "we have work to do. This place is under our stewardship now. Let us show the idle west how it should be done."

But Korfax was not listening. He gazed instead at the closed gates. He suddenly felt awfully alone, like he had when he had first entered the seminary of the Dar Kaadarith.

Days passed and little happened. The watch was kept and Korfax spent his time either standing on the wall, studying or meditating. Occasionally he would watch as Ralir duelled with some of the Branith, tutoring them under the stern but approving eye of Onizim. So when it was announced that a rider was approaching he was up and on to the wall in moments.

It was the first excitement since he had arrived. But better was to come. When he looked down from the parapet he saw immediately who it was. It was Orkanir. He clutched at the stone and all but laughed in gladness.

Though he had not seen Orkanir in seven years, he would have known that face anywhere. The memory of the desperate fight at Losq filled him even as his eyes filled with tears. He turned back to find Ralir watching him.

"Who is it? Who comes?" Ralir asked.

Korfax laughed happily in answer.

"It is Orkanir! Branvath Orkanir! He was the one who saved my life at Losq."

Korfax leapt down the stairs and on to the courtyard. And there he waited, barely containing himself, as they opened the gates. Then Orkanir rode in upon his great white ormn.

They saw each other immediately and Orkanir was off his steed and before Korfax in an instant. They grasped arms and stared at each other before both bursting out in laughter.

"By The Creator, look at you!" cried Orkanir at last. "How you have grown! You are taller than I am!"

Korfax put his head on one side.

"Or maybe it is you that has shrunk?" he suggested.

They both laughed before embracing again. Finally Orkanir stepped back.

"It is so good to see you again, Noren, so good." Then he checked himself. "Or rather, should I say 'Geyad'."

Korfax smiled in blissful happiness.

"Just Korfax will do," he said.

Orkanir offered a wry smile in return.

"I do not think Enay Onizim would entirely approve."

He glanced about.

"And where is the Enay? I have messages for him."

Korfax gestured at the tower.

"He is inside. I will take you to him. It is so good to see you again."

They left together whilst another stabled Orkanir's ormn. Ralir watched them go, still standing upon the wall with a strange look in his eyes. So that was Orkanir, was it? He had heard Korfax mention Orkanir many times. Son of Ocholor, son of a duellist of the Nazad Esiask and said to be the best with a blade in all the north. Korfax had named him as such and Ralir now found himself wondering how he could test that assertion.

The arrival of Orkanir seemed to have a strange effect on Korfax. He suddenly found the ritual of the days stifling and felt in need of something else to break the rhythm. Despite the warning of Angalam he decided to take a ride into the old forest.

Without permission, he left the fortress and soon found himself deep in amongst the trees. He rode slowly, revelling in its immensity. Angalam had been right – this was indeed a wonderful place. The trees here were huge, ancient with moss, their aged scent filling the air about them. He breathed deeply and smiled. Here was balm for the soul.

He came upon a grotto set in the midst of a rocky outcrop, one of many that he had passed, an ancient spur of weathered stone born of the hills above. At its deepest part there was a cave. The great trees had coiled their roots about its opening, giving it an air of mystery, inviting mystery. Korfax wondered what its history might be. No doubt, during the wars, this would have been a good place to hide.

He approached the cave mouth, intending to put up his lance and draw out his kabadar to provide some light, but when something inside the cave growled back at him he reigned in his steed and tilted his lance downwards again.

A dim form reared up slowly, shadows moving within shadows. Something huge was there, shifting slowly this way and that. There was something else, too, something smaller and quicker, a crouching form that gleamed with a dim grey light.

Korfax drew his steed back further, his heart beating hard in his chest. He could already guess what he had found. A thrill of fear coursed through him as he remembered back to that terrible day when he had fled with his mother from demons. Then he had been a helpless child. He tightened his grip upon his lance at the thought. He was a helpless child no longer.

Almost as if they had been summoned by his thought, the shadows came forward, a rider and its mount, both snarling at him through wicked teeth.

Korfax stared at the headless rider for a moment, an unpleasant mingling of fear and disgust swirling inside, but then he looked at the Agdoain's steed and felt the burn of bile at the back of his throat. Here was the very creature that Angalam had seen.

Like its squatting master above, the beast was a sick nightmare. Grey, ever grey, it came forward slowly on four muscular limbs set at each corner of its thick, wide body. Each limb ended in a great paw adorned with huge curving claws that left deep gouges in the soil. There was a tail, long and meaty, stretching out from its hind quarters and tipped with a great knotted fist of bone like a hammer, and as the beast ambled slowly forward so the tail waved back and forth with impatient violence.

Much of the beast was covered in a thick hide, a seeping patchwork like that of its rider, but on its back two huge bones had punched their way through the skin to make a saddle, a pair of immense lips that met in the exact centre, frozen for ever in an obscene kiss for the rump of its rider.

But even now that was not the worst of it, for just like its master the thing had no head. All Korfax could see was a mouth, a great mouth that stretched out from between its immense shoulders, a huge mouth filled with long and curving teeth like gutting knives.

Korfax did not wait, he could not. He wanted the thing gone from his sight. Forgetting his stave entirely he tilted his lance and charged. Such was the fury of his attack that it was over before it had truly begun. His lance went through the beast even as it reared, then through its rider.

Korfax let go of his lance, pulled his ormn back and drew his sword, his eyes wide, his teeth bared. The Agdoain was pinned to the ground by its mount, crushed to the earth, whilst its steed bellowed weakly and waved its limbs in the air. Korfax was mesmerised by the gruesome spectacle.

The Agdoain reached out with its sword of bone and pointed it at Korfax. It snarled and its mouth moved oddly as though trying to form words with which to curse him. Korfax felt another surge of disgust. Such abominations should not be allowed to live, they should be put out of their misery, but he could not move. Instead, a strange thought came to him, something from his lessons in the Umadya Semeiel.

There were tales from the Wars of Unification of the odd chances of battle. At the time he had thought little of them, but now that he had his foe helpless before him he considered again how advantage could be gained from the dying of demons.

It was said that whenever a demon died, whenever it passed beyond, sometimes one of the Urenith had managed to find her way back to the summoner by following the demon's energies as they returned to their source. Always there was a summoning circle, and if the Uren was sharp enough, she might see the summoner themselves before the demon died. Korfax was no Uren, but he had learnt something of the technique from his teachers at the seminary. One followed the trail of energy with one's mind.

The moment came. The Agdoain uttered its last rattling gasp, and Korfax, eager with audacity, breathless with fear, made his attempt. He hurled his mind into that of his foe and sought out its summoner.

He dived as deeply as he dared but encountered no overriding will. Instead he felt waves of energy beating against him like a tide of corrosion. He grappled with it for a moment and then felt the thread of life snap even as he grasped at it – a breaking, crushing sound that assailed him from every side. Then, with its last unformed thoughts screaming in his mind, Korfax felt it flee the world at last, dragging him along with it.

Down ever darkening tunnels he plummeted, following a formless vapour of grey that twisted and turned, a failing flame that stuttered at the edges of existence.

Into the depths he went, down into the grey depths, the fear ever-mounting the deeper he went. But he was held by it, in thrall to it, compelled to follow and compelled to see.

Finally the walls about him fell away and he came upon a vaguer place. Wisps of almost nothing floated by, the grey following the grey. He was adrift in a fog-bound void.

Though the fear was overwhelming, he knew there was something worse here, something below him. Though he dreaded it, he looked down. There it was, a portal onto an abyss so featureless that he could not describe it at all.

He realised, almost as if the emptiness had answered his unspoken question, that to enter the portal was to cease to exist. Now the fear became terror. Never, not even in his darkest dreams, had he ever imagined anything as terrifying as that which lay before him now.

He felt the essence of the Agdoain, such as it was, enter the nothingness. He felt it vanish, erased, ceasing to be. It almost pulled him in with it, but he stopped himself at the borders and resisted the urge to fall further. He should not be here, he told himself, this was no place to be. So he turned about and tried to go back the way he had come. But he could make no headway.

The nothingness pulled at him. Korfax fought the blind force with all his might, turning his back upon the hungry grey, but even as he moved he felt a dim stirring. Something below had turned upon itself and now looked back up at him, something immense.

He understood. He had trespassed where he should not have. His presence had disturbed the illimitable grey. His life, its flame, was as a thorn in its side, and the nothingness had awoken from its terrible sleep of oblivion, swelling the abyss below as it crawled its way slowly upwards from its depths.

Korfax fought not to see it, fought with all his strength not to see that which came for him. He pulled himself slowly away in an ecstasy of fear. It was like climbing an impossible hill, hand over hand, foot over foot, whilst something, some unseen and as yet unimagined horror, crept up from behind, gaining all the while.

Then came the sudden moment, delirium or nightmare, as he fled the reaching grey, flying upwards into the light whilst the void receded behind him, reverberating to the echo of mighty wings like drums of regret.

He found himself back in the glade again, still astride his ormn, whilst his enemy's body and that of its steed crumbled into the ground and decayed at last.

Korfax breathed a long sigh of relief. That had been close. He shuddered again and looked about avidly, drinking in the world around him as though starved of sight and sound and sensation. But the grey abyss still sat in his mind as though he had brought it back with him.

It took all his self-control to suppress a sudden urge to run. It was there in his mind, the seeds of a panic planted deep, right there in his mind, demanding that he run, and run and run. Korfax thrust it away from him, sending his fear back down deep inside. But he could remove neither the taint of the grey nor the sense of foreboding that came with it.

He reclaimed his lance, turned his steed away and rode back to the tower, whilst in his mind he pondered what had happened. The demon had fallen into an abyss and at the end it had surrendered its life with a strange eagerness, before returning to its genesis. He thought unwillingly of the grey nothingness into which it had fallen and wondered what it was that he had disturbed therein.

"This was not well done."

Korfax bowed his head slightly.

"And did you know that the enemy possess cavalry?"

Onizim scowled.

"That is not the point."

"I disagree," said Korfax. "You now have intelligence that you did not have before."

"And you went out into the old forest against the advice of your elders and betters," returned Onizim.

"And discovered something not known before."

"You disobeyed an edict."

"An edict written in ignorance."

Onizim stood up and smashed his fist into the table.

"Arrogant youth! Do you believe that you know all ends? Only your gift of knowledge has assuaged my wrath at this time – that and the fact that you are the son of your father. But if you step outside my bounds again, believe me when I say that I shall be waiting for you. And I will not be so gracious a second time! You may leave."

Ralir was waiting for Korfax outside.

"I heard what you did. Many think you were right to do it."

"But Enay Onizim does not."

Ralir offered a careful smile.

"Maybe so, but you have proven yourself in battle. Many here applaud your courage. I certainly do."

Korfax smiled unhappily.

"It was not courage. I had to face them again. I *needed* to face them again. I needed to see them and to assuage my fear of them."

Ralir frowned.

"I understand. All know the story of what happened at Umadya Losq."

Korfax looked up.

"All?"

Ralir looked surprised for a moment.

"Well, only that you suffered siege and were rescued by your father."

He leaned in closer.

"I haven't mentioned what you told me to anyone else."

Korfax looked down again.

"I'm sorry, I did not mean to imply that. It is just that I am feeling a little unsettled. I think I have traded one fear for another."

Korfax hurled himself from his bed and staggered to the window. He clutched at the sill to steady himself and stared out at the night, eyes wide with fear. He had never had such a dream before, so terrifying and yet so real. He shivered, but not from the cold.

The clouded light of the moon gave the world outside a grey cast, wiping out detail and leaving only a vague copy behind as though everything it touched it corroded. Korfax blinked. Even the Branith that marched along the walls were affected by its taint, their faces erased and their limbs strangely warped.

Korfax shuddered and turned away. It wasn't the moonlight that did this, but the acid touch of his dream. He sat upon his bed and held his head in his hands whilst his dream sat in his mind and grinned back out at him.

He had found himself back at Losq, standing in the main hall where the great table had once stood. Only now the great table lay in ruins and its detritus was scattered across the darkened floor in a chaos of broken pieces.

Korfax stared at the wreckage, bereft, mute. The hall, the tower, stank of abandonment. The air felt dead about him and his breath steamed, rising up to gather in the vaulted ceiling above like so many coiling webs. A crawling sense of fear filled him. What had happened to his ancient home?

He looked this way and that, but there was nothing else to see. The only occupant of the great hall was the broken table. He felt a thrill of desperation. What should he do? Should he explore? Should he try to find out what had occurred here? But he had to explore, he had to see; he had no choice. Reluctantly he took to the stairs.

When he gained the first landing he noticed that the windows were shuttered. He wondered whether he should look outside, but as soon as he reached for the latch he knew that he did not want to do so. It was dark out there, dark and grey, and he was suddenly certain that he did not want to see what lay beyond the confines of the tower.

The further he went, the deeper the fear became. Dust and rubble lay everywhere, and the little furniture he came upon was either broken or rotting. Even the tower itself was not unaffected, for the walls dripped with a slimy fluid as though the stones themselves bled, and here and there, in the darker corners, shapeless bundles crouched, glistening excrescences that had taken root in the dank shadows. Korfax peered briefly at them as he passed on by, but he did not approach too closely. They reeked of putrefaction.

When he came to the door that led to the upper balcony he stopped. He tried to work up enough courage to step outside, telling himself that he must see what had to be seen, but now that he stood before the closed door he found that he dared not open it. Something was out there, something appalling.

It took him long moments to summon up the courage to peer through the cracks, but all he saw was a dark-grey fog that lay across his rotting home like a shroud. He drew back again and dreaded the thought that some sound might eventually come to him from out of the blank encroaching grey.

Continuing his climb, he headed onwards to the very top. But it was as he reached his old room that he became aware of a sound at last. Though faint, it seemed shockingly loud in that shrouded place. Someone was crying inside his room. He closed his eyes and swallowed. The sound almost paralysed him with fear.

The cry was weak, barely audible through the rotting door, but it was also strangely penetrating, as though the bleeding stones repeated it, echoing it in their distress.

Listening to that cry Korfax thought of something long-drowned that sobbed, filling the world about it with its sunken grief, cold and liquid and altogether piteous to hear. He wanted to turn away and leave it far behind him, but his feet moved him on as though compelled.

He entered his room and found it almost bare of any furniture at all. His bed had gone and only a single chair remained – an empty chair with a broken leg – in the centre of the room. Somehow the chair seemed to mock him as it sat there, tilting like the insane world about it. Korfax turned away. He did not like the mocking chair.

The crying sound came again, and Korfax looked back. It came from the darkest corner, where another of those shapeless glistening bundles lurked. But this one was different. This one moved.

He felt his heart hammer against the wall of his chest as he approached the decaying shape. The cries that came from it were both pitiable and vile, reluctantly wrenched from its unhappy mass as it rocked gently back and forth. Korfax came closer and then drew back again. Were those hands he could see, clasped to something that resembled a head? He wished he could be certain, but the rocking thing seemed to defeat his sight in some way as though its contours vanished into realms he could not penetrate. He stared. Those were hands, surely they were, but everything else about the rocking thing seemed to be in flux, continuously changing, its substance dribbling into the air or running down into the floor.

He leaned closer, he could not help it. Though utterly repelled, he had to see. He reached out to touch the dim form, slowly, tentatively. Then, with a sick, sucking sound, one of the hands moved, peeling slowly away from the face that it covered. Korfax looked at the hand and saw that the fingers were fused together as though the flesh had melted. He looked up at what they had uncovered and saw the decaying face of his father. He screamed. The face sobbed back at him and melted as it sobbed.

Korfax fell backwards and staggered out of his room. Down the stairs he ran, staggering away from each dark lump he passed, not daring to think what it might once have been. His flight through the tower became a fevered thing, a nightmare of dripping stone and grey light that flickered past him as he tumbled down the stairs in his mad rush to escape.

To the main door he came, running through it to stand beyond the threshold. And there he met the grey fog, curling past him as though eager to enter the tower. He felt its cold touch and recoiled, realising his mistake, but it was already too late. His legs would no longer work and he was stuck where he was. The trap was sprung.

The fog circled about him as though waiting for its moment to strike, but Korfax knew that it was just the medium through which the real horror would come. He had no choice; he had to wait while the fear mounted until it was all but intolerable. Then he felt it, coming towards him through the fog, something immense.

He could not move. It came closer, ever closer, and with every moment the panic increased, until, in a complete and utter frenzy of fear, he hurled himself out of the dream and back into the waking world.

· He breathed deeply and waited for calm to return, but it was a long time coming. This is it, he found himself thinking, this is the purpose – the Agdoain will come and they will swallow the world.

And that single thought remained with him for the rest of the sleepless night.

He was sitting alone, his first meal of the day untouched before him, when Boavor marched smartly by, stopping before Onizim at one of the other tables.

"There is a force of Agdoain outside, Enay. We estimate their number to be a thousand at least. More are arriving with every moment."

Onizim looked up.

"Are they on foot?"

"Not all, Enay. Some are on foot, but others ride great beasts much like those Geyad Korfax described."

Onizim frowned.

"Well now! Here is a new play. Who would have thought that they would change their tactics so? Ambush and stealth have been the way of it up until now, not open battle. What is their aim? What new purpose fires their evil hearts?"

He looked across to Korfax and his eyes hardened.

"Did you cause this?" he asked. "Did you stir them into action?"

Korfax had nothing to say. The previous night's dream still occupied his thoughts. Onizim was about to say something more when Boavor interjected.

"Maybe this is happening all across the north? Maybe we are but seeing a small part of a greater campaign."

Onizim did not take his eyes from Korfax.

"I am waiting, Geyad! What do you know of this? This is something to do with your encounter yesterday, isn't it?"

Korfax swallowed.

"I cannot say, Enay, not yet at least."

"But something troubles you. I can see it. I would know what it is."

Korfax took a while to answer.

"I had a dream last night."

Onizim raised an eyebrow.

"A dream? An admonishment from The Creator, perhaps?"

Korfax looked darkly back at Onizim.

"Do you mock?"

"I do not, but dreams and visions are the province of the Exentaser. Are you such a one? Leave your dreams in the place reserved for them. I require you in the here and the now and in no other place."

Korfax did not answer.

"So, I ask you again. Do you have anything else to say?"

Korfax said nothing further. If Onizim was not prepared to listen to the particulars then Korfax found himself equally loath to expand upon them. He looked down at the food before him and felt instead a heat behind his eyes.

Onizim continued to look at Korfax for a moment as if seeking something, but then he gestured to Boavor.

"So be it! Let us go out and see what we may see. Come, all of you."

Korfax followed, but even after the admonishment of Onizim the dread from his dream did not leave him. Instead, it mounted. With each step he took towards the wall, he felt dim weights falling into his mind as though a heavy and impenetrable fog were descending upon him. It almost felt as if the hungry grey was coming for him once more.

They reached the battlements and looked out, or rather Onizim and Boavor looked out, while Korfax merely peered briefly at the Agdoain below before turning away again.

What had only been a mere guess beforehand seemed an utter certainty now. Each headless horror was here because of him. He could feel them, a sense of seeking in the air, a malignant swarm of wordless thoughts.

Onizim glanced at Boavor.

"Have they attempted to parley at all?"

Boavor looked back in surprise.

"Parley, Enay? These are demons! They have never done such a thing before."

Onizim smiled grimly.

"I know, but neither have they laid siege before. And remember! Even Karmaraa spoke with the Agedobor before the end, or have you forgotten your history? These Agdoain have changed their tactics once already, so why not again?"

Korfax looked up in shock, surprised in spite of his dread. The Agedobor? Not many knew that tale. But Onizim had not noticed. He was still staring down at the Agdoain as if he already knew everything that he needed.

"The Agdoain are both organised and cunning," he announced, "much like the Agedobor were. I know, I have studied them. And I have studied our histories, so I will not make the mistake of underestimation. But this place is not like the others that they have attacked. They now threaten a fortress in posture of war. We have a full complement of arms within these walls and I think that the Agdoain, or their master, would like to test our resolve."

Korfax pondered that notion. Onizim was wrong, he was certain of it. He had to say something, to warn him.

"I do not think so," he announced.

Both Onizim and Boavor turned to look at him.

"They will attack," he said, "but only when they feel that there are enough of them. I do not think they are here to test our resolve at all; instead, I think they are here because of what happened yesterday. I think you are right, Enay. I think they are here because of me."

Onizim narrowed his eyes.

"There is a connection certainly. What have you not told me?"

"I would rather not say."

"You would rather not say? But I demand an answer. Tell me, Geyad! Tell me what you know!"

"I told you of what happened yesterday. I tried to divine the source of the Agdoain."

"And?"

"I had a dream last night."

"That again?"

"Yes!"

"A dream, is it? So tell me your dream then!"

"I would rather not. It is difficult."

"Then how can I accept your counsel? Either your insight is relevant or it is not."

"But I am a Geyad of the Dar Kaadarith."

"And what is that to me now? You are here to serve, so serve!"

Korfax found the tale difficult and he was glad to be done with it. Telling it was like reliving it again. Boavor looked sympathetic, but not Onizim.

"Is that all?" Onizim asked.

"All? And when was the last time you had a dream like that?"

Onizim waited a long while with an unreadable expression on his face. Then he turned away, looking below whilst taking a long, slow breath. He seemed to relax a little as he turned back to Korfax again, and his eyes were somewhat gentler then before.

"What dreams have I had?" he asked. "Korfax, you are young. You are new-made and you been have thrust suddenly into a place of testing before you were ready. Knowing your experience, or lack thereof, I questioned your coming here, but I was denied. Given what has now happened, I see that I was right to do so. You have had only two encounters with this foe. One was yesterday, the other was when you were but a child. Now you have had a dream? Who here has not had a dream? I have had several, and none of them were pleasant. I saw what happened at Tohus. I saw what happened to my people. Are you going to tell me now that you know this enemy better than I, or that you know what they will or will not do better than I? You are young and untried, Geyad Korfax, whereas I have been fighting these demons for the last six years. So I say to you again that I am a better judge of this matter than you, whatever the Geyadel may think."

Onizim drew in another deep breath.

"You look pale, Geyad. I am not unmindful of such things, or of what you might have seen in your time, but I suggest that you harden your heart and forget about your dreams and your memories. Concentrate instead upon the moment at hand. You are inexperienced and unmindful, as are all the young. But that can be remedied. Think rather of how your father would act. Cast your dreams and your imaginings aside, for you have no need of them here. They are a distraction and they will bring nothing but ruin upon you."

Onizim placed a firm hand upon his shoulder and then turned and strode away, quickly followed by Boavor. Korfax watched them go and then reluctantly looked back over the wall. The Agdoain were gathering well out of bow shot, massing in the deeper valley amongst the trees flanking the two great horns of rock that guarded the only approach to Piamossin. But it was as he turned away that he noticed a vague taste riding the air, a taste like cold rot. No doubt it was the Agdoain he could smell, but it made him think back to his dream. He shuddered at the recollection and felt sick with fear.

Orkanir and Ralir came to stand beside him. Ralir looked almost eager to pit his blade against the enemy, his step jaunty, his eyes alight, but Orkanir was more deliberate and his expression was altogether more careful.

Korfax remembered his blade at Losq and how many Agdoain had fallen before it. He fingered his stave. He thought of the things he could do, the summoning of earth and air and of fire and water, but neither seemed adequate in the face of the milling hordes below.

Ralir gave him a keen look.

"So what does Enay Onizim think?"

Korfax glowered.

"He thinks we should wait and see what they will do."

Ralir shrugged.

"They will attack, surely?"

Korfax looked away.

"I believe so, but Enay Onizim remains cautious."

Orkanir agreed.

"His caution has served him well for many years, though no one, to my knowledge, has ever had to suffer siege before in this strange affair. In the past, it has all been stealth and ambush."

How reassuring Orkanir sounded as he echoed what Onizim had said. It brought back to Korfax the world as he had known it at Losq, predictable and safe, all ways known, where even speech together became a ritual, full of the repetitions and the reaffirmations of accepted truths. But now the Agdoain were here, breaking the hallowed rites of the Ell like the deadly hand of chaos. He felt his fear again and rested his head against the cold stone of the wall. Orkanir came closer.

"Korfax, are you all right?"

"I had a restless night," he said.

"Is that all?" Ralir said. "Easy enough to remedy! I recommend at least one flagon of the excellent Nouriss that Enay Bienchir left behind in his hurry to leave this place. Drink of that and you will sleep on the other side of the river until the morning, at the very least."

Orkanir looked at Ralir with displeasure.

"And be of absolutely no use to anyone until midday," he chided.

Ralir wagged a finger in response.

"Not so. The healing ministrations of one of the Faxith is all that are required if the body remains unwilling."

"I fear you are already beyond help, Napei," sighed Orkanir.

Ralir laughed quietly but did not answer.

It happened, even as they stood there. The Agdoain advanced in small bands, to this part of the wall or that. They came in a rush, and many stared down in horrified fascination as the leaders flung themselves upon the stone, bodies shuddering as they grappled with its unyielding surface. The look was the same on many a face. What were they doing? Then their flesh unravelled.

Vines grew, vines of skin and bone that sped upwards, rooting themselves to the wall with thin claws. Those behind swarmed up the vines to their limit – and then they too unravelled in turn.

Onizim gave the order and a hail of arrows lanced down. Many Agdoain were slain, but the vines remained. Then a hail of darts was shot back, another surprise. It seemed that a few of the Agdoain were not armed with blades at all but with hollowed fists instead. The darts were spat from these, bouncing off the stone or biting into flesh wherever they found it. Some on the wall staggered and dropped as the grey darts caught them. It had begun.

Korfax backed away. He felt ill. There was a fear inside him now like the upsurge of deep waters, and he fell away from the world and down into silence. All he could think of was the horror, his dream, the enemy, the face of his father as it slowly rotted. Events around him slowed to a crawl.

He watched unmoving as the Agdoain scrambled up their vines, getting closer and closer with each assault, until they were touching the very edges of the battlements and leaping over them. He watched as the Branith of the tower rushed forward to meet them, fury in their faces, their swords catching the sunlight. Bodies clashed, weapons met and the dying cried out or screamed. But it was another world, another place, and Korfax felt himself retreating from it all, drowning at last in grey mists as silent images battled ponderously above him like giants.

"Korfax! KORFAX!"

Sound returned to him, the sound of battle. Around him lay prostrate forms, and in front of him many of the Branith still held the Agdoain at bay whilst their hideous vines yet pulsed upon the wall. Someone was shaking him. It was Enay Onizim, staring into his face.

"Wake up, youth! There are deeds to be done here!"

He turned about and strode off to the wall, his great sword raised above his head like a standard.

Korfax felt as though he had just stepped out from some fevered nightmare, his thoughts still slow within him. Someone barged into him from behind and he turned about. It was another of the Branith coming to reinforce the defence of the wall. Korfax watched the Branith go, shield one side, sword the other, but as soon as he reached the battlements a grim grey blade pierced him and he fell dead upon the stones. Korfax stared at his face in horror. The world stopped at last and he entered the timeless place.

A hand caught his shoulder and turned him about. He awoke to find Onizim before him again, flushed with exertion.

"What are you doing? What are you thinking? They were nearly over the wall here. If Branvath Orkanir and those under his command had not fought like enraged Vovin, the Agdoain would have been in the tower by now. I want more from you than your dreams!"

Korfax felt dim horror clutch at him. He could not answer. Onizim was about to speak again when Orkanir came forward to stay his hand. Behind him, Korfax could see the others putting up their weapons. There was a sense of relief in the air, like the passing of a storm. The attack had been beaten off and many times many of the Agdoain had been slain. Orkanir spoke.

"Enay, I saw what happened here and I think I understand this matter better than you."

Onizim stiffened but said nothing. Orkanir continued.

"Korfax was at Losq. He was only a child. He witnessed the massacre. Anyone can succumb to such horrors, Enay, if they are unprepared for them. Both you and I know how it is. You saw the aftermath of Tohus. But one thing I do know, Korfax will not allow it to happen again. He is the son of his father."

Onizim stared at Orkanir for a long moment.

"So be it. I will accept what you say, Branvath Orkanir, but only for now. See to it that Korfax realises what his weakness has cost us this day. Weakness in battle is fatal."

He strode off. Korfax sank to his knees and shook. Orkanir looked down at him and then crouched beside him.

"Are you all right?" he asked.

"Once again you rescue me," Korfax answered. "But this time I feel that I do not deserve it. And I doubt I shall ever get back in favour with Enay Onizim again," he conceded.

Orkanir smiled.

"Do not think on it. Onizim is a lot like Napeiel Valagar; a foe to those that do not do their duty, a friend to those that do. I know which of those you are. Now, come back to the wall with me. We need you. We have to find a way to remove those vines."

It was odd, but Orkanir's simple faith in him had stirred something inside. There was a fire there now where none had been before. He thought back to other moments in his life, moments of triumph. He thought again of his duel with

Simoref. That was what he needed now, that rage, rage enough to beat back his fear.

He went to the wall with Orkanir, only to discover that the Agdoain had regrouped and were advancing again, this time all of them, a mass of teeth, swords and shields. What could he do? Fire was his only answer.

Korfax raised his stave. Here it came. The test. He reached inside and his stave hummed angrily as he called up fire of air. He was suddenly amazed at how easy it was.

The Branith around him fell back as red destruction blossomed in the air above them. Then Korfax leaned out over the wall and let his fire descend.

The vines of the Agdoain burned, the Agdoain upon them burned, and Korfax's fire scoured both the wall and the rocks below, from end to end. Charred bodies fell like rain, and for a moment it seemed as though Piamossin itself was enveloped in a surging tide of flame and that each of its stones burned with its own fiery light. Then Korfax pulled back again and dropped his power, breathing hard. The fire diminished as quickly as it had come. The rest of the Agdoain withdrew back into the forest.

He stepped back slowly from the wall. He had been far too extravagant. Not only had he burnt the vines and the Agdoain, he had scorched the stone as well. But even as he regained his composure he felt a change in the air about him. The others, the Branith, were all staring at him in utter astonishment. There was a great silence for a moment and then they saluted him, all of them, a swelling chorus of praises and gratitude. Then they began to cheer him, holding up their swords to honour him. They named him great and praised his power.

Korfax bowed his head to them all until a heavy hand landed upon his shoulder. He looked up and came face to face with Enay Onizim. There was a smile on his lips now, and a grateful light flickered in each eye.

"Now I see before me a true son of the house of the Farenith. Now I see your worth."

Onizim bowed his head and the Branith cheered again. Korfax bowed in return and felt an immense gratitude fill him almost to the brim. But deeper inside he felt something else stir, something darker and more lustful: '*Do it again,*' it said, '*kill again and fill the world with fire.*' Korfax looked out over the wall and frowned in the very midst of his victory. Where would this take him now?

He walked the walls, unable to sleep. The Agdoain had retreated but they had not departed. Now it became a waiting game. No one could leave the tower without fear of assault, but the Agdoain could not approach either for fear of fire.

Korfax thought of his dream the night before, but now that he had struck a blow against the Agdoain, denying them with his power, he found the dream's hold on him lessened.

Even he felt stunned by what he had done. He had killed many times many with a single blow. Every so often as he walked the wall he stared at the stave in his hands, marvelling at how potent it was, how truly miraculous. But there was the rub. He also remembered what his teachers had told him towards the end, just before his making.

Forbear, they had said, and do not let the power control you. He fully understood them now. It was the last temptation, the last test, the one that would remain with him for the rest of his life. Only when he had finally passed into the river could he truly say that he was victorious. He controlled an awesome power and he must never submit to its siren call. He must never try to solve all his problems with power. It would corrupt him.

He looked out over the wall. The Agdoain were still there, in the lower forest below, far beyond the reach of lance or bow. They were not easy to see, but the moonlight occasionally caught one or two of them, shifting shapes of grey lurking in the shadows. They had not given up yet, even though many had perished during his onslaught. Instead they were waiting for something. He had stopped them, but their intent had not been blunted. Something was happening, another change had occurred and the Agdoain had shifted once more.

As luck would have it, Korfax was asleep when the alarm was raised. He almost tumbled from his cot as he woke up to the sound of the great bell, grabbing for his robes whilst trying to stand up all at the same time.

Once he was fully awake and properly attired, he ran outside. There was a gathering upon the wall and Enay Onizim was there. Korfax ran up the stairs.

"Ah, Geyad, you have come. Good! Look there."

Korfax looked where Onizim pointed. The hillocks beyond the two great horns of rock below the walls literally seethed with Agdoain. Korfax felt a shiver of fear. There were at least ten times the foe that there had been the previous day.

Ralir looked down at the swelling numbers.

"Now those are not fair odds at all!" he announced.

All heads turned. Onizim's face was a picture of approbation.

"And that will be quite enough of that, Napei."

Ralir merely smiled pleasantly in return. He seemed utterly unconcerned. Onizim looked back to the Agdoain.

"We do not have enough on this watch to hold the wall. I want everyone awake and ready."

The tower bell was rung again and runners were sent to each of the sleeping rooms. From each watch a single Bransag leapt down one of the many stairs to wake those that slept below. The others remained upon the battlements, their swords and shields before them.

Watching from the wall Korfax considered his options. Fire of air was the most likely for offence, as he had already proved, but he also needed to give some thought to defence. For that, earth of air was said to be the best, but he did not feel confident that he could cover the entire wall. He thought of winds and fogs, water of air, or of treacherous grounds, water of earth, but nothing seemed adequate. And it was his decision, his alone.

No other could tell a Geyad what was best in any given situation, and Korfax was acutely aware of how lonely his position actually was. This was the other side to that of temptation – the loneliness of power. All his teachings seemed to fall in upon him at once, each crushed to a point. If he took the wrong course, made the wrong decision, if he used his powers injudiciously, then he placed Piamossin and all who dwelt within its walls in jeopardy.

He decided at last. His was a stave of fire and he was a Geyad of fire, so he would use fire in both offence and defence. Fire of air was the easiest, and certainly the most flexible, of all the powers at his disposal. He could make a fiery wall, an incandescent cloud like a shield, or he could direct a shaft of lightning and so burn the foe piecemeal. Those were enough for this fight.

It was just before dawn that it happened. There was no signal, no visible sign, but with one single heave the Agdoain began their advance. They swarmed in from every side and from their ranks hail after hail of grey darts were spat at the lower wall.

Korfax stood back from the edge and hurled his fire where he could, but the Agdoain were attacking every side of the tower, all at once, and he could only defend one place at a time. The Branith cut down any that dared peer over the battlements, but if anyone showed themselves over the wall they were met by a hail of darts. There were just too many of the foe.

Korfax burnt the vines from the wall as fast as he could, but the speed with which they grew back again made the task almost impossible. The Agdoain would breach the defences through sheer force of numbers.

As Rafarel rose up to the east and the first light of day brushed the high tops behind the tower, the Agdoain forced their way over the southern side of the wall. Though they were driven back by the second line of defence, the defenders found themselves getting fewer and further between. Many already understood the brutal equation. For every three Agdoain that fell, a Bransag was likely to be slain as well. The trade was unequal, for the foe outnumbered the defenders by at least ten to one.

Korfax ran to help, calling up a great cloud of fire and throwing it over the wall. Many Agdoain were burnt by the summoning, whilst their climbing vines were turned to ash, but ever more grew up in their place and many more Agdoain clambered eagerly up their still writhing limbs. Beyond and below the ground still heaved with the foe, surging forward as they discharged their grey darts through the air.

Cries came from the other side, cries of warning. The Agdoain had broken through to the north and now poured over the walls in ever-increasing numbers.

Korfax ran back to the breach, summoning fire of air as he went, and by the time he had reached the scene of the attack, his stave was almost incandescent with force.

All he could see before him was chaos. The defenders had been forced off the wall and now fought in the courtyard below, Agdoain dancing where they would, teeth and swords flashing. He could not use his power there, as it would be far too indiscriminate. On the wall above, though, grey bodies flowed over the stone like a cataract, so he hurled his fire there. He stemmed the flood for a long moment, his blast of power leaving behind it a great charred hole, but almost immediately the hole was filled again with more of the grinning foe.

He changed the nature of his summoning and called up a scythe of lightning instead, burning through flesh and bone as he swung his stave in great arcs. He slew the foe by the dozen with each pass, until he could summon fire no more. Then, as his power failed, so the Branith who waited behind him seized their chance and surged forward, attacking with shield and sword. The breach was closed.

Korfax came wearily back to his position on the higher wall, stave held before him. He could do little more for the moment except hope that the Branith below could contain the enemy. He felt exhausted. There were fewer Agdoain now, he was sure of it, but how many had already entered the tower? He did not know.

He reached the top and stared down. He cursed silently to himself. Whilst he had tried to stem the breach to the north, another had been in progress to the south. This one was smaller, and the defenders had managed to beat it back but at a terrible price. Few were left upon that wall now. Korfax looked beyond the tower and out into the valley below. Except for their beasts, there were no Agdoain remaining that he could see. They had committed all their forces to the attack.

He heard shouts from behind him. He looked about. The cries were coming from the tower itself. He looked up at its curving stone and almost immediately saw the shadows of headless forms as they danced by one of the windows. He ran back to the tower along the upper bridge, hoping against hope that he could do something to help. Now the siege had become a battle for possession of the tower itself.

Korfax ran into the corridor and found Boavor leaning heavily against the wall. Around him lay many bodies, mostly the guard of Enay Onizim. Then Korfax saw that Boavor cradled the head of his lord in his lap. Onizim was already dead.

Lying about them both were the remnants of many Agdoain, liquid heaps of thinning bone and running flesh. Korfax went to Boavor's side and knelt.

"You have taken hurt?" he said.

Boavor leaned heavily on Korfax and smiled.

"Geyad? Good, you are here. You can say the rites."

Boavor hissed with pain.

Korfax saw the blood across his chest. There was a hole there, a great ragged hole made by a sword. Korfax winced at the sight.

"I will fetch a healer," he ventured.

Boavor made a passing gesture with one of his hands.

"There are no more healers," he answered. "The Agdoain overran their quarters before we could stop them."

Korfax clutched at Boavor. The memory of his father saving Orkanir came to him.

"But you are still amongst the living. I can help you."

Boavor coughed, and blood dribbled from his lips.

"No, Geyad. I am here for the moment only. A few of them got through my guard, though they paid for the privilege."

Boavor sagged. Korfax helped him sit back up, keeping his back against the wall.

"It cannot be helped, not now. My time has come. I can feel it. My Enay has gone on ahead and I shall follow him. Save what remains of the command and then leave here whilst you still can. Get to Ralfen! Warn your father!"

His head dropped and did not rise again. Korfax dashed his stave to the floor in helpless rage and then wept like a child.

Ralir was the last upon the wall, fighting for his life against the last of the foe. There were five of them but the way was narrow, so they could only come at him singly or in pairs. The first two were easy enough to dispatch, his sword in them and through them before they could counter. The next two divided, one leaping up onto the parapet itself, but Ralir leapt and span, taking away its legs before crashing into the other and knocking it down from the wall and into the courtyard below. It smashed upon the hard stone and did not move. The fifth waited its moment and then caught Ralir against the stone, shield against shield, blade against blade. Ralir drew back as it extended its mouth, its teeth reaching for his face. He pushed hard with his sword, twisting it, and felt the sword of his enemy break upon the stone. The Agdoain howled and leapt back, striking Ralir full on with its shield. Ralir's sword flew out of his hand and over the wall. But as he backed away, looking about for another weapon, so the Agdoain hissed and extended the stump of its sword like a threat.

Ralir stared in fascinated horror as the Agdoain's arm swallowed what remained of its sword with a sick, sucking sound. There was a mouth now at the end of its arm, a puckered slobbering hole, and as the last of the sword vanished inside, so the mouth vomited up something else instead, a great knobbed club of grey bone. In mere moments the club had assumed full size. The Agdoain gave a liquid roar, raising its mouth to the sky as if caught in the arms of some foul ecstasy, and then advanced again, its long tongue licking its teeth with horrid anticipation.

Ralir found himself being beaten back as the club threatened to smash his shield with every single blow. The Agdoain punched its clubbed limb like a battering ram, fast and furious, and it was all that Ralir could do to keep the demon at bay.

With dented shield he staggered back slowly along the wall. The continuous rain of blows numbed his arm and it was beginning to look desperate. There were no other weapons here. The only idea that came to mind was to throw himself from the wall and take his enemy down with him.

Then he heard the Agdoain gurgle. He looked over his shield and saw a blade protruding from its breast. The Agdoain fell back and off the wall, crashing with a sodden thump on the distant ground. Ralir stared after it and then looked back at his saviour. It was Orkanir. Ralir breathed a sigh of relief.

"You possess a most excellent sense of timing," he said.

Orkanir smiled and bowed his head slightly.

"I was on my way here when I caught your sword play from beyond the tower. When I saw you lose your weapon with that last one, I came here as fast as I could."

Ralir leant against the wall.

"And very glad I am that you did."

Orkanir looked down at the slowly disintegrating Agdoain below.

"Curious, I have never seen an Agdoain armed with a club before."

Ralir shuddered.

"I have not seen one, either. But it grew the unholy thing right in front of me, after I broke off its sword."

Orkanir looked back at Ralir, questions in his eyes.

"It grew it?"

Ralir looked down. An expression of distaste crossed his face as he remembered what he had seen.

"A most disgusting sight, I can assure you."

"That explains a few things," said Orkanir.

Ralir gave him a puzzled look.

"What do you mean?" he asked.

"For a start, how they were able to knock down the stone doors at Losq. Then there are those darts they can fire at us. I do not believe that we have seen all that they are."

"On that we are very much in agreement," replied Ralir with feeling. "They seem more than able to pull dark miracles out of the air to aid them. I shudder to think what they will get up to next."

Orkanir didn't answer for a moment but continued to stare down at the remains of the Agdoain below. His mouth twisted slightly for a moment and his gaze tightened. He turned back to Ralir.

"Come," he said. "Let us see who else has survived."

Ralir reached across and held Orkanir's arm for a moment.

"How many have we lost? There were ten of us here, but as you can see, I am the only one left."

He gestured over the wall.

"The others had no saviour."

Orkanir sighed.

"Only a few," he said.

"Not enough to see off another attack then."

Orkanir gestured back the way he had come.

"No, come! Let us find Korfax. We need to decide what to do next."

They ran back along the wall.

Korfax looked about him. Everywhere he saw the dead. There had been more than a thousand here, and they had fought off ten times that number, but their losses were such that they could no longer keep this place. Of all the defenders of Piamossin only some thirty or so remained.

He looked over the wall. There was no sign of the foe. They were either dead or gone. He went to find the others so that they could prepare for what they had to do now.

All the bodies that could be found were placed in the room set aside for the dead, the Tar Telloajes. There was no time for anything more elaborate.

Korfax stood by the great door, looking down the steps into the shadow and waiting to say the words that would bid the souls of the departed enter the great river. He felt tired as never before. The others waited behind him, each holding an ormn, ready to mount. As soon as the rites of passage were performed, they would leave.

Korfax spoke the words, making the sign of Zinznagah with his stave. He had just enough strength left to create a fiery trail in the air, drawing the requisite words in fire. The others answered him at each appropriate moment, and then, all too quickly, it was done.

Ralir closed the door, sealing it by its locking stone. Heat mounted within, a rising flame that would reduce the dead to ash. Korfax bowed his head for a moment and then mounted the ormn Orkanir held for him. He looked back at the others. All eyes were on him now, sad but resolute, and they regarded him with more respect than he felt he deserved.

True, the Agdoain had been defeated, but at what cost? Onizim was dead! Boavor was dead! Korfax felt a sudden and terrible guilt envelop him. He was Geyad! He should have been able to save them all, as in the old tales. But he had not been able to. Instead, he felt the presence of all those who would never leave this place like a weight around his neck.

16

MESSAGES AND MEETINGS

Zor-gei-ord Nis-uran-big
Chi-alkar Krih-lim-dril-drm
Lap-maonkao Bag-levas-jo
Zor-dohim Odmon-odman
Raz-ial-prg Odzam-ranjo
Si-lon-ohr Od-iam-pibor
Bai-a-vim Odnis-sotoh

They rode to Ralfen, following the wide road that would take them around Zlminoaj on its northern side. The land felt quiet and downcast, like the aftermath of a storm.

Korfax felt quiet also, subdued like the land, and tired, so very tired. He had expended himself in fire, burnt himself with his power, but still found himself wanting. Too many had died because he was not strong enough.

Orkanir watched him for a long while, before finally speaking.

"Korfax, you torture yourself for no good reason."

"Do I?" asked Korfax. "This has been death's day!"

"And you are not the first Geyad to travel this road. Many have been where you are now. Besides, if it hadn't been for you, no one would have escaped from Piamossin at all."

"Is that supposed to make me feel better? Almost two parloh have been slain and Piamossin is abandoned. I should have done more. Or perhaps less."

"What do you mean?" Orkanir asked.

"I stirred them up," Korfax told him. "They attacked because of me."

"They would have attacked sooner or later," said Orkanir, "given their numbers. Perhaps you forced their hand and they attacked before they were ready. We did beat them after all."

"But at what cost?"

"And do not blame yourself for this, either. Onizim was right in what he said. No sooner do you become Geyad than you are thrown into battle. This situation was not foreseen by any. Up until now the Agdoain have been satisfied only with stealth and ambush. Who would have guessed that they would have attacked in such numbers and with such ferocity?"

"This has happened before, though. What about Losq?"

Orkanir frowned.

"Not quite the same."

"So what of Tohus and the slaughter that occurred in the Umadya Beltanuhm?"

"And we don't know precisely what happened. There were no survivors. But this is different. A siege? The Agdoain have done nothing like it in all the intervening years. Think of it. We were besieged by ten thousand of the foe. No one knew there were so many! So I ask you again, who could have foreseen it?"

Korfax looked away.

"I should have done more."

"What you feel is what you should feel. Those who survive the trial always feel guilty afterwards. Why am I here when the others are not? My father taught me this. How do you think I feel about his death at Losq? It is the way of things. Besides, they will return to us again from the great river."

Korfax bowed his head in acknowledgement but kept his silence.

They passed between the hills on the north side of Zlminoaj and went on towards Ralfen. The road was high, twisting its way downwards in great curves. To the north more hills spread themselves out over the land like so many ships upon a wide sea. But they did not move. Only the heavens moved, clouds rushing from the east, grey curtains of rain passing in the distance.

Ralir breathed deeply as he looked about him.

"I like this land," he said. "So many shades, so unlike the south."

Korfax turned to stare at his friend.

"How can you think of such things at a time like this?"

Ralir stared back.

"You aren't still thinking about Piamossin, are you?"

"They are dead, Ralir, all of them."

"And cursing yourself for it is not going to bring them back. What's done is done. It is why we are here. We put ourselves in harm's way because that is our calling."

Korfax felt a hand on his arm. He turned. It was Orkanir.

"Listen to him, Korfax."

Once more Korfax did not answer.

They rode on through the night. The clouds passed just as dawn came, and they found themselves approaching Ralfen at first light. All the others looked with gladness at the sight, but Korfax felt only dread. Here it came. Here he would have to answer for what had happened.

They entered Ralfen and were met by a number of the guard led by Lasidax, Bienchir and Angalam.

They dismounted and bowed. Lasidax waited, a look of astonishment on his face.

"Why are you here?" he asked. "What has happened?"

Korfax took a deep breath.

"There was an attack upon Piamossin. The Agdoain laid siege to the tower. We defeated them, but at great cost. Only a few of us survived."

Lasidax looked utterly stunned.

"Siege?"

Lasidax turned to Orkanir.

"It is as Geyad Korfax says," said Orkanir.

"When?"

"Two days ago."

Lasidax looked at all the others and then back at Bienchir. Bienchir had nothing to say either; he seemed just as shocked as Lasidax. They were all at a loss, all except for Angalam. He came forward, smiled and placed a hand upon Korfax's shoulder.

"You look exhausted," he said. He turned to the others. "All of you do. Come inside and rest, this tale can wait a little longer."

Lasidax turned.

"No, it cannot. I demand to know what has happened."

"No, Enay," said Angalam. "Look at them – they are exhausted. Hard battle then a hard ride to warn us here? Consider instead your command. What are your imperatives?"

Bienchir stepped forward. He looked angry now.

"Imperatives be damned," he said. "I also would like to know what has happened. Piamossin was in good order when I left it. I would like to know how my command was so swiftly overthrown. What? Did you all run at the first sight of the foe? How is it that two parloh can be reduced to only a handful? This smells of cowardice to me!"

Ralir drew his sword and had it at Bienchir's throat in a moment. Guards surged forward. Orkanir pulled Ralir back.

"Gently, Napei, gently."

Ralir shook him off.

"I will not stand idly by whilst some idle fool from the idle west questions the valour of the dead."

He turned back to Bienchir.

"Cowardice, is it? A thousand died at Piamossin whilst you were here, filling yourself with wine. I call you out, Bienchir."

Korfax looked behind. All the others from Piamossin had their hands on their swords and were ready to step up beside Ralir. Bienchir's eyes were wide in shock. He clearly could not believe how far Ralir was prepared to go. Lasidax did not move either, obviously at a complete loss as well. There was only one thing to do. He stepped between the two sides.

"Enough, all of you," he said.

He turned to Bienchir.

"If you want someone to blame, blame me. It was my fault."

There were muffled protests from behind. Both Ralir and Orkanir would have said something but Korfax held up his hand to stop them.

"Against better judgement I went exploring," he continued. "In my travels I came upon one of the Agdoain. It was riding some kind of beast, the same kind that Angalam encountered. I fought it and killed it, and this, I believe, is what stirred them up. They attacked Piamossin with a force ten thousand strong, both cavalry and infantry, and we lost everyone but those that you see here. Though we all agreed that Piamossin was no longer defensible, it was my decision to abandon it. I thought it best to come here so that we could warn the rest of you that the Agdoain have risen up."

Bienchir had nothing to say and neither did Lasidax. Both were still trying to come to terms with it all. Korfax turned to Angalam, who glanced at the others and then smiled.

"I have a feeling that there is far more to this tale than you are telling us, Korfax. And from the reaction of those that follow you I believe they do not share your belief that you are responsible for this turn of events."

He turned to Lasidax. His voice had an edge to it now.

"Since it is clear to me that a decision needs to be made, I suggest that the tower prepares itself for siege. Whilst that is being dealt with I will hear the full tale from Korfax."

He turned to Bienchir.

"I also suggest that messages be sent as soon as possible. We need to warn everyone else. It seems our little war here in the north has just become somewhat larger."

Korfax sat with Angalam in his room. There was wine and food upon the table. Korfax only availed himself of the wine.

Angalam had listened quietly as Korfax told his tale, but his first question was not what Korfax had expected at all.

"So fire of air is effective."

"Utterly."

Angalam leaned back.

"Your father never speaks of Losq, or of any other encounter he has had. For myself I have never had to use my stave in anger against the foe. It is good to know that it is efficacious."

He looked long at Korfax as though measuring something.

"It was not your fault," he said.

"I started it."

"Korfax, at some point this had to happen. Any one of us could have been in your position! A chance to discover more about the foe? Who would not have leapt at it?"

"But it was costly."

"Most things in war are, as your father will tell you. He is due to return tomorrow."

He glanced at the food.

"Now eat and then rest."

Sazaaim rode in through the gates, an entire parloh behind him. He stopped and dismounted as soon as he saw Orkanir.

"Orkanir? What are you doing here?"

Then he saw Korfax. He stared at his son. Korfax waited, they all did. Without the wind in the trees it would have been utterly silent.

Sazaaim took a step forward.

"What has happened?" he asked.

"Siege and battle," said Korfax. "The Agdoain attacked Piamossin. Only a handful of us survived."

Sazaaim went dark. There was a terrible look on his face now, almost savage. Korfax could not look for long. He bowed his head, but then his father came forward and embraced him.

"My son, my son."

After long moments Sazaaim drew back. His face was gentler now, but there was still a look in his eyes, a dangerous look of suppressed rage.

"That you are here is all that matters," he said.

He took a long breath, calming himself further.

"Now tell me the tale."

Korfax kept his head down.

"It is a long story."

"Look at me, Korfax."

Korfax looked up. This meeting should have been other than it was. It should have been joyous. If only the circumstances were better.

"Did the Agdoain take Piamossin?" his father asked.

"No, they were defeated."

"Is Onizim here?"

"He died."

Sazaaim glanced at Orkanir.

"You must tell me everything." He looked back at his son. "Both of you."

After the tales were told yet again, and more messages sent, Sazaaim walked with his son along the outer wall of Ralfen.

"All the others speak very highly of you, those that survived."

He smiled.

"They say you slaughtered the foe by the hundred, that victory would not have been possible if you had not been there."

"Victory would not have been necessary if I had not been there," said Korfax.

"No!" exclaimed his father. "This was inevitable. It was only a matter of time. Whether their hand was pushed or not is irrelevant – the Agdoain were intent upon it. This was inevitable."

"As everyone keeps saying. So what will happen now?"

"Bienchir will be sent back to Piamossin to secure it again. Angalam will go with him, as will double the force that was sent before."

"Bienchir?"

"If nothing else it will preserve his life. I understand Ralir still wants to meet him upon the field of combat."

Korfax smiled.

"He called us cowards. I am the only one worthy of that accusation."

Sazaaim took his son by the shoulders and looked fully into his eyes.

"Orkanir told me about that, too. You must not blame yourself. Do you think that fear in the face of battle is dishonourable. It is not. You mastered your fear. You are no coward, Bienchir is a fool. Think nothing of his words."

Korfax looked down. Sazaaim sighed.

"I know how you feel. This is how it was when I came upon Tohus."

"What is to happen now?" asked Korfax.

"You will stay here for the moment. Messages have been sent. Let us see what replies come back."

The replies came quickly. One of them was from the Geyadel with orders that Korfax was to return to Othil Zilodar to deliver his report in person. Sazaaim smiled darkly when he read that. He went to his son and told him.

"It seems the Geyadel wishes to make amends," he said.

"Father?"

"He sent you here. He knows it was unprecedented, but he did it anyway. No doubt he now feels a certain guilt at his actions."

"But who else was there to send?" Korfax asked. "I am of the north. I was the best available choice."

Sazaaim's smile became even darker.

"Your loyalty does you credit, but I should be a little less eager to defend the Geyadel, if I were you. There were others Abrilon could have sent, many others, but his eye turned to you. I am not sure why he is watching you, but you should take care. Abrilon is hard. He is good at spending others in the name of his will, but he pays less attention to their needs than he should. I still have not forgiven him for hazarding the life of my son."

Korfax looked down.

"But that was my fault."

"No, it was not. Abrilon was the one that sent you north before you were truly ready. I agree with Ponodol in this."

"Ponodol?"

"Who do you think had Ralir go with you? He sent messages to me telling me what he had done. That is why I sent Orkanir to Piamossin. I wanted you as safe as you could be."

Korfax kept his head down. He suddenly felt angry.

"I am no child, not any more. I want to play my part."

He looked up again.

"Do not shield me."

Sazaaim looked back gently.

"I would do no such thing, but neither will I stand idly by whilst you are placed in needless peril. I am the one that should be at risk, not you. I am the past. You are the future. I want you to survive what is coming."

"And what is coming?"

"War! That is why I approve of your orders. Perhaps you will succeed where I have failed for all these years. Make the case for war. Abrilon may listen to you more readily than he does to me. The Dar Kaadarith should be ready. The Nazad Esiask should be ready. The deluge is coming."

Abrilon sat at the table and stared into its well-polished depths.

"Though I read many of the dispatches that come down from the north, hearing of your experiences in person is worse, far worse. This is grim news, Korfax, grim news."

He looked up.

"I fear we may be hard pressed if what you experienced at Piamossin is a sign of what is yet to come."

Korfax looked glumly out of the window. Grim news. Yes, and he found himself hoping that this would be the last time he had to tell of it. He had told it to Raxen Liexar on the sky ship to Leemal, he had told it to his mother and then he had spoken before the lord of the city and his counsellors, escorted to and from the great hall of the Garad by no less a personage than Brandril Fizur himself, commander of the city guard. Not only that, but it seemed that everyone in the city had turned out to stare at him as he went by. Did any of them have sons at Piamossin, he wondered. Did they blame him for their deaths?

Now he had told his tale again, this time to Abrilon. He thought of his father's words. Make the case for war! He dreaded the prospect. How foolish his notions were as a child. War was a horror.

But the furthest north needed reinforcements. Only four of the Geyadith walked the lands beyond Leemal, and they were not enough. The furthest north was wide and desolate. Entire armies could be hidden there. Korfax looked back at Abrilon.

"When do I set forth again?"

Abrilon looked kindly at Korfax.

"Not yet, my young Geyad, not yet. By all accounts you have exhausted yourself. The defence of Piamossin was a sore trial for you. Others have marked it and I can see it for myself. No, you need rest for the moment, rest and recovery. I have arranged for another twenty of our guild to be sent north. Six of them will meet up with your father at Ralfen, six more will go to Piamossin and the others will stay in Leemal until called for. Napeiel Valagar himself is coming north, as are many more of the Nazad Esiask. Your father has been proven right in this matter. So now we are going to war. The threat of the Agdoain will finally be met with overwhelming force. We cannot have another Piamossin; we cannot have that at all."

Korfax bowed his head in relief. Twenty more of the Dar Kaadarith was a different matter entirely. He looked carefully up again.

"But what of me, Geyadel? I should help, surely."

Abrilon smiled.

"No! As I have already said, you need rest."

Abrilon stood up and walked about the table. He clasped his hands before him.

"I have to return to Emethgis Vaniad in seven days' time, but Samafaa and Ponodol will remain here, to speak for the council and to order the disposition of our forces. I am currently staying with Geyadril Fokisne. Have you ever been inside his tower?"

"No, Geyadel, I have not."

Abrilon's eyes glinted.

"Then it is high time that you did. I will arrange it. He has some of the finest works of art ever created under his care. You should see them, I think. Beauty heals the soul."

Abrilon turned for a moment and then suddenly looked back at Korfax with brighter eyes.

"Yes... beauty heals the soul."

Korfax bowed to the Geyadel, but inside he suddenly felt very uncertain. He was sure there was a double meaning in what the Geyadel said. He thought again of his father's words, that Abrilon was hard, spending others as he saw fit. But sitting here it did not seem that way to him at all. Abrilon seemed to care a great deal.

Geyadril Fokisne came quickly at the summons.

"Geyadel?"

"Fokisne! I have a favour to ask of you."

"I live to serve."

Abrilon raised his eyebrows.

"And to increase your collection, I think. I noticed several new pieces when I went through the west hall this morning. I think the works you now possess rival even those of the Velukor!"

"Not so," said Fokisne. "I have heard it said that Audroh Usdurna and Tabaud Zamferas can show better."

Abrilon smiled and Fokisne bowed his head slightly.

"So, Geyadel, what are your requirements?" he asked.

"I would very much like it if Korfax stayed with you whilst here in Othil Zilodar. I want him close by. I wish to watch him for a while."

"Korfax? I have heard much concerning him. The first of us to withstand siege since the wars themselves? Most impressive for one so young. I understand that he is powerful but still somewhat uncertain. Not much like his father, then. Now there is certainty."

"You compare the hammer with the chisel? Be careful, Fokisne! The hand that wields them both is almost exactly the same. As you said, he is young. Certainty comes with experience and Korfax has a long way to travel yet."

"Oh?"

"I believe Korfax has a destiny."

Abrilon held up a clear crystal goblet, half-filled with pale Nomzas. Fokisne watched the Geyadel and waited. It was wise to do so with Abrilon. One never knew exactly where the conversation would go.

Abrilon cast a glance at Fokisne.

"You know me well," he said.

He placed the goblet back down, exactly in the same position it had formerly occupied. Abrilon could not resist precision.

"I shall speak as plainly as I may," he continued. "I have reviewed what we know of the Agdoain and a thing has come to light that bothers me. It bothers Asvoan also."

Fokisne offered the Geyadel a sour look.

"In this I am with Samafaa. We do not need to consult continually with the Exentaser. It is like staring into a mirror."

"And have you never considered how instructive a reflection can be?"

Fokisne drew back.

"So what is it you wish to tell me?"

"Only this! The Agdoain first attacked Losq. Who was there? Korfax! Who, by his association with Dialyas, identified Ovuor for us? Korfax! Who first endured sustained siege by the Agdoain? Korfax!"

"No, I do not see it," said Fokisne. "It is coincidence born of circumstance, surely?"

"I would be inclined to agree with you if I believed in coincidences," returned Abrilon, "but I do not. I sent Korfax to Piamossin on purpose. That, though, is not the point I wish to make."

Abrilon looked speculatively at Fokisne.

"I have come to believe that Korfax is a focus for events, the stone that starts the avalanche, so to speak. We tried to have Dialyas removed to Lonsiatris for many years, but he always remained one step ahead of us, ever skirting the boundaries of the law but never quite stepping over them. He was clever, and his many arguments in his defence on the exact nature of heresy and free will left the rest of us fuming in frustration. But then, suddenly, along comes Korfax and Dialyas finds himself ensnared by circumstances outside his control. His long fall finally comes to its sorry end and he is gone from us within the space of a few seasons!"

"But surely that was an isolated event? Dialyas consorted with heresy, so it was merely a matter of time before he overreached his aim."

"Overreached his aim, you say? It was not heresy brought him down, but circumstance! Who recognised Ovuor? By all rights Korfax should never have been present at that meeting at all."

"Very well, I will grant you that at least. But what of the other occurrences?"

"Have you heard about Korfax's experiences at Piamossin? He had a vision there. He saw something monstrous, something terrible, and by looking he stirred the foe into action. Something tells me that Korfax is vital in our war with the Agdoain."

"That may very well be, but you have not yet explained to me what happened at Losq. And unless I am very much mistaken, Korfax was not the target there."

Abrilon smiled.

"You think? Look at this!"

Abrilon held up an oanadar and placed it upon the table. He touched it, thinking the requisite thoughts, and a map was projected into the air above it, a map of the northernmost tip of Lukalaa.

"The Agdoain that first attacked Losq ignored many other places nearby."

Abrilon pointed to the right-hand side of the map, where a long and imbricated coastline wound its way up to the northern-most tip of land.

"If they came from the east," he said, "they had to skirt the Faor Leor and the Faor Golor. Neither was attacked."

Abrilon pointed to the bottom of the map.

"If they came from the south," he continued, "they would have had to pass through the vale of Gieris. There were many targets for them there, many easy targets – all far easier than Losq."

Now Abrilon gestured at the left-hand side of the map.

"And if they came from the west they would have had to pass by the Faor Saqorris and the Faor Illifor. So you see, there are no ways that are empty and there were plenty of easier targets. Yet the Agdoain chose to attack Umadya Losq itself. Surely the lesser houses would have been easier to subdue than a fully fortified tower?"

Fokisne frowned as he studied the map.

"But then again, one of the Argedith would have counted a Geyad the biggest threat!"

"Indeed! That thought crossed my mind also. But one of the Argedith would also have known the rhythms of the seasons. Why attack during the exact time when Sazaaim would be absent?"

Fokisne had no answer. Abrilon smiled his coldest smile yet.

"I have spoken with others concerning this issue, but only a few."

Fokisne bowed his head.

"I am honoured that you would share this with me."

Abrilon bowed in return.

"I am telling you because you are the first Geyadril of this city. This may affect you. I have also spoken to Zildaron, to Samafaa and to Ponodol."

Fokisne frowned, a gesture that did not go unnoticed by Abrilon.

"You do not like Ponodol, do you?" he asked.

Now Fokisne looked uncomfortable.

"It is just that I have never been able to get his former association with Dialyas out of my mind."

Abrilon suddenly looked less than pleased.

"And that will be enough of that!" he admonished. "It is ancient history, gone and no more. Besides, you should know that Ponodol could even have been Geyadel after Gemanim, if circumstances had been otherwise. It would be foolish to discount such experience and ability. You should look deeper than you do, Fokisne! All the Geyadrilith should."

After the meeting Fokisne decided to take Abrilon's advice to heart. If the Geyadel wanted him to look deeper then look deeper he would. He went searching for Ponodol and soon found him standing upon a high bridge overlooking one of the many pools scattered throughout the tower gardens, staring down into the water.

"Ponodol!"

Ponodol looked up.

"Fokisne? What an unexpected pleasure! And what can I do for you?"

Fokisne did not miss the forced joviality.

"I require answers to hard questions."

Ponodol smiled gently in response.

"How direct you have become! How unlike yourself! What answers?"

Not a flicker of expression crossed Fokisne's face.

"I know your history, Ponodol, as you know mine, so play no games with me. That we do not like each other is well known, and I would not normally seek you out, but I have recently had a conversation with the Geyadel and find that I must talk to you."

"Ah," Ponodol said, "Korfax."

Fokisne watched carefully. Ponodol kept the same gentle smile as if nothing of any consequence had occurred at all.

"Well?" he said.

Ponodol offered up the mildest expression that he could muster.

"I imagine that the Geyadel has told you all that you need to know. I doubt I can add anything of worth."

Fokisne was not to be put off.

"Nevertheless, I wish to hear what you have to say."

Ponodol made to turn away.

"Do you? And what if I think otherwise?"

Fokisne took Ponodol by the arm.

"No, I will not be denied! I am sure that Abrilon gave the tutelage of Korfax to you for a reason. There are many things I would like to know, but the reasons behind that decision will do for now – especially in the light of your association with Dialyas. This affects us all; we are going to war."

Ponodol shrugged Fokisne away.

"So the first is no longer the Geyadel? He is merely Abrilon now?"

Fokisne drew himself up.

"I have already told you not to play games with me, Ponodol. Tell me what I want to know."

Ponodol remained still, but there was a subtle hint of anger about him now, something in the air, something dangerous.

"Games, Fokisne? You think we play games here? You may well be the first Geyadril in Othil Zilodar, and a close friend of the Geyadel no less, but you still have much to learn."

Ponodol took a deep breath.

"The Geyadel did not ask me to tutor Korfax, I took it upon myself to do so. But I had the Geyadel's blessing, once he understood my reasoning."

"And what was your reasoning?"

"Dialyas!"

"But that is the thing I do not understand."

"You should. I worked with him. I knew him from the very first. I helped him make the Kapimadar, as did Sazaaim and Virqol, but the three of us rejected his interpretation of the result. At the end he gave us little choice. We had to denounce him. And that was why I took it upon myself to watch over Korfax. It was vital Korfax suffer no taint from his association."

"Taint? But why should he? Dialyas was nothing but an arrogant heretic!"

Ponodol mused for a moment.

"You think so? Ah! But I am forgetting. You weren't there, were you?"

"What was so special about him?"

A hint of indulgence crept over Ponodol's face.

"Think of him as a star," he said, "dragged from its place in the heavens and given flesh. Think to yourself that the fire of The Creator burned within his breast."

Fokisne drew back.

"That is profane!"

"Profane? And are you saying that The Creator made no stars of ill omen?"

Fokisne paused. This was not going the way he had thought it would. Perhaps the answers he sought were not the ones he wanted after all.

"And what do you mean by that?" he asked.

"Only that you should not go looking for answers without first understanding what it is you are actually seeking," Ponodol replied. "Some questions are dangerous, Fokisne. Some questions reveal more than the questioner seeks. Would you really like to discover the truth of it all? I suddenly find myself wondering whether you really would. You see, once the bottle is opened the stopper never fits so well again."

"I don't understand."

"The Geyadel does."

"He was the one that told me to look deeper."

Ponodol changed his demeanour completely. He stared intently at Fokisne for a moment.

"The Geyadel said that to you?"

"He did."

"I see."

Ponodol looked down at the water.

"Very well then, let me set you on the path."

He looked back at Fokisne.

"Here is a question for you: would you know temptation if it lurked within salvation?"

"What are you talking about now?"

"I thought it simple enough: would you know temptation if it lurked within salvation?"

"I do not understand!"

"Fokisne, we know the rightness of a thing by its feel, by its very essence. Or so we think in our ignorance. But if we were offered salvation, and that salvation contained within it the very thing that would damn us, would we know it for what it truly was?"

"Now you go too far! Nothing is that devious!"

"And there you are wrong, Fokisne. There you are so utterly wrong! Why do you think Dialyas attracted so much attention? Why do you think Dialyas escaped banishment for so long? You wish to understand? Read the records from his trial."

And with that, Ponodol turned about and went back to the tower. Fokisne watched him go and found himself wondering whether he actually wanted to pursue this at all.

Korfax entered the main tower at the behest of the Balzarg and was directed to the entrance hall. His meagre belongings had already been taken by another and were no doubt secreted in a room somewhere above. He waited while the Balzarg went off to find his lord.

The entrance hall, even taken by itself, was utterly magnificent. It was as Abrilon had said. Geyadril Fokisne possessed an eye for the rare and the beautiful and, being wealthy, had managed to gain whatever that eye coveted. Everywhere that Korfax looked he saw works by masters, sculptures of great delicacy, paintings of great sensitivity. Much beauty was on display here, much dangerous beauty.

He went closer to one of the paintings and gazed up at it. There was a name etched in its bottom left-hand corner, almost carved into the pigment. Voangah! Korfax stepped back and swallowed. This was an original and not some careful copy. Above him, like a giant, was a Napei, standing beside a proud steed of the most brilliant white, both waiting timelessly beneath the spreading branches of a huge and magnificent peis. Korfax stepped further back and took a moment to collect his thoughts. The portrait had such power, such might. The eyes gazed down at him with gentle fire, whilst the steed seemed to glow as though fresh from battle. Every leaf was outlined in light, whilst each knuckle of bark reached proudly outwards, almost protruding from the painting itself.

Unlike Leidaroh, or even Peimoz, Voangah preferred a broader brush so that he could almost mould his thought into being, layering the paint onto his canvas with such vigour and passion that it fairly leapt out into the air beyond. But even though his strokes seemed coarser, each line was just as carefully placed. There was no great attention to detail, for that had not been Voangah's way; there was only the captured moment, like the impression from a long-held memory. But how startling the result! Voangah dared to capture the very spirit itself and display it in all its glory, stripping away the walls of substance that obscured it so that it could stand naked before the world. 'Resurrect no true image' was the commandment, but Korfax was certain Voangah would have broken even that stricture if it meant exposing the underlying truth. Voangah was dangerous.

He turned to the next picture and smiled. He was on safer ground here. This one had been painted by Manneh, if his eyes did not deceive him. He stepped closer to study it.

Manneh was much like Voangah, not so much an artist with an eye for detail but more an artist with an eye for the moment. However, he was altogether gentler than Voangah, and the fire of his imagination was a much subtler affair.

Here was another portrait, one of the Balt Kaalith, the distillation of a Noqvoanel, or so Korfax guessed from the clothing. Only the upper body was visible, face beatific, hands raised in prayer. But Korfax found himself studying the eyes. They were cold and glinted like ice. He stood back from the painting. Had the Balt Kaalith been pleased when they eventually saw the finished article? Korfax decided that they would have been. All the Balt Kaalith seemed to be carved from the very same stone, and judging by this work alone it certainly seemed that Manneh had agreed with that summation.

He was about to move on when a voice came from behind him like a hidden satisfaction.

"Geyad Korfax! You are here at last! Good! Most good! And how do you like my little collection?"

Korfax turned about and bowed as Geyadril Fokisne stepped out of the shadows. Fokisne was smiling and Korfax thought it somewhat smug, but he kept his expression careful. It was not his place to judge.

"My apologies, Geyadril," he answered. "I was distracted."

Fokisne laughed.

"Nonsense, you have an eye for beauty, much like your father, I think. Whenever he comes here, he always stops to gaze at that particular piece. Though I believe he also has a liking for the Rendaran which hangs in my dining hall."

Korfax looked down.

"I was asked to come..."

Fokisne raised a hand.

"Of course, of course, I know you were. But allow yourself a little time between duties, Korfax. Admire beauty when you see it. It enriches the soul, it revitalises and rejuvenates. And from what I have heard of your adventures, you have much need of such things."

Korfax felt a sudden clench take him. He shook it off with difficulty. He hoped Fokisne would not demand another retelling.

"My time at Piamossin was not what I expected it to be," he said. "Many died."

Fokisne looked away. It was his turn to look uncomfortable now.

"I know that, young Geyad, I know. But you survived the trial and that is all that need be said of the matter. Did not Karmaraa suffer defeat before the end?"

Then Fokisne smiled warmly and gestured to the far door.

"But now is not the time for pain, Korfax, now is the time for reflection and restoration. And you need restoration, as I said before. Beauty is a great restorer. And speaking of beauty, you must come with me now, for the Geyadel and his daughter await us both."

They went through the tower, through halls, through corridors, until they reached a door into the gardens. Here was Abrilon. Beside him was another, tall and robed as an Uren. Abrilon smiled as Korfax approached.

"Korfax!" he announced, looking back at him brightly. "May I present my daughter. Here is Uren Kallus Pasen Obelison."

Abrilon looked proudly from Korfax to his daughter, but she kept her eyes down. Abrilon smiled slightly and spoke again.

"Obelison? This is Geyad Faren Noren Korfax, of whom I spoke. He is one of the best of us, a fighter of demons, one of the very few and a certain candidate for the Geyadrilith, I think."

Korfax bowed low, glancing at the Geyadel as he did so. Geyadril? That was the first he had heard of it. He had only just become Geyad! But when he looked at Obelison again and met her eyes, all other thoughts fled his mind.

He wondered what he could say to her, but there seemed nothing that he could. There was no expression on her face, but it seemed to him then that he knew her, everything there was to know, all at once.

Abrilon smiled slightly, his eyebrows raised. He looked from one to the other and back again, his eyes gleaming with pleasure.

"By the powers, I have never seen the like before. Are both of you struck dumb? Do neither of you retain the power of speech at all? Maybe if I leave you together and come back after my duties permit, the pair of you will have recovered your composure somewhat."

Korfax dropped his gaze at last and blushed. Abrilon laughed quietly and laid a light hand on Korfax's shoulder. There was a look to his eyes now, a fond look that reminded Korfax of his father. He suddenly found himself uncomfortable under that gaze. It was far too familiar.

"My daughter has not seen the gardens here yet. I am sure she would like an escort and a guide, but what do you say, my young Geyad?"

Korfax swallowed. He had never seen the gardens either.

"I would be honoured, Geyadel."

He said the words without thinking. Abrilon smiled warmly.

"Then I shall leave the jewel of the house of Kallus in your care. Obelison will be in the safest of hands, I am sure. But I and Fokisne will expect you both for refreshment between the hours of Safaref and Ialaxan. You will find us in the south hall."

They walked through a scented realm as though they were a single being. Even if he had been alone, Korfax would have enjoyed the garden, but now he felt himself transported to some mythical place of delight. With Obelison at his side, it was as though he had crossed the great divide and now walked beyond the great river itself, adrift in the blessed realms.

Obelison did not say a word, and neither did Korfax, but their minds touched and through no fault of their own became entangled. Like a stream rushing headlong to the sea, like the fall of snow upon the mountain, it seemed altogether inevitable. Korfax had never known the like before.

At the end, when they came to the door of the south hall, he bowed to her and she to him. But their eyes met again and they both suddenly drowned in the sight. In all that time not a word had been spoken. There had been no need.

For the next few days Korfax spent all the time that he could with Obelison. When he was not with her, he ached to be at her side. When he was with her, he ached whenever he looked at her. Her beauty pierced him, a pain he almost could not endure and yet greatly desired. Heedless of the world around him, he found her to be the only world that he wanted. And, wonder of wonders, he knew she felt the same.

Abrilon watched, as he always did, from a high window, watching his daughter with Korfax. She was happy, he could see it, the light filling her, gentle fires behind her eyes, and that pleased him more than he could say. He blessed her and he blessed Korfax for bringing her that joy. Occasionally Fokisne would stand with him, watching also, summoning up the courage to speak. Eventually Abrilon gave him the excuse he needed.

"This is more than I could have hoped for," said Abrilon, gazing down.

"Are you not being somewhat precipitate?" Fokisne dared. "What will Sazaaim say? Or Tazocho?"

Fokisne wondered if he had dared too much, but Abrilon merely smiled.

"It is not up to them. It is up to Korfax and Obelison."

Then Abrilon looked sad.

"Would that her mother were here to see it! It would have pleased her so much. One of the Farenith. She would have laughed at the joy of it. Fate was ever inscrutable."

Fokisne agreed.

"Your daughter is like her mother in many ways," he said. "Enay Zirad was a rare jewel, one of the rarest."

But Abrilon did not answer and his eyes were suddenly hard.

Obelison sat alone, deep in thought. The last few days had been wonderful. She had not imagined that it could be like this. What was it about him? Why him? And yet it was obvious, inevitable, a thing beyond words. They had not needed to speak. They seemed to know everything there was to know about each other. But now she was scared.

A vision had come to her, unsought, demanding and powerful. She had been taught how to seek – that was the primary ability of an Uren – and she was good at it, but a vision that came of itself? That was another matter entirely.

This was her first. Her tutors had explained it, one even describing it from a personal perspective, but to experience it was another matter entirely. It was as though the world had unfolded before her, drawing back to reveal what lay underneath.

She thought about Korfax. He had already faced great danger in his life following the attack upon Losq and the siege of Piamossin, but now she would cause him to face even more. Though what she had seen was stark, she had no choice. This was her calling.

She had to record the vision, pass it on and have it verified whilst it was still fresh in her mind, so she took out a blank uranadar and touched it with her thought. The clear stone darkened and began to pull at her. It wasn't a pleasant sensation. She had to stop the stone from taking anything other than her vision, otherwise it would be meaningless. The stone pulled at her blindly, mindless and unthinking, and she resisted except for the requisite memories, ordering them and then releasing them piece by piece. It took a long while and she was tired by the end of it, very tired, but she had done it. She held up the uranadar. It was opaque. Her first vision.

She felt split in two. She was proud of what she had just achieved, but scared for herself and for Korfax. How she cared for him. It was as though he had become a part of her, a most necessary part. She thought of her choices. Should she share this vision? But it was no choice. She had to share, it was vital. No one had ever seen anything like this at all.

She went straight to the Tower of Sight in Othil Zilodar and sought out Nimagrah, first Urendril of the city. Nimagrah looked up as Obelison entered. She saw the signs and was immediately on her guard. The set of Obelison's features, her posture, the look of clarity in her eyes – Obelison had had an unsought vision.

She was very young for this to have befallen her. It was not unknown, but it wasn't common, and given the way that she looked it had clearly been demanding. Obelison came to Nimagrah and knelt before her. Clutched in her hand was a clouded uranadar. Nimagrah turned to the others and flicked a hand. They left immediately.

She came forward and with a quick thought bade Obelison stand.

"A vision!" she said.

"Yes, Urendril, within the last hour," replied Obelison, looking more than usually perturbed. Such things could be greatly upsetting, but Nimagrah could already feel that this was important.

"Show me," she said.

Obelison gave her the stone. Nimagrah pulled at the vision and drank it down. She staggered and then released it. She stared back at Obelison for a long moment and then took a deep breath.

"Come with me," she said. "Your father must see this now. We cannot delay."

Samafaa looked at the Geyadel and sighed.

"What are you doing now, Abrilon?"

"Whatever do you mean?"

Samafaa drew himself up to his fullest height.

"You know full well what I mean! Why do you persist in sending Korfax into the fire? There are many others more experienced. He may be powerful, he may have ridden out the storm of Piamossin, but many will question this, more than the last time."

Abrilon waved a hand in dismissal.

"You have already answered yourself. Korfax has proven himself against the foe. That is why he is here."

Samafaa glowered.

"What game are you playing?"

"No game."

"Then explain this to me!"

Abrilon turned. His face was dark.

"It was my daughter had the vision."

Samafaa drew back.

"I will say no more then."

"That would be wise."

Abrilon took a deep breath, calming himself again. Samafaa did not deserve such approbation.

"I am sorry, my friend, but all will become clear soon enough. To that end I want you to be the one to tell Korfax of his mission. You sent him to Piamossin. You will send him north this time as well."

Samafaa started.

"Why me?"

Abrilon smiled.

"I do believe that I have surprised you at last."

Samafaa sighed.

"Were Sazaaim here," he said, "he would have something to say about this!"

"Sazaaim knows his duty!"

"And I shirk no duty."

"That was not what I meant."

"Then why do you ask me to do this again?"

"Because you are not me! Korfax, like all the others of our order, expects nothing but duty from you! Besides, I am too close. She is my daughter, after all. Kommah is one thing, but this is quite another."

"Is it kommah? They are both very young."

"It is, I have seen it. Nimagrah has seen it, too."

Samafaa looked down.

"Well, if that is what it is, then so be it!"

He looked up again.

"I will do as you ask."

Abrilon smiled and then held up his hand.

"One other thing. Korfax must not know of the latest developments in the north."

"Now what are you doing? Why should he not know that no other tower has been attacked? Why should he not hear that even Angalam has seen neither hair nor hide of the foe? Surely he will wonder when he learns of it."

"He will believe what you tell him. It could simply be that the Agdoain are regrouping. After all, they suffered a great defeat at his hand. Korfax will appreciate that, I think. But I do not want him to know what I suspect."

"What?"

"That he is the stone that starts the avalanche!"

Samafaa scowled.

"I have never agreed with you on this matter. There is no pattern here, merely circumstance. The Agdoain attacked Piamossin because they were commanded to do so. And they have not attacked anywhere else because they were defeated there."

"No," said Abrilon. "That is not how it is at all. The Agdoain react to him, I am certain of it. And since you do not believe it, you are the best one to tell him, for you can tell him the truth as you see it."

"Then I have a question for you."

"And what is that?"

"What troubles you? You are concerned, I can see it."

"And I am not sure that I should tell you this. There were worrying things in the vision, dangerous and disturbing."

Samafaa spread his hands wide in the gesture of service.

"A burden shared is a burden halved."

Abrilon smiled at the thought.

"Have I ever told you how much I value your support?"

"You are the Geyadel. You do not have to say anything."

"Thank you for that, my friend, thank you greatly."

Korfax received the summons late. It was almost the time he was supposed to appear before Samafaa. He ran all the way to the Spire of Duty. Samafaa was waiting for him.

"Korfax, good, you are here at last!"

Korfax bowed hastily.

"My apologies, Geyadril. I did not receive word until a few moments ago..."

Samafaa held up a hand.

"Do not concern yourself with excuses on my account. I am not interested in such things. That you are here, now, should be all that matters."

Korfax bowed again, more slowly this time.

"Good," said Samafaa. "I have summoned you because I have a task for you."

"A task, Geyadril?"

"We have intelligence that these Agdoain are coming from a single place, somewhere to the far north-west. We want you to find this place and destroy it. This will be a mission of stealth, so only a few will travel with you."

Korfax frowned.

"Given what happened at Piamossin, would it not be better to march into the north-west with an army?"

Samafaa smiled grimly.

"No, that was not foreseen."

Korfax paused. Foreseen? The Exentaser were involved?

"There was a vision then?"

Korfax waited, but Samafaa said nothing. He kept his face still and waited as well. If this had come from the Exentaser, why hide the fact? He looked expectantly at Samafaa, but Samafaa still did not move. It was well known that Samafaa did not approve of the Exentaser, so perhaps he did not approve of this? Korfax decided he would wait for his answers.

"Who shall go with me?" he asked.

Samafaa seemed to relax ever so slightly. It was the right move. What would Samafaa do next?

"Only a few. Who would you trust on such a mission?"

That was easy and required little thought. His choices were obvious.

"Those that I know. Branvath Orkanir and Napei Ralir come to mind. Orkanir knows the north better than most and Ralir is the best with a sword I have ever seen. I would trust either of them with my life."

Samafaa looked somewhat unsettled, and Korfax could guess why.

"They were in the vision also, weren't they?" he said.

Samafaa's reaction told him all that he needed to know. There had been a vision. He remembered what his mother had told him regarding such matters. The more specific the vision was, the more dangerous it was to ignore. Samafaa was testing the vision.

"Geyadril, if I may ask? Why is it that you do not trust the Exentaser?"

Samafaa reared up, his eyes blazing.

"And that will be enough of that!"

"I should know everything, Geyadril. What one does not know can be fatal."

Samafaa receded a little.

"It is simply that I do not trust what I do not understand. Their visions are like the touch of chaos. Every time they speak it is as if they overturn the order of the world."

Korfax could appreciate that much, at least. Samafaa enjoyed certainty. Visions were uncertain, even the best of them, hiding more than they revealed. One could follow the path and yet find it taking you to quite unexpected places. Some even considered them malicious in the way they twisted the outcome.

Samafaa sighed.

"You are right, of course. You should know everything. Urendril Nimagrah told us about it first."

Korfax was careful to keep his face neutral, but Samafaa was on his guard as well. As much as he enjoyed certainty, he hated subterfuge, especially in others.

"So what I am about to tell you now goes no further. Do you understand?"

Korfax bowed his head.

"Of course, but I never discuss the business of our order with others anyway."

Samafaa seemed somewhat satisfied with that, but something was clearly bothering him still. They regarded each other for a moment and then Samafaa scowled.

"And if you think you can read me as easily as that then perhaps I no longer need to tell you anything more."

Korfax was tempted to withdraw, but then he decided he would be bold instead. Plain speech was the best way to Samafaa's heart.

"I have seen the truth this far, have I not?"

Samafaa glared for a moment, but then suddenly gentled.

"Korfax, I will tell you something. I like you. We have seen each other, you and I. You have seen that I do not like to hide things and I have seen that you seek the truth at all times. I find that good! Indeed, I find that excellent! We are of a kind, you and I. We respect what is. We respect the unalloyed truth."

Korfax bowed his head in acknowledgement.

"It was as I was taught," he said. "When someone lies, they murder a part of the world."

Samafaa smashed his fist upon the table. It was so quick and unexpected that Korfax all but jumped back.

"EXACTLY!" Samafaa roared. "And you do not know how glad I am to hear you say it. I thought our order buried under layers of obfuscation until the Agdoain came. Now that we have a true enemy, true purposes are revealed at last. Ask your questions, I will hold nothing back that you need to know. Damn the consequences!"

Korfax relaxed. He was inside.

"Visions of the north are rare," he said. "My mother told me that she sees nothing, literally nothing, when she looks. The only other who has seen anything at all is an Uren called Payoan, but she is still in Emethgis Vaniad, or so I thought."

"This vision is not hers. Instead it was Abrilon's daughter who saw this. Who else did you think it could be?"

Korfax started. Samafaa clearly knew about him and Obelison. Was everything he did common knowledge? He leaned forward and glared at Samafaa.

"Am I being spied on?" he asked.

Samafaa glared back.

"Of course not! There are no spies in the Dar Kaadarith, as you well know. You have merely been observed, that is all."

Samafaa leaned forward himself.

"Is that anger I see?"

Korfax did not move.

"And are you surprised?" he returned quietly.

"No," said Samafaa. "I would feel much the same as you do now."

They both looked at each other. Korfax was the first to break the silence.

"I seem to have been 'observed' all my life. I had hoped that by becoming a Geyad I would have earned some measure of trust from those around me."

Samafaa offered up the merest hint of a smile in response.

"But you are wrong, Korfax," he said. "That is not how it is at all. You are trusted, greatly. But do you not appreciate how unique you are? I know of no other Geyad who has experienced the things you have, nor had the hand of fate point at him as it points at you. Of course there are many who watch you! Who would not? But I shall tell you this also. In this matter only a few are privileged to know, the veriest few."

Korfax bowed his head and swallowed. The hand of fate – Samafaa was right. Things did indeed seem to happen to him. Not for the first time he found himself wondering why that was.

"Then I apologise for my anger," he said.

Samafaa smiled.

"There is no need. I understand entirely and I thoroughly approve of your displeasure. I would not like to be in your position either, but that is how it is. To each is given their due."

Korfax took a deep breath.

"So then, what are the details?" he enquired.

"That you are to cross the Adroqin Vohimar in the furthest north. That you will find mighty ruins set within a dark land. And there you will find the genesis of the Agdoain."

"Just that?"

"Just that."

"It seems perilously little to go on. The furthest north is far larger than many realise. On the west side of the mountains it is wild and little travelled. There are no great ruins either. The only thing left of any consequence is the Forujer Allar, and I am told there is precious little left even of that."

"No," said Samafaa, "nor is there anything on the maps either, not even those that were made before the wars. It is a mystery. But that is the vision."

"Could Obelison not be mistaken? She has only just become Uren, after all."

Samafaa folded his arms.

"I may not approve of the involvement of the Exentaser, but I have to respect their abilities and their powers. I have to, as too many times have they shown us the way. I am told that this vision is strong, very strong, and Nimagrah herself was shaken by it. But even so, we should err on the side of caution. Since it is clear that something is going on in that part of the world, we should investigate. If we send in a large force, no doubt it will not find anything. A small force, though, a few individuals? They might go unnoticed and so uncover the truth."

"What of a sky ship?"

"Also not seen."

Korfax waited. Samafaa seemed curiously coy about the details.

"May I see the vision?"

"No," said Samafaa, "you may not. Even I haven't seen it. Nimagrah gave Abrilon the uranadar directly, and he has shown it to no one else. I do not know why."

Korfax took a step forward. It was involuntary, perhaps, but his stave was now before him. Samafaa held up both hands to halt him.

"Peace, Korfax. I know this is difficult, but you must remember that Obelison is his daughter. It is for him to say. There may have been things of a personal nature in the vision, things that neither you nor I nor any other should know."

Korfax subsided. That was true enough. He looked out of the window and then back at Samafaa.

"Are there no further directions? Must I trawl the furthest north until I find what I am looking for?"

"Perhaps, but then again, perhaps not. There is a brief glimpse in the vision of a most strange place. Abrilon told me that he had never seen anything like it before. There was a great wilderness of hills and valleys, and all the hills were topped by strange spires of stone."

Korfax looked up.

"A wilderness of hills topped by spires?"

He smiled.

"Ask any of the north and they will tell you exactly where that is – the Leein Patinalad, it can be no other."

Samafaa returned the smile.

"Well, if nothing else I am easier in my mind. You complement the vision."

"Yes," said Korfax, "and I can tell you something more. That far north there are only two passes over the Adroqin Vohimar: the Pisea Gruen and the Pisea Fal. That narrows things down even further."

He took a deep breath.

"When do I leave?"

"As soon as everything is in place. Once all is set a sky ship will take you to Leemal."

"But what of Orkanir and Ralir? They should be told."

Samafaa paused for a moment.

"Messages will be sent. I will make sure that the order goes through and that they will be ready when you join them."

"No need, just tell them who it is that asks. Ralir will do it because he is my friend and Orkanir will do it because my life already belongs to him. He saved it once before."

"I know," said Samafaa. "The trust of good friends is sometimes worth more than an entire army at one's beck and call."

Korfax stood up to leave but then Samafaa held up a hand.

"One other thing."

"Yes, Geyadril?"

"You are to take qasadar with you. They also were seen in the vision and they will, apparently, be vital to your success."

"Qasadar?"

"Indeed."

Destroying stones? That was unprecedented. Korfax pondered their nature. Difficult to make, difficult to use – everything about qasadar was difficult. They had not been used in anger since the end of the last war. With hearts of pent-up

426

fury they were the most potent weapons of offence made by the Dar Kaadarith, and the most dangerous to wield. Once set in motion they could not be unset again and they would do exactly what their name implied. They would destroy everything within their range. And their range was very great.

"Are they here?"

"We wait for them," said Samafaa. "Given how long they take to make it was thought best to send some here from Emethgis Vaniad rather than embark upon a forging. Luckily there were four still in the archives. Once they arrive you will be off to Leemal."

Samafaa placed a heavy hand against the table and sighed. He had not told Korfax everything, but then he had been told not to. What would Korfax have made of the tale of the guiding hand? Or of Obelison's insistence that she accompany him? That was in the vision also, but Nimagrah had been less than forthcoming about the details. Abrilon, of course, had said nothing at all. Samafaa scowled. Visions? They were the very touch of chaos!

17

NORTH

Ur-ho-drm Krih-ipaj-ooch
Vix-a-von Odtal-ahan
Iamho-ask Od-avdoa-luj
Zak-od-ran Oded-pei-ihd
Nihon-lai Lon-pi-inarm
Rit-hus-tol Sorar-ged-vep
Ur-ia-a Sor-lim-usith

Korfax arrived in Leemal to find Ralir already waiting for him.

"You received the message then?"

"Yes, Orkanir and I have been getting everything ready – the steeds, the provisions... the wine. We are ready to go."

Korfax looked up.

"The wine?"

"A jest, Korfax."

"I hope so, for your sake."

There was little time for talk. Ralir went to join Orkanir and Korfax went to see his mother.

"This is how it is with your father," she said. "I see him briefly and then he is gone."

"I am sorry, I have a mission."

"I know."

He paused.

"Mother, I need to tell you something before I go. I have... met someone."

She looked at him fully, that seeing look he knew all too well.

"I know about that, too," she said.

"You do?"

She smiled, a strange smile, almost wistful.

"I know all about Obelison, my son. You have been spending much time with her, I hear."

"But who told you?"

"Can you not guess? It is why I know of your mission. Why do you think Ralir and Orkanir were ready for you when you arrived? Messages have been passing backwards and forwards ever since Obelison had her vision. It is no small matter."

"Does everybody discuss everything that I do?"

"No, not everything and not everyone; only the things that matter."

She went to him and placed her hands on his arms, holding them firmly.

"Do not think on it. Just make sure that you return safely. Be well, my son."

"Be well, my mother."

They embraced and he left. She watched him go and pondered on his leaving.

He went to the wall garrison, where he found his steed waiting for him. Orkanir and Ralir were also ready and waiting. It was time to leave.

They took the high road to the north, not the low as they had when aiming for Piamossin. There was a strong wind against them, strong and cold as though it wished to impede their progress. In the sky above dark clouds swept over them, covering the land from horizon to horizon, a rush of tumbling forms.

Ralir looked about him.

"This could be a hard land if it wished, I think," he said.

Orkanir agreed.

"It has its moods, but even in its rage it still has beauty."

Ralir smiled.

"And you will not find me arguing with that," he said.

It was as they came to the long rise before the Leein Patinalad that Orkanir called a halt. He had occasionally hung back from time to time, watching the road behind as if he saw, or felt, something to be there. Korfax watched this with quiet puzzlement, but he knew enough not to ask. Ralir also watched, making no comment either, but Korfax wondered whether his silence was due to some other reason.

"We are being followed," Orkanir told Korfax at last.

Korfax stared back the way they had come.

"How many?"

"One rider."

"Balt Kaalith?"

"I don't think so. This one rides well and tracks us properly, but she is not as careful as she could be."

"She?"

"I have seen her."

"And?"

"She hides herself well enough, but to me she now stands out like a star in the night. Only the Balt Kaalith are as careful as those trained by the Nazad Esiask."

"So who can it be then?"

"I cannot say. It is not for me to guess."

Korfax frowned at Orkanir. Orkanir glanced at Ralir. Ralir frowned back. Korfax looked at them both.

"Well? Tell me! What have I missed now?"

Ralir looked reluctant.

"Knowing your involvement, Orkanir thought it would be better if I was the one to point you in the right direction. But I can't say that I like the prospect. You have a fearsome temper, Korfax, and a fearsome power in that stave of yours. I would not like to suddenly find myself on the receiving end of your wrath."

Korfax sighed.

"Just tell me the worst, will you? This mission was given to me."

Ralir bowed his head.

"Of course, but first let me ask you a question. Whose vision was it that sent the three of us into the north?"

Korfax stared at the ground at his feet. Then he looked up again and glared at each of them in turn.

"Damn the pair of you. Both of you could have said it straight out, without the need for hint and evasion."

He looked back over his shoulders.

"And damn her also. What is she doing here? This is her vision. Doesn't she trust it?"

Ralir leaned across his saddle.

"May I suggest that we wait? Four together are better than one alone, after all."

Korfax turned away.

"And spare me such comfort," he said. "If it is her then Abrilon will have me over a slow fire for this, merely on principal."

The rider approached. Orkanir was right. Even at this distance Korfax could tell who it was. He could see her as if she was standing immediately before him. It was as though there was not a single thing about her that he did not know. She danced in his dreams.

The rider passed him by and Korfax stood up from his hiding place, lifting the silence in his mind. He stepped out into the road and announced his presence.

"Turn about, Obelison. Turn about and explain yourself. This is not well done."

She stopped and drew back her hood. She looked at Korfax and their eyes met. How wonderful the sensation! They met and they merged, mind with mind, thought with thought. His anger could not compete. It shattered upon her shores and crumbled back into his depths. She mastered him, even as he mastered her. He reached out a hand to touch her and she did the same, only for them both to be interrupted by Ralir.

"Yes, not well done at all, really."

Korfax blinked and looked back at Ralir. Obelison had already dismounted and now stood beside her ormn.

"Well done or not, I am here," she said. "This vision was mine, mine alone, and still they denied me."

Korfax turned to her.

"Denied you? Whatever are you talking about? Am I not here? They did not deny you at all."

"But they did," she insisted. "I told them how it should be, but they chose to ignore me."

"And what do you mean by that?"

"In my vision I accompanied you."

Korfax frowned.

"That was not what I was told at all."

Obelison smiled drily.

"And do they tell you everything?"

Korfax turned to the others.

"Did either of you know anything of this?"

"Not at first," Orkanir said. Then he glanced at Ralir. Korfax turned to Ralir and glared at him.

"Ralir?"

Ralir held up his hands.

"What can I say?"

Korfax looked dark now.

"I am in no mood, Ralir, no mood at all."

Ralir offered up the most careful smile that he could.

"Geyadril Samafaa may have mentioned something concerning it, but I wasn't really paying too much attention at the time," he said as he smiled his most winning smile. "You know me, always looking for the next bottle."

Obelison stepped up beside Korfax.

"So they would rather tell a drunken sword than a Geyad? How wise is that?"

Korfax would have answered, but Ralir was quicker.

"Be careful how you insult others, Uren. You are here against better judgement."

Obelison stepped forward as if to do more than answer, but Korfax drew her aside before turning to Ralir himself.

"And you did not think to tell me of this?"

"I was told not to."

He glanced from Korfax to Obelison and back again.

"It all seemed pointless, all of it. Why not say what should be said and be done with it? But I was given strict orders."

Korfax turned away for a moment.

"Trust!" he spat.

Ralir shrugged, suddenly serious.

"Who ever trusts the young? The young are rash."

"But they trusted you!" Korfax muttered, and then he walked away.

Now it was Obelison's turn to glare at Ralir.

"So you decided to keep this to yourself," she accused.

Ralir frowned back at her.

"I did what I was told to do."

"And what of this quest?" she cried. "What of the decisions Korfax will have to make? Do you care nothing for the truth? He has not been told everything, and such a lack of knowledge could mean the difference between success and failure! Did that ever occur to you?"

Ralir gave her a colder look.

"That is how you see it. It is your vision, after all. But have you considered that others might see things somewhat differently?"

"I am of the Exentaser. There is no other perspective. We are the guardians of the sight."

Now Ralir laughed and he did not hold back his contempt.

"Strange as it may seem to you, you are not the world and neither is your order. There are others that are not of the Exentaser and they make up the majority, I believe. Small and insignificant we may be compared to the guardians of the sight, but quite often the rest of us see things that you in your high and mighty towers do not."

Obelison gasped.

"Do you deny our sovereignty in this matter?"

Ralir snorted.

"Of course I do. You think you are the world. I think you are not. Vision is a guide, no more and no less. Nothing is written in stone!"

She placed her hand on the hilt of her sword.

"And for that I will have satisfaction."

Ralir folded his arms.

"Will you now?" he scoffed.

She drew her sword so quickly that she caught Ralir completely off his guard. The sword passed within a hand's breadth of his neck and he staggered back.

"By the pit, lady, careful with your blade."

She assumed the ready stance, sword high above her head, eyes glaring. Ralir stared back at her in complete disbelief. He looked at Korfax.

"Did you see that? Did you see what she just did?"

Korfax came back to stand between them both.

"Enough of this! We have no time for any of it."

"But what of her?"

"Whether I agree or not is no longer the issue. She is here now. She should stay with us."

"What? After that? You saw what she did. Damn near took my head off."

"You heard me! Besides, you suggested this yourself. Four together are better than one alone, remember?"

Ralir gave Obelison a hard look.

"I have been known to be wrong," he said.

Korfax turned to Orkanir.

"What do you think?"

"We cannot send her back on her own. She has been lucky so far, but she cannot trust to luck for ever. The Agdoain roam these lands."

Orkanir turned to Obelison.

"We should take her back. She won't go on her own."

Obelison put up her sword and folded her arms.

"I am here, you know. You can speak to me."

"Then I will say it your face," said Orkanir. "We should take you back."

"No!" she insisted. "Time is of the essence. I feel it. I know it. We must continue."

Korfax frowned.

"But you should go back!"

"And in my vision I accompanied you!"

He looked at the others. Ralir threw up his hands and walked away. Orkanir watched him go and then turned to Korfax.

"It is your decision."

Korfax sighed.

"Then I suppose I must place my trust in the vision. If this was the way it was meant to be, then this must be the way that it is."

He turned to Obelison.

"It was your father, wasn't it? He was the one that refused you."

She did not answer for a long moment.

"I am his care," she finally admitted. "What father would not act so?"

Korfax sighed. What father would not act so, he repeated to himself.

"So," he announced, "here we are then."

She turned back to her steed.

"One last thing," said Korfax.

She looked back.

"How is it you are here? You were in Othil Zilodar. There were no other sky ships coming north."

"I stowed away on yours."

"You stowed away? Steed and all? That should not have been possible."

"I am Uren."

Korfax paused.

"You had help?"

Silence.

"You aren't going to explain it, are you?"

"No," she said. And that was that.

They made camp by a deep river running down from the heights of the Leein Patinalad to the west. The ancient bones of the world lay exposed upon their dark shoulders, rocky masses shaped by long years into coiled and flattened spires. All gazed up at them, eyes drawn to their very strangeness, but Ralir stared the longest, an odd expression on his face. Korfax watched him carefully for a moment, before catching Orkanir's eye and gesturing back towards Ralir. Orkanir bowed his head slightly and walked to where Ralir stood.

"What is it?" he asked. "What do you see? I see nothing up there but the high stones. What are you looking at, Ralir?"

Ralir gestured to the heights.

"The north has suddenly become far stranger than I had ever thought it could be. When we rode to Piamossin we followed the low road and these great heights were hidden from our sight. Then we came to Piamossin, set amongst mountains and forests, and I thought them little different from those that I had seen elsewhere. The north is colder, too, but that is no great surprise either. These strange heights, though..." He gestured at the crouching rocks that waited on each summit above. "I have never seen their like before."

Orkanir smiled to himself.

"Well now, if you think this place strange, wait until we have cleared the Agdoain from the north. Then I will show you the Piral Nodil. If ever there was a land where the mystery of The Creator was made manifest, that is it."

"The Piral Nodil? I have not heard of that either."

Orkanir looked at Ralir with a certain satisfaction.

"Few not born of these lands have. It is a mystery reserved only for those that dwell here. But I warn you. Once seen, it will haunt you for the rest of your life. It is a place of shared covenant."

Orkanir gestured northwards.

"There are hills there that did not grow but were instead shaped by some great hand. They rear up like the prows of mighty ships, ploughing through the sea of the earth, heading ever northwards."

Korfax joined them both.

"I would like to see the Piral Nodil again, but more than that I would like to see the Lee Izirakal once more."

Now it was the turn of Obelison. She came to stand beside Korfax, taking his arm in hers.

"And I would like to see them with you," she said. "To have your home taken from you..."

But she had said too much. Korfax suddenly glared at her, before shrugging her hand away and walking off. Obelison frowned and made to follow, but Orkanir stopped her.

"Do not," he said. "You are here under sufferance. You have added to his cares just by your presence, so do not deepen his wounds further. The Farenith have become a house without a home and few understand what that really means, unless they experience it for themselves. Be careful what you say next, or you will awaken a fire so fierce that even you will be unable to quench it."

The crossing of the Leein Patinalad took them two days, which was better even than Orkanir had expected. Though they seemed to be for ever climbing one long rise after another, they made very good time. They were also fortunate with the weather, for it remained unseasonably mild.

Usually, at that time of year, the heights would be hidden in cloud whilst the valleys in between would be whipped by torrential rain. So it was with some relief that they came to the edge of the western flanks of the Leein Patinalad just as a storm swept in behind them, tumbling its lowest clouds across the wide plateau they had just vacated.

As they dropped to the lowlands the dark clouds increased their grip upon the high hills, covering them in curling mists. The ancient summits of twisted stone looked black now, stark silhouettes set against the sky. It was not long before grey curtains of rain erased them entirely.

The lowlands took another day to cross, the old track leading them through sparse woodland and over rock-strewn moors, and though the going was good, Korfax began to feel a creeping sense of unease. The land about them seemed far too quiet. Where were all the beasts? Since the crossing of the Leein Patinalad they had seen none, either of the earth or the air. Come midday, after he had scanned the wide horizons once again, looking for some sign of movement, he could stand it no longer.

"Where are all the beasts that once lived here? This land was abundant with them. Where have they all gone? They cannot all have hidden themselves away."

Only Obelison answered him.

"I feel nothing," she said.

Korfax looked about him again. There was no further need for words. He knew the others could feel it, for the silence seemed to close in about them, stifling both sound and thought.

They remained on edge all the way to the Peisith Tatanah, but nothing came near, and nothing except an unsteady wind from the east disturbed the quiet lands around them.

Eventually they arrived at the borders of a great forest, which stretched before them like a wall. Orkanir gestured.

"Here it is at last – the Peisith Tatanah. It will take us at least another day to pass through it."

Ralir stared up at the great green ramparts.

"I am with Korfax on this. It is too quiet. The forests of the south are alive with sound, but this place is silent."

Orkanir smiled.

"That, at least, is as it should be. This has always been a place of silence. It is the abode of trees. Little else lives here. Only trees hold sway in Tatanah."

Then he gestured. "Come, let us go on. For one day at least we will not have to fear the weather. Tatanah is yet a sanctuary for the Ell."

They rode through deep darkness. Above them stretched the green whilst below them lay the soft fall of years uncounted. Each footfall was silent, and each tongue also, for the green darkness about them would let nothing disturb its slumber.

They made their way through vast and shadowed halls, children crossing the abode of giants, daring now and again to marvel at each mighty pillar of bark.

They slept in a sheltered glade, safe within the shadows and guarded by the watchful green. They leant against the mighty boles whilst their steeds stood over them, and each entertained a fantasy, thinking that it was theirs alone. But it was not, for they all shared a single vision that the forest still possessed a power to deny even the grey demons. Like an entrenched army it defended its borders with coiled root and weighty limb. Let the foe dare its unsighted boundaries, and the long slow growth of ages would awaken.

They emerged from the great forest the following day and found the Adroqin Vohimar rearing its greater walls before them, low shoulders rising to hard ridges and hard ridges rising to snow-capped summits. A mightier forest than the green perhaps, and far less forgiving, but such was the nature of stone.

They crossed to the foothills and made camp by one of the noisy streams that tumbled down from the heights. It was pleasant, despite the silence, and they relaxed with the fading light of day.

It happened so suddenly that all of them were taken unawares. One moment the peace of the evening surrounded them, seducing them with quiet contemplation; the next, they were engulfed in chaos.

The Agdoain must have crept up silently. It was a small band, no more than sixteen perhaps, but they made up for their lack of numbers by sheer surprise.

As soon as their steeds started screaming, Korfax was up and ready. In moments he had the enemy in his sights, brilliant fire pouring from his stave. The others were only just behind him, their blades drawn, but they did not need to act. None of the Agdoain survived the flames.

The damage, though, had already been done. Only one of the steeds still lived, struggling feebly as it tried to get up. The others were dead, their throats and bellies ripped out. The ground was awash with blood.

Korfax grimaced at the carnage and walked over slowly to the one remaining survivor. But even as he approached Obelison rushed past him and fell by its side, cradling its neck as she sobbed her denial. It was her ormn that she held, Gahlus. He understood and wished that he did not. For all her certainty, for all her defiance, this would be her first real experience of the bloody reality of war. He reached out to touch her, but then withdrew his hand as though fearing she would break.

436

"The wounds are mortal," he told her as gently as he could. "Come away now, I will do what needs to be done."

Obelison only held Gahlus tighter. Gahlus stared upwards, wide eyes full of shock and incomprehension. The ormn's breath came in shudders and her great chest heaved. Korfax turned to Orkanir.

"Please!" he implored. Orkanir bowed his head and came forward. He took Obelison gently aside. Then Korfax knelt beside Gahlus and touched her head with his hand.

"I am sorry," he said. And, as if she understood the words, Gahlus lay still under his touch. Korfax raised his stave and placed it over the ormn's heart. Then he closed his eyes. His power came and went and Gahlus lay still at last.

Korfax stared down with sudden fury in his face. Gahlus had been Obelison's favourite, light of foot, strong and proud. Now Gahlus was dead, blank of eye, still of heart.

Obelison wept long, berating herself over and over again for not foreseeing what would happen. Korfax would have comforted her but he had another task to perform, so Orkanir kept her aside whilst he burned the bodies. Ralir stood beside him during the burning, reciting the prayer of all beasts, but Korfax said nothing at all; his face was set in stone and his eyes were dark.

Orkanir gestured at the last four packs. The others he had hidden beneath a large rock, wrapped and shielded from the damp in cloth of oil.

"Ralir and I have divided the supplies," he said. "We have enough, I think, but the road from here onwards will not be easy. We have to cross the Adroqin Vohimar on foot and then find our way through the lands beyond. It is not an easy journey even by ormn, but on foot it will be especially difficult. I think it will take us many days, and without our steeds we can only carry a little of what might be needed for the return journey. We must be frugal from this time onwards."

Korfax looked at Orkanir and then sat down beside Obelison. Her head was still bowed and she did not acknowledge him. Orkanir looked at them both as though he wished he could say something comforting. After a moment, though, he pointed to the way ahead.

"I should also warn you that there is little shelter in the mountains and nothing beyond. If you wished to find the wildest parts of Lukalaa, you could do no worse than pick where we are now."

Korfax reached out to Obelison and touched her shoulder gently.

"You are certain that it is this way?"

She wiped her eyes and looked up at last.

"I am. This is the way that we should go."

"Even though there is nothing in this region?"

"But I saw ruins, mighty ruins. A shadow lay over them and the genesis of the Agdoain was there."

"I do not doubt your vision," said Korfax, "but I cannot think of any ruins on the other side of the mountains. No one has lived there since the time of the wars. This land was emptied. The old towers were destroyed and all trace of them was removed. Even the stones of the roads were ripped up and scattered. The Iabeiorith were quite thorough in their intent. No one was to use what they had abandoned, so they destroyed it all. All they left behind them were bare bones and old scars. It took a very long time to heal."

Orkanir bowed his head in agreement.

"Only the Forujer Allar remains, but that is now a mere stump of shattered stone. I know, I have seen it."

Obelison suddenly lit up like a beacon and her hands were at her breast as if in prayer. They all stared at her.

"Of course," she sighed, "I should have realised. The Forujer Allar! Now I know why it felt so familiar."

Korfax glanced at Orkanir, but Orkanir was saying nothing. He turned back to Obelison.

"I don't understand," he said.

"But don't you see?" she told him. "Sondehna's birthplace? Where else should one call up the horrors of the Mahorelah but from there?"

"You said great ruins, though!"

"Yes!" she said. "There is a picture in my father's house, a picture by Kasyal. It is entitled 'The Cursing'."

She paused as if that was all that she needed to say, but seeing that all of them were still waiting on her words, her expression tightened somewhat and she carried on.

"Then since you do not know of it, I will tell you how it is. In it stands Anolei, the seventh Velukor, casting the stones of the Forujer Allar down into the sea. The ruins around him are mighty and the earth at his feet fumes as if from recent fire."

Her eyes glinted.

"In its day the tower must have been powerful indeed, fit only for princes, but Anolei was its equal, his stave a thing of fire and his power irresistible. All around him the world was in tempest. The seas were up, wind scoured the land and lightning shattered the sky, but in the midst of the ruins, from out of its very foundations, a black shadow with terrible eyes had risen up, even mightier than he, and it lofted a terrible clawed fist as though to smite him."

She shivered and looked back at Korfax.

"It always scared me as a child. If ever I had to pass through the corridor in which it hung I would always run as quickly as I could, but they took it away after my mother died. I think it was because my father did not want such darkness to remain in the tower. Instead he filled the walls with brightness so that he could imagine her in a better place."

Korfax looked away.

"I did not know that. You never told me."

She looked at him carefully.

"No one outside our house knew it before now, but here, in this place, you need to understand. This is what I saw. It is to the Forujer Allar that my vision is leading me. I just did not make the connection before."

"But it cannot be there!" Korfax said. "It cannot be the Forujer Allar!"

He turned to Orkanir.

"My father went there! Angalam went there! You went there!"

He glanced at Obelison.

"No one saw or felt a thing. It cannot be that place!"

Orkanir bowed his head in agreement but Obelison remained unmoved.

"I do not know the reason why, but that is where my vision has told me to go. There is something in my mind, something to do with time, something about rhythms and seasons."

She looked down.

"I do not know why no one else has found anything there, but of all the places in all these wide lands, does not the Forujer Allar seem to be the likeliest choice?"

Korfax watched her for a moment.

"There is something else, isn't there? Something you have not told us."

"No," she said, but Korfax could already see that was not so.

There was a long silence. Finally Orkanir lifted up one of the packs.

"Well, since we are to go, let us go indeed."

Ralir looked to the heights above.

"So do we take the Pisea Gruen or the Pisea Fal?"

Orkanir looked to the south and then to the north.

"Neither seems promising," he said. "Both are snowbound and the fall looks heavy, even for this time of year. I think our good fortune with the weather has ended."

Obelison looked to where Orkanir pointed, her gaze flicking, like his, from the south to the north and back again. Finally she pointed.

"We take the northerly route," she said.

"You are sure?" Korfax asked.

"Yes," she answered.

Korfax bowed his head to her.

"Then that is the way we should go. The Pisea Fal it is."

Ralir gestured to the south.

"Korfax, is this wise? The southerly route is lower, if the maps are right. If a storm should come in we might fare better if we crossed to the south."

Obelison gave Ralir a scornful look.

"Wise? It is certainly not wise to ignore the counsel of an Uren if you have one with you!"

Ralir matched her scorn with his own.

"You have already missed two things to my knowledge, so I would have thought the answer obvious, but seeing the obvious has never been a trait you of the Exentaser were overly burdened with. You would sooner mistake error for chaos and call it the will of The Creator rather than admit that you were ever wrong!"

Obelison bridled.

"And what do you know of it? I don't remember ever seeing you in the Umadya Zedekel."

"No plan ever survives its execution," he told her, "but I would rather give it all the chances that I could than set it against an obstacle too hard to surmount. I would rather this mission succeeded."

"Well, it certainly won't if you ignore my counsel."

She turned to the others. Orkanir looked troubled, Korfax likewise, though he tried to hide it.

"Do you all doubt me? Is that it?"

Korfax held up his hands in the gesture of placation.

"I trust you, of course I do, but it is obvious that you are also holding something back. Perhaps if you explained? I know that vision is a compelling thing – you fear to say too much, or too little..."

Obelison ignited with rage.

"You know, do you? And when did you study the Namad Soygah?"

Korfax took a deep breath.

"My mother has been one of the Urenith much longer than you. She entered the realm of sight over a hundred years ago. Can you say the same? She has had many visions in her time, and she has tried to explain it to me on more than one occasion. I know more than you think!"

But Obelison was not to be put off.

"Even so, have you experienced this thing for yourself?"

Now it was his turn to look angry.

"Strange as it may seem to you, I also know what it is like to follow a single path. I did so at Piamossin, ignoring the advice of others, and look what happened there. I hope that this journey does not teach you so bitter a lesson as the one I learned. For your sake I hope that you are right. I hope that we do find the genesis of the Agdoain at the Forujer Allar, but you should also prepare yourself for other eventualities, failure not the least."

Korfax stood in front of her and looked deep into her eyes.

"Just as there are things I do not know about you," he said, "there are things you do not know about me."

She would have remonstrated. Had their minds not met? Had their souls not entangled? But Korfax was now somewhere else, somewhere she could not reach.

"Ask yourself one simple question," he said. "Why are we here? Is it not because of your vision? I have already agreed to support you in this matter."

He pointed a finger at her.

"But," he told her, "you have defied. There will be a price." He looked away again. "There is always a price," he muttered.

She did not mistake the bitterness in his voice.

"And what price might that be?" she asked, daring him to answer, but when he looked back at her again there was flame in his eyes. She felt herself go cold inside.

"What price, you ask? A thousand died at Piamossin because I defied an edict and stirred up the enemy. Now they haunt my dreams."

He held up his hand in warning.

"You have defied the will of your father. Now you must abide by the consequences, be they good or ill."

She tried to face him down, even on this point, but he did not flinch and she was the one to turn away at last. He had hurt her, more than he had intended to perhaps, but rather than berate him she suddenly found herself cursing her own choices. He had been where she had yet to go.

They climbed the long ridge, following a wide but uneven path. Only its flatness kept them on the right track, for little else remained of what must have once been a mighty road. The Iabeiorith had been utterly ruthless in their retreat it seemed, removing everything behind them, even the road, as they withdrew to their ancient fastnesses at the edges of the world.

To Korfax it felt as though they were stepping ever further back into the deeps of time, walking slowly, inexorably, into the unrepentant heart of evil. They struggled now across the veriest foothills, the last of the gentle lands before the unscalable heights that guarded the last stronghold of shadow.

Here was the only part of the north that had never been made over by the victorious west. Almost every other city, tower or house had been rebuilt after the wars, rebuilt from the destruction and rebuilt as new. The roads had been remade, and every void left by the ancient darkness had been filled again with light, except for here. And the only reason that the Forujer Allar had survived at all was because it still had one last purpose to serve. It remained as a reminder, one of the very few, of what had once been. Like some recrudescent nightmare its horrid bulk became the brief focus for the ritual of the cursing, briefly done and then forgotten, until the seasons turned and turned again, seven times seven.

The cursing. It was the ritual of reaffirmation. Every forty-nine years the Velukor or his representative would come to curse the last black stones of that ancient fortress. Then, ceremonially, another part of its crumbling foundations would be tipped into the sea below to be washed clean of its evil, and from what Orkanir had said there was precious little now that remained of anything.

They arrived at the end of the long ridge and so came to the beginning of the pass itself. The climb before them was both steep and forbidding, turning slowly to their right as it wound its way up into the mountains beyond. They stood upon the last shoulder for a moment, pausing and marking the way to go. Orkanir looked back as if to bid the lower heights farewell, but then he roundly cursed their fortune. The others looked at him and he pointed upwards. They looked where he pointed. Words were unnecessary.

A great line of black cloud covered the sky behind them, stretching from the furthest north to the uttermost south, whilst beneath it hung a dark curtain of deepest grey. A great storm was sweeping in, a furious storm out of the east.

The dark edge of the cloud passed quickly over their heads and a howling wall of snow followed in its wake. The cold of the wind cut them like phantom knives, and its passing chilled them to the bone, even through their heavy cloaks. Korfax raised his stave and called up both heat and shelter, heat from his stave and a net of winds to surround them all. He smiled in gratitude as his power held the tempest at bay, a bright sphere of warmth against the oncoming night. So they drew in about him and walked on, shielded from the storm whilst the air grew dark and the snow ever deepened underfoot.

Into the darkening night they made their way, through the mounting storm, but by the early hours of the morning Korfax found himself beginning to struggle. Each step he took became shorter than the previous one, and each breath he took was more ragged than the last. The sheath of winds he held about them started to weaken, and the heat from his stave diminished by equal moments.

All of them made attempts to persuade him to rest but he refused. Every time he glanced at Obelison he reminded himself that time was of the essence and that they must keep going. He had to be strong now, he had to endure.

It was as he approached exhaustion that Obelison finally got him to pause.

"This is no good," she said. "You will kill yourself if you continue. You have been at it for half the night and we have still to reach the head of the pass."

Orkanir agreed.

"You really should rest. We will find shelter somewhere, back below the edge of this rise perhaps."

Korfax bowed his head and his voice came back to them as little more than a hiss of pain.

"But there is nothing here. There is nowhere to hide. There is no place to shelter. You have looked. Ralir has looked. We must travel the Pisea Fal. We have no choice. We must pursue this vision."

Obelison looked at him with dawning horror.

"Do you do this because of me? Do you intend to teach me consequences now?"

Korfax dropped to his knees, and as he sank to the ground so his power fell away entirely. His net of winds died and bitter cold swept in about them all.

"No," he whispered hoarsely. "I do not, but your vision is what drives this quest. You said that it was a matter of time, so I begrudge any that is lost. I failed at Piamossin. I refuse to fail here."

"But by doing this you have cost us! Who else can use the qasadar?"

"And this is your vision. Is there something you have not told the rest of us?" he murmured, bowing his head.

She drew back from him and looked at the others. Neither Ralir nor Orkanir spoke, but their eyes shone with an identical light. Consequences indeed.

Orkanir and Ralir made a shelter of sorts, raising up the snow about them in a circular wall. Obelison brought out a purgadar and set it in motion. It held the cold at bay somewhat with its heat, but the unthinking malice of the storm howled in the air about them and did not relent.

Korfax sat before the heat stone and shivered as he hugged himself. Even wrapped in his heavy cloak he was cold. He had lost too much of himself to his power. His face felt as if it had been reduced to mere ice, brittle and unmoving, but down inside, deep down, he felt the ghost of a rueful smile.

Obelison handed a meal cake each to Orkanir and Ralir as they came back from their labours to sit before the heat stone. Then she took one for herself and one for Korfax. She offered it to him.

"In a little while," he whispered. "Give it to me in a little while. I am too tired yet. I need to rest."

Korfax closed his eyes and felt a sudden drowsy warmth fill him. Obelison reached forward and shook him.

"No, Korfax! Do not sleep! Not here! Not now! You must eat!"

He struggled with himself. How good it would be to surrender to the weariness. How good it would be to sleep, but then he remembered that the cold would take him if he did and he would never awaken again, despite the comfort of the heat stone.

"Eat!" she insisted.

Korfax forced himself to take a bite. He chewed. He swallowed. Then, after a moment, his eyes brightened a little. So she held him up and helped him eat the meal cake, little by little. And as he ate, the pain returned.

Orkanir knelt beside her and watched, his eyes glistening. Ralir watched Orkanir and felt jealous as never before. Korfax was his friend, his friend of friends, but Orkanir had a prior claim he could never surmount.

Obelison held Korfax tight and tried to bolster his will with her own.

"He is drifting away," she said. "I cannot counter this, not here."

She looked up in panic at Orkanir.

"Help me, please."

He knelt beside her.

"Keep him warm. Hold him close. This night, this cold, it cannot last for ever. Keep him warm. Keep him with us."

She sent her mind back into his, but it was hard work. He had barriers about him, cold barriers she could not penetrate. He had all but succumbed to weariness. She took out another purgadar and held it against him, touching him with its warmth as she touched him with her thought. *Stay with me*, she implored.

"I am trying," he answered faintly.

So she held him close, battling against the flood and feeding his failing fire, hoping against hope that another answer would present itself.

It was not long after that Orkanir stood up and peered into the storm for a moment.

"Ralir?" he said "I think you should see this! There is a light out there."

Ralir stood up.

"A light? Are you certain?"

"Yes, look! Do you see? There! It comes towards us, I think."

Ralir joined Orkanir and stared out into the rushing darkness. It took him a moment, but then he caught it, a dim and flickering orb bobbing this way and that, fighting its way through the unremitting malice of the storm. And as Ralir watched it, so it grew brighter and larger. It was indeed approaching.

"I thought you said that none travelled these parts."

"I did."

"So what is this then?"

"It is a light that is being carried, so perhaps you should ask a different question: not what, but who?"

Ralir looked darkly at Orkanir.

"Then do you know 'who' it is?"

A pained look crossed Orkanir's face.

"No, of course I don't!"

Ralir turned back to the approaching light. For a moment he glowered at it, but then he glanced back at Obelison.

"So she was right after all," he said under his breath.

Orkanir looked at him in surprise.

"What do you mean by that?"

"Nothing," Ralir answered, drawing his sword.

The bearer of the light came forward. Broader rather than tall, his width was accentuated by many layers of thick furs. Only his eyes were visible, narrow slits that glinted in the deep darkness. He seemed completely impervious to the cold.

"Your companion needs help, I'm thinking," he announced, gesturing towards Korfax. "And maybe you do, too. The Pisea Fal is no place for the unwary, whether they be of the mind, the stone or the sword. This land does not look kindly upon those that treat its perils lightly."

"And who are you?" Ralir asked, his sword before him.

The stranger brushed the sword aside with an easy gesture and stepped forward to look closer at Korfax.

"He has exhausted himself, almost to the death. Foolish and extravagant, I'm thinking, but also brave. How many would dare defy such a storm?"

The stranger turned back to Ralir.

"I heard his unquiet power all the way from the Orpaeith. Proud I thought it, arrogant even, but when I felt it fail I knew that I was needed."

"Who are you?" Ralir repeated, reaching out an arm and grasping the stranger. The stranger shook him off for a second time and laughed. He held up his light. It was an ornate box with crystal sides in which something flickered.

"Trespassers should ever declare themselves first, I'm thinking. I live here. You do not."

The stranger shook his light at Ralir.

"You are trespassers," he accused, but then he lowered his light and looked at Korfax.

"But you are also in need," he muttered, as if need was something he found offensive. For a moment he waited, but then he turned to Ralir again and his eyes were fierce.

"So I grant you a boon. I will give you my name first, if that is what it will take to placate you, but then you will give me yours in return. And if you do not..." He gestured vaguely at the swirling snow around them all.

None missed the implication. Orkanir drew his sword as well.

"You threaten us?"

The stranger turned to Orkanir.

"This storm threatens you, fool! If you do not accept my help then this storm will eat you."

Orkanir lowered his sword again. The stranger bowed slightly as if satisfied and then looked at all of them in turn.

"I am called Mathulaa," he announced, "and that is all you will know of it. I belong to no house, not now."

He looked at each of them again.

"Give me your names then. Once I have them then I will help you, but that is the only way it shall be."

Ralir frowned. This Mathulaa spoke oddly, as though he had fallen through some crack in the world from times long gone. There were kamliadar in the Umadya Madimel filled with voices that were somewhat similar; but to hear dead words imprisoned in stone was one thing, to hear them in the flesh was quite another. Ralir looked hard at Mathulaa and found himself wondering who he really was. Nobody else spoke.

Mathulaa put his box down and folded his arms, fixing Ralir all the while with his angry stare.

"Well now, I have told you who I am and what I require, but all I see yet are four nameless souls in need of succour, unwilling even to pay for it with their very own names. Are you all so lacking in courtesy?"

Ralir sighed.

"I'm sorry, but you are a surprise in this place. I was told..." here he glanced at Orkanir, "...it was believed that none dwelt here now."

Mathulaa snorted.

"Pah! All I am hearing yet is ignorance, and I knew of your ignorance long before I ever met you. So I will only ask once more. Your names?"

There was a sense of finality to the question, so Ralir bowed his head at last.

"Of course," he said. "I am Napei Ralir and this is Branvath Orkanir."

Orkanir inclined his head slightly.

"Here is Uren Obelison."

Mathulaa gave her a knowing smile, but she only frowned back. His gaze was far too familiar for her liking.

"And our companion," continued Ralir, "whose power you seemingly felt, is Geyad Korfax."

Mathulaa looked away from Obelison at last and considered Korfax. His smile faded and a strange gleam came into his eyes.

"Geyad is it? So, I was right – an adept of the stone!"

He paused and then looked hard at Ralir.

"Do you lead?"

"I do not," said Ralir.

"Then who does?" Mathulaa asked.

Reluctantly Ralir pointed at Obelison.

"We follow her vision," he replied.

Mathulaa looked at her for a long time. Eventually she looked away. He smiled, bowed his head and then turned to the others and encompassed them all with a gesture.

"Well now, a flock indeed! One of the mind, one of the stone and two of the sword! And all of them lost on the high passes of the Adroqin Vohimar! Such snowbound achir as yourselves need a guide, I'm thinking."

Here he glanced at Obelison again, before turning away and lifting his light back up.

"So pick up your companion and follow me. There is a cave not far from here where he can be tended and where you will all find warmth and food."

They would not have known the cave was there even if they had passed within seven paces of it. The snow-laden rocks enclosing its entrance looked like every other outcrop that lay scattered over the wide hillside, old and worn and clustered about each other as if for comfort, but in between two of the largest there was an opening, if one stood in the right place. It was not a large entrance, but it was easy enough to pass through, if they entered in single file.

First the floor dropped, following a low downwards passage that went deep into the ground, smooth and well worn. Then, after a fair distance, the passage levelled out again, opening onto a large and well-lit expanse. The cave was almost circular, curving walls of rough-hewn stone reflecting the ruddy light of a large fire in the centre.

Everywhere they looked they saw the signs of occupancy and the trappings of old comfort. Furs covered the larger ledges that dotted the walls, whilst pots and containers filled the smaller ones. There were more furs draped over flat boulders for chairs, and many shadowed objects dangled from the ceiling – implements, dried bunches of herbs and less discernible shapes, all in equal measure. In one corner of the room there was a great pile of dead wood, no doubt set there to feed the fire. There was a hole in the roof, a vent to the world above. Smoke coiled lazily up into it.

All of them looked at the fire with mixed feelings. It was an anachronism, a relic from more distant times, but its luxuriant warmth could not be denied and the glow it gave to the cave was welcoming. In its way it reminded them of the Peisith Tatanah, another remnant of older days that had seemingly strayed far beyond its time.

At the direction of Mathulaa, Orkanir and Ralir lowered Korfax onto a large mass of furs that looked like a bed. Ralir straightened himself back up and breathed deeply.

"I think that your master needs to lose some weight, Orkanir. He has indulged himself in far too much good living."

Orkanir cast a weary eye at Ralir.

"I do not think that Korfax is at fault here; rather, I think the cold has taken its toll upon us all."

Obelison came between them and placed her hand on Korfax's brow.

"He is drifting. He should never have overextended himself like that."

Mathulaa barged his way past them all and touched Korfax on the brow himself. He looked at Obelison and offered her another knowing smile.

"Do not be troubled," he murmured. "I will heal your beloved."

Obelison stood back.

"Who are you?" she hissed.

"You know full well who I am," he whispered, even as he turned, bent like a root. Then he drew himself upright and his face became hard again.

"Now!" he announced. "Let me be about my business."

He pointed his finger at them all.

"And let none of you interfere."

Mathulaa worked quickly and with such facility that Obelison could not follow half the things that he did, despite her training.

Dried herbs were taken from many pots in rapid succession – flowers, leaves and stems, each crushed in his hands and mixed roughly together in a larger pot in seemingly random quantities. One pinch of this, two of that, three of the other. Then water was added and the pot was hung over the fire. While the contents began to cook, Mathulaa placed his hand at Korfax's throat. For a long moment he remained still, breathing deeply and slowly, but then, almost as though he had been prodded with a knife, he stood up and turned to the pot again. He took it from the fire and sniffed the vapours that now rose from within. He grimaced and reached up for something on a shelf above. From amongst many dim curling forms he extracted a strange and oddly shaped root, coiled and twisted as though it had fought back when pulled from the earth.

The root was placed quickly into the pot and the pot was quickly hung back over the fire again as if time was suddenly of the essence. Heady fumes began to fill the cave and Obelison could feel the edges of her senses slipping away. This was some strange drug that Mathulaa prepared. She raised her hand, about to question, but Mathulaa, seemingly sensible of her attention, silenced her with a fiery look. Remembering his earlier warning she did not interrupt again.

After another long moment Mathulaa took the strange root back out from the pot. Obelison could see that the shrivelled thing had swollen, for it looked glossy and fat now, a headless torso set about with strange and fattened limbs. Mathulaa grimaced at it as though it offended him in some way, but then he took the root up and bit it in half. He chewed carefully whilst keeping his hand at Korfax's throat. Then he let out a long sigh and became very still.

A strange sense of heat began to emanate from him, as though he was the one in fever, not Korfax. Obelison finally understood. Mathulaa was doing what the Faxith did. He was passing healing energies into Korfax. Though he was not using an apiladar as a Langar would, the effect was just the same. The essences from the prepared root quickened the energies of life, and Mathulaa was using them to heal Korfax.

Eventually Mathulaa stood up and walked away, rubbing his shoulders with both hands. He stretched for a moment and then sank into a convenient mass of furs. He closed his eyes. He appeared tired but not weary. Obelison glanced back at Korfax. He was sleeping, or insensible, but she did not know which. She looked at Mathulaa again and he opened his eyes, locking them with hers.

"I know what it is that you seek," he told her. "It is the reason I decided to help you. You and I share common cause, I'm thinking. The grey demons killed those that I loved also, killed all of them except for me, but fate has something else in mind for Mathulaa."

He smiled darkly at the thought.

"Though my flock were slaughtered, I was spared. Such things do not happen by chance."

He looked away from her and into the fire, and the flames drew shadows across his face. His eyes stared hard at the flickering red tongues, but no light was reflected back from them; they were wholly dark.

"Your flock?" she asked.

"My people!"

"I'm sorry for your loss, when did this happen?"

Mathulaa did not move.

"Five years past, on the eve of the fourth day of Ahaneh, when Gahburel was but a thin sliver in the heavens. The grey demons fell upon them all and scattered them to the four horizons, but all of them were slaughtered in the end."

Then, as if the memory had poisoned him, Mathulaa passed a venomous glance over his guests.

"And why should any of you care? None of you knew that we even existed. You do not strike me as those that would weep for strangers."

He looked away again and Obelison frowned.

"But why should we not? Your people were slain. Is that not reason enough?"

Mathulaa snarled silently at the fire and his voice became distant as though he had not heard her at all.

"At the end of Adolin under Bataivah they fell upon us, like a pack of mad risson. I should have seen it, I should have felt it, but I did not. Life was good. I had forgotten everything important in my old comfort. I had forgotten that Ahaneh was ever the time of the hunter."

No one spoke for a long while. They watched him carefully, unsure what to say. Finally Obelison leaned forward and managed to catch his attention.

"So what is it that we seek?"

Mathulaa turned to her again and stared back. There was an odd look to his face now, something altogether unfathomable. Obelison felt curiously unsettled by it, as she did every time that he looked at her. It was as though she was continuously being placed at a disadvantage. She held Mathulaa's gaze as best as she was able, though she was far from comfortable doing so. Then, unexpectedly, he was the one to look away first. He laughed quietly to himself.

"You've strength in you, young follower of Nalvahgey, I will allow you that much at least. Your companions are well served by it, but you lack the one thing you need most, I'm thinking."

He held up a long finger and then curled it like a hook.

"Knowledge!" he announced. "Knowledge is what you need. What are the grey demons, yes? Where do they come from? They come out of the wilderness, out of the north-west, creeping over the land to butcher the unwary. And nearly – nearly, mark you – all the way to Leemal they have gone, going where they will and doing what they would as if they already owned the land, but then they disappear again like phantoms. So where do they come from and where do they go? What is their purpose and what are they called?"

Orkanir raised his head slightly.

"We do not know their name. We have called them Agdoain," he said in answer to Mathulaa's question.

Mathulaa turned back to the fire and smiled harshly.

"So, some wisdom lingers yet in the outer world. I also have considered them nameless, but that has not helped me in the end, for whether you remember it or not, one has no power over that which cannot be named. All words are useless in the face of such a foe."

He lowered his voice.

"And they devour both the living and the dead. Abominations!"

Orkanir looked down.

"That has long been known," he said.

Mathulaa smiled unpleasantly in return.

"Have you seen them at their leisure then?"

Orkanir scowled.

"I have not and nor do I wish to, but that was what my Enay found in Umadya Beltanuhm. I was with him and I saw for myself what had been done."

Mathulaa grunted in grudging assent. Obelison watched him for a moment and then pressed him once more.

"So what is it that we seek?"

Mathulaa's eyes flashed.

"Their origin," he said.

"Yes," agreed Obelison. "We believe it to be some unknown pit from the depths of the Mahorelah."

Mathulaa smiled as if at a secret joke.

"No, that is not so. They do not come from that place."

Obelison started.

"But they must! How can you say that they do not?"

Mathulaa looked crafty now.

"Because, child, I have some experience in the matter. More than you, I'm thinking. Can you not guess, young mistress of the mind? We are caught within your vision after all."

Obelison stared hard at Mathulaa, trying to see his thoughts, but the old Ell kept them hidden away. Then Obelison looked inwards, caught by the moment or perhaps the memory. Something that Mathulaa had just said came back to her. 'One has no power over that which cannot be named.' She felt herself wreathed in shadows. She focused on Mathulaa again and he smiled. He was clearly waiting for her to say something.

A movement from behind disturbed them all. Korfax was awake. He was even sitting up. Obelison went to him, holding him to her as if avid for his touch. He returned her embrace, even smiling a little, but all too soon he looked past her to Mathulaa.

"You healed me!"

It sounded almost like an accusation.

Mathulaa shrugged.

"It was easy enough. You had exhausted yourself. I merely fed your fire a little."

"I thank you for it."

"Do you?"

"Yes."

Mathulaa sneered.

"I wonder."

Korfax sat straighter.

"As I awoke, just now, I heard something of what you said."

"You did?"

"Yes, no news of your loss came south."

"Did it not? How strange!"

"You do not fool me."

"And why would I even care to try?"

"So that you can hide what you really are."

"And what have you seen?"

"Perhaps more than my companions."

Mathulaa glanced back at Obelison for a moment and then turned to Korfax.

"Perhaps, perhaps indeed. So now we come to it, young master of stone, the time of testing. Let us see your quality. Let us see who you are."

No one moved and Mathulaa looked back at the others. He broadened his smile into something a little more mocking.

"And how did I find you?" He held up his arms. "And how did I escape the grey demons?" he continued with widening eyes.

Mathulaa made many passes in the air with his hands, a flickering dance of fingers. For a moment, the briefest moment, glowing shapes like the sparks from a fire left a trail in the air as his hands passed this way and that. Strange and threatening sigils glowed briefly and then were gone again, evanescent words that only he understood perhaps. He looked back at Korfax again and his wide smile darkened.

"So know this, young master of stone. I am the last of my kind. There are none now that can follow me, for no other survived, but with your coming the fear of discovery has been lifted from my soul and I no longer care for the consequences. For why should I? The nameless are finally here and we are beset by true demons at last."

Mathulaa dropped his smile altogether and his eyes were now an unlit darkness, a reflection of gleams in shadowed pits.

"And did you really think that there was nought else but a well of souls?"

Korfax drew back from that black stare and Mathulaa laughed as he did so, short and contemptuous, but then he dropped his gaze and looked away.

"You have seen them, I'm thinking. You know of what I speak. You have seen the grey void, just as I have. You have seen the infinite nothing, the place of dissolution. I saw it within you even as I healed you. Its servants have come amongst us at last: the foul, the vile, the upwelling spume. They are the unending hunger, the very heavings of Zonaa itself."

Mathulaa blinked slowly and his eyes became fearsomely bright. If Korfax could have backed further away he would have, but intransigent rock lay behind him and it denied his retreat. Obelison clutched at her seer stone and the colour drained from her face. Both Ralir and Orkanir stared at them both until the truth finally dawned upon them as well. Then they drew their swords and turned to Mathulaa. Korfax did not need to look at his companions, for he could already feel Obelison preparing her shields and defences and he could hear Ralir and Orkanir assume their stances. He stared at Mathulaa and lent his gaze all the power that he could.

"You are one of the Argedith. You follow the Namad Mahorelah. I once swore an oath to destroy such as you."

Mathulaa did not move. Instead he swept his gaze over all of them in turn, his black eyes glittering with contempt even as they burned.

"Blind! Blind!" he accused. "You are blind, all of you! History has buried you. Unthinking tradition has trodden its way across your souls and entombed you in its sightless darkness."

He held up his hands in mock supplication and cried at the hidden heavens.

"Suffer not the Argedith to live?"

He stayed there for a moment, but then dropped his hands again and spat into the fire. He stared at the low flames for a moment. Part of the fire settled and a few small sparks flew upwards.

"And is this how you repay charity?" he muttered. "Is this how you pay for shelter and healing?"

Korfax sighed.

"I swore an oath. We all did, though I think none of us ever thought that we should find ourselves in a situation such as this."

"Your oaths are nothing to me."

"But they should be. If I were to honour mine it would mean your death."

Mathulaa looked long and hard at Korfax.

"And what do you say of your healing?"

"I thank you."

"Is that all?"

"It is all that I can spare for now. I will be held answerable for this."

Then he turned to Obelison.

"As will you. Now I know why you said nothing."

She started.

"All I saw was that help would be granted. I knew that we would find a guide."

She glanced at Mathulaa.

"I just did not know the manner of it. Or the cost."

Orkanir started.

"You saw this?" he asked.

"Yes."

"And you did not tell us!"

"I could not."

"Why?"

"There is a danger in saying too much," she said.

"And one in saying nothing at all!" he retorted.

"You do not understand. It is a difficult path that I walk."

Orkanir looked at her for a moment as if weighing possibilities and then he turned on Ralir.

"Now I see. They gave you the entire vision, didn't they? You knew about this right from the very beginning."

Ralir looked into the fire.

"And what makes you say that?"

"I heard what you said back in the storm. I am not an idiot, Ralir."

Obelison clenched her fists as she glared at Ralir.

"You?" she exclaimed. "They gave you my vision?"

Ralir turned to her.

"I was given explicit orders. I was to act in your stead."

"But... my vision?"

"I was not given all of it, I am sure," he told her. "Only what was needed. Between the pair of us, Orkanir and I could have guided Korfax in the seeking."

"But you do not believe in the vision," she said.

Ralir glanced at Mathulaa.

"I do now."

"Meaningless!" she exclaimed. "If I had not followed, this mission would have been doomed from the start. Korfax would have been led astray!"

"Then blame your father!" Ralir spat back. "It was his insistence that this would be the way of it. What was I supposed to do? Disobey the Geyadel himself?"

Korfax watched Obelison, saw her distress. He understood. She was fighting her way through her love for her father and the thought that Korfax would have failed in his mission if she had not disobeyed. It was a hard place she occupied now. Consequences indeed! Korfax thought again of his own father's words. Abrilon spends others to do his will, Sazaaim had said, but not his own daughter, it would seem.

"There is fault on all sides," he said at last. "Choices have been made and we will all have to live with what ensues, but we are here now and the vision still stands. I may not agree with what has been done, but neither will I judge it. My own judgement awaits me, and that is a far more serious matter."

Here he looked meaningfully at Mathulaa, who scowled for a moment as if he did not understand what Korfax meant, but then he laughed quietly.

"Well said, young master of stone. Come the end we all must pay for our choices. You understand after all. As evil is its own reward, no good deed goes unpunished either."

"What are you talking about?" Obelison asked.

"My oath," Korfax answered. "You heard it from his lips: 'Suffer not the Argedith to live.' It is the word of Karmaraa. By accepting the aid of Mathulaa, by letting him live, I will have broken my oath. And the decision is mine. This is my mission. I will be held to account for that, no matter the outcome."

Mathulaa bowed his head slightly and then stood up.

"Well, you may have allied yourself with me, but you still condemn me in your heart. So, what of your lore?"

"The forces that I commune with were given to us by The Creator," Korfax answered. "They are as natural to us as the stone, the wind, the fire and the water that make up our world. They serve us because they are meant to do so. They are not dragged unwillingly from their place of being and made to act against their nature. The creatures that dwell in the abyss may be unlovely to our eyes, but they do not deserve enslavement and humiliation."

Mathulaa snarled and his eyes burned.

"And yet you of the Dar Kaadarith were ever ready to destroy that which was summoned, I'm thinking, rather than learn how to send it back."

Korfax raised his head up, eyes suddenly imperious.

"We preserve," he said, "we do not destroy. Only when no other course presents itself do we take such drastic action. Only during the war, when each summoning became as a madness upon the land, despoiling and destroying, did we take the dark path of destruction. Better the demons die than our own people, I think."

Mathulaa tightened his expression, looking more like an outraged root now than mere flesh and blood.

"So righteous you are, so very certain of your superiority. And yet what were the Wars of Unification? Now there was a blood-letting upon a scale to terrify the imagination. Few stones were left unturned by that conflagration, or so I was told. Entire peoples vanished as if the ground had opened up and swallowed them whole. And if that was not enough, the Velukor's forces swept across the emptied land like a flood, the songs of death ever in their hearts. Why do you think my people hid themselves away?"

Korfax leaned forward and grabbed Mathulaa by the arm.

"And do you wonder at it? What of Sondehna? What crime did he not commit? Was there ever a truer prince of darkness? What horror did he not summon from the abyss? What degradation did he not heap upon those who dared to deny his will? What lengths would he not go to slake his lust for dominion? Do you truly ally yourself with him?"

Mathulaa threw Korfax off.

"I was not speaking of the Black Heart," he spat back. "Do you always judge others by such absolutes? Not all that followed the Namad Mahorelah believed as that one did – far from it, in fact. Many in the north welcomed the news of his ending, rejoicing that his mad ambition and his lust-darkened heart were ended at last."

Mathulaa seemed to ignite for a moment, his eyes raging.

"Yes, the darkest of the dark was dead, burned by the brightness of the Rising Saviour. What rejoicing there was, what feasts! But then new truths supplanted the old and the all-conquering west proved itself almost as bad. Few had mercy from the forces of the Saviour when they came north in the wake of their great victory!"

He drew back again and his expression became strangely mild.

"So tell me, Geyad, you are from the north. Have you ever seen the ruins of Peis-homa?"

Korfax looked back carefully. The question was far more than it appeared to be, he was certain.

"I have," he answered, "and I am somewhat surprised to hear you mention them. If ever there was a lasting monument to the folly of the Namad Mahorelah, then surely it must be Peis-homa. That was the worst crime of all, the very worst!"

Mathulaa smiled unkindly. Carefully, very carefully, as though he did not wish to disturb the air, he gestured about him.

"Peis-homa was the worst of it you say?" he asked. "You think that her people did not merit their fate? So what would you say to those that still keep the memory of that horror alive?"

Korfax narrowed his eyes, even as he realised how he had been caught. He had just walked into the jaws of a trap, and now he could feel those jaws closing about him.

"What do you mean?" he dared, fearing the worst.

Mathulaa reached inside his robes and drew out an iridescent form. It sat in his hand like a piece of night, ever flickering with the rush of luminous clouds.

"This is an apnoralax," he announced, "a stone of the abyss, filled with stories. In here are many collected lives, all taken from the city of Peis-homa. It has been in the keep of my family ever since they fled that place. I keep it next to my heart always, to remind myself of who I am and from whence I came."

He laughed quietly.

"So, young master of stone, would you like to witness its truth?"

Korfax felt the world tilt about him. A stone of memories from the Mahorelah? What dark pit had he uncovered now?

"Your people fled Peis-homa? But the histories said that none survived."

Mathulaa reared his head in contempt.

"Then the histories know nothing," he snarled, before leaning closer and holding up the iridescent form before him. Its strange light flickered in each of his eyes like a warning.

"We of Peis-homa followed the Namad Mahorelah, just as many others did in that time, but we were innocent of the crimes ascribed to us. And remember, young one, we had been there, in that place, since before the times of memory. Though we held no allegiance to any other we were no threat to them either. We eschewed violence, even during the Black War. Ours was the way of passive resistance. We created; we did not destroy. We spoke with the denizens of the abyss; we did not summon them to work our will regardless. If work needed doing, we asked; we did not compel. And if we were refused then that was the end of it and another way was sought. Peis-homa was the one shining example of what could be, until

Sondehna and his perverted slaves tore it apart and slew its children. Do you wish to see, follower of the Namad Dar? Do you wish to see what few have ever seen since the ending of the Black Heart?"

Without waiting for an answer, Mathulaa made a pass with his hand over the gleaming form and Korfax was enveloped in a swirling vapour. He felt himself falling downwards, down, ever down, as though his body was being sucked into a deep and bottomless pit, but then light grew about him and brightness rose up from below to greet him. There was a rush of sound, a blast of winds, and he suddenly found himself standing in the streets of a city, a city he did not recognise but which looked strangely familiar nonetheless.

Peis-homa reared tall and proud and her aged towers gleamed in the light of the failing year as though remembering golden times long past. Korfax looked about him in sudden wonder, this way and that, taking in all the strange yet familiar sights. He would have stayed there too, caught in the vision, had not someone pulled at his arm to gain his attention.

There was a child beside him, a smiling, laughing child who pulled at his sleeve, beckoning him on, on through the slow and stately crowds and up onto the city walls themselves.

Once there, Korfax found himself looking out over a fertile land, a land rich with orchards and fields. He could have stayed there for a long while, breathing the fragrant air and feeling the light upon his face, but the child did not let him linger. It had a purpose. And so Korfax found himself under a strange compulsion, compelled both to see and to know.

He was taken on a tour, a tour that rushed by like a dream, a fragmented journey through the life of the people of Peis-homa. It was a life, but for the lore that they practised, he found he understood all too well.

Everywhere he looked he saw a people at peace with themselves and at peace with the world, both the seen and the unseen. The conjurations he witnessed were the conjurations of energies only, of heat and cold, of light and dark. How strangely like the Namad Dar it suddenly was.

He saw a mother singing her child to sleep with soft and ancient songs whilst sorcerous lights glided to and fro above the infant's head, beguiling it with the wonder of dreams. He saw an artisan, eyes intent and mind alight, filled to the brim with infinite possibilities as he coaxed a fluted vase of the purest crystal from out of his furnace, summoning its shape with cunning energies gleaned from the abyss below. He saw the city elders, a council of the wise and the just, ever considerate, ever careful, as they made this judgement or that, smoothing the way of those that they served and easing the passage of life throughout their care, the care that was the city of Peis-homa.

Korfax thought of Leemal. Remove the sorcery and it was as though he looked upon Leemal's twin, but he was not allowed to watch for very long, for the child pulled him ever on, back again to the wall and to the unfolding story.

In his absence the view from the wall had changed, for now, out on the wide plain beyond and in the distance, a vast army had encamped itself, blackening the air as though it fumed.

From that dark army a delegation rode up to the city walls to beat imperiously upon her gates with the pommels of their black swords. They waited impatiently for their answer, and their expressions were set ever harder as the moments lengthened.

Eventually, a few of the council emerged from the city and spoke with the dark emissaries. Those of the council were calm and quiet as they offered up their answers, but then their eyes opened wide with alarm as further demands were visited upon them. The council looked at each other and then held up their hands in denial. They refused.

The emissaries snarled with anger and their leader, the herald of their lord, raised up his black sword. Korfax felt the hairs on the back of his neck stand up, for the blade that the herald lofted coiled and writhed in the air above his head like a living thing. It was a qorihna, a demon sword, darkening the dying day with its shadowed radiance.

The world shifted around him as a door, unbidden, opened in his head. He suddenly heard a song of blood and a place of red mists loomed, beckoning to him. The pause was like a blink, a memory within a memory. He closed his eyes and opened them again, even as the unfolding story awaited his attention. He knew what he saw even as the door closed again – the black sword at Losq. The slaying of demons.

So that was the answer! He felt a deeper darkness inside him. His family possessed such a periapt? Why? Why keep it at all? But he could not answer that question here; instead, he must let this tale move on. The memory receded, his attention moved outwards again and the story continued.

With a single movement the herald swept his qorihna down and all but sliced the first of the council in half. Blood erupted, burning blood, a red fountain shot through with inconstant gold. Then each half of the tumbling body crumbled slowly to ash and the heat of its passing was outlined in fire. Mayhem ensued.

The rest of the council erected barriers, thin vapours that steamed upwards from the ground at their feet, barring the invaders even while the ash of their first fell to the earth, but the herald was not done yet. He held up his qorihna again, and that blade elongated to strike at the council's defence. It moaned and whined as it poked and probed, and then it sighed at last as it found its way through the barrier, attacking the nearest with its hungry tip. Through her heart it went, tearing her open as it twisted and writhed within. She danced briefly upon its metal tongue and then fell to the ground in smoking ruin. The others fled back to the gates.

The gates opened and closed, locks were thrown, doors were bolted, energies were summoned and the walls of Peis-homa filled with her sons and daughters, fearful but resolute, armed with sorceries and swords, all now ready to defend her to the death.

Korfax looked to his side and met the gaze of the child, who looked grimly back up at him and gestured at the forces on the wall, before pointing out at the greater forces waiting on the plain below as if to say 'there is no hope.' Korfax stared at where the child pointed and the world flickered about him as though caught upon a flame.

Time became a fluid thing, the acts of days compressing into moments, but even so, Korfax still witnessed the full horror of it all. He saw the fall of Peis-homa.

Sondehna's forces surrounded her, uncounted pavilions of black chased in scarlet, each surmounted by a pennant burning with the crest of the Iabeiorith, a red field and a black Vovin rampant. Scattered amongst these were other, darker tents, wholly black, whose standard was the gyre of the Haelok Aldaria, black upon black, the warrior elite, those who spoke with the will of their master.

Korfax saw sorcerous forms erupt from the encampments, each circling into the sky as though smoke had suddenly discovered purpose. Then, pausing only to solidify, each slipped away from its place of summoning and sped towards the wall.

The defenders fought valiantly, erecting barriers and traps that undid the vaporous forms, but occasionally, just occasionally, one would get through to wreak havoc amongst the luckless defenders. For the vaporous forms froze their victims from the inside out, bursting their bodies with unbearable cold.

Finally, and after much trouble, the things of smoke and cold were vanquished at last and the defenders of Peis-homa breathed a collective sigh of relief, but the respite was brief, for now other forms fell out of the cruel air and shambled towards the city over the plain itself.

Korfax recognised them immediately and shuddered. He knew what these creatures were, for he had seen them before. They were Pataba, unthinking brutes the size of many Ell. Armoured with an all but impenetrable hide and claws like blunt axes, they could scale the walls or even topple the gates, for their strength was like that of living rock itself.

To the walls they came, clambering up them by gouging holes in the hard stone. It looked altogether hopeless to Korfax, but the defenders of Peis-homa had an answer even to this peril. They opened holes in the air above the heads of the Pataba and pulled bright liquids out of the abyss, fuming liquids that tumbled down upon the demons below. The liquids undid the Pataba, corroding and dissolving them, driving them screaming back down onto the plain to die in searing agony. Even then, some of the Pataba managed to reach the edge of the wall itself and so clamber onto the wide causeway that ran around its top. Many of the defenders in those places were torn limb from limb or crushed into the stone or hurled back over the wall, until these last few could be slain as well.

Eventually the Pataba were repulsed, but yet another summoning occurred, and another after that, until the walls of Peis-homa were guarded by those who were not so strong, nor so expert in the marshalling of the city's defence, but none of the forces encamped beyond the walls advanced to the attack, for while they could spend their slaves, the summoned of the Mahorelah, what did it matter? The city would fall eventually, and then her citizens would know the full horror of the abyss before their eventual and inevitable end.

So it continued. Demon horde after demon horde rampaged across the plain to the city walls, or polluted its skies with shapes of nightmare, visiting ever darker horrors upon the city. Korfax watched the faces around him as if now in a wakeless dream from which he could not escape. It was all here – the dread, the hopelessness, the grief. For even if the survivors wanted to surrender, they could not, not now. They were to be an example, held up before the whole world as a sign of what would happen to those foolish enough to defy the will of the Haelok, the will of Sondehna.

So it finally came, when children, their mothers, the old and the last few able to defend the city yet stood upon the walls, when the streets and the towers had been scorched and burned, when all the stones had been drenched in blood, that Korfax witnessed the last terrible pause in the destruction of Peis-homa, that moment when each and every one of its remaining people knew that this was to be their very last day of life.

Towards the city walked a single Ell, clothed all in black except for a burning red jewel that hung at his breast. He was huge, larger than any Korfax had ever seen before. Taller even than Usdurna, broader even than Valagar, this one was a giant amongst the Ell. And across his back was a sword, a great black sword of uncommon size, a blade that Korfax instinctively knew was a qorihna of exceptional power.

Dressed in black, all in black, black armour from head to foot, the great Ell flickered as he walked, like a flame dancing upon a wick. Ripples of energy rode the air about him, clouds that came and went like a continuous summoning. Black and armoured feet planted themselves carefully upon the receding earth, and with each tread the earth fumed.

With a shock Korfax realised who this was, understood exactly who it was that walked alone and unescorted up to the very walls of Peis-homa itself, and he felt the air freeze in his breast. This was it. He would see the ultimate evil at last. It could be no other. Here was Sondehna himself, the Black Heart, the prince of darkness.

But despite all that he had seen and witnessed, all the lessons of his life, all the admonitions and the warnings, Korfax still found himself marvelling, even now, at the grace, the power and the sheer arrogance. Who else would cross such a battlefield alone?

Sondehna walked with that especial care that only the very strongest ever showed, carefully and adroitly as though trying not to wound the world with his passing. Sondehna was mighty, both in the flesh and the spirit. This was no monster of history. This was a living, breathing Ell, true in every line, almost perfect in both his power and his poise.

Though Korfax could not see the face clearly, he was suddenly certain that Sondehna would be uncommonly beautiful, straight of back and clean of limb, a true prince of the Ell.

Finally he halted, just out of bow shot, and for a moment all was still. Nothing moved; nothing dared. Then he raised his right hand and the dead of Peis-homa rose up in answer as if dragged up by chains. Within the city and without, they stood up. In whatever state they happened to be, they raised themselves up and bared their teeth. Burnt, eaten, torn or ripped, they all stood up, warped and decaying, swaying to the music of their summoner's will, their dead eyes burning with mad fire. Then they all turned about and fell, one after another, upon the survivors and tore them apart.

Fathers ate daughters, mothers ate sons and Korfax turned away. He could not witness such sights. He could not. The dead stalked the living. He closed his eyes and vomited up a dream of his revulsion upon the stones at his feet. In Peis-homa, and out of it, the broken dead stalked the living.

After the long screams had stopped, after the horrid lust for flesh had been sated, the world fell silent again. Every last living thing in Peis-homa was dead.

Finally, as the last life ended, so Sondehna dropped his right hand. The dead fell back down again, falling back to the blood-stained earth in a tumble of rot, dead teeth piercing dead flesh, all still wrapped in the cerements of passing.

Sondehna turned away and went back to his army, walking easily over the still fuming earth whilst his slaves dismantled his tents and pavilions, making ready to depart in a sudden fury of fear. And when he arrived back amongst his slaves he mounted his great black steed and rode away to the south, letting his followers creep after him like a plague, whilst at his back Peis-homa reared its ruin to the overcast sky, a broken place at last.

But it was not over yet, for the child had other things to show his guest. He took Korfax into the heart of the city, through streets scattered with the slain and the summoned dead. In the central tower the child took Korfax down, down into the very deepest room, where a circular chamber awaited them. In the centre of the chamber's floor was a motif chased in faded colours, old stone worn out by the passage of time.

The child touched something upon the wall and a part of the floor opened, its singular motif dropping down upon hidden levers before splitting into four parts sliding away into cunning recesses. Where the motif had been the entrance to a tunnel now yawned.

Korfax followed the child down into the earth. The stairs in the tunnel were treacherous, cracked and covered in loose chips, or slick with damp moulds. Through the nighted depths they went until, after what seemed an age, they started to climb.

The climb seemed almost as interminable as the tunnel, but eventually it came to an end. Now Korfax found himself in a shallow cave set in the low hills that overlooked the western side of Peis-homa. Standing at the lip of the cave were a few hundreds, the last of its people, nearly all of them children. There they stood, staring down at their lost city and weeping as though their tears were infinite.

Korfax awoke from the dream and stared back at Mathulaa. He breathed the free air again. He understood.

"Those were your people?" he asked.

"They were," Mathulaa said. "The mothers and the fathers, the daughters and the sons. They were the Korith Peis. Alone, independent, at war with nothing and with no one until the very last days and the coming of the Black Heart."

Obelison looked from one to the other for a moment and then she reached out to Korfax.

"What happened? What did you see?"

He took her hand and bowed his head.

"The fall of Peis-homa," he said. "All of it."

Ralir gestured.

"All of it? All I saw was a shadow pass and then it vanished. You were still for only a moment."

Korfax looked back at Ralir.

"It felt a lot longer than that."

There was another long silence. Korfax stared downwards, clearly shaken. Obelison stood beside him waiting, while neither Ralir nor Orkanir moved. Mathulaa was the first to speak.

"So, now that you have seen it, will you follow me? Will you tread paths untrodden by any others but me and my folk? Will you trust Mathulaa?"

Korfax gave Mathulaa a cautious look.

"I have to, we all do – I do not think we have a choice. I think that this way lies our only chance of success."

Mathulaa looked at Obelison.

"I know that also. I have seen it. That is the other reason I chose to aid you. There is only one path to take and only one vision to follow. She knows."

Obelison looked away from them both. Korfax watched her for a moment.

"Choices," he muttered.

Mathulaa bowed in return and his expression gentled somewhat.

"Choices indeed! I thank you Korfax, for you have repaid my trust in full."

As they made to leave the cave Orkanir turned to Ralir.

"And when were you going to tell me what was in the vision?" he asked.

"I was hoping I would not have to," Ralir told him. "I do not like this any more than you do."

"It is not my place to like or dislike," said Orkanir. "I serve, that is all, but it would have been better if you had shared the knowledge. I know these lands. You do not."

Ralir turned away.

"I was told to keep it to myself."

Orkanir passed him an unreadable glance and then left the cave without another word. Ralir looked after him for a moment and then back at the fire. It was low now, and its red light threw black shadows across the stone.

"Damn orders!" he said to himself. "Damn orders, damn ritual, damn tradition and damn service!"

A voice echoed down to him from far up the tunnel.

"Ralir? Are you coming?"

He shrugged.

"It seems I have been coming all my life, but when do I get to arrive? That is what I want to know."

He looked about again.

"Wonderful, now I am talking to myself."

He went to the tunnel and left the cave. Behind him the last embers of the fire died and the cave darkened into featureless night.

18

AWAKENINGS

Bor-i-arm Nis-hul-zonjiz
Dis-degrah Baade-nimin
Ech-eilim Thilji-pat-ix
Or-imop Oalzien-ris-jir
Kas-urqnis Torzon-qorith
Mol-get-qao Zia-gar-zumnil
Odzid-vi Nalvor-krg-ul

They dropped down from the Adroqin Vohimar by following a path even Orkanir had not known was there, taking them quickly beyond the snow and the cold and on to warmer regions. Even though the way was unfamiliar to him, Orkanir still knew the land they travelled through, naming the mountains to the south and pointing out where the Pisea Fal would have brought them. Mathulaa, though, said nothing.

They crossed hill and vale, passed through woodland and ravine, following the line of hills to their north. It took them the best part of two days to reach the last of them, but even as they skirted its summit they could see for the first time the narrow peninsular where the Forujer Allar was said to be. Mathulaa pointed.

"There it is – the accursed place. The ruins lie beyond that low ridge. We are in good time."

"Good time for what?" Ralir asked.

"You will see," Mathulaa smiled grimly.

It took them all night to reach the low ridge. Mathulaa would not stop. When asked, all he would say was that they would understand come the dawn. Other than that, he would say nothing.

Mathulaa led them carefully, not following the high ground where the walking was easiest but taking instead a slower and more tortuous path through low woodland and across wild heathland. And when they reached the low ridge at last, he took them up a narrow path that stopped just below the highest point. There they halted, hidden from any foe that might be lurking on the other side. Light grew in the east, silhouetting the Adroqin Vohimar. Ridges and peaks cut sharply into the pale sky. Dawn approached.

They crept cautiously to the lip and looked out over the land below. The light was enough. They could see everything. Mathulaa turned to Korfax with a mocking smile.

"There now, young Geyad of the Dar Kaadarith, there it is at last. Behold the Forujer Allar! Look upon its majesty and despair."

Korfax looked at the failing land beyond the ridge. Here it was, the old heart of darkness, but it was a dead darkness now, a broken darkness, the merest of foundations, the barest of bones. Little remained of the might and splendour that must once have been.

A wide expanse stretched out before him, rising up to a vast promontory, a great throne of rock. Many hollows lay here and there, all filled with grey soil, loose and dusty and settling where the wind would let it. Nothing grew, nothing at all, except for the blackest of stones, all squatting in the dead earth like stunted things.

On the last edge, clinging to the stubborn cliffs, lay the shattered ruins of the Forujer Allar – Sondehna's birthplace and the birthplace of all the princes of the Iabeiorith before him.

There was little left of the mighty towers that had once threatened the heavens – a few low walls, broken teeth in shrunken gums – but the foundations still remained, sunk deep in the earth like roots, and though the weight of six thousand years of cursing lay upon their sullen stones, they had power enough in them yet to still defy the light.

Korfax stared down. Here was the edge of the world, waiting to fall at last into limitless night. Here was the place where stone failed, where all was dead and ashen, where even the mightiest limb of land was reduced to pale fragility by the sheer weight of evil that had been piled upon it. This land had lived once, but with the coming of war it had died. The last gasp of the Iabeiorith, their final act, had cursed it and it was irredeemably broken. It was not how he had imagined it would be at all. He felt sick inside.

Ralir grimaced at the dead land beyond the rise.

"Well, here we are at last, but I see nothing."

"Then those of the south are blind."

Ralir looked at Mathulaa and scowled.

"You keep saying things like that, but I see nothing that warrants such an accusation. I see the cursed land, I see the cursed ruins, but I do not see any cursed evidence that we have come to the right place at all."

Mathulaa laughed quietly.

"So wait a moment, impatient youth, and then you will."

Mathulaa moved closer and bared his teeth.

"And afterwards, young sword, you will wish that you had not!"

He paused a moment, smiling darkly, before turning to the east.

"Rafarel is about to rise. Now comes the moment. You are about to see that which none have ever witnessed save myself."

"And how do you know?" Ralir asked.

"Because the required number of days has passed. We are here at the requisite time."

"But how can that be?"

"The thing that you seek only appears when the time is right, and it only appears when it is ready to appear. There is a rhythm by which it is ruled, a progression of numbers. You might ponder that, child, when you have a moment, but that is unimportant now. Dawn approaches. Wait and watch."

And with his last words Rafarel rose from behind the mountains to the east and flooded the sky with his generous light, but even as the far snows of the Adroqin Vohimar caught fire so a darker dawn boiled up from the foundations of the Forujer Allar to greet it.

Out of the black foundations it grew, a seething greyness, like some hasty rot. Where all had been barren and sterile, there was life once more, but it was a horrid life.

Swollen limbs groped, crawling roots fattened and all fastened upon the broken stones from which they swelled, breaking them further in their eagerness to be. Onwards they went until all was strong enough to swarm upwards into the retreating sky.

Two great limbs boiled heavenwards, huge and meaty and uncouth, all but dragging their lesser siblings with them. Up into the air they squirmed, twin pillars of bloated flesh. They reached up and up until they could go no further and then they leaned in towards each other, heaving towers of grey fusing in fervent embrace. Now there was only an arch, a great circular arch, pulsing and writhing, swelling and fattening upon the ruins.

For a moment it stretched and then it drooped as if its weight had become too much. Now it sagged like a tired mouth, heaving to the rhythm of its long, slow contractions and gleaming as though beslimed.

Through the puckered opening, where sky and land should have been visible, something grew, an absence of both colour and form that hurt the eyes. Slow moiling shapes twisted and coiled behind thin veils, whilst beyond lay a pale evanescence like a concealment.

None of them could look at it for very long. After it had grown and formed they soon turned away and dropped back below the ridge. No one spoke.

Korfax closed his eyes. He could feel the void within it, before it and behind it, and he no longer knew up from down or left from right. He was caught again in the fog, the limitless fog, and grey despair rooted him to the spot. He was back in that wooded glade again, his foe pinned to the ground with a lance. He was following the grey to its genesis, daring to peer into the abyss, daring to know the horror. This, though, was worse.

He looked up at the pure light of Rafarel as though to replenish himself. He remembered back to his making. He had sworn oaths that day, oaths he thought he had understood, only to realise afterwards that he did not. Now he was made over again. Before he had been an innocent. Now he was one no longer. He understood. Sorcery must be destroyed, no matter the cost. As it had been in the days of the war, so it was once more. Karmaraa suddenly stood at his shoulder and told him what he must do.

Orkanir was the first to speak. He raised his head and looked back over the ridge. His face was twisted in dismay.

"What is that unholy thing?"

Korfax would have answered but Ralir was quicker, his breath hissing over his teeth like a curse.

"Isn't it obvious? It is sorcery! It stinks of the Agdoain."

Obelison turned away. She looked pale and shaken.

"But it isn't as simple as that," she said.

Korfax looked to her. She looked ill and sickened, as though the mere sight of the thing in the ruins had infected her with its poison, but what had she said? It wasn't simple? What did she mean? Was there more to this? But what more could there be? Surely they had seen it all?

"What is it?" he asked. "What did you see?" *What have the rest of us missed*, he asked in his mind.

She closed her eyes and shuddered. She already understood his deeper meaning.

"That thing back there, it is like a violation," she said. "I am wrong, it is not a doorway, at least not in any sense that we might imagine. My vision was incomplete. It is... something else."

"Something else?" he pressed. "What else can it be?"

Mathulaa answered for her.

"She knows, though she does not trust herself enough to say it."

They all looked at Mathulaa, but he only had eyes for Obelison, his expression curiously grateful.

"She has seen the truth. You are fortunate indeed to have such a one amongst you, one who dares walk in the very footsteps of Nalvahgey herself. Listen to her, you will learn much."

Obelison glared at Mathulaa, but Mathulaa merely smiled in return.

"She knows," he said, letting his smile harden as he gestured back at the ruins. "She knows what that thing out there really is, what it is that grows and shrinks, that pulses alone amongst the evil ruins and swells with evil blood when the time is right. She knows what it is, though she dare not say it."

Korfax went to Obelison and put his arm about her as if to shield her. He glared back at Mathulaa.

"You are harsh," he accused.

"The world is harsh."

"So you tell me then, you tell me what it is."

"It is a womb."

Korfax did not hide his shock. Mathulaa merely bowed his head in response.

"Now you begin to see! Have you not witnessed the grey? A womb? That was my exact thought when I first discovered the truth, but I know of what I speak. I have seen it give birth."

He looked away, his innate ire subsumed by his revulsion. Hate was written there as well as appalled disgust.

"Out they tumble," he hissed, "wet, struggling, denying yet desiring, all thrashing at their collective caul even as they are born, but they are not as all other things are, for they arrive in the world full-grown. To see even one enter this life is more than enough, but to see thousands of them, each piling up upon the other as they are spat out like unwanted filth? Such things should never be seen at all, never witnessed, never known. It is too much, even for this dark place. To see them is to be tainted, and to be tainted is to know abomination."

Korfax narrowed his eyes.

"But this is your world," he said, "not mine. This is sorcery!"

"It is not!" Mathulaa snapped back. "Did you ever hear of anything like that before? Do you truly believe that such things are born of the Mahorelah? Any of the Argedith, even the least of them, were they here now would soon tell you otherwise."

Korfax looked at Mathulaa for a moment and wondered. Was this horror the product of other places and not of the abyss at all? Other places? That was a fiction, surely. Where else could such a monstrosity have come from if not from the pit? Korfax crouched by a stone and ran his hand over it as though seeking for answers on its stubborn surface. He did not know, but knowledge could wait, he had a duty to perform. He looked up again.

"I cannot judge in this matter. I think one thing, Mathulaa clearly thinks another, so I will say nothing except this. Not even in the accounts of the Wars of Unification was such a thing ever described. None of the forces of the abyss I have ever heard of do anything like this."

Korfax looked uneasily at Mathulaa.

"How long has it been here? Is this the only one or are there more?"

Mathulaa raised an eyebrow.

"So, you admit to things of which you are ignorant! How unlike the mighty Dar Kaadarith!"

Korfax scowled.

"I have already admitted my fallibilities. So tell me, what of yours?"

Mathulaa made a sour face.

"I have many, but to speak is easy. To do, though? That carries far more weight."

He gave Korfax one more unreadable look and then straightened.

"After they attacked my people, after I escaped, I sought them out with sorceries.

Plagues I sent upon them, choking mists and corroding rains. I killed but a few, a few trees taken from an ever-swelling forest. So I looked for their genesis, thinking to smite that instead. I found this place."

Korfax looked carefully at the aged Arged.

"So why did you not try to destroy it?"

Mathulaa snarled back.

"You think I did not? I tried many things but it survived them all. It is surpassing strong. To destroy it you would need something of uncaring might."

"This is all well and good," Ralir said, "but how did it get there?"

Mathulaa smiled craftily.

"Now that is a better question than perhaps you know. It hasn't always been there. It comes and it goes, following its own strange cycle of decay and renewal, but one thing is certain. It was placed there, deliberately, many years ago."

Korfax leaned forward.

"What do you really know?"

"Is that suspicion I see?"

"You sound very certain!"

Mathulaa shrugged.

"There is always the possibility that I could be wrong. I have made many mistakes in my life. Am I making another one now?"

"I cannot say. Are you?"

Mathulaa took a deep breath.

"It was placed there. By whom or by what I do not know, for it happened before I was even aware of the danger, but it was placed there deliberately – of that, at the very least, I am quite certain."

Mathulaa gestured back towards the ruins.

"It has been nestling within the ruins of the Forujer Allar for more than seven years, rising up at each appointed time to vomit up its spawn. And each time it has arisen it has thrown up ever more of its progeny, for each eruption is greater than the one preceding it. More and more have been coming through each time, though where most of them go I have not been able to discover. They hide themselves in impenetrable mists, fogs that cloud the mind and the soul. They sink into the land as though into a featureless mire and then they disappear. A few, a mere handful, roam the lands, causing mayhem and confusion as is their wont, but the rest of them simply vanish away. Where they have gone I do not know, but there must be a vast army of them by now, sleeping and waiting for a time yet to come."

Korfax felt staggered by what Mathulaa said. More than seven years? That matched almost exactly with the very first attack upon Losq, but surely this doorway, this 'womb' as Mathulaa called it, would have been seen before now. His father had been here, his mother had been here, and not a few others as well. The Forujer Allar would have been one of the first places any Geyad would have looked. He stared hard at Mathulaa.

"I don't understand. That rotten thing out there should have been seen before now. This place has been visited many times. Such powers leave marks behind them."

Mathulaa grinned back at him with happy contempt.

"And have you not seen the truth of it yet?"

He pointed back at the ruins.

"It hides. They hide. They are the masters of hiding. Have you ever tried to seek for nothing? You cannot! To see it you have to know what you are looking for or when it deigns to show itself. It isn't always here, or have you wilfully misunderstood all that I have told you? It grows and then it fails again, dying away, feeding the unholy root that made it. Only at certain times will you see it, times like now. It follows its own rhythm, one that it took me a long time to discover, though I still do not understand the whys and the wherefores. But I understand enough now, enough to be very frightened indeed. For by my reckoning a new army of grey demons will be coming out of it very soon. Each birthing is many times greater than the one before it, as I have already told you. So here is what you face if you do nothing. The next delivery will be of a size to drown the entire north in blood, if the last was anything to go by."

Mathulaa looked back at Korfax and licked his lips in anticipation.

"So, if you are truly intent upon destroying it, you should do so now!"

Korfax held up one of the four qasadar that he had brought with him and stared at it intently. He had already awoken it somewhat, stirring the dim fires of its heart with his mind, and now it flickered unevenly in his hand, waiting for that final touch that would release the last locks and swing wide the inner gates.

Imbalance was the key. Though the outer form of a qasadar might appear smooth and unblemished, within each stone an asymmetrical madness sat, a deep pool of caged energies potent enough to tear the very substance of the world asunder if they were ever allowed expression.

"Have you ever used one of those before?"

Korfax looked up in sudden surprise. It was Ralir.

"No, I haven't," he answered quietly. "But the practice stones I trained with felt much as this one does now."

"Practice stones?"

"They did nothing. They merely felt like qasadar. One could awaken them and see nothing more than a brief flash of light. They were harmless. This, though," said Korfax as he looked at the qasadar cupped in his hand, "is another matter entirely."

Ralir looked warily at the unquiet crystal.

"I do not trust it. A weapon should be tested before it is used."

Korfax frowned and looked back at Ralir.

"And which part of Lon-Elah do you consider expendable?" he asked. "The Dar Kaadarith do not run blithely across the land destroying it upon a whim. We are here to preserve."

He held up the qasadar and its chaotic light threw strange and inconstant shadows across his face.

"This is a weapon, a terrible weapon. It is filled almost to overflowing with the energies of destruction. And such energies are indiscriminate. The walls of the Forujer Allar were shattered by such power, the first and the last to be so."

He gestured at the ruins.

"You can judge the results for yourself. We of the Dar Kaadarith do not call up such forces unless we have no choice. So I ask you again, which part of Lon-Elah would you sacrifice so that you too can know what I do already? I know my lore, Ralir; it is what I was trained for."

Orkanir reached forward and pulled Ralir away.

"It is as Korfax says. It is not for us to question this. Qasadar were sanctioned by Anolei himself. Let Korfax do now what he needs to. This rot must be excised from the land and only the holiest of fires will burn it from the world."

Ralir relented, allowing Orkanir to lead him back down while Mathulaa and Obelison waited below. Korfax found himself suddenly caught by their unequal expressions. Obelison's was one of hope, but Mathulaa's was one of fear. Korfax swallowed in a mouth gone dry. For all his proud words he suddenly felt very uncertain. And he was running out of time.

Without further ado, he turned back again. Clutching his stave tightly with his left hand he summoned up a net of winds. He wrapped the qasadar in walls of air even as he threw the gleaming crystal aloft. Then he guided it on its way with his mind and his stave, sending it to its intended target. On it flew, its light waxing as its inner energies began to break through the walls of their prison.

Korfax found the expression of his lore oddly calming. With one part of his mind he controlled a bubble of air, an enclosing net of squalls that he for ever fuelled with energies from his stave; and yet, with another part of his mind, he gradually loosened the chains that constrained the power of the qasadar. Order and chaos battled within, each fighting for supremacy, and it took all his concentration to balance them so that the qasadar could fly to its final resting place. In this, at least, he was the master. Nothing happened but that which he decided. The world outside would go the way that it would, but inside, within himself, he was his own god.

The great circular archway of bloated vines suddenly shuddered and squirmed. Korfax frowned. Had the vile thing sensed the oncoming threat? But even as he asked himself the question the great archway began to shrink away. Korfax clenched his fists about his stave and quickened his purpose, but he did not need to, for the flight of the qasadar was already faster than the stoop of a vabazir, and before the great, sick arch of grey flesh could withdraw itself any further, the qasadar reached it.

There was light, a blinding flash of intolerable brilliance that hid both the earth and the sky. Korfax had already turned away, dropping below the ridge whilst shielding his eyes with his arm. He had been warned that qasadar could be fierce, but he had never imagined how fierce. Then he discovered that he had not yet experienced its full fury.

With the qasadar fully unleashed, the elements erupted in response. The earth shuddered, the wind howled and the ocean was pushed back from the shore by a vast, unseen hand. White fire shouted at the heavens and the clouds fled its touch. The forces of destruction rampaged across the edges of the world and tore its last remaining ramparts down. Rock burned, water steamed and fires lit the firmament.

The force of it threw everyone to the ground. Korfax lay still for a moment before looking back. The ridge had preserved them, though vapours now rose from its cracked and broken summit. He stood up and brushed the dust from his cloak and his armour. He went back up to the ridge and looked beyond.

The promontory had been shattered, and its stone had been hurled down into the sea. Great cracks crossed the land that remained and they fumed. Of the ruins of the Forujer Allar there was little left except for the dark smear of its lowest foundations. A great hole had been torn from the surrounding stone and all that remained were the very dregs, exposed at last to heaven's gaze.

Of the gateway there was nothing. Korfax smiled grimly at the shattered rock beyond. He had done it. He felt a sudden rush of pride. He was the first of the Dar Kaadarith to use a qasadar in anger since the Wars of Unification themselves.

But then the smile slipped from his face when he saw at what price the destruction had been bought, for from the turbulent sea an avenging tide of grey was rising up. Though the ocean still heaved angrily at the shattered cliffs, they rose up from within it and strode through its fury. They swarmed up and over the broken promontory, rolling in from the left and the right, grinning and headless as they climbed over the still fuming stone. They had awoken even as he had unleashed his power and they had heard him. They had felt his touch and they had understood who it was that had spoken. Now they would come for him again, as they had before, wave upon wave of them, many times many, rising up from their deeps, scrambling over the stone and dancing over the ashen earth, rising from their hidden places like a hungry and gleeful flood.

Korfax stepped backwards, holding his stave up before him like a barrier. The others came to his side, all of them, to see what it was that he saw. Orkanir and Ralir drew their swords, Mathulaa cursed and Obelison clutched at Korfax as if for dear life, but the oncoming foe did not pause at all, for they were awake now and hungry, and their gleaming teeth filled all horizons.

They ran, and behind them came the Agdoain, an indistinguishable seething of forms. Far back they may have been, very far to the rear, but they were slowly gaining, a silent swarm of shields, swords and mouths.

Further back lurched greater shapes, war beasts foul and meaty, each surmounted by a rider squatting gleefully upon its obscene saddle. Through the swarming ranks came the misshapen cavalry, faster by far, a hideous surge from the rising flood.

Obelison glanced back at Korfax. He felt her thought, felt the fear in her. She looked behind him to the distant hordes and he knew what she was thinking. They had three more qasadar.

He looked about him. Away from the Forujer Allar the land was good, filled with bushes and trees of many and varied sorts. It was spare but vital. Korfax felt a quick rush of reluctance and then guilt. The land here deserved more than a mere glance, but the tyranny of his need drove him. He closed his eyes and hardened his heart. He had to. He had no choice. His task was before him and he heard again the words of Karmaraa.

'And this too shall pass away.'

If those words had once seemed gentle, they were harder than stone now. Mortality laid bare in a few well-chosen syllables.

He took out another qasadar, showing it to her as he did so. She looked grateful in return, almost as if he had already saved her, but Korfax was no longer so innocent.

He raised the qasadar up and stared at it. It glinted in his hand, an almost gentle glimmer, but he saw it now with new eyes. This, after all, was a weapon. It was not blessed, it was not cursed – it merely was.

With an angry snarl he threw it aloft and let it fly back on summoned winds to meet the pursuing Agdoain. He felt its flight, felt it land deep amongst the distant foe, a bouncing spangle of incoherence that was all but ignored by the grey upheaval that trampled over it. Then he touched it with his mind and let it fulfil its purpose.

For the second time that day light shattered the world. Korfax turned away from the glare even as he felt himself raised up by mighty hands of air, raised high and floating, only to be discarded again as if in disgust, thrown back to the ground like some piece of refuse.

For a moment he could neither move nor breathe. Choking dust, hot dust, boiled around him, but then he remembered himself enough to calm the air with his stave. The tormented fire passed him by and he waited for stillness before staggering back to his feet again.

He looked behind, back the way they had come, and saw only desolation. All the Agdoain nearby, and all their beasts, were gone, but so too were the bushes and the trees. The dark and fertile earth had suddenly become ash, and a great fuming pit, wide and deep, had been gouged out of the ground. Korfax shuddered. With one swift stroke he had broken the land. He felt dark. Was this where he was destined to go? How much more was he doomed to destroy in the name of his need? He felt Obelison pulling at him. They had to go on, for more Agdoain had appeared in the distance, rising up and pouring heedlessly over the ash of their brethren.

Twice more Korfax hurled destruction back at the swarming enemy behind. And each time it was the same. The earth was blasted and nothing that lived survived the onslaught, but, with each attack, he found his guilt less than it had been, not more. He did not like what that told him.

They reached the edges of the hills and Mathulaa took them along another path. All looked ahead, none behind, except for Korfax. He glanced back over his shoulder from time to time, and that was only because a dark shadow had been growing in his mind. So he was the first to glimpse the following forms, grey and darting, scampering movements hidden in shadow, fleeting shapes that passed between the boles of distant trees, swarming forwards in relentless pursuit. The Agdoain had caught up with them again.

Mathulaa led them into a steep-sided valley that gradually became a ravine, grassy slopes giving way to sheer walls of rock. He brought them to a crossroads of sorts, a place where the ravine they followed was intersected by another, a place of wide grassy levels and high sheer cliffs, all-enclosing, all-dominating.

Korfax stopped at the edge of the ravine from which they had emerged. He turned about. The Agdoain were close now, he could feel them. He must stop them, and if he were to do so, then the best place to do it would be here. The ravine had become like the neck of a bottle. To pass, everything had to flow through it.

The others, seeing Korfax had stopped, turned about as well. Ralir looked at Orkanir, unspoken questions in his eyes, but Orkanir said nothing. Obelison and Mathulaa, though, felt the building of forces. Obelison turned to explain.

"He is summoning power!" she told them, but even as she spoke Korfax held up his stave and pulled energies out from its depths, mighty energies. He called up earth of air, that crystalline condensation of the spirit of air, less potent than qasadar perhaps, but just as indiscriminate.

Korfax stood back, his face pale, his stave aloft, as a series of sharp reports like icy crepitations rang from his stave, echoing this way and that between the walls of the ravine. Then, from the tip of his stave, a great mass of crystalline forms blossomed, a sudden squall of huge snowflakes. He gestured at the vague forms with his stave, and they scattered this way and that as if caught by a sudden wind. Now they wandered ponderously to and fro across the lip of the ravine, serried ranks ordered by his power.

It was a wall, a high and thick wall of great flat crystals, seven times seven deep, many overlapping layers wandering back and forth over the ground or drifting through the air within the ravine but never crossing its boundaries.

Obelison saw almost immediately what he had done, and she all but laughed in acknowledgement. Korfax had been cunning. Earth of air was a defence that was also an attack, for it was a shifting wall of many independent pieces, a wall whose individual components would crush anything with which they came into contact.

They could not be passed. Even a mountain would find itself sorely taxed if it ever came this way. Earth of air could crush even stone.

Korfax breathed deeply and turned around to join his companions. Obelison smiled gladly at him as he came forward.

"That was a mighty working," she told him.

Korfax bowed his head to her in acknowledgement.

"And let us hope that I do not have to do such a thing again for a very long while yet. I am suddenly quite tired."

Orkanir pointed beyond the vague airy forms.

"They have come," he said.

All of them turned, watching as the Agdoain approached the head of the valley, their distorted forms stretched into even more bizarre shapes through the many lenses of crystalline air.

Mathulaa looked quizzically at Korfax.

"What will this defence achieve?"

Korfax offered Mathulaa a faint smile.

"It will forbid their advance."

"And if they try to push it aside?"

Korfax darkened his smile.

"Then it will crush them," he returned.

Mathulaa smiled back.

"Good!" he replied, and his eyes filled with expectant malice, but even as Korfax looked at the old Arged, one of the Agdoain came forward to test itself against the ephemeral shapes. It prodded one of the crystals with its sword, then it fell, gurgling and hissing as the vague crystalline form it had touched, touched it in return. Air solidified, and like some lethal fabric the crystal folded itself about the luckless Agdoain, covering it completely in a shimmering blanket. Then it collapsed, releasing the energies of its making.

The Agdoain was reduced to liquid in moments, its flesh squeezed and its bones powdered. The others stopped and snarled as their companion was crushed back down to nothingness. There was a brief gust of wind and then the crystal was gone, but that which it had crushed was gone as well.

The rest of the Agdoain stood before the barrier and squirmed this way and that as though unsure what to do next. Korfax watched them for a moment and then offered them a mocking bow. He turned to his companions.

"Come, let us move on. This will hold them for a good while yet. They have many layers to penetrate. Let them try its numbers. One crystal can destroy as many as touch it and they have all been set to fill the empty spaces."

And so, guided by Mathulaa, they ran on, following the ravine, their breath streaming behind them, whilst at their backs a few more Agdoain experimentally prodded Korfax's defence with their swords, only to find themselves crushed back to oblivion for their temerity.

The ravine gentled, its cliffs eroding and its slopes receding. Finally it failed and they found themselves running through softer valleys.

They passed through thick groves of high bushes, leard for the main part, its thick leaves now darkening with the onset of the end of the year. And as they ran, Mathulaa took a moment to speak with Korfax.

"How long will that defence last?" he asked.

Korfax looked back.

"No more than a day," he said. "They can try to go around it but that will take time. They can try to go through it, but they will pay for the privilege. Nothing that lives can survive earth of air. The only flaw is that each crystal they touch diminishes the defence."

Mathulaa snorted.

"There were many Agdoain after us, many hundreds."

"I know," Korfax replied. "Though I did not tell the others I doubt that I have actually bought us more than a long hour at most. I created as many crystals as I could, but even I cannot say whether I created enough."

Mathulaa looked down.

"All power is a two-edged sword, whether you practice the Namad Dar or the Namad Mahorelah."

Korfax said nothing in return, but he looked hard at the old Arged as he remembered back to his vision in the cave.

It was as they came to the end of the valley, just before the foothills of the Adroqin Vohimar really began, that Ralir caught Korfax by the arm and gestured to the rear.

"I'm sorry, Korfax, but our friends have caught up with us again. Look behind!"

Ralir pointed at the low bushes they had just left. Something stood in the shadows there, on the path, something stooped and grey and headless. Then, almost as if it knew it had been sighted, it stepped out of the darkness and revealed itself.

It bared its teeth back at them, even as they saw it, rearing up and widening its hideous maw in a yawn of lust. It hissed briefly for a moment, a gesture of defiance perhaps, but then it leant back upon its haunches and howled at the heavens.

The sound was monstrous, a gargling roar that echoed from one side of the valley to the other. Obelison came to Korfax, drawing her sword.

"What is it doing?" she asked quietly. "What does that mean? Does it signal its brethren? What is its intent?"

Korfax unsheathed his stave. He understood. This was it. His time had come. They could not all flee for ever. He felt a sudden sadness he knew he could never put into words. Here lay his last purpose. The Agdoain pursued him, not the others. It was as plain as Great Rafarel in the sky. He looked back at Obelison and let his gaze linger, but he did not let her see his thought.

"That is no signal," he said. "I have never seen them talk to one another. They do not speak in any fashion whatsoever. They have never offered up a word, or a sign or any semblance of communication that I know of, but I am sure that they comprehend nonetheless. I believe that what one knows, they all know. And if I were to hazard a guess, it would be that this one merely gives vent to its lust. They desire our flesh, all of them, every single one of them. All you are hearing is the sound of their endless hunger."

For a moment Obelison stared at him in dismay, but then she backed away. Korfax suddenly found himself wishing that he had not spoken at all. He had said far more than he had intended, horrifying her rather than comforting her. She shrank from him now and he would have reached out to her, but then the others would see where his choices were about to take him – and that would not do at all.

He caught Mathulaa's glance. Mathulaa even deigned to smile back gently, offering up his sad approval instead of his ever-present scorn.

"Indeed, young master of stone. Hunger it is! There is nothing else. That is all that they have: hunger! But sometimes there comes a delicacy, rich and fine, that will assuage them for a while. I salute your insight, Korfax of the Farenith. You have proven yourself a worthy witness to the fall of Peis-homa."

Korfax glanced at Mathulaa and their eyes met. Mathulaa gave him the slightest of bows, all he would allow. They suddenly understood each other completely.

The lone Agdoain finished its howling and now waited instead, grinning, ever grinning. Korfax gestured at Mathulaa.

"Get my companions to safety. I will erect another defence."

The gentleness in Mathulaa suddenly hardened. He bowed his head in acquiescence and then gestured to the others, but they did not move.

"What are you waiting for?" he cried. "We move on."

Obelison stayed where she was.

"We do not," she said. "Where Korfax stands, I stand also."

Orkanir joined her.

"I stand beside Korfax as well. I will ward him."

Ralir stepped forwards.

"Then I suppose that makes three of us, even though I seem to have come a little late to the feast."

Mathulaa pointed at Korfax.

"But did you not hear what he said?"

Ralir smiled.

"Yes I did, but does that mean that any of us should abandon him?"

Mathulaa snarled, the hard lines of his face falling back into their accustomed places.

"Then you are fools, all of you. He uses powers that you do not. He will kill them in droves. What can you do?"

Ralir was about to answer, but Orkanir was quicker.

"We can stand beside him and we can ward him."

Korfax turned to them all.

"Enough of this, I will create another defence. None of you can help. You must all go on. I will follow when I can. Do it!"

Ralir and Orkanir exchanged glances, a flicker of questions, and Obelison watched them. Then she saw it. The others had not quite divined it yet, but she could see it now. Korfax had only spoken half the truth. He had no intention of following at all. She looked at Mathulaa. He understood and he approved, which was why he had urged them to leave as well. She cursed him silently. She, at least, had no intention of letting Korfax sacrifice himself.

"No, Korfax!" she said. "I say that we all go on, or that none of us do."

Korfax saw the resolution in her eyes and her resolve to fight. He looked away and clenched his teeth in chagrin. When it came to the point, she controlled herself better than he did. He could not hide from her.

"But knowledge of this must get back," he insisted, his last gasp.

"And I am a seer," she said. "I have seen beyond these days. You trusted my vision once, almost to the point of death. Are you so unwilling to trust it again?"

Korfax bowed his head. She had seen beyond these days? Whatever did that mean? He dropped his shoulders. Even in this, even in his final choice, he had doubts, but she was right, of course. He should continue to trust to her vision. She had been proven right up to now.

Korfax called up more earth of air, but it was hard work. The lone Agdoain remained where it was, grinning its vile grin back at him as if it also understood. Korfax had the sudden and unpleasant feeling that it knew exactly what he was up to, and that it and its brethren had already come up with an answer.

With nothing to do except wait, his companions watched, Mathulaa with ill-concealed hatred, the others with varying degrees of distaste.

More Agdoain arrived, even as the summoning was completed, whilst even more swarmed in their wake, until the valley was filled with many hundreds. Then, though no signal passed between them, they all advanced, all together.

Korfax watched as they approached. They are mechanisms, he thought to himself, mechanisms made flesh. Spirit drawn down into the world, stolen from the distant places, from beyond the river, from beyond Zinznagah, and cruelly trapped, its light dimmed, its purity for ever defiled and doomed to oblivion in the all-consuming void.

The Agdoain came forward like a wall and then spread themselves out. Korfax frowned for a moment, wondering what they were doing, but when they started to dig into the ground with their shields, he felt his world collapse about him. His work, all of it, had been utterly in vain.

Their answer to his defence was obvious. Using their shields like scoops they dug down into the earth, pulling out rocks and great masses of soil, which they then threw at the floating crystals, forcing them to dissipate.

Korfax yelled a wordless cry of thwarted rage and unleashed fire of air. A red flood of boiling flames spilled around the earth of air and burned the Agdoain beyond, incinerating many, but ever more followed in their wake, and more after them. Soon there was a veritable maelstrom of rock and soil beyond his wall, hundreds of Agdoain throwing whatever they could, diminishing his defence piece by piece.

Korfax felt a moment of brief regret. This, at least, was the one advantage a practitioner of the Namad Mahorelah had over a practitioner of the Namad Dar. According to record, summoned energy from the Mahorelah took little account of the summoner, and the energy could in many cases be reclaimed and turned to other purposes, but it was not so with the Namad Dar. Once the energy was out and in the world at large, it could never be called upon again. Korfax suddenly wished he could dismantle his defence and use it against the foe, but that was not how it worked.

He was tiring. The fire he summoned burned just as brightly as before, but he could feel his strength waning all the while. He did not know how long he could continue to call it up from his stave, but whilst the Agdoain remained heedless of their own lives he had no choice but to match them.

Despair threatened. The Agdoain were too absolute to be dissuaded or put aside, too single-minded to consider their own preservation. They were the ultimate foe – implacable, unswerving and for ever hungry. Horror grew inside him as he thought of their existence and how it must be. No individuals existed; they were a force with but a single mind, a being of many bodies, each intent upon a single goal, the extermination of the Ell. If they could spend themselves by the thousand to kill just one, then they would do so.

A warning cry came from behind. He glanced about, just in time to see a band of Agdoain leap down from the sloping cliffs to his left whilst another band dropped down to his right. They had scaled the heights and crossed his defences by other means. It was suddenly all too obvious. Whilst he had concentrated on those that attacked his defence, these others had been free to stalk him from above.

Down they now came, straight for him. He splashed them with fire, burning them off the rock. Some tumbled onto the remaining earth of air, some burned where they stood, but some got through, and they were enough.

Korfax ducked as the first to reach him swept its blade at him, striking for his head, but then a second came at him from his left and thrust a long limb at his side. Something jolted him and he staggered. He looked down and saw a grey limb touching him, a long grey limb with a long grey blade buried in his side. Then the long grey limb drew back, pulling its blade out from his flesh, slick with his very own blood.

His side suddenly burned with a vile heat as though he had been stabbed with acid. Korfax gasped and staggered, trying to bring his stave to bear, but before he could do anything else, his attackers fell back, one howling, the other dead. The tip of a sharpened staff emerged from the chest of the first, while the other fell apart, its limbs parting company with its body. Behind them both stood Obelison and Mathulaa, he with his staff and she with her sword, while Ralir and Orkanir attacked the others in a flicker of blades.

Korfax sank to the floor, clutching at his side. He drew back his hand and stared at it in shock. It was not merely stained with blood, it was drenched, and the precious fluid dripped from each finger like the draining of his life. For a moment he felt his mind drift over a pit of darkness, and then the world faded about him altogether.

Korfax awoke to find Orkanir and Ralir leaning over him. Someone else was worrying at his side. He looked there and watched as Obelison bound him about with many wrappings. He felt a fire where she touched him, as though she were branding him with hot metal. He looked at her and she smiled back at him gratefully.

"Thank The Creator! You are back with us at last."

Korfax swallowed.

"How bad is it?"

"The wound was deep, but at least it was clean. Mathulaa stopped the bleeding and found me some niltham to pack the bindings with. It will hold so long as you do not pull at it. You really should rest, but we cannot stay here."

Korfax looked up at Mathulaa.

"I am in your debt once more," he said.

Mathulaa cocked his head to one side.

"As I am in yours. Can you stand?"

Korfax tried to do so but then staggered back as searing pain flared in his side. It all but crippled him. For long moments he could not move at all.

Finally, after a number of attempts, he managed to stand up, leaning carefully on Obelison and Mathulaa as he found a way around his pain. He looked at the others.

"What of the Agdoain?" he asked.

Ralir gestured behind him at the still wandering wall of earth of air drifting lazily over the fuming earth.

"All dead. You've a fearsome power in that stave of yours, my friend. There were only a handful left for us to deal with at the end, but I have an unpleasant feeling that these were only a scouting party. We should move on now before the rest attach themselves to our tail."

Obelison looked appalled.

"Only a scouting party? You did not say that before. There were hundreds of them!"

Ralir smiled unhappily in return.

"And when that gateway was destroyed, I suspect that they all awoke, all at once. Do not ask me how or why, but a sense of them has been growing on me ever since the Forujer Allar. They are coming for us, all of them, every single one. While you were tending Korfax, Orkanir and I went up onto the top and looked behind. We saw what we think is a sign. Far away they might have been, but both of us are fairly certain. These Agdoain will not relent, will not stop, will not turn aside. If it takes them an eternity, and their numbers are all but infinite, they will spend all that they are to stop us."

Korfax glanced at Ralir.

"You feel it also?"

Ralir looked uncomfortable.

"And what did I just say?" he answered. "But if we do not move on soon, none of us will feel anything ever again."

They ran as best they could whilst behind them grew a rumour, and then more than a rumour, of pursuit. There were brief glimpses of grey, the briefest flashes of movement far back across the trail. The Agdoain had caught up with them again.

For Korfax the pursuit became a nightmare. What with the extravagant use of his power and the wound in his side, every step he took seemed worse than the last. He would never have believed before this moment that he could feel so weary.

Up ahead frowned the final foothills that guarded the high passes of the Adroqin Vohimar, but Korfax did not think he would ever make the long climb, even as Mathulaa pointed the way that they should go.

"We must climb up onto the left-hand ridge. That one will be easier to defend."

Ralir did not look convinced. The ridge was high with sheer sides. There was only one way up and it was very steep.

"That is all well and good," he said, "but once we gain the ridge will we be in a fit state to defend it? Unlike us, our pursuers never seem to tire."

Orkanir looked back behind.

"And they are gaining," he said.

Mathulaa pointed emphatically at the ridge above.

"Let me worry about such things. Your task is to ward. Each to his own, adept of the sword. We go to the left-hand ridge."

They passed through dense foliage, following a winding path that Mathulaa seemed to know all too well. And though it went this way and that, the path appeared to take them by the easiest route to the slope ahead. Behind them the Agdoain took all the available ways, following every route through the green maze, and if they came upon a dead end then they merely slashed their way through to the other side. It slowed the pursuit a little, but not by much. By the time they reached the ridge the Agdoain would most likely be upon them.

Eventually the land started to rise sharply and the low trees that had been their shelter gave way to even lower bushes of orkim, a diminishing garden of leafy domes around which they passed as quickly as they could. Before them reared the final slope, one single rise without pause, a straight climb that would take them all the way up to the ridge above.

They clambered up the only path and Korfax struggled through an ever-deepening nightmare. He fought against the steepness, he fought against his fatigue, he fought against his pain and he fought against himself.

He felt Obelison pulling him forward and Ralir pushing him from behind. Ahead of them Mathulaa led the way whilst behind them Orkanir guarded their rear, his sword now slick with Agdoain fluids. Korfax glanced back wearily.

The Agdoain swarmed below, snarling and hissing, each pressing forward on the narrow and precipitous slope, ever hurling themselves onto Orkanir's sword in mad rushes. Orkanir had the advantage yet and slew all that came within his reach with economy and dispatch, but even his breath was coming hard now.

Ralir finally broke the struggling silence.

"How is it with you, Orkanir?"

Orkanir was a while in answering.

"I have had better days."

"Do you wish me to take your place yet?"

"Not yet. I am still determined to teach these monsters at least some respect for Ell sword craft."

Korfax smiled even as he turned back. There was no despair yet. Orkanir remained as immovable as Ralir was eager. That, at least, gave him some hope. He, though, inhabited a sea of pain and his wounds were like acid in his mind, corroding his will and sapping what little strength he had left. He barely heard the words of encouragement Obelison murmured to him as she pulled him on. Instead he dreamed of rest, of a blessed surcease to his torment. He longed to lie down so that he could simply sleep. Was that really so much to ask?

As they reached the lip of the ridge, Ralir saw Mathulaa smiling down at him from beside the huge boulder that stood at its edge like a sentinel.

"Help me here! Leave your friend and help me push this over. There is a surprise under this stone, a surprise for our pursuers."

Ralir frowned.

"What surprise?"

Mathulaa gestured at the boulder.

"All we need do is move this."

Ralir stared back at him in disbelief. The boulder was at least four times as tall as Mathulaa and almost three times as broad. From the look of it, it had been glowering down from the edge of the hill ever since this part of the world had been made. It looked far too well planted in the earth to be moved by the mere touch of a hand.

"Move that? You jest!"

Mathulaa dropped his smile and all but spat.

"Hurry, fool, whilst our rear guard climbs up to join us. He can help us when he gets here."

Ralir joined Mathulaa. He placed a grudging hand against the boulder, if only to humour Mathulaa, but then suddenly drew back again in surprise when he felt it shift.

"How?" he asked.

"Assist me and you will see a thing," came the reply.

Ralir called down to Orkanir.

"Orkanir? I think you might want to join us as quickly as you can. Good Mathulaa here has prepared a little surprise for our followers." He looked at the great boulder and gave it another push. "It certainly surprised me," he muttered to himself.

The boulder shifted ever further as they pushed, and Ralir could now see the why of it, for from the crevice created by its movement he could see that the boulder was balanced carefully upon a fulcrum of power, a barely flickering cache of slumbering energy that waited to send it down the slope. Ralir could feel its potency, for it beat against him now like the heat from a furnace.

Orkanir came at last to his side and Mathulaa hissed at them both.

"Now, both of you, push it hard and leap clear of the edge as it falls. The power it holds in place will do the rest."

They did so, jumping back to where Korfax now lay with Obelison.

The boulder tilted and fell, and as it fell the entire side of the hill fell with it. Energies awakened and erupted, and the slope shattered. The Agdoain that were on it were all swept back down to the valley below in a tumble of soil and stone. Many were crushed and buried. Mathulaa walked to the new edge of the hill and leaned over it. He laughed.

"There are not many such traps left in these parts, so we were fortunate to have been so close to this one. I have been killing the grey demons with such stratagems for years."

Ralir joined him.

"I wondered why you wanted to come this way. Clever!"

Orkanir went to the other side of the ridge and looked back in the direction they had come from.

"Yes, clever indeed, but I think any victory celebration should be put off for now. Our pursuers have received reinforcements. Will this never end?"

Ralir and Mathulaa looked to where he pointed and both of them cursed, Ralir under his breath, Mathulaa openly. More Agdoain were arriving, the remnant of those that had been caught by the avalanche now joined by a force ten times their number. And many were mounted. Ralir grimaced.

"There must be as many down there now as there were at Piamossin," he said. Then he gestured at the broken slope of loose stone and soil with his sword.

"What do you think? Can those beasts of theirs climb even this?" he asked.

But before Orkanir had time to reply, the newly arrived Agdoain urged their mounts onwards to the hill, and the beasts began to climb indeed, their great claws digging into the loose soil and broken rock, their great mouths thrust forward in bestial imitation of their masters. Ralir drew back from the edge.

"It seems I have my answer," he said. "There is no choice left to us then. We must go on."

Ralir turned to leave, as did Orkanir, but Mathulaa remained where he was. There was a strange look upon his face now, something almost regretful. Ralir gestured.

"Come Mathulaa, we must cross this hill. You know the way on from here. Come! Lead us!"

Mathulaa remained where he was and his face was strangely gentle, his smile almost kind.

"No," he said. "It is my turn now."

He looked back at Korfax.

"Your friend, the young master of stone, look at him. He has spent himself for the rest of us, and he has spent himself selflessly. I cannot ignore such sacrifice. So now I must spend myself in turn. Like does for like, after all. Like for like, lore for lore, debt for debt. I shall hold them here whilst the rest of you escape."

Mathulaa then pointed at Obelison.

"She has seen this, I know. I have seen it also. You should follow her vision as you have ever done before. That is the way you should go."

He pointed at the mountains beyond, towards the heights. Then he looked at Ralir.

"Go and warn the world. Tell them what you have found and tell them what you have seen. And at the end, tell them all how the last of the Korith Peis chose to spend himself."

Ralir came back to Mathulaa and grabbed at him.

"But this is madness! You cannot hold back such numbers alone!"

Mathulaa shook off Ralir, who staggered for a moment but then held his sword before him. Mathulaa merely laughed at the gesture, even as his face became grim again.

"Obey or die? Is that it?"

He drew himself up and a sudden sense of power informed him.

"I will spend the last moments of my life in any way that I see fit, young sword! Like your friend of the stone I have reached my limit. I no longer wish to run before them like driven cattle. It is time they learned the true price of their folly."

He leaned forward and his eyes were brilliant.

"For folly it is. I am Arged!"

He turned back again, shielding his light so as to regard the slowly advancing masses below. He looked down at them as if they were already dead.

"And have no fear, young sword, I shall not be alone."

His face twisted into a snarl of dismissal, but Ralir still remained where he stood. "What are you saying?" he asked.

Now it was the turn of Mathulaa to grab at Ralir, and neither was he gentle. Mathulaa turned around and advanced upon Ralir, clutching at him and lifting him high into the air. Then he threw him with all his strength and Ralir, too surprised to react, tumbled away from Mathulaa over the thin grass.

"Go, you fool!" Mathulaa cried. "Have you no wits left to you at all? Take your friends and leave whilst you still can. I shall summon aid." He raised up a single finger in warning. "And you do not want to be here when that aid arrives."

Orkanir helped Ralir stumble away as Mathulaa turned to face the Agdoain again. He waited a moment, gathering himself up as though about to leap from the edge of the hill itself, but then he tilted his head back and flung his arms wide. Strange words were sent up into the sky, his voice roaring and moaning, demands and pleas in equal measure, whilst weird echoes drifted back from the surrounding hills like uncertain answers.

A wind out of nowhere suddenly coiled itself about him and dim shapes seemed to dance within it, pulling at his robes, pulling at his flesh, mocking him with spectral laughter. He swatted them aside with brief flicks of his hands.

Perturbed, Ralir and Orkanir drew back further, only stopping at last when they reached where Korfax and Obelison now waited, some distance away.

"What is this?" Ralir asked. "What is Mathulaa doing? Is this sorcery?"

Korfax closed his eyes.

"Yes," he answered quietly. "This is sorcery. He attempts a summoning."

"But what will he summon?"

"I do not know, but I fear the worst. Be ready to run."

The wind died down again and the dim mocking shapes vanished away as the last words were uttered. The world held its breath and all the Agdoain, even those upon the slopes, paused for a moment as they tasted the change about them on their long grey tongues, daring to wonder perhaps what this sudden stillness might portend.

All of them – Korfax, Ralir, Orkanir and Obelison – looked up at the blue vault, expecting at any moment to see strange and monstrous shapes fall out of the sky, but it was not to be.

They came from below the hill, not above it. Three great and silent shapes, wings outstretched and jaws agape, flew up and over the ridge and then followed its undulating contours with contemptuous ease.

Korfax gasped in terrified astonishment even as he caught sight of them. He pointed, his outstretched finger following their curving flight as if he had pierced them with its very tip, but they were far beyond his reach and their great bodies turned this way and that in the sky above, swooping, soaring, each slow beat of each great wing a heavy throb of air.

Involuntary tears filled his eyes. The Agdoain, the peril, the pain, all were forgotten as he gazed with unrepentant awe at the majestic forms Mathulaa had dared call to his side. For here, before him, disported the mightiest of the mighty, the greatest ever to take wing under the gaze of The Creator. Korfax shuddered in an ecstasy of guilty delight, for a childhood dream was suddenly fulfilled, and that surely was the strangest thing of all.

"Vovin!" Korfax cried at the great shapes, naming them with his heart.

"He has summoned Vovin," he now whispered, as if he dared not name the crime. The others did not answer. They crouched behind him like spellbound children, watching wide-eyed all together as a sudden and terrible legend displayed itself above as if for their amazement.

The three Vovin were huge, larger by far than even rumour had made them, and they hurled themselves through the air as though born of storms and fury. One, the largest, flew directly above Mathulaa, where it circled, lowering its head in a grudging bow. The other two waited above, hot eyes staring downwards with ill-concealed rage. Mathulaa raised his arms almost in supplication, but the gesture seemed altogether futile. The Vovin, all of them, were utterly unmoved.

Korfax could feel them, could feel the anger that boiled inside them, even from where he lay. On an impulse he reached out to them, daring to know their thoughts, but the instant he touched them he withdrew again as though scalded. He understood their rage now, understood it all too well.

How dare this puny thing call to them, they told him, how dare it hold them with its insignificant purposes! How dare it!

But they could not deny the summons nor ignore it, for greater words held them, words that were mightier than they, words they resented deeply. They were chained for the moment, their lethal passions prowling the limits of their bondage, but let flesh fall and will fail and it would be a different story altogether.

Korfax lay back, catching his breath. Such savagery, such majesty! If he had been standing, he would have fallen to his knees. If he had been kneeling, he would have prostrated himself, but even so, as weary as he was, he bowed his head to them, for they surpassed his imagination altogether.

Now he understood what Mathulaa had done, the length of it, the breadth. And, even in the midst of his wonder and awe, he felt a terrible fear. Mathulaa had doomed himself. As Korfax had intended to fight the Agdoain until he died, so Mathulaa now did the same, but whereas Korfax had escaped, Mathulaa's end was all but inevitable, and Korfax knew that nothing could prevent it.

Mathulaa hissed in pain and pointed at the Agdoain. The Vovin that circled above him looked down slowly and bared their teeth. Even in enslavement, their disdain was imperial.

Mathulaa gasped as he flung his arms wide again. The Vovin stared at him, all of them, their eyes flames in their heads, burning with rage, but then they looked down reluctantly again at the proffered sacrifice, even as it heaved itself up from below. They would have recoiled from such filthy meat if they had possessed the choice, but now they merely rattled the bars of their cage. They had to accept the charge, for it was written in their blood. They had no choice at all. So they unsheathed their claws, opened their jaws and fell from the sky like vengeance unleashed.

The nearest of the Agdoain was plucked upwards, the rider and the mount crushed and pierced by mighty claws. Then each was torn apart, even as they were lofted into the air, eviscerated almost with a bloody joy. The parts and the pieces fell back down again, a spent and grisly rain.

Like an icon of retribution Mathulaa remained upon the brow of the hill, body straight and arms aloft, whilst the Vovin swooped and dived and dived again, tearing great clawfuls of corrupted flesh from the side of the hill, before ripping it all apart and dropping it back down upon the land below.

Korfax watched as the Vovin went about their bloody work and began to feel an itch in his mind, like the beginnings of a worrisome question. Surely there was more to their savagery than this? Many beasts were armed with both tooth and claw, and many could rend their prey with equal ferocity. Surely the Vovin had more inside them than this? There were thousands of Agdoain down there.

Then he realised what Mathulaa was doing. This was but a prelude. He was letting the Vovin play, letting them build themselves up, stoking the fires of their enslaved anger with violence and carnage.

The air around them began to change, a gathering of forces like a storm, so he felt rather than saw, the moment when Mathulaa unleashed the last movement of his summoning. Almost immediately, all three of the Vovin threw back their heads and spat the wish of their hearts down upon the enemy below.

Three great shafts of liquid fire, impossibly bright, impossibly powerful, lanced down like slow lightning. They struck the hillside almost as one and their collected fires exploded upwards in great balls of heaving, rolling flame. With brief and hideous screams all of the Agdoain that were touched by the fire failed in but a single moment, caught in intolerable torment as summoned flame washed greedily over them, eating their flesh and consuming their bones. The eaters became the eaten.

The Vovin roared and spat as they would, calling up the final dance of destruction and expelling their power downwards, ever downwards upon the sea of grey.

The valley beyond the hill erupted in red and gold as a rising storm of fire eclipsed the land. The flames rose up and up again as the Vovin rained their flesh-born fire downwards, fire upon fire and fire upon fire again, until all became an earthbound tempest, a coiling fury that hurled its heat back up into the sky whilst stark against its flickering holocaust the silhouette of Mathulaa remained alone, held in place by the very powers he had dared call up. Korfax shuddered.

"How many Agdoain were there?" he asked.

Orkanir stared at the fire.

"Probably as many as there were at Piamossin," he said.

"And the Vovin have slain them all?"

Orkanir could only bow his head. Korfax looked horrified.

"I do not suffice. The Namad Dar does not suffice."

Obelison looked at him in shock.

"But you cannot say that. Karmaraa defeated Sondehna. What more proof do you need?"

Korfax bowed his head.

"Then I am inadequate," he said.

Orkanir laid his hand on Korfax's shoulder.

"Korfax, you are far too hard upon yourself. You have warded us all the way. How many others of the Dar Kaadarith could do what you have done? How many of them have done what you have done?"

"But Mathulaa has surpassed me. He has called up Vovin. I cannot match him. I cannot match them," Korfax answered.

No one spoke again as they watched the land beyond the edge of the hill burn. The forests burned, the grasses burned and even the rocks burned. It was as if the flames of the first glory had come, to burn the world beyond the hill into a wilderness of ash and molten stone. And still the Vovin circled, hurling their rage at the ground.

Ralir turned to Korfax, his face a mixture of shock and wonder.

"I still do not understand any of this. Why did Mathulaa tell us to leave? If the Vovin slay the Agdoain then we are safe, aren't we?"

Korfax leant back against a rock, Obelison holding him on one side, Orkanir the other. He spoke slowly.

"In the Umadya Semeiel there are many stones that detail the acts of the Argedith, and amongst them all there is a stark warning. There are three summonings that should never be attempted: the summoning of the gods of the lower deeps, the summoning of the Gaaha and the summoning of Vovin."

Korfax turned his gaze to the vast circling forms above.

"It is said that once the summoning is over a Vovin will turn upon its summoner and tear them apart, visiting upon them in return the pain inflicted by the summoning. And there is no way of stopping it. The pain is real. I have felt it. I have seen it. Vovin ill-endure domination, and to summon them is to violate them. Mathulaa has damned himself by saving us."

Ralir and Orkanir stood up, swords at the ready, but Korfax stopped them with a raised hand.

"Do not even think to go to his aid. You would die before he does. Can you honestly stand against such might?"

Orkanir drew back again, but Ralir turned upon Korfax, disbelief written on his face.

"But he saved us! We must try to save him in return!"

Korfax sighed.

"I am exhausted," he said. "If I could summon power enough to protect him, don't you think I would be over there now, at his side?"

Ralir snarled. A look of contempt replaced his disbelief.

"But that isn't the answer, is it? Mathulaa follows the Namad Mahorelah. And that is the real reason, isn't it? That is why you are so willing to leave him to his fate!"

Obelison gasped. Korfax looked up, pained surprise written on his face. Orkanir grabbed Ralir roughly by his arm.

"Withdraw your accusation!" he said. "Korfax would never do such a thing. He is of the Farenith. You saw how he intended to sacrifice himself for the rest of us! Does that mean nothing to you now? None of us have studied this lore as Korfax has. You should listen to what he says."

Ralir shrugged off Orkanir and stepped back.

"Should I? And what is the creed of the Dar Kaadarith?"

He pointed back at Mathulaa.

"From his own lips you heard it. You shall not suffer the Argedith to live!"

He looked at them all.

"You can prostrate yourselves before the altar of dogma all you like, but I go to give aid to an ally. Stay here and bathe in your self-righteous duplicity, if you will."

Without another word Ralir turned away and headed back towards Mathulaa, but he did not reach him.

With the ending of the last of the Agdoain, the Vovin wheeled their way up from the valley and back into the sky above whilst Mathulaa lowered his arms as if in utter defeat.

Then, released at last from the power of the summoning, each of the Vovin turned in the air and swooped down again, down upon Mathulaa in blind fury. The largest of the three reached him first and swept him violently up in an outstretched claw, its mouth wide in unfettered rage. Then it flew low across the ridge whilst its companions followed eagerly in its wake.

Over the ridge they came, low to the ground, eyes aglow, mouths agape.

Ralir dived behind a great rock as one of the trailing Vovin came for him. Sparks erupted from the rock as it split in two, sliced in half by an adamantine claw. There was a rush of wings and a hiss of chagrin, but none of the Vovin turned away from their flight. They understood their peril also. The Ell were here, and the Ell had ever been hunters. So they continued to the heights above, weaving between the peaks as though evading attack, and as the three vanished into the far distances a limp bundle could just be seen below the largest, a limp bundle dangling from mighty claws.

Korfax pulled himself up to his feet, leaning heavily on Orkanir. He watched the dwindling forms as they flew to the northern heights and said a silent prayer for the last of the Korith Peis.

Ralir came back and stared long at Korfax. Then he looked away.

"Why?" he demanded, almost spitting the word out.

Korfax breathed deeply.

"Vovin abhor dominion. Mathulaa was already dead when he started the summoning. If I had known what he had intended to do then I would have tried to stop him, but I do not know the Namad Mahorelah. I am not versed in its application. Until recently the lore was thought to be all but dead. All the grimoires were burned long ago and all the practitioners were put to death, as it was written. And you know as well as I that even the contemplation of the art is considered profane. Now you have seen why. Summoning any creature into dominion is evil. The Vovin Mathulaa summoned had to defeat the Agdoain. They had no other choice; the summoning bound them. They might have died in the attempt, but that is the price they had to pay. The end always justifies the means."

Korfax leaned heavily on his stave. Obelison came to his side.

"You should rest," she said.

"Not yet," he told her. "We need to move on. Mathulaa has bought us time enough to escape. We should not waste it. His death should not be without meaning."

He walked off, following the path of the ridge, using his stave as a prop. Obelison went after him to help and the others followed her. And as Korfax went, he told a tale.

"There was a story I heard a long time ago, before I became a Geyad, the story of the Arged of Unchir. For a long time she held her land, but eventually she was beaten back to her fastness. First she tried to threaten her besiegers with hostages she had taken. That did not work, so she set about summoning up forces, fires and winds, for her defence. When that failed she sent out the last of the Haelok Aldaria that served her, and they all perished. Finally, in desperation, she summoned the most powerful allies that she could, beings called Gaaha."

Orkanir frowned.

"You mentioned them earlier. I have not heard that name before. What are these Gaaha?"

Korfax did not answer for a while. Instead he walked on, looking into the distances, trying to remember all that he had heard and read. When he answered at last his voice was as distant as his gaze.

"Only the Dar Kaadarith preserve their memory. We have no physical record of their likeness, just a few personal accounts. They are said to be ferocious, almost unstoppable."

"Outside the keep of the Arged were five hundred of the Nazad Esiask along with a Geyad of the Dar Kaadarith, a Geyad by the name of Achoin. The Arged summoned a company of Gaaha, as many as she could manage, and as she did this

Achoin was able to breach the walls of her keep. In rode the Branith of the Nazad Esiask. Victory was seemingly at hand, but what followed next was a slaughter, of a kind. Over the course of the next hour, those Gaaha managed to wipe out almost three quarters of Achoin's forces. Think of it, over three hundred slain. Only Achoin could keep the Gaaha at bay, and then only with great difficulty. At the end, as the Arged's strength failed her, the demons relented and turned upon her instead. They killed her, much like the Vovin did to Mathulaa. Then they returned whence they came."

"I do not see the point," Ralir said.

Korfax smiled grimly.

"The tale comes in two parts. I was told one tale when I first came to the Umadya Semeiel, but then I was told another. This account was far more disturbing. From what Achoin related he was the only one they could not close with, so after a long and weary hour they finally turned upon their summoner instead, and before they returned to the abyss they left behind a message."

"Which was?"

"Don't ever summon us again."

"That was their message?"

"Yes!"

"And how do you know this? It could be that they were just unthinking animals doing whatever it was they were supposed to do, like the Vovin."

"And if you think the Vovin are unthinking then you clearly do not know as much about such beasts as you think you do, but that is not the point I am trying to make. There was one last damning piece of evidence. The Gaaha left a message on the floor of the room into which they had been summoned. And they wrote it in the blood of their summoner. It was written in Logahithell. I know of no beast that can do such a thing."

Korfax stared back at Ralir for a moment.

"So let me ask you this in return. If someone snatched you from this world, without asking first, and compelled you to hazard your life in the name of a cause you did not understand, what would you think?"

Ralir breathed deeply.

"I would not be happy, I can tell you that much."

"Exactly, and that is how it is with those who follow the Namad Mahorelah. The end always justifies the means. So what if a few demons from the abyss are destroyed? There is an almost unlimited supply of them, isn't there? And if there isn't, then we can use some other summoned force, can't we?"

Korfax winced as he turned back again. His wound made him stiff.

"A long time ago," he said, "someone brought a few Vovin here from the Mahorelah. Whoever did it was either astonishingly powerful or incredibly lucky, because the Vovin remained. Normally a summoned entity will return whence it came, but not the Vovin. They remained here and bred, much as they do in the abyss. They have become part of our world now, but that was by no design of The Creator. They are not meant to be here. This isn't their natural habitat and they were born to dwell elsewhere. If The Creator had wanted Vovin here, The Creator would have put them here."

"I see the point you are making," Ralir told him, "but it is not something we of the south tend to think over much on. Why though does that mean we should not have leapt to Mathulaa's aid?"

"Because we also needed to honour his choice!"

"His choice?"

"Yes, it was Mathulaa's choice! I would have given my life to save the rest of you in that valley, but you all decided otherwise and the moment passed, but there may again come a time when I am required to lay down my life so that others may live. Orkanir knows what I am talking about. And I thought, as a sword of the Nazad Esiask, you would, too."

Ralir looked down.

"He helped us!"

It was a moment before Korfax spoke again.

"But once he was committed to the path we could not help him," he said.

19

JUDGEMENTS

Vors-luhkal Orim-azil
Ipzar-krih Torzu-brj-jo
Nio-isag Ang-od-tranun
Qu-ipul Zumvi-butith
Thil-q-uhm Ipaj-temihs
Nihon-bad Krg-fel-thilarp
Pim-pi-je Od-ald-onun

They traversed the ridge as quickly as they could, but with Korfax wounded their progress was slow. The only good thing was that they saw no further sign of the enemy at all.

As they reached the last summit on the ridge, they came to a high valley, the briefest of respites before the great walls and peaks of the Adroqin Vohimar began in earnest. Somewhere up ahead and somewhat to the south lay the Pisea Fal. There was no other way that they could go or any other way of which they knew.

Korfax was not looking forward to the climb. Though the storms had been and gone, it would take at least another two days to cross the mountains, and who knew how the weather would change in the meantime? The Pisea Fal was not the easiest of paths and there was no longer any Arged of the Korith Peis to come to their aid.

It was as they rested that Obelison saw it, a glint in the sky, a reflection of brilliant light high up above the clouds. She pointed to it and laughed. There was only one thing that it could be.

"Look!" she cried. "A sky ship! There is a sky ship up there!"

Orkanir and Korfax looked up with smiles, but Ralir could only frown.

"And how will that help us? They are up there, we are down here."

Obelison gave him a fierce look, but Korfax laid a hand upon her arm and looked reprovingly at Ralir.

"You forget; I can send up a signal."

He drew out his stave and summoned fire of air from the emptiness within. Though it hurt him greatly, he could do that much at least. A single shaft of light flew from his stave and up into the heavens. The clouds parted at its touch and the sky ship was revealed. And so, of course, were they.

It was not long before the sky ship circled and came back in answer to the call. They watched as it approached. It was one of the smaller kind, and the ridge on which they now waited was just large enough to accept it.

It glided over the ridge and circled around before rearing up before them, halting itself upon a sudden updraft. It then folded its great wings away and landed gently. For a moment all was still, then its doors opened and several figures emerged.

Orkanir was the first to come to its side. The sky master had already disembarked and now stood there with five Branith spread to either side. Behind them waited a Noqvoan. Orkanir bowed to them all in gratitude.

"May the light of The Creator shine upon you," he said

"And upon you, Branvath Orkanir," said the sky master, bowing in return.

Orkanir smiled.

"Raxen Liexar. It is good to see you."

"And you."

He looked at all the others.

"You are all here? Good! You are lucky that you saw us. Though it was not the nature of our mission, I had hoped we would find you."

He gestured to the Noqvoan behind, as if that answered every question, but the Noqvoan was not looking at either of them. Instead he had eyes only for Korfax, and his expression was a curious mixture of anger and regret.

"Yes, fortunate indeed," said the Noqvoan. "If you had continued this way you would have come upon the Agdoain even as you achieved the other side of the Adroqin Vohimar."

"And who are you?" Korfax asked.

"I am Noqvoan Kalas Nar Odoiar and am here at the express command of the Noqvoanel. You should board now. Time is of the essence."

They boarded the ship and it was soon up in the air again, circling as it gained height.

Korfax turned to Odoiar.

"You said that we would come upon the Agdoain beyond the mountains, but the only Agdoain that we have seen were all behind us, and they were not following such a path."

Odoiar looked critically at Korfax's stave.

"We saw your fire and came to investigate. Though you may have put down many times many as you fled into the hills, my guess would be that they were but a few roving bands, the outriders of a far greater storm."

"What storm? What do you mean?"

Odoiar looked back at Liexar.

"Are we there yet?" he asked.

"We are just approaching our last position, Noqvoan," returned Liexar.

Odoiar beckoned to Korfax.

"Come with me, 'Geyad', and let me show you a thing."

Korfax limped after Odoiar, leaning as ever upon Obelison. Both Orkanir and Ralir had offered to help, but she would let no other touch him now; he had become her concern and hers alone. So Ralir and Orkanir came behind. Odoiar had not invited them, but they followed all the same. At the rail of the balcony they all stopped and looked down.

A grey mist partially obscured the land below, and though it lay across the valleys and all the low places, it seemed to be flowing ever upwards, like an incoming tide. This was a mist with a purpose.

The others frowned but Odoiar did not change his expression at all.

"This is what I was observing when Liexar saw your sign. We heard rumour of it only this morning, the rising of great mists across the whole of the furthest north."

He hardened his gaze.

"It is as I and many others of my order feared. Your mission to destroy the genesis of these demons has stirred them up, all at once. Now they will wage open war against us. Their hand has been forced."

Korfax glanced at the Noqvoan.

"But I was ordered to destroy their way into this world," he said. "I was told to do so by the Geyadel himself, and by no lesser personage."

"So I was informed," said Odoiar. "But when my order learned of this, many considered it a step too far."

Korfax clutched at his stave and stepped forward.

"You dare to judge the Geyadel?"

Obelison held him back gently. Odoiar looked at her for a moment as if her intervention was totally unnecessary, before turning back to contemplate the mist below. He had an air of weariness about him now, as though he was dealing with reluctant children.

"I dare nothing," he said. "I merely state the facts."

Ralir stepped forward.

"You heard what Mathulaa said," he said to Korfax. "You know how long that gateway had been at the Forujer Allar. Who knows how many Agdoain have tumbled through it, hiding themselves away in all the dark places? This land is wide and empty. It is the one reason why the Wars of Unification took so long to end. Who knows all the secret ways? No one now. If Mathulaa and his people could have hidden from us for all this time, imagine what the Agdoain could do."

Odoiar frowned at what Ralir had revealed.

"And who is this Mathulaa?"

"He helped us," answered Ralir. "We encountered him on our travels. He died to preserve us."

Ralir gestured downwards.

"Many of the enemy followed us after the gateway was destroyed, and Korfax killed them with the last of his qasadar, but I have found myself wondering how many were left behind. The gateway through which they have come has been sitting there for seven years at least."

Odoiar did not move. He gave the impression that little would satisfy him.

"Yes," he said, "how many indeed! Well, the answer lies below you. Follow those mists back, follow them all and you will find that they cover all the country hereabouts, all the empty places as you say. And the mist keeps growing as though welling up from many springs. If an army travels beneath it then they are still emerging from whatever holes they have been sleeping in."

Then Odoiar laughed bitterly to himself.

"Army? What am I saying? That is no mere army down there; that is a flood, a deluge, an irresistible tide. May The Creator have mercy upon any that stand in its path, for they will be swept away and drowned."

He turned to Liexar.

"Take us back now, I think we have seen enough."

They came to the great towers of Ralfen as night enfolded the land about them in shadows.

The sky ship landed upon the wide swath set aside for it, inside the outer wall and just beyond the northernmost tower. They disembarked and stood upon the verdant lawns of Ralfen. Each in their own particular way breathed easier at the sight. Korfax bowed his head, Obelison watched gently, Orkanir stood straighter and Ralir smiled the most careless smile that he could. They had returned once more to a tamer place, one made over in the image of the Ell.

Many Branith came forward to form an honour guard, and many looked on in expectation as Korfax, leaning ever on Obelison, walked slowly towards them whilst Orkanir and Ralir followed behind. In front, though, at his own insistence, walked Odoiar, his face as hard as ever, looking neither left nor right as he led them all to the great doors.

The slam of the great doors behind them was both music and a warning to their ears. They were safe at last, but judgement awaited them and outside it was getting dark.

In the apartments of the Faxith, Korfax's wound was tended and swiftly healed. There was no poison in it and though deep it was declared clean by the healers in attendance, but a better healing awaited him, for his father was already in the tower and it was not long before Sazaaim came to see his son.

He came with shining eyes, Orkanir at his side like a herald. Korfax and Sazaaim embraced for long moments and then Sazaaim stared intently at his son whilst Orkanir looked on proudly.

"That you are safe and well is as great a joy to me than any I have known these past few seasons. And that you were successful in the task that was given to you merely tips the flame. I do not know when I have been as happy or as proud as I am now. You have honoured your house in so many ways. I am so proud of you, my son."

Korfax could say nothing. His eyes filled with tears and they embraced again. Finally Sazaaim drew back.

"Orkanir tells me that you have discovered something more of the nature of the Agdoain," he said.

"The gateway that they used was like nothing I have ever seen before," Korfax told him. "This is a threat from realms of which we have no knowledge at all."

Sazaaim sighed.

"That is also what I have come to believe. Nothing of the old learning applies."

He turned away for a moment, his eyes distant, but then he turned back again and smiled his rare smile. "Now tell me everything and leave nothing out. I must know your tale. I must know how my son honours his calling."

Korfax bowed his head but his father laughed in return. How clean the sound, how honest! His father took his arms and held them.

"No, my son, I do not say such things lightly. This is twice now that you have proven your valour, and twice that Orkanir and Ralir have seen you do it, but now I would hear it in full, from you and from no other."

So Korfax told all that had happened, of the following of Obelison, of the loss of their steeds and the help of Mathulaa, even what he saw of Peis-homa, and at the end he was surprised to see a sad look on his father's face. Now it was Sazaaim's turn to bow his head.

"So the last of the Korith Peis chose to perish in order to save you. That is a sad end indeed, but noble."

He looked up again.

"You truly saw Peis-homa?" he asked.

"As though I were there."

Korfax was surprised to see the sadness in his father's face replaced by a sudden look of guilt.

"Such a terrible thing," Sazaaim said. "So terrible."

Korfax turned to Orkanir.

"Would you leave us? There are some questions I must ask my father."

Orkanir bowed and left. Sazaaim looked at his son carefully.

"What is it?"

"Where is Obelison?"

"With those of her order; they will not let her see another until they are done with her."

Korfax surged to get up, but his father pushed him back down again.

"Do not interfere. It is no longer your concern, despite what you may believe. She has disobeyed. She must now answer for her defiance."

Then Sazaaim smiled again.

"So she is the one you have chosen?"

"Yes," Korfax replied, instantly on edge. "We would not have succeeded if not for her. They should not have denied her vision."

His father looked on for a moment, watching and feeling the air with his thoughts. "I do not think you should be overly concerned," he said at last. "They may disapprove of what she did, but they cannot deny the outcome. She has been vindicated, and they cannot argue with that."

Then he leaned in closer.

"You have chosen well," he said.

Korfax smiled at his father's approval. Then he lay back and thought for a moment, before turning back to his father once more.

"Father, there is something else, something I saw in the vision of Peis-homa."

"What is it?"

"Black swords – the Haelok Aldaria wielded black swords."

Sazaaim bowed his head.

"I know the question that burns you. Why? I asked my father the very same thing at the end, and he told me the truth, but I will not give you this burden, my son, not yet. Let it remain with me until my time is up. It is as I said to you at the beginning: we are guardians, you and I. That is our calling. The Farenith are guardians."

"But why not destroy it?"

Sazaaim smiled sadly.

"Because we are caught between the cliff and the sea. I will not tell you the reason for that either, so let us say no more about it. Forget it, my son, forget it until the time comes when you must know. Let us think instead about the now."

Then he became stern as though he had gathered himself up and now shrouded himself in his duty once more.

"No doubt Ralir has also told this tale, as has Obelison. Many will know that you let one of the Argedith live. I fear there will be trouble for you because of that."

"But he saved us! He allied himself to us. He was part of the vision."

"I know that, my son, I know. And not a few will honour him for it, but there are others that will not."

"What do you mean?"

"History, it seems, desires ever to repeat itself. You have entered a time of testing, much as I did at your age, but do not surrender to them, do not admit to acts that you did not commit, nor to things that you did not witness. You spared this Mathulaa precisely because he chose to aid you in your need. You saw him for what he was, not what others might call him. You saw his truth, but there are some on the council, in our order even, who only bow before the altar of expediency. Beware of them, beware them all, for they will try to use this to bring down our house. They have tried it before, as you well know. They will say that you broke your oaths, that you diminished your calling, but you must pay them no heed, none of them. They are but voices in the wind, and how often does the wind blow where it will? You must be as strong as you were at your forging. You have many powerful friends, and though you may not realise it, the mightiest of them can turn aside even the wrath of the west. Let no harsh words trouble you, my son, for you are well loved."

Wrapped about by the words of his father, Korfax walked the great wall of Ralfen and bowed in turn as each Bransag of the watch bowed to him as he passed. He felt stronger now, able to walk unaided, though he lent upon his stave somewhat more than was customary. However, his stave was unbreakable and harder than any substance known to the Ell, so his only danger lay in damaging the stone of the wall.

Somewhere, in one of the towers, Obelison was still enduring the wrath of her order. He missed her. He had not seen her since they had come to Ralfen and he found himself aching to see her again, but Obelison had been hustled away as soon as they had declared themselves within the gates, lost to sight in a swirl of enclosing robes.

Even his father was gone from him now, deep in discussion with Enay Lasidax and Noqvoan Odoiar, debating what action it was best to take next. Korfax wondered what they would decide.

Odoiar passed his hands through the many maps that hung in the air over the great table.

"They travel the land in great roving bands," he said, "tens of thousands strong. Two such armies have I seen, both heading south, though I imagine there are many more like them scattered across the furthest north. But behind this ragged vanguard seethes a force I would not have thought possible before now. It is as though the entire north-west, from Tohus all the way to the Forujer Allar, has erupted with the foe. I think they have been waiting in all the empty places, beneath the earth, deep in cave or lake..."

Lasidax leaned forward and stared hard at Odoiar.

"Lake? Whatever do you mean, my good Noqvoan?" he questioned.

Odoiar narrowed his gaze.

"I saw them myself. Before we came upon Geyad Korfax I saw them rise up out of the waters of Zlminoaj, clambering out of the south end, a seemingly endless stream. It was fortunate indeed that we flew past at the apposite time, or we would not have seen them at all."

Odoiar breathed deeply before continuing.

"Do you know how long Zlminoaj is, how wide and how deep? One could sink all the beasts of the world in its waters and never see the bodies again. Our foe has arisen at last. This mission given to Korfax, this mission to destroy their way into our world, has been like a beacon of war to these creatures. They will fight us openly now, and with all their strength. And why? They have no choice! We have forced their hand. They have no place of retreat."

Odoiar became grimmer, if such a thing were possible, and he stared at the table as though it suddenly appalled him.

"Neither have we seen all that they are. I am certain that they possess stratagems we do not yet comprehend."

Lasidax lost all of his customary mannerisms at last and stood as still as a statue.

"And what do you mean by that?" he asked quietly.

The light from the stones upon the table lent Odoiar's face a sepulchral cast as he leaned forward.

"There were many shapes that crawled their way out of Zlminoaj," he answered, "and not all of them were like the creatures that we have come to know. I saw tall thin things, quick and fast and dancing. I only caught a glimpse of them, for they were distant and covered by obscuring mists, but what I saw was enough to fill me with disquiet. And then there were the others, vast lumbering shapes as huge as towers. What they might be I do not know, but I fear that we will rue our ignorance ere the end."

Odoiar placed his clenched fists upon the table and gazed downwards.

"But around these stranger shapes swarmed a force I recognised all too well. I saw the Agdoain and their mounts, in numbers so vast that I could not even begin to count them."

Lasidax now leaned across the table himself and looked intently at Odoiar.

"I do not believe what I am hearing. Do you have any idea of their strength at all, or is it your unhappy intent to horrify the rest of us into silence with the power of your imagination?"

Odoiar narrowed his eyes but did not look up.

"And that will be enough of that, Enay! In the Umadya Levanel I was trained to observe, objectively and impassively. I was not trained to imagine. And when I underwent my training I had no peer in the Balt Kaalith in either the estimation of numbers or in the disposition of forces."

He suddenly glared back at Lasidax, impassioned at last.

"And this is no idle boast, Enay! Consider it instead another simple fact, one of many and utterly verifiable. Do I have any idea of their strength? You do not know what you are asking! The rise of the Agdoain is so great in number that it chills my blood merely to think of it."

He drew away from the table and stared at each in turn as though to mark them in his mind. Finally he took the gaze of Lasidax and held it.

"Enay, there are so many of the foe that no place in the north can withstand them. They will crush everything in their path. Every tower and every city that lies between them and Othil Zilodar they will conquer. It is all but a certainty. And though it might seem inconceivable to you, they may very well take Othil Zilodar also, before finally marching down upon Emethgis Vaniad."

Sazaaim looked sadly at Odoiar.

"So that is it then. It is decided. There is no other choice before us. We abandon all the places hereabouts and make for Othil Zilodar. We make our stand there."

Lasidax looked up, his thin face contorted in outrage.

"It is NOT decided! Who has authority here? Last time I looked it was Lasidax, not Sazaaim, who commanded this stone."

Sazaaim drew himself up to his full height and his gaze was fiery. He took out a cloth set with the seal of the high council of the Dar Kaadarith. The cloth wrapped a kamliadar. He held that up.

"Here is the will of Abrilon, Geyadel of the Dar Kaadarith."

Sazaaim handed the crystal to Lasidax.

"Take this stone and hear the words within it."

Lasidax took the crystal but did not set it in motion. Sazaaim waited a moment and then hardened his gaze.

"Set the stone in motion, Lasidax, so that all here may bear witness."

Lasidax drew back and touched the kamliadar as he was bidden. The blue light within waxed brightly and a voice spoke out of it, the unmistakable voice of Abrilon.

"Hear now the will of Geyadel Kallus Enay Abrilon. In times of peril I give Geyad Faren Enay Sazaaim my full authority, to speak with my voice and to stand in my place. He is to be obeyed in all ways unless one of the high council be present. So say I, Abrilon, Geyadel of the Dar Kaadarith, in the service of the Velukor, blessed be his name."

Lasidax threw the crystal down as though it had burned him. He scowled back at Sazaaim.

"So I am to abandon my command without even showing a token of resistance? How easily is Ralfen to be bought?"

Sazaaim all but ignited.

"And do you, Lasidax, think it was easy for me to abandon Losq? My family, my forebears, have dwelt there since the days of Anolei, blessed be his name. How much greater is my loss than yours?"

There was a stunned silence until Odoiar reached out and picked up the stone. He handed it back to Sazaaim.

"I concur," he said. "We should leave as soon as possible. I suggest we head for Leemal. From there the word will spread more quickly."

Sazaaim chose as many as possible to accompany him to Leemal, but the single sky ship could not take more than a hundred, so the rest were to head east under the command of Angalam and Lasidax.

Lasidax was clearly not happy, but he did not argue. Angalam, though, was grateful. They would head for Peinothar, his home, and that meant he had a chance to help preserve it. Everyone else boarded the sky ship.

They flew across the wide hills and fields of the north, heading south. From the balcony of the sky ship Korfax watched it all go by with a disquieting sense of fearful familiarity. The land below was far too empty for his comfort.

There were no beasts in the fields or on the hillsides. No one was on the road, and all the towers and the houses that they passed over reeked of abandonment. It was like the land on his journey to the Forujer Allar. Only the trees and the grass remained.

Odoiar came up beside him.

"You see it, don't you?" he said.

"See what?" asked Korfax.

"Below – a sign of what is to come. You see how empty it is down there."

Korfax looked down again.

"These lands were evacuated a long time ago on my father's orders, after the slaughter at the Umadya Beltanuhm."

"That is so," Odoiar agreed. "But what you are looking at is what will happen elsewhere now. The north will clear of life before the oncoming flood, and those who escape its hunger will become as spirits of regret. We have been forced to abandon our world to demons."

"Until we claim it back again."

Odoiar looked back darkly at Korfax.

"No doubt you comfort yourself with such hopes," he said, "but I am of another temper. I have already divined the truth here. The Agdoain intend to remove us from this life, and your rash actions and those of your order have caused them to act before the rest of us were ready."

Having said his piece he turned about and walked away again. Korfax watched him go and scowled at his receding back. He felt Obelison come to his side. He put an arm about her and held her close. She leaned her head against his shoulder.

"I do not like him," she said, meaning Odoiar.

Korfax looked down at her gently and stroked her arm.

"All the Balt Kaalith are carved from such stone," he said, but the words were no comfort. Odoiar had already divined the truth here, much as Korfax had: 'The Agdoain intend to remove us from this life.' That was what he had said, and Korfax knew it to be true.

There were many upon the viewing balcony as they came closer to Leemal, waiting to see the safety of their city. First the high top of Lee Par slowly emerged from behind its neighbours, swiftly followed by its companion, Lee Nor, and between them both Leemal was finally revealed. Faces fell at the sight. There was silence. War had already passed this way.

Some of the towers looked burnt and broken and many of the inner walls appeared to have been beaten down. Thin grey mists rose up into the sky from within the city walls like the ghosts of spent pyres and there were black stains, like scorches, scattered here and there upon the pale stone. Leemal looked utterly abandoned.

Korfax clutched at the rail even as he looked. He stared at the ruined city and felt his heart go dead inside him. Fair Leemal, the fairest city of the furthest north, was fair no longer.

Odoiar came to stand beside him. The look on his face was not quite one of satisfaction or quite one of vindication, but something in between. He gestured at the city.

"Do you see now what you have begun? I told you that this would happen, but you refused to believe it. Only now do you begin to appreciate the price others will pay for your order's lack of judgement. Siege and slaughter have become your gifts to the world."

Korfax did not stop to think. He turned and struck Odoiar full upon his face with a clenched fist. Odoiar fell back, flew back even, before crashing to the deck in a sprawl. Others came forward to restrain Korfax, but he threw them aside, even as they lay hold of him. Eventually there were too many and he was held down, though they had much difficulty keeping him there.

"LET GO OF ME!" he roared. "LET GO! HE SHALL PAY FOR HIS WORDS."

Obelison ran forwards and knelt before him, taking his raging face in her hands. She sent her mind into his and soothed his fire. He stared back at her for a moment, the fire boiling in his eyes, but then he gradually calmed, and as he subsided so the others gradually released him.

Odoiar was back on his feet by now, rubbing his face as blood dribbled from his nose and his lips. He wiped the blood away and looked at its stain on his hand. Then he looked back at Korfax.

"I will have satisfaction for this, at the very least," he said.

Korfax glared back and stood up. Then he raised a fist and shook it.

"Name the place and the time! I already look forward to meeting you there."

Sazaaim arrived and stepped between them both.

"Enough! There is no time for this, none at all."

Korfax pointed at Odoiar.

"He came to me. When he saw the city he mocked me. He spoke of siege and slaughter as if he relished such things."

Korfax gestured at Leemal and his eyes were suddenly clenched with pain.

"Mother was down there!"

Sazaaim stared at Korfax for a moment and then turned back slowly to Odoiar.

"Is this true? Did you mock?"

Odoiar held up his hands in the gesture of denial.

"I only pointed out to your son what his actions have wrought. It is your order that has brought us to this ruin, your lack of judgement that has brought this about."

Sazaaim took a step forward. Odoiar took a step back.

"Do you dare question the will of the council of the Dar Kaadarith? My son was told to seek out the gateway of the Agdoain. This he did. My son did his duty as befits a Geyad of the Dar Kaadarith, and he did it bravely and with much sacrifice."

"But when disaster ensues I would question the judgement of any for not having foreseen it," said Odoiar. He pointed at Korfax. "And as for your son's duty? Many know his tale now. He allowed one of the Argedith to live."

Korfax folded his arms and glared back.

"Mathulaa saved my life," he answered. "Mathulaa saved the life of all of us who sought to destroy the Agdoain gateway. He fought with us against the Agdoain. And there is more. This was no reluctant alliance on his part – he relished it. He spat whenever the name of the Black Heart was spoken. He was the last of the Korith Peis, the last of the people of Peis-homa. Do you remember the tale of Peis-homa, Odoiar? He helped us because of that, not despite it. I spared his life? Of course I did. Who would not?"

Odoiar looked disgusted.

"You spared his life?" he hissed. "What are the words of Karmaraa? From your very own mouth you are condemned. You are an oath breaker!"

Oath breaker? Korfax paused. He had no answer to that. Many around him now wore frowns of concern, but Sazaaim did not; instead, he rounded on Odoiar in sudden fury.

"And can you see all ends, Noqvoan? My son was both merciful and considerate, but you it seems have never been of such a temper. You of the Balt Kaalith were ever quick to judge, ever quick to call up the immutable law to your defence, but you reinvent yourselves easily enough when you see advantage in it. How many times have I seen your policies bend with the wind? More than I care to remember. You and yours have no honour in my eyes!"

Sazaaim drew himself taller and his eyes glittered.

"Live in your dream of self-righteous purity, if you will, but leave the rest of us to deal with the real world."

Sazaaim pointed at the wreck of Leemal.

"The love of my life was in that place, Odoiar, down there in that smouldering ruin. Would you mock her death before me? Would you? Dare you?"

Sazaaim drew out his stave and held it up. Energies flashed within it and at each of its tips. Everyone backed away now, even Korfax. He watched his father with amazement and with growing pride. Let Odoiar and his ilk answer his father's wrath!

Though Odoiar stood his ground, his breath came hard as he steeled himself for the killing blow. He understood his peril now, all too well. Let Sazaaim speak with his power and he would cease utterly to be.

"I did not mock," he said quietly.

"Then why did my son strike you?" asked Sazaaim.

"Because I wounded his pride!"

Korfax surged forwards again but Sazaaim stopped him with an upraised hand.

"Do not. This one is not worthy."

He turned back to Odoiar.

"I see more than you, Odoiar of the Balt Kaalith. I know the real reason my son struck you. He struck you not for his pride but for your own. I have seen enough of you now to know what kind of creature you are. Your kind are rife within your order. You believe that your way is the only way, and you treat the rest of the world with contempt! I will tolerate you no more. If we survive what comes next I will have your obeisance and your contrition – and that of your order – or I will call you out upon the duelling field myself, along with every other Noqvoan that dares stand beside you."

There was dead silence now. Sazaaim looked around him.

"Now let this be an end to it. The rest of you should be about your tasks. We have a duty to those in the city below, and that duty we shall perform. This matter will not be spoken of again on this journey."

And that was that. Sazaaim turned away and took Korfax with him. Obelison followed closely and the rest of those on the viewing platform turned away. Odoiar was left alone, hard eyes filled with a brittle light and a dark swelling growing upon his cheek.

They landed outside the walls.

Sazaaim chose many of the Branith to go with him into the city itself, but to ride at his side he picked Orkanir, and Orkanir alone. Neither Korfax nor Ralir were to go. Korfax would have protested but Ralir held him back.

"Do as your father says," he counselled.

Korfax rounded on him and his eyes were furious.

"This is not your concern."

Ralir remained mild.

"Oh, but it is. Your father gave me orders, orders I do not think I would care to disobey."

Korfax dropped some of his anger.

"What orders?"

"Only that you are to remain on board and under my eye. Besides, we don't want you putting our resident Noqvoan to the sword in a moment of ill-considered rage, now do we?"

"It is the best thing for him as far as I am concerned."

Ralir smiled.

"Come on, come with me. Let your father do what he needs to do. Orkanir is with him, so your father is already warded by one of the very best."

Korfax bowed his head at last and let Ralir lead him back into the sky ship. Obelison was waiting for them both.

"What happens now?" she asked.

Ralir looked over his shoulder.

"Geyad Sazaaim said that we should remain aloft until they have ridden through the city and taken account of the dead and the damage."

Korfax looked down and his eyes all but boiled.

"If my mother is one of them..."

He let the words hang in the air. Obelison took his arm.

"Come, Korfax, please, come and sit with me. You must not dwell on that. There is always hope."

Ralir gestured ahead.

"I know of a quiet place. I was going to take Korfax there anyway. Raxen Liexar has been given his orders also. We will remain aloft until such time as we are called back down again."

It was a long time before the sky ship landed again, but when it did so, Sazaaim, Orkanir and the others were already waiting outside.

Korfax watched his father dismount. What news would he bring? Korfax suddenly found himself not wanting to hear it. Then he saw that his father was smiling, even as he approached, and his demeanour was far happier than it had been before.

"Not all died, it seems," he said. "Some escaped and your mother was amongst them. She left word for us where she knew I would find it."

Korfax breathed a sigh of relief but then looked back at the city.

"What happened? Where are the foe?"

"They have not lingered. It appears they continued east. From what your mother told me in her message it was her intent to run south, following the high road over the hills."

His father came forward and held him.

"Baschim will be with her. His sword will ward her."

Korfax drew back and looked hard at the city once more.

"This is my fault. This would not have happened but for me."

His father grasped him by the shoulders.

"No, my son. This would have happened whether they arose now or a year from now. If you had not destroyed their gateway imagine how much worse this would be. How many more of the foe would now fill the north?"

Sazaaim turned to the Liexar.

"We fly south and follow the hills. We look for survivors."

They flew on, taking a long curving flight to the south-west in the hope of finding those that had escaped the wreck of Leemal.

It was as they reached the last failing line of the long hills of the Leein Ises that they saw the riders. There were many chariots as well, old relics that had been drafted back into service. When the riders saw the sky ship many on the viewing platform heard their grateful cries rising up from below.

The sky ship landed beyond them, upon the high green sward of a wide hill.

All those inside came out, waiting to offer aid or looking for loved ones. Sazaaim looked at Liexar as he disembarked.

"Do we have any room at all?"

Liexar looked doubtful.

"We are almost full to capacity as it is. There are the lower holds, of course, but it will be difficult to take even a few. This ship was built for speed, not for cargo."

"Then we will do what we can," Sazaaim said. "At least there is no sign that the Agdoain follow in pursuit. We must leave behind as few as is possible, and those must be fast and able to defend themselves. The road to Othil Zilodar may be long, but at least it is easy."

The riders came to the sky ship. There were many hundreds. A Geyad led them and there was a Brandril by his side. Korfax looked at them both for a moment but only recognised the Brandril. It was Fizur, the commander of Leemal's forces and one of the highest of the Belenith. He had been proud and strong when Korfax had seen him last, but now he looked strangely fragile, as though something inside him had broken.

Korfax continued to search the faces until he finally saw her, his mother. He ran to her and they embraced. Then he stood aside as his father came to her, and as they embraced he turned to find Baschim standing there as well. They smiled gladly at each other and then hugged at last.

"It is good to see you again, Noren."

"And you, Baschim, and you."

"A hard road."

"But a glad ending."

After the joys and disappointments, the meetings and the debates, Korfax found himself with his mother on a long bench in the lower holds of the sky ship.

Earlier he had watched as she met Obelison for the first time.

"So you are the one that has claimed my son's heart?" she enquired coldly.

Obelison kept herself still, not knowing what to expect.

"He has claimed mine also," she answered.

"I am also told that you rebelled."

"They denied me."

Obelison looked hard now, matching the hardness of Tazocho, but then Tazocho seemed to fill with light and warmth and she came forward and embraced Obelison.

"Bless you!" she said. "Bless you for your bravery and for bringing my son back to me. You are worthy of all the praise I can give you."

Obelison was clearly surprised and gladdened, but then Tazocho drew back once more and looked piercingly into her eyes.

"Never give in," Tazocho told her. "Follow your vision always, and know that it will always be true."

Korfax felt a deep surge of happiness as he watched his mother and Obelison embrace once more. She approved, as did his father. That was good.

Now they sat alone, mother and son, tales ready to be told. Though they were crowded about by many, a subtle space was left around them. They were effectively alone.

"Do you wish to speak of it?" he asked.

She looked at him for a moment but then quickly looked away. She sighed and stared at the floor.

"To brood in silence darkens the heart," she murmured. Then she looked back at him again. "But to find both you and your father once more? Such things can banish even the darkest fears."

She laid her hand in his and smiled as best she could.

"When the enemy came upon the city in the night I thought my world already ended. It was like Losq all over again, just like Losq – the chaos, the disbelief, the horror – but a thousand times worse."

She closed her eyes. "Would that I could forget it." She opened them again. "Do you really wish to hear about it?" she asked.

"I wish only to hear whatever you choose to tell me," he answered.

She looked carefully at him now, her eyes searching his.

"I am not the only one that has travelled a hard road, I think. I see scars, scars and dark bruises."

Now it was his turn to look away, to look down.

"I was successful in my mission, but many now question my judgement."

She drew back a little, frowning ever so slightly. Then she smiled more fully and turned his head back towards her with her left hand.

"Then here is the way it shall be. I will tell you my tale and then you will tell me yours."

Korfax agreed.

"You should hear what I have to say anyway," he told her. "It will help when others offer harsher opinions."

Tazocho paused for a moment, searching his face again, and then she began her tale.

"I awoke in the early hours to the sound of warning bells. I went to my door but found Baschim already there. His face was grave. He told me that Agdoain had climbed over the walls and that there was fighting in the city. I dressed quickly and went to find Enay Paoahz. Paoahz, when I came to him, was alone, apart from Bomian. You remember Bomian, don't you? As silent as the hills and just as unreadable. He was a lot like Baschim in many ways, never shirking his duty, always as solid as stone.

"Bomian did not move when I entered, neither greeting nor dismissing, but as soon as Paoahz saw me he told me what was occurring and what I should do. The Agdoain had poured in from the west and had swarmed up the walls so quickly and in such numbers that the Branith of the watch could do little or nothing to hold them back. He told me that a tower of flesh had fallen against the wall and that the Agdoain had climbed up this. How such a thing was possible I do not know, and I can say nothing more on the matter as I did not witness it. Geyad Jerrah and Geyad Zenapil were the first to rally a defence, along with Brandril Fizur, but by the time they engaged the foe the city was already doomed. There were tens of thousands of them and they filled the western quarter. We faced a flood of swords and teeth. They swarmed through the streets, all but irresistible. Of the Branith sent to stop them only a handful survived. Zenapil spent himself so that Jerrah and Fizur could escape. He even burned the stone of the city at the end, so much force he called up.

"Paoahz had already ordered the evacuation when I came to him. He ordered me from the city. I understood his intent. He would remain and Bomian would stay with him. Just as Paoahz could not bear to leave his city, Bomian could not bear to leave his master's side.

"I left with Baschim. He is gifted with foresight, that one. He had already prepared a number of old ceremonial chariots kept in the Garad for just such an occasion as this, so by the time I got back from Paoahz, we were ready to leave. We then fled to the east side of the city and events moved quickly after that. I left a stone for your father in a certain place, hidden under a marker, telling him what had happened. Whilst I was with Paoahz, Baschim told the other servants what they should do, just in case. So it was with a fleet of fast and well-stocked chariots that we arrived at the east gate.

"At the east gate I met with Jerrah and Fizur. Jerrah, though wounded, was still strong, but Fizur had been reduced to a walking ghost. I do not think he could believe how quickly his command had been overthrown.

"Seeing how the Agdoain were so intent about their business I suggested that we ride around the walls whilst they were within and make our escape to the south and the west, taking the road over the Leein Ises. I even told Jerrah that I saw good fortune in it, though little was certain by that time. Thank The Creator both sight and luck were with me that night.

"A few hundreds joined us, the last of the city. Those that were wounded we set in the chariots. Then we left signs saying where we had gone so that others might follow, intending to leave before the Agdoain saw us. I also had some of the others of my order hide copies of my stone for any that followed, just in case.

"We rounded the walls and took to the road. A few roving bands of Agdoain were circling the wall, but the Branith with us swept them all aside. Brief vengeance was taken, though it was poor recompense for our losses. Then we rode hard into the hills and made our escape through the darkness. The Agdoain took the rest of the city, feasting as they went. Then they went east, every single one of them. One lone Bransag remained behind so that he could bear witness. Then he followed us and told us all that we were safe for now. Jerrah relaxed somewhat after that and thanked me greatly for my advice. He also turned to Baschim and blessed him for his foresight. No other had been so prepared."

She smiled to herself.

"Baschim had ordered the packing of much food and supplies. I am so grateful that he was there. When this is over we should honour him. He knows how to serve."

Korfax was silent for a long while. Eventually, he spoke.

"So out of great defeat a little hope still rises."

"A little, but only a little. We have yet to come to the main test, it seems. What amasses now out upon the northern plains is still to be faced."

"You have not told me everything, I think," Korfax said.

"Nor shall I," she answered, "not here at least. Some tales should never be told in the dark."

Then Korfax told her what he could of his mission and tried to be as sparing as his mother had been, but he could not evade the darker moments, the revelations, the horrors and the terrible price of victory.

Now it was Tazocho's turn to be silent. It had become a dance of revelations between them both, one following the other until no more could be said. She looked long at her son at the end and then she put her arms about him and held him tight. She said no words, but the passion with which she clung to him told him everything that he needed to know.

Sazaaim stood before Baschim.

"Now that all has been ordered and we have some time between us for smaller matters, I must ask you this. How did you know to prepare the chariots?"

Baschim bowed his head.

"It was a fear, Enay, a fear that grew on me when I heard of the Noren's mission to the north. My thoughts kept turning back to Losq, warning me that we should be prepared. I have never known such a thing, and the more I ignored it, the worse it became. So I set about ordering the preparation of the chariots. Many wondered why I was doing it, but all I could say was that we needed to be prepared. It was as though some watchful spirit had planted that very thought in my head. Save as many as possible, it said to me, and I saw it all again, in my mind if you will, the dead littering the city streets, just as they had littered the stones of Losq."

"Well, whatever the reason, it was well done."

Sazaaim smiled. Then he looked carefully at his servant.

"And did you bring aught else with you from Leemal?"

Baschim kept his head down.

"But that was the strangest thing, Enay. It was the first thing that I preserved, almost as if it had told me what to do. Nor could I gainsay it."

Sazaaim stared at his servant for a long time. His face darkened.

"I see," he said at last. "Then no more shall be said on the matter."

Othil Zilodar was reached quickly, and the news from the north spread out from the landing field like a plague. War was marching south. Korfax had expected to deliver his report to Geyadril Samafaa as soon as he arrived, but almost within the hour he was summoned to stand before the Tabaud himself for summary judgement. It seemed that Odoiar had wasted no time in bringing his accusations to bear.

Korfax stood as calmly as he could before a hastily assembled council of seven, but inside he was on fire.

The high lord of the city, Tabaud Abinax, sat before him, in the middle, as his judge. On either side sat six others, three to the left and three to the right, a sharp curve of advisers hurriedly assembled for this all but unprecedented council.

On the left were Geyadril Ponodol, Geyadril Samafaa and Geyadril Fokisne, whilst on the right were Urendril Nimagrah, Noqvoandril Tiarapax and Enay Orphahan, first counsellor to the Tabaud.

Looking at them all, seeing them all arrayed in their robes of office, Korfax remembered back to other times and other places. He had been here before. It was almost as if he was back in the seminary of the Dar Kaadarith again, standing once more for judgement, but though he had escaped lightly then, he did not consider that he would do so here. He had now broken one of the most solemn oaths of all.

Abinax stood up and looked at each of the others in turn. He then turned to Korfax as though reluctant, as if he did not want to be standing in judgement at all.

"Geyad Korfax," he said, "do you understand why you are here?"

Korfax bowed his head.

"Noqvoan Odoiar!"

Abinax offered a careful smile in response.

"Such an economical answer," he returned. "You have learnt brevity in your short life."

Abinax then frowned, but even his frown was careful.

"Noqvoan Odoiar has made a particularly serious charge against you," he continued. "I presume you know what it is?"

Korfax bowed again.

"Yes, Tabaud. That I did willingly allow one of the Argedith to live."

Abinax looked almost sad now.

"So tell me the tale, Korfax, and leave nothing out. Then we shall see what we shall see."

Korfax spoke. No one interrupted, but as the narrative moved on its way, so the faces before him began to change. Concern, disbelief, horror and pride all flickered this way and that. Even the glacial Tiarapax seemed moved at times.

When Korfax was done, Abinax sat back in his chair.

"I have never heard anything like it in all my life. Astonishing, utterly astonishing."

Samafaa stood up, his face glowing with rage as he turned upon Tiarapax.

"This council should not be sitting at all. Withdraw the charges."

Tiarapax stood also and met the gaze of Samafaa with ease. He was just as tall but sparely built. He looked both strong and capable and his eyes were piercingly bright. Looking at him now Korfax felt daunted, despite himself. Tiarapax was one of the highest in the Balt Kaalith, on its high council no less, and rightly so by his demeanour. He exuded both force and purpose as though they were a second skin in which he had clothed himself.

"I will not," he said. "You heard the testimony. The charge is oath breaking. How can I possibly withdraw it, given what we have just heard?"

Samafaa folded his arms across his chest.

"The letter of the law but not its spirit, is that how it is now?"

Tiarapax would not be moved.

"The law is the law. An oath has been broken."

Abinax raised his stave and tapped it lightly upon the floor. The sound echoed sharply.

"Sit, both of you. Who sits in judgement here?"

Samafaa bowed to Abinax and sat himself back down. Tiarapax also sat but did not bow.

Abinax turned back to Korfax.

"So what do you say, Korfax?"

Korfax swallowed. Here it came. He could only tell the truth.

"It is true that I spared the life of Mathulaa, and it is true that he was of the Argedith, but he also saved my life, even though he knew what I was and what I was sworn to do."

"But could he not have done this in order to gain your trust?" Abinax asked.

"No," Korfax answered. "He sought us out willingly. He did not have to do anything that he did, but he did it nonetheless. He aided us and then gave his life to save ours. I think that shows something of his measure. Also he was the last of the Korith Peis, and that is no small matter either."

Abinax waited a moment and then let his gaze become a little harder.

"But is it not written in the Logah Dar that one shall not permit the Argedith to live?"

Korfax bowed his head but did not speak.

"And did you not swear, by The Creator, to uphold the words of Karmaraa?" continued Abinax.

Korfax closed his eyes.

"Yes," he said, and his voice shook.

"Then you have broken your oath, have you not?"

"Yes," Korfax said again, but this time he all but whispered it. Tiarapax sat back in his seat, folded his arms and looked satisfied at last. Abinax glanced at him for a moment and then turned back to Korfax.

"But in doing so you were successful in your mission to destroy the genesis of the Agdoain, were you not?"

Tiarapax unfolded his arms and glared at Abinax. Korfax took a long breath.

"I was," he answered.

"And who laid this mission upon you?"

"The Geyadel."

"And why did he give it to you?"

"Because his daughter saw it in a vision, it was her vision that guided us."

"She is one of the Exentaser, is she not?"

"Yes."

"So you were following the vision of an Uren?"

"Yes, I was."

Now Abinax looked at Tiarapax and Tiarapax all but scowled in return. Abinax leaned forward.

"Do you see where this leads, Noqvoandril?"

Tiarapax let out a long hiss.

"Very clever, Abinax, very clever indeed, but let us not forget the point in hand. An oath has been broken, an oath taken before The Creator."

"Yes, that is true," Abinax agreed, "but only in part, for did not Karmaraa also say that even evil may be made to serve the purposes of The Creator and in the end be seen as good? Or did you misunderstand the lesson of the Vovin? You are far too narrow in your vision, Tiarapax, you and the Balt Kaalith. I am beginning to wonder whether the breaking of oaths is the only reason you have asked for a council of judgement. Have not the Balt Kaalith been accused in return? Are you not now nursing your wounded pride?"

"This is no mere piece of theatre, Tabaud. The law has been broken."

"And did you not hear what I just said? Good from evil, as it is written. If it was only that, you still would not have a case to answer, but the Exentaser have also spoken. Or do you now deny that their word takes precedence over all others in such matters? Obelison was there, alongside Korfax, defending her vision. Would you have her come here and explain herself? Or do you now question the presence of Urendril Nimagrah? She did, after all, assay this vision. This was prophecy, Noqvoandril, and you know full-well that even Karmaraa bowed before prophecy and changed his policies accordingly."

Tiarapax stood up. He glanced at the rest of the council and then glared back at Abinax.

"You already knew what your judgement would be even before this council was assembled. You could have saved us all much time and preparation if you had revealed yourself beforehand."

He deepened his gaze.

"You accuse us of narrowness, but should we not accuse you in turn? Your friendship with Enay Sazaaim is well known."

Abinax tapped his stave lightly on the floor again, but now it had a dangerous sound to it. Tiarapax took a step back. Abinax held his stave before him and energies flickered dimly inside it.

"Beware, Noqvoandril! Do not provoke me! I find the tale of Korfax, Ralir, Orkanir and Obelison to be worthy of nothing but praise and song. They saw what needed to be seen. They acted with their hearts and with their heads. They endured great hardship and were both brave and compassionate. They did what had to be done and a great service to all of Lon-Elah was performed. These charges brought by Odoiar are born of spite, Tiarapax. Do you hear me? Spite! They are born of spite and envy and overweening pride. I find the Balt Kaalith wanting. Consider who you are, Tiarapax, and who you serve. Is it the greater good or the unyielding law?"

Tiarapax drew himself up for a moment, almost as if he meant to strike the high lord of the city with his stone scroll of office, but then he turned about and strode from the chamber.

Korfax waited before Abinax, his head still bowed. Abinax looked at each of the others in turn and met only agreement. He smiled and bowed to them all. Then he turned back to Korfax.

"You may go now, Korfax. There are no charges to answer here, none whatsoever. I have seen your heart, as have the others that remain beside me. Go now and serve the Dar Kaadarith again, as you have so ably done before. You are without stain."

Korfax bowed to the Tabaud and then left the chamber.

As Korfax entered the outer chamber he found his mother and father already waiting for him. Sazaaim stepped forward, as did Tazocho, and they both reached out for him, he on the left, she on the right. They touched him almost at the very same instant. His father spoke first.

"We just saw Tiarapax leave in a storm of fury. What happened?"

Korfax turned away. There was a fire in him somewhere, a great and burning fire.

"The Tabaud has said that there were no charges to answer. He bid me serve as I have ever done. I am without stain."

Korfax lowered his head like a penitent, but inside he shook with frustrated rage. How many times must he endure this? How many times must he justify himself in this way?

His mother came closer to him and held him tight. They stood there for a moment, two as one, whilst Sazaaim watched. Then Tazocho drew back again and smiled up at her son. Sazaaim smiled also as if everything was complete.

"Come," he announced, "let us leave this place. We have better things to occupy our time with."

Sky ships flew across the northern skies in well-ordered procession, coming and going, receiving and leaving. Many peoples entered the city and then left again.

The great and the powerful descended upon Othil Zilodar – Geyadel Abrilon to confront his daughter, Urenel Asvoan to see the peril for herself and Noqvoanel Vixipal to ask the many questions that vexed him. As soon as he arrived he went to the chambers of Tiarapax, not acknowledging anyone else until he stood before the Noqvoandril at last.

"Well, Tiarapax, and what was that council of judgement all about?"

"Did you not listen to my report?"

"I did, but now I am asking you to explain it to me in person."

Tiarapax kept his displeasure in abeyance. It was wise to do so with Vixipal, as one never knew where the Noqvoanel's attention was really focused.

"Noqvoan Odoiar cited charges against Korfax. He laid them before the Tabaud himself without consulting me. From that moment on my hand was forced."

Vixipal looked back coolly.

"I was told that you were most displeased by the verdict. That does not sound like reluctance to me."

Tiarapax held up a finger.

"I do not like to be made a fool of. When I heard that Leemal had fallen and that Sazaaim had spoken openly against the Balt Kaalith, I was angry. Besides, the charges were of the utmost seriousness. Here was one of the Dar Kaadarith, not only sparing the life of one of the Argedith, but also causing an army of demons to rise up and march down from the north to besiege the city where I was born. I was displeased at the end because Abinax had already decided which way his sword would fall."

Tiarapax glowered.

"I dislike mummery, Noqvoanel, especially when I am its unwitting victim."

Vixipal glowered back.

"Whilst I am appalled that one of the Farenith should spare the life of one of the Argedith, this is not a course of action I would have chosen at all."

Tiarapax started. That was not the answer he had expected, either.

"And just what do you mean by that?"

Vixipal stared at his hand, the one that was caressing the stone of the table.

"I had plans for Korfax," he said. "I had intended to woo him. He could have given us much-needed patronage. After all, he was the one that caused the exile of Dialyas, but now? We shall have to step most carefully in the future."

Tiarapax took a long, slow breath to calm himself down.

"If I had known your will in this matter I might have been more circumspect, but there are also the words of Sazaaim to consider. Harsh words were given to Odoiar, and they were heard by many. That tale is also being told. We are not held in high favour at the moment. Many side with Sazaaim."

"Yes, I have heard that, too, and it does not improve my mood."

Tiarapax held up a hand in warning.

"Do not think to confront him on this," he said, "or you will awaken too fierce a fire, I fear."

Vixipal offered the gesture of dismissal.

"You need have no concern for that. I know much concerning the Enay of Losq. He had the ear of the last Velukor. He wed with the Velukor's cousin after all. Many are in awe of his house and many are in awe of him, but he is already set in his ways, already intractable. Zafazaa saw to that."

Now Tiarapax was thoroughly mystified.

"What has Audroh Zafazaa to do with this?"

"A tale for another day, I think," said Vixipal.

"Then make that day soon. The Agdoain are on their way here."

"They will be repulsed."

"Odoiar does not think so."

"Odoiar? Thank you for reminding me. He has shown himself to be far too absolute, far too precipitate. He has spoiled my plans for Korfax. Korfax could have been a good friend to us, but now matters are worse and it is all due to Odoiar. I shall punish him, I think."

Abrilon looked down at his daughter and sighed.

"When I learned that you had gone missing it near broke my heart," he said.

Obelison kept her head bowed and did not answer. He narrowed his eyes.

"Have the Exentaser given you their judgement?" he asked.

"Yes," she answered quietly.

"And?"

His voice was imperious. She remained subdued.

"After much deliberation they approved. I was exonerated by my vision. It was agreed that the mission would have in all likelihood failed had I not been there."

Abrilon sighed again and stepped forward. He placed his hands upon her shoulders, caressing them, owning them.

"Oh, my child!" he returned. "Oh, my only!"

He closed his eyes entirely as he finally held her to him.

"Never, ever do such a thing again," he admonished. "I cannot lose you, too, I cannot. That would be too much to bear."

Obelison returned his embrace, clutching at him even as he held her. She let one single tear fall down her left cheek, one single tear, all she would spare. The others she buried away deep inside.

Abrilon held himself locked in sad pain as he held his daughter, his arms a wall about her. Choices, he thought to himself, and cost! He understood all too well.

They held a council in the great debating hall, all whose care was the world. They took their seats in turn, a wide circle of the powerful, the spiritual and the temporal.

Abinax held up his stave and tapped it seven times upon the floor. The others bowed and Abinax bowed in return.

"Let the deliberations begin," he announced.

There was a brief silence before Abrilon stood up. Abinax gestured.

"Geyadel."

Abrilon smiled.

"Tabaud, the preparations for the upcoming siege are already well in hand. The city fills with swords and empties of those that cannot fight, even as we speak. The Dar Kaadarith are prepared for any eventuality. There is little else to do now but continue our preparations and await the foe."

Now Vixipal stood up. Abinax bowed to him.

"Noqvoanel," he said.

Vixipal smiled.

"Tabaud, I have a concern."

"Say on."

"Would we be in this situation at all if it were not for the actions of the Geyadel?"

Abrilon raised an eyebrow.

"And how many more of the foe would you like to face? We acted as soon as we learned of the gateway. The mission of Korfax stopped yet another incursion of Agdoain into our world. There comes a time, Noqvoanel, when only action will suffice."

Vixipal bowed his head.

"I agree," he said. "But the Agdoain have been stirred up nonetheless. I always thought that divide and conquer was the better strategy. It was, after all, how the Wars of Unification were won. Deal with your enemy piecemeal. Good advice, I think, but now you have given these Agdoain no choice at all. Now they have come together as one, one single and overwhelming force."

Abrilon grimaced.

"But Korfax said that he was just in time to stop yet another eruption of these creatures."

"On the word of an Arged? Please! On this matter Korfax trusted a little too readily, I feel."

"And what do you mean by that?"

"Innocence is the province of youth. It takes time and experience to learn to see through masks. The Argedith have never been trustworthy."

Vixipal noted many sour expressions scattered about the table and smiled to himself inside. Abrilon, though, looked thoroughly scandalised.

"You judge far too harshly, Vixipal. Korfax followed the vision of Obelison. She saw the peril also, or do you deny the word of the Exentaser now?"

Vixipal did not withdraw.

"I do not," he said. "Though sent for judgement, Korfax has been exonerated. I have seen him, I have heard the tale of his deeds and I find his service to the Velukor worthy of nothing but praise. Mercy is a noble quality, one I am glad that he possesses in abundance. No doubt he will make a fine and noble Enay one day, but mercy, like idealistic youth, is also sometimes blind. Evil comes in many forms and has many masks. It even misleads itself at times. That is not the point that I wish to make, though. The hand that acts cannot be held accountable for the will that orders it."

Abrilon leaned forward.

"Say what it is you wish to say, Vixipal. No more circumlocutions, if you please. This is battle and siege we face here."

"And who was it that brought it upon us?"

Now Samafaa surged to his feet.

"I have heard enough of this! The peril was seen and was dealt with," he snapped.

Vixipal all but dismissed Samafaa with a wave of his hand.

"But we have an even greater peril before us now. Leemal has fallen and the north is all but abandoned. I think the actions of your order ill-considered at best. You acted far too hastily and most certainly did not account for the consequences."

Samafaa snorted and folded his arms across his chest like a buttress.

"And you did?"

Vixipal offered a harder smile in return.

"We were not even consulted. We have been following intelligence of the foe ever since the very first days that they appeared, covertly and carefully, and we have shared our observations with the rest of you, but what did the mighty Dar Kaadarith share with us in return?"

Samafaa scowled.

"And your point is?"

"One acts when one knows what one's actions will achieve. You have acted rashly and so caused this current crisis. You should have been subtler. Divide and conquer I said."

Samafaa stabbed a finger at Vixipal.

"How wise it is to look back over your shoulder and criticise the unsighted past."

Vixipal again waved his hand in dismissal.

"And what do you think my order has been doing? We have been seeking out each nest, each gathering place of the foe. And we had many of them. That knowledge should have been used to good effect, I think, whilst the demons still slept, but what do we have now? They have been stirred up all together and we have all but lost our advantage."

Another stood up. It was Enay Orpahan.

"Is this true? Did you really have knowledge of all their hiding places?"

"Many of them," Vixipal replied, "or so I am informed."

"But I have heard nothing of this. Did any other know?"

No one answered. Orpahan fixed Vixipal with as hard a stare as he could muster. "You kept this to yourself?"

Vixipal smiled as if to a child.

"One does not act until one's intelligence is complete. We would have found them all in time. Then we could have destroyed them with one swift and coordinated strike."

Samafaa scoffed.

"So that was your strategy, was it? Then it is a shame that you did not tell the rest of us what it was that you were about."

Vixipal sighed heavily.

"And we were wise not to do so, seeing how rashly you acted when presented with a mere vision."

Abrilon rested both hands upon the table and glared angrily at Vixipal.

"Enough!" he hissed. "I will not stand here and listen to such twisted justifications. Nor will I be held to account for my actions by those who wilfully conceal theirs. You dare criticise us for not sharing when you have done exactly the same!"

Abinax tapped the floor with his stave.

"This debate is in danger of becoming stale, I think. One does not act upon what could have been, but only upon what is. We now face siege by uncounted numbers of the foe. What is needed here is knowledge of where we are, where we intend to be and what we face."

Abrilon took a deep breath and then bowed.

"Then, in that case, I have already given my assessment. The Dar Kaadarith are prepared to face whatever comes down against us out of the north."

He gave Vixipal a brief look of contempt and then sat back down again, quickly and precisely. Samafaa sat also, but he descended upon his chair as though to punish it with his disapproval. Orpahan followed suit, sitting down hard as well, but he was no Samafaa. Vixipal looked at them all for a moment and then sat down as deliberately as he could. He carefully insinuated himself into his seat, before smiling back at Abrilon. Abrilon did not smile in return.

Korfax walked the great wall of the city. He had done the same for the last forty-nine days, gazing north, ever north, waiting, ever waiting, for the foe to finally arrive.

Every so often he would catch a glance from one of the Branith that stood on guard along its edge, a look of curiosity, a gleam of interest. He was grateful for that at least. There was no animosity, and from what he had heard, from what he had been told, most thought him merciful, daring to play the compassion of his heart against the wrath of the mighty.

But what of his order? Fokisne had been as friendly as ever, Ponodol had been full of quiet pride, Samafaa full of unspoken approval and Abrilon the most understanding and conciliatory of all.

He had stood before the Geyadel and they had discussed everything he had seen and done, and then the Geyadel had smiled upon him and thanked him for the safe return of his daughter. Abrilon had even told him that he was indebted.

It was as his father had said. He was well loved, but there were doubts in him still. Leemal had fallen and the north was abandoned – all because of him. The Agdoain reacted to him, he was certain of it, and now, standing here upon the wall, he felt the chill of their malevolence. They were coming south, all of them, all at once. War was marching south.

He looked again to the horizon, to the north. The reports he had heard had the enemy travelling slowly, but their speed was difficult to estimate, as they always hid themselves under grey mists which changed shape and size and sometimes even vanished unexpectedly, revealing nothing underneath. One thing was certain, though – they were close and getting closer, the main bulk of the mists covering the far and wide plains from end to end, but what did the mists hide? What walked under their cloak? Rumour made that force immense, a flood, a deluge, a tide of numbers uncounted, but what was the truth?

It was on the eve of the hundredth day that the last refugees came to Othil Zilodar, the last tributary of a greater river that had escaped the horror in the north. Along the wide road they came, each holding up a piradar, a long line of wavering stars, tired but proud.

Korfax went out to watch them as they came into the city, but he continued to look back across the plain. In the last few hours a grey mist had risen up in the far distance, far away to the north. Korfax decided he did not like it.

Turning his ormn about he rode back up to the end of the column, back to the summit of the low rise over which the column had passed. There he found others surveying the very same mist, each peering back to the horizon, much as he had.

Orkanir and Baschim both seemed carved of stone, the last rays of Rafarel painting their faces in light and shade. They had suddenly become oddly alike, as if a single spirit had invested them as they stared to the north, steadfastly awaiting the approach of the foe. Korfax found himself caught by their profiles: so fine, so proud, so resolute. He involuntarily squared his shoulders, hoping all the while that he shared something of the quality they now projected. Then he glanced at his father and stopped where he was.

Sazaaim gazed to the north also, but the light that fell about him seemed softer somehow, as if it had been slowed by the sudden fall of ages. Lines crossed his face, lines Korfax had never seen before. Like an ancient cliff, the weathered stone of his father's face looked down upon the world as if all too aware that it also would crumble at last. Korfax had never seen his father look so sad, or so mortal.

Shaken, he clutched at the pommel of his saddle to steady himself and then turned back to the north. He suddenly felt a terrible mixture of fear and hatred;

hatred for the grey mist that now swallowed the horizon, but fear for the future. What had his father seen that had escaped the others?

"Come," said his father, turning away. "We must make sure that these last few are not assaulted as they enter the city. Ward them well."

All wheeled their steeds about and followed him back down the path, all except for Korfax. He remained where he was, still caught in his vision. So he remained until Orkanir came back to find him. Further down the path waited the dim forms of others, the last few of the Branith by their silhouettes.

"Korfax? Why are you still out here?" Orkanir asked.

Korfax started and looked back.

"I was lost in thought. I am sorry."

Orkanir leaned forward and touched his arm.

"What troubles you?"

Korfax smiled.

"Nothing, nothing. I was thinking about what was and what might be, that is all."

Orkanir looked at him carefully for a moment but then looked back at the city.

"Well, if that is all that it is, then let us be away from here at last. They will need to close the gates soon. It is getting dark."

Korfax followed Orkanir down past the waiting Branith. To the end of the line of refugees they went, while far out on the pale horizon the grey mist lingered.

20

SIEGE

Av-drilix Ban-alk-urq-ja
Gon-homin Ipooch-teos-u
Bantra-in Torz-fo-raxne
Iks-honan Zinim-fijir
Tol-akim Q-ad-dr-pan
Tol-alkar Doroln-qahl-jo
Bitem-jiz Faabaa-ana

Sazaaim and Ponodol sat together in a small room overlooking a verdant courtyard set deep within the Umadya Romok.

"I find myself starting to believe the words of Abrilon," said Ponodol.

"What words?" asked Sazaaim.

"That Korfax has become the axis about which this war turns."

Sazaaim looked up and his brow furrowed.

"My son?"

"He was the one who recognised Ovuor from Payoan's vision, after all. He was at Piamossin when the Agdoain attacked openly for the very first time and he was the one sent to find and destroy the Agdoain gateway. It all turns about him, I think."

Sazaaim looked back down again.

"And he was there when the Agdoain first appeared," he murmured.

"Just so," said Ponodol, "though it might have all been so very different if you had not got back to Losq when you did. You rescued the day there, I think, but in every other confrontation Korfax has been pivotal."

Sazaaim looked away in obvious unease. Ponodol watched for a moment.

"What is it? What have I said?" he asked.

"Nothing," Sazaaim said, "you said nothing. Ever since we began preparing for this siege I have had a presentiment of doom, that is all. It has sat upon me ever since the fall of Leemal. Black wings circle me."

Ponodol leaned forward and gently touched Sazaaim's hand.

"That may well be, my friend, but when we spoke of Losq, I am certain that was not what you were thinking at all. Tell me, what is it? We have shared much in our lives, both the good and the troublesome. Share this with me. Lighten your load."

Sazaaim looked up again and Ponodol was disconcerted to see a sudden look of fear cross his old friend's face, a fleeting shadow of fear, before it hid itself away again.

"It is nothing, nothing at all," Sazaaim answered. "You see things that are not there. I have lost the ancient home of my fathers, my son and heir is in peril and my world is threatened by forces I do not comprehend. Why should I not be troubled?"

Ponodol offered his friend the gentlest, most careful smile that he could.

"Sazaaim, please, I have known you for far too long. Something hangs over you, I know it, I feel it, and I have felt its presence ever since the day your father returned to the river. You changed then, and it wasn't until the birth of your son that you became something more like the Sazaaim I used to know, but then, all too soon, the Agdoain arrived to wreak havoc upon us, and that dreadful spirit returned to haunt you once more. It is twice now, twice since I first met you, that you have become a closed door."

Ponodol sighed and looked away.

"But have no fear that any other has seen this. They have not."

Ponodol looked back again and his eyes were bright and hopeful.

"Your secret is safe with me. Only one repentant old heretic has ever dared guess that there is another tale to tell here, and only I have ever wagered that it has something to do with Gemanim and your refusal to become Geyadril."

Sazaaim took a deep breath and closed his eyes. His face alternated between pain and contentment, as if each emotion now battled for possession of his body. Ponodol watched the contest carefully, but as quickly as the duel had risen up, it all too quickly sank back down again and Sazaaim suddenly looked old beyond his years – an ancient sea, weary of tempests at last. Finally he opened his eyes once more, but now they were hard, harder than Ponodol had ever seen them before. They glinted like ice, and behind their windows a dark flame flickered.

"And what if I say to you that there is no tale to tell?" Sazaaim said. "What if I say to you that you see phantoms?" Sazaaim leaned forward and his teeth glistened between parted lips. "You see nothing, Ponodol!"

For a moment the room darkened. Maybe it was Ponodol's shock at the sudden transformation, and maybe it was not, but it seemed to him then that a vast shadow reared up behind Sazaaim, something immense and threatening. Ponodol felt a great chill course through his body, his soul, but then Sazaaim broke the moment, turning away and holding up his stave before him.

"It is long past time that I looked to our defences," he announced. "Those of the Geyadith that are now upon the wall will need a strong hand to guide them. Few of them have faced the foe yet. I shall see once more to their instruction."

Ponodol, suddenly reckless, sent his thought at Sazaaim with all the force that he could muster. He struck a wall of stone. A brief flicker of contempt passed over Sazaaim's face.

"And if you wish to keep my friendship, Ponodol, never, ever do that again!"

Ponodol bowed his head.

"You should have been one of the Geyadrilith, Sazaaim. How did we lose you?"

Sazaaim turned away and went to the door, but he paused a moment at the threshold and looked back over his shoulder. He spoke, and his voice froze the air, so cold it was.

"You did not lose me, you gained me! I am of the Geyadith! And be thankful that I am! I could have taken other paths, but none of them would have led into the light. I have chosen the only course that I could, so be grateful for that and ask no more."

Then he left.

Ponodol looked at the empty space where Sazaaim had stood for a long time, as though trying to divine strange truth from it. Eventually he admitted defeat and left the room as well. Behind him the room lay empty at last, like an omen of the end.

At the edges of the city, behind the wall, they began to gather. A hundred thousand swords, a hundred thousand steeds, the armed and the armoured, each helm gleaming, each lance bright. Never had such a sight been seen before in or out of living memory, and many stood upon this balcony or that just to stare down at the assemblage of so much proud might.

Before each parloh went a Branvath, cloaked in scarlet. And at each Branvath's side rode a Geyad of the Dar Kaadarith, cloaked in purple, a crystal stave held before him.

Above them and around them stood the defenders of Othil Zilodar, upon the walls or in the towers, blade and bow at the ready, helms and shields gleaming in the light of morning, but those that stood at the edges did not look back at the assembling masses below; instead, they gazed out over the great plain of Zilodar, staring out to the distant horizon where the enemy now lurked.

Out beyond the city, out beyond the furthest marker, the foe gathered. Out there, in the distant mist, a vast grey horde grew, building its numbers by gradual degrees, covering the horizon from the furthest east to the uttermost west.

But they did not assemble in stillness; instead, they boiled in frustration, dim forms moving this way and that, partly hidden by shadow or by the vaporous exhalations that welled up around them. Occasionally one of them would reveal itself in stark silhouette, like a threat or a promise of what was yet to come.

There would be a brief scream of claws as some great war beast or other reared itself above its neighbours, thrashing at the air as though weary of the wait whilst its headless rider would dance upon its heaving flanks so that it could brandish its flesh-born sword at the heavens.

Further back, beyond the seething masses, other shapes waited, fainter and vaster by far, siege towers for the wall, or so many guessed. Tall they were, twisted and tapering monstrosities, looking not so much as if they had been built but rather as if they had been grown instead, though from what cold womb they had fallen few dared speculate. But there they were, dim grey shapes leaning over the distant horizon, all pointing obliquely at the heavens.

Vixipal stood beside Valagar upon the northernmost watchtower and looked out at the foe. Both bore sword and shield, both wore armour, Vixipal in dark green and Valagar in bright red.

"So you will attack?" Vixipal asked.

"No, we will wear them down in defence," said Valagar. "As it is written."

"But is that the best strategy? Look at what happened at Piamossin. A cautious defence may not serve you so well here."

"This is not Piamossin. Besides, the hasty stroke often goes astray. We do not know how many of them there are. They could outnumber our forces by twenty to one, by forty, by a hundred. They have infantry, they have cavalry and they have towers for the wall. Who knows what else they might have hidden away within their ranks."

"But they do not have the Dar Kaadarith riding with them. Let the Geyadith clear a path for you."

"No!" commanded Valagar. "If it is not clear in your mind, then let me tell you how it will be again. This is how it is written in the Namad Alkar. Defend and weaken! That is the way of it. We have food enough to last for many seasons. We have water, we have air. We stand upon the wall, and from there we will smite them with fire. And when the retreat comes at last, when we have beaten them back and reduced their strategy to rubble, then and only then will we ride out and strike them down!"

Korfax went to his appointed place upon the wall and waited. Beside him stood another, a Branvath of the watch. He turned to the Branvath.

"It is Branvath Achanin, is it not? I was told you are of the Belenith."

Achanin smiled proudly.

"Yes, Geyad, and I am proud to serve alongside one of the Farenith at last!"

Korfax smiled back.

"And I am proud to stand beside you also. Have you served in Leemal or Ralfen?"

"No, Geyad," answered Achanin. "I have been here since the clearances, unable to wield my blade."

Korfax thought he caught a brief glimpse of frustration. He gestured towards the north with his stave.

"You will get your chance soon enough, I think," he said.

Now Achanin looked eager.

"I am ready," he said. He looked to the horizon again, fingering the hilt of his sword for a moment before turning back to Korfax.

"Geyad, I must tell you a thing. Of those under my command, many are from the farthest north. I gathered them to a purpose. We have here some of the Saqorrisith, some of the Gruadith and even some of the Aelith Golor and the Aelith Leor."

Korfax looked back at Achanin in surprise.

"Truly? I had not heard that any had sent their sons here. It would indeed be an honour to stand beside the pride of the furthest north."

Achanin seemed to swell at the words.

"But the honour is all ours, Geyad. When it was known that you would be upon the wall beside us, many wanted to be here also. You are of the Farenith. We will know victory with you at our side."

Korfax bowed his head and smiled as best he could, but inside he was troubled. Some had said the same to him at Piamossin when he had first arrived. Few of them had survived what followed.

It came to it at last. Having assembled, the enemy advanced. The thunderous sound of innumerable feet stamping forwards in union echoed over the plain and through the stone.

Abinax sat upon his great throne in the northernmost watchtower and looked to the far horizon, fingering his stave. He stared at the advancing grey and listened to the sound of them. Even at this great distance they did not sit easily within the eye. Soon though it would be worse, much worse, for that turbulent horde, that chaos of limb and blade, would march right up to the walls of the city and, if not stopped, climb up and over, an endless hunger for flesh pulsing in its foetid heart.

Orpahan watched the high lord of the city with unease. Like all the others he could feel the pounding, could feel it in his bones, even as it echoed up from below. He leaned forward.

"Tabaud, should you not be away from here?"

Abinax frowned.

"I stay upon the walls of my city," he said.

Orpahan looked back to the north. How the ground reverberated to the footfall of the foe! He turned back to Abinax.

"But Tabaud, surely it would be prudent."

Abinax smiled back proudly.

"Do not worry, my friend. My city is surrounded by the mightiest walls that have ever been built. None have ever breached her stone."

Orpahan looked down awkwardly.

"I know, Tabaud, but none have ever tried."

Abinax looked away. No one else spoke. Orpahan suddenly wished that he had remained silent after all.

The siege towers of the Agdoain advanced, unsettling silhouettes still obscured by mists, but Korfax had no doubt what it was that he saw. Something his mother had told him sat in his mind, how the Agdoain had scrambled up a tower of flesh to gain the city of Leemal. He looked back at the swaying forms and their crowns of slowly waving limbs. The order of the world seemed turned upon its head, for forms better suited to the oceans' depths now walked upon the land.

At the base of each tower travelled an escort, also dimly seen. Many Agdoain, a mob of forms walking or mounted on a snarling war beast, moving as the tower moved, lurching towards the wall. Korfax looked down at them and thought of Odoiar's description. An incoming tide indeed, but one sluggish with piled up filth. He shuddered and turned back to Achanin.

"There are so many of them," he said.

Achanin held his sword before him.

"More than I would like to see," he said.

Korfax hefted his stave. It was not time yet. The enemy had to reach the outer markers and then he could act.

The closer the towers came, the thinner the mists became, and soon movement could be seen, a great heaving movement at the base of each. There was no longer any doubt. The siege towers lived, walking on great coiling limbs that wound their way about a paler core, all rising to a writhing apex, an unwholesome flowering of flesh and bone.

"So there it is," he said to no one in particular. "Living siege towers! I wonder what else the Agdoain have done with their flesh?"

Achanin did not answer – no one did; they all watched in horrified fascination as each tower made its ponderous way to the city walls, marching unevenly on their vast and limb-lithe roots.

The Branith upon the walls waited steadfastly, but Korfax could feel the fear rising about him now like a cloud. Few of those that defended Othil Zilodar had ever seen battle before, yet here they all were, standing upon a high wall above a monstrous foe that swarmed towards them in almost limitless numbers.

These creatures had driven the whole of the north before them like cattle, eating their way across the land like a plague. They had taken both city and fortress in their mad rush south, swarming across the stone of the Ell as if it was of no consequence at all. No wonder fear occupied the air.

Korfax held up the first of his quotient of qasadar and awaited the signal. These were smaller than the ones he had used at the Forujer Allar, more exact. Freshly forged, they gleamed with a brighter light. He smiled. One of his teachers from the seminary had made these – Asakom. Since the destruction of the gateway Asakom had become something of an expert in their making. Being a master of air and a careful forger, the capacity for such stone came easily to him, so he had come north with Abrilon to share his skill. Now he was closeted away in the Umadya Romok, making more with the aid of Geyadril Fokisne.

As the nearest tower crossed the first marker the seventh horn upon the seventh gate sent out its call, long and deep and shivering. Its single note hung in the air as it swept along the wall, and Korfax stood taller at the sound. How potent it was, and how compelling. Then each of the other horns over each of the other gates sent out its own call in acknowledgement, and soon the whole of Othil Zilodar rang to the sound. That was the signal. The horns had spoken. Let battle commence.

Korfax launched his qasadar at the siege tower nearest to his position, whilst the Branith about him watched avidly as he wrapped it in a net of winds, gazing at the strange summoning of powers and taking heart from the very mystery of it.

Korfax concentrated carefully as his summoned winds carried the qasadar towards the siege tower, guiding them, fuelling them all the while with his mind and his stave. As his qasadar sped towards its target he wondered briefly to himself how all the others of the Geyadith were finding the experience. Did they also feel the strange conflict betwixt chaos and discipline? Or was it something more personal, like the communication with the void within each stone? He could not say. He was the only one here that had ever done anything like this before.

He watched as his qasadar shot through the air, a gleaming shard of chaos spinning on the turbulent winds that ever kept it aloft. It was as close now to eruption as he dared let it become. He gave a quick glance to his left and to his right. His qasadar was but one amongst many, for a quickly expanding arc of flickering stars now flew out from the city walls, each one aimed at a siege tower. Korfax allowed himself a brief smile. Who had ever seen this before? This was a new world, and a new way to wage war.

It was as his stone neared its target that Korfax began to feel a numbing sensation in his mind, as though another force fought to put aside his purpose. Something was trying to halt the flight of his qasadar, trying to stop the winds that surrounded it and trying to turn it aside. Korfax frowned. This had not happened when he had destroyed the Agdoain gateway. He thought furiously even as he struggled for control. Was the tower repelling him? Or was it something else?

He clenched his power like a fist about his qasadar and punched it through the opposing force. The force gave way reluctantly, but it did not relent. Instead it grew, and neither did it grow smoothly. Rather it seemed to increase in rapid jerks, as though great weights, one after another, were being dropped into his mind. He fought back, increasing the width of his summoned energies, but the power that opposed him kept pace, increasing even as he did.

It was like wading through mud. The power mounted moment by moment, and Korfax began to find it increasingly difficult. Then came the crisis point when he could go no further, so whilst the qasadar still answered his will he released its energies.

A blinding flash lit up the plain of Zilodar, throwing everything into stark relief by its brilliance. Korfax shielded his eyes as a white flickering dome of flame, like a sphere of earthbound lightning, flashed outwards and upwards in front of him. Elsewhere, at almost exactly the same moment, similar eruptions occurred to either side, eruptions of force that shattered the air and the earth. A great white arc of negation blossomed around the entire northern wall of the city.

Korfax breathed deeply for a moment before looking back at his intended target. He had missed it, but only by the smallest of margins. His qasadar had still done its worst. It had erupted somewhat short of the siege tower, but the blast of its ending had torn a vast hole in the siege tower's side and had burnt away the grey mist completely, leaving everything underneath naked to heaven's gaze.

The tower had been stopped in its tracks and sick grey fluids now flowed in torrents from the burning wound that was its body. Korfax watched its demise with disgust. Most of the Agdoain that had been escorting the tower were gone, erased from the world by the qasadar's eruption, whilst those few that had miraculously survived the blast either lay feebly twitching or staggered this way and that as though the qasadar had shattered their purposes as well.

The burning siege tower held itself upright for a moment longer and then toppled backwards slowly, its great weight breaking it into pieces as it collapsed. A brief eruption followed, thick grey fluids flying upwards and outwards, the last upsurge of its essential ichor, before it lay still at last, rotting with indecent haste into the soil of the plain.

Korfax looked beyond his kill and saw that more than half the siege towers that had advanced towards the walls had suffered the same fate. They had either been completely destroyed or were now crippled beyond redemption. One in particular caught his eye, a broken thing that tottered in ever-decreasing circles, going round and round over the same shrinking ground as though unable to stop. He stared at it, mesmerised. Mechanisms made flesh, he thought.

He took a deep breath and held himself ready again. Beyond the decaying wreckage of the first assault another line of siege towers was already lurching towards the walls, whilst behind them waited more towers, and yet more behind them. Korfax stared at the receding lines. They suddenly seemed all but infinite.

He turned about and looked at Branvath Achanin behind him. Achanin did not smile, but he looked back proudly at Korfax.

"You destroyed it, Geyad," he said.

"Yes, but I was opposed," Korfax answered.

Achanin frowned.

"Opposed? I do not understand. What do you mean?"

"They have the ability to oppose my will. Doubtless all of the Geyadith know this by now, but send a message to Napeiel Valagar and to Geyadel Abrilon anyway. Meanwhile, we must endeavour to continue. Only when there are no more siege towers left will the Agdoain have to resort to other means to take this city. There is still the matter of their climbing vines."

Korfax took out another qasadar and hurled it at the next siege tower as it came into range. As before he felt the same opposing force, but this time he thought it had lessened. Or perhaps it was only that he was stronger, more prepared, no longer weakened by his surprise. Whichever way it was, his qasadar reached its target full-on this time. Then the siege tower all but vanished in the bursting light, the smouldering remnants of its shattered bulk falling back down onto the plain and its inner fluids boiling outwards like some slow volcano of slime.

So it continued. The walls of Othil Zilodar echoed and re-echoed to the sounds of shattering stone and erupting towers, whilst the Branith even began to cheer as each tower crumbled into the plain beyond. It all became the rhythm of the day.

First came the shattering of the qasadar, a light bright enough to erase the sky. Then came the dull crepitation, felt rather than heard; a wave of force that shook the air and shivered the ground. Then came the destruction of the tower, a sliding roar as it slumped back down onto the plain. Then came the cheer of the Branith, hailing each vanquished monstrosity with raised swords and rising voices.

Then the Agdoain changed their tactics. Now the towers advanced alone and their escort followed at a discreet distance behind. And when each tower was destroyed, the escorting Agdoain scurried back to follow in the wake of another.

Korfax frowned. Now what did this mean? Were their forces that depleted? Surely not! Up until now the Agdoain had been heedless of their lives. Now it seemed they were conserving their forces, spending only their towers.

He began to wonder whether the Agdoain were deliberately trying to deplete the supply of qasadar. Certainly qasadar were difficult to make, a long and slow process, which was why many were back at the furnaces aiding Asakom and not upon the wall. Only the skilled could make them safely.

The moment arrived. There were no more qasadar, but also there were very few siege towers left, and these were not advancing. Korfax looked out over the wall and had an unpleasant thought. The numbers were too well-matched. Was it really just a coincidence, or was it something more? He turned to Achanin.

"They are not advancing!" he announced.

Achanin gestured.

"They appear to have only a few towers left to them. Perhaps they wish to conserve them?"

Korfax was not convinced.

"They do not think like that," he said. "Besides, they have their climbing vines. Do not forget those."

"Can they climb even these walls?"

"I cannot say, but that is how it was at Piamossin."

Korfax looked to the far horizon. Would it really be that easy? Had the siege been turned aside? Korfax decided that he did not trust it. The Agdoain did not give up so easily. He remembered Piamossin. There they had attacked, withdrawn and then attacked again with everything that they had. They never gave up, not until they were all dead.

Soon it was clear. The Agdoain were retreating, withdrawing back to the north. Many cheered that they had been beaten off so swiftly, but Korfax did not join in.

The numbers were too precise. It had almost been one qasadar for every siege tower. He wondered if he was alone in his doubts. He turned to Achanin.

"Send a message to the Napeiel. This has to be a ploy. The Agdoain do not give up so easily."

"Would not the Napeiel think of this?"

"But I have fought the Agdoain. I know how they fight, and they do not give up. Ask the survivors of Piamossin or my companions on the quest to destroy the Agdoain gateway. This is not how the Agdoain fight."

Korfax walked away.

"No," he said. "I will go myself. They must be made to understand the peril."

Korfax rode around the wall to the northernmost watchtower where Valagar stood. There were many others with him, including Abrilon.

"Korfax! What are you doing here?"

Korfax pointed at the Agdoain.

"Geyadel, this has to be a ploy. They did not do this at Piamossin."

"I understand your fears," said Abrilon, "but this is not Piamossin. Besides, it is for Napeiel Valagar to decide."

Valagar, hearing his name spoken, came over himself, flanked by one of his aides.

"Geyad Korfax, is it?"

Korfax bowed.

"Napeiel."

"I have read your report of Piamossin, along with all the others. I read your conclusions, that Agdoain fight until the end, but in this case I cannot concur. Their siege has failed and they know this only too well."

"But Napeiel, what if it is their intent to draw us out?"

"I do not think so. Do you see how many siege towers they have left?"

"But look to the north," implored Korfax. "There is still a mist there. What if they are hiding more forces under that?"

"A possibility, but not persuasive. We will do this as it is written. Now go back to your place upon the wall."

"But how is it that they withdraw precisely at the moment that they have depleted our stocks of qasadar?"

"A coincidence, nothing more. Go!"

Valagar turned away. Korfax looked at Abrilon, who pointed back along the wall.

"You heard the Napeiel: as it is written. Return to your place upon the wall."

Korfax turned about with a sinking feeling. This was wrong, he could feel it.

Ralir waited with silence in his heart. He was one of the first in line, one of the first that waited to ride out through the gates. Beside him waited Geyad Hladon, strong and powerful, almost as young as he was, eagerly clutching his stave of water. Behind them both was the largest mounted force ever assembled since the end of the Wars of Unification.

Ralir could feel the tension in the air about him, a strange mingling of fear, eagerness, expectancy and dread. He fingered his lance.

For many the waiting was the worst part, but not so for Ralir. For him it was a simple matter. His teachers had impressed it upon him time and time again. One waited with a stilled awareness, they had said, ready to unleash the ever-tightening circle and so turn aside the foe like the coiling wind of the plains. So simple to say, but so difficult to do. It had taken time, years of it, but Ralir had finally understood the lesson.

So he did not smile as he waited. He had already forgotten himself. Instead, in his mind, he considered a flight of seeds caught upon a curling breeze, each flying through the air on a dozen whirling blades. And in his mind, reduced to motedom, he span past those blades in a greater circle, and sliced each off at the root.

Up on the walls the last of the qasadar were being spent. Every so often a dull explosion would reach his ears, a dim pulse that echoed through the streets as another destroying stone unleashed its pent-up energies. For a moment, the merest moment, Ralir found himself wondering how the Agdoain could sustain such losses. Just how many of them were there anyway? But then he turned again to his meditations. It was of little import now.

In his darker moments he had wondered whether there weren't a limitless supply, but he knew from whence such fears came. They came from the Urq, the black reflection that sat inside everyone. Nothing was infinite, nothing but the circle. And the circle was holy; it came from The Creator.

Word came down from above. Make ready. So Ralir mounted his steed and felt rather than heard all the others about him do the same. He smiled. It was coming at last. The Agdoain had failed in their attempt upon the wall. The Dar Kaadarith had undone them. Soon he would ride out and then the besiegers would become the besieged.

It happened. The cry went up. The Agdoain were retreating. They were withdrawing back to the north. That was it, as it was written. Though it seemed to take an age, the signal was eventually given and the great gates were swung open silently. Through the ever-increasing gap, Ralir could see the enemy, a distant greyness shifting upon the horizon. He smiled and raised his lance. The others behind him watched it, their eyes, his lance, all joined as one. He held it aloft for a moment, mesmerised by its gleaming tip. Then he dipped it and the charge began.

The three most northerly of the city gates opened, slowly at first, but then with gathering speed. Out of them poured wave upon wave of riders whose cloaks streamed behind them as they raced out onto the plain.

Korfax watched it all from above. Ralir was in there somewhere, leading the charge, no doubt. He could see the head of each column; two riders in front for each five hundred, one cloaked in red, the other in purple.

He suddenly wished he was at his friend's side, not stuck up here upon the wall. He glanced at Branvath Achanin and marked the wistful look on his face. Achanin was thinking the very same thing. He, too, would have preferred to thunder out of the city, lance in one hand and shield in the other, astride a great steed of war, ready to cast the enemy down and trample them underfoot.

A chaos of sound and fury enveloped Ralir as he rode out from the gates. His lance and shield were before him, aimed ever at the enemy. At his side Hladon held up his stave, raising it high above his head and shouting something into the maelstrom. His words were all but lost in the thunder. Ralir glanced up at the stave and saw the light within it, remote but constant, like the long drawn out light of a distant star.

Ralir looked to either side. He rode now at the tip of a great wedge, one of many, great lances of force hurled from the city at the foe. Here they were, huge formations of riders and steeds, each thundering out across the plain in a well-planned dance. He looked ahead. Grey mist enveloped the foe, but above the reek reared the delirious shapes of the last remaining towers, nightmarish forms that lurched drunkenly from side to side as they tried desperately to retreat.

Ralir had the odd impression that he now rode towards the last surviving remnants of a vast and monstrous forest, each tree suddenly unseated from its roots as it tried to escape the oncoming axe, tottering this way and that in panic whilst below it the very earth fumed in revulsion. He shuddered. That such perversions should see the light of day! He was suddenly glad that he was an axe, ready to chop down such unclean growth.

He tightened his grip upon his weapons, before loosening it again. The grey mists came slowly closer, vague forms milling uncertainly within. Ralir concentrated upon the shifting forms and sought out a target.

Korfax watched it all from the wall's edge. The riders were far from the city now, many great wedge formations designed to split the enemy ranks, but the Agdoain had stopped their retreat and now waited where they were, waiting imperturbably beside their last few siege towers. Korfax felt a sudden sense of misgiving. He was certain that the Agdoain knew what was coming next and had already prepared for it.

Ralir threw down his lance. On the end of it lay one of the Agdoain, skewered to its mount even as its mount was skewered to the ground. They had broken through the lines. He uncaged his sword and held it aloft. Now it began in earnest.

Hladon hurled liquid fire about him, this way and that, golden shafts of slowly coiling flames that undid the grey mists and enveloped the enemy beyond. Ralir laughed. The circle was here.

Each of the great wedges had split into many hundreds, each attacking the foe along its wide and retreating lines. Only those with a Geyad attacked the last remaining siege towers. Ralir looked behind him and to the side. His command thundered around him, a veritable forest of sword and lance.

In the heaving chaos beyond he glimpsed the distant unleashing of powers, lightning, coiling winds, crystalline forms pulled out from the very air itself. As yet it was still a battle of powers, but Ralir did not delude himself that it would remain so. The Agdoain had a nasty habit of producing surprises.

They arrived at their intended destination, a huge tower surrounded by many hundreds of the foe. Hladon hurled his fire, and the tower began to burn. Ralir and his command rode into the ranks on either side and then chaos erupted.

Korfax watched as the two forces clashed in a distant eruption of dust. Energies flickered through the haze and the far off sound of battle drifted back slowly to the city walls. Then, one by one, the last few remaining towers of the Agdoain fell to the ground, tumbling backwards into the plain as they burned. Cheers went up from the walls, cheers that mounted with each fall.

Korfax watched and waited. Was he wrong to doubt? Would it really be this easy? He stared out at the distant battle, waiting to see if the forces of Othil Zilodar could indeed turn the siege into a rout.

Ralir fought upon a field of demons, and his ormn, brave Rokallor, fought with him. Rokallor's single horn glistened as it reared, whilst its hooves, each shod with well-tempered laidrom, trampled the failing bodies of the foe down into the mire even as Ralir's sword, Ilpazar, flickered above and below, to and fro, undoing the flesh of the enemy in liquid arcs.

Somewhere nearby, beside the disintegrating tower of the Agdoain, Hladon was hurling his astonishing bolts of fire, surrounded by a wall of swords as he battled with whatever demons lurked there.

Ralir hoisted his shield to catch the downward swing of an Agdoain sword. Its weight as it fell, despite his shield, jarred his shoulder and numbed his arm, but then he returned the compliment and caught his opponent across its midriff, almost unseating it from its mount. Rokallor finished the task, pounding both Agdoain and war beast into the earth with its armoured hooves, whilst around them both the melee continued. Claws reached and swords thrust or swung in great arcs, whilst bodies fell, an endless falling, down, ever downwards, into the pit of death.

For a moment he felt a wonderful sense of invulnerability, that nothing could stand before him, that victory was within his grasp, but then a shadow crossed the field of battle, and the Agdoain grew. Every which way that he looked he saw horror mount upon horror as the enemy rose up again, becoming stronger by the moment. Suddenly they were a river whereas before they had only been a trickle. Then they became a torrent, then a deluge, unending waves of flesh and bone, a tide of gaping maws, teeth like curling knives, all rushing heedlessly forward and conquering by sheer weight of numbers alone.

Ralir watched, unable to act, as Numenur, his very own Branvath, was pulled from his steed by tongues shot out from between the immense teeth of encircling war beasts, teeth enough to tear him apart before he even touched the ground. Ralir turned about again, just in time to see grey horrors erupt beneath the steeds of his honour guard and rip open their bellies with their claws, whilst the riders above found themselves tumbling down onto endless swords of grey.

Ralir found himself alone, enmeshed within a circle of foes, a grinning circle of teeth. He turned. There was no one else. He was alone. He spurred Rokallor on and his steed leapt, vaulting the sudden snare. Ralir let his sword arm wreak its havoc where it would, even as they leapt, but the foe pursued him and would not relent.

Enveloped in grey, the day's fire had turned to nightmare. On and on he rode, this way and that, but found only the enemy. Mad with battle fever, he fought the rising tide, his sword arm drenched in the blood of war. Then, finally, out of the madness a face came at him, a face that he knew. It was Hladon, and others were with him.

"Ralir, we must leave, we must leave now. We must retreat. It was a feint. They have outdone us. There are too many of them."

Ralir stared at Hladon as if he had suddenly become incomprehensible, lost in another language. Hladon reached over and shook him.

"Ralir, hear me! We must flee. This retreat was a feint!"

Rising as if to breach the surface of some distant sea, he finally understood what he was being told. He clasped Hladon's arm in return and then he raised his arm and gave the command.

"Back to the walls," he cried, "Back to the walls."

The cry was taken up by those around him and then those further out, all the way out to the edges and beyond. So they all turned back, fighting their way free of the grey mist. Ralir raced away, looking back at Hladon with a fierce smile, but the smile froze upon his lips even as he turned and it faded away to horror.

A grey sword impaled the receding Geyad, whilst several others impaled his steed. Like the vengeful void that had birthed them, the Agdoain hurled themselves upon Hladon. Claws reached and mouths gaped even as Hladon fell, diminishing, falling slowly down onto the waiting mouths below. And they took him, both him and his steed, and they tore them apart with their teeth.

Grey like the mist about him, Ralir stared back at it all with stunned disbelief whilst Rokallor, wise to danger and to horror, carried Ralir back to Othil Zilodar as fast as he could manage.

Eventually, from the grey mists, one column emerged into view, racing hard. Another did the same, followed by another and then another, but their numbers looked few and Korfax clutched at the wall. It was not the Agdoain that had suffered a rout but the forces of Othil Zilodar instead. The riders came back to the city in ragged formations, riding heedlessly over the plain at breakneck speed whilst the foe followed, emerging from their dust like remorseless echoes.

Column after column of Agdoain war beasts galloped after the fleeing riders. Korfax felt despair fill him as the Agdoain overtook the fleeing columns and engaged them. The clash of arms could be heard, even at this distance, along with the thunder of hooves. Dim roaring sounds echoed across the plain as the Agdoain swept across the forces from the city and threw them down. Few seemed likely to escape.

More columns of riders appeared, each ragged and wayward, riding back to the city in disarray. And each had to fight its way through the sudden masses of Agdoain soldiery. The few that got through made it to the gate, escorted by sorties sent out to succour their comrades. From the towers on the walls lightning fell, warding the fleeing Branith and burning their pursuers.

Ralir raced madly across a field of the slain. Everywhere he glanced he saw the dead or the dying. Agdoain horrors crumbled into the ground, melting into the earth, flesh and bone liquescent as they oozed their foul marrow.

But here also lay the last of the cavalry. He could see them, all of them, even as he swept on by, steeds lying forlornly, great hearts stilled, eyes like wet crystal. With them their riders, bereft of life, features unmoving, each gazing blindly at the heavens or down into the battle-stained earth. So many dying, so many dead, whilst here and there, hopping eagerly from this place to that, lone Agdoain danced like fiends, sating their boundless appetite and filling their wide mouths with flesh.

Ralir heard himself groan. He faced to the front and tried not to look back again. He had no time for the dead now. He must get back to the city, but as he raced to the walls, he became aware of a growing sense that he was being pursued, and the further he went, the more certain he became. It came to it at last when he could resist the temptation no longer, and he looked back over his shoulder. His heart almost failed at the sight.

A tide of grey lashed at his heels. Behind him reared a monstrous wave, filled to bursting with glittering teeth and gleaming bone. The Agdoain war beasts strode shoulder to shoulder, their mouths thrust forward and their jaws agape, their barbed tongues licking against their ragged teeth. Ralir stared back at them and could not tell where one beast ended and another began. They had become a single creature, a many-limbed monster, charging across the world in a single line of unbroken flesh. And they howled, a continuous and dismal ululation that filled Ralir with a nameless dread.

Upon their flanks stood their masters, each pointing their flesh-grown weaponry at him as though to curse. He could feel them in his mind, a chasm of lust pulling at him like a great weight, eager to pull him down so that it could eat him and end him and erase him from the world.

Ralir closed his eyes and rode on. He was certain that he was the last to leave the field, certain that he now had the entire might of the Agdoain army raging in behind him. He was alone upon the field, mere moments away from death. Rokallor, still strong, yet out-paced the reaching foam of claws, but if he stumbled or fell it would be over. The Agdoain would achieve them both and they would cease utterly to be. So Ralir stared resolutely ahead, reins in one hand, sword in the other and his shield upon his back whilst the walls of Othil Zilodar crawled slowly towards him.

Korfax looked down at the few that limped back through the gates. From what he could see, most of them looked dazed and bloody, barely able to hold on to their steeds. Of the tens of thousands that had ventured forth, barely a handful were returning.

The word was that they had killed double their own number, maybe even more, toppling the last of the siege towers and wreaking havoc amongst the ranks of the enemy, but that was but a drop in the ocean. Inconceivable as it seemed, there were even more of the foe lurking beyond the horizon. Rumour had it that the whole of the north now seethed with the Agdoain.

The messenger that had passed on this news then paused and looked directly at Korfax. His eyes looked dead as he said that not a single one of the Dar Kaadarith had made it back. Korfax felt himself go still inside, and suddenly the prospect that the Agdoain might actually take the city did not seem so fanciful. He wondered whether Ralir had survived, but looking at the sad few that were gathered behind the closed gates, he doubted that his friend had made it back. For a moment he felt dead himself. Ralir? Gone? He turned away, cursing the tears that suddenly threatened his eyes. Now, not only did he know fear and sorrow, but he also knew the possibility of despair.

Ralir rode delirium's dark road whilst his enemies ever clutched at his heels. He raced across an unending surface, unreachable sanctuary ahead, receding even as it beckoned.

His pursuers wanted his soul. He could hear their calls, could hear their hungry sound as though nothingness ached within their breasts, sucking at the substance of the world through the portals of their mouths. Grey forms lurched to his left, to his right or in his fevered mind. He had been fleeing for ever, or so it seemed, clutching with desperation at the tiny ledge that had become his life, whilst below, down in the grey, things waited for him to fall – wet things, things with teeth.

Something shot past his shoulder whilst another object bounced off the shield on his back. He glanced behind again, wide eyes staring. One of the Agdoain was spitting darts at him from its hollowed fist. Ralir spurred his steed on. Another dart shot past his head and he heard again that vile sucking sound he had first heard on the ramparts of Piamossin. He dared another glance and saw that every Agdoain, every single one of them, had swallowed its sword and grown a hollowed fist instead. Now they grinned down at him, down the length of their arms as they took careful aim, a veritable forest of poisoned thorns to lay him low at last. Ralir closed his eyes and awaited the inevitable.

A sudden heat fell about him. He opened his eyes but could only see brilliance. Was this what it felt like to die? He looked back in time to see his pursuers erased in a storm of fire. He looked up. It was almost as if The Creator had spoken on his behalf. Power eclipsed the skies like a shield and fell down from on high. Protected by its might Ralir passed through the closing gates. They boomed shut behind him and he all but fell from his steed. He was safe. Comforting hands caught him and he thanked them. He was still alive and he thanked a merciful Creator that it was so, but even though the gates had shut behind him, even though it seemed he was safe, he could not stop himself from looking over his shoulder, just in case, just to make sure that the emptiness had not followed him inside.

21

LOSS

Najil-khs Thilarp-ith-jo
Vim-im-ih Ifen-qas-ji
Zad-od-nor Biamirk-trathil
Kap-maobas Gilan-deral
Far-us-eof Taqu-torzu
Imvix-kal Tolul-ial-je
Pir-karan Dohgel-ithihs

The day drew on, growing long. The last survivors of the charge were back within the walls and the gates were closed again. No further tales came up from below, but many on the wall glanced ever and anon back into the city, wondering what had been seen or endured out amongst the foe.

More siege towers tottered towards the city, many more. Korfax watched and waited, his stave ready in his hand. Was it his imagination or were these even larger than the ones that had advanced before? He stilled himself but could not help wondering what else the enemy would reveal. It seemed that they understood the Ell far too well. The charge had been a complete waste of time – as the Agdoain had intended it should be. They were cunning, these mechanisms made flesh. First they had tested the resolve of the defence and then they had absorbed all the qasadar, before feigning a retreat and swallowing the cavalry. Now they attacked again with redoubled vigour. It was as though they could read the minds of their enemies.

Korfax held himself in readiness as a tower lurched towards his position on the wall, mists rising up around it carrying a stench like suffocation.

He could smell it now: vile, rotten, as though its inner workings had already slumped down into a lake of putrefaction deep inside.

He waited whilst behind him waited many of the Branith, each ready with sword and shield, a few of them wrinkling their faces in disgust at the stink. Before them, at the wall, archers darted between the battlements, trying to pick off the Agdoain at the base of the tower, but every time someone revealed themselves to the advancing forces below, a hail of grey darts were hurled upwards in retaliation.

Korfax had already seen a number find their targets, faces and limbs filled with barbed darts that buried themselves greedily into both flesh and bone. And even the darts seemed to have purpose, for they gradually ate their way inside and they were poisonous. They decayed in the wound and their substance spread throughout their host like a fever.

The tower was close now, its hidden flanks already swarming with Agdoain, each waiting eagerly for the moment when it eventually achieved the wall. They did not have long to wait.

With a sick, wet sound, the tower fell against the wall itself, root-like fibres shooting out from the main mass, each fingered end squirming across the rock of the wall, eager for purchase.

This was the moment Korfax had been waiting for. He stood up and unleashed fire of water, the most potent force of offence in a Geyad's armoury, but probably the most difficult to control. Like a river of translucent lava it boiled from his stave, enveloping both the Agdoain and the siege tower, burning its way downwards. The tower slumped and crumbled away from the wall. It tipped over and fell backwards onto the masses below, crushing them. From its charred crown liquid fire spilled in red torrents, adding to the carnage about it. The surviving Agdoain withdrew, retreating as ever to regroup around another tower.

Korfax took a deep breath. That had been harder than he would have liked. He could not do that again for a long moment. He was about to turn back to Achanin when a heavy hand landed upon his shoulder. It was Geyadril Samafaa.

"That was impressive, Geyad Korfax, most impressive, but be sparing with your strength. Fire of water takes much out of the wielder."

Korfax bowed.

"Yes, Geyadril," he said.

Samafaa offered the briefest smile back.

"You were right, it seems. We have been outplayed."

"I find myself wishing I was not."

"You and many others, but that is not what we should be thinking about now. This battle has a long way to go yet, and the foe have sent only a tithe of their strength to test us. So keep something in reserve. Use fire of air in future."

"Yes, Geyadril."

Korfax paused.

"Geyadril? When will there be more qasadar?"

Samafaa looked troubled.

"Not yet. It seems that we sorely underestimated the task at hand. More are being made and even Abrilon has gone to help, but the first of them will not be ready for at least another hour."

Then Samafaa smiled fully at Korfax.

"But whilst we have the likes of you upon the wall, what need is there for qasadar?"

Samafaa moved on. Korfax watched him go and wished he felt as confident.

The Agdoain attacked again and another phalanx of lumbering towers crossed the plain of Zilodar. Their tactics were obvious now. Having absorbed the qasadar and the cavalry, the Agdoain now concentrated on weakening the defence. One only had to look out from the walls to see how the plain beyond the city was filled once more with the foe. Whatever else was true, one thing was certain. The Agdoain had numbers to burn this day.

Without qasadar, Korfax had to wait, along with Achanin, until the towers were close to the wall. Unlike last time he now used fire of air, hurling incandescent sheets of lightning from his stave. Though not as potent as fire of water, it was far easier to control and had a much greater range. He burned the Agdoain that swarmed below in droves. Around him, others fought with more conventional weapons – shields parried poisoned darts and arrows flew in swarms to bury themselves in the enemy. All Korfax could hear were the shouts of his companions, the hissing snarls of the Agdoain and the dim roar of the fire he unleashed from his stave.

He aimed at a tower as it came close, but then something halted his flame. A grey flicker in the air, like a bubble of grimy water, appeared over the tower. Korfax hurled his fire in ever-increasing torrents, but he could not make headway against the opposing power.

Something denied him, something with a mind. He drew back. What was this? He remembered back to the force that had tried to turn aside his qasadar, but this felt different again, more directed and intimate.

A shape came into view, a long thin form that strode confidently over the top of the lurching tower. Korfax stared up at it in horrified amazement. What was this?

It looked somewhat like one of the Agdoain, but it was taller, much taller, and it was long and thin, not squat and crouching like its brethren. Its bones jutted sharply from its emaciated body, and its long limbs were held coiled against its narrow chest as though each was waiting to spring out and rend the unwary with hidden claws. Even as Korfax saw it, it perceived him as well. It stopped and bent its shoulders forward so that it could bare its thin mouth in a snarl of wickedly narrow teeth. Then it drew out its arms from within the hollow of its famished breast and held both of them up before it, like a display, like a threat.

The left arm was a nightmare. Though it ended in a set of long curling claws like hooks, there were also many bony blades set along its length. It had but to sweep that limb about it and anything caught in its path would be sliced and shredded, but for Korfax the right arm was worse.

Instead of a right forearm the creature held aloft a long grey crystal grown obscenely from its flesh and bone. At the crystal's centre was a long thin rupture through which a sickly light bled, dribbling back out into the surrounding air as though it could barely escape.

Korfax could not move. He could not think. All the rules by which he had lived his life were suddenly overturned. He knew what that crystal was, knew its purpose, for he could feel it, even from where he stood. He understood what he saw and he wished that he did not.

The crystal was a stave – corrupted and polluted, but a stave nonetheless. He could almost taste the fevered glimmers of power within it. He was appalled. This was altogether too much. The Agdoain understood the Namad Dar?

Then came the final blow, for the creature before him was also in his mind, snarling at him from within his own head. The void was with it, here and now, and it saw him.

"What in the name of all creation is that?" hissed Achanin at his side.

But Korfax could not answer. He was still grappling with his horror. He tried desperately to fight the thing back out of his head, but it would not leave. A void yawned, a hungry abyss, and it was Piamossin all over again. The grey fog was here, around him, circling him, hemming him in. He felt something immense stirring within the grey, peering back out at him. He tried to retreat but there was nowhere to go. It was already here.

He stepped backwards and the thin and twisted abomination above advanced in turn, stalking him as it snarled down the long length of its misbegotten limb. Korfax stopped. He must not retreat. He pulled himself together and summoned one single scream of power that his monstrous opponent could not parry. The fire took it and erased it, along with the top of the tower, and they both fell back and away from the wall. Grey bodies tumbled and the ruin of it all slumped down into the plain.

Korfax breathed again. Hands were laid upon his shoulders and voices were lifted in praise. Achanin stepped in front of him.

"Samafaa would be proud, Geyad. That was a mighty stroke, but what did you slay?"

"I would rather not say," answered Korfax.

He breathed deeply for a moment and then collected himself.

"But I must. Send a message to the others around the wall. Our enemy has just revealed itself again."

"Do you know what that thing was?"

"Yes! It was one of the Agdoain, but of a kind we have not seen before. Up until now, we have seen only their warriors, their equivalent of the Nazad Esiask, if you will, but that thing I just killed? It knew the Namad Dar. The Agdoain comprehend the Namad Dar."

"But surely not! The Namad Dar is holy."

"No, Achanin, it is holy no longer. As with everything else they have touched, the Agdoain have corrupted that as well."

All along the wall other battles still raged. Grey towers staggered against stone, each replete with their cargo of Agdoain and each eagerly waiting their chance to attack, only to be repulsed by fire and by sword. Korfax watched the courier ride off with his message of warning for Ponodol and Samafaa.

He turned to survey the plain of Zilodar and saw that yet more towers were advancing, and yet more behind them, but whereas before they had attacked the entire northern side of the city, now they had changed direction. Every tower that had not yet reached the wall had turned about. They were coming, all of them, to the exact same spot where he now stood.

He swallowed in a throat suddenly gone dry. They were coming for him, all of them, great and staggering forms lurching imperturbably forwards. And behind them came the rest. Like the upwelling of some dark ocean, like a surging tide suddenly driven by a purposeful wind, the entire mass of the Agdoain army flowed in behind, following in the wake of their towers.

Korfax felt his heart go dead inside him. There were so many towers, so many Agdoain. And, as at the Forujer Allar, they were all coming for him.

Sazaaim dismounted and looked at his son.

"They are all coming here, it seems."

Korfax agreed.

"Yes, and I know why."

Sazaaim returned a hardened look.

"You do?"

"I am here," Korfax said.

"No, my son," said Sazaaim. "I have heard this tale before. You are not the cause. You are not the stone that starts the avalanche."

Korfax pointed at the approaching towers.

"Then perhaps you will tell me why they have all suddenly decided to attack this part of the wall only?"

His father looked oddly unbalanced by the question.

"An arbitrary choice," he insisted. "They have decided to attack here with all their might. One single and devastating blow! It is as simple as that."

"No!" Korfax returned. "As it was at Piamossin and at the Forujer Allar, so here it is again. I am their target. I have seen them and they have seen me. The third times pays for all, as it ever has. They come for me at last."

Sazaaim could not help it. All his fears and all his concerns now flooded his face all at once.

"No, my son!" he said. "No! You had a dream! That was all!"

But Korfax would not relent.

"Then tell me why the power that halted the qasadar revealed itself to me and to me alone? It perceived me even as I perceived it."

"What do you mean?"

"It was here. It stood upon its tower and it challenged me."

"But what?"

"You have felt it, haven't you, like great weights dropping into your mind? The Agdoain we have seen up until now were mere warriors, but they have brethren, taller, thinner and far more evil. I have seen one of them. Where their right hands should be they have staves instead. They have minds of power, Father. They can summon earth and wind, fire and water. I know, I have fought one of them. The Agdoain are our opposites in all things. They comprehend the Namad Dar."

Another Geyad thrust himself forward. Korfax did not recognise him.

"What fantasy is this?" the Geyad asked, his outrage written in every line of his body.

"It is no fantasy," Korfax answered. "They exist. Call them Ageyad, if you will, for I can think of no better name."

Sazaaim drew back and looked with consternation at his son.

"Ageyad? Do you know what you are implying?"

"Yes, I do! And I am as certain of this as I have ever been of anything in my life."

The other laughed, short, sharp and full of derision.

"What insanity is this?" he demanded. "Demons using the Namad Dar? Ageyad? Have you lost your mind?"

Achanin stepped forward and answered before Korfax could.

"No, Geyad, he has not! It is as he has said! I saw it also! It had a stave, grown from its very flesh no less. I witnessed this, as did all these others."

The Geyad took a step back. Achanin had his sword before him and he was pointing it at the Geyad. "And if you would call Korfax a liar, then you must call me a liar also. I was there, as were all these under my command. Everyone here saw it. Are we all liars then?"

The Branith behind Achanin surged forward as if suddenly called to arms, their swords held up and at the ready. Sazaaim held up his stave and it flashed with a commanding light.

"PEACE!" he cried.

There was silence. The force in Sazaaim's voice stopped them all where they stood.

Sazaaim turned upon the Geyad.

"Boranil! You will withdraw your accusations! My son knows more of this than you."

"But he is young..."

"And what has that to do with it? Have you not felt them in your mind also? Was not each qasadar that you threw at the enemy opposed? And did the opposition not increase with each passing moment?"

"Yes, but..."

Sazaaim drew himself up at last and gave Boranil his full attention.

"And who here amongst us has fought the Agdoain as my son has? You, Boranil? Were you there at Piamossin? Did you destroy the Agdoain gateway? Did you slaughter them by the hundred as you fled from the Forujer Allar? If my son says there are Ageyad, then there are Ageyad. Or do you wish to doubt me as well?"

Boranil bowed his head and withdrew.

"Good!" Sazaaim said.

Then he turned to Achanin.

"And you, Branvath, you will apologise for your insurrection."

Achanin bowed promptly and offered up his sword.

"Of course! My sword is yours, if you wish it, Geyad."

Sazaaim smiled slightly.

"No need for that now. Keep your sword, Branvath; you will be needing it, I think."

Sazaaim looked at them all.

"Now," he said at last, "let us end this argument. All will make ready. Shall the Agdoain come to this wall and find us still engaged in heated debate?"

No one answered.

"The Geyadith will form defences and assaults, whilst the Branith will wait in readiness behind them," said Sazaaim. "Othil Zilodar will be won or lost in this place. Here comes the final play."

No one moved. Sazaaim almost erupted with the power that was in him.

"DO IT!" he roared.

They all ran to obey.

"Korfax!" he called. "Come here!" he ordered.

Korfax did as he was told. He knew that voice, but when he stood before his father Sazaaim came close and bowed his head so that only Korfax could hear his words.

"You have not told me everything, I think. What have you seen?"

"The grey void is here again," he answered. It was all that he could manage.

Sazaaim closed his eyes and placed his hands upon his son's shoulders.

"You are not alone, my son, not now. Whatever you have seen, whatever you have endured, do not endure it alone. I am here. Let this burden fall to me instead. Let me ward you at the last. Allow the father to save the son!"

Sazaaim held Korfax tight for a moment and then drew back again. The preparations around them both seemed to fall silent as Sazaaim and Korfax looked into each other's eyes. Then they saw each other as never before. Sazaaim let his eyes light up with hope, whilst Korfax saw his father's love for him, a single and unquenchable flame.

Even as reinforcements began to head for that part of the wall, those that were behind Sazaaim, Geyad or Bransag, aligned themselves along the barricade and prepared themselves. Some of the Geyad wove defences out of the air, shields of earth of air, crystalline forms that billowed out from the wall, whilst others readied themselves to strike at the wedge of advancing siege towers. Korfax was amongst the latter, standing beside his father and waiting to summon fire of air and hurl it down upon the advancing foe. And behind the Dar Kaadarith waited the Branith with Achanin at their head. They waited for the attack to begin, ready in case the Dar Kaadarith failed.

Samafaa and Ponodol arrived and conferred briefly with Sazaaim. Sazaaim and Ponodol joined the defence, leaving Samafaa to command. Brief orders flickered through the ranks, confirming Sazaaim's plan. Then they waited.

The siege towers came within range at last and Samafaa gave the mental signal. The air tensed about them all and then they unleashed their power. Shafts of fire shot out at the living towers, pouring out through sudden openings in the defences.

But the fires did not reach their targets. Instead, they splashed upon grey globes of force, great and greasy spheres of energy that both surrounded and protected the advancing towers.

Korfax could feel the bite of his fire, feel his summoned energies gnawing at the tenebrous defences that the Ageyad had erected. He felt his flame lick at the many surfaces, avid to find some way in, some small way in, but it was not to be. For the moment, he and the others were being denied.

The towers lurched ever onwards, eating up the short distance between themselves and the wall. Then they began to grow and extend as if they suddenly sensed the nearness of stone, suddenly hungry for its touch. And all the while the Dar Kaadarith that were upon the wall poured down their fire, a grim battle of energies, a grim battle of wills, for the Ageyad could now be felt in each and every mind, a snarl of opposition like the screech of tearing metal. Under the assault the great defensive spheres began to give way. The power flickered, retreated and contracted, and all of the Geyadith clenched their power ever tighter. Some gave vent to their satisfaction, daring to smile, but as it had ever been before, so it was again.

The counterstrike took them all by surprise. Suddenly, on the many tops of the many advancing towers, a great number of thin shapes rose up and many of the Geyad paused in astonishment.

They were exactly as Korfax had described them. They were Agdoain and yet they were unlike any that had ever been seen before. They were tall, emaciated and vicious and each was armed with a sick grey crystal where its right forearm should be. The pause was brief, for even as the Ageyad revealed themselves they unleashed a collective bolt of force, a single pulsing wave of nullity that erupted from their crystalline limbs. It flew through the trembling air, brushing aside the shields of wind and crystal and consuming them utterly before smashing like a hammer against the defences that stood upon the top of the wall.

The defences shattered.

They had no choice.

One moment Korfax was hurling his fire at the foe, the next he was tumbling through the air like wind-blown scrap. How he managed to save himself he did not know, but when his world stopped spinning, he found himself hanging precariously from the tip of a carving on the inner side of the wall. His right hand had miraculously caught it and now both carving and arm bore his weight. Pain racked his body.

He could hear nothing but a wailing sound. The force of the blast had overwhelmed his ears and he could feel himself bleeding, his neck already slick with blood. He shook his head, trying to clear it. Vague sounds came to him, penetrating the phantom wailing like muffled words. What were they, or were they anything at all? Was it all just his imagination, or was it more than that? Through the chaos he heard a distant sucking sound. He recognised that at least. The Agdoain made sounds like that. Did it mean that they were already upon the wall?

He cursed his weakness and his pain as he slowly pulled himself back up to the wall road, reaching at the edge, seeking purchase, struggling with its smoothness, but just as he gained the top he all but let go again, for there before him was his worst nightmare of all.

The towers had fallen against the outer wall almost as one, clamping themselves to the stone, cracking and breaking it with their slowly strangling limbs. A few prone bodies lay here and there, and those unfortunate enough to be still lying against the wall were caught and crushed where they lay. All the others were gone, scattered to the four winds by the force of the Agdoain attack.

The Ageyad were standing at the edge, all along the wall, line upon line of them, their crystal limbs before them as if triumphant, and in the middle of the wall road, right at its very centre, one single defender remained, bloodied but unbowed. Where all the others had fallen, this one had stood his ground. He alone remained in defiance, holding up his red stave in readiness as the Ageyad leered down at him from the lip of the parapet. They all but leaned over him, a grey wave tipped with grinning teeth, but he defied them still, daring them, all of them, to cross the final boundary. Korfax felt a terrible and helpless despair well up inside, for the lone figure was his father.

Something clawed at him, a delirium of panic that told him to rise, to act, to stretch out his hand, to stop what was about to happen, but his fear smothered it in a choking cloud. He could not move.

The Ageyad stepped a single pace forward from their accursed towers and onto the sacred stone of the wall itself. They raised their crystal limbs in horrid unison and Korfax saw each mouth widen with anticipation. He saw his father tighten his grip upon his stave as he drew himself up, his face now filled with an all but indomitable defiance. He became a stone, a cliff, a mighty and forbidding barrier.

Power rippled along the length of his stave and fire of water filled the air around him, a great and incandescent storm, and the summoning was so fast that Korfax could only gasp in astonishment, for barely had the fire been called up than it was sent on its way. A wall of flame, a veritable flood, filled the air in all directions and the Ageyad that stood upon the wall were undone in a single instant, burned where they were, burned before they could act.

Ash fell across the wall. There was silence. Korfax bowed his head and then raised it again. He would have cried out in happy disbelief, but innumerable others had already stepped over the burnt remnants of their brethren and taken their place. Unconcerned and unstoppable, like the fall of night, they were inevitable.

With equal speed they raised their limbs, unleashing grey fire in answer, a hungry flickering that sped through the air as one.

Korfax saw the bolts fail, each held at the barrier, caught upon the wick of his father's power even as they were consumed, but the flood was already here, a deluge beyond all hope, a rise of numbers uncounted. The abyss opened its maw and the Ageyad howled. Grey fires filled the air. The defences shattered, overwhelmed at last by sheer force of numbers. The lone defender staggered as three fingers of force touched him.

Korfax watched wordlessly as his father failed. He cried out, a silent shout of denial, as if such unspoken sounds alone could deny fate itself, but nothing could do so. His father's body convulsed, jerking this way and that as each fire caught him in turn. For a moment he seemed to pause at the portals of the world, blinking in and out of existence as curtains of force rippled this way and that across his body, erasing his flesh and his life. Then he fell, outlined by dying fires, and by the time he reached the ground the energies of the Agdoain had done their worst, riving away his life and leaving nothing behind at all.

Korfax watched his father tilt like a broken statue, watched him lie still, watched as he broke upon the stone of the wall, watched the stillness, watched the death.

He screamed a silent denial and his mind went blank. Some part of him still saw the Agdoain, the wall, the siege towers, the scattered bodies and the dead, but the rest of him stared at his father's body as if it and it alone had been the reason for his life.

His father was dead.

It became his truth, the one single truth that wrote itself in black words across the landscape of his mind, but rather than being an end, his father's death became a beginning, a terrible beginning that filled him up from his infinite deeps to his unscalable heights.

Despair pierced him, impaling him upon the bitterest of blades. Denial and horror engulfed him in a choking cloud, but they were only heralds, the merest presage of the storm that followed in their wake.

From some lightless place below, from some unlit cavern long-sealed, dark rage surged upwards like the rise of unlimited fire, turning aside everything else that he was. Like the onset of death, his rage took him beyond himself and on to another place entirely, a place where only absolutes held sway. Once more he dwelt in a land of red mists whilst the distant sound of battle came to his ears, but now it was his body that was the battleground.

Across his red soul his rage and his grief struggled for supremacy – one a black sword, the other a white shield. His rage battered his grief, beating, hammering, crushing, until only it remained. Then it lifted its lonely head and howled at the bloody heavens.

Out of him it came, an eruption like the end of everything. Unthinking, it rose above him; uncaring, it filled the air with unseen flame. Then it turned about and sought for prey.

There were the foe, still standing, still gloating over the dead remains of their victim, frozen in place and in time. Mad ire took it and turned the ever darkening fire of its heart upon them.

The Ageyad turned, almost as one, even as Korfax approached his father's side. They raised their limbs accordingly, quickly and with dispatch, but what happened next was swifter by far.

With a terrible look upon his face, a mask of rage emptier than the emptiness of his enemy, Korfax stood over father's body and raised up his father's stave. Then, with the clouds of war drifting into the sky above, he unleashed the fire of his stricken heart, and day turned to night as Rafarel hid his face.

Dark fire, black fire, darker than the pit itself, flew out at the foe and the Agdoain upon the wall all but vanished at its touch. Nor did they simply burn. They ceased utterly to be, as though they were caught upon a flame so hot their flesh was all but undone in an instant, leaving not even ash behind.

The wall emptied of Agdoain, one brief shout of power clearing the way. Korfax paused, staring sightlessly ahead as if he had forgotten everything, his eyes red brilliance, his stave rippling with black heat. Then he strode like a giant to the wall's edge and stood upon it like judgement, turning the infinite within upon the innumerable without.

The siege towers that clung to the wall below him all but collapsed under the fury of his fire, its dark torment burning through them as if they were already ghosts, whilst the Agdoain that hung upon their flanks vanished in screams of smoke and vapour.

With their assault suddenly failing, the Agdoain turned back in confusion and disarray, but Korfax did not stop. He could not. He sent his black fire this way and that along the wall and over the ground beyond. Any siege tower that he touched collapsed almost immediately, slumping into itself, a boiling morass of burning flesh and failing bones that quickly turned to ash. The Agdoain, their mounts, those that milled around and in between barely flickered as the black fire passed over them.

Soon, very soon, all about him were consumed, but still he did not stop, for the darkness within would not relent. He held out his father's stave, out beyond the wall like a standard, and let the fires of hatred build within it. Waves of black, coruscating tides of force, flew from end to end, building, multiplying and growing. The force began to spill outwards, black lightning spitting up into the sky or out along the wall, but still it was not enough. The air about him began to shake, the wall under him began to shake, and the ground under the wall began to shake.

Darkness eclipsed the stave, black oblivion held within a single burning fist; it eclipsed his body and only his eyes remained to pierce the gloom, twin beams of blood-lit light that caught everything in their gaze and pinned it to the world. Then, at last, the stave was lowered and the fire within it was unleashed.

A terrible black finger lashed out from the walls of Othil Zilodar, and all that it touched was utterly erased. The Agdoain tried to flee, but few escaped. Only those that were at the edges, out upon the horizon and beyond, were left unscathed, and only then because they dropped over the very limb of the world in their extremity.

To those that watched, staring spellbound from tower or wall, it seemed as though The Creator had suddenly stepped down amongst them, the fire of endings pouring from an upraised hand.

A single black figure stood at the edge, naked and alone, a single piece of elemental night cut into the very fabric of the world. It stood upon the wall like a hole, a gateway upon the heights, hurling its black fire ever downwards, ever downwards, a fire so hot that even light itself was consumed. On and on it went – destruction, endings, oblivion. Beyond the walls of the city the world burned and hurled its ashes at the sky.

And when the enemy had been burnt back to the nothingness from which it had so rashly risen, when the spheres had turned and turned again and the land had been scoured from horizon to horizon, the flame began to fail. What had been briefly given was taken back and the flame stuttered, guttering upon its wick as though reluctant to leave. It flashed for a moment, a dim thunder that rolled across the city, and then went out.

The darkness lifted and Rafarel showed his face again, emerging from the ragged cloud of war like a hope of salvation. Light crossed the city and the burning land both. Smoke and vapour drifted slowly upwards, caught in the sudden brightness, shapeless shrouds for the departed. The world bowed its head and everything was silent.

They found Korfax beside his father's body.

After the fire, after the astonishment, Samafaa and Ponodol were the first to master themselves. Ponodol was nursing a broken arm and blood dripped from a wound on Samafaa's head. Both came upon the bodies together, but Ponodol held back while Samafaa knelt between them both, touching first Sazaaim's brow and then the brow of Korfax. He bowed his head.

"And now we know the price for our deliverance! The Salman Farenith are no more. They are both dead!"

Ponodol dropped to his knees. He looked at Sazaaim, then at Korfax and then back at Sazaaim again.

"Though many have died this day, sons and fathers both, I count this the worst loss of all."

Tears filled his eyes.

"They were ever the straight path."

Ponodol looked long at Sazaaim, his eyes shining. Then he turned away.

"Good bye, old friend," he whispered. He bowed his head.

Samafaa placed a gentle hand on Ponodol's shoulder and then turned away himself. Eyes unused to tears shed them now. A mountain wept.

It was not long before others came, one of the Faxith amongst them. She glanced at Ponodol and Samafaa both, bowing her head and lowering her eyes in acknowledgement of their grief. Then she approached the bodies to complete the rites of confirmation.

She touched both Sazaaim and Korfax upon the crowns of their heads and a look of resignation crossed her face, but then she paused and looked again at Korfax. She reached out and felt the top of his head as before, but this time she touched his brow, then his throat and then his chest, working her way down to his loins. The seven centres spoke to her. She looked back at Samafaa.

"Do not grieve yet," she said. "This one at least has not passed into the river, though he is as close to it as any I have ever seen. I have never felt so little life left in one not yet dead."

Samafaa drew himself up and looked at her as if she had become marvellous, while Ponodol reached out a hand and clutched at her.

"Korfax lives?"

She removed his hand gently.

"Yes, he lives. I have fed the energies in him a little, but we must get him to the Umadya Birax immediately or he will die indeed. He needs all the ministration that we can give."

Samafaa surged forward, but Ponodol caught him.

"Gently, my friend, gently. Let the Faxith do what they must. This tale is not yet over, Creator be praised."

On the healer's instructions, some of the others quickly made a bier upon which to carry Korfax. The healer then turned her attentions to the stave still clutched in Korfax's hands. She sighed.

"These hands are badly burned. Almost they are welded to this stave. This also will need a great deal of time to heal."

As she examined the burns, Ponodol gasped with astonishment despite his grief and his joy.

"Samafaa! The stave! Look at the stave!"

Samafaa frowned.

"But it is white. Where did it come from?"

"That is not my stave," said Ponodol. "Is it yours?"

"No, mine is lying down there somewhere," he said as he pointed beyond the wall. "It was blown from my hand."

They both stared at each other in shock. Samafaa was the first to speak.

"Is it possible?"

Ponodol carefully knelt beside the healer and looked at it. It was indeed white, except for one of its ends. There its substance had darkened and the tip was almost completely black. He reached out and touched the crystal, closing his eyes as he felt within. After a moment he staggered. Then, without a word, he went over to the ramparts where he leant heavily against the battle-burned stone.

Samafaa touched the stave and probed it just as Ponodol had. For a moment he thought that it would deny him but then he felt what it was inside, and the deeper he went so he caught more of the echo of what it had been. Then he fell heavily against the wall himself, shocked beyond any further capacity to speak. Ponodol watched him sadly for a moment and then sank back again into his own thoughts.

The healer directed the bier carriers to take Korfax to the Tower of Ministration. Then, with a brief but puzzled bow to both Ponodol and Samafaa, she left as well.

Samafaa finally spoke.

"By The Creator!" he exclaimed. "I never thought I would witness such a thing."

Ponodol bowed his head.

"A great deed has been done this day. Driven to extremity, he surpassed himself."

Samafaa looked up.

"Surpassed himself? There has never been an act like it."

Samafaa placed his head in his hands.

"Once this day is done and all are accounted for, we must convene the council. They must be told."

Ponodol bowed again.

"Without a doubt!"

He sighed as he watched more Branith arrive to take away the bodies of the slain. He watched as a bruised and bloodied Branvath limped over to Sazaaim's body and carefully, oh so carefully, lifted it up so that it could be borne in honour down into the city. The Branvath made the sign of light as they took Sazaaim away. Then he turned to Ponodol with eyes full of hard tears.

"I saw what happened," he said. "Though I fell, I did not fall all the way. I saw it all."

He held both Ponodol and Samafaa with his gaze, almost as if he was daring them to see what he had seen. They stared back at him, awaiting his words with eager dread.

"He saved the city," said the Branvath. "The Agdoain would have been over this wall with all their strength if he had not destroyed them."

The Branvath looked down for a moment but quickly looked up again, his eyes brighter than ever before.

"I saw it all. He avenged his father's death. He took his father's stave and he turned it white. He is Karmaraa come back to us, returning at the very moment of our need."

The Branvath then staggered and was caught by others. They took him away, back towards the towers of healing. Samafaa and Ponodol followed them both with their eyes. Ponodol breathed deeply.

"It is true then."

Samafaa looked troubled.

"But who will believe it? Or him? This has suddenly become a thing of fantasy."

Ponodol laughed bitterly.

"But what a fantasy it is! Let them look out at the plain of Zilodar. Let them explain the destruction of the Agdoain. Let them tell us what mighty power it was that stood upon this very wall with the fire of The Creator pouring from its upraised hand. Believe us? They will have no choice!"

"But what about that Branvath? What did he say? Karmaraa? Karmaraa has come again?"

"No! Korfax is not Karmaraa!"

"But he turned his father's stave white nonetheless. No other has ever done such a thing. You felt it. I felt it. The Branvath makes an apt comparison. Only Karmaraa ever achieved such grace."

Then Samafaa smiled.

"Well, if nothing else, we have a victory this day. Rejoice in that at least."

Ponodol looked down.

"Rejoice? I will count the dead first, and the grief to the living. Let others praise The Creator as they may; this has been a costly day."

He opened his eyes slowly. It was difficult for a time, but he managed it at last. He did not know who he was or where he was – he knew only that he existed and that he was enclosed in comfort. Softness and warmth wrapped him. Was he a child? Was he a helpless child? There were no answers.

For a long moment he stared upwards at the ceiling above, running his eyes over the soothing, self-repeating patterns. A memory, like a fleeting cloud, wandered the contours of his mind. There had been a struggle, a conflict, but it all seemed like a dream. Or was it? He wrestled briefly with the conundrum, but even as he sought for an answer his mind fell back into the depths. Weariness covered him like a smothering blanket and he sank back down into darkness.

When he opened his eyes next he saw the same ceiling as before, but now there were others in the room about him, familiar faces that held him with their eyes. He looked dimly at each in turn, trying to remember who they were and what they meant, but the task was beyond him. Briefly he marked their concern, some open, others masked, their passions obscured. What a puzzle it all was.

There was one face that drew him, and he almost reached out to touch it as he fought so very hard to remember where he had seen it before, but even that proved too much, even as the face reached out for him in turn, and he fell away from the world again, back down to his comforting depths.

Over the next few days Korfax surfaced again and again from his healing deeps, a little more aware each time, as though his mind was learning his body anew. Always Tazocho was at his side, and he looked at her the longest as the memories started to return one by one. He knew her face, of course, but not who she was.

He saw her sadness and the broken grief that haunted her eyes, and he found himself wondering at it and at the echo of pain that rose up inside him as if in answer.

Obelison was there also, almost as much as Tazocho, but when he saw her and her hope, he found his heart leaping within him. She gave him strength, as if she was impelling him to remember some long-buried glory, and she became the first to make him smile.

Many faces came to stand before him, looks of hope and puzzlement, but there was one other that stood out. There was a look to this one, a look of lost joy, as though he had witnessed dark things and had been scarred by them. Korfax felt an echo of that darkness within himself and wondered what it all meant.

So it went on. Each time he awoke, more was added to the puzzle that had been his life, the pieces slotting themselves back into place: names, places, people, experiences, but he could not speak of them yet, as it was too soon. And when the day came that he almost had it all in place he awoke again and sat up slowly, grimacing at the weakness in his body.

He was fully awake at last, back within himself, finally remembering what he had been and what he had wanted to be. He looked about the room he occupied, but there was no one else there.

He dropped his head.

Had it all been a dream?

He looked up again.

The room had a late glow to it, the sunlight painting the walls about him with warm colours. He tried to rise from his bed, but it took him longer to gain his feet than he expected it to do.

He was not used to being so frail. He looked briefly at the robe he wore. It was a healing robe, coloured with gentle shades and soothing patterns. He turned and looked out of the window. He knew that view.

He was in Othil Zilodar. That was where he was. He could be in no other place. And from his vantage point he guessed that he was high up in the Umadya Birax, looking down across the fifth road that led all the way up to the high lord's tower itself, the Umadril Detharzi.

Korfax looked along the great road. It was packed with people – tiny, brightly coloured dots moving this way and that – whilst in their midst a greater column of shapes moved – riders, many riders, the light glinting on their polished helms, a light breeze fluttering their many banners.

Korfax turned away and walked slowly to the door. He opened it and came face to face with his mother. Caught by her sudden appearance, he drew back again, but she came after him and caught him in turn, holding him fast. He bowed his head.

So it was true after all, all of it, all the things that he remembered. He felt the sudden upsurge of a long and waiting grief. He returned her embrace, holding her tighter and tighter yet as the grief consumed him. And so they remained together, bound by their grief, for a very long while.

Korfax sat upon the bed and gazed out of the window, but he saw nothing of the world beyond. Tears blurred his vision. Tazocho sat beside him, her eyes filled with the very same tears that he now shed as she told him all that had happened since the death of his father.

He had turned the tide. The vast army of the Agdoain had been all but destroyed and the last survivors had fled in ragged disarray. There was not a trace of them left anywhere nearby. Forays into the land far around Othil Zilodar had not discovered even a single one of them. Sky ships had even gone as far as the wreck of Leemal, but whilst that city remained broken, it also remained utterly empty. The lands between were quiet and the enemy had hidden itself away again or had fled the world entirely.

Of the forces that went out of the city during the height of the siege, few had returned. Korfax felt a tinge of relief as his mother told him that Ralir had been one of the few, but she also told him that Ralir had been hurt by the things he had seen, things that as yet he had told no one else. Some horror still lay upon him, some tale still waiting to be told, but Ralir would not speak of it. He had been the only sword to make it back to the city alive; all the others had been slain and consumed. None of the Dar Kaadarith that went out had survived, either. Both the Nazad Esiask and the Dar Kaadarith had paid a heavy price for the salvation of Othil Zilodar.

But there was more. The Velukor himself had come to Othil Zilodar. He had come to celebrate the victory and to honour the dead. Her tale complete, Tazocho looked at her son.

"What do you remember?" she asked.

He did not answer for long moments. Even though he had them once more, his memories were still too raw to expose to the light of day. He tested them, tried them, but he could not go near them. They were altogether too much. He would have to tell a simpler tale.

"I remember rage," he said. "I remember an anger the like of which I have never, ever known before. And there was a pain, a burning pain in my hands and in my head. All I remember is rage and agony."

He glanced at his hands.

"You said that I was burnt?"

"Yes, but they healed you."

He continued to look at his hands, studying them, looking for scars, any sign of the all-consuming pain, but he saw nothing. They were his hands, as they had always been.

"There are no scars," he murmured to himself. "There should be scars."

He looked up again.

"You said something about the Velukor. He is here?"

She offered him a sad smile.

"Yes, the city is full of imperial Branith, full of court officials. Everyone is here. All the highest of the land have come to Othil Zilodar to celebrate a glorious victory. They have come to honour you."

Korfax looked away. He did not miss the bitterness in her voice. He understood all too well.

"Me? Is that all that they can think of? What of him?"

Her smile became gentler as she cupped his face with her hand and turned it back.

"But you are the hero, my son. You turned the battle. You destroyed the Agdoain." Her eyes were suddenly brilliant. "And you destroyed them with such a display of power as has never been seen before. You are a hero, a mighty hero, gifted by The Creator."

Korfax dropped his head.

"I am no hero," he said. "All I remember is a battle of rage and grief. Was that a gift of The Creator also?"

He looked back up and Tazocho felt a cold wind rush through her as she caught the dark heat of his gaze.

"Why do they not honour him?" he suddenly raged. "He stood alone. Him! If it had not been for him, I would not even be here at all!"

Korfax looked down again.

"But I could not save him. I am no hero. All the others were scattered or killed by the power the Agdoain unleashed, but he stood his ground. I tried to climb back up onto the wall, but I was already too late. They killed him. I could not stop it. It is my fault that he is dead."

Tazocho reached out and shook him, her eyes full of fearful contrition.

"That is a lie, and I will not have you thinking it. It is not your fault. Your father, were he here now, would tell you the very same. Never think it your fault. Never, ever think that. He stood before you. It was his right. The father ever preserves the son."

Korfax bowed his head and wept once more. Tazocho held him against her, and her tears fell silently to the floor, joining with his.

They came together in the great council hall, where they sat in a circle. From the city came Tabaud Abinax and Enay Orpahan. From the Dar Kaadarith came Geyadel Abrilon with three of the Geyadrilith, Fokisne, Ponodol and Samafaa. From the Exentaser came Urenel Asvoan with three of the Urendrilith, Nimagrah, Kukenur and Andispir. From the Nazad Esiask there came Napeiel Valagar, Napeidril Gersim and Napeidril Zuroin, whilst from the Balt Kaalith came Noqvoanel Vixipal, Noqvoandril Uchanir and Noqvoandril Tiarapax. And last of all came the Velukor himself, Onehson, the heir of Karmaraa.

In the centre of the circle was a table of highly polished Pidai, azure as the deepest sky, upon which lay a long white stave, dull and blackened at one end as though its substance had been almost burnt away. They all sat around the table, around the stave, and looked at it with troubled eyes.

"And this was Sazaaim's, you say?"

Onehson gestured at the stave.

"Indeed, my Velukor," answered Abrilon.

Samafaa gestured as well.

"Both Ponodol and I felt it, my Velukor. There was a sense in it, a sense of what it had once been, but there is something else. There is a witness. Branvath Belen Rom Achanin saw the transition. Though he lay wounded many paces away, he still saw what happened. He saw Sazaaim fall. He saw Korfax pick up his father's stave and he saw Korfax turn it white."

Onehson pointed at the darkened end.

"But what does this discolouration mean? I have never seen anything like that before, and there is no record that I know of that speaks of such a thing."

"We are still investigating the blackening, my Velukor," said Abrilon, "but it appears that the power Korfax hurled through this stave almost destroyed the substance of which it was made. As Korfax called up more power, and more beyond that, so that power began to consume its very substance. This stave has been rendered all but useless. The fracture within it is almost closed."

There were many gasps around the table. Abinax was the first to speak.

"What are you saying?" he asked.

Abrilon looked back carefully at Abinax.

"I am saying that we do not yet fully understand what has occurred here. What Korfax did should not have been possible, given our current understanding of the Namad Dar, but it happened nonetheless."

Onehson frowned for a moment.

"And where is Korfax now?"

Abrilon spread his hands out upon the table.

"In the hands of the Faxith, my Velukor. I have been to see him. He has finally returned to himself. His body is healed and his mind is clear, but he cannot remember what he did or how he did it. All he remembers is rage and grief. And his grief is very great. He blames himself for the death of his father."

There was a long silence. Onehson looked down, staring into his lap. Then he turned to Asvoan.

"And what do the Exentaser think of this?"

Asvoan widened her eyes for a moment and looked hard at the stave.

"It is difficult to know what to think, my Velukor. We stand upon the other side of an act of almost unprecedented power, but I think our judgement can wait for now."

Onehson drew back and raised an eyebrow.

"How so?"

Asvoan merely smiled.

"Do we not have a victory to celebrate, my Velukor, and a hero to honour? Whatever the reason for our deliverance, a great and terrible enemy has been defeated in this place. Othil Zilodar has been saved and the Agdoain, as far as we can tell, are now a spent force."

With that, everyone around the table relaxed and smiled or bowed in agreement. All except for Onehson. He continued to look at Asvoan for a moment and then looked back at the stave. He frowned at it.

"That, at least, is true," he said.

Onehson paused for a moment and then smiled, looking up again.

"Yes, we have a victory. And when Korfax is ready, we shall honour him. There we shall stand, all of us, apparelled in ornaments of brightness, to praise those that are gone and those that still dwell amongst us by the grace of The Creator."

There was a brief light upon, or within, his face as he said this, but then he darkened again as he pointed at the stave.

"But," he said, "there are more questions before us now than there were before. I would like to understand what has occurred here, because whoever, or whatever, our enemy is, I am sure that we have not heard the last of them. I would have us ready for the next onslaught. I fear we have a long road ahead of us."

He stood up and swept from the room, sucking the Imperial Branith into his wake. All around the table rose to their feet and bowed, but Onehson did not acknowledge them. They all sat back down again with varying degrees of discomfort on their faces. No one had expected him to leave so soon.

For a moment there was little movement, but then it began in earnest and eyes flickered left and right, each waiting to see who would speak first. Enay Orpahan decided he would be the one to do it.

"The Velukor does not seem so very pleased, I think," he said.

Noqvoanel Vixipal turned and looked at Orpahan carefully.

"You think so?"

Orpahan gestured at the vacant seat.

"I have but to look with my eyes and listen with my ears," he scolded.

Abinax regarded his fingers.

"I think I know what Orpahan means. The Velukor holds great store in the pre-eminence of his house, but look at what is before us. Any descendant of Karmaraa would be unsettled by such an unprecedented turn of events."

Vixipal leaned forward.

"An interesting choice of words, Tabaud."

"Interesting?" asked Abinax. "You think so? Then perhaps it is now your turn to explain yourself."

Vixipal gestured behind him.

"I was merely thinking of the tales that are now running hither and thither across the land. Korfax turning his father's stave white? That act is not as unprecedented as some here seem to think. There is one other that achieved such a feat."

Abinax frowned.

"Everyone around this table knows exactly what I mean," he said.

Abinax gestured at the stave.

"The Velukor is young, freshly come to power, just at the very moment when we are beset by an enemy we have never encountered before, an enemy that can match us upon the battlefield and even dares usurp our holiest lore. And we are only saved from that enemy by an act of astonishing power, an act that mirrors the one act that began everything we now know. Who would not be shaken by it?"

Vixipal smiled.

"Thank you, Tabaud. You have, I believe, put your finger upon it."

He turned to Abrilon.

"So?"

Abrilon gave Vixipal a cool look.

"You have heard our words already," Abrilon said. "We are still investigating, but I will say this at least." He looked around the table, meeting every eye in turn with his hardest gaze, but only Asvoan endured it. All the others had to bow their heads or look away. They all knew where the real power lay. Abrilon withdrew his gaze and smiled lightly. "Korfax, when he is ready, shall be tested once more, and, Creator willing, I expect him to become Geyadril shortly thereafter."

There were scattered intakes of breath around the table. Vixipal looked less than pleased.

"That wasn't the answer I was expecting," he said. "Are you not being somewhat precipitate? Does he not have to prove himself for an entire season of years before he can even be considered at all?"

Abrilon became very still and met the gaze of the Noqvoanel again, but now Vixipal found himself caught by it. Abrilon's eyes were suddenly far too bright and far too piercing. Vixipal leaned away from the table and tried to put as much distance between himself and the Geyadel as he possibly could.

"And does the Noqvoanel now think himself competent to decide policy for the Dar Kaadarith?" Abrilon demanded.

Vixipal could feel the force of Abrilon's mind just beyond the boundaries of his own. It hovered there like some great vice, ready to squeeze at the slightest provocation. Vixipal understood the threat all too well, but there were always other ways to turn such power aside. With more effort than he would have liked, he extricated himself from Abrilon's grip and turned to Asvoan instead.

"And what of the Exentaser?" he asked. "Do you have anything further to add?"

Asvoan did not hide her amusement.

"You heard our answer to the Velukor well enough, Noqvoanel, or have you suddenly become hard of hearing?"

Vixipal glanced left and right, but surprised no smiles. He was sure they were there, though. Mockery floated on the air.

"This is nothing to do with us," Asvoan continued. "The matter lies entirely in the purview of the Dar Kaadarith, but if you are asking whether any of us have seen harm in it, we have not. Korfax is the son of his father, heir to the Salman Farenith, one of the most loyal houses in the whole of Lukalaa, if not the whole of Lon-Elah itself."

Vixipal bowed his head to her.

"Thank you for reminding me," he returned. None missed his asperity. He looked around the table.

"Does no one have anything else they would like to say?" he asked.

Orpahan snorted.

"Korfax saved my city, so I for one wish him joy and long life. Needless to say he shall be proclaimed the hero of Zilodar, though I think any celebration on his part will be tempered by the loss of his father. I mourn with him. Sazaaim was the best of us."

Vixipal pursed his lips.

"That was not what I was asking!"

Orpahan slapped both hands upon the table.

"Have you no heart, Noqvoanel? Do you feel no grief for his loss?"

Vixipal drew back again.

"Of course I mourn the loss of Sazaaim, as I mourn for all the others that have left us. Who would not? But my concern at this moment is for the future, not for what has gone before."

Orpahan narrowed his eyes for a moment, gathering himself for a retort perhaps, but then he seemed to think better of it. He leaned back from the table.

"I have said all that I am going to say," he told Vixipal. "I will say no more upon the matter."

Then he looked hard at the Noqvoanel.

"But tell me this, Vixipal, tell me this. Why are you so eager? Why do you worry at this issue like a risson at a bone?"

Now it was Vixipal's turn to lean back from the table. He steepled his hands under his nose and smiled inside. Orpahan had gone to the one place the others had not. There was always one that would ask the right question. He had achieved that much at least.

"Why do I pursue this?" he asked gently. "Why does it obsess me?" he smiled. "Does no one else here look beyond their own borders? Abinax seems to be the only one here who has seen the same thing as I."

Abinax frowned slightly, but Vixipal was not looking his way. He was looking instead at Abrilon.

"This stave has become the sudden drip of water onto an otherwise still pool, but unlike in a pool, these ripples do not diminish. They gather up and gain momentum, an ever growing threat of uncertainty. And as I am sure you are aware, the Velukor can feel that uncertainty all about him now, for it rocks the vessel of his rule. Questions are being asked, and it will not be long before many start to demand answers."

Vixipal made the gesture of warning.

"We take the lessons of the past and apply them to the present. We take the confluences and seek comfort in them, especially in times of trouble." He turned to Asvoan. "When was the last time a sword was seen in the sky?"

Asvoan started.

"A sword? Where are you going with this, Vixipal?"

"Indulge me!"

"The last such conjunction was twenty-one years ago, at the birth of the Velukor."

"Who else was born at that time?"

There were murmurs about the table. Asvoan narrowed her eyes; she did not look pleased.

"Many were, scattered over the entire world. Many chose to have their children at that time. It is considered especially propitious to be born at the same time as the Velukor."

"But there was one in particular, was there not?"

"Everyone here knows that Korfax also entered the world at that time. I fail to see why you are making such an issue of this," Asvoan said.

"As I said before," Vixipal reminded her, "indulge me."

He drew himself up and his eyes darkened.

"So when was the last time before that a sword was seen in our skies?"

Asvoan stood up.

"Have a care, Vixipal!" she warned. "The Weave of Heaven is not your concern!"

Vixipal folded his arms.

"All things are my concern if they affect the rule of the Velukor."

Vixipal held up a single finger, curled like a hook.

"Let me state the facts as clearly as I may," he began. "The last time a sword was seen was at the birth of Karmaraa and Sondehna! Korfax was born under a sword. Korfax is of the blood. Korfax has done a thing no other has done since the time of Karmaraa."

Many around the table stood now, looks of outrage on their faces. Vixipal stood also and held up both hands again in the gesture of warning.

"May I remind you all that war is upon us once more, a war that threatens our very existence?"

He paused.

"Some are already proclaiming Korfax as Karmaraa come back to us. Do you see my meaning now? If we do not find answers soon, it will be too late and the matter will be out of our hands. The people will decide for us. This is not the time for us to be divided."

Abrilon leaned forward and snatched up the stave.

"You say you wish to calm the waters of the Velukor's rule?" he hissed across the table. "Then why are you so intent on stirring them up? Speak out! Proclaim that the Velukor is the Velukor, that nothing threatens his rule! That is what I intend to do!"

Vixipal leaned forward also.

"Really? Your intent? Must I throw your own words back at you? Was it not you that said Korfax is the stone that starts the avalanche?"

Abrilon looked stunned. Satisfied, Vixipal passed his glance about the table.

"Think long and hard, all of you. This matter of the stave goes beyond mere victory. It is of the unknown, it is the touch of chaos. It strikes at the very heart of us, eroding us from within and sowing doubt and confusion amongst us all."

Vixipal turned back to Abrilon again.

"You heard the Velukor – he requires answers. Do not take too long, or answers will be found in spite of you."

He turned and left the room. There was complete silence until Abrilon moved at last.

"Nonsense!" he said, to no one in particular. Then he, too, left the room.

The others gradually followed in ones and twos, silent knots of doubt, until only Samafaa and Ponodol were left at the great table. Samafaa turned to Ponodol.

"Now we see where this goes."

Ponodol sighed.

"We must find a way to blunt the teeth of the Balt Kaalith. This play of Vixipal's is fraught with danger."

"But what of Korfax?" asked Samafaa. "I don't often agree with Vixipal, but he is right in that at least. Korfax is far too young to become Geyadril."

"But he has chosen himself. He turned his father's stave white."

"I had not forgotten it, but no one becomes Geyadril until they have passed the first season of their lives."

Ponodol looked hard at Samafaa.

"So tradition tells us, but now we know him for what he is – stronger than any other of our order. Shall we waste that strength? I know what Abrilon fears. We must keep him with us. Do not let us lose him as we lost his father. Sazaaim should have become Geyadril. It is still a mystery to me as to why that never happened. He never told me, not even at the end."

"A mystery, you say?" Samafaa growled. "You and every other member of the Dar Kaadarith have ever wondered at it, but we shall never know the truth of it now. Both Gemanim and Sazaaim have taken the secret back with them into the river."

Ponodol looked down.

"And it is my fear that we shall never see Sazaaim's like again."

Here ends

LAND OF THE FIRST
- SERVANT OF FIRE -

The tale continues in

LAND OF THE FIRST
- SERVANT OF LIES -